THE BOOKS OF E

The City of Ember

An ALA-ALSC Notable Children's Book

★ "An electric debut!" —*Publishers Weekly,* Starred

★ "The cliffhanger ending will leave readers clamoring for the next installment." —*Kirkus Reviews,* Starred

★ "Science fiction for those who do not like science fiction." —*Voice of Youth Advocates,* Starred

The People of Sparks

★ "DuPrau clearly explores themes of nonviolence and when to stand up for oneself." —*School Library Journal,* Starred

"A thought-provoking novel about brinkmanship and the way societies can plant the insidious seeds of war." —*Publishers Weekly*

"This fast-paced tale of post-Apocalyptic strife will resonate with new and returning fans alike." —*Kirkus Reviews*

The Prophet of Yonwood

"Apropos to what is happening in the world today." —*Booklist*

"This novel has a great deal of immediacy in light of current world events. It sharply brings home the idea of people blindly following a belief without questioning it." —*School Library Journal*

"DuPrau effectively depicts a community in the grip of a millennial fever. . . . A provocative read with an appealingly conflicted protagonist." —*Kirkus Reviews*

Jeanne DuPrau

THE BOOKS OF EMBER

THE CITY OF EMBER
The First Book

THE PEOPLE OF SPARKS
The Second Book

THE PROPHET OF YONWOOD
The Third Book

RANDOM HOUSE NEW YORK

Published in the United States by Random House Children's Books,
a division of Random House, Inc., New York.
The Books of Ember comprises
The City of Ember, The People of Sparks, and *The Prophet of Yonwood,*
published separately by Random House Children's Books,
a division of Random House, Inc., New York,
in hardcover in 2003, 2004, and 2006, respectively.

Dust mite photograph courtesy of
the American Academy of Allergy, Asthma & Immunology.
Chang and Eng photograph courtesy of Picture History.

Visit us on the Web! www.randomhouse.com/kids

Educators and librarians, for a variety of teaching tools, visit us at
www.randomhouse.com/teachers

www.booksofember.com

Library of Congress Cataloging-in-Publication Data is available upon request.
ISBN 978-0-375-85116-2

Cover design and map by Chris Riely
Front cover photo by Jason Reed/Getty Images

Printed in the United States of America
10 9 8 7 6 5 4 3 2
First Omnibus Edition

Contents

The City of Ember 1

The People of Sparks 279

The Prophet of Yonwood 625

THE CITY
OF
EMBER

Contents

The Instructions 7
1. Assignment Day 10
2. A Message to the Mayor 23
3. Under Ember 46
4. Something Lost, Nothing Found 60
5. On Night Street 76
6. The Box in the Closet 90
7. A Message Full of Holes 99
8. Explorations 119
9. The Door in the Roped-Off Tunnel 127
10. Blue Sky and Goodbye 138
11. Lizzie's Groceries 146
12. A Dreadful Discovery 161
13. Deciphering the Message 172
14. The Way Out 184
15. A Desperate Run 199
16. The Singing 219
17. Away 232
18. Where the River Goes 244
19. A World of Light 256
20. The Last Message 264

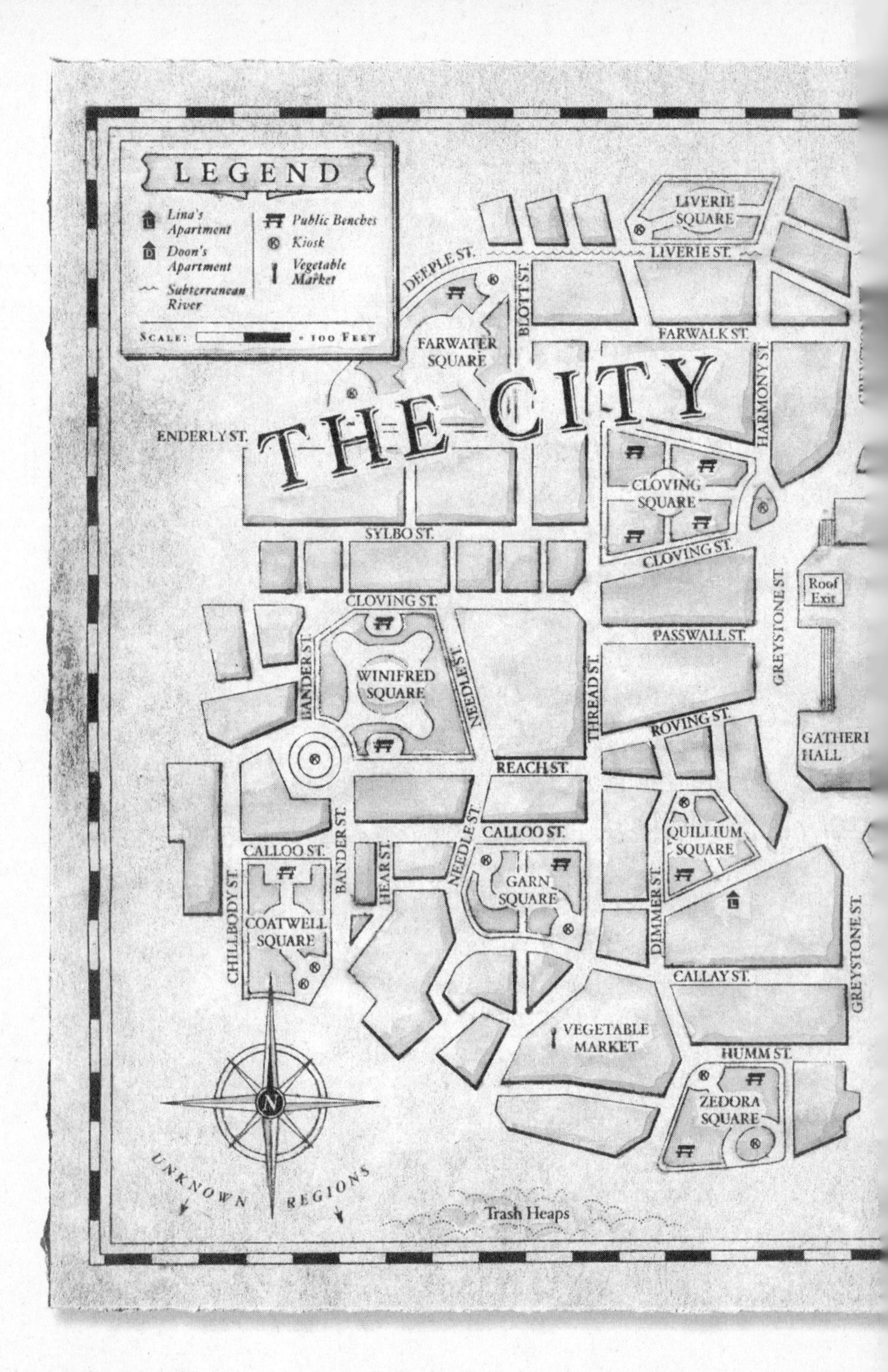
THE CITY
LEGEND
Lina's Apartment
Doon's Apartment
Subterranean River
Public Benches
Kiosk
Vegetable Market
SCALE: = 100 FEET
LIVERIE SQUARE
LIVERIE ST.
DEEPLE ST.
BLOTT ST.
FARWALK ST.
FARWATER SQUARE
HARMONY ST.
ENDERLY ST.
CLOVING SQUARE
SYLBO ST.
CLOVING ST.
GREYSTONE ST.
Roof Exit
PASSWALL ST.
WINIFRED SQUARE
BANDER ST.
NEEDLE ST.
THREAD ST.
ROVING ST.
GATHERI
HALL
REACH ST.
CALLOO ST.
QUILLIUM SQUARE
HEAR ST.
GARN SQUARE
CHILLBODY ST.
COATWELL SQUARE
DIMMER ST.
CALLAY ST.
VEGETABLE MARKET
HUMM ST.
ZEDORA SQUARE
N
UNKNOWN REGIONS
Trash Heaps

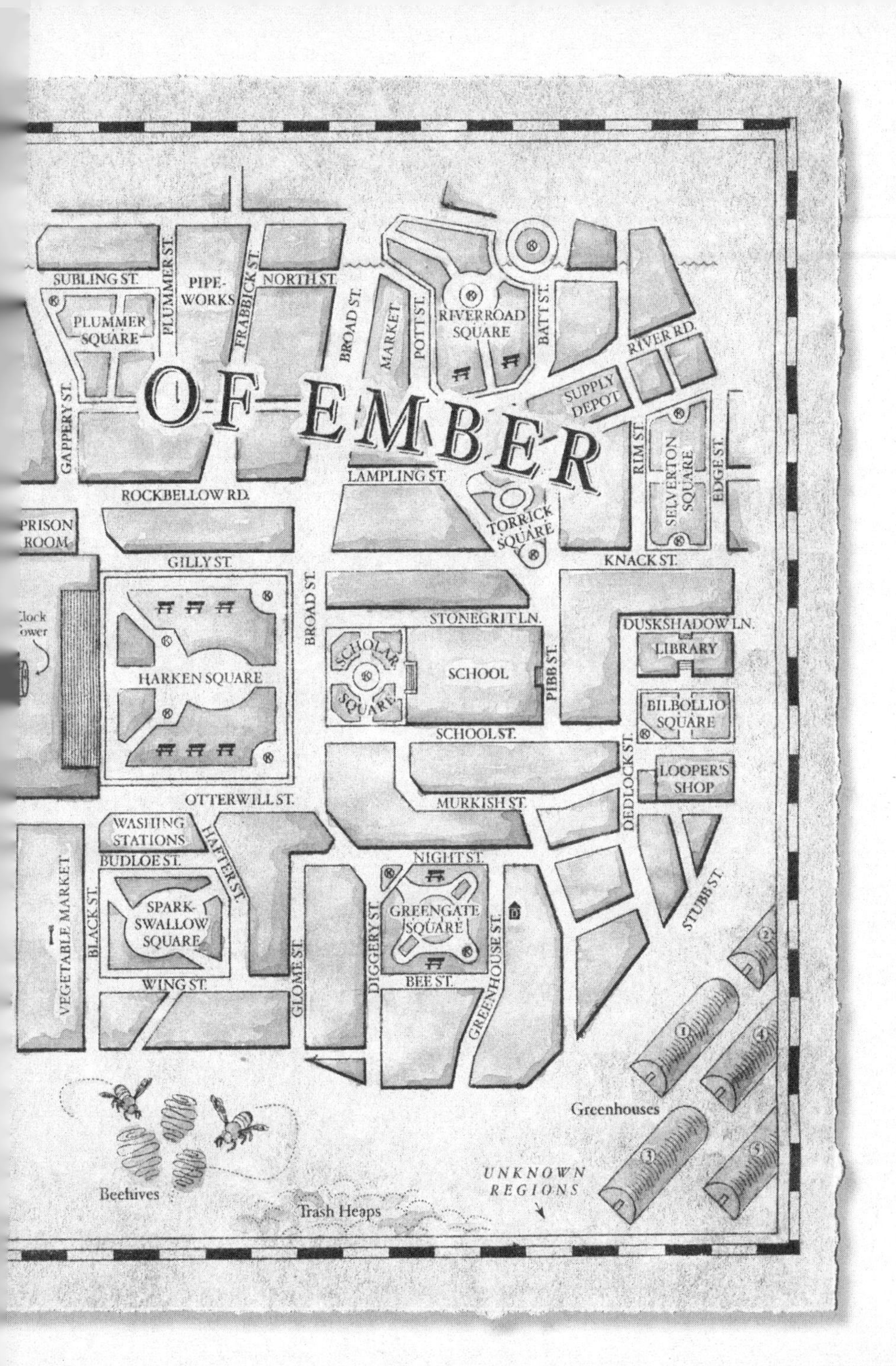

OF EMBER
SUBLING ST.
PLUMMER ST.
PIPE-WORKS
FRABBICK ST.
NORTH ST.
BROAD ST.
MARKET
POTT ST.
RIVERROAD SQUARE
BATT ST.
RIVER RD.
PLUMMER SQUARE
GAPPERY ST.
SUPPLY DEPOT
RIM ST.
SELVERTON SQUARE
EDGE ST.
LAMPLING ST.
ROCKBELLOW RD.
TORRICK SQUARE
PRISON ROOM
GILLY ST.
KNACK ST.
STONEGRIT LN.
DUSKSHADOW LN.
LIBRARY
HARKEN SQUARE
SCHOLAR SQUARE
SCHOOL
PIBB ST.
BILBOLLIO SQUARE
SCHOOL ST.
DEDLOCK ST.
LOOPER'S SHOP
OTTERWILL ST.
MURKISH ST.
WASHING STATIONS
HAFTER ST.
BUDLOE ST.
NIGHT ST.
VEGETABLE MARKET
BLACK ST.
SPARK-SWALLOW SQUARE
GLOME ST.
DIGGERY ST.
GREENGATE SQUARE
GREENHOUSE ST.
STUBB ST.
WING ST.
BEE ST.
Greenhouses
Beehives
Trash Heaps
UNKNOWN REGIONS

The Instructions

When the city of Ember was just built and not yet inhabited, the chief builder and the assistant builder, both of them weary, sat down to speak of the future.

"They must not leave the city for at least two hundred years," said the chief builder. "Or perhaps two hundred and twenty."

"Is that long enough?" asked his assistant.

"It should be. We can't know for sure."

"And when the time comes," said the assistant, "how will they know what to do?"

"We'll provide them with instructions, of course," the chief builder replied.

"But who will keep the instructions? Who can we trust to keep them safe and secret all that time?"

"The mayor of the city will keep the instructions," said the chief builder. "We'll put them in a box with a timed lock, set to open on the proper date."

"And will we tell the mayor what's in the box?" the assistant asked.

"No, just that it's information they won't need and must not see until the box opens of its own accord."

"So the first mayor will pass the box to the next mayor, and that one to the next, and so on down through the years, all of them keeping it secret, all that time?"

"What else can we do?" asked the chief builder. "Nothing about this endeavor is certain. There may be no one left in the city by then or no safe place for them to come back to."

So the first mayor of Ember was given the box, told to guard it carefully, and solemnly sworn to secrecy. When she grew old, and her time as mayor was up, she explained about the box to her successor, who also kept the secret carefully, as did the next mayor. Things went as planned for many years. But the seventh mayor of Ember was less honorable than the ones who'd come before him, and more desperate. He was ill—he had the coughing sickness that was common in the city then—and he thought the box might hold a secret that would save his life. He took it from its hiding place in the basement of the Gathering Hall and brought it home with him, where he attacked it with a hammer.

But his strength was failing by then. All he managed to do was dent the lid a little. And before he could return the box to its official hiding place or tell his successor about it, he died. The box ended up at the back of a closet, shoved behind some old bags and bundles. There it sat, unnoticed, year after year, until its time arrived, and the lock quietly clicked open.

CHAPTER 1

Assignment Day

In the city of Ember, the sky was always dark. The only light came from great flood lamps mounted on the buildings and at the tops of poles in the middle of the larger squares. When the lights were on, they cast a yellowish glow over the streets; people walking by threw long shadows that shortened and then stretched out again. When the lights were off, as they were between nine at night and six in the morning, the city was so dark that people might as well have been wearing blindfolds.

Sometimes darkness fell in the middle of the day. The city of Ember was old, and everything in it, including the power lines, was in need of repair. So now and then the lights would flicker and go out. These were terrible moments for the people of Ember. As they came to a halt in the middle of the street or stood stock-still in their houses, afraid to move in the utter blackness, they were reminded of something they preferred not to think about: that someday the lights of the city might go out and never come back on.

But most of the time life proceeded as it always had. Grown people did their work, and younger people, until they reached the age of twelve, went to school. On the last day of their final year, which was called Assignment Day, they were given jobs to do.

The graduating students occupied Room 8 of the Ember School. On Assignment Day of the year 241, this classroom, usually noisy first thing in the morning, was completely silent. All twenty-four students sat upright and still at the desks they had grown too big for. They were waiting.

The desks were arranged in four rows of six, one behind the other. In the last row sat a slender girl named Lina Mayfleet. She was winding a strand of her long, dark hair around her finger, winding and unwinding it again and again. Sometimes she plucked at a thread on her ragged cape or bent over to pull on her socks, which were loose and tended to slide down around her ankles. One of her feet tapped the floor softly.

In the second row was a boy named Doon Harrow. He sat with his shoulders hunched, his eyes squeezed shut in concentration, and his hands clasped tightly together. His hair looked rumpled, as if he hadn't combed it for a while. He had dark, thick eyebrows, which made him look serious at the best of times and, when he was anxious or angry, came together to form a straight line across his forehead. His brown corduroy jacket was so old that its ridges had flattened out.

Both the girl and the boy were making urgent wishes. Doon's wish was very specific. He repeated it over and over again, his lips moving slightly, as if he could make it come true by saying it a thousand times. Lina was making her wish in pictures rather than in words. In her mind's eye, she saw herself running through the streets of the city in a red jacket. She made this picture as bright and real as she could.

Lina looked up and gazed around the schoolroom. She said a silent goodbye to everything that had been familiar for so long. Goodbye to the map of the city of Ember in its scarred wooden frame and the cabinet whose shelves held *The Book of Numbers, The Book of Letters,* and *The Book of the City of Ember.* Goodbye to the cabinet drawers labeled "New Paper" and "Old Paper." Goodbye to the three electric lights in the ceiling that seemed always, no matter where you sat, to cast the shadow of your head over the page you were writing on. And goodbye to their teacher, Miss Thorn, who had finished her Last Day of School speech, wishing them luck in the lives they were about to begin. Now, having run out of things to say, she was standing at her desk with her frayed shawl clasped around her shoulders. And still the mayor, the guest of honor, had not arrived.

Someone's foot scraped back and forth on the floor. Miss Thorn sighed. Then the door rattled open, and the mayor walked in. He looked annoyed, as though *they* were the ones who were late.

"Welcome, Mayor Cole," said Miss Thorn. She held out her hand to him.

The mayor made his mouth into a smile. "Miss Thorn," he said, enfolding her hand. "Greetings. Another year." The mayor was a vast, heavy man, so big in the middle that his arms looked small and dangling. In one hand he held a little cloth bag.

He lumbered to the front of the room and faced the students. His gray, drooping face appeared to be made of something stiffer than ordinary skin; it rarely moved except for making the smile that was on it now.

"Young people of the Highest Class," the mayor began. He stopped and scanned the room for several moments; his eyes seemed to look out from far back inside his head. He nodded slowly. "Assignment Day now, isn't it? Yes. First we get our education. Then we serve our city." Again his eyes moved back and forth along the rows of students, and again he nodded, as if someone had confirmed what he'd said. He put the little bag on Miss Thorn's desk and rested his hand on it. "What will that service be, eh? Perhaps you're wondering." He did his smile again, and his heavy cheeks folded like drapes.

Lina's hands were cold. She wrapped her cape around her and pressed her hands between her knees. Please hurry, Mr. Mayor, she said silently. Please just let us choose and get it over with. Doon, in his mind, was saying the same thing, only he didn't say please.

"Something to remember," the mayor said, holding up one finger. "Job you draw today is for three years. Then, Evaluation. Are you good at your job? Fine. You may keep it. Are you unsatisfactory? Is there a greater need elsewhere? You will be re-assigned. It is *extremely important,*" he said, jabbing his finger at the class, "for all . . . work . . . of Ember . . . to be done. To be *properly* done."

He picked up the bag and pulled open the drawstring. "So. Let us begin. Simple procedure. Come up one at a time. Reach into this bag. Take one slip of paper. Read it out loud." He smiled and nodded. The flesh under his chin bulged in and out. "Who cares to be first?"

No one moved. Lina stared down at the top of her desk. There was a long silence. Then Lizzie Bisco, one of Lina's best friends, sprang to her feet. "I would like to be first," she said in her breathless high voice.

"Good. Walk forward."

Lizzie went to stand before the mayor. Because of her orange hair, she looked like a bright spark next to him.

"Now choose." The mayor held out the bag with one hand and put the other behind his back, as if to show he would not interfere.

Lizzie reached into the bag and withdrew a tightly folded square of paper. She unfolded it carefully. Lina couldn't see the look on Lizzie's face, but she could hear the disappointment in her voice as she read out loud: "Supply Depot clerk."

"Very good," said the mayor. "A vital job."

Lizzie trudged back to her desk. Lina smiled at her, but Lizzie made a sour face. Supply Depot clerk wasn't a bad job, but it was a dull one. The Supply Depot clerks sat behind a long counter, took orders from the storekeepers of Ember, and sent the carriers down to bring up what was wanted from the vast network of storerooms beneath Ember's streets. The storerooms held supplies of every kind—canned food, clothes, furniture, blankets, light bulbs, medicine, pots and pans, reams of paper, soap, more light bulbs—everything the people of Ember could possibly need. The clerks sat at their ledger books all day, recording the orders that came in and the goods that went out. Lizzie didn't like to sit still; she would have been better suited to something else, Lina thought—messenger, maybe, the job Lina wanted for herself. Messengers ran through the city all day, going everywhere, seeing everything.

"Next," said the mayor.

This time two people stood up at once, Orly Gordon and Chet Noam. Orly quickly sat down again, and Chet approached the mayor.

"Choose, young man," the mayor said.

Chet chose. He unfolded his scrap of paper. "Electrician's helper," he read, and his wide face broke into a smile. Lina heard someone take a quick breath. She looked over to see Doon pressing a hand against his mouth.

You never knew, each year, exactly which jobs would be offered. Some years there were several good jobs, like greenhouse helper, timekeeper's assistant, or messenger, and no bad jobs at all. Other years, jobs like Pipeworks laborer, trash sifter, and mold scraper were mixed in. But there would always be at least one or two jobs for electrician's helper. Fixing the electricity was the most important job in Ember, and more people worked at it than at anything else.

Orly Gordon was next. She got the job of building repair assistant, which was a good job for Orly. She was a strong girl and liked hard work. Vindie Chance was made a greenhouse helper. She gave Lina a big grin as she went back to her seat. She'll get to work with Clary, Lina thought. Lucky. So far no one had picked a really bad job. Perhaps this time there would be no bad jobs at all.

The idea gave her courage. Besides, she had reached the point where the suspense was giving her a stomach ache. So as Vindie sat down—even before the mayor could say "Next"—she stood up and stepped forward.

The little bag was made of faded green material, gathered at the top with a black string. Lina hesitated a moment, then put her hand inside and fingered the bits of paper. Feeling as if she were stepping off a high building, she picked one.

She unfolded it. The words were written in black ink, in small careful printing. PIPEWORKS LABORER, they said. She stared at them.

"Out loud, please," the mayor said.

"Pipeworks laborer," Lina said in a choked whisper.

"Louder," said the mayor.

"Pipeworks laborer," Lina said again, her voice loud and cracked. There was a sigh of sympathy from the class. Keeping her eyes on the floor, Lina went back to her desk and sat down.

Pipeworks laborers worked below the storerooms in the deep labyrinth of tunnels that contained Ember's water and sewer pipes. They spent their days stopping up leaks and replacing pipe joints. It was wet, cold work; it could even be dangerous. A swift underground river ran through the Pipeworks, and every now and then someone fell into it and was lost. People were lost occasionally in the tunnels, too, if they strayed too far.

Lina stared miserably down at a letter B someone had scratched into her desktop long ago. Almost anything would have been better than Pipeworks laborer. Greenhouse helper had been her second choice. She imagined with longing the warm air and earthy smell of the greenhouse, where she could have worked with Clary, the greenhouse manager, someone she'd known all her life. She would have been content as a doctor's assistant, too, binding up cuts and bones. Even street-sweeper or cart-puller would have been better. At least then she could have stayed above ground, with space and people around her. She thought going down into the Pipeworks must be like being buried alive.

One by one, the other students chose their jobs. None of them got such a wretched job as hers. Finally the last person rose from his chair and walked forward.

It was Doon. His dark eyebrows were drawn together in a frown of concentration. His hands, Lina saw, were clenched into fists at his sides.

Doon reached into the bag and took out the last scrap of paper. He paused a minute, pressing it tightly in his hand.

"Go on," said the mayor. "Read."

Unfolding the paper, Doon read: "Messenger." He scowled, crumpled the paper, and dashed it to the floor.

Lina gasped; the whole class rustled in surprise. Why would anyone be angry to get the job of messenger?

"Bad behavior!" cried the mayor. His eyes bulged and his face darkened. "Go to your seat immediately."

Doon kicked the crumpled paper into a corner. Then he stalked back to his desk and flung himself down.

The mayor took a short breath and blinked furiously. "Disgraceful," he said, glaring at Doon. "A childish display of temper! Students should be *glad* to work for their city. Ember will prosper if all . . . citizens . . . do . . . their . . . best." He held up a stern finger as he said this and moved his eyes slowly from one face to the next.

Suddenly Doon spoke up. "But Ember is *not* prospering!" he cried. "Everything is getting worse and worse!"

"Silence!" cried the mayor.

"The blackouts!" cried Doon. He jumped from his seat. "The lights go out all the time now! And the shortages, there's shortages of everything! If no one does anything about it, something terrible is going to happen!"

Lina listened with a pounding heart. What was wrong with Doon? Why was he so upset? He was taking things too seriously, as he always did.

Miss Thorn strode to Doon and put a hand on his shoulder. "Sit down now," she said quietly. But Doon remained standing.

The mayor glared. For a few moments he said nothing. Then he smiled, showing a neat row of gray teeth. "Miss Thorn," he said. "Who might this young man be?"

"I am Doon Harrow," said Doon.

"I will remember you," said the mayor. He gave Doon a long look, then turned to the class and smiled his smile again.

"Congratulations to all," he said. "Welcome to Ember's work force. Miss Thorn. Class. Thank you."

The mayor shook hands with Miss Thorn and departed. The students gathered their coats and caps and filed out of the classroom. Lina walked down the Wide Hallway with Lizzie, who said, "Poor you! I thought *I* picked a bad one, but you got the worst. I feel lucky compared to you." Once they were out the door, Lizzie said goodbye and scurried away, as if Lina's bad luck were a disease she might catch.

Lina stood on the steps for a moment and gazed across Harken Square, where people walked briskly, bundled up cozily in their coats and scarves, or talked to one another in the pools of light beneath the great streetlamps. A boy in a red messenger's jacket ran toward the Gathering Hall. On Otterwill Street, a man pulled a cart filled with sacks of potatoes. And in the buildings all around the square, rows of lighted windows shone bright yellow and deep gold.

Lina sighed. *This* was where she wanted to be, up here where everything happened, not down underground.

Someone tapped her on the shoulder. Startled, she turned and saw Doon behind her. His thin face looked pale. "Will you trade with me?" he asked.

"Trade?"

"Trade jobs. I don't want to waste my time being a messenger. I want to help save the city, not run around carrying gossip."

Lina gaped at him. "You'd rather be in the *Pipeworks*?"

"Electrician's helper is what I wanted," Doon said. "But Chet won't trade, of course. Pipeworks is second best."

"But why?"

"Because the generator is in the Pipeworks," said Doon.

Lina knew about the generator, of course. In some mysterious way, it turned the running of the river into power for the city. You could feel its deep rumble when you stood in Plummer Square.

"I need to see the generator," Doon said. "I have . . . I have ideas about it." He thrust his hands into his pockets. "So," he said, "will you trade?"

"Yes!" cried Lina. "Messenger is the job I want

most!" And not a useless job at all, in her opinion. People couldn't be expected to trudge halfway across the city every time they wanted to communicate with someone. Messengers connected everyone to everyone else. Anyway, whether it was important or not, the job of messenger just happened to be perfect for Lina. She loved to run. She could run forever. And she loved exploring every nook and cranny of the city, which was what a messenger got to do.

"All right then," said Doon. He handed her his crumpled piece of paper, which he must have retrieved from the floor. Lina reached into her pocket, pulled out her slip of paper, and handed it to him.

"Thank you," he said.

"You're welcome," said Lina. Happiness sprang up in her, and happiness always made her want to run. She took the steps three at a time and sped down Broad Street toward home.

CHAPTER 2

A Message to the Mayor

Lina often took different routes between school and home. Sometimes, just for variety, she'd go all the way around Sparkswallow Square, or way up by the shoe repair shops on Liverie Street. But today she took the shortest route because she was eager to get home and tell her news.

She ran fast and easily through the streets of Ember. Every corner, every alley, every building was familiar to her. She always knew where she was, though most streets looked more or less the same. All of them were lined with old two-story stone buildings, the wood of their window frames and doors long unpainted. On the street level were shops; above the shops were the apartments where people lived. Every building, at the place where the wall met the roof, was equipped with a row of floodlights—big cone-shaped lamps that cast a strong yellow glare.

Stone walls, lighted windows, lumpy, muffled shapes of people—Lina flew by them. Her slender legs felt immensely strong, like the wood of a bow that flexes and springs. She darted around obstacles—broken furniture left for the trash heaps or for scavengers, stoves and refrigerators that were past repair, peddlers sitting on the pavement with their wares spread out around them. She leapt over cracks and potholes.

When she came to Hafter Street, she slowed a little. This street was deep in shadow. Four of its streetlamps were out and had not been fixed. For a second, Lina thought of the rumor she'd heard about light bulbs: that some kinds were completely gone. She was used to shortages of things—everyone was—but not of light bulbs! If the bulbs for the streetlamps ran out, the only lights would be inside the buildings. What would happen then? How could people find their way through the streets in the dark?

Somewhere inside her, a black worm of dread stirred. She thought about Doon's outburst in class. Could things really be as bad as he said? She didn't want to believe it. She pushed the thought away.

As she turned onto Budloe Street, she sped up again. She passed a line of customers waiting to get into the vegetable market, their shopping bags draped over their arms. At the corner of Oliver Street, she dodged a group of washers trudging along with bags of laundry, and some movers carrying away a broken table. She passed a street-sweeper shoving dust around with his broom. I am so lucky, she thought, to have the job I want. And because of Doon Harrow, of all people.

When they were younger, Lina and Doon had been friends. Together they had explored the back alleys and dimly lit edges of the city. But in their fourth year of school, they had begun to grow apart. It started one day during the hour of free time, when the children in their class were playing on the front steps of the school. "I can go down three steps at a time," someone would boast. "I can hop down on one foot!" someone else would say. The others would chime in. "I can do a handstand against the pillar!" "I can leapfrog over the trash can!" As soon as one child did something, all the rest would do it, too, to prove they could.

Lina could do it all, even when the dares got wilder. She yelled out the wildest one of all: "I can climb the light pole!" For a second everyone just stared at her. But Lina dashed across the street, took off her shoes and socks, and wrapped herself around the cold metal of the pole. Pushing with her bare feet, she inched upward. She didn't get very far before she lost her grip and fell back down. The children laughed, and so did she. "I didn't say I'd climb to the top," she explained. "I just said I'd climb it."

The others swarmed forward to try. Lizzie wouldn't take off her socks—her feet were too cold, she said—so she kept sliding back. Fordy Penn wasn't strong enough to get more than a foot off the ground. Next came Doon. He took his shoes and socks off and placed them neatly at the foot of the pole. Then he announced, in his serious way, "I'm going to the top." He clasped the pole and started upward, pushing with his feet, his knees sticking out to the sides. He pulled himself upward, pushed again—he was higher now than Lina had been—but suddenly his hands slid and he came plummeting down. He landed on his bottom with his legs poking up in the air. Lina laughed. She shouldn't have; he might have been hurt. But he looked so funny that she couldn't help it.

He wasn't hurt. He could have jumped up, grinned, and walked away. But Doon didn't take things lightly. When he heard Lina and the others laughing, his face darkened. His temper rose in him like hot water. "Don't you dare laugh at me," he said to Lina. "I did better than you did! That was a stupid idea anyway, a stupid, stupid idea to climb that pole. . . ." And as he was shouting, red in the face, their teacher, Mrs. Polster, came out onto the steps and saw him. She took him by the shirt collar to the school director's office, where he got a scolding he didn't think he deserved.

After that day, Lina and Doon barely looked at each other when they passed in the hallway. At first it was because they were fuming about what had happened. Doon didn't like being laughed at; Lina didn't like being shouted at. After a while the memory of the light-pole incident faded, but by then they had got out of the habit of friendship. By the time they were twelve, they knew each other only as classmates. Lina was friends with Vindie Chance, Orly Gordon, and most of all, red-haired Lizzie Bisco, who could run almost as fast as Lina and could talk three times faster.

Now, as Lina sped toward home, she felt immensely grateful to Doon and hoped he'd come to no harm in the Pipeworks. Maybe they'd be friends again. She'd like to ask him about the Pipeworks. She was curious about it.

When she got to Greystone Street, she passed Clary Laine, who was probably on her way to the greenhouses. Clary waved to her and called out, "What job?" and Lina called back, "Messenger!" and ran on.

Lina lived in Quillium Square, over the yarn shop run by her grandmother. When she got to the shop, she burst in the door and cried, "Granny! I'm a messenger!"

Granny's shop had once been a tidy place, where each ball of yarn and spool of thread had its spot in the cubbyholes that lined the walls. All the yarn and thread came from old clothes that had gotten too shabby to be worn. Granny unraveled sweaters and picked apart dresses and jackets and pants; she wound the yarn into balls and the thread onto spools, and people bought them to use in making new clothes.

These days, the shop was a mess. Long loops and strands of yarn dangled out of the cubbyholes, and the browns and grays and purples were mixed in with the ochres and olive greens and dark blues. Granny's customers often had to spend half an hour unsnarling the rust-red yarn from the mud-brown, or trying to fish out the end of a thread from a tangled wad. Granny wasn't much help. Most days she just dozed behind the counter in her rocking chair.

That's where she was when Lina burst in with her news. Lina saw that Granny had forgotten to knot up her hair that morning—it was standing out from her head in a wild white frizz.

Granny stood up, looking puzzled. "You aren't a messenger, dear, you're a schoolgirl," she said.

"But Granny, today was Assignment Day. I got my job. And I'm a messenger!"

Granny's eyes lit up, and she slapped her hand down on the counter. "I remember!" she cried. "Messenger, that's a grand job! You'll be good at it."

Lina's little sister toddled out from behind the counter on unsteady legs. She had a round face and round brown eyes. At the top of her head was a sprig of brown hair tied up with a scrap of red yarn. She grabbed on to Lina's knees. "Wy-na, Wy-na!" she said.

Lina bent over and took the child's hands. "Poppy! Your big sister got a good job! Are you happy, Poppy? Are you proud of me?"

Poppy said something that sounded like, "Hoppy-hoppyhoppy!" Lina laughed, hoisted her up, and danced with her around the shop.

Lina loved her little sister so much that it was like an ache under her ribs. The baby and Granny were all the family she had now. Two years ago, when the coughing sickness was raging through the city again, her father had died. Some months later, her mother, giving birth to Poppy, had died, too. Lina missed her parents with an ache that was as strong as what she felt for Poppy, only it was a hollow feeling instead of a full one.

"When do you start?" asked Granny.

"Tomorrow," said Lina. "I report to the messengers' station at eight o'clock."

"You'll be a famous messenger," said Granny. "Fast and famous."

Taking Poppy with her, Lina went out of the shop and climbed the stairs to their apartment. It was a small apartment, only four rooms, but there was enough stuff in it to fill twenty. There were things that had belonged to Lina's parents, her grandparents, and even *their* grandparents—old, broken, cracked, threadbare things that had been patched and repaired dozens or hundreds of times. People in Ember rarely threw anything away. They made the best possible use of what they had.

In Lina's apartment, layers of worn rugs and carpets covered the floor, making it soft but uneven underfoot. Against one wall squatted a sagging couch with round wooden balls for legs, and on the couch were blankets and pillows, so many that you had to toss some on the floor before you could sit down. Against the opposite wall stood two wobbly tables that held a clutter of plates and bottles, cups and bowls, unmatching forks and spoons, little piles of scrap paper, bits of string wound up in untidy wads, and a few stubby pencils. There were four lamps, two tall ones that stood on the floor and two short ones that stood on tables. And in uneven lines up near the ceiling were hooks that held coats and shawls and nightgowns and sweaters, shelves that held pots and pans, jars with unreadable labels, and boxes of buttons and pins and tacks.

Where there were no shelves, the walls had been decorated with things of beauty—a label from a can of peaches, a few dried yellow squash flowers, a strip of faded but still pretty purple cloth. There were drawings, too. Lina had done the drawings out of her imagination. They showed a city that looked somewhat like Ember, except that its buildings were lighter and taller and had more windows.

One of the drawings had fallen to the floor. Lina

retrieved it and pinned it back up. She stood for a minute and looked at the pictures. Over and over, she'd drawn the same city. Sometimes she drew it as seen from afar, sometimes she chose one of its buildings and drew it in detail. She put in stairways and streetlamps and carts. Sometimes she tried to draw the people who lived in the city, though she wasn't good at drawing people—their heads always came out too small, and their hands looked like spiders. One picture showed a scene in which the people of the city greeted her when she arrived—the first person they had ever seen to come from elsewhere. They argued with each other about who should be the first to invite her home.

Lina could see this city so clearly in her mind she almost believed it was real. She knew it couldn't be, though. *The Book of the City of Ember,* which all children studied in school, taught otherwise. "The city of Ember was made for us long ago by the Builders," the book said. "It is the only light in the dark world. Beyond Ember, the darkness goes on forever in all directions."

Lina had been to the outer border of Ember. She had stood at the edge of the trash heaps and gazed into the darkness beyond the city—the Unknown Regions. No one had ever gone far into the Unknown Regions—or at least no one had gone far and returned. And no one had ever arrived in Ember from the Unknown Regions, either. As far as anyone knew, the darkness *did* go on forever. Still, Lina wanted the other city to exist. In her imagination, it was so beautiful, and it seemed so real. Sometimes she longed to go there and take everyone in Ember with her.

But she wasn't thinking about the other city now. Today she was happy to be right where she was. She set Poppy on the couch. "Wait there," she said. She went into the kitchen, where there was an electric stove and a refrigerator that no longer worked and was used to store glasses and dishes so Poppy couldn't get at them. Above the refrigerator were shelves holding more pots and jars, more spoons and knives, a wind-up clock that Granny always forgot to wind, and a long row of cans. Lina tried to keep the cans in alphabetical order so she could find what she wanted quickly, but Granny always messed them up. Now, she saw, there were beans at the end of the row and tomatoes at the beginning. She picked out a can labeled Baby Drink and a jar of boiled carrots, opened them, poured the liquid into a cup and the carrots into a little dish, and took these back to the baby on the couch.

Poppy dribbled Baby Drink down her chin. She ate some of her carrots and poked others between the couch cushions. For the moment, Lina felt almost perfectly happy. There was no need to think about the fate of the city right now. Tomorrow, she'd be a messenger! She wiped the orange goop off Poppy's chin. "Don't worry," she said. "Everything will be all right."

* * *

The messengers' headquarters was on Cloving Street, not far from the back of the Gathering Hall. When Lina arrived the next morning, she was greeted by Messenger Captain Allis Fleery, a bony woman with pale eyes and hair the color of dust. "Our new girl," said Captain Fleery to the other messengers, a cluster of nine people who smiled and nodded at Lina. "I have your jacket right here," said the captain. She handed Lina a red jacket like the one all messengers wore. It was only a little too large.

From the clock tower of the Gathering Hall came a deep reverberating bong. "Eight o'clock!" cried Captain Fleery. She waved a long arm. "Take your stations!" As the clock sounded seven more times, the messengers scattered in all directions. The captain turned to Lina. "Your station," she said, "is Garn Square."

Lina nodded and started off, but the captain caught her by the collar. "I haven't told you the rules," she said. She held up a knobby finger. "One: When a customer gives you a message, repeat it back to make sure you have it right. Two: Always wear your red jacket so people can identify you. Three: Go as fast as possible. Your customers pay twenty cents for every message, no matter how far you have to take it."

Lina nodded. "I always go fast," she said.

"Four," the captain went on. "Deliver a message

only to the person it's meant for, no one else."

Lina nodded again. She bounced a little on her toes, eager to get going.

Captain Fleery smiled. "Go," she said, and Lina was off.

She felt strong and speedy and surefooted. She glanced at her reflection as she ran past the window of a furniture repair shop. She liked the look of her long dark hair flying out behind her, her long legs in their black socks, and her flapping red jacket. Her face, which had never seemed especially remarkable, looked almost beautiful, because she looked so happy.

As soon as she came into Garn Square, a voice cried, "Messenger!" Her first customer! It was old Natty Prine, calling to her from the bench where he always sat. "This goes to Ravenet Parsons, 18 Selverton Square," he said. "Bend down."

She bent down so that her ear was close to his whiskery mouth.

The old man said in a slow, hoarse voice, "My stove is broke, don't come for dinner. Repeat."

Lina repeated the message.

"Good," said Natty Prine. He gave Lina twenty cents, and she ran across the city to Selverton Square. There she found Ravenet Parsons also sitting on a bench. She recited the message to him.

"Old turniphead," he growled. "Lazy old fleaface. He just doesn't feel like cooking. No reply."

Lina ran back to Garn Square, passing a group of Believers on the way. They were standing in a circle, holding hands, singing one of their cheerful songs. It seemed to Lina there were more Believers than ever these days. What they believed in she didn't know, but it must make them happy—they were always smiling.

Her next customer turned out to be Mrs. Polster, the teacher of the fourth-year class. In Mrs. Polster's class, they memorized passages from *The Book of the City of Ember* every week. Mrs. Polster had charts on the walls for everything, with everyone's name listed. If you did something right, she made a green dot by your name. If you did something wrong, she made a red dot. "What you need to learn, children," she always said, in her resonant, precise voice, "is the difference between right and wrong in every area of life. And once you learn the difference—" Here she would stop and point to the class, and the class would finish the sentence: "You must always choose the right." In every situation, Mrs. Polster knew what the right choice was.

Now here was Mrs. Polster again, looming over Lina and pronouncing her message. "To Annisette Lafrond, 39 Humm Street, as follows," she said. "My confidence in you has been seriously diminished since I heard about the disreputable activities in which you engaged on Thursday last. Please repeat."

It took Lina three tries to get this right. "Uh-oh, a

red dot for me," she said. Mrs. Polster did not seem to find this amusing.

Lina had nineteen customers that first morning. Some of them had ordinary messages: "I can't come on Tuesday." "Buy a pound of potatoes on your way home." "Please come and fix my front door." Others had messages that made no sense to her at all, like Mrs. Polster's. But it didn't matter. The wonderful part about being a messenger was not the messages but the places she got to go. She could go into the houses of people she didn't know and hidden alleyways and little rooms in the backs of stores. In just a few hours, she discovered all kinds of strange and interesting things.

For instance: Mrs. Sample, the mender, had to sleep on her couch because her entire bedroom, almost up to the ceiling, was crammed with clothes to be mended. Dr. Felinia Tower had the skeleton of a person hanging against her living room wall, its bones all held in place with black strings. "I study it," she said when she saw Lina staring. "I have to know how people are put together." At a house on Calloo Street, Lina delivered a message to a worried-looking man whose living room was completely dark. "I'm saving on light bulbs," the man said. And when Lina took a message to the Can Café, she learned that on certain days the back room was used as a meeting place for people who liked to converse about Great Subjects. "Do you think an Invisible Being is watching over us all the time?" she heard someone ask. "Perhaps," answered someone else. There was a long silence. "And then again, perhaps not."

All of it was interesting. She loved finding things out, and she loved running. And even by the end of the day, she wasn't tired. Running made her feel strong and big-hearted, it made her love the places she ran through and the people whose messages she delivered. She wished she could bring all of them the good news they so desperately wanted to hear.

Late in the afternoon, a young man came up to her, walking with a sort of sideways lurch. He was an odd-looking person—he had a very long neck with a bump in the middle and teeth so big they looked as if they were trying to escape from his mouth. His black, bushy hair stuck out from his head in untidy tufts. "I have a message for the mayor, at the Gathering Hall," he said. He paused to let the importance of this be understood. "The mayor," he said. "Did you get that?"

"I got it," said Lina.

"All right. Listen carefully. Tell him: Delivery at eight. From Looper. Repeat it back."

"Delivery at eight. From Looper," Lina repeated. It was an easy message.

"All right. No answer required." He handed her twenty cents, and she sprinted away.

The Gathering Hall occupied one entire side of Harken Square, which was the city's central plaza. The square was paved with stone. It had a few benches bolted to the ground here and there, as well as a couple of kiosks for notices. Wide steps led up to the Gathering Hall, and fat columns framed its big door. The mayor's office was in the Gathering Hall. So were the offices of the clerks who kept track of which buildings had broken windows, what streetlamps needed repair, and the number of people in the city. There was the office of the timekeeper, who was in charge of the town clock. And there were offices for the guards who enforced the laws of Ember, now and then putting pickpockets or people who got in fights into the Prison Room, a small one-story structure with a sloping roof that jutted out from one side of the building.

Lina ran up the steps and through the door into a broad hallway. On the left was a desk, and at the desk sat a guard: "Barton Snode, Assistant Guard," said a badge on his chest. He was a big man, with wide shoulders, brawny arms, and a thick neck. But his head looked as if it didn't belong to his body—it was small and round and topped with a fuzz of extremely short hair. His lower jaw jutted out and moved a little from side to side, as if he were chewing on something.

When he saw Lina, his jaw stopped moving for a moment and his lips curled upward in a very small smile. "Good day," he said. "What business brings you here today?"

"I have a message for the mayor."

"Very good, very good." Barton Snode heaved himself to his feet. "Step this way."

He led Lina down the corridor and opened a door marked "Reception Room."

"Wait here, please," he said. "The mayor is in his basement office on private business, but he will be up shortly."

Lina went inside.

"I'll notify the mayor," said Barton Snode. "Please have a seat. The mayor will be right with you. Or pretty soon." He left, closing the door behind him. A second later, the door opened again, and the guard's small fuzzy head re-appeared. "What *is* the message?" he asked.

"I have to give it to the mayor in person," said Lina.

"Of course, of course," said the guard. The door closed again. He doesn't seem very sure about things, Lina thought. Maybe he's new at his job.

The Reception Room was shabby, but Lina could tell that it had once been impressive. The walls were dark red, with brownish patches where the paint was peeling away. In the right-hand wall was a closed door. An ugly brown carpet lay on the floor, and on it stood a large armchair covered in itchy-looking red material, and several smaller chairs. A small table held a teapot and some cups, and a larger table in the middle of the room displayed a copy of *The Book of the City of*

Ember, lying open as if someone were going to read from it. Portraits of all the mayors of the city since the beginning of time hung on the walls, staring solemnly from behind pieces of old window glass.

Lina sat in the big armchair and waited. No one came. She got up and wandered around the room. She bent over *The Book of the City of Ember* and read a few sentences: "The citizens of Ember may not have luxuries, but the foresight of the Builders, who filled the storerooms at the beginning of time, has ensured that they will always have enough, and enough is all that a person of wisdom needs."

She flipped a few pages. "The Gathering Hall clock," she read, "measures the hours of night and day. It must never be allowed to run down. Without it, how would we know when to go to work and when to go to school? How would the light director know when to turn the lights on and when to turn them off again? It is the job of the timekeeper to wind the clock every week and to place the date sign in Harken Square every day. The timekeeper must perform these duties faithfully."

Lina knew that not all timekeepers were as faithful as they should be. She'd heard of one, some years ago, who often forgot to change the date sign, so that it might say, "Wednesday, Week 38, Year 227" for several days in a row. There had even been timekeepers who forgot to wind the clock, so that it might stand at noon or at midnight for hours at a time, causing a very long day or a very long night. The result was that no one really knew anymore exactly what day of the week it was, or exactly how many years it had been since the building of the city—they called this the year 241, but it might have been 245 or 239 or 250. As long as the clock's deep boom rang out every hour, and the lights went on and off more or less regularly, it didn't seem to matter.

Lina left the book and examined the pictures of the mayors. The seventh mayor, Podd Morethwart, was her great-great—she didn't know how many greats—grandfather. He looked quite dreary, Lina thought. His cheeks were long and hollow, his mouth turned down at the corners, and there was a lost look in his eyes. The picture she liked best was of the fourth mayor, Jane Larket, who had a serene smile and fuzzy black hair.

Still no one came. She heard no sounds from the hallway. Maybe they'd forgotten her.

Lina went over to the closed door in the right-hand wall. She pulled it open and saw stairs going up. Maybe, while she waited, she'd just see where they went. She started upward. At the top of the first flight was a closed door. Carefully, she opened it. She saw another hallway and more closed doors. She shut the door and kept going. Her footsteps sounded loud on the wood, and she was afraid someone would hear her and come and scold her. No doubt she was not supposed to be here. But no one came, and she climbed on, passing another closed door.

The Gathering Hall was the only building in Ember with three stories. She had always wanted to stand on its roof and look out at the city. Maybe from there it would be possible to see beyond the city, into the Unknown Regions. If the bright city of her drawings really did exist, it would be out there somewhere.

At the top of the stairs, she came to a door marked "Roof," and she pushed it open. Chilly air brushed against her skin. She was outside. Ahead of her was a flat gravel surface, and about ten paces away she could see the high wall of the clock tower.

She went to the edge of the roof. From there she could see the whole of Ember. Directly below was Harken Square, where people were moving this way and that, all of them appearing, from this top-down view, more round than tall. Beyond Harken Square, the lighted windows of the buildings made checkered lines, yellow and black, row after row, in all directions. She tried to see farther, across the Unknown Regions, but she couldn't. At the edges of the city, the lights were so far away that they made a kind of haze. She could see nothing beyond them but blackness.

She heard a shout from the square below. "Look!" came a small but piercing voice. "Someone on the roof!" She saw a few people stop and look up. "Who is it? What's she doing up there?" someone cried. More people gathered, until a crowd was standing on the steps of the Gathering Hall. They see me! Lina thought, and it made her laugh. She waved at the crowd and did a few steps from the Bugfoot Scurry Dance, which she'd learned on Cloving Square Dance Day, and they laughed and shouted some more.

Then the door behind her burst open, and a huge guard with a bushy black beard was suddenly running toward her. "Halt!" he shouted, though she wasn't going anywhere. He grabbed her by the arm. "What are you doing here?"

"I was just curious," said Lina, in her most innocent voice. "I wanted to see the city from the roof." She read the guard's name badge. It said, "Redge Stabmark, Chief Guard."

"Curiosity leads to trouble," said Redge Stabmark. He peered down at the crowd. "You have caused a commotion." He pulled her toward the door and hustled her down all three flights of stairs. When they came out into the waiting room, Barton Snode was standing there looking flustered, his jaw twitching from side to side. Next to him was the mayor.

"A child causing trouble, Mayor Cole," said the chief guard.

The mayor glared at her. "I recall your face. From Assignment Day. Shame! Disgracing yourself in your new job."

"I didn't mean to cause trouble," said Lina. "I was

looking for you so I could deliver a message."

"Shall we put her in the Prison Room for a day or two?" asked the chief guard.

The mayor frowned. He pondered a moment. "What is the message?" he said. He bent down so that Lina could speak into his ear. She noticed that he smelled a little like overcooked turnips.

"Delivery at eight," Lina whispered. "From Looper."

The mayor smiled a tight little smile. He turned to the guard. "Just a child's antics," he said. "We will let it go this time. From now on," he said to Lina, "behave yourself."

"Yes, Mr. Mayor," said Lina.

"And you," said the mayor, turning to the assistant guard and shaking a thick finger at him, "watch visitors much . . . more . . . carefully."

Barton Snode blinked and nodded.

Lina ran for the door. Outside, the small crowd was still standing by the steps. A few of them cheered as Lina came out. Others frowned at her and muttered words like "mischief" and "silliness" and "show-off." Lina felt embarrassed suddenly. She hadn't meant to show off. She hurried past, out into Otterwill Street, and started to run.

She didn't see Doon, who was among those watching her. He had been on his way home from his first day in the Pipeworks when he'd come across the cluster of people gazing up at the roof of the Gathering Hall and laughing. He was tired and chilly. The bottoms of his pants legs were wet, and mud clung to his shoes and smeared his hands. When he raised his eyes and saw the small figure next to the clock tower, he realized right away that it was Lina. He saw her raise her arm and wave and hop about, and for a second he wondered what it would be like to be up there, looking out over the whole city, laughing and waving. When Lina came down, he wanted to speak to her. But he knew he was filthy-looking and that she would ask him questions he didn't want to answer. So he turned away. Walking fast, he headed for home.

CHAPTER 3

Under Ember

That morning, Doon had arrived at the Pipeworks full of anticipation. This was the world of serious work at last, where he would get a chance to do something useful. What he'd learned in school, and from his father, and from his own investigations—he could put it all to good purpose now.

He pushed open the heavy Pipeworks door and stepped inside. The air smelled strongly of dampness and moldy rubber, which seemed to him a pleasant, interesting smell. He strode up a hallway where yellow slickers hung from pegs on the walls. At the end of the hallway was a room full of people, some of them sitting on benches and pulling on knee-high rubber boots, some struggling into their slickers, some buckling on tool belts. A raucous clamor filled the room. Doon watched from the doorway, eager to join in but not sure what to do.

After a moment a man emerged from the throng. He thrust out a hand. "Lister Munk, Pipeworks director," he said. "You're the new boy, right? What size feet do you have—large, medium, or small?"

"Medium," said Doon, and Lister found him a slicker and a pair of boots. The boots were so ancient that their green rubber was cracked all over, as if covered with spiderwebs. He gave Doon a tool belt, too, in which were wrenches and hammers, spools of wire and tape, and tubes of some sort of black goop.

"You'll be in Tunnel 97 today," Lister said. "Arlin Froll will go down with you and show you what to do." He pointed at a short, delicate-looking girl with a white-blond braid down her back. "She may not look like an expert, but she is."

Doon buckled his tool belt around his waist and put on his slicker, which, for some reason, smelled like sweaty feet. "This way," said Arlin, without saying hello or smiling. She wove through the crowd of workers to a door marked "Stairway" and opened it.

Stone steps led so far down that Doon couldn't see the end of them. On either side was a sheer wall of dark reddish stone, glistening with dampness. There was no railing. Along the ceiling ran a single wire from which a light bulb hung every few yards. Water stood in shallow pools on each stair, in the hollow worn into the stones by years of footsteps.

They started down. Doon concentrated on his

feet—the clumsy boots made it hard not to stumble. As they went deeper, he began to hear a low roar, so low he seemed to hear it more with his stomach than his ears. It grew louder and louder—was it a machine of some kind? Maybe the generator?

The stairway came to an end at a door marked "Main Tunnel." Arlin opened it, and as they stepped through, Doon realized that the sound he had been hearing wasn't a machine. It was the river.

He stood still, staring. Like most people, he had never been really sure what a river was—just that it was water that somehow flowed on its own. He'd imagined it would be like the clear, narrow stream that came out of the kitchen faucet, only bigger, and horizontal instead of vertical. But this was something entirely different—not a stream of water, but endless tons of it pouring by. Wide as the widest street in Ember, churning and dipping and swirling, the river roared past, its turbulent surface like black, liquid glass scattered with flecks of light. Doon had never seen anything that moved so fast, and he had never heard such a thunderous, heart-stopping roar.

The path they stood on was about six feet wide and ran parallel to the river for farther than Doon could see in both directions. In the wall along the path were openings that must lead, Doon thought, to the tunnels that branched everywhere below the city. A string of lights like the one in the stairway hung high up against the arched ceiling.

Doon knew he was standing beneath the north edge of Ember. In school, you were taught to remember the directions this way: north was the direction of the river; south was the direction of the greenhouses; east was the direction of the school; and west was the direction left over, having nothing in particular to mark it. All the Pipeworks tunnels branched off from the main tunnel to the south, toward the city.

Arlin leaned toward Doon and shouted into his ear. "First we'll go to the beginning of the river," she said. She led him up the main tunnel for a long way. They passed other people in yellow slickers, who greeted Arlin with a nod and glanced curiously at Doon. After fifteen minutes or so, they came to the east edge of the Pipeworks, where the river surged up from a deep chasm in the ground, churning so violently that its dark water turned white and filled the air with a spray that wet Doon's face.

In the wall to their right was a wide double door. "See that door right there?" Arlin shouted, pointing.

"Yes," Doon shouted back.

"That's the generator room."

"Can we go in?"

"Of course not!" said Arlin. "You have to have special permission." She pointed back down the main tunnel. "Now we'll go to the end of the river," she said.

She led him back, past the stairway door, all the way to the west edge of the Pipeworks. There the river flowed into a huge opening in the wall and vanished into darkness.

"Where does it go?" Doon asked.

Arlin just shrugged. "Back into the ground, I guess. Now let's find Tunnel 97 and get to work." She pulled a folded piece of paper from her pocket. "This is the map," she said. "You have one in your pocket, too. You have to use the map to find your way around in here." The map looked to Doon like an immense centipede—the river arched across the top of the page like the centipede's body, and the tunnels dangled down from it like hundreds of long, long legs all tangled up with each other.

To get to Tunnel 97, they followed a complicated route through passageways lined with crusty, rusted pipes that carried water to all the buildings of Ember. Puddles stood on the floor of the tunnel, and water dripped in brown rivulets down the walls. Just as in the main tunnel, there was a string of bulbs along the ceiling that provided dim light. Doon occupied his mind by calculating how far underground he was. From the river to the ceiling of the main tunnel must be thirty feet or so, he thought. Above that were the storerooms, which occupied a layer at least twenty feet high. So that meant he was fifty feet underground, with tons of earth and rock and buildings above him. The thought made him tense up his shoulders. He cast a quick glance upward, as if all that weight might collapse onto his head.

"Here we are," said Arlin. She was standing next to a leak that spurted a stream of water straight out from the wall. "We have to turn the shut-off valve, take the pipe apart, put on a new connector, and stick it back together again."

With wrenches, hammers, washers, and black goop, they did this, getting soaked in the process. It took them most of the morning and proved to Doon that the city was in even worse shape than he'd suspected. Not only were the lights about to fail and the supplies about to run out, but the water system was breaking down. The whole city was crumbling, and what was anyone doing about it?

When the lunch break came, Arlin took her lunch sack from a pocket in her tool belt and went off to meet some friends a few tunnels away. "You stay right here and wait until I get back," she said as she left. "If you wander around, you'll get lost."

But Doon set out as soon as she disappeared. Using his map, he found his way back to the main tunnel, then hurried to the east end. He wasn't going to wait for special permission to see the generator. He was pretty sure he could find a way to get in on his own, and he did. He simply stood by the door and waited for someone to come out. Quite soon, a stout woman carrying a lunch sack pushed open the door and walked away. She didn't notice him. Before the door could close again, Doon slipped inside.

Such a horrendous noise met him that he staggered backward a few steps. It was an earsplitting, growling, grinding, screaming noise, shot through with a hoarse *rackety-rackety* sound and underscored with a deep *chugga-chugga-chugga.* Doon clapped his hands over his ears and stepped forward. In front of him was a gigantic black machine, two stories high. It was vibrating so hard it looked as if it might explode any second. Several people wearing earmuffs were busy around it. None of them noticed him come in.

He tapped one of them on the shoulder, and the person jumped and whirled around. He was an old man, Doon saw, with a deeply lined brown face.

"I want to learn about the generator!" Doon screamed, but he might as well have saved his breath. No one could be heard in the uproar. The old man glared at him, made a shooing motion with his hand, and turned back to work.

Doon stood and watched for a while. Beside the huge machine were ladders on wheels that the workers pushed back and forth and climbed up on to reach the high parts. All over the room, greasy-looking cans and tools littered the floor. Against the walls stood big bins holding every kind of bolt and screw and gear and lever and rod and tube, all of them black with age and jumbled together. The workers scurried between the bins and the generator or simply stood and watched the thing shake.

After a few minutes, Doon left. He was horrified. All his life he had studied how things worked—it was one of his favorite things to do. He could take apart an old watch and put it back together exactly as it had been. He understood how the faucets in the sink worked. He'd fixed the toilet many times. He'd made a wheeled cart out of the parts of an old armchair. He even had a hazy idea of what was going on in the refrigerator. He was proud of his mechanical talent. There was only one thing he didn't understand at all, and that was electricity. What was the power that ran through the wires and into the light bulbs? Where did it come from? He had thought that if he could just get a look at the generator, he would have the clue he needed. From there, he could begin to work on a solution that would keep the lights of Ember burning.

But one glimpse of the generator showed him how foolish he was. He'd expected to see something whose workings he could understand—a wheel turning, a spark being struck, some wires that led from one point to another. But this monstrous roaring thing—he wondered if *anyone* understood how it worked. It looked as if all they were doing was trying to keep it from flying apart.

As it turned out, he was right. When the day was over and he was upstairs taking off his boots and slicker, he saw the old man from the generator room and went to talk to him. "Can you explain to me about the generator?" he asked. "Can you tell me how it works?"

The old man just sighed. "All I know is, the river makes it go."

"But how?"

The man shrugged. "Who knows? Our job is just to keep it from breaking down. If a part breaks, we got to put on a new one. If a part freezes up, we got to oil it." He wiped his hand wearily across his forehead, leaving a streak of black grease. "I been working on the generator for twenty years. It's always managed to chug along, but this year . . . I don't know. The thing seems to break down every couple minutes." He cracked a wry smile. "Of course, I hear we might run out of light bulbs before that, and then it won't matter if the generator works or not."

Running out of light bulbs, running out of power, running out of time—disaster was right around the corner. That's what Doon was thinking about when he stopped outside the Gathering Hall on his way home and saw Lina on the roof. She looked so free and happy up there. He didn't know why she was on the roof, but he wasn't surprised. It was the kind of thing she did, turning up in unexpected places, and now that she was a messenger, she could go just about anywhere. But how could she be so lighthearted when everything was falling apart?

He headed for home. He lived with his father in a two-bedroom apartment over his father's shop in Greengate Square—the Small Items shop, which sold things like nails, pins, tacks, clips, springs, jar lids, doorknobs, bits of wire, shards of glass, chunks of wood, and other small things that might be useful in some way. The Small Items shop had overflowed somewhat into their apartment above. In their front room, where other people might display a nice teapot on a tabletop or a few attractive squashes or tomatoes on a shelf, they had buckets and boxes and baskets full of spare items for the shop, things Doon's father had collected but not yet organized for selling. Often these items spilled over onto the floor. It was easy to trip over things in this apartment, and not a good idea to go barefoot.

Today Doon didn't stop in at the shop to see his father before going upstairs. He wasn't in the mood for conversation. He removed two buckets of stuff from the couch—it looked like mostly shoe heels—and flopped down on the cushions. He'd been stupid to think he could understand the generator just by looking at it, when other people had been working on it their entire lives. The thing was, he had to admit, he'd always thought he was smarter than other people. He'd been sure he could learn about electricity and help save the city. He wanted to be the one to do it. He had imagined many times a ceremony in Harken Square, organized to thank him for saving Ember, with the entire population in attendance and his father beaming from the front row. All Doon's life, his father had been saying to him, "You're a good boy and a smart boy. You'll do grand things someday, I know you will." But Doon hadn't done much that was grand so far. He ached to do something truly important, like finding the secret of electricity, and, as his father watched, be rewarded for his achievement. The size of the reward didn't matter. A small certificate would do, or maybe a badge to sew on his jacket.

Now he was stuck in the muck of the Pipeworks, patching up pipes that would leak and break again in a matter of days. It was even more useless and boring than being a messenger. The thought made him suddenly furious. He sat up, grabbed a shoe heel out of the bucket at his feet, and hurled it with all his might. It arrived at the front door just as the door opened. Doon heard a hard *thwack* and a loud "Ouch!" at the same moment. Then he saw the long, lean, tired-looking face of his father in the doorway.

Doon's anger drained away. "Oh, I hit you, Father. I'm sorry."

Doon's father rubbed the side of his head. He was a tall man, bald as a peeled potato, with a high forehead and a long chin. He had kind, slightly puzzled gray eyes.

"Got me in the ear," he said. "What *was* that?"

"I got angry for a second," said Doon. "I threw one of these old heels."

"I see," said his father. He brushed some bottle tops off a chair and sat down. "Does it have to do with your first day at work, son?"

"Yes," said Doon.

His father nodded. "Why don't you tell me about it," he said.

Doon told him. When he was finished, his father ran a hand across his bald head as if smoothing down the hair that wasn't there. He sighed. "Well," he said, "it sounds unpleasant, I have to admit. About the generator, especially—that's bad news. But the Pipeworks is your assignment, no way around it. What you get is what you get. What you *do* with what you get, though . . . that's more the point, wouldn't you say?" He looked at Doon and smiled, a bit sadly.

"I guess so," Doon said. "But what can I do?"

"I don't know," said his father. "You'll think of something. You're a clever boy. The main thing is to pay attention. Pay close attention to everything, notice what no one else notices. Then you'll know what no one else knows, and that's always useful." He took off his coat and hung it from a peg on the wall. "How's the worm?" he asked.

"I haven't looked at it yet," said Doon. He went into his room and came out with a small wooden box covered with an old scarf. He set the box on the table and took the scarf off, and he and his father both bent over to look inside.

A couple of limp cabbage leaves lay on the bottom of the box. On one of the leaves was a worm about an inch long. A few days before school ended, Doon had found the worm on the underside of a cabbage leaf he was slicing up for dinner. It was a pale soft green, velvety smooth all over, with tiny, stubby legs.

Doon had always been fascinated by bugs. He wrote down his observations about them in a book he had titled *Crawling and Flying Things.* Each page of the book was divided lengthwise down the center. On the left he drew his pictures, with a pencil sharpened to a needle-like point: moth wings with their branching patterns of veins; spider legs, which had minute hairs and tiny feet like claws; beetles, with their feelers and their glossy armor. On the right, he wrote what he observed about each creature. He noted what it ate, where it slept, where it laid its eggs, and—if he knew—how long it lived.

This was difficult with fast-moving creatures like moths and spiders. To learn anything about them, he had to catch what glimpses he could as they lived their lives out in the open. If he put them in a box, they scrambled around for a few days and then died.

This worm, though, was different. It seemed perfectly happy to live in the box Doon had made for it. So far, it did only three things: eat, sleep (it looked like sleeping, though Doon couldn't tell if the worm closed its eyes—or even if it had eyes), and expel tiny black poop balls. That was it.

"I've had it for five days now," said Doon. "It's twice as big as it was when I got it. It's eaten two square inches of cabbage leaf."

"You're writing all this down?"

Doon nodded.

"Maybe," said his father, "you'll find some interesting new bugs in the Pipeworks."

"Maybe," said Doon. But to himself he said, No, that's not enough. I can't go plodding around the Pipeworks, stopping up leaks, looking for bugs, and pretending there's no emergency. I have to find something important down there, something that's going to help. I have to. I just *have* to.

CHAPTER 4

Something Lost, Nothing Found

One day when Lina had been a messenger for several weeks, she came home to find that Granny had thrown all the cushions from the couch onto the floor, ripped up a corner of the couch's lining, and was pulling out wads of stuffing.

"What are you doing?" Lina cried.

Granny looked up. Wisps of sofa stuffing stuck to the front of her dress and clung to her hair. "Something is lost," she said. "I think it might be in here."

"What's lost, Granny?"

"I don't quite recall," said the old woman. "Something important."

"But Granny, you're ruining the couch. What will we sit on?"

Granny tore a bit more of the covering off the couch and yanked out another puff of stuffing. "It doesn't matter," she said. "I'll put it back together later."

"Let's put it back now," Lina said. "I don't think what's lost is in there."

"You don't know," said Granny darkly. But she sat back on her heels, looking tired.

Lina began cleaning up the mess. "Where's the baby?" she asked.

Granny gazed at Lina blankly. "The baby?"

"You haven't forgotten the baby?"

"Oh, yes. She's . . . I think she's down in the shop."

"By herself?" Lina stood up and ran down the stairs. She found Poppy sitting on the floor of the shop, enmeshed in a tangle of yellow yarn. As soon as she saw Lina, Poppy began to howl.

Lina picked her up and unwound the yarn, talking soothingly, though she was so upset that her fingers trembled. For Granny to forget the baby was dangerous. Poppy could fall downstairs and hurt herself. She could wander out into the street and get lost. Granny had been forgetful lately, but this was the first time she'd completely forgotten about Poppy.

When they got upstairs, Granny was kneeling on the floor gathering up the white tufts of stuffing and jamming them back into the hole she'd made in the couch. "It wasn't in there," she said sadly.

"*What* wasn't?"

"It was lost a long time ago," said Granny. "My father told me about it."

Lina sighed impatiently. More and more, her grandmother's mind seemed caught in the past. She could explain the rules of pebblejacks, which she'd last played when she was eight, or tell you what happened at the Singing when she was twelve, or who she'd danced with at the Cloving Square Dance when she was sixteen, but she would forget what had happened the day before yesterday.

"They heard him talking about it when he died," she said to Lina.

"They heard who talking?"

"My grandfather. The seventh mayor."

"And what did they hear him say?"

"Ah," said her grandmother with a faraway look. "That's the mystery. He said he couldn't get at it. 'Now it is lost,' he said."

"But what *was* it?"

"He didn't say."

Lina gave up. It didn't matter anyway. Probably the lost thing was the old man's left sock, or his hairbrush. But for some reason, the story had taken root in Granny's mind.

The next morning on her way to work, Lina stopped in at the house of their neighbor, Evaleen Murdo. Mrs. Murdo was brisk in her manner, and in her person thin and straight as a nail, but she was kind in her unsmiling way. Until a few years ago, she'd run a shop that sold paper and pencils. But when paper and pencils became scarce, her shop closed. Now she spent her days sitting by her upstairs window, watching people in the street with her sharp eyes. Lina told Mrs. Murdo about her grandmother's forgetfulness. "Will you look in on her sometimes and make sure things are all right?" she asked.

"I will, certainly," said Mrs. Murdo, nodding twice, firmly. Lina went away feeling better.

That day Lina was given a message by Arbin Swinn, who ran the Callay Street Vegetable Market, to be delivered to Lina's friend Clary, the greenhouse manager. Lina was glad to carry this message, though her gladness was mixed a little with sadness. Her father had worked in the greenhouses. It still felt strange not to see him there.

The five greenhouses produced all of Ember's fresh food. They were out past Greengate Square, at the farthest edge of the city. Nothing else was out there but the trash heaps, great moldering, stinking hills that stood on rocky ground and were lit by a few floodlights high up on poles.

It used to be that no one went to the trash heaps but the trash collectors, who dumped the trash and left it. Now and then a couple of children might go there to play, scrambling up the side of the heaps and tumbling down. Lina and Lizzie used to go when they were younger. They'd pull out the occasional treasure—some empty cans, maybe an old hat or a cracked plate. But not anymore. Now there were guards posted at the trash heaps to make sure no one poked around. Just recently, an official job called trash sifter had been created. Every day a team of people methodically sorted through the trash heaps in search of anything that might be at all useful. They'd come back with broken chair legs that could be used for repairing window frames, bent nails that could become hooks for clothes, even filthy rags, stiff with dirt, that could be washed out and used to patch holes in window blinds or mattress covers. Lina hadn't thought about it before, but now she wondered about the trash sifters. Were they there because Ember really was running out of everything?

Beyond the trash heaps there was nothing at all—that is, only the vast Unknown Regions, where the darkness was absolute.

From the end of Diggery Street, Lina could see the long, low greenhouses. They looked like big tin cans that had been cut in half and laid on their sides. Her breath came a little faster. The greenhouses were a home to her, in a way.

She knew that she was most likely to find Clary somewhere around Greenhouse 1, where the office was, so that was where she headed first. A small toolshed stood beside the door to Greenhouse 1; Lina peeked into it but saw only rakes and shovels. So she opened the greenhouse door. Warm, furry-smelling air washed over her, and all her love for this place came rushing back. Out of habit, she gazed up toward the ceiling, as if she might see her father there on his ladder, tinkering with the sprinkler system, the temperature gauges, and the lights.

The greenhouse light was whiter than the yellowish light of the Ember streetlamps. It came from long tubes that ran the length of the ceiling. In this light, the leaves of the plants shone so green they almost hurt Lina's eyes. On the days when she'd come here with her father, Lina had spent hours wandering along the gravel paths that ran between the vegetable beds, sniffing the leaves, poking her fingers into the dirt, and learning to tell the plants apart by their look and smell. There were the beans and peas with their curly tendrils, the dark green spinach, the ruffled lettuce, and the hard, pale green cabbages, some of them as big as a newborn baby's head. What she loved best was to rub the leaves of the tomato plant between her fingers and breathe in their pungent, powdery smell.

A long, straight path led from one end of the building to the other. About halfway down the path, Clary was crouching by a bed of carrots. Lina ran toward her, and Clary smiled, brushed the dirt from her hands, and stood up.

Clary was tall and solid, with big hands and knobby knuckles. She had a square jaw and square shoulders, and brown hair cut in a short, squarish way. You might have thought from looking at her that she was a gruff, unfriendly person—but her nature was just the opposite. She was more comfortable with plants than with people, Lina's father had always said. She was strong but shy, a person of much knowledge but few words. Lina had always liked her. Even when she was little, Clary did not treat her like a baby but gave her jobs to do—pulling up carrots, picking bugs off cabbages. Since her parents had died, Lina had come many times to talk to Clary, or just to work silently beside her. Clary was always kind to her, and working with the plants took Lina's mind off her grief.

"Well," said Clary. She smiled at Lina, wiped her hands on her already grimy pants, and smiled some more. Finally she said, "You're a messenger."

"Yes," said Lina, "and I have a message for you. It's from Arbin Swinn. 'Please add four extra crates to my order, two of potatoes and two of cabbages.'"

Clary frowned. "I can't do that," she said. "At least, I can send him the cabbages, but only one small crate of potatoes."

"Why?" asked Lina.

"Well, we have a sort of problem with the potatoes."

"What is it?" asked Lina. Clary had a habit of answering questions in the briefest possible way. You had to keep asking and asking before she would believe you really wanted to know and weren't just being polite. Then she would explain, and you could see how much she knew, and how much she loved her work.

"I'll show you," she said. She led the way to a bed where the green leaves were spotted with black. "A new disease. I haven't seen it before. When you dig up the potatoes, they're runny inside instead of hard, and they stink. I'm going to have to throw out all the ones in this bed. There are only a few beds left that aren't infected."

Most people in Ember had potatoes at every meal—mashed, boiled, stewed, roasted. They'd had fried potatoes, too, in the days before the cooking oil ran out.

"I'd hate it if we couldn't have potatoes anymore," Lina said.

"I would, too," said Clary.

They sat on the edge of the potato bed and talked for a while, about Lina's grandmother and the baby, about the trouble Clary was having with the beehives, and about the greenhouse sprinkler system. "It hasn't worked right since . . ." Clary hesitated and glanced sideways at Lina. "For a long time," she said. She didn't want to say "since your father died." Lina understood that.

She stood up. "I should go," she said. "I have to

take Arbin Swinn the answer to his message."

"I hope you'll come again," said Clary. "You can come whenever . . . you can come any time." Lina said thank you and turned to go.

But just outside the greenhouse door, she heard running footsteps and a strange, high, sobbing sound. Or rather, she heard sobs and then a wail, sobs and then a shout, and then more sobs, getting louder. She looked back toward the rear of the greenhouses, toward the trash heaps. "Clary," she called. "There's something . . ."

Clary came out and listened, too.

"Do you hear it?"

"Yes," said Clary. She frowned. "I'm afraid it's . . . it's someone who . . ." She peered toward the crying noise. "Yes . . . here he comes." Her strong hand gripped Lina's shoulder for a moment. "You'd better go," she said. "I'll take care of this."

"But what is it?"

"Never mind. Just go on."

But Lina wanted to see. Once Clary had walked away, she ducked behind the toolshed. From there she watched.

The noise came closer. Out beyond the trash heaps, a figure appeared. It was a man, running and stumbling, his arms flopping. He looked as if he was about to fall over, as if he could hardly pick up his feet. In fact, as he came closer he *did* fall. He tripped over a hose and crumpled to the ground as if his bones had dissolved.

Clary stooped down and said something to him in a voice too low for Lina to hear.

The man was panting. When he turned over and sat up, Lina saw that his face was scratched and his eyes wide open in fright. His sobs had turned into hiccups. She recognized him. It was Sadge Merrall, one of the clerks in the Supply Depot. He was a quiet, long-faced man who always looked worried.

Clary helped him to his feet. The two of them came slowly toward the greenhouse, and as they got closer Lina could hear what the man was saying. He spoke very fast in a weak, trembly voice, hardly stopping for breath. ". . . was sure I could do it. I said to myself, Just one step after another, that's all, one step after another. I knew it would be dark. Who doesn't know that? But I thought, Well, dark can't hurt you. I'll just keep going, I thought. . . ."

He stumbled and sagged against Clary. "Careful," Clary said. They reached the door of the greenhouse, and Clary struggled to open it. Without thinking, Lina darted out from behind the toolshed and opened it for her. Clary shot her a quick frown but said nothing.

Sadge didn't stop talking. ". . . But then the farther I went the darker it was, and you can't just keep walking into black dark, can you? It's like a wall in front of you. I kept turning around to look at the lights of the city, because that's all there was to see, and then I'd say to myself, Don't look back, keep moving. But I kept tripping and falling. . . . The ground is rough out there, I scraped my hands." He held up one hand and stared at the red scratches on it, which oozed drops of blood.

They got him into Clary's office and sat him down in her chair. He rambled on.

"Be brave, I said to myself. I kept going and going, but then all of a sudden I thought, Anything could be out here! There could be a pit a thousand feet deep right in front of me. There could be . . . something that bites. I've heard stories . . . rats as big as garbage bins . . . And I had to get out of there. So I turned around and I ran."

"Never mind," said Clary. "You're all right now. Lina, get him some water."

Lina found a cup and filled it from the sink in the corner. Sadge took it with a shaking hand and drank it down.

"What were you looking for?" Lina asked. She knew what *she* would have been looking for if she'd gone out there. She'd thought about it countless times.

Sadge stared at her. He seemed to have to puzzle over her question. Finally he said, "I was looking for something that could help us."

"What would it be?"

"I don't know. Like a stairway that leads somewhere, maybe. Or a building full of . . . I don't know, useful things."

"But you didn't find anything? Or see anything?" Lina asked, disappointed.

"Nothing! Nothing! There is nothing out there!" His voice became a shout and his eyes looked wild again. "Or if there is, we can never get to it. Never! Not without a light." He took a long, shaky breath. For a while he stared at the floor. Then he stood up. "I think I'm all right now. I'll be going."

With uncertain steps, he went down the path and out the door.

"Well," said Clary. "I'm sorry that happened while you were here. I was afraid you might be scared, that's why I told you to go."

But Lina was full of questions, not fear. She had heard tales of people who tried to go out into the Unknown Regions. She had thought about it herself—in fact, she'd wondered the same things as Sadge. She had imagined making her way out into the dark and coming to a wall in which she would find the door to a tunnel, and at the end of the tunnel would be the other city, the city of light that she had dreamed about. All it would take was the courage to walk away from Ember and into the darkness, and then to keep going.

It might have been possible if you could carry a light to show the way. But in Ember, there was no such thing as a light you could carry with you. Outside lights were fixed to their poles, or to the roofs of houses; inside lights were set into the ceiling or had cords that had to be plugged in. Over the course of Ember's history, various clever people had tried to invent a movable light, but all of them had failed. One man had managed to ignite the end of a stick of wood by holding it against the electric burner on his stove. He'd run across the city with the flaming stick, planning to use it to light his journey. But by the time he got to the trash heaps, his torch had gone out. Other people latched on to his idea—one woman who lived on Dedlock Street, very near the edge of the city, managed to get into the Unknown Regions with her flaming stick. But the stick burned quickly, and before she could go far, the flame singed her hands and she threw it down. Everyone who had tried to penetrate the Unknown Regions had come back within a few hours, their enterprise a failure.

Lina and Clary stood by the open door of the greenhouse and watched Sadge shuffle toward the city. As he neared the trash heaps, two guards who had been sitting on the ground got to their feet. They walked over to Sadge, and each of them took hold of one of his arms.

"Uh-oh," said Clary. "Those guards are always looking for trouble."

"But Sadge hasn't broken any law," said Lina.

"Doesn't matter. They need something to do. They'll get some fun out of scaring him." One of the guards was shaking his finger at Sadge and saying something in a voice almost loud enough for Lina to hear. "Poor man," said Clary with a sigh. "He's the fourth one this year."

The guards were marching Sadge away now, one on either side of him. Sadge looked limp and small between them.

"What do you think is out in the Unknown Regions, Clary?"

Clary stared down at the ground, where the light from the greenhouse was casting long, thin shadows of them both. "I don't know. Nothing, I guess."

"And do you think Ember is the only light in the dark world?"

Clary sighed. "I don't know," she said. She gave Lina a long look. Her eyes, Lina thought, looked a little sad. They were a deep brown, almost the color of the earth in the garden bed.

Clary put a hand in her pocket and drew something out. "Look," she said. In the palm of her hand was a white bean. "Something in this seed knows how to make a bean plant. How does it know that?"

"I don't know," said Lina, staring at the hard, flat bean.

"It knows because it has life in it," said Clary. "But where does life come from? What *is* life?"

Lina could see that words were welling up in Clary now; her eyes were bright, her cheeks were rosy.

"Take a lamp, for instance. When you plug it in, it comes alive, in a way. It lights up. That's because it's connected to a wire that's connected to the generator, which is making electricity, though don't ask me how. But a bean seed isn't connected to anything. Neither are people. We don't have plugs and wires that connect us to generators. What makes living things go is *inside* them somehow." Her dark eyebrows drew together over her eyes. "What I mean is," she said finally, "something is going on that we don't understand. They say the Builders made the city. But who made the Builders? Who made *us*? I think the answer must be somewhere outside of Ember."

"In the Unknown Regions?"

"Maybe. Maybe not. I don't know." She brushed her hands together in a time-to-get-back-to-work way.

"Clary," said Lina quickly, "here's what I think." Her heart sped up. She hadn't told this to anyone before. "In my mind, I see another city." Lina watched to see if Clary was going to laugh at her, or smile in that overly kind way. She didn't, so Lina went on. "It isn't like Ember; it's white and gleaming. The buildings are tall and sort of sparkle. Everything is bright, not just inside the buildings but all around them, too, even up in the sky. I know it's just my imagination, but it feels real. I think it *is* real."

Clary said, "Hmmm," and then she said, "Where would such a city be?"

"That's what I don't know. Or how to get to it. I keep thinking there's a door somewhere, maybe out in the Unknown Regions—a door that leads out of Ember, and then behind the door a road."

Clary just shrugged her shoulders. "I don't know," she said. "I have to get back to work. But here—take this." She handed Lina the bean seed, took a little pot from a shelf, scooped some dirt into it, and handed the pot to Lina, too. "Stick the bean in here and water it every day," she said. "It looks like nothing, like a little white stone, but inside it there's life. That must be a sort of clue, don't you think? If we could just figure it out."

Lina took the seed and the pot. "Thank you," she said. She wanted to give Clary a hug but didn't, in case it would embarrass her. Instead, she just said goodbye and raced back toward the city.

CHAPTER 5

On Night Street

Granny's mind was getting more and more muddled. Lina would come home in the evenings and find her rifling through the kitchen cupboards, surrounded by cans and jars with their lids off, or tearing the covers off her bed and trying to lift up the mattress with her skinny arms. "It was an important thing," she would say, "the thing that was lost."

"But if you don't know what it was," said Lina, "how will you know when you've found it?"

Granny didn't try to answer this question. She just flapped her hands at Lina and said, "Never mind, never mind, never mind," and kept on searching.

These days, Mrs. Murdo spent a great deal of time sitting by their window rather than her own. She would tell Granny she was just coming to keep her company. "I don't want her to keep me company,"

Granny complained to Lina, and Lina said, "Maybe she's lonely, Granny. Let her come."

Lina rather liked having Mrs. Murdo around—it was a bit like having a mother there. She wasn't anything like Lina's own mother, who had been a dreamy, absent-minded sort of person. Mrs. Murdo was mother-like in quite a different way. She made sure they all ate a good breakfast in the morning—usually potatoes with mushroom gravy and beet tea. She lined up the vitamin pills by each person's plate and made sure they were swallowed. When Mrs. Murdo was there, shoes got picked up and put away, spills were wiped off the furniture, and Poppy always had on clean clothes. Lina could relax when Mrs. Murdo was around. She knew things were taken care of.

Every week, Lina—like all workers between age twelve and age fifteen—had Thursday off. One Thursday, as she was standing in line at the Garn Square market, hoping to get a bag of turnips for stew that night, she overheard a startling conversation between two people standing behind her.

"What I wanted," said one voice, "was some paint for my front door. It hasn't been painted for years. It's gray and peeling, horrible. I heard a store over on Night Street had some. I was hoping for blue."

"Blue would be nice," said the other voice wistfully.

"But when I got there," the first voice continued, "the man said he had no paint, never had. Disagreeable man. All he had were a few colored pencils."

Colored pencils! Lina had not seen colored pencils in any store for ages. Once she'd had two red ones, a blue one, and a brown one. She'd used these for her drawing until they were stubs too small to hold. Now she had only one plain pencil left, and it was rapidly growing shorter.

She longed to have colored pencils for her pictures of the imaginary city. She had a feeling it was a colorful place, though she didn't know what its colors might be. There were other things, of course, on which her money would be better spent. Granny's only coat was full of holes and coming apart at the seams. But Granny rarely went out, Lina told herself. She was either at home or in her yarn shop. She didn't really need a new coat, did she? Besides, how much could a few pencils cost? She could probably get a coat for Granny *and* some pencils.

So that afternoon she set out for Night Street. She took Poppy with her. Poppy had learned how to ride piggyback—she wrapped her legs around Lina's waist and gripped Lina's throat with her small, strong fingers.

On Budloe Street, people were standing in long lines with their bundles of laundry at the washing stations. The washers stirred the clothes in the washing machines with long poles. In days past, the machines themselves had whirled the clothes around, but not one of them worked anymore.

Lina turned up Hafter Street, where the four streetlamps were still out and a building crew was repairing a partly collapsed roof. Orly Gordon called out to her from high on a ladder, and Lina looked up and waved. Farther on, she passed a woman with bits of rope and string for sale and a man pulling a cart full of carrots and beets to the grocery stores. At the corner, a cluster of little children played catch with a rag ball. The streets were alive with people today. Moving fast, Lina threaded her way among them.

But as she went into Otterwill Street, she saw something that made her slow down. A man was standing on the steps of the Gathering Hall, shouting and howling, and a crowd of people had gathered around him. Lina went closer, and when she saw who it was, her insides gave a lurch. It was Sadge Merrall. His arms flailed wildly, and his eyes were stretched wide open. In a high, rapid voice, he wailed out a stream of words: "I have been to the Unknown Regions!" he cried. "There is nothing, nothing, nothing there! Did you think something out there might save us? Ha! There's only darkness and monsters, darkness and terrible deep holes, darkness forever! The rats are the size of houses! The rocks are sharp as knives! The darkness sucks your breath out! No hope for us out there, oh no! No hope, no hope!" He went on like this for a few minutes and then crumpled to the ground. The people watching him looked at each other and shook their heads.

"Gone mad," Lina heard someone say.

"Yes, completely," said someone else.

Suddenly Sadge sprang up again and resumed his terrible shouting. The crowd stepped back. Some of them hurried away. A few of them approached Sadge, speaking in calming voices. They took him by the arms and led him, still shouting, down the steps.

"Who dat? Who dat?" said Poppy in her small, piercing voice. Lina turned away from the miserable spectacle. "Hush, Poppy," she said. "It's a poor, sad man. He doesn't feel good. We mustn't stare."

She headed toward Night Street, which ran along Greengate Square. There a stringy-haired man sat cross-legged on the ground playing a flute made out of a drainpipe, and five or six Believers circled him, clapping and singing. "Soon, soon, coming soon," they sang. What's coming soon? Lina wondered, but she didn't stop to ask.

Two blocks beyond, she came to a store that had no sign in its window. This must be the one, she thought.

At first it looked closed. Its window was dark. But the door opened when she pushed on it, and a bell attached to its doorknob clanked. From the back room came a black-haired man with big teeth and a long neck. "Yes?" he said.

Lina recognized him. He was the one who'd given her the message for the mayor on her very first day of work. His name was Hooper—no, Looper, that was it.

"Do you have pencils for sale?" she asked. It seemed doubtful. The shop's shelves were empty except for a few stacks of used paper.

Poppy squirmed on Lina's back and whimpered a little.

"Sometimes," said Looper.

Poppy's whimper became a wail.

"All right, you can get down," Lina said to her. She set her on the floor, where she tottered about unsteadily.

"What I'd like to see," said Lina, "are your colored pencils. If you have any."

"We have a few," said Looper. "They are somewhat expensive." He smiled, showing his pushy teeth.

"Could I see them?" said Lina.

He went into the back room and returned a moment later, carrying a small box, which he set down on the counter. He took the lid off. Lina bent forward to look.

Inside the box were at least a dozen colored pencils—red, green, blue, yellow, purple, orange. They had never even been sharpened; their ends were flat. They had erasers. Lina's heart gave a few fast beats.

"How much are they?" she said.

"Probably too much for you," the man said.

"Probably *not,*" said Lina. "I have a job."

"Good, good," the man said, smiling again. "No need to take offense." He picked up the yellow pencil and twirled it between his fingers. "Each pencil," he said, "five dollars."

Five dollars! For seven, you could buy a coat—it would be an old, patched coat, but still warm. "That's too much," Lina said.

He shrugged and began to put the lid back on the box.

"But maybe . . ." Lina's thoughts raced. "Let me look at them again."

Once more the man lifted the lid and Lina bent over the pencils. She picked one up. It was painted a deep clear blue, and on its flat top was the blue dot of the lead. The pink eraser was held on by a shiny metal collar. So beautiful! I could buy just one, Lina thought. Then I could save a little more and buy a coat for Granny *next* month.

"Make up your mind," said the man. "I have other customers who are interested, if you aren't."

"All right. I'll take one. No, wait." It was like hunger, what she felt. It was the same as when her hand sometimes seemed to reach out by itself to grab a piece of food. It was too strong to resist. "I'll take two," she said, and a faint, dazzly feeling came over her at the thought of what she was doing.

"Which two?" the man said.

There were more colors in that box of pencils than in all of Ember. Ember's colors were all so much the same—gray buildings, gray streets, black sky; even the colors of people's clothes were faded from long use into mud green, and rust red, and gray-blue. But these colors—they were as bright as the leaves and flowers in the greenhouse.

Lina's hand hovered over the pencils. "The blue one," she said. "And . . . the yellow one—no, the . . . the . . ."

The man made an impatient noise in the back of his throat.

"The green one," said Lina. "I'll take the blue and the green." She lifted them out of the box. She took the money from the pocket of her coat and handed it to the man, and she put the pencils in her pocket. They were hers now; she felt a fierce, defiant joy. She turned to go, and that was when she saw that the baby was no longer in the store.

"Poppy!" she cried. She whirled around. "Did you see my little sister go out?" she asked the man. "Did you see which way she went?"

He shrugged. "Didn't notice," he said.

Lina darted into the street and looked in both

directions. She saw lots of people, some children, but no Poppy. She stopped an old woman. "Have you seen a little girl, a baby, walking by herself? In a green jacket, with a hood?" The old woman just stared at her with dull eyes and shook her head.

"Poppy!" Lina called. "Poppy!" Her voice rose to a shout. Such a little baby couldn't have gone far, she thought. Maybe down toward Greengate Square, where there were more people walking around. She began to run.

And then the lights flickered, and flickered again, and went out. Darkness slammed up in front of her like a wall. She stumbled, caught herself, and stood still. She could see absolutely nothing.

Shouts of alarm came from up and down the street, and then silence. Lina stretched her arms out. Was she facing the street or a building? Terror swept through her. I must just stand still, she thought. The lights will come on again in a few seconds, they always do. But she thought of Poppy alone in the blackness, and her legs went weak. *I must find her.*

She took a step. When she didn't bump into anything, she took another step, and the fingers of her right hand crumpled against something hard. The wall of a building, she thought. Keeping her hand against it, she turned left a little and took another step forward. Then suddenly her hand touched empty air. This would be Dedlock Street. Or had she passed Dedlock Street already? She couldn't keep the picture of the streets clear in her mind. The darkness seemed to fill not just the city around her but the inside of her head as well.

Heart pounding, she waited. Come back, lights, she pleaded. Please come back. She wanted to call out to Poppy, to tell her to stand still, not to be afraid, she would come for her soon. But the darkness pressed against her and she couldn't summon her voice. She could hardly breathe. She wanted to claw the darkness away from her eyes, as if it were someone's hands.

Small sounds came from here and there around her—a whimpering, a shuffling. In the distance someone called out incoherently. How many minutes had gone by? The longest blackout ever had been three minutes and fourteen seconds. Surely this was longer.

She could have endured it if she'd been on her own. It was the thought of Poppy, lost, that she couldn't stand—and lost because she had been paying more attention to a box of pencils. Oh, she'd been selfish and greedy, and now she was so, so sorry! She made herself take another step forward. But then she thought, What if I'm going *away* from Poppy? She began to tremble, and she felt the sinking and dissolving inside her that meant she was going to cry. Her legs gave way like wet paper and she slid down until she was sitting on the street, with her head on her knees. Trembling, her mind a wordless whirl of dread, she waited.

An endless time went by. A moan came from somewhere to the left. A door slammed closed. Footsteps started, then stopped. Into Lina's mind floated the beginning of the worst question: What if the lights never . . . ? She squeezed her arms around her knees and made the question stop. Lights come back, she said to herself. Lights come back, come back.

And suddenly they did.

Lina sprang up. There was the street again, and people looking upward with their mouths hanging open. All around, people started crying or wailing or grinning in relief. Then all at once everyone started to hurry, moving fast toward the safety of home in case it should happen again.

Lina ran toward Greengate Square, stopping everyone she passed. "Did you see a little girl walking by herself just before the lights went out?" she asked. "Green jacket with a hood?" But no one wanted to listen to her.

On the Bee Street side of the square stood a few people all talking at once and waving their arms. Lina ran up to them and asked her question.

They stopped talking and stared at her. "How could we have seen anyone? The lights were out," said Nammy Proggs, a tiny old woman whose back was so bent that she had to twist her head sideways to look up.

Lina said, "No, she wandered away *before* the lights went out. She got away from me. She may have come this direction."

"You have to keep your eye on a baby," Nammy Proggs scolded.

"Babies need watching," said one of the women who'd been singing with the Believers.

But someone else said, "Oh, a toddler? Green jacket?" and he walked over to an open shop door and called, "You have that baby in there?" and through the door came someone leading Poppy by the hand.

Lina dashed to her and lifted her up. Poppy broke into loud wails. "You're all right now," said Lina, holding her tightly. "Don't worry, sweetie. You were just lost a moment, now you're all right. I've got you, don't worry." When she looked up to thank the person who'd found her, she saw a face she recognized. It was Doon. He looked the same as when she'd last seen him, except that his hair was shaggier. He had on the same baggy brown jacket he always wore.

"She was marching up the street by herself," he said. "No one knew who she belonged to, so I took her into my father's shop."

"She belongs to me," Lina said. "She's my sister. I was so afraid when she was lost. I thought she might fall and hurt herself, or be knocked over, or . . . Anyway, thank you *so much* for rescuing her."

"Anyone would have," said Doon. He frowned and looked down at the pavement.

Poppy had calmed down and was curled up against Lina's chest with her thumb in her mouth. "And your job—how is it?" Lina asked. "The Pipeworks?"

Doon shrugged his shoulders. "All right," he said. "Interesting, anyway."

She waited, but it seemed that was all he was going to say. "Well, thank you again," she said. She hoisted Poppy around to her back.

"Lucky for you Doon Harrow was around," said Nammy Proggs, who'd been watching them with her sideways glare. "He's a good-hearted boy. Anything breaks at my house, he fixes it." She hobbled after Lina, shaking a finger at her. "You'd better watch that baby more carefully," she called.

"You shouldn't leave her alone," the flute player added.

"I know," said Lina. "You're right."

When she got home, she put the tired baby to bed in the bedroom they shared. Granny had been taking an afternoon nap in the front room and hadn't noticed the blackout at all. Lina told her that the lights had gone out for a few minutes, but she didn't mention anything about Poppy getting lost.

Later, in her bedroom, with Poppy asleep, she took

the two colored pencils from her pocket. They were not quite as beautiful as they had been. When she held them, she remembered the powerful wanting she had felt in that dusty store, and the feeling of it was mixed up with fear and shame and darkness.

CHAPTER 6

The Box in the Closet

It was strange how people didn't talk much about the blackout. Power failures usually aroused lively discussion, with clumps of people collecting on corners and saying to each other, "Where were you when it happened?" and "What's the matter with the electricians, we should kick them out and get new ones," and that sort of thing. This time, it was just the opposite. When Lina went to work the next morning, the street was oddly silent. People walked quickly, their eyes on the ground. Those who did stop to talk spoke in low voices, then hurried on their way.

That day, Lina carried the same message twelve times. All the messengers were carrying it. It was simply this, being passed from one person to another: Seven minutes. The power failure had been more than twice as long as any other so far.

Fear had settled over the city. Lina felt it like a cold chill. She understood now that Doon had been speaking the truth on Assignment Day. Ember was in grave danger.

The next day a notice appeared on all the city's kiosks:

TOWN MEETING

ALL CITIZENS ARE REQUESTED TO ASSEMBLE
IN HARKEN SQUARE AT 6 P.M. TOMORROW
TO RECEIVE IMPORTANT INFORMATION.
MAYOR LEMANDER COLE

What kind of important information? Lina wondered. Good news or bad? She was impatient to hear it.

The next day, people streamed into Harken Square from all four directions, crowding together so close that each person hardly had room to move. Children sat on the shoulders of fathers. Short people tried to push toward the front. Lina spotted Lizzie and called a greeting to her. She saw Vindie Chance, too, who had brought her little brother. Lina had decided to leave Poppy at home with Granny. There was too much danger of losing her in a crowd like this.

The town clock began to strike. Six vibrating bongs rang out, and a murmur of anticipation swept through the crowd. People stood on tiptoe, craning to see. The door of the Gathering Hall opened, and the mayor came out, flanked by two guards. One of the guards handed the mayor a megaphone, and the mayor began to speak. His voice came through the megaphone both blurry and crackly.

"People of Ember," he said. He waited. The crowd fell silent, straining to hear.

"People of Ember," the mayor said again. He looked from side to side. The light glinted off his bald head. "Our city has experienced some slight diff-cushlaylie. Times like this require gresh peshn frush all."

"What did he say?" people whispered urgently. "What did he say? I couldn't hear him."

"Slight difficulties," someone said. "Requires great patience from us all."

"But I stand here today," the mayor went on, "to reassure you. Difficult times will pass. We are mayg effn effuff."

"What?" came the sharp whisper. "What did he say?"

Those near the front passed word back. "Making every effort," they said. "Every effort."

"Louder!" someone shouted.

The mayor's voice blared through the megaphone louder but even less clear. "Wursh poshuling!" he said. "Pank. Mushen pank. No rrrshen pank."

"We can't hear you!" someone else yelled. Lina felt

a stirring around her, a muttering. Someone pushed against her back, forcing her forward.

"He said we mustn't panic," someone said. "He said panic is the worst possible thing. No reason to panic, he said."

On the steps of the Gathering Hall, the two guards moved a little closer to the mayor. He raised the megaphone and spoke again.

"*Slooshns!*" he bellowed. "*Arbingfoun!*"

"Solutions," the people in front called to the people in back. "Solutions are being found, he said."

"*What* solutions?" called a woman standing near Lina. People elsewhere in the crowd echoed what the woman had said. "What solutions? What solutions?" Their cry became a chorus, louder and louder.

Again Lina felt the pressure from behind as people moved forward toward the Gathering Hall. Jostling arms poked her, bulky bodies bumped her and crushed her. Her heart began to pound. I have to get out of here! she thought.

She started ducking beneath arms and darting into whatever space she could find, making her way toward the rear of the crowd. Noise was rising everywhere. The mayor's voice kept coming in blasts of incomprehensible sound, and the people in the crowd were either shouting angrily or yelping in fear of being squashed. Someone stepped on Lina's foot, and her scarf was half yanked off. For a few seconds she was afraid she was going to be trampled. But at last she struggled free and ran up onto the steps of the school. From there she saw that the two guards were hustling the mayor back through the door of the Gathering Hall. The crowd roared, and a few people started hurling whatever they could find—pebbles, garbage, crumpled paper, even their own hats.

At the other side of the square, Doon and his father battled their way down Gilly Street. "Move fast," his father said. "We don't want to be caught up in this crowd." They crossed Broad Street and took the long way home, through the narrow lanes behind the school.

"Father," said Doon as they hurried along, "the mayor is a fool, don't you think?"

For a moment his father didn't answer. Then he said, "He's in a tough spot, son. What would you have him do?"

"Not lie, at least," Doon said. "If he really has a solution, he should have told us. He shouldn't pretend he has solutions when he doesn't."

Doon's father smiled. "That would be a good start," he agreed.

"It makes me so angry, the way he talks to us," said Doon.

Doon's father put a hand on Doon's back and steered him toward the corner. "A great many things make you angry lately," he said.

"For good reason," said Doon.

"Maybe. The trouble with anger is, it gets hold of you. And then you aren't the master of yourself anymore. Anger is."

Doon walked on silently. Inwardly, he groaned. He knew what his father was going to say, and he didn't feel like hearing it.

"And when anger is the boss, you get—"

"I know," said Doon. "Unintended consequences."

"That's right. Like hitting your father in the ear with a shoe heel."

"I didn't mean to."

"That's exactly my point."

They walked on down Pibb Street. Doon shoved his hands into the pockets of his jacket and scowled at the sidewalk. Father doesn't even *have* a temper, he thought. He's as mild as a glass of water. He can't possibly understand.

Lina was running. She'd already dismissed the mayor's speech from her mind. She sped by people on Otterwill Street going back to open their stores and overheard snatches of conversation as she passed. "Expects us to believe . . . ," said one voice. "He's just trying to keep us quiet," said another. "Heading for disaster . . . ," said a third. All the voices shook with anger and fear.

Lina didn't want to think about it. Her feet

slapped the stones of the street, her hair flew out behind her. She would go home, she would make hot potato soup for the three of them, and then she would take out her new pencils and draw.

She climbed the stairs next to the yarn shop two at a time and burst through the door of the apartment. Something was on the floor just in front of her feet, and she tripped and fell down hard on her hands and knees. She stared. By the open closet door was a great pile of coats and boots and bags and boxes, their contents all spilled out and tangled up. A thumping and rattling came from inside the closet.

"Granny?"

More thumps. Granny's head poked around the edge of the closet door. "I should have looked in here a long time ago," she said. "This is where it would be, of course. You should *see* what's in here!"

Lina gazed around at the incredible mess. Into this closet had been packed the junk of decades, jammed into cardboard boxes, stuffed into old pillowcases and laundry bags, and heaped up in a pile so dense that you couldn't pull one thing out without pulling all the rest with it. The shelf above the coatrack was just as crammed as the space below, mostly with old clothes that were full of moth holes and eaten away by mildew. When she was younger, Lina had tried exploring in this closet, but she never got far. She'd pull out an old scarf that would fall to pieces in her hands, or open a box that proved to be full of bent carpet tacks. Soon she would shove everything back in and give up.

But Granny was really doing the job right. She grunted and panted as she wrenched free the closet's packed-in stuff and tossed it behind her. It was clear that she was having fun. As Lina watched, a bag of rags came tumbling out the door, and then an old brown shoe with no laces.

"Granny," said Lina, suddenly uneasy. "Where's the baby?"

"Oh, she's here!" came Granny's voice from the depths of the closet. "She's been helping me."

Lina got up from the floor and looked around. She soon spotted Poppy. She was sitting behind the couch, in the midst of the clutter. In front of her was a small box made of something dark and shiny. It had a hinged lid, and the lid was open, hanging backward.

"Poppy," said Lina, "let me see that." She stooped down. There was some sort of mechanism on the edge of the lid—a kind of lock, Lina thought. The box was beautifully made, but it had been damaged. There were dents and scratches in its hard, smooth surface. It looked as if it had been a container for something valuable. But the box was empty now. Lina picked it up and felt around in it to be sure. There was nothing inside at all.

"Was there something in this box, Poppy? Did you

find something in here?" But Poppy only chortled happily. She was chewing on some crumpled paper. She had paper in her hands, too, and was tearing it. Shreds of paper were strewn around her. Lina picked one up. It was covered with small, perfect printing.

CHAPTER 7

A Message Full of Holes

It was the printing that sparked Lina's curiosity. It was not handwriting, or if it was, it was the neatest, most regular handwriting she had ever seen. It was more like the letters printed on cans of food or along the sides of pencils. Something other than a hand had written those words. A machine of some kind. This was the writing of the Builders. And so this piece of paper must have come from the Builders, too.

Lina gathered up the scraps of paper from the floor and gently pried open Poppy's fists and mouth to extract the crumpled wads. She put all this into the dented box and carried it to her room.

That evening, Granny and the baby were both asleep by a little after eight. Lina had nearly an hour to examine her discovery. She took the scraps from the box and spread them out on the table in her bedroom. The paper was thick; at each torn edge was a fringe of tangled fibers. There were many little pieces and one big piece with so many holes that it was like lace. The chewed bits were beyond saving—they were almost a paste. But Lina spread out the big lacy piece and saw that on one edge of it, which was still intact, was a column of numbers. She collected all the dry scraps and puzzled over them for a long time, trying to figure out where they fit into the larger piece. When she had arranged them as well as she could, this was what she had:

Instru r Egres

This offic doc in stric
secur period of ears.
prepara made for
inha city.
as foll

1. Exp
riv ip ork .
2. ston marked with E by r
dge
3. adde down iverb nk
to edge appr eight
low.
4. acks to the
wat r, find door of bo
ker. Ke hind small steel

pan the right . Rem
ey, open do .

5. oat, stocked with
nec uip ent. Bac
ont s eet.

6. Usi opes, lowe
ter. Head dow st . Us pa
av cks and assist over rap .

7. approx. 3 hours. Disem
. Follow pat .

Lina could make sense of only a few words here and there. Even so, something about this tattered document was exciting. It was not like anything Lina had ever seen. She stared at the very first word at the top of the page, "Instru," and she suddenly knew what it must be. She'd seen it often enough at school. It had to be the beginning of "Instructions."

Her heart began knocking at her chest like a fist at a door. She had found something. She had found something strange and important: instructions for something. But for what? And how terrible that Poppy had found it first and ruined it!

It occurred to Lina that this might be what her grandmother had been talking about for so long. Perhaps *this* was the thing that was lost. But of course not knowing what had been lost, Granny wouldn't have recognized the box when she saw it. She would have tossed it out of the closet just as carelessly as she tossed everything else. Anyhow, it didn't matter whether this was the thing or not the thing. It was a mystery in itself, whatever it was, and Lina was determined to solve it.

The first step was to stick the scraps of paper down. They were so light that a breath could scatter them. She had a little bit of glue left in an old bottle. Painstakingly, she put a dot of glue on each of the scraps and pressed each one into its place on one of her precious few remaining whole sheets of paper. She put another piece of paper on top of this and set the box on top to flatten everything down. Just as she finished, the lights went out—she'd forgotten to keep an eye on the clock on her windowsill. She had to undress and get in bed in the dark.

She was too excited to sleep much that night. Her mind whirled around, trying to think what the message she'd found might be. She felt sure it had something to do with saving the city. What if these instructions were for fixing the electricity? Or for making a movable light? That would change everything.

When the lights went on in the morning, she had a few minutes before Poppy wakened to work at the puzzle. But there were so many words missing! How could she ever make sense of such a jumble? As she pulled on her red jacket and tied the frayed and knotted laces of her shoes, she thought about it.

If the paper was important, she shouldn't keep it to herself. But who could she tell? Maybe the messenger captain. She would know about things like official documents.

"Captain Fleery," Lina said when she got to work, "would you have time to come home with me later on today? Just for a minute? I found something I'd like to show you."

"Found what?" asked Captain Fleery.

"Some paper with writing on it. I think it might be important."

Captain Fleery raised her skinny eyebrows. "What do you mean, important?"

"Well, I'm not sure. Maybe it isn't. But would you look at it anyway?"

So that evening Captain Fleery came home with Lina and peered at the bits of paper. She bent down and inspected the writing. "Foll?" she said. "Acks? Rem? Ont? What kind of words are those?"

"I don't know," said Lina. "The words are all broken up because Poppy chewed on them."

"I see," said Captain Fleery. She poked at the paper. "This looks like instructions for something," she said. "A recipe, I suppose. 'Small steel pan'—that would be what you use to cook it with."

"But who would have such small, perfect writing?"

"That's the way they wrote in the old days," said Captain Fleery. "It could be a very *old* recipe."

"But then why would it have been kept in this beautiful box?" She showed the box to Captain Fleery. "I think it was locked up in here for some reason, and you wouldn't lock up something unless it was important. . . ."

But Captain Fleery didn't seem to have heard her. "Or," she said, "it could be a school exercise. Someone's homework that never got turned in."

"But have you ever seen paper like this? Doesn't it look as if it came from someplace else—not here?"

Captain Fleery straightened up. A look of puzzlement came over her face. "There *is* nowhere but here," she said. She put both her hands on Lina's shoulders. "You, my dear, are letting your imagination run away with you. Are you overtired, Lina? Are you anxious? I could put you on short days for a while."

"No," said Lina, "I'm fine. I am. But I don't know what to do about . . ." She gestured toward the paper.

"Never mind," said Captain Fleery. "Don't think about it. Throw it away. You're worrying too much—I know, I know, we all are, there's so much to worry about, but we mustn't let it unsettle us." She gave Lina a long look. Her eyes were the color of dishwater. "Help is coming," she said.

"Help?"

"Yes. Coming to save us."

"Who is?"

Captain Fleery bent down and lowered her voice, as if telling a secret. "Who built our city, dear?"

"The Builders," said Lina.

"That's right. And the Builders will come again and show us the way."

"They will?"

"Very soon," said Captain Fleery.

"How do you know?"

Captain Fleery straightened up again and clapped a hand over her heart. "I know it here," she said. "And I have seen it in a dream. So have all of us, all the Believers."

So that's what they believe, Lina thought—and Captain Fleery is one of them. She wondered how the captain could feel so sure about it, just because she'd seen it in a dream. Maybe it was the same for her as the sparkling city was for Lina—she *wanted* it to be true.

The captain's face lit up. "I know what you must do, dear—come to one of our meetings. It would lift your heart. We sing."

"Oh," said Lina, "thank you, but I'm not sure I . . . maybe sometime . . ." She tried to be polite, but she knew she wouldn't go. She didn't want to stand around waiting for the Builders. She had other things to do.

Captain Fleery patted her arm. "No pressure, dear," she said. "If you change your mind, let me know.

But take my advice: forget about your little puzzle project. Lie down and take a nap. Clears the mind." Her narrow face beamed kindness down at Lina. "You take tomorrow off," she said. She raised a hand goodbye and went down the stairs.

Lina took advantage of her day off to go to the Supply Depot to see Lizzie Bisco. Lizzie was quick and smart. She might have some good ideas.

At the Supply Depot, crowds of shopkeepers stood in long, disorderly lines that stretched out the door. They pushed and jostled and snapped impatiently at each other. Lina joined them, but they seemed so frantic that they frightened her a little. They must be very sure now that the supplies are running out, she thought, and they're determined to get what they can before it's too late.

When she got close to the head of the line, she heard the same conversation several times. "Sorry," the clerk would say when a shopkeeper asked for ten packets of sewing needles, or a dozen drinking glasses, or twenty packages of light bulbs. "There's a severe shortage of that item. You can have only one." Or else the clerk would say, "Sorry. We're out of that entirely." "Forever?" "Forever."

Lina knew that it hadn't always been this way. When Ember was a young city, the storerooms were full. They held everything the citizens could want—so much it seemed the supplies would never run out.

Lina's grandmother had told her that schoolchildren were given a tour of the storerooms as part of their education. They took an elevator from the street level to a long, curving tunnel with doors on both sides and other tunnels branching off it. The guide led the tour down the long passages, opening one door after another. "This area," he would say, "is Canned Goods. Next we come to School Supplies. And around this bend we have Kitchenware. Next come Carpentry Tools." At each door, the children crowded against each other to see.

"Every room had something different," Granny told Lina. "Boxes of toothpaste in one room. Bottles of cooking oil. Bars of soap. Boxes of pills—there were twenty rooms just for vitamin pills. One room was stacked with hundreds of cans of fruit. There was something called pineapple, I remember that one especially."

"What was pineapple?" asked Lina.

"It was yellow and sweet," said Granny with a dreamy look in her eyes. "I had it four times before we ran out of it."

But these tours had been discontinued long before Lina was born. The storerooms, people said, were no longer a pleasure to look at. Their dusty shelves stood mostly empty now. It was rumored that in some rooms nothing was left at all. A child seeing the rooms where powdered milk had been stored, or the rooms that stored bandages or socks or pins or notebooks, or—most of all—the dozens of rooms that had once held thousands of light bulbs—would not feel, as earlier generations of children had, that Ember was endlessly rich. Today's children, if they were to tour the storerooms, would feel afraid.

Thinking about all this, Lina waited in the line of people at Lizzie's station. When she got to the front, she leaned forward with her elbows on the counter and whispered, "Lizzie, can you meet me after you're through with work? I'll wait for you right outside the door." Lizzie nodded eagerly.

At four o'clock, Lizzie came trotting out the office door. Lina said to her, "Will you come home with me for a minute? I want to show you something."

"Sure," said Lizzie, and as they walked, Lizzie talked. "My wrist is killing me from writing all day," she said. "You have to write in the tiniest letters to save paper, so I get a terrible *cramp* in my wrist and my fingers. And people are so *rude*. Today they were worse than ever. I said to some guy, 'You can't have fifteen cans of corn, you can only have three,' and he said, 'Look, don't tell me that, I saw plenty of cans in the Pott Street market just yesterday,' and I said, 'Well, that's why there aren't so many left today,' and he said, 'Don't be smart with me, carrot-head.' But what am I supposed to do? I can't *make* cans of corn out of thin air."

They passed through Harken Square, around the Gathering Hall, and down Roving Street, where three of the floodlights were out, making a cave of shadow.

"Lizzie," said Lina, interrupting the flow of talk. "Is it true about light bulbs?"

"Is what true?"

"That there aren't very many left?"

Lizzie shrugged. "I don't know. They hardly ever let us go downstairs into the storerooms. All we see are the reports the carriers turn in—how many forks in Room 1146, how many doorknobs in 3291, how many children's shoes in 2249 . . ."

"But when you see the report for the light bulb rooms, what does it say?"

"I never get to see that one," said Lizzie. "That one, and a few other ones like the vitamin report, only a few people can see."

"Who?"

"Oh, the mayor, and of course old Flab Face." Lina looked at her questioningly. "You know, Farlo Batten, the head of the storerooms. He is so *mean,* Lina, you would just hate him. He counts us late if we come in even two minutes after eight, and he looks over our shoulders as we're writing, which is awful because he has bad breath, and he runs his finger over what we've written and says, 'This word is illegible, that word is illegible, these numbers are illegible.' It's his favorite word, illegible."

When they came to Lina's street, Lina ducked her head in the door of the yarn shop and said hello to Granny, and then they climbed the stairs to the apartment. Lizzie was talking about how hard it was to stand up all day, how it made her knees ache, how her shoes pinched her feet. She stopped talking long enough to say hello to Evaleen Murdo, who was sitting by the window with Poppy on her lap, and then she began again as Lina led her into her bedroom.

"Lina, where were you when the big blackout came?" she asked, but she went right on without waiting for an answer. "I was at home, *luckily.* But it was scary, wasn't it?"

Lina nodded. She didn't want to talk about what had happened that day.

"I hate those blackouts," Lizzie went on. "People say there's going to be more and more of them, and that someday—" She stopped, frowned, and started again. "Anyway, nothing bad happened to me. After that, I got up and figured out a whole new way to do my hair."

It seemed to Lina that Lizzie was like a clock wound too tightly and running too fast. She'd always been a little this way, but today she was more so than ever. Her gaze skipped from one spot to another, her fingers twiddled with the edge of her shirt. She looked paler than usual, too. Her freckles stood out like little smudges of dirt on her nose.

"Lizzie," said Lina, beckoning toward the table in the corner of her room. "I want to show you—"

But Lizzie wasn't listening. "You're so lucky to be a messenger, Lina," she said. "Is it fun? I wish I could have been one. I would have been so good at it. My job is so boring."

Lina turned and looked at her. "Isn't there *anything* you like about it?"

Lizzie pursed her lips in a tiny smile and looked sideways at Lina. "There's one thing," she said.

"What?"

"I can't tell you. It's a secret."

"Oh," said Lina. Then you shouldn't have mentioned it at all, she thought.

"Maybe I'll tell you someday," said Lizzie. "I don't know."

"Well, I like *my* job," Lina said. "But what I wanted to talk to you about was what I found yesterday. It's this."

She lifted the box away and took up the piece of paper covering the patched-together document. Lizzie gave it a quick look. "Is it a message someone gave you? That got torn up?"

"No, it was in our closet. Poppy was chewing on it, that's why it's torn up. But look at the writing on it. Isn't it strange?"

"Uh-huh," said Lizzie. "You know who has beautiful handwriting? Myla Bone, who works with me.

You should see it, it's got curly tails on the y's and the g's, and fancy loops on the capital letters. Of course Flab Face hates it, he says it's illegible. . . ."

Lina slid the piece of paper back over the pasted-down scraps. She wondered why she had thought Lizzie would be interested in what she'd found. She'd always had fun with Lizzie. But their fun was usually with games—hide-and-seek, tag, the kinds of games where you run and climb. Lizzie never had been much interested in anything that was written on paper.

So Lina quietly put the document back in its place, and she sat down with Lizzie on the floor. She listened and listened until Lizzie's chatter ran down. "I'd better go," Lizzie said. "It was fun to see you, Lina. I miss you." She stood up. She fluffed her hair. "What was it you wanted to show me? Oh, yes—the fancy writing. Really nice. Lucky you to find it. Come and see me again soon, all right? I get so bored in that office."

Lina made beet soup for dinner that night, and Poppy spilled hers and made a red lake on the table. Granny stared into her bowl, stirring and stirring the soup with her spoon, but she didn't eat. She didn't feel quite right, she told Lina; after a while she wandered off to bed. Lina cleaned up the kitchen quickly. As soon as her chores were out of the way, she could get back to studying her document. She washed Poppy's clothes. She sewed on the buttons that had come off her messenger jacket. She picked up the rags and sacks and boxes and bags that Granny had tossed out of the closet. And by the time she had done all this and put Poppy to bed, she still had almost half an hour to study the fragments of paper.

She sat down at her desk and uncovered the document. With her elbows on either side of it and her chin resting in her hands, she pored over it. Though Lizzie and Captain Fleery had paid it no attention, Lina still thought this torn-up page must be important. Why else would it have been in such a cleverly fastened box? Maybe she should show it to the mayor, she thought reluctantly. She didn't like the mayor. She didn't trust him, either. But if this document was important to the future of the city, he was the one who should know about it. Of course, she couldn't ask the mayor to come to her house. She pictured him puffing up the stairs, squeezing through the door, looking disapprovingly at the clutter in their house, recoiling from Poppy's sticky hands—no, it wouldn't do.

But she didn't want to take her carefully patched-together document to the Gathering Hall, either. It was just too fragile. The best thing to do, she decided, was to write the mayor a note. She settled down to do this.

She found a fairly unspoiled half-piece of paper, and, using a plain pencil (she wasn't going to waste her colored ones on the mayor), she wrote:

Dear Mayor Cole,

I have discovered a document that was in the closet. It is instructions for something. I believe it is important because it is written in very old printing. Unfortunately it got chewed up by my sister, so it is not all there. But you can still read some bits of it, such as:

marked with E
find door of bo
small steel pan

I will show you this document if you want to see it.

Sincerely yours,
Lina Mayfleet, Messenger
34 Quillium Square

She folded the note in half and wrote "Mayor Cole" on the front. On her way to work the next morning, she took it to the Gathering Hall. No one was sitting at the guard's desk, so Lina left the note there, placed so that the guard would see it when he arrived. Then, feeling that she had done her duty, she went off to her station.

Several days went by. The messages Lina carried were full of worry and fear. "Do you have any extra Baby Drink? I can't find it at the store." "Have you heard what they're saying about the generator?" "We can't come tonight—Grandpa B. won't get out of bed."

Every day when she got home from work, Lina asked Granny, "Did a message come for me?" But there was nothing. Maybe the mayor hadn't gotten her note. Maybe he'd gotten it and paid no attention. After a week, Lina decided she was tired of waiting. If the mayor wasn't interested in what she'd found, too bad for him. *She* was interested. She would figure it out herself.

Twice during the week, when Poppy and Granny were both asleep, she'd had a little free time. She'd spent this time making a copy of the document, in case anything happened to the fragile original. It had taken her a long time. She used one of her few remaining pieces of paper—an old label, slightly torn, from a can of peas. The copy was as accurate as she could make it, with the missing bits between the letters carefully indicated as dashes. She had tucked it under the mattress of her bed for safekeeping.

Now she finally had a whole free evening. Poppy and Granny were both asleep, and the apartment was tidy. Lina sat down at her table and uncovered the patched-together document. She tied back her hair so it wouldn't keep falling in her face, and she put a piece of paper next to her—blank except for a little bit of Poppy's scribbling—to write down what she decoded.

She started with the title. The first word she'd already figured out. It had to be "Instructions." The next word could be "for." Then came "Egres"—she wasn't sure about that. Maybe it was someone's name. Egresman. Egreston. "Instructions for Egreston." She decided to call it "The Instructions" for short.

She went on to the first line. "This offic doc" probably meant "This official document." Maybe "secur" meant "secure." Or "security." Then there were the words "period" and "ears" and "city." But after that, so much was missing.

She studied the line next to the number 1. *Exp.* That could be *Expect* or *Expert* or so many things. She moved on to *riv.* That might be part of a word like "drive" or "strive." What could *ip* and *ork* possibly be? They were so close together, maybe they were part of one word. What ended with *-ip*? *Whip,* Lina thought. *Trip. Slip.* What ended with *-ork*? *Fork* came to mind immediately. *Tripfork. Slipfork.* Nothing she could think of made sense.

Maybe it wasn't *fork.* What else ended in *-ork*? Starting at the beginning of the alphabet, Lina went through all the words that rhymed with *fork.* Most of them were nonsense: *bork, dork, gork, hork, jork. . . .* This isn't going to work, she thought miserably. Oh . . . *work*! The word could be *work.*

Then what would the first part be? *Tripwork? Flipwork?* But maybe there was a letter between the p and the w. *Dipswork? Pipswork?*

Suddenly it came to her. Pipeworks. Pipeworks!

That had to be it. Something in this message was about the Pipeworks!

Lina looked back at *Exp* and *riv*. *Riv!* That could be *river*! Rapidly she ran her eyes down the page. In line 3, she saw *iverb nk*—that looked like *riverbank*. The word *door* jumped out at her from line 4, whole on its scrap of paper. Lina took a quick breath. A door! What if it was the one she'd wished for, the one that led to the other city? Maybe her city was real after all, and these were instructions for finding it!

She wanted to leap from her chair and shout. The message had something to do with the river, a door, and the Pipeworks. And who did she know who knew about the Pipeworks? Doon, of course.

She pictured his thin, serious face, and his eyes looking out searchingly from beneath his dark eyebrows. She pictured how he used to bend over his work at school, holding his pencil in a hard grip, and how, during free time, he was usually off by himself in a corner studying a moth or a worm or a taken-apart clock. That was one thing, at least, that she liked about Doon: he was curious. He paid attention to things.

And he cared about things, too. She remembered how he'd been on Assignment Day, so furious at the mayor, so eager to trade his good job for her bad one so he could help save the city. And he'd taken Poppy inside his father's shop on the day of the blackout so she wouldn't be afraid.

Why had she stopped being friends with Doon? She vaguely recalled the incident of the light pole. It seemed silly now, and long ago. The more she thought about Doon, the more it seemed he was the very person—the *only* person—who might be interested in what she had found.

She placed the plain sheet of paper over the Instructions and put the box on top. I'll go and find Doon, she thought. Tomorrow was Thursday—their day off. She would find him tomorrow and ask for his help.

CHAPTER 8

Explorations

Doon had taken to wandering the Pipeworks alone. He would go to his assigned tunnel and do his job quickly—once you got good at using your wrenches and brushes and tubes of glue, it wasn't hard. Most of the workers did their jobs quickly and then gathered in little groups to play cards or have salamander races or just talk and sleep.

But Doon didn't care about any of that. If he was going to be stuck in the Pipeworks, he would at least not waste the time he had. Since the long blackout, everything seemed more urgent than ever. Whenever the lights flickered, he was afraid the ancient generator might be shuddering to a permanent halt.

So while the others lounged around, he headed out toward the edges of the Pipeworks to see what he could see. "Pay attention," his father had said, and that's what he did. He followed his map when he could, but in some places the map was unclear. There were even tunnels that didn't show up on the map at all. To keep from getting lost, he dropped a trail of things as he walked—washers, bolts, pieces of wire, whatever he had in his tool belt—and then he picked them up on his way back.

His father had been at least a little bit right: there were interesting things in the Pipeworks if you paid attention. Already he had found three new crawling creatures: a black beetle the size of a pinhead, a moth with furry wings, and the best of all, a creature with a soft, shiny body and a small, spiral-patterned shell on its back. Just after he found this one, while he was sitting on the floor watching in fascination as the creature crept up his arm, a couple of workers came by and saw him. They burst into laughter. "It's bug-boy!" one of them said. "He's collecting bugs for his lunch!"

Enraged, Doon jumped up and shouted at them. His sudden motion made the creature fall off his arm to the ground, and Doon felt a crunch beneath his foot. The laughing workers didn't notice—they tossed a few more taunts at him and walked on—but Doon knew instantly what he'd done. He lifted his foot and looked at the squashed mess underneath.

Unintended consequences, he thought miserably. He was angry at his anger, the way it surged up and took over. He picked the bits of shell and goo off the sole of his boot and thought, I'm sorry. I didn't mean to hurt you.

In the days that followed, Doon went farther and farther into the Pipeworks, holding on to the hope that he might find something not only interesting but important. But what he found didn't seem important at all. Once he came upon an old pair of pliers that someone had dropped and left behind. Twice he found a coin. He discovered a supply closet that appeared to have been completely forgotten, but all it held were some boxes of plugs and washers and a rusty box containing shriveled bits of what must once have been someone's lunch.

He found another supply closet at the far south end of the Pipeworks—at least, he assumed that's what it was. It was at the end of a tunnel with a rope strung across it; a sign hanging from the rope said, "Caved In. No Entry." Doon entered anyway, ducking under the rope. He found no sign of a cave-in, but there were no lights. He groped his way forward for twenty steps or so, and there the tunnel ended in a securely locked door—he couldn't see it, but he felt it. He retraced his steps, ducked back under the rope again, and walked on. A short distance away, he found a hatch in the ceiling of the tunnel—a square wooden panel that must lead, he thought, up into the storerooms. If he'd had something to stand on, he could have reached it and tried to open it, but it was about a foot above his upstretched hand. Probably it was locked anyhow. He wondered if the Builders had used openings like this one during the construction of the city to get more easily from one place to another.

On days when his job was near the main tunnel, he sometimes walked along the river after he'd finished working. He stayed away from the east end, where the generator was; he didn't want to think about the generator. Instead, he went the other way, toward the place where the river rushed out of the Pipeworks. The path grew less level at this end, and less smooth. The river here was bordered with clumps of wrinkled rock that seemed to grow out of the ground like fungus. Doon liked to sit on these clumps, running his fingers along the strange creases and crevices that must have been carved somehow by running or dripping water. In some places there were grooves that looked almost like writing.

But as for things of importance, Doon found none. It seemed that the Pipeworks was no use after all to a person who wanted to save the city. The generator was hopeless. He would never understand electricity. He used to think he could use electricity to invent a movable light, if he studied hard enough. He took apart light bulbs; he took apart the electric outlets on the wall to see how the wires inside wound together and in the process, got a painful, vibrating jolt all through his body. But when he tried to wind wires of his own together in exactly the same way, nothing happened. It was what came *through* the wires that made the light, he finally understood, and he had no idea what that was.

Now he could see only two courses of action: he could give up and do nothing, or he could start to work on a different kind of movable light.

Doon didn't want to give up. So on his day off one Thursday, he went to the Ember Library to look up fire.

The library occupied an entire building on one side of Bilbollio Square. Its door was at the end of a short passage in the middle of the building. Doon went down the passage, pushed open the door, and walked in. No one was there except for the librarian, ancient Edward Pocket, who sat behind his desk writing something with a tiny pencil clutched in his gnarled hand. The library had two big rooms, one for fiction, which was stories people made up out of their imaginations, and the other for fact, which was information about the real world. The walls of both rooms were lined with shelves, and on most of the shelves were hundreds of packets of pages. Each packet was held together with stout loops of string. The packets leaned against each other at angles and lay in untidy stacks. Some were thick, and some were so slim that only a clip was needed to hold them together. The pages of the oldest packets were yellowed and warped, and their edges were uneven rows of ripples.

These were the books of Ember, written over the years by its citizens. They contained in their close-written pages much that was imagined and everything that was known.

Edward Pocket looked up and nodded briefly at Doon, one of his most frequent visitors. Doon nodded back. He went into the fact room, to the section of shelves labeled "F." The books were arranged by subject, but even so, it wasn't easy to find what you wanted. A book about moths, for instance, might be under "M" for moths, or "I" for insects, or "B" for bugs. It might even be under "F" for flying things. Usually you had to browse through the entire library to make sure you'd found all the books on one subject. But since he was looking for "fire," he thought he might as well start with "F."

Fire was rare in Ember. When there was a fire, it was because there had been an accident—someone had left a dishtowel too close to an electric burner on a stove, or a cord had frayed and a spark had flown out and ignited curtains. Then the citizens would rush in with buckets of water, and the fire was quickly drowned. But it was, of course, possible to start a fire on purpose. You could hold a sliver of wood to the stove burner until it burst into flame, and then for a moment it would flare brightly, giving off orange light.

The trick was to find a way to make the light last. If you had a light that would keep going, you could go out into the Unknown Regions and see what was there. Finding a way to explore the Unknown Regions was the only thing Doon could think of to do.

He took down a book from the "F" shelf. *Fungus,* it was called. He put it back. The next book was called *How to Repair Furniture.* He put that back, too. He went through *Foot Diseases, Fun with String, Coping with Failure,* and *Canned Fruit Recipes* before he finally found a book called *All About Fire.* He sat down at one of the library's square tables to read it.

But the person who had written the book knew no more about fire than Doon. Mostly the book described the dangers of fire. A long section of it was about a building in Winifred Square that had caught fire forty years ago, and how all its doors and all its furniture had burned up and smoke had filled the air for days. Another part was about what to do if your oven caught on fire.

Doon closed the book and sighed. It was useless. *He* could write a better book than that. He got up and wandered restlessly around the library. Sometimes you could find useful things just by choosing randomly from the shelves. He had done this many times—just reached out and grabbed something—in the hope that by accident he might come upon the very piece of information he needed. It would be something that another person had written down without understanding its significance, just a sentence or two that would be like a flash of light in Doon's mind, fitting together with things he already knew to make a solution to everything.

Although he'd often found something interesting in these searches, he'd never found anything *important.* Today was no different. He did come across a collection called *Mysterious Words from the Past,* which he read for a while. It was about words and phrases so old that their meanings had been forgotten. He read a few pages.

Heavens above
 Indicates surprise. What "heavens" means is unclear. It might be another word for "floodlight."
Hogwash
 Means "nonsense," though no one knows what a "hog" is or why one would wash it.
Batting a thousand
 Indicates great success. This might possibly refer to killing bugs.
All in the same boat
 Means "all in the same predicament." The meaning of "boat" is unknown.

Interesting, but not useful. He put the book back on the shelf and was about to leave when the door of the library opened, and Lina Mayfleet came in.

CHAPTER 9

The Door in the Roped-Off Tunnel

Lina saw Doon immediately—he was reaching up to set a book back on its shelf. He saw her, too, when he turned around, and his dark eyebrows flew up in surprise as she hurried over to him.

"Your father told me you were here," she said. "Doon, I found something. I want to show it to you."

"To me? Why?"

"I think it's important. It has to do with the Pipeworks. Will you come to my house and see it?"

"Now?" Doon asked.

Lina nodded.

Doon grabbed his old brown jacket and followed Lina out of the library and across the city to Quillium Square.

Granny's shop was closed and dark when they arrived, and so Lina was surprised when they went upstairs and saw Evaleen Murdo sitting in her place by the window. "Your grandmother's in her bedroom," Mrs. Murdo said. "She didn't feel well, so she asked me to come."

Poppy was sitting on the floor, banging a spoon on the leg of a chair.

Lina introduced Doon, then led him into the room she shared with Poppy. He looked around, and Lina felt suddenly self-conscious, seeing her room through his eyes. It was a small room with a lot crammed into it. There were two narrow beds, a very small table that fit into a corner, and a four-legged stool to sit on. On the wall, clothes hung from hooks, and more clothes were strewn untidily on the floor. Beneath the window was a brown stain made by the bean seed in its pot on the windowsill. Lina had been watering it every night because she'd promised Clary she would, but it was still nothing but dirt, flat and unpromising.

A couple of shelves beside the window held Lina's important possessions: the pieces of paper she'd collected for drawing, her pencils, a scarf with a silver thread woven through it. On the parts of the wall that had no hooks and no shelves, she had pinned up some of her pictures.

"What are those?" Doon asked.

"They're from my imagination," Lina said, feeling slightly embarrassed. "They're pictures of . . . another city."

"Oh. You made it up."

"Sort of. Sometimes I dream of it."

"I draw, too," said Doon. "But I draw other kinds of things."

"Like what?"

"Mostly insects," said Doon. He told her about his collection of drawings and the worm he was currently observing.

To Lina, this sounded far less interesting than an undiscovered city, but she didn't say so. She led Doon over to the table. "Here's what I want to show you," she said. She lifted the metal box. Before she could reach for the papers underneath, Doon took the box and started examining it.

"Where did this come from?" he asked.

"It was in the closet," Lina said. She told him about Granny's wild search and about finding the box with its lid open and Poppy with paper in her mouth. As she talked, Doon turned the box over in his hands, opened and closed its lid, and peered at the latch.

"There's some sort of odd mechanism here," he said. He tapped at a small metal compartment at the front of the box. "I'd like to see inside this."

"Here's what was in the box," said Lina, lifting the covering paper from her patchwork of scraps. "At least, it's what's left of what was in there."

Doon bent over, his hands on either side of the paper.

Lina said, "It's called 'Instructions for Egreston.' Or maybe 'Egresman.' Someone's name, anyhow. Maybe a mayor, or a guard. I just call it 'The Instructions.' I told the mayor about it—I thought maybe it was important. I wrote him a note, but he hasn't answered. I don't think he's interested."

Doon said nothing.

"You don't have to hold your breath," said Lina. "I glued the pieces down. Look," she said, pointing. "This word must be *Pipeworks.* And this one *river.* And look at this one—*door.*"

Doon didn't answer. His hair had fallen forward, so Lina couldn't see the expression on his face.

"I thought at first," Lina went on, "that it must be instructions for how to do something. How to fix the electricity, maybe. But then I thought, What if it's instructions for going to another place?" Doon said nothing, so Lina went on. "I mean someplace that isn't here, like another city. I think these instructions say, 'Go down into the Pipeworks and look for a door.'"

Doon brushed the hair back from his face, but he didn't straighten up. He gazed at the broken words and frowned. "Edge," he murmured. "Small steel pan. What would that mean?"

"A frying pan?" said Lina. "But I don't know why there'd be a frying pan in the Pipeworks."

But Doon didn't answer. He seemed to be talking

to himself. He kept reading, moving a finger along the lines of words. "Open," he whispered. "Follow."

Finally he turned to look at Lina. "I think you're right," he said. "I think this *is* important."

"Oh, I was sure you'd think so!" Lina cried. She was so relieved that her words poured out in a rush. "Because you take things seriously! You told the truth to the mayor on Assignment Day. I didn't want to believe it, but then came the long blackout, and I knew—I knew things were as bad as you said." She stopped, breathless. She pointed to a word on the document. "This door," she said. "It has to be a door that leads out of Ember."

"I don't know," said Doon. "Maybe. Or a door that leads to *something* important, even if it isn't that."

"But it *must* be that—what else could be important enough to lock up in a fancy box?"

"Well . . . I suppose it could be a storage room with some special tools in it or something—" A look of surprise came over his face. "Actually, I *saw* a door where I didn't expect to see one—out in Tunnel 351. It was locked. I thought it was an old supply closet. I wonder if that could be it."

"It must be!" cried Lina. Her heart sped up.

"It wasn't anywhere near the river," Doon said doubtfully.

"That doesn't matter!" Lina said. "The river goes

through the Pipeworks, that's all. It's probably something like, 'Go down by the river, then go this way, then that way . . .'"

"Maybe," said Doon.

"It *must* be!" Lina cried. "I *know* it is! It's the door that leads out of Ember."

"I don't know if that makes sense," said Doon. "A door in the Pipeworks could only lead to something underground, and how could that . . ."

Lina had no patience for Doon's reasoning. She wanted to dance around the room, she was so excited. "We have to find out," she said. "We have to find out right away!"

Doon looked startled. "Well, I can go and try the door again," he said. "It was locked before, but I suppose . . ."

"I want to go, too," said Lina.

"You want to come down into the Pipeworks?"

"Yes! Can you get me in?"

Doon thought for a moment. "I think I can. If you come just at quitting time and wait outside the door, I'll stay out of sight until everyone has gone, and then I'll let you in."

"Tomorrow?"

"Okay. Tomorrow."

Lina stopped at home the next day only long enough to change out of her messenger jacket, and then she dashed across town to the Pipeworks. Doon met her just outside the door, and she followed him inside, where he handed her a slicker and boots to put on. They descended the long stone stairway, and when they came out into the main tunnel, Lina stood still, staring at the river. "I didn't know the river was so big," she said, after she found her voice.

"Yes," said Doon. "Every few years, they say, someone falls in. If you fall in, there's no hope of fishing you out. The river swallows you and sweeps you away."

Lina shivered. It was cold down here, a cold that she felt all the way through, cold flesh, cold blood, cold bones.

Doon led her up the path beside the water. After a while they came to an opening in the wall, and they turned into it and left the river behind. Doon led the way through winding tunnels. Their rubber boots splashed in pools of water on the floor. Lina thought how awful it would be to work down here all day, every day. It was a creepy place, a place where it seemed people didn't belong. That black river . . . it was like something in a bad dream.

"You have to duck here," said Doon.

They had come to a roped-off tunnel. "But there's no light in there," Lina said.

"No," said Doon. "We have to feel our way. It isn't far." He ducked under the rope and went in, and Lina did the same. They stepped forward into the dark. Lina kept a hand against the damp wall and placed her feet carefully.

"It's right here," said Doon. He had stopped a few feet ahead of Lina. She came up behind him. "Put your hands out," he said. "You'll feel it."

Lina felt a smooth, hard surface. There was a round metal knob, and below the knob, a keyhole. It seemed an ordinary door—not at all like the entrance to a new world. But that was what made things so exciting—nothing was ever how you expected it to be.

"Let's try it," she whispered.

Doon took hold of the knob and twisted. "Locked," he said.

"Is there a pan anywhere?"

"A pan?"

"The instructions said 'small steel pan.' Maybe that would have the key in it."

They felt around, but there was nothing—just the rocky walls. They patted the walls, they put their ears to the door, they jiggled the knob and pulled it and pushed it. Finally Doon said, "Well, we can't get in. I guess we'd better go."

And that was when they heard the noise. It was a scuffling, scraping noise that seemed to be coming from somewhere nearby. Lina stopped breathing. She clutched Doon's arm.

"Quick," Doon whispered. He made his way back toward the lighted tunnel, with Lina following.

They ducked under the rope and rounded a turn, then stopped, stood still, and listened. A harsh scraping sound. A thud. A pause . . . and then the sound of an impact, a short, explosive breath, and a muttered word in a gruff, low voice.

Then slow footsteps, getting closer.

They flattened themselves against the wall and stood motionless. The footsteps stopped briefly, and there was another grunt. Then the steps continued, but seemed to be fading. In a moment, from a distance, there was another sound: the chink of a key turning in a lock, and the click of a latch opening.

Lina made an astonished face at Doon. Someone had gone down the roped tunnel and opened the door! She put her mouth close to Doon's ear. "Shall we try to see who it is?" she whispered.

Doon shook his head. "I don't think we should," he said. "We should go."

"We could just peek around the corner."

It was too tempting not to try. They crept forward to the place where the tunnel turned. From there they could see the entrance to the roped tunnel. Holding their breath, they watched.

And in a minute, they heard a thump and click—the door closing, the lock turning—and footsteps once again, this time quick. A long leg stepped over the rope, and the person it belonged to turned and walked away. All they saw was his back—a dark coat, dark untidy hair. He walked with a lurching motion that struck Lina as somehow familiar. In a few seconds, he had vanished into the shadows.

When they came up out of the Pipeworks, they stripped off their boots and slickers and hurried out into Plummer Square, where they flopped down on a bench and burst into furious talk.

"Someone got there before us!" said Lina.

Doon said, "He was walking slowly when he went in—as if he was looking for something. And he walked fast when he came out . . ."

"As if he'd *found* something! What *was* it? I can't stand not to know!"

Doon jumped up. He paced back and forth in front of the bench.

"But how did he get the key?" he asked. "Did he find Instructions like the ones you found? And how did he get into the Pipeworks? I don't think he works there."

"There's something familiar about the way he walks," said Lina. "But I don't know why."

"Well, anyhow, he opened that door and we can't," said Doon. "If it *does* go somewhere, if it *does* lead out of Ember, he'll be telling the whole city pretty soon. He'll be a hero." Doon sat down again. "If he's found the way out, we'll be glad, of course," he said glumly. "It doesn't matter who finds it, as long as it helps the city."

"That's right," Lina said.

"It's just that I thought *we* were going to find it," said Doon.

"Yes," Lina said, thinking how grand it would have been to stand before all of Ember, announcing their discovery.

They sat without talking for a while, lost in their own thoughts. A man pulling a cart full of wood scraps went by. A woman leaned from a lighted window on Gappery Street and called out to some boys playing in the square below. A couple of guards, in their red and brown uniforms, ambled across the square, laughing. The town clock rang out six deep booms that Lina could feel, like shudders, beneath her ribs.

Doon said, "I guess what we do now is wait to see if there's an announcement."

"I guess so," said Lina.

"Maybe that door is nothing special after all," said Doon. "Maybe it's just an old unused supply closet."

But Lina wasn't ready to believe that. Maybe it wasn't the door out of Ember, but it was a mystery nevertheless—a mystery connected, she was sure, to the bigger mystery they were trying to solve.

CHAPTER 10

Blue Sky and Goodbye

Lina slept restlessly that night. She had frightening dreams in which something dangerous was lurking in the darkness. When the lights went on in the morning and she opened her eyes, her first thought was of the door in the Pipeworks—and then right away she felt a thud of disappointment, because the door was locked and someone else, not her, knew what was behind it.

She went in to wake Granny. "Time to get up," she said, but Granny didn't answer. She was lying with her mouth half open and breathing in a strange hoarse way. "Don't feel too good," she finally said in a weak voice.

Lina felt Granny's forehead. It was hot. Her hands were very cold. She ran for Mrs. Murdo and after that to Cloving Square to tell Captain Fleery she would not be coming to work today. Then she ran to Oliver Street, to the office of Dr. Tower, where she banged on the door until the doctor opened it.

Dr. Tower was a thin woman with uncombed hair and shadows under her eyes. When she saw Lina, she seemed to grow even more tired.

"Dr. Tower," Lina said, "my grandmother is sick. Will you come?"

"I will," she said. "But I can't promise to help her. I'm low on medicine."

"But come and look. Maybe she doesn't need medicine."

Lina led the doctor the few blocks to her house. When she saw Granny, the doctor sighed. "How are you, Granny Mayfleet?" she asked.

Granny looked at the doctor blearily. "I think ill," she said.

Dr. Tower laid a hand across her forehead. She asked her to stick out her tongue, and she listened to her heart and her breathing.

"She has a fever," the doctor told Lina. "You'll need to stay home with her today. Make her some soup. Give her water to drink. Put rags in cool water and lay them across her forehead." She picked up Granny's bony hand in her rough, reddish one. "What's best for you is to sleep today," she said. "Your good granddaughter will take care of you."

And all day, that's what Lina did. She made a thin soup of spinach and onions and fed it to Granny a spoonful at a time. She stroked Granny's forehead, held her hand, and talked to her about cheerful things. She kept Poppy as quiet as she could. But as she did all this, in the back of her mind was the memory of the days of her father's illness, when he seemed to grow dim like a lamp losing power, and the sound of his breathing was like water gurgling through a clogged pipe. Though she didn't want to, she also remembered the evening when her father let out one last short breath and didn't take another, and the morning a few months later when Dr. Tower emerged from her mother's bedroom with a crying baby and a face that was heavy with bad news.

In the late afternoon, Granny got restless. She lifted herself up on one elbow. "Did we find it?" she asked Lina. "Did we ever find it?"

"Find what, Granny?"

"The thing that was lost," Granny said. "The old thing that my grandfather lost . . ."

"Yes," said Lina. "Don't worry, Granny, we found it, it's safe now."

"Oh, good." Granny sank back onto her pillows and smiled at the ceiling. "What a relief," she said. She coughed a couple of times, closed her eyes, and fell asleep.

Lina stayed home from work the next day as well. It was a long day. Granny dozed most of the time. Poppy, delighted to have Lina at home to play with, kept toddling over with things she found—dust rags, kitchen spoons, stray shoes—and whacking them against Lina's knees, saying, "Play wif dis! Play wif dis!" Lina was glad to play with her, but after a while she'd had enough of spoon-banging and rag-tugging and shoe-rolling. "Let's do something else," she said to Poppy. "Shall we draw?"

Granny had drunk a full cup of soup for dinner and was falling asleep again, so Lina got out her colored pencils and two of the can labels she'd been saving—they were white on the back and made good enough drawing paper, if you flattened them out. With their sharpest kitchen knife, she whittled the pencils into points. She gave the green pencil and one can label to Poppy, and she herself took the blue pencil and smoothed out the other can label on the table.

What would she draw? Taking hold of a pencil was like opening a tap inside her mind through which her imagination flowed. She could feel the pictures ready to come out. It was a sort of pressure, like water in a pipe. She always thought she would draw something wonderful, but what she actually drew never quite matched the feeling. It was like when she tried to tell a dream—the words never really captured how it felt.

Poppy was grasping the pencil in her fist and making a wild scribble. "Lookit!" she cried.

"Lovely," said Lina. Then, without even a clear idea of what it was to be, she began her own picture. She started on the left side of the can label. First she drew a tall, narrow box—a building. Then more boxes next to it—a cluster of buildings. Next she drew a few tiny people walking on the street below the buildings. It was what she nearly always drew—the other city—and every time she drew it, she had the same frustrating feeling: there was more to be drawn. There were other things in this city, there were marvels there—but she couldn't imagine what they were. All she knew was that this city was bright in a different way from Ember. Where the brightness came from she didn't know.

She drew more buildings and filled in the windows and doors; she put in streetlamps; she added a greenhouse. All the way across the paper, she drew buildings of different sizes. All the buildings were white, because that was the color of the paper.

She set her pencil down for a moment and studied what she'd done. It was time to fill in the sky. In the pictures she'd done with regular pencils, the sky was its true color, black. But this time she made it blue, since she was using her blue pencil. Methodically, as Poppy scratched and scribbled beside her, Lina colored in the space above the buildings, her pencil moving back and forth in short lines, until the entire sky was blue.

She sat back and looked at her picture. Wouldn't it be strange, she thought, to have a blue sky? But she liked the way it looked. It would be beautiful—a blue sky.

Poppy had started using her pencil to poke holes

in her paper. Lina folded up her own picture and took Poppy's away from her. "Time for dinner," she said.

Sometime deep in the night, Lina woke suddenly, thinking she'd heard something. Had she been dreaming? She lay still, her eyes open in the darkness. The sound came again, a weak, trembling call: "Lina . . ."

She got up and started for Granny's room. Though she had lived in the same house all her life, she still had trouble finding her way at night, when the darkness was complete. It was as if walls had shifted slightly, and furniture moved to new places. Lina stayed close to the walls, feeling her way along. Here was her bedroom door. Here was the kitchen and the table—she winced as she stubbed her toe on one of its legs. A little farther and she'd come to the far wall and the door to Granny's room. Granny's voice was like a thin line in the dark air. "Lina . . . Come and help . . . I need . . ."

"I'm coming, Granny," she called.

She stumbled over something—a shoe, maybe—and fell against the bed. "Here I am, Granny!" she said. She felt for Granny's hand—it was very cold.

"I feel so strange," said Granny. Her voice was a whisper. "I dreamed . . . I dreamed about my baby . . . or someone's baby . . ."

Lina sat down on the bed. Carefully she moved her hands over the narrow ridge of her grandmother's body until she came to her shoulders. There her fingers tangled in the long wisps of Granny's hair. She pressed a finger against the side of Granny's throat to feel for her pulse, as the doctor had shown her. It was fluttery, like a moth that has hurt itself and is flapping in crooked circles.

"Can I get you some water, Granny?" Lina asked. She couldn't think what else to do.

"No water," Granny said. "Just stay for a while."

Lina tucked one foot underneath her and pulled part of the blanket over her lap. She took hold of Granny's hand again and stroked it gently with one finger.

For a long time neither of them said anything. Lina sat listening to her grandmother's breathing. She would take a deep, shuddering breath and let it out in a sigh. Then there would be a long silence before the next breath began. Lina closed her eyes. No use keeping them open—there was nothing to see but the dark. She was aware only of her grandmother's cold, thin hand and the sound of her breathing. Every now and then Granny would mumble a few words Lina couldn't make out, and then Lina would stroke her forehead and say, "Don't worry, it's all right. It's almost morning," though she didn't know if it was or not.

After a long time, Granny stirred slightly and seemed to come awake. "You go to bed, dear," she said.

"I'm all right now." Her voice was clear but very faint. "You go back to sleep."

Lina bent forward until her head rested against Granny's shoulder. Granny's soft hair tickled her face. "All right, then," she whispered. "Good night, Granny." She squeezed her grandmother's shoulders gently, and as she stood up a wave of terrible loneliness swept over her. She wanted to see Granny's face. But the darkness hid everything. It might still be a long time until morning—she didn't know. She groped her way back to her own bed and fell into a deep sleep, and when, hours later, the clock tower struck six and the lights came on, Lina went fearfully into her grandmother's room. She found her very pale and very still, all the life gone out of her.

CHAPTER 11

Lizzie's Groceries

Lina spent all that day in Mrs. Murdo's house, which was just like theirs, only neater. There was one couch, and one fat chair covered in fuzzy striped material, and one big table, only Mrs. Murdo's table wasn't wobbly like theirs. On the table was a basket, and in the basket were three turnips, each of them lavender on one end and white on the other. Mrs. Murdo must have put them there, Lina thought, not just because she was going to have them for dinner, but also because they were beautiful.

Lina sat sideways on the couch with her legs stretched out, and Mrs. Murdo covered her with a soft gray-green blanket. "This will keep you warm," she said, tucking it around Lina's legs. Lina didn't really feel cold but she did feel sad, which was in a way the same. The blanket felt good, like someone holding her. Mrs. Murdo gave Poppy a long purple scarf to play with and made a creamy mushroom soup with potatoes, and all day Lina stayed there, snuggled under the blanket. She thought about her grandmother, who had had a long and mostly cheerful life. She cried some and fell asleep. She woke up and played with Poppy. The day had a strange but comforting feel to it, like a rest between the end of one time and the beginning of another.

On the morning of the next day, Lina got up and got ready to go to work. Mrs. Murdo gave her beet tea and spinach hash for breakfast. "The Singing's coming up soon," she remarked to Lina as they ate. "Do you know your part?"

"Yes," said Lina. "I remember it pretty well from last year."

"I rather like the Singing," said Mrs. Murdo.

"I love it," Lina said. "I think it's my favorite day of the year." Once a year, the people of the city came together to sing the three great songs of Ember. Just thinking of it made Lina feel better. She finished her breakfast and put on her red jacket.

"Don't worry about Poppy, I'll take care of her," said Mrs. Murdo as Lina headed for the door. "When you come back this evening, we'll talk about how to proceed."

"Proceed?" said Lina.

"Well, you can't live by yourselves, just the two of you, can you?"

"We can't?"

"Certainly not," said Mrs. Murdo sternly. "Who's to take care of Poppy while you go off delivering messages? You must move in here with me. I have an empty bedroom, after all, and quite a nice one. Come and look."

She opened a door at the far end of the living room, and Lina peeked in. She had never seen such a beautiful, cozy room. There was a big, lumpy bed covered with a faded blue blanket, and at its head four plump pillows. Next to the bed was a chest of drawers with drawer handles shaped like teardrops and a mirror attached to the top. The carpets on the floor were all different shades of blue and green, and in the corner was a sturdy square table and a chair with a back like a ladder. "This will be your room," said Mrs. Murdo. "Yours and Poppy's. You'll have to share the bed, but it's big enough."

"It's lovely," Lina said. "You're so kind, Mrs. Murdo."

"Well," said Mrs. Murdo briskly, "it's just common sense. You need a place. I have one. You go on now, and I'll see you this evening."

Three days had passed since Lina and Doon had seen the man in the Pipeworks, and there hadn't been any special announcements. So if that man had discovered a way out of Ember, he was keeping the news to himself. Lina couldn't understand why.

As Lina ran through the city with her messages on her first day back to work, it seemed to her that the mood of the people was even gloomier than before. There were long, silent lines at the markets, and knots of people gathered in the squares, talking in low voices. Many shops—more each day, it seemed—displayed signs in their windows saying "Closed" or "Open Mon. Tues. only." Every now and then, the lights flickered, and people stopped and looked up in fright. When the flickering ended and the lights stayed lit, people just took a breath and walked on.

Lina delivered her messages as usual, but inside she felt strange. Everywhere she ran, she heard the same words, like a drumbeat, in her mind: *alone in the world, alone in the world.* It wasn't exactly true. She had Poppy. She had friends. And she had Mrs. Murdo, who was somewhere between a friend and a relative. But she felt as if she had suddenly gotten older in the last three days. She was a sort of mother herself now. What happened to Poppy was more or less up to her.

As the day went on, she stopped thinking *alone in the world* and began thinking about her new life at Mrs. Murdo's. She thought about the blue-green room and planned how she would arrange her pictures on the walls. The one she'd drawn with her blue pencil would look especially nice, because it would match the color of the rugs. She could bring her pillows from home and add them to the ones on the bed, and then she'd have six altogether—and maybe she could find some old blue dresses or shirts and make pillow covers for them. The blue-green room, the orderly apartment, the meals cooked, and the blankets tucked in cozily at night—all this gave her a feeling of comfort, almost luxury. She was grateful for Mrs. Murdo's kindness. I am not ready yet to be alone in the world, she thought.

Late that afternoon, Lina was given a message to take to Lampling Street. She delivered the message and, as she was coming back out onto the street, caught sight of Lizzie coming out the door of the Supply Depot—her orange hair was unmistakable. "Lizzie!" Lina called out.

Lizzie must not have heard her. She kept on going. Lina called again. "Lizzie, wait!" This time it was clear that Lizzie had heard, but instead of stopping, she walked faster. What's the matter with her? Lina wondered. She ran after her and grabbed the back of her coat. "Lizzie, it's me!"

Lizzie stopped and turned around. "Oh!" she said. Her face was flushed. "It's you. Hi! I thought it was . . . I didn't realize it was you." She smiled brightly, but there was a distracted look in her eyes. "I was just going home," she said. Her arms were wrapped around a small bulging sack.

"I'll walk with you," said Lina.

"Oh," said Lizzie. "Oh, good." But she didn't look pleased.

"Lizzie, something sad has happened," Lina said. "My grandmother died."

Lizzie gave her a quick sideways glance, but she didn't stop walking. "That's too bad," she said absently. "Poor you."

What was wrong with her? Lizzie was ordinarily so interested in other people's misfortunes. She could be sincerely sympathetic, too, when she wasn't wrapped up in her own troubles.

Lina changed the subject. "What's in the sack?" she asked.

"Oh, just some groceries," said Lizzie. "I stopped at the market after work."

"You did?" Lina was confused. She had seen Lizzie not two minutes ago leaving the storeroom office.

Lizzie didn't answer. She began walking and talking quite fast. "It was so busy today at work. Work is so hard, isn't it, Lina? I think work is much harder than school, and not as interesting. You do the same thing every day. I get so *tired,* don't you, running around all day?"

Lina started to say that she liked running and hardly ever got tired, but Lizzie didn't wait for her to answer.

"Oh, well, at least there are some good things about it. Guess what, Lina? I have a boyfriend. I met him at work. He really likes me—he says my hair is the exact color of a red-hot burner on a stove."

Lina laughed. "It's true, Lizzie," she said. "You look like your head is on fire."

Lizzie laughed, too, and lifted one hand to fluff her hair. She puckered her lips and fluttered her eyelashes. "He says I'm as beautiful as a red tomato."

They were crossing Torrick Square now. It was crowded in the square. People had just left work and were lining up at the shops and hurrying along with packages. A cluster of children sat on the pavement, playing some sort of game.

"Who is this boyfriend?" asked Lina.

But just at that moment, Lizzie tripped. She'd been strutting along being beautiful, not paying attention to her feet, and the edge of her shoe caught on an uneven place in the pavement. She staggered and fell, and as she fell she lost her grip on the sack. It hit the ground and toppled sideways, and some cans spilled out. They rolled in all different directions.

Lina reached for Lizzie's arm. "Did you hurt yourself?" she asked, but Lizzie went scrambling after the cans so quickly it was clear she wasn't hurt. Wanting to help, Lina went after the cans, too. Two had rolled under a bench. Another was going toward the children, who were on their feet now, watching Lizzie's wild spider-like motions. Lina picked up the cans under the bench, and for a second her breath stopped. One of them was a can of peaches. "Peaches," it said right on it, and there was a picture of a yellow globe. No one she knew had seen a can of peaches in years. She looked at the other one. It was just as amazing—"Creamed Corn," it said. Lina remembered having creamed corn once, as a thrilling treat, when she was five years old.

There was a shout. She looked up. One of the children had picked up a can. "Look at this!" he cried, and the other children gathered around him. "Applesauce!" he said, and the children murmured, "Applesauce, applesauce," as if they had never heard the word before.

Lizzie was on her feet. She had all the cans except for the two in Lina's hands and the one the child had picked up. She stood there for a moment, her eyes flicking back and forth from Lina to the children. Then she smiled, a bright fake-looking smile. "Thanks for helping me," she said. "I found these on a back shelf at the market. What a surprise, huh? You can keep those." She waved the back of her hand at the children, waved again at Lina, and then took off, holding the sack by its neck so it hung beside her and banged against her legs.

Lina didn't follow her. She walked home, thinking about Lizzie's sack of cans. You simply did not find cans of peaches and applesauce and creamed corn on the back shelves of markets. Lizzie was lying. And if the cans hadn't come from a market, where had they come from? There was only one answer: they had come from the storerooms. Somehow, Lizzie had gotten them because she worked in the storeroom office. Had she paid for them? How much? Or had she taken them without paying?

Mrs. Murdo had cooked a dinner of beet-and-bean stew for them that night. When Lina showed her the two cans, she gasped in astonishment. "Where did you get these?" she asked.

"From a friend," said Lina.

"And where did your friend get them?"

Lina shrugged. "I don't know."

Mrs. Murdo frowned slightly but didn't ask any more questions. She opened the cans, and they had a feast: creamed corn with their stew, and peaches for dessert. It was the best meal Lina had had in a very long time—but her enjoyment of it was tainted just a little by the question of where it had come from.

The next morning, Lina headed for Broad Street. Before she started delivering messages today, she was going to have a talk with Lizzie.

She spied her half a block from the storeroom office. She was sauntering along looking in shop windows. A long green scarf was wound around her neck.

Lina ran up swiftly behind her. "Lizzie," she said.

Lizzie whirled around. When she saw Lina, she flinched. She didn't say anything, just turned around and kept walking.

Lina caught hold of one end of the green scarf and jerked Lizzie to a halt. "Lizzie!" she said. "Stop!"

"What for?" Lizzie said. "I'm going to work." She tried to pull away, but she didn't get far, because Lina had a firm grip on her scarf.

Lina spoke in a low voice. There were people all around them—a couple of old men leaning against the wall, a group of chattering children just ahead, workers going toward the storerooms—and she didn't want to be overheard. "You have to tell me where you got those cans," she said.

"I told you. I found them on a back shelf at the market. Let go of my scarf." Lizzie tried to wrench her scarf out of Lina's grip, but Lina held on.

"You didn't," Lina said. "No market would just forget about things like that. Tell me the truth." She gave a yank on the end of the scarf.

"Stop it!" Lizzie reached out and grabbed a handful of Lina's hair. Lina yelped and pulled harder on the scarf, and the two of them scuffled, snatching at each other's hair and coats. They knocked against a woman who snapped at them angrily, and finally they toppled over, sitting down hard on the pavement.

Lina was the first one to laugh. It was so much like what they used to do in fun, chasing each other and screaming with laughter. Now here they were again, nearly grown girls, sitting in a heap on the pavement.

After a moment, Lizzie laughed, too. "You dope," she said. "All right, I'll tell you. I sort of wanted to anyway." Lizzie leaned forward with her elbows on her knees and lowered her voice. "Well, it's this," she said. "There's a storeroom worker named Looper. He's a carrier. Do you know him? He was two classes ahead of us. Looper Windly."

"I know who he is," said Lina. "I took a message for him on my first day of work. Tall, with a long skinny neck. Big teeth. Funny-looking."

Lizzie looked hurt. "Well, I wouldn't describe him *that* way. I think he's handsome."

Lina shrugged. "Okay. Go on."

"Looper explores the storerooms. He goes into every room that isn't locked. He wants to know the *true situation*, Lina. He's not like most workers, who just plod along doing their jobs and then go home. He wants to find things out."

"And what has he found out?" Lina asked.

"He's found out that there's still a little bit left of some rare things, just a few things in rooms here and there that have been forgotten. You know, Lina," she said, "there are *so many* rooms down there. Some of them, way out at the edges, are marked 'Empty' in the ledger book, and so no one ever goes there anymore. But Looper found out that they're not all empty."

"So he's been taking things."

"Just a few things! And not often."

"And he's giving some to you."

"Yes. Because he likes me." Lizzie smiled a little smile and hugged her arms together. I see, Lina thought. She feels *that* way about Looper.

"But Looper's stealing," said Lina. "And Lizzie—he isn't just stealing things for you. He has a store! He steals things and sells them for huge prices!"

"He does not," said Lizzie, but she looked worried.

"He does. I know because I bought something from him just a few weeks ago. He has a whole box of colored pencils."

Lizzie scowled. "He never gave me any colored pencils."

"He shouldn't be giving you anything—or selling things. Don't you think everyone should know about this food he found?"

"No!" Lizzie cried. "Because listen. If there's only one can of peaches left, only one person gets to have it, right? So why should everyone know? They'd just end up fighting over it. What good would that be?" Lizzie reached out and put a hand on Lina's knee. "Listen," she said. "I'll ask Looper to find some good stuff for you, too. I know he will, if I ask him."

Before she had time to think, Lina heard herself saying, "What kind of good stuff?"

Lizzie's eyes gleamed. "There's two packages of

colored paper, he told me. And some cough medicine. And there's three pairs of girls' shoes."

It was treasure. Colored paper! And cough medicine to cure sickness, and shoes . . . she hadn't had new ones for almost two years. Lina's heart raced. What Lizzie said was true: if everyone knew there were still a few wonderful things in the storerooms, people would fight each other trying to get them. But what if no one knew? What difference would it make if she had the colored paper, or the shoes? She suddenly wanted those things so badly she felt weak. A picture arose in her mind's eye—the shelves at Mrs. Murdo's house stocked with good things, and the three of them happier and safer than other people.

Lizzie leaned closer and lowered her voice. "Looper found a can of pineapple. I was going to split it with him, but I'll give you a bite if you promise not to tell."

Pineapple! That delectable long-lost thing that her grandmother had told her about. Was there anything wrong with having a bite of it, just to see what it was like?

"I've already tasted peaches, applesauce, and a thing called fruit cocktail," said Lizzie. "And prunes and creamed corn and cranberry sauce and asparagus . . ."

"All *that*?" Lina was astonished. "Then there's a lot of special things like that still?"

"No," said Lizzie. "Not a lot at all. In fact, we've finished all those."

"You and Looper?"

Lizzie nodded, smiling smugly. "Looper says it's all going to be gone soon anyway, why not live as well as we can right now?"

"But Lizzie, why should *you* get all that? Why you and not other people?"

"Because we found it. Because we can get at it."

"I don't think it's fair," said Lina.

Lizzie spoke as if she were talking to a not-very-bright child. "You can have some, *too.* That's what I'm *telling* you. There are still a few good things left."

But that wasn't the unfairness Lina was thinking of. It was that just two people were getting things that everyone would have wanted. She couldn't think how it should have been done. You couldn't divide a can of applesauce evenly among all the people in the city. Still, something was wrong with grabbing the good things just because you *could.* It seemed not only unfair to everyone else but bad for the person who was doing it, somehow. She remembered the hunger she'd felt when Looper showed her the colored pencils. It wasn't a pleasant feeling. She didn't *want* to want things that way.

She stood up. "I don't want anything from Looper."

Lizzie shrugged. "Okay," she said, but there was a look of dismay on her small pale face. "Too bad for you."

"Thanks anyway," said Lina, and she set off across Torrick Square, walking fast at first and then breaking into a run.

CHAPTER 12

A Dreadful Discovery

About a week after he and Lina had seen the man come out the mysterious door, Doon was assigned to fix a clog in Tunnel 207. It turned out to be easy. He undid the pipe, rammed a long thin brush down it, and a jet of water spurted into his face. Once he'd put the pipe back together, he had nothing else to do. So he decided to go out to Tunnel 351 and take another look at the locked door. It was strange, he thought, that no announcement about a way out of Ember had come. Maybe that door had not been what they thought it was.

So he set out for the south end of the Pipeworks. When he came to the roped-off passage in Tunnel 351, he ducked in and walked along through the dark, feeling his way. He was pretty sure the door would be locked as usual. His mind was on other things. He was thinking of his green worm, which had been behaving oddly, refusing to eat and hanging from the side of its box with its chin tucked in. And he was thinking about Lina, whom he hadn't seen for several days. He wondered where she was. When he came to the door, he reached absently for the knob, and what he felt startled him so much that he snatched his hand back as if he'd been stung. He felt again, carefully. There was a *key* in the lock!

For a long moment, Doon stood as still as a statue. Then he took hold of the doorknob and turned it. Very slowly, he pushed on the door. It swung inward without a sound.

He opened it only a few inches, just enough to peer around the edge. What he saw made him gasp.

There was no road, or passage, or stairway behind the door. There was a brightly lit room, whose size he could not guess at because it was so crowded with things. On all sides were crates and boxes, sacks and bundles and packages. There were mounds of cans, heaps of clothes, rows of jars and bottles, stacks of light-bulb packages. Piles rose to the low ceiling and leaned against the walls, blocking all but a small space in the center. In that small space, a little living room had been set up. There was a greenish rug, and on the rug an armchair and a table. On the table were dishes smeared with the remains of food, and in the armchair facing Doon was a great blob of a person whose head was flopped backward, so that all Doon could see of it was an upthrust chin. The blob stirred and muttered, and Doon, in the second before he stepped back and pulled the door closed, caught a glimpse of a fleshy ear, a slab of gray cheek, and a loose, purplish mouth.

That day, Lina had more messages to carry than ever. There had been five blackouts in a row during the week. They were all fairly short—the longest was four and a half minutes, Lina had heard—but there had never been so many so close together. Everyone was nervous. People who might ordinarily walk to someone's house were sending messages instead. Often they didn't even come out into the street but beckoned to a messenger from their doorway.

By five o'clock, Lina had carried thirty-nine messages. Most of them were more or less the same: "I'm not coming to the meeting tonight, decided to stay home." "I won't be in to work tomorrow." "Instead of meeting me in Cloving Square, why don't you come to my house?" The citizens of Ember were hunkering down, burrowing in. Fewer people stood around talking in groups under the lights in the squares. Instead, they would pause briefly to murmur a few words to each other and then hasten onward.

Lina was on her way home to Mrs. Murdo's—she and Poppy had moved in with all their things—when she heard rapid footsteps. Startled, she turned and saw Doon racing toward her.

At first he was so out of breath he couldn't speak.

"What is it? What *is* it?" said Lina.

"The door," he panted. "The door in 351. I opened it."

Lina's heart leapt. "You did?"

Doon nodded.

"Is it the way out?" Lina whispered fiercely.

"No," Doon said. He glanced behind him. Clutching Lina's arm, he pulled her into a shadowy spot on the street. "It doesn't lead out of Ember," he whispered. "It leads to a big room."

Lina's face fell. "A room? What's in there?"

"Everything. Food, clothes, boxes, cans. Light bulbs, stacks of them. Everything. Piles and piles up to the ceiling." His eyes grew wide. "And someone was there, in the middle of it all, asleep."

"Who?"

A look of horror passed over Doon's face. "The mayor," he said. "Conked out in a big armchair, with an empty plate in front of him."

"The mayor!" Lina whispered.

"Yes. The mayor has a secret treasure room in the Pipeworks."

They stared at each other, speechless. Then Doon suddenly stamped hard on the pavement. His face flushed red. "*That's* the solution he keeps telling us about. It's a solution for *him*, not the rest of us. He gets everything he needs, and we get the leftovers! He doesn't care about the city. All he cares about is his fat stomach!"

Lina felt dizzy, as if she'd been hit on the head. "What will we do?" She couldn't think, she was so stunned.

"Tell everyone!" said Doon. He was shaking with anger. "Tell the whole city the mayor is robbing us!"

"Wait, wait." Lina put a hand on Doon's arm and concentrated for a minute. "Come on," she said at last. "Let's go sit in Harken Square. I have something to tell you, too."

At the north end of Harken Square stood a circle of Believers, clapping their hands and singing one of their songs. Lately they seemed to be singing more loudly and cheerfully than ever. Their voices were shrill. "Coming soon to save us!" they wailed. "Happy, happy day!"

Near the Gathering Hall steps, something unusual was happening. Twenty or so people were pacing around and around, carrying big signs painted on old planks and on big banners made of sheets. The signs said "WHAT solutions, Mayor Cole?" and "We want ANSWERS!" Every now and then the demonstrators would yell these slogans out loud. Lina wondered if the mayor was paying any attention.

Doon and Lina found an empty bench on the south side of Harken Square and sat down.

"Now, listen," said Lina.

"I *am* listening," said Doon, though his face was still red and the look on his face was stormy.

"I saw Lizzie coming out of the storerooms yesterday," Lina said. She told him about the cans, and Lizzie's new friend, Looper, and what Looper was doing.

Doon pounded his fist on his leg. "That's *two* of them doing it, then," he said.

"Wait, there's more. Remember how I thought there was something familiar about the man who came out the door? I've remembered what. It was that way he walked, sort of dipping over sideways, and also that hair, that black hair all unbrushed and sticking out. I've seen him twice. I don't know why I didn't remember who it was right away—maybe because I've only seen him from the front. I took a message for him on my first day."

Doon was jiggling with impatience. "Well, who was it, *who was it*?"

"It was Looper. Looper, who works in the storerooms. Lizzie's boyfriend. And Doon—" Lina leaned forward. "It was a message to the *mayor* that he gave me, and it was this: 'Delivery at eight.'"

Doon's mouth dropped open. "So that means . . ."

"He's taking things from the storeroom for the mayor. And he's giving some to Lizzie, and selling some in his store."

"Oh!" cried Doon. He slapped his hand against his head. "Why didn't I get it before? There's a hatch in the ceiling near Tunnel 351. It must go right up into the storerooms. Looper comes through there! *That's* what we heard that day, remember? A sort of scraping—that would have been the hatch opening. Then a thud—his sack of stuff dropping through—and then a sound like someone jumping down and landing hard on the ground."

"And then walking slowly—"

"Because he was carrying a load!"

"And walking quickly on the way out because he'd left it all for the mayor." Lina took a deep breath. Her heart was drumming and her hands were cold. "We have to think what to do," she said. "If this were an ordinary situation, the mayor would be the one to tell."

"But the mayor is the one committing the crime," said Doon.

"So then we should tell the guards, I guess," said Lina. "They're next in authority to the mayor. Though I don't like them much," she added, remembering how she'd been so roughly hustled down the stairs from the roof of the Gathering Hall. "Especially the chief guard."

"But you're right," Doon said. "We should tell the guards. They'll go down into the Pipeworks and see for themselves that we're telling the truth. Then they can arrest the mayor and have all the stuff put back in the storerooms, and *then* they can tell the city what's been going on."

"That's a much better idea," said Lina. "Then you and I can get back to what's more important."

"What?"

"Figuring out the Instructions. Now that we know that the door we found wasn't the right one, we have to *find* the right one."

"I don't know," said Doon. "We might be all wrong about those Instructions. They could just be about some old Pipeworks tool closet." He made a sour face. "'Instructions for Egreston.' Who's Egreston? Or Egresman? Or whoever it was? Why couldn't he have been just an especially stupid Pipeworks guy who needed instructions to find his way around?" He shook his head. "I don't know. I think maybe those Instructions are just hogwash."

"Hogwash? What's that?"

"It means nonsense. I read it in a book in the library."

"But they can't be nonsense! Why would they have been kept in a box like that? With the strange lock?"

But Doon didn't want to think about the Instructions right then. "We'll figure it out tomorrow," he said. "Right now, let's go find the guards."

"Wait," said Lina, catching hold of the sleeve of his jacket. "I have one more thing to tell you."

"What?"

"My grandmother died."

"Oh!" Doon's face fell. "That's so sad," he said. "I'm sorry." His sympathy made tears spring to Lina's eyes. Doon looked startled for a moment, and then he took a step toward her and wrapped his arms around her. He gave her a squeeze so quick and tight that it made her cough, and then it made her laugh. She realized all at once that Doon—thin, dark-eyed Doon with his troublesome temper and his terrible brown jacket and his good heart—was the person that she knew better than anyone now. He was her best friend.

"Thanks," she said. "Well." She smiled at him. "Let's go and talk to the guard."

They crossed the square and climbed the steps of the Gathering Hall. Sitting at the big reception desk outside the door of the mayor's office was the assistant guard, Barton Snode, the same one Lina had encountered her first time here. Snode looked bored. His elbows were on the desk, and his chin was moving very slowly from side to side.

"Sir," said Doon, "we need to speak with you."

The guard looked up. "Certainly," he said. "Go right ahead."

"In private," said Lina.

The guard looked puzzled. His small eyes darted back and forth. "This is private," he said. "No one here but me."

"But anyone could come along," said Doon. "What

we have to say is secret, and very important."

"Very important?" said Snode. "Secret?" His face brightened. Grunting, he raised himself up from his chair and motioned them into a narrow hallway off to the side of the main hall. "What is it?" he said.

They told him. As they spoke, interrupting each other to make sure they got in all the details, the guard's eyebrows gradually lifted higher and higher over his eyes. "You *saw* this room?" he said. "This is true? Are you sure?" He was chewing faster now. "You mean the mayor . . . you mean the mayor is . . ."

At that moment, a little way down the hall, a door opened. Through it came three more guards, including—Lina spotted him by his beard—the chief guard. They strode forward, talking to each other in low voices, and as they passed, the chief guard threw a quick glance at Lina. Does he recognize me? Lina wondered. She couldn't tell.

Barton Snode finished his sentence in a husky whisper. "You mean . . . the mayor is *stealing*?"

"That's right," said Doon. "We thought you should be informed, because who else can arrest the mayor? And once you've done that, the guards can put all the things he's stolen back where they came from."

"And then tell the city that a new mayor has to be found," added Lina.

Barton Snode leaned heavily against the wall and rubbed a hand over his chin. He seemed to be thinking. "Something must be done," he said. "This is shocking, shocking." He started back toward his desk, and Doon and Lina followed. "I will make a note," he said, taking a pencil from the desk drawer. Lina watched as he wrote slowly on a scrap of paper: "Mayor stealing. Secret room."

When he'd finished, he let out a satisfied breath. "Very good," he said. "Action will be taken, you may be sure. Some sort of action. Quite soon."

"Good," said Doon.

"Thank you," said Lina, and they turned to leave.

The three guards were standing by the main door of the Gathering Hall as Doon and Lina went out. The chief guard moved aside to make way for them, and they went through the door and out onto the wide front steps. Lina glanced over her shoulder. Before the door swung closed, she saw the chief guard striding toward the reception desk, where Barton Snode was standing up, leaning forward, his eyes shining with important news.

CHAPTER 13

Deciphering the Message

Doon headed for home, and Lina went in the opposite direction across Harken Square. The little group of Believers had gone, but the protesters with their signs continued to pace back and forth. A few of them were still shaking their fists in the air and yelling, but most of them tramped silently, looking tired and discouraged. Lina felt a bit that way, too. Once Doon said he'd seen a door, she was sure that the door he'd found and the door in the Instructions were the same. She had had such hopes for that door in the Pipeworks. But hoping so hard had made her jump to conclusions. She'd gone a little too fast. She always went fast. Sometimes it was a good thing and sometimes not.

Now Doon thought the Instructions were nothing important after all. She didn't want him to be right. She didn't believe he was, even now. But her thoughts felt like a mess of tangled yarn. She needed someone wise and sensible to help her sort things out. She headed for Glome Street.

Though it was nearly six o'clock, she found Clary still in her workroom, at the far end of Greenhouse 1. It was a small, crowded room. Pots and trowels cluttered a high table at one end. Above the table were shelves full of bottles of seeds, and boxes of string, wire, and various kinds of powders. Clary's desk was a rickety table, littered with scraps of paper, all of them covered with notes in her neat, round handwriting. Two rickety chairs went with the rickety table, one on each side. Lina sat down facing Clary. "I have to tell you some important things," she said. "And they're all secret."

"All right," said Clary. "I can keep secrets." She was wearing a patched shirt that had faded from blue to gray. Her short brown hair was tucked behind her ears, and a bit of leaf clung to it on the right-hand side. She folded her arms in front of her on the desk. She looked square and solid.

"The first thing is," Lina began, "that I found the Instructions. But Poppy had chewed them up."

"The Instructions," said Clary. "I'm not familiar with them."

Lina explained. She went on to explain everything—how she'd shown the Instructions to Doon, what they had figured out, how he'd searched the Pipeworks and found the door, and what he'd seen when he opened the door.

Clary made an unhappy sound and shook her head. "This is very bad," she said. "And sad, too. I remember when the mayor was first starting out. He has always been foolish, but not always wicked. I'm sorry to know that the worst side of him has won out." Clary's dark brown eyes seemed to grow deeper and sadder. "There is so much darkness in Ember, Lina. It's not just outside, it's inside us, too. Everyone has some darkness inside. It's like a hungry creature. It wants and wants and *wants* with a terrible power. And the more you give it, the bigger and hungrier it gets."

Lina knew. She had felt it in Looper's shop as she hovered over the colored pencils. For a moment, she felt sorry for the mayor. His hunger had grown so big it could never be satisfied. His huge body couldn't contain it. It made him forget everything else.

Clary let out a long breath, and a few of the scraps of paper on her desk fluttered. She ran her fingers through her hair, felt the bit of leaf, and plucked it out. Then she said, "About these Instructions."

"Oh, yes," said Lina. "They might be important, or they might not be. I don't know anymore."

"I'd like to see them, if you'd let me."

"Of course you can see them—but you'll have to come home with me."

"I'll come now, if that's all right," said Clary. "There's plenty of time before lights out."

Lina led Clary up the stairs and into her new bedroom at Mrs. Murdo's. "Nice room," Clary said, looking around with interest. "And I see you have a sprout."

"A what?" said Lina.

"Your bean," said Clary, pointing at the little pot of dirt on the windowsill.

Lina bent to see what Clary was talking about. Sure enough, the dirt was heaving up a little. She touched the pushed-up part, brushed away the dirt, and discovered a pale green loop. It looked like a neck, as if a creature in the bean were trying to escape but hadn't yet managed to pull its head out. Of course she already knew that plants grew from seeds. But to have put that flat white bean in the dirt, to have almost forgotten about it, and now to see it forcing its way up into the air . . .

"It's doing it!" she said. "It's coming to life!"

Clary nodded, smiling. "Still amazes me every time I see it," she said.

Lina brought out the Instructions, and Clary sat down at the table to study them. She puzzled over the patchwork of scraps for a long time, tracing the lines with her finger, murmuring the parts of words.

"What you've figured out so far seems right to me," she said. "I think 'ip ork' must be 'Pipeworks.'

And 'iverb nk' must be 'riverbank.' So this bit must be 'down riverbank'—then there's a big space here—'to edge.' Edge of what, I wonder? And does it mean 'down riverbank' as in 'walk alongside the river'?"

"Yes, I think so," Lina said.

"Or does it mean go down the riverbank itself, down the bank toward the water? Maybe 'edge' means 'edge of the water.'"

"It couldn't mean that. The bank goes straight down like a wall. You couldn't go down to the edge of the water, you'd fall in." Lina pictured the dark, swift water and shivered.

"This word," said Clary, putting a finger on the paper. "Maybe it isn't 'edge,' maybe it's something else. It could be 'hedge.' Or 'pledge.' Those don't make much sense. But it could be 'ledge' or 'wedge.'"

Lina saw that Clary was no better at deciphering the puzzle than she was. She sighed and sat down on the end of her bed. "It's hopeless," she said.

Clary straightened up quickly. "Don't say that. This torn-up piece of paper is the most hopeful thing I've ever seen. Do you know what this word is?" She pointed to the word at the top of the paper, *Egres.*

"Someone's name, isn't it? The title would be 'Instructions for Egreston,' or maybe 'Egresman,' or something like that. The person the instructions were for."

"I don't think so," said Clary. "If you add an s to

this word, right where this tear in the paper is, you get 'Egress.' Do you know what that means?"

"No," said Lina.

"It means 'the way out.' It means 'the exit.' The title of this document is 'Instructions for Egress.'"

When Clary left, there was still over an hour before lights out. Lina raced across the city to Greengate Square. She glanced in the window of the Small Items shop, where Doon's father was reaching for something on a shelf, and then she dashed up the stairs and knocked on the door of Doon's apartment. Right away, she heard quick steps and Doon opened the door.

"I have something exciting to tell you," Lina said breathlessly.

"Come in, then."

Lina went across the cluttered room to stand by a lamp. She pulled from her pocket a tiny piece of paper on which she had written "Egres." "Look at this word," she said.

"It's from the title of the Instructions. Someone's name," said Doon.

"No," said Lina. "It's meant to be 'Egress,' with two s's. I showed the Instructions to Clary, and she told me. It means 'the way out.'"

"The way out!" cried Doon.

"Yes! The way out. The exit. It's instructions for the way out of Ember!"

"So it *is* real," Doon said.

"It is. We have to figure out the rest. Or as much of the rest as possible. Can you come now?"

He darted into his room, emerged with his jacket, and they ran.

"All right," said Lina. They were on the floor of the blue-green room at Mrs. Murdo's. "Let's take the first line." She moved her finger along it slowly.

1. Exp
riv   ip   ork .

"We know that 'ip ork' is Pipeworks," she said. "'Exp' could be 'expand,' or 'explore,' or 'expose' . . ."

"There's a big space between 'Exp' and the rest," said Doon. "There must be more words in there."

"But who knows what they are? Let's move on." Lina swept her straggly hair impatiently back from her face. "Look at number two."

2.   ston   marked with E by r
dge

Lina put her finger on *ston*. "What could that be?"

"Maybe 'piston,'" said Doon. "That's part of a machine, like the generator. Or maybe it's 'astonish.' Or it could be . . ."

"I bet it's just plain 'stone,'" said Lina. "There's a lot of stone in the Pipeworks."

Doon had to admit this was probably right. "So then," he said, "it would be 'stone marked with E. . . .'" He frowned at the next bit. "This must be 'river's edge.' 'Stone marked with E by the river's edge.'"

They looked at each other in delight. "E for Egress!" cried Lina. "E for Exit!"

They bent over the document again. "There's not much left of this next line," said Doon.

3. adde down iverb nk
to edge appr eight
low.

"Just this part—which must say, 'down riverbank to edge' . . . something."

"'Edge of water' would make sense. But right after 'edge' there's 'app.' What would that be?" Doon sat back on his heels and gazed up at the ceiling, as if the answer might be there. Lina muttered, "down riverbank to edge, edge." She thought of Clary's guesses about that line. "Maybe it's 'ledge,'" she said. "'Down riverbank to ledge.' There could be a ledge down near the water."

"Yes, that must be right. There's a stone marked with E, and down the riverbank at that point there's a ledge. I think we're getting it."

Once again they crouched over the page, their heads close together. "Okay," Doon said. "Line 4."

4. acks to the
wat r, find door of bo
ker. Ke hind small steel
pan the right . Rem
ey, open do .

"This is where it says 'door,'" Lina said. "Somehow the door is by the ledge. Does that make sense?"

"And there's that 'small steel pan'—what can that mean? What would a pan have to do with anything?"

"But look, but look." Lina tapped the paper urgently. "Here it says 'ke' and here it says 'ey.' It's talking about a key!"

"But what is it a door *to*?" said Doon, sitting back. "Remember, we thought about this before. A door in the bank of the river would lead *under* the Pipeworks."

Lina pondered this. "Maybe it leads to a long tunnel that goes way out beyond Ember, and then gradually up and up until it comes out at the other city."

"What other city?" Doon glanced up at the drawings tacked to the walls of Lina's room. "Oh," he said. "You mean *that* city."

"Well, it could be."

Doon shrugged. "I suppose so. Or it could be another city exactly like this one."

That was a gloomy thought. Both of them felt their spirits sink a little at the idea. So they turned back to the task of deciphering.

"Next line," said Lina.

But Doon sat back on his heels again. He stared into the air, half smiling. "I have an idea," he said. "If we *do* find the way out, we'll need to announce it to everyone. Wouldn't it be splendid to do it during the Singing? Stand up there in front of the whole city and say we've found it?"

"It would be," Lina said. "But that's only two days away."

"Yes. We have to hurry."

They were bending again over the glued-down fragments when Doon remembered that he should check the time. It was a quarter to nine. He barely had time to get home.

"Come again tomorrow," said Lina. "And while you're at work, look for the rock marked with E."

That night, Doon had trouble sleeping. He couldn't find a comfortable position on his bed. It seemed to be made up of nothing but lumps and wrinkles, and it squeaked and groaned every time he moved. He flailed around so much that the noise woke his father, who came to his room and asked, "What *is* it, son? Nightmares?"

"No," said Doon. "Just can't sleep."

"Are you worrying? Frightened of anything?"

Doon wanted to say, Yes, Father. I'm worried because the mayor of our city is taking for himself the things that people need, and I'm afraid because any day our lights could go out forever. I'm worried and afraid a lot of the time, but I'm also excited because I think there *is* a way out, and we might find it—and all those feelings are whirling around in my head, which makes it hard to sleep.

He could have told his father everything. His father would have plunged in with great enthusiasm. He would have helped them decipher the Instructions and expose the mayor's thievery; he would even have come down into the Pipeworks and helped search for the rock marked with E. But Doon wanted to keep these things to himself for now. Tomorrow, the guards would announce that an alert young boy had uncovered the mayor's crime, and his father, hearing the announcements along with the rest of Ember, would turn to the person next to him and say, "That's my son they're talking about! My *son*!"

So in answer to his father's question, he simply said, "No, Father, I'm all right."

"Well, then, see if you can't lie still," said his father. "Good night, son," he added, and closed the door.

Doon smoothed out his covers and pulled them up to his chin. He closed his eyes. But still he couldn't sleep.

So he tried a method that had often worked for him before. He would choose a place he knew well—the school, for instance—and imagine himself walking through it, picturing it as he went in minute detail. Often his thoughts would wander, but he would always bring them back to the imaginary journey, and something about doing this would often make him sleepy. This night he decided to retrace his explorations of the Pipeworks. He held his mind to the task for a long time, picturing, with all the clarity he could muster, everything he had seen in that underground realm—the long stairway, the tunnels, the door, the path along the river, the rocks along the path. He felt sleep drawing closer, a heaviness in his limbs, but just as he was about to give in to it, he saw in his mind's eye the wrinkled rocks that bordered the river at the west end of the Pipeworks, the rocks whose strange ridges and creases had reminded him of writing. His eyes flew open in the dark, his heart began to hammer, and he gave up on sleeping and lay in a state of terrible impatience for the rest of the night.

CHAPTER 14

The Way Out

The next day was Song Rehearsal Day. Everyone was let off from work at twelve o'clock to practice for the Singing. It was a slow morning for messages. Lina had a lot of time to sit at her station in Garn Square and think. She put her elbows on her knees, rested her chin in her hands, and stared down at the pavement in front of the bench, which was worn smooth by the many feet that had passed there. She thought about the mayor, down in his room full of plunder, gorging on peaches and asparagus and wrapping his huge body in elegant new clothes. She thought of his great stack of light bulbs and shook her head in bewilderment. What was he thinking? If he still had light bulbs when everyone else in Ember had run out, would he enjoy sitting in his lit room while the rest of the city drowned in darkness? And when the power finally ran out for good, all his light bulbs would be useless. Possessions couldn't save him—how could he have forgotten that? He must be thinking the same way as Looper: everything was hopeless anyhow, so he'd live it up while he could.

She leaned back against the bench, stretched her legs out, and took a long breath. Very soon, the guards would storm into the secret room and seize the mayor as he sat stuffing himself on stolen goodies. Maybe they already had. Maybe today the stunning news would come: Mayor Arrested! Stealing from Citizens! Maybe they'd announce it at the Singing, so everyone could hear it.

No one came with any messages to be delivered, so after a while Lina left her station and found a step to sit on in an alley off Calloo Street. She pulled back her hair and braided it to keep it from sliding around. Then she took from her pocket the copy of the Instructions she'd made just after she sent her note to the mayor. She unfolded it and began to study it.

This is what she was doing when, a little before twelve o'clock, she looked up to see Doon running toward her. He must have come straight from the Pipeworks—he had a big damp patch of water on one leg of his pants. He spoke in an excited rush. "I've been looking all over for you!" he said. "I've found it!"

"Found what?"

"The E! At least it looks like an E. It *must* be an E, though you wouldn't know it if you weren't looking for it. . . ."

"You mean the rock marked with an E? In the Pipeworks?"

"Yes, yes, I found it!" He stood breathing hard, his eyes blazing. "I'd seen it before, but I didn't think of it as an E then, just a squiggle that looked like writing. There are all these rocks that look like they're covered with writing."

"Which rocks? Where is it?" Lina was on her feet now, bouncing with excitement.

"Down at the west end of the river. Near where it goes into that great hole in the Pipeworks wall." He paused, trying to catch his breath. "And listen," he said. "We could go there right now."

"Right now?"

"Yes, because of rehearsals. Everyone's going home, so the Pipeworks will be closed and empty."

"But if it's closed, how will we get in?"

Grinning, Doon produced a large key from his pocket. "I ducked into the office on my way out and borrowed the spare key," he said. "Lister—he's the Pipeworks director—was in the bathroom practicing his singing. He won't miss the key today. And tomorrow, everyone will be off work." He did an impatient shuffle. "So come on," he said.

The town clock struck the first of its twelve noontime booms. Lina stuffed her copy of the Instructions back in her pocket. "Let's go."

The Pipeworks was empty and silent. Lina and Doon went up the hallway past the rows of boots and the slickers hanging on their hooks. They didn't take any of these for themselves. This was not a Pipeworks tunnel they were about to enter, they were sure; it wouldn't be dripping with water or lined with spurting pipes.

They went down the long stairway and out into the main tunnel, where the river thundered alongside the path, its dark surface strewn with flecks of light.

Doon led the way along the river's edge. As they neared the west end, Lina saw the rocky outcroppings Doon had described to her. They were strange bulging shapes creased with lines like the faces of the very old. Not far beyond, Lina could see the place where the river disappeared into a great hole in the Pipeworks wall.

Doon knelt down beside a clump of stones. He ran a finger over their convoluted surface. "Look here," he said. Lina stooped down and peered at the deeply carved lines. It was hard to see the E at first, because it was surrounded by such a tangle of other lines, and because she was expecting it to be an E drawn with straight strokes. But once she saw it—an E drawn with curving lines, a script E—she was sure it had been carved on purpose: it was centered on its stone, and its lines were deep and even.

"So from here we should look down at the river," said Doon. "That's what the Instructions said, 'down riverbank to ledge.'"

He lay on his stomach next to the rock and inched forward until his head hung out over the edge of the path. Lina watched him anxiously. His elbows stuck up on either side of him, and his head, bent down, was nearly invisible. He stayed that way for long seconds. Then he shouted, "Yes! I see something!" and scrambled to his feet again. "You do it," he said. "Look at the riverbank right below us."

Lina did as he had. She lay down and pulled herself forward until her head was over the edge. Eight feet or so below her, she saw the black water churning by. She tucked her chin in and looked at the riverbank. It was a sheer rock wall, straight up and down and slick with spray, and at first that was all she saw. But she kept looking and before long could make out short iron bars bolted into the bank, one below the next, almost directly below her. They were like the rungs of a ladder. They *were* a ladder, she realized. The bars provided a way to climb down the riverbank. Not a very appealing way—the bars looked slippery, and the water below was so terribly fast. And because of the dimness and the flying spray, she couldn't actually see if there was a ledge at the bottom or not. But the E was clearly an E, and the bars were clearly a ladder. This must be the right place.

"Who'll go first?" said Doon.

"You can," Lina said, getting to her feet and stepping away.

"All right." Doon turned so that his back was to the river, and he eased himself carefully over the rocks, feeling for the first rung with his foot. Lina watched as he sank out of sight, little by little. After a few moments his voice called up from below: "I'm down! Now you come!"

Lina inched backward, just as Doon had, letting one foot dangle over the edge, lower and lower, until it touched the first rung of the ladder. She shifted her weight to that foot, clinging with cold fingers to a ridge in the rock, and lowered herself slowly until she was standing on the rung with both feet. Her heart was beating so hard she was afraid it would shake her fingers loose from their grip.

Now she had to move downward. She felt for the next rung with her foot, found it, let herself down. It would have been easy if it hadn't been for the river waiting below to swallow her.

"You're almost here!" called Doon. His voice came from right below her. "There's a ledge—one more rung and you'll feel it."

She did feel it, solid beneath her foot. For a second, she stood there, still clutching the ladder. The surging water was only inches below her now. Don't think about it, she told herself. She moved sideways two steps to stand next to Doon, and there in front of them was a rectangular space carved out of the river wall, rather like the entry hall of a building. It was perhaps eight feet wide and eight feet high, and would havc been invisible from anywhere else in the Pipeworks. You had to have climbed down the riverbank to see it.

They stepped into this entry hall and walked a few steps. Enough light to see by came from the tunnel behind them.

Lina stopped. "There's the door!" she said.

"What?" said Doon. The water roared so loudly they had to shout to be heard.

"The door!" Lina yelled happily.

"Yes!" Doon yelled back. "I see it!"

At the end of the passage was a wide, solid-looking door. It was dull gray, mottled with greenish and brownish blotches that looked like mildew. Lina put her palms against it. It was metal, and it felt cold. The door had a metal handle, and just below the handle was a keyhole.

Lina reached into the pocket of her pants for her copy of the Instructions. She unfolded it, and Doon looked over her shoulder. Together they squinted at the paper in the dim light from the main tunnel.

"This is the part, right here," she said, pointing:

3. adde down iverb nk
to edge appr eight
low.
4. acks to the
wat r, find door of bo
ker. Ke hind small steel
pan the right . Rem
ey, open do .

Lina ran her finger along line number 3. "This must say, 'Something something down riverbank to ledge approximately eight feet below.' That's what we've just done. Then four is something about . . . 'backs to the water, find door . . . something.' And then 'Ke hind'—that must be 'key behind,' and then there's the small steel pan. Do you see a small steel pan?"

Doon was still studying the paper. "It says 'right.' We should look to the right of the door."

And quite easily they found it. It wasn't a pan at all, but a small square of steel embedded in the wall. "A steel *panel,*" said Lina. She ran her fingers across it and felt a dent at one side. When she pressed there, the panel sprang open easily and silently, as if it were glad to have been finally found. Inside, a silver key was hanging on a hook.

Lina reached for it and then drew her hand back. "Shall I do it?" she said. "Or shall you?"

"You do it," said Doon.

So she took the key from its hook and put it in the keyhole. She turned it and felt a click. She grasped the door handle and pushed, but nothing happened. She pushed harder. "It won't budge," she said.

"Maybe it opens outward," said Doon.

Lina pulled. The door still didn't move. "It *has* to open," she said. "We unlocked it!" She pulled and pushed and hauled on the handle—and the door moved, not inward or outward but sideways. "Oh, *this* is how it goes!" cried Lina. She pulled the handle to the left, and with a deep rasping sound, the door slid away, into a slot in the wall. Behind it was a space of utter darkness.

They stared. Lina had expected to see something when the door opened. She had thought there would be light behind it, and a path or road.

"Shall we go in?" said Lina.

Doon nodded.

Lina stepped across the threshold. The air had a dank, stuffy smell. She turned to the right and put her right hand against the wall. It was smooth and flat. The floor, too, was smooth.

"There might be a light switch," she said. She patted the wall just inside the door, from the floor to as high as she could reach, but found nothing.

Doon turned left and felt on the other side, with the same result. "Nothing," he said.

Very slowly, keeping a hand to the wall and tapping the floor cautiously with their feet before every step, Doon and Lina made their way in opposite directions. Each of them soon came to a corner and turned again. Now they were going deeper into the dark. They both had the same thought: Is the way out of Ember a long dark tunnel? Must we go mile after mile in absolute darkness?

But suddenly Lina gave a yelp of surprise. "Something's here on the floor," she said. Her foot had banged against a hard object. She knelt down and touched it cautiously with her hands. It was a metal cube, about a foot square. "It's a box, I think. Two boxes," she added as she explored farther.

Doon took a step toward her in the darkness, and his knees banged into a hard edge. "There's something else here, too," he said. "Not a box." He ran his hands along it. "It's big and has a curved edge."

"The boxes are small enough to lift," said Lina. "Let's take them out where it's lighter and see what they are. Come and help."

Doon made his way to Lina and picked up one of the boxes. They walked back through the door and set the boxes down a few feet from the river's edge. They were made of dark green metal and had gray metal handles on top and a kind of latch on the side. The latches opened easily. Lina and Doon raised the hinged lids and looked inside.

What they saw puzzled and disappointed them. Lina's box was full of smooth white rods, each about ten inches long. At the end of each one, a little bit of string poked out. In Doon's box were dozens of small packets wrapped in a slippery material. He opened one and found a lot of short wooden sticks, each with a blue blob on the end. Both boxes had a label on the inside of the lid. The label on Lina's box said "Candles." The label on Doon's said "Matches," and under it was a white, inch-wide strip of some kind of rough, pebbly material.

"What does 'Candles' mean?" Lina said, puzzled. She took out one of the white rods. It felt slick, almost greasy.

"And what does 'Matches' mean?" said Doon. "Matches what?" He took one of the small sticks from its packet. The blue stuff on the end was not wood. "Could it be something to write with? Like a pencil? Maybe it writes blue."

"But what's the point of a whole box of tiny pencils?" asked Lina. "I don't understand."

Doon frowned at the little blue-tipped stick. "I don't see what else it could be," he said finally. "I'll try writing something with it."

"On what?"

Doon looked around. The floor was too damp from the spray of the river to write on. "I could try it on the Instructions," he said. Lina handed them to him. Carefully, he rubbed the blue end of the stick along the edge of the paper. It didn't leave a mark. He rubbed it along his arm. No mark there, either.

"Try this white stuff," Lina said, pointing to the white strip inside the lid of the box.

He scraped the blue tip across the rough surface. Instantly, the end of the stick burst into flame. Doon cried out and flung the stick away. It landed on the floor a few feet off, where it burned brightly for a moment and then sputtered out.

They stared at each other, their mouths open in astonishment. There was a strange sharp smell in the air that smarted in their noses.

"It makes fire!" said Doon. "And light!"

"Let me try one," said Lina. She took a stick from the box and ran it across the rough strip. It blazed up fiercely, but she managed to hold on to it for a moment. Then she felt the heat on her fingers and let go, and the flaming stick dropped over the ledge and into the river.

"Fire sticks," said Doon. "Are they what saves Ember?"

"I don't see how they could be," said Lina. "They're so small. They go out too fast." She shivered. This was not turning out the way she'd thought it would. She held up one of the white things. "Anyway, what are these for?"

Doon shook his head in bewilderment. "Maybe a candle is a kind of handle," he said. "Maybe you tie the stick on with the string, and then you can hold it longer while it burns."

"It would still go out just as fast," Lina said.

"Yes," said Doon. "But it's all I can think of. Let's try it."

With a great deal of effort, they looped the string of a rod around one of the sticks. Lina held the rod while Doon scraped the blue tip into flame. They watched the stick flare brightly, making shadows jump up behind them. The wood turned black, and the charred firestick crumbled and dropped to the ground. But the light didn't go out. The string itself had caught fire. As they watched, it sputtered and smoked and then burned steadily, filling the little room with a warm glow.

"It's the movable light," said Doon in awe.

All Lina's excitement flooded back. "And now, and now—" she said, "we can go back into the room and see what's there."

They went back down the passage to the doorway and stepped inside. Lina held the movable light at arm's length before her. In its flickering glow they saw something made of silvery metal. They walked slowly around, examining it. It was long and low, filling up the center of the room. One end of it came to a point. The other end was flat. Across the open middle stretched two metal strips. Four stout ropes were attached to the outside, one at each end and one on each side. And on the floor of the thing were two poles, each flattened at one end.

"Look," said Lina. "There's a word on its side." They squatted at the pointed end and held the flame near the word. It said, in square black letters, "BOAT."

"Boat," repeated Doon. "What does that mean?"

"I don't know," said Lina. "And here's another word, on these poles: 'Paddles.' The only paddle I know is the one Mrs. Polster uses on kids who misbehave in school."

Once again, she took her copy of the Instructions from her pocket and consulted it, holding it in the light of the flame. "Look," she said, "right here: 'oat' must be 'boat.'"

5. oat, stocked with
nec uip ent. Bac
ont s eet.

"And the next part must say, 'stocked with necessary equipment,'" said Doon. "That must be what's in the boxes."

"Then there's this." Lina ran her finger along the next line.

> 6. Usi opes, lowe
> ter. Head dow st . Us pa
> av cks and assist over rap .

"This word must be 'ropes,'" she said. "Then 'lower' . . . and then . . . would this word be 'downstairs'? Maybe it says, 'head downstairs'?"

"That doesn't make sense," said Doon. "There aren't any stairs, except the ones that go up." He frowned at the word, and then he took a short, sharp breath. "Downstream," he said. "The word must be 'downstream.' It must say something like, 'Use the ropes to lower the boat, and head downstream.'" He looked up at Lina and spoke in a voice full of wonder. "The boat goes on the water. It's something to ride in."

They stared at each other in the flickering light, realizing what this meant. There was no tunnel leading out of Ember. The way out was the river. To leave Ember, they must go on the river.

CHAPTER 15

A Desperate Run

"But this can't be right," said Doon. "If the river is the way out of Ember, why is there just one boat? It's only big enough for two people."

"I don't know," said Lina. "It *is* strange."

"Let's look around some more."

They stood up. Doon went back to where they'd left the boxes and got another candle. He brought it into the boat room and lit it, and the room grew twice as bright. Right away they saw what they hadn't noticed before: in the back wall was a door almost as wide as the whole room. When they went up to it they could see that it, too, was a sliding door. Doon took hold of the handle that was on the right and pulled sideways, and the door rolled smoothly open to reveal more darkness.

They stepped in. They could guess from the echoing sound of their voices when they spoke that they were in a tremendous room, though the ceiling was low—they could see it just over their heads. The candlelight glinted off something shiny, and as they went in farther they could see that the room was filled with boats, row upon row of them, all just like the one in the first room. "There must be hundreds," Lina whispered.

"Enough for everyone, I suppose," said Doon.

They wandered around a bit, but there wasn't really much to see. All the boats were the same. Each one contained two metal boxes and two paddles. The room was cold, and the air felt heavy in their lungs. The candle flames burned weakly. So they went back to the small room and slid the door closed behind them. "I guess," said Lina, "that this first boat is meant as a sort of sample. We learn what's what on the one that has signs. 'Boat.' 'Paddles.' 'Candles.' 'Matches.'"

They went back out to the river's edge. Lina blew out her candle and began closing up the boxes they'd opened.

Doon blew out his, too. "I'm going to take my candle with me," he said, "to look at later. I want some matches as well." He took a packet of matches from the box and tucked it inside his shirt.

Lina returned the boxes to the boat room and slid the door closed. Then she and Doon stood together on the ledge and gazed down. Less than a foot below, the river rushed by. A short distance downstream it plunged into the dark mouth in the wall and disappeared.

"Well," he said, "we've found it."

"We've found it," Lina repeated, wonderingly.

"And tomorrow, at the start of the Singing," said Doon, "we'll stand up in Harken Square and tell the whole city."

When they came up out of the Pipeworks, it was nearly six o'clock. They hadn't realized they'd been down there so long; both Doon's father and Mrs. Murdo would be wondering where they were. They stood for a moment under a lamppost, just long enough to agree on a time to meet the next day and plan their announcement. Then they hurried home. When Doon's father asked why he was so late, he said his song rehearsal had gone long. He wanted to shout out to his father, *We've found the way out! We're saved!* But he held himself in for the sake of his moment of glory. Tomorrow, when his father saw him on the steps of the Gathering Hall, he would be so overcome with surprise and pride that he would go weak in the knees, and the people standing next to him would have to catch him and hold him up.

And the announcement about the thieving mayor! That would probably happen tomorrow, too. Doon had almost forgotten it in the excitement of finding the boats. The mayor's arrest and the city's rescue, both at once! It was going to be an amazing day. Racing thoughts kept Doon awake almost until morning.

The day of the Singing was a holiday for the entire city; all the stores and other businesses were closed. This meant that Doon didn't have to go to the Pipeworks. His father didn't have to go to his shop, either, but he was going to go anyhow. If he wasn't in his shop, fussing with his merchandise, he didn't know what to do with himself.

Doon dawdled over his breakfast of carrot sticks and mashed turnips, waiting for his father to go. He wanted to get ready for the journey down the river. They probably wouldn't leave for a few days—he and Lina would make their announcement tonight, and people would need time to get organized before they could leave the city—but he was too excited to sit around doing nothing.

As soon as his father left, Doon slipped the case off his pillow. This would be his traveling pack. He put in the candle and the matches. He put in the key he'd borrowed from the Pipeworks office. He put in a good-sized piece of rope that he'd found at the trash heaps and had been saving for years and a bottle for water. He put in an ancient folding knife that his father had given him, which had come down through generations of his family and which he used to chop off his bangs when they got so long they tickled his eyelids. He put in some extra clothes, in case he got wet, and some paper and a pencil, so that he could write a record of the journey. Along with these things, he crammed in a small blanket—it might be cold in the new city—and a packet of food: six carrots, a handful of vitamins, some peas and mushrooms wrapped in a lettuce leaf, two boiled beets, and two boiled turnips. That should be enough. Surely, when they got to where they were going, the people who lived there would give them something to eat. He tied the top of the pillowcase in a knot, and then he untied it again. He might want to add something else.

He stood in the middle of the apartment and looked around at the jumble of stuff. There was nothing else here that he wanted to take with him—no, there was one thing. He went back into his room. From beneath his bed he pulled out the pages of his bug book. He leafed through it. The white spider. The moth with the zigzag pattern on its wings. The bee, striped brown and yellow on its rear end. He looked at his drawings for a long time, memorizing their beauty and strangeness. Tiny fringes of hair, minute claws, jointed legs. Should he take this with him? There might not be creatures like this where they were going. He might never see such things again.

But no, he'd leave it behind—his pack should be small and light. He put the bug book back under his bed and pulled out the box where he kept the green worm. He drew back the scarf to check his captive one more time. Several days before, the worm had done a curious thing: it had wrapped itself up in a blanket of threads. Since then it had hung motionless from a bit of cabbage stem. Doon had been watching it carefully. Either it was dead, or it was undergoing the change that he'd read about in a library book but could hardly believe was true—the change from a crawling thing to a flying thing. So far, the bundled-up worm had shown no signs of life.

But now he saw that it was wriggling. The whole wrapped-up bundle, which was shaped like a large vitamin pill, bent slightly from side to side, then was still, then bent back and forth again. Something was pushing at the top end of it, and in a moment the threads there split apart and a dark furry knob emerged. Doon watched, holding his breath. Next came two hairlike legs, which clawed and plucked at the blanket. In a few minutes the whole creature was out. Egress, thought Doon with a smile. The creature's wings were crushed flat against its body at first, but soon they opened, and Doon saw what his green worm had become: a moth with light brown wings. He lifted the box and carried it to the window. He opened the window and held the box out into the air. The moth waved its feathery feelers and took a few steps along the wilted cabbage leaf. For several minutes, it stood still, its wings trembling slightly. Then it fluttered up into the air, rising higher and higher until it was just a pale spot against the dark sky.

Doon watched until the moth disappeared. He knew he had seen something marvelous. What was the power that turned the worm into a moth? It was greater than any power the Builders had had, he was sure of that. The power that ran the city of Ember was feeble by comparison—and about to run out.

For a few minutes he stood by the window, looking out over the square and thinking again about what to pack for his journey. Should he put in anything like nails or wire? Would he need money? Should he take some soap?

Then he laughed and struck a hand against his head. He kept forgetting that the entire population of the city would be with him on the trip. If he needed something he didn't have, someone would surely be able to supply it.

So he tied a knot in his pillowcase and was about to close the window when he caught sight of three burly men wearing the red and brown uniform of the city guards striding into the square. They stopped and looked around for a moment. Then one of them confronted old humpbacked Nammy Proggs, who was standing not far from the entrance to the Small Items shop. The guard towered over her, and she twisted her head sideways and squinted up at him. Doon could hear the guard's voice clearly: "We're looking for a boy named Harrow."

"Why?" said Nammy.

"Spreading vicious rumors" was the answer. "Do you know where he is?"

Nammy hesitated a moment, and then she said, "Went off to the trash heaps just a minute ago." The guard nodded curtly and beckoned to his companions. They marched away.

Spreading vicious rumors! Doon was so stunned that he stood still as stone for a long minute. What could they possibly mean? But there was only one answer. It had to be what they'd told the assistant guard about the mayor. Why were they calling it a vicious rumor? It was the truth! He didn't understand it.

He did understand, though, that Nammy Proggs had done him a favor. She must have seen that the guards meant him no good. She had protected him, at least for the moment, by sending the guards to the wrong place.

Doon forced his mind to slow down and think. Why did the guards think he and Lina were lying? Obviously, they hadn't investigated the room in Tunnel 351. If they had, they'd have known he and Lina were telling the truth.

He could think of only one other possibility. The guards—at least some of them—already knew what the mayor was doing. They knew about it and wanted it to stay a secret. And why? It was clear: the guards, too, were getting things from the storerooms.

It had to be the answer. For a moment, the fear he'd felt when he saw the guards was replaced by rage. The familiar hot wave rose in him, and he wanted to grab a handful of his father's nails or pot shards and throw them against the wall. But all at once he remembered: if the guards were after him, they'd be after Lina, too. He had to warn her. He dashed down the stairs, his anger turning into power for his running feet.

After discovering the room full of boats, Lina had come home to Mrs. Murdo's with the sound of the river still in her ears. It was like a huge, powerful voice, roaring at the top of its lungs. Deep inside herself Lina felt an answering call, as if she, too, contained a drop of the same power. She would ride on the river—she could hardly believe it—and it might take her to the shining city she had dreamed of, or it might drown her. What she had imagined before—the smooth, gently sloping path leading out—now seemed childish. How could the way into a new world be so easy? She dreaded going on the river, but she was ready for it, too. She longed to go.

She slept that night in the beautiful blue-green room, in the big, lumpy bed with Poppy next to her.

She felt safe here. Mrs. Murdo came in and tucked the covers around her. She sat on the edge of the bed and sang an odd little song to Poppy—something about rock-a-bye baby, in the treetops. "What are treetops?" Lina asked, but Mrs. Murdo didn't know. "It's a very old song," she said. "It's probably nonsense words."

She said good night and went out into the living room, where Lina could hear her humming quietly as she tidied up. She was so orderly. She never left her stockings draped over the back of a chair, or her sewing spread out all over the table. Lina closed her eyes and waited for sleep.

But her thoughts kept tumbling around. So much was going to happen tomorrow—the whole city would be in an uproar. People would stream down into the Pipeworks to see the boats. They'd be excited, shouting and laughing and crying, packing up their belongings, and surging through the streets. If they couldn't all fit into the boats, there would be fights. Some people might get hurt. It was going to be a mess. She'd have to keep her little family close around her—Poppy, Mrs. Murdo, and Doon, and perhaps Doon's father and Clary. Through it all, she would hold tight to Poppy so no harm could come to her.

It seemed she had barely closed her eyes when she felt Poppy's hard little heels banging against her shins. "Time-a get up! Get up!" Poppy chirped.

She got out of bed and dressed herself and Poppy. In the kitchen, Mrs. Murdo was mashing potatoes for breakfast. How lovely, Lina thought, to have breakfast cooked for her—to hear water bubbling in the pot, and to find a bowl and a spoon set out on the table, and vitamins lined up neatly beside a cup of beet tea. I could live here forever, Lina thought, before she remembered that in a day or two they would all be leaving.

There was a sudden banging on the front door. Mrs. Murdo dried her hands and went to answer it, but before she'd taken three steps the banging came again. "I'm coming, I'm coming," Mrs. Murdo cried, and when she opened the door, there was Doon.

His face was flushed, and he was breathing hard. He had a bulging pillowcase slung over his shoulder.

He looked past Mrs. Murdo to Lina. "I have to talk to you," he said. "Right now, but . . ." He threw a doubtful glance at Mrs. Murdo.

Lina scrambled up from the table. "In here," she said, towing him toward the blue-green room.

When she had closed the door, Doon told her what had happened. "They'll come for you, too," he said, "any minute. We have to get out of here. We have to hide from them."

Lina could hardly make sense of what he was saying. They were in *trouble*? Her legs went shaky at the knees. "Hide?" she said. "Hide where?"

"We could go to the school—no one would be there today—or the library. It's almost always open, even on holidays." He hopped impatiently from foot to foot. "But we have to go *fast,* we have to go *now.* They have *signs* up about us all over the city!"

"Signs?"

"Telling people to report us if they see us!"

Lina felt as if a swarm of insects was inside her head, buzzing so loudly she couldn't think. "How long do we have to hide? All day?"

"I don't know—we don't have time to think about it. Lina, they could be outside the door *this minute.*"

The urgency in his voice convinced her. On the way through the living room she gave Poppy a quick kiss and called, "Bye, Mrs. Murdo. We have some emergency work to do. If anyone comes asking for me, say I'll be back later." They were down the stairs before Mrs. Murdo could ask any questions.

Once in the street, they ran. "Where to?" Lina said.

"The school," Doon answered.

They took Greystone Street, staying within the shadows as much as they could. As they passed the shoe shop, Lina saw a white piece of paper stuck up on the window. She glanced at it and her heart gave a wild jump. Her name and Doon's were written on it in big black letters:

A Desperate Run

DOON HARROW AND LINA MAYFLEET

WANTED FOR SPREADING VICIOUS RUMORS

IF YOU SEE THEM,

REPORT TO MAYOR'S CHIEF GUARD.

BELIEVE NOTHING THEY SAY.

REWARD

She snatched the poster off the window, crumpled it up, and tossed it into the nearest trash can. In the next block, she tore down two more, and Doon ripped one off a lamppost. But there were too many to get them all, and they didn't have time to waste.

They ran faster. On this holiday, people slept late, and because the stores were closed, the streets were nearly empty. Still, they took the long route all the way out by the beehives to avoid Sparkswallow Square, where a few people might be standing around and talking. They ran past the greenhouses and up Dedlock Street. As they crossed Night Street, Lina glanced to her left. Two blocks away, a couple of guards were crossing to Greengate Square. She tapped Doon's shoulder and pointed. He saw, and they ran faster. Had they been noticed? Lina thought not; they would have heard a shout if the guards had seen them.

They got to the school and went in through the back door. In the Wide Hallway, their footsteps echoed on the wooden floor. It was strange to be here again, and to be here alone, without the clatter and chatter of other children. The hallway with its eight doors seemed smaller to Lina than it had when she was a student, and shabbier. The planks of the floor were scuffed gray, and there was a cloud of finger smudges around the doorknob of every door.

They went into Miss Thorn's room and, out of habit, sat at their old desks. "I don't think they'll look for us here," said Doon. "If they do, we can crawl into the paper cabinet." He set his pack down next to him on the floor.

For a while they just sat there, getting their breath back. They hadn't turned the light on, so the room was dim—the only light came from beneath the blind over the window.

"Those posters," Lina said after a while.

"Yes. Everyone will see them."

"What will they do to us if they catch us?"

"I don't know. Something to keep us from telling what we know. Put us in the Prison Room, maybe."

Lina ran her finger along the B carved in the desktop. It felt like a very long time since she'd last sat at this desk. "We can't hide in here forever," she said.

"No," said Doon. "Just until it's time for the Singing. Then when everyone is gathered in Harken Square, we'll go and tell about the boats and the mayor. Won't we? I haven't really thought about it—I haven't had a chance to think at all this morning."

"But the guards are always there at the Singing, standing next to the mayor," said Lina. "They'd grab us as soon as we opened our mouths."

Doon's eyebrows came together in a dark line. "You're right. So what will we do?"

It was like finding yourself on a dead-end street, Lina thought. There was no way out. She stared blankly at the things that had once been her daily companions—the teacher's desk, the stacks of paper, *The Book of the City of Ember* on its special shelf. The old words ran through her head: "There is no place but Ember. Ember is the only light in the dark world." She knew now that this wasn't true. There *was* someplace else—the place where the boats would take them.

As if Doon had read her thoughts, he looked up. "We could go."

"Go where?" she said, though she knew right away what he meant.

"Wherever the river leads," he said. He gestured to the pillowcase sack. "I packed up my bag this morning—I'm all ready. I'm sure I have enough for you, too."

Lina felt her heart shrink a little. "Go by ourselves?" she said. "Without telling anyone?"

"We *will* tell them." Doon was on his feet now. He went to the cabinet and got a sheet of paper. "We'll write a note explaining everything—a note to someone we trust, someone who'll believe us."

"But I can't just leave," said Lina. "How could I leave Poppy? And not even say goodbye to her? Not know where I'm going, or if I'm ever coming back? How could *you* go without saying goodbye to your father?"

"Because," said Doon, "once they find the boats, the rest of Ember will follow us. It's not as if we're leaving them forever." He strode across the room and rummaged in Miss Thorn's desk. "Who shall we write the message to?"

Lina wasn't sure about this idea, but she couldn't, at the moment, think of a better one. So she said, "We could write it to Clary. She's seen the Instructions. She'll believe what we say. And she lives close by—just up in Torrick Square."

"Okay," said Doon. He pulled a pencil from the desk drawer. "Really," he said, "this is a perfect idea. We can get away from the guards and leave our message behind us. *And* we can be the first ones to arrive in the new city! We *should* be the first, because we discovered the way."

"Well, that's true." Lina thought for a minute. "How long do you think it will take before the rest of them find the boats and come? It's a lot of people to get organized." She numbered on her fingers the things that would have to happen. "Clary will have to get the head of the Pipeworks to go down with her and find the boats. Then she'll have to make the announcement to the city. Then everyone in Ember will have to pack up their things, troop down to the river, get all those boats out of that big room, and load themselves in. It could be a big mess, Doon. Poppy will need me." She pictured frenzied crowds of people, and Poppy tiny and lost among them.

"Poppy has Mrs. Murdo," said Doon. "She'll be fine. Really. Mrs. Murdo is very organized."

It was true. The thought of taking Poppy with her on the river, which had darted into Lina's mind, darted out again. I'm only being selfish, she thought, to want to have her with me. It's too dangerous to take her. Mrs. Murdo will bring her in a day or two. This seemed the most sensible plan, though it made her so sad that it cast a shadow over the thrill of going to the new city. "What if something goes wrong?" she said.

"Nothing will go wrong! It's a good plan, Lina. We'll be there ahead of everyone else—we can welcome them when they come, we can show them around!" Doon was bursting with eagerness. His eyes shone, and he jiggled up and down.

"Well, all right," Lina said. "Let's write our message, then."

Doon wrote for a long time. When he was finished, he showed what he'd written to Lina. He'd explained how to find the rock with the E, how to go down to the boat room, even how to use the candles.

"It's good," she said. "Now we have to deliver it."

She paused a moment to see if she had any courage inside her. She found that she did, along with sadness and fear and excitement. "I'll deliver it," she said. "I'm the messenger, after all. I know back ways to go, where no one will see me." An idea struck her. "Doon, maybe Clary will be home! Maybe she would keep us safe and help us tell what we know, and we won't *have* to leave right now."

Doon quickly shook his head. "I doubt it," he said. "She's probably with her singing group, getting ready. You'll just have to leave the note under her door."

Lina could tell from his tone of voice that Doon didn't really want Clary to be home. She supposed he had his heart set on their going down the river by themselves. Doon glanced up at the clock on the schoolroom wall. "It's a little after two," he said. "The Singing begins at three. After that, everyone will be in Harken Square and the streets will be empty. I think we can get to the Pipeworks safely then—why don't we leave about a quarter after three."

"You still have the key?"

Doon nodded.

"So after I've delivered the note to Clary, I'll come back here," said Lina.

"Yes. And then we'll wait until three-fifteen, and then we'll go."

Lina got up from the cramped desk and went to the window. She moved the blind a little and peered out. There was no one in the street. The dusty schoolroom was very quiet. She thought about Doon's father, who would be frantic when he saw his son's name on those posters and then realized later that Doon had disappeared. She thought about Mrs. Murdo, who might already have seen the posters, and who would be frightened if guards came looking for Lina and terrified if Lina didn't come home by nightfall. She tried not to think about Poppy at all; she couldn't bear it.

"Give me the note," she said to Doon at last. She folded the piece of paper carefully and put it in the pocket of her pants. "Back soon," she said, and went out of the room and down the hall to the rear door of the school.

Doon went to the window to watch her go. He moved the blind aside just enough to see out into Pibb Street. There she was, running in that long-legged way, with her hair flying. She started across Stonegrit Lane. Just before she reached the other side, Doon's breath stopped in his throat. Two guards rounded the corner from Knack Street, directly ahead of her. One of them was the chief guard. He leapt forward and shouted so loudly Doon could hear him plainly through the glass: "That's her! Get her!"

Lina reversed her direction in an instant. She raced back down Pibb Street, turned down School Street toward Bilbollio Square, and vanished from Doon's sight. The guards ran after her, shouting. Doon watched, sick with horror. She's much faster than they are, he told himself. She'll lose them—she knows places to hide. He stood frozen next to the window, hardly breathing. They won't catch her, he thought. I'm sure they won't catch her.

CHAPTER 16

The Singing

When Lina heard the guards shout, terror shot through her. She ran faster than she ever had before, her heart pounding wildly. Behind her, the guards kept up their shouting, and she knew that if other guards were nearby they would come running. She had to find a hiding place. Ahead of her was Bilbollio Square—was there a spot she could duck into? And like an answer, Doon's words came back to her: "The library. It's almost always open, even on holidays." She didn't have time to think. She didn't ask herself whether Edward Pocket would be willing to hide her, or whether there would even *be* a good place to hide in the library. She just ran for the passageway that led to the library door and darted down it.

But the library door wouldn't open. She turned the knob frantically, she pulled and pushed, and then, at the same time that she heard the running footsteps of the guards coming into the square, she saw the small handwritten sign stuck to the door: "Closed for the Singing." The guards were very near now. If she ran, they would see her. She flattened herself against the wall, hoping they wouldn't think to look in the library passage.

But they did. "Here she is!" yelled one of the guards. She tried to shoot past him, but the passage was too narrow, and he caught her by the arm. She pulled and twisted and kicked, but the chief guard had her now, too. He gripped her other arm with fingers that felt like iron. "Stop your struggling!" he shouted.

Lina reached up and grabbed a handful of his wiry beard. She pulled with all her might, and the chief guard roared, but he didn't let go. He yanked her forward, almost off the ground, and the two guards dragged her across the square at an awkward, lopsided pace that made her stumble over her own feet.

"You're hurting me!" Lina said. "Don't hold so tight!"

"Don't you tell us what to do," said the chief guard. "We'll hold you tight till we get you where you're going."

"Where is that?" said Lina. She was so enraged at her bad luck that she almost forgot to be afraid.

"You're going to see the mayor, missy," said the chief guard. "He'll decide what to do with you."

"But I haven't done anything wrong!"

"Spreading vicious rumors," said the guard. "Telling dangerous lies calculated to cause civic unrest."

"It's not a lie!" she said. But the guard gripped her arm even more tightly and gave her a shove so she stumbled sideways.

"No talking," he said, and they walked the rest of the way in grim silence.

A few people had already gathered in Harken Square, though the workers were still getting it ready for the Singing. Street-sweepers crossed the square back and forth, pushing their brooms. Someone appeared at a second-floor window of a building on Gilly Street and unfurled one of the banners that was always displayed for the Singing—a long piece of red cloth, faded after years of use but still showing its design of wavy lines, representing the river, the source of all power. That was for "The Song of the River." There would be a banner on the Broad Street side of the square, too, this one deep yellow-gold with a design like a grid to represent "The Song of the City," and another banner on the Otterwill side for "The Song of Darkness," perfectly black except for a narrow yellow edge.

The guards marched Lina up the steps of the Gathering Hall and through the wide doorway. They took her down the main corridor, opened the door at the end, and gave her one last push, a push that caused her to stagger forward in an undignified way and bump up against the back of a chair.

It was the same room she'd been in that other, much happier day—her first day as a messenger. Nothing had changed—the frayed red curtains, the armchairs with the upholstery worn thin, the hideous mud-colored carpet. The portraits on the wall looked down at her sorrowfully.

"Sit there," said the chief guard. He pointed at a small, hard-looking chair that faced the large armchair. Lina sat. Next to the chair was the small table she remembered from before, with the china teapot and a tray of china teacups with chips around their edges.

The chief guard left the room—to find the mayor, Lina supposed. The other one stood silently with his arms folded across his chest. Nothing happened for a while. Lina tried to think about what she would say to the mayor, but her mind wouldn't work.

Then the door to the front hall opened, and the mayor came in. It was the first time Lina had seen him up close since she had delivered Looper's message to him. He seemed even more immense. His baggy face was the color of a mushroom. He wore a black suit that stretched only far enough across his vast belly for one button to connect with its buttonhole.

He moved ponderously across the room and settled into the armchair, filling it completely. Next to his chair was a table, and on the table was a brass bell the size of a fist. The mayor gazed for a moment at Lina with eyes that looked like the openings of tunnels, and then he turned to the guard.

"Dismissed," he said, waving the back of his hand at him. "Return when I ring the bell."

The guard left. The mayor swung his gaze back to Lina. "I am not surprised," he said. He lifted one arm and pointed a finger at Lina's face. "You have been in trouble before. Going where you shouldn't."

Lina started to speak, but the mayor held up his hand. It was an oddly small hand, with short fingers like ripe pea pods.

"Curiosity," said the mayor. "A dangerous quality. Unhealthy. Especially regrettable in one so young."

"I'm twelve," said Lina.

"Silence!" said the mayor. "I am speaking." He wriggled slightly from side to side, wedging himself more firmly into the chair. He'll need to be pried out of it, Lina thought.

"Ember, as you know," the mayor went on, "is in a time of difficulty. Extraordinary measures are necessary. This is a time when citizens should be most loyal. Most law-abiding. For the good of all."

Lina said nothing. She watched how the flesh under the mayor's chin bulged in and out as he spoke, and then she turned her eyes from this unpleasant sight and looked carefully around the room. She was thinking now, calculating, but not about what the mayor was saying.

"The duties of a mayor," said the mayor, "are . . . complex. Cannot be understood by regular citizens, particularly children. That is why . . . ," he went on, leaning slightly forward so that his stomach pushed farther out along his lap, "certain things must remain hidden from the public. The public would not understand. The public must have faith," said the mayor, once again holding up his hand, this time with a finger pointing to the ceiling, "that all is being done for their benefit. For their own good."

"Hogwash," said Lina.

The mayor jerked backward. His eyebrows came down over his eyes, making them into dark slits. "*What?*" he said. "Surely I heard you incorrectly."

"I said hogwash," said Lina. "It means—"

"Do not presume to tell me what it means!" the mayor cried. "Impudence will make things worse for you." He was breathing heavily, and his words came out with spaces between them. "A misguided child . . . such as yourself . . . requires . . . a forceful lesson." His short fingers gripped the arms of the chair. "Perhaps," he said, "your curiosity has led you to wonder . . . about the Prison Room. What could it be like, eh? Dark? Cold? Uncomfortable?" He made the smile that Lina remembered from Assignment Day. His lips pulled away from his small teeth; his gray cheeks folded. "You will have a chance to find out. You will become . . . closely acquainted . . . with the Prison Room. The guards will escort you there. Your accomplice—another known troublemaker—will join you, as soon as he is located."

The mayor turned to look for the bell. This was the moment when Lina had planned to make a dash for freedom—she thought she had a slim chance to succeed if she moved fast enough—but something happened in that instant that gave her a head start.

The lights went out.

There was no flicker this time, just sudden, complete darkness. It was fortunate that Lina had already planned her move and knew exactly which way to go. She leapt up, knocking over her chair. With her arm, she made a wide swipe and knocked over the table next to the chair as well. The furniture thumping to the floor, the teapot shattering, and the mayor's enraged shouts made a clamor that covered the sound of her footsteps as she dashed to the stairway door. Was it unlocked? She reached for the knob. Grunts and squeaks told her that the mayor was struggling to rise from his chair. She turned the knob and pulled, and the door sprang open. She closed the door behind her and leapt upward two steps at a time. Even in the pitch dark, she could climb stairs. In the room, the bell clanged and clanged, and the mayor bellowed.

When she got to the first landing, she heard the

guards shouting. There was a crash—someone must have fallen over the toppled chair or table. "Where is she?" someone yelled. "Must have run out the door!" Did they know which door? She didn't hear footsteps behind her.

If she could make it to the roof—and if from the roof she could jump to the roof of the Prison Room and from there to the street—then maybe she could escape. Her lungs were on fire now, her breath was burning her throat, but she climbed without stopping, and when she came to the top, she burst through the door to the roof and ran out.

And that was when the lights came back on. It was as if the blackout had been arranged especially for her. I am so lucky, she thought, so extremely lucky! Ahead of her was the clock tower. She went around to the other side of it. No dancing on the roof this time.

A low wall ran along the edge of the building. Lina approached it cautiously and peered out over the swarm of people assembling in Harken Square. Directly below her was the entrance of the Gathering Hall, and as she watched, two guards dashed out the door and down the steps. Good—they had gone the wrong way! They must think she'd escaped into the crowd. For the moment, she was safe. The clock in the tower began to chime. Three great booms rang out. It was time for the Singing to begin.

Lina gazed down at the people of Ember, gathered

to sing their songs. They stood so close together that she could see only their faces, which were lifted up toward the sky, with the hard bright lights shining down on them. They were silent, waiting for the Songmaster to appear on the Gathering Hall steps. There was a strange hush, as if the city were holding its breath. Of the whole Ember year, Lina thought, this hush before the Singing was one of the most exciting moments. She remembered other years, when she had stood with her parents, too short to see the Songmaster's signal, too short to see anything but people's backs and legs, and waited for the first note to thunder out. She felt her heart move at that moment, every year. The sound would rise in waves around her like water, almost as if it could lift her off the ground.

Now suddenly the moment came again. From hundreds of voices rose the first notes of "The Song of the City," deep and strong. She felt as she had all the years before: a quivering inside, as though a string under her ribs had been plucked, and a rush of joy and sadness mixed together. The deep, rumbling chords of the song filled Harken Square. Lina felt that she might step off the edge of the building and walk across the air, it seemed so solid with sound.

"The Song of the City" was long—there were verses about "streets of light and walls of stone," about "citizens with sturdy hearts," about "stored abundance never-ending." (Not true, Lina thought.) But at last,

"The Song of the City" wound down to its end. The singers held the final note, which grew softer and softer, and then there was silence again. Lina looked out at the lighted streets spreading away in every direction, the streets she knew so well. She loved her city, worn out and crumbling though it was. She looked up at the clock: ten minutes after three. Doon would be getting ready to leave for the Pipeworks. She didn't know whether he'd seen her being captured—if he had, he would be wondering if she'd been locked into the Prison Room. He'd be wondering if he should try to rescue her, or if he should go down the river by himself.

She should be hurrying to join him—but a sadness held her back, like a heavy stone in her chest. She bent her face into the palms of her hands and pressed hard against her closed eyes. How could she go away from Ember and leave Poppy behind? Because if she went, she must leave Poppy behind, mustn't she? How could she take her on a journey of such danger?

"The Song of the River" startled her when it began—the men's voices, low and rolling, swelling with power, and then the women's voices coming in above with a complicated melody that seemed to fight the current. Lina listened, unable to move. "The Song of the River" made her uneasy—it always had. With its rolling, relentless rhythm, it seemed to urge her onward, saying, Go down, go away, go now. The more she listened, the more she felt something like the motion of the river in her stomach, a churning, sickening feeling.

Then came "The Song of Darkness," the last of the three songs, and the one most filled with longing and majesty. The soul of Ember was in this song. Its tremendous chords held all the sorrow and all the strength of the people of the city. The song reached its climax: "Darkness like an endless night," sang the hundreds of voices, so powerfully the air seemed to shiver.

And at that moment, the lights once more went out. The voices faltered, but only for an instant. Then they rose again in the darkness, stronger even than before. Lina sang, too. She stood up and sang with all her might into the deep, solid blackness.

The last notes echoed and faded into a terrible silence. Lina stood utterly still. Will it end like this, she thought, at the finish of the last song? She felt the cold stone of the clock tower behind her back. She waited.

Then an idea came to her that made her skin prickle. What if she were to shout into the silence right now? What if she were to say, *Listen, people! We've found the way out of Ember! It's the river—we go on the river!* She could announce the astounding news, just as she and Doon had planned to do, and then—and then what would happen? Would the guards rush to the roof and seize her? Would the people in the square think her news was just a child's wishful thinking, or would they listen and be saved? She could feel the words pushing upward in her throat, she wanted so much to say them. She took a deep breath and leaned forward.

But before she could speak, a rumble of voices arose below. Someone shouted, "Don't move!" and someone else shrieked. The rumble rose to a roar, and then cries flew into the darkness from everywhere. The crowd was erupting into panic.

There was no hope of being heard now. Lina clutched the edge of the clock tower as if the tumult below might cause her to fall. She strained her eyes against the darkness. Without light, she could go nowhere. Lights, come back on, she prayed. Come back on.

Then she saw something. At first, she thought her eyes were tricking her. She closed them tightly and opened them again. It was still there: a tiny point of light, moving. As she watched, it moved along slowly in a straight line. Then it turned and moved in a straight line again. Was it on River Road? She couldn't tell. But suddenly she knew what it was. It was Doon, with a candle. Doon, going toward the Pipeworks in the dark.

And she wanted to go, too. She could feel it all through her, the urge to run and meet him and find the way out of Ember, to the new place. She listened to the shouts and wails of the terrified people in the square below. She thought of Mrs. Murdo down there in the dark, being bumped and pushed, with her arms wrapped tightly around Poppy, trying to protect her, and all at once everything seemed clear. Lina knew what she would do—if only the lights would come back on, if only this was not the very last blackout in the history of Ember. Watching the tiny light following its steady course, she made a wish with the whole force of her heart and mind.

Then the floodlights flickered—there was a great cry of hope from the crowd—and the lights came on and stayed on. Lina ran to the back edge of the roof, dropped easily down onto the roof of the Prison Room, and, seeing no guards in the crowd that was now streaming into the street, she jumped from there to the ground and joined the throng of people. She made her way down Greystone Street, going at the same pace as everyone else so she wouldn't stand out. When she came to the trash-can enclosure behind the Gathering Hall, she squatted down and hid. Her heart was beating fast, but she felt strong and purposeful now. She had her plan. As soon as she spotted Mrs. Murdo and Poppy on their way home, she'd put it into action.

CHAPTER 17

Away

At three-twenty, Doon took his pillowcase pack, left the school by the back door, and started up Pibb Street. He went fast—the lights had gone out for a few minutes just before three, and he was nervous about being outside. He planned to take the long way to the Pipeworks, out at the very edge of the city, to avoid any guards that might still be looking for him.

He was filled with dread about Lina. He wouldn't know what had happened to her until he got to the Pipeworks and she either showed up or didn't. All he could do now was run.

He raced down Knack Street. It was strange to be out in the city with the streets so utterly deserted. Without the people passing back and forth, the streets seemed wider and darker. Nothing moved but himself, his shadow, and his fleeting reflection in shop windows he passed. In Selverton Square, he saw a kiosk where the poster with his and Lina's names on it had been pinned up. Everyone in the city must have seen these posters by now. He was famous, he thought wryly, but not in the way he'd wanted. There would be no glorious moment on the Gathering Hall steps after all. Instead of making his father proud, he would cause him dreadful worry.

This thought made him so sad that his knees felt suddenly wobbly. How could he just vanish without a word? But it was too late now, he couldn't go back. If only there was some way to send him a message—and in a moment, he realized there was. He stopped, fished in his pack for the paper and pencil he had brought, and scribbled on it, "Father—We have found the way out—it was in the Pipeworks after all! You will know about it tomorrow. Love, Doon." He folded this in quarters, wrote "Deliver to Loris Harrow" in big letters on the outside, and pinned it to the kiosk. There! That was the best he could do. He would have to trust that someone would deliver it.

In the distance, he heard the faint sound of singing. He listened—it was "The Song of the River," just ending. *"Far below, like the blood of the earth, From the center of nowhere rushing forth,"* he sang under his breath. Like everyone in Ember, he knew the words of the three songs by heart. He sang along softly with the faraway singers:

> *"Making the light for the lamps of Ember,*
> *Older than anyone can remember,*
> *Faster than anything anyone knows,*
> *The river comes and the river goes."*

Up Rim Street now to River Road. He was halfway there. The singers were starting on "The Song of Darkness." It was his favorite, with its powerful, deep harmonies—he was a little sorry to be missing it. He went up the Pott Street side of empty Riverroad Square, where another poster hung crookedly on the kiosk, and he was headed toward North Street when suddenly the lights flickered and went out.

He jolted to a stop. Stand still and wait—that was his automatic response. In the distance he heard a dip in the sound of the singing, some startled voices breaking the flow, but then the song rose again, defying the darkness. For a moment all thoughts vanished from Doon's mind; there was nothing but the fearless words of the song:

> *"Black as sleep and deep as dreaming,*
> *Darkness like an endless night.*
> *Yet within the streets of Ember*
> *Bright and bravely shines our light."*

He sang, standing still in the blackness. When the song ended, he waited. The lights would surely come back soon. For a few minutes there was silence, and then, far away but piercingly clear, he heard a scream. More screams and shouts followed, the sounds of panic. He felt the panic himself, like a hand taking hold of him, making him want to leap up and fling himself against the dark.

But suddenly, with a flash of joy, he remembered: he didn't have to wait for the lights to come back on. He had what no citizen of Ember had ever had before—a way to see in the dark. He set his pack down, untied the knot at the top, and groped around inside until he felt the candle. Down in a corner, he found the little packet of matches. He scraped a match against the pavement, and it flared up instantly. He held the flame to the string on the candle, and the string began to burn. He had a light. He had the only light in the entire city.

The candle didn't cast its light very far, but it was enough to see at least the pavement in front of him. He went slowly along Pott Street, then turned left on North Street. At the end of the street was the wall of the Pipeworks office.

When he got to the Pipeworks entrance, no one was there. A little cloud of moths came to flutter around the flame of his candle, but otherwise nothing moved in Plummer Square. There was nothing to do but wait. Doon blew the candle out—he didn't want to use it all up in case the lights stayed off a long time—and squatted down on the pavement, setting down his bundle and leaning against one of the big trash cans. He waited, listening to the distant shouts—and at last the lights blinked, blinked again, and came on.

Lina was nowhere in sight. If the guards had found her and taken her . . . But Doon preferred not to think about that yet. He would wait for a while—she would have been delayed by the blackout if she was on her way. He couldn't see the clock tower from here, but it was probably not quite four o'clock.

What if she didn't come? The Singing was over, the people were dispersing throughout the city, and the guards, no doubt, would soon resume their search for him. Doon clasped his arms together and pressed them hard against his stomach, trying to stop the queasy fluttering.

If she didn't come, Doon had two choices: he could stay in the city and do what he could to save Lina, or he could go in the boat by himself and hope Lina could somehow free herself and tell the people of Ember about the way out. He didn't like either of these plans; he wanted to go down the river, and he wanted to go with Lina.

Doon stood up and hoisted his sack again. He was too restless to keep sitting. He walked down to Gappery Street and looked in both directions. Not a single person was in sight. He walked to Plummer Street, thinking that perhaps Lina was coming by way of the city's edge, as he had, to avoid being seen. But no one was there; he didn't even see anyone when he went past Subling Street to the very end of the city. He had to decide what to do.

He went and stood in the doorway of the Pipeworks. Think, he said to himself. Think! He was not even sure he *could* make the river journey by himself. How would he get the boat into the water? Could he lift it without help? On the other hand, how could he help Lina if she was in the hands of the mayor's guards? What could he possibly do that would not just get himself caught, too?

He felt sick. His hands were cold. He stepped out of the doorway and scanned the square once again. Nothing moved but the moths around the lights.

And then down Gappery Street Lina came running. She came slantwise across the square, and he dashed to meet her. She was hugging a bundle to her chest.

"I've come, I'm here, I almost didn't make it," she said, breathing so hard she could barely talk. "And look." She folded back the blanket of her bundle. Doon saw a curl of brown hair and two wide frightened eyes. "I've brought Poppy."

Doon was so glad to see Lina that he didn't mind

at all that Poppy was coming with them, making a risky journey even riskier. Relief and excitement flooded through him. They were going! They were going!

"Okay," he said. "Come on!"

With his borrowed key, he opened the Pipeworks door, and they hurried past the yellow slickers on their hooks and the lines of rubber boots. Doon dashed into the Pipeworks office long enough to replace the key on its hook, and then they pulled open the stairway door and started down. Lina stepped slowly because of Poppy, and Poppy clung to her neck, unusually quiet, sensing the strangeness and importance of what was happening. At the bottom of the stairs, they came out into the main tunnel and walked down the path to the west until they came to the marked rock.

"How are we going to get Poppy down there?" Doon asked.

Lina said, "I'll fasten her to my chest." Setting Poppy down, Lina took off the coat and the sweater she was wearing. With Doon's help, she made her sweater into a sling for Poppy, tying its sleeves behind her neck. Then she put her coat back on and buttoned it up.

Doon looked doubtfully at this bulky arrangement. "Will you be able to climb down, carrying her like that? Will you be able to reach around her and hold on to the rungs?"

"Yes," said Lina. Now that she had Poppy with her, she felt brave again. She could do whatever she needed to.

Doon went down first. Lina followed. "Stay very still, Poppy," she said. "Don't squirm." Poppy did stay still, but even so it was not easy going down the ladder with her extra weight. Lina's arms were just long enough to reach past Poppy and hold on to the ladder. She descended very slowly. When she got to the ledge, she stepped sideways, gripped the hand Doon held out for her, and, with a deep breath of relief, came into the entryway.

They walked to the back of the entry hall, and Doon opened the steel panel and took out the key. He slid aside the door to the room where the single boat was, and they went in. Doon took his candle from his sack and lit it. Lina unwrapped Poppy and sat her down at the back of the room. "Don't move from there," she said. Poppy put her thumb in her mouth, and Doon and Lina set to work.

Doon's sack went in the pointed end of the boat, which they decided must be the front. They put the boxes of candles and matches into the rear of the boat. It was clear they'd been designed to go there; they fit snugly.

The poles labeled "Paddles" were a mystery. Lina thought maybe they were weapons, meant for fending off hostile creatures. Doon thought they might fit across the boat somehow to make railings to brace yourself against, but he couldn't get them to work in this way. Finally they decided just to leave the paddles in the bottom of the boat and figure out what they were for as they went along.

Doon dripped a bit of wax on the floor and stood his candle up in it, so he'd have both hands free. "Let's see if we can lift the boat," he said.

With Doon at the rear and Lina at the front, they found they could lift the boat with ease. It was amazingly light, even with the boxes and pack inside it. They set it down again. The next step was to get it in the water somehow, and then get in it themselves.

"We can't just drop it in," Lina said. "The river would grab it right away."

"That must be what the ropes are for," said Doon. "We lower it in by holding on to the ropes. And tie the ropes to something to keep it from moving."

"To what?"

"They must have put a peg or something in the wall to tie it to." Doon went back out to the edge of the river and got down on his knees. Leaning over, he felt with one hand along the bank below. At first there was only smooth, slippery rock. He moved his hand slowly back and forth, up and down. River water splashed against his fingers. At last he felt something—a metal rod attached to the river wall, like the rungs of the ladder they had climbed down. "I've found it," he called.

He got up again and went back to the boat room. "Let's carry the boat out," he said. He and Lina lifted it and, taking small steps, moved it forward. As they went out the door, Poppy began to wail.

"Don't cry!" Lina called to her. "Stay right there! We'll be back in a second."

They carried the boat right to the edge of the water and set it down carefully, its front end pointing downstream. Doon knelt again, feeling for the metal rod. "Hand me the end of the rope," he said.

Which rope? Lina thought for a second. She realized it had to be the one attached to the side of the boat nearest her—that would be the side closest to the riverbank when they put the boat in. She uncoiled the rope, ran it around the boat, and handed its end down to Doon, who lay on his stomach with his head hanging over the edge and knotted the rope to the metal rung in the wall. He got to his feet again, wiping water from his face.

"Now," Doon said, "we can put the boat in the water."

Another wail came from the boat room. "I'm coming," Lina called, and dashed back for Poppy. She hoisted her up and spoke into her ear, in the voice she used for announcing an exciting game: "We're going on an *adventure,* Poppy. We're going for a *ride,* a ride in the water! It will be fun, sweetie, you'll see." She blew out the candle Doon had left and carried Poppy to the river's edge.

"Are we ready?" said Doon.

"I guess we are." Goodbye to Ember, Lina thought. Goodbye to everyone, goodbye to everything. For a second, a picture of herself arriving in the bright city of her dreams flashed into her mind, and then it faded and was gone. She had no idea what lay ahead.

She set Poppy down against the wall of the entry passage. "Sit here," she told her. "Don't move until I tell you to." Poppy sat, her eyes wide, her plump legs sticking out in front of her.

Lina took hold of the rope at the rear of the boat. Doon took hold of the rope at the front. They heaved the boat up and stretched sideways to swing it out over the water. It tipped alarmingly from side to side. "Let it down!" yelled Lina. They both let the ropes slide through their hands, and the boat fell and hit the water with a slap. It bounced and rocked and pulled against its tether, but Doon's knot held. The boat stayed in place, waiting for them.

"Here I go!" Doon cried. He bent over, gripped the rim of the boat with one hand, turned backward, and stepped in. The boat tipped sideways under his weight. Doon staggered a step, and then found his balance. "All right!" he yelled. "Hand me Poppy!"

Lina lifted Poppy, who began to howl and kick at

the sight of the bucking boat and the churning water. But Doon's arms were right there, and Lina thrust her into them. A second later, she jumped in herself, and then all three of them were tossed to the floor of the boat by its violent rocking.

Doon managed to get to his feet. He hauled on the rope that held the boat to the bank until he was close enough to reach the knot. He struggled with it. Water splashed into his face. He yanked at the knot, loosened it, pulled the rope free—and the boat shot forward.

CHAPTER 18

Where the River Goes

For a second, Lina saw the banks of the river streak by. Ahead was the opening of the tunnel, like an enormous mouth. They plunged into it and left the light of the Pipeworks behind. In complete darkness, the boat pitched and rolled, and Lina, in the bottom of it, banged from side to side, gripping Poppy with one arm and grabbing with the other hand for anything to hold on to. Doon slid into her, and she slid into the boxes. Poppy was shrieking wildly.

"Doon!" Lina shouted, and he shouted back, "Hold on! Hold on!" But she kept losing her grip on the edge of the boat and being flung sideways. She was terrified that Poppy would slam into the metal bench, or be torn from her arms and tossed into the river.

The boat hit something and shuddered, then raced on. It felt like being swallowed, this rushing through the dark, with the river roaring like a thousand voices.

Lina's legs were tangled with Doon's, and Poppy's arms were so tight around her neck that she could hardly breathe. But it was the dark that was most terrible—going so fast into the dark.

She closed her eyes. If they were going to smash into a wall or plunge into a bottomless hole, there was nothing she could do about it. All she could do was hold tight to Poppy. She did that, for what seemed a long time.

And then at last the current slowed, and the boat stopped thrashing about so wildly. Lina managed to sit up, and she felt Doon moving, too. Poppy's shrieks turned to whimpers. The darkness was still complete, but Lina sensed space above and around her. Where were they? She had to *see.*

"Doon!" she said. "Are you all right? Can you find us a candle?"

"I'll try," Doon said. She felt him scramble past her to the back of the boat, and she heard a scrape as he pulled a box out from its place under the bench. "Can't find the latch!" Doon said. Then a second later, "There, I've got it. This is the matches, so this one must be candles." More scraping and banging. The boat lurched, Lina slid forward. Doon slid, too, and slammed into her back. He gave a yell of rage.

"Dropped the match! Hold on, I almost had it." Long seconds of scrambling and clattering. Then a light flared up, and Doon's shadowed face appeared above it. He touched the match to a candle, and the light grew steadier.

It was only a small flame, but it cast glints of light on the tunnel walls and the silky surface of the water. The tunnel had an arched ceiling, Lina saw, like the tunnels of the Pipeworks, but it was much wider than those tunnels. The river ran through it like a moving road.

"Can you light another?" Lina asked. Doon nodded and turned back to the boxes, but once again the boat struck something, causing a spray of water to slap into them and put the candle out.

It was several minutes before Doon managed to light it again, and more before he finally had two burning at once. He jammed one of them into a space between the bench and the side of the boat, and he held the other in his hand. His hair was flattened against his forehead, and dripping. His brown jacket was torn at the shoulder. "That's better," he said.

It was better—not only did they have light to see by, but the current was slower, and the boat sailed more smoothly. Lina was able to unwrap Poppy from her neck and look around. Ahead she could see that the tunnel curved. The boat swung into the curve, banged against the wall, straightened itself, and sped on. "Hand me a candle, too," she said.

Doon gave Lina the candle he was holding and lit another. They found places to wedge all three candles into the frame of the boat, so they could keep their hands free. For a while they rushed along almost silently, the river having become nearly as smooth as a sheet of glass.

Then suddenly the current slowed even more, and the tunnel opened out. "We've come into a room," said Lina. Far overhead arched a vaulted ceiling. Columns of rock hung down from it, and columns of rock rose from the water, too, making long shadows that turned and mingled as the boat floated among them. They glimmered in the candlelight, pink and pale green and silver. Their strange lumpy shapes looked like something soft that had frozen—like towers of mashed potatoes, Lina thought, that had hardened to stone.

Now and then the boat bumped into one of these columns, and they found that they could use a paddle to knock themselves free again. In this way they crossed the room to the other side, where again the passage narrowed and the current ran faster.

Much faster. It was as if the boat were being pulled forward by a powerful hand. The water grew rough again, and splashes of spray put out their candles. Lina and Doon huddled in the bottom of the boat with Poppy between them, their arms clasped around her.

They clenched their teeth and squeezed their eyes shut, and soon there was nothing in their minds but the roll and plunge of the boat and nothing in their bodies but the effort not to be thrown out. Once, the sound of the river rose to a crashing, and the front of the boat tipped downward, and they were pitched about so violently that it seemed they were tumbling down stairs—but that lasted only a few seconds, and then they were streaming onward as before.

Lina lost track of time. But a while later, maybe a few minutes, maybe an hour, the current slowed. The candles they'd stuck in the boat had been knocked overboard, so Doon lit new ones. They saw that they had come to another pool. There were no lumpy columns of rock here; nothing interrupted the wide flat surface of the water, which stretched out before them in the flickering light from their candles. The ceiling was smooth and only about ten feet above their heads. The boat drifted, as if it had lost its sense of direction. Using a paddle to poke against the walls, Doon guided the boat around the edge of the pool.

"I don't see where the river goes on," said Doon. "Do you?"

"No," said Lina. "Unless it's there, where it flows into that little gap." She pointed to a crack in the wall only a few inches wide.

"But the boat can't go there."

"No, it's much too small."

He poled the boat forward. Their shadows moved with them along the wall.

"Wanna go home," said Poppy.

"We're almost there," Lina told her.

"We certainly can't go back the way we came," said Doon.

"No." Lina dipped a hand in the water. It was so cold it sent an ache up her arm.

"Could this be the end?" said Doon. His voice sounded flat in this closed-in place.

"The end?" Lina felt a shiver of fear.

"I mean the end of the trip," Doon said. "Maybe we're supposed to get out over there." He pointed to a wide expanse of rock that sloped back into the darkness on one side of the pool. Everywhere else, the walls rose straight out of the water.

He poled the boat over to the rock slope. The boat scraped bottom here—the water was shallow. "I'll get out and see if this goes anywhere," said Lina. "I want to be on solid ground again, anyway." She handed Poppy to Doon and stood up. Holding a candle, she put one foot over the edge of the boat and into the cold water, and she waded ashore.

The way did not look promising. The ground sloped upward, and the ceiling sloped downward. As she went farther back she had to stoop. A few yards in, a tumbled heap of rocks blocked the way. She inched around them, turning sideways to squeeze through the narrow space, and crept forward, holding the candle out in front of her. This goes nowhere, she thought. We're trapped.

But a few steps farther along, she found she could stand up straight again, and a few steps beyond that she turned a corner, and suddenly the candlelight shone on a wide path, with a high ceiling and a smooth floor. Lina gave a wild shout. "Here it is!" she cried. "It's here! There's a path!"

Doon's voice came from far away. She couldn't tell what he was saying. She made her way back toward the boat, and when it came in sight she yelled again, "I found a path! A path!"

Doon scrambled out and waded ashore, carrying Poppy. He set her down, and then he and Lina took hold of the boat and hauled it as far as they could up the slope of rock. Poppy caught the excitement. She shouted gleefully, waving her fists like little clubs, and stomped around, glad to be on her feet again. She found a pebble and plunked it into the water, crowing happily at the splash it made.

"I want to see the path," said Doon.

"Go up that way," Lina told him, "and around the pile of rocks. I'll stay here and take things out of the boat."

Doon went, taking another candle from the box in the boat. Lina sat Poppy down in a kind of nook formed by a roundish boulder and a hollow in the wall. "Don't move from here," she said. Then she pulled Doon's bundle from under the seat of the boat. It was damp, but not soaked. Maybe the food inside would still be all right. She was hungry all of a sudden. She'd had no dinner, she remembered. It must be the middle of the night by now, or maybe even morning again.

She carried Doon's bundle ashore, along with the boxes of candles and matches, and as she set them down, Doon came back. His eyes were glowing, the reflection of a tiny flame dancing in each one. "That's it for sure," he said. "We've made it." Then his eyes shifted. "What's Poppy got?" he asked.

Lina whipped around. In Poppy's hands was something dark and rectangular. It wasn't a stone. It was more like a packet of some kind. She was plucking and pulling at it. She lifted it to her mouth as if to tear it with her teeth—and Lina jumped to her feet. "Stop!" she shouted. Poppy, startled, dropped the packet and began to cry.

"It's all right, never mind," Lina said, retrieving what Poppy had been about to chew on. "Come and have some dinner now. Hush, we're going to have dinner. I'm sure you're hungry."

In the light of Doon's candle, with Poppy squirming on Lina's lap, they examined Poppy's find. The packet was wrapped in slippery, greenish material and bound up with a strap. It wasn't wrapped very well; it looked as if someone had bundled it up quickly. The material was loose, and blotched with whitish mold.

Lina edged the strap off carefully. It was partly rotten; on the end of it was a small square buckle, covered with rust. She folded back the wrapping.

Doon took a sharp breath. "It's a book," he said. He moved his candle closer, and Lina opened the brown cover. The pages inside had faint blue lines across them, and someone had written along these lines in slanted black letters, which were not neat like the writing in the library books, but sprawling, as if the writer had been in a hurry.

Doon ran his finger under the first line. "It says, *They tell us we* . . . learn? . . . No, leave. *They tell us we leave tonight.*"

He looked up and met Lina's eyes.

"Leave?" said Lina. "From where?"

"From Ember?" Doon asked. "Could someone have come this way before us?"

"Or was it someone leaving the other city?"

Doon looked down at the book again. He riffled through the pages—there were many of them.

"Let's save it," said Lina. "We'll read it when we get to the new city."

Doon nodded. "It'll be easier to see there."

So Lina wrapped up the book again and tied it securely into Doon's bundle. They sat on the rock shelf for a while, eating the food Doon had brought. The candles wedged in the boat still shone steadily, and their light was cozy, like lamplight. It made golden shapes on the still surface of the pond.

Doon said, "I saw the guards run after you. Tell me what happened."

Lina told him.

"And what about Poppy? What did you tell Mrs. Murdo?"

"I told her the truth—at least I hope it's the truth. I caught up with her on her way home after the Singing. She'd seen the posters—she was terrified—but before she could ask questions, I just said she must give Poppy to me. I said I was taking her to safety. Because that's what I suddenly realized on the roof of the Gathering Hall, Doon. I'd been thinking before that I *had* to leave Poppy because she'd be safe with Mrs. Murdo. But when the lights went out, I suddenly knew: There *is* no safety in Ember. Not for long. Not for anyone. I couldn't leave her behind. Whatever happens to us now, it's better than what's going to happen there."

"And did you explain all that to Mrs. Murdo?"

"No. I was in a terrible hurry to get to the Pipeworks and meet you, and I knew I had to go while there were still crowds in the street, so it would be harder for the guards to see me. I just said I was taking Poppy to safety. Mrs. Murdo handed her over, but she sort of sputtered, 'Where?' and 'Why?' And I said, 'You'll know in a few days—it's all right.' And then I ran."

"So you gave her the note, then?" said Doon. "The one meant for Clary?"

"Oh!" Lina stared at him, stricken. "The message to Clary!" She put her hand in her pocket and pulled out the crumpled piece of paper. "I forgot all about it! All I was thinking of was getting Poppy and getting to you."

"So no one knows about the room full of boats."

Lina just shook her head, her eyes wide. "How will we get back to tell them?"

"We can't."

"Doon," said Lina, "if we'd told people right away, even just a few people . . . if we hadn't decided to be grand and announce it at the Singing . . ."

"I know," said Doon. "But we didn't, that's all. We didn't tell, and now no one knows. I did leave a message for my father, though." He told Lina about pinning his last-minute message to the kiosk in Selverton Square. "I said we'd found the way out, and that it was in the Pipeworks. But that's not much help."

"Clary has seen the Instructions," Lina said. "She knows there's an egress. She might find it."

"Or she might not."

There was nothing to be done about it, and so they

put the supplies back into Doon's pillowcase and got ready to go. Lina used Doon's rope to make a leash for Poppy. She tied one end around Poppy's waist and the other around her own. She filled her pockets with packs of matches, and Doon put all the remaining candles in his sack—in case they arrived in the new city at night. He filled his bottle with river water, lit a candle for himself and one for Lina, and thus equipped, they left the boat behind and crept up the rocky shelf to the path.

CHAPTER 19

A World of Light

As they squeezed past the rocks at the entrance to the path, Doon thought he saw the candlelight glance off a shiny place on the wall. He stopped to look, and when he saw what it was, he called out to Lina, who was a few steps ahead of him. "There's a notice!"

It was a framed sign, bolted to the stone, a printed sheet behind a piece of glass. Dampness had seeped under the glass and made splotches on the paper, but by holding their candles up close, they could read it.

Welcome, Refugees from Ember!
This is the final stage of your journey.
Be prepared for a climb
that will take several hours.
Fill your bottles with water from the river.
We wish you good fortune,
The Builders

"They're expecting us!" said Lina.

"Well, they wrote this a long time ago," Doon said. "The people who put it here must all be dead by now."

"That's true. But they wished us good fortune. It makes me feel as if they're watching over us."

"Yes. And maybe their great-great-great-grandchildren will be there to welcome us."

Encouraged, they started up the path. Their candles made only a feeble glow, but they could tell that the path was quite wide. The ceiling was high over their heads. The path seemed to have been made for a great company of people. In some places, the ground beneath their feet was rutted in parallel grooves, as if a wheeled cart of some kind had been driven over it. After they had walked awhile, they realized that they were moving in long zigzags. The path would go in one direction for some time and then turn sharply and go the opposite way.

As they went along, they talked less and less; the path sloped relentlessly upward, and they needed their breath just for breathing. The only sound was the light *pat-pat* of their footsteps. Lina and Doon took turns carrying Poppy on their backs—she had gotten tired of walking very soon and cried to be picked up. Twice, they stopped and sat down to rest, leaning against the walls of the passage and taking drinks from Doon's bottle of water.

"How many hours do you think we've been walking?" Lina asked.

"I don't know," Doon said. "Maybe two. Maybe three. We must be nearly there."

They climbed on and on. Their first candles had long ago burned down to the last inch, as had their second candles. Finally, when their third ones were about halfway gone, Lina began to notice that the air smelled different. The cold, sharp-edged rock smell of the tunnel was changing to something softer, a strange, lovely smell. As they rounded a corner, a gust of this soft air swept past them, and their candles went out.

Doon said, "I'll find a match," but Lina said, "No, wait. Look."

They were not in complete darkness. A faint haze of light shone in the passage ahead of them. "It's the lights of the city," breathed Lina.

Lina set Poppy down. "Quick, Poppy," she said, and Poppy began to trot, keeping close at Lina's heels. The strange, lovely smell in the air grew stronger. The passage came to an end a few yards farther along, and before them was an opening like a great empty doorway. Without a word, Lina and Doon took hold of each other's hands, and Lina took hold of Poppy's. When they stood in the doorway and looked out, they saw no new city at all, but something infinitely stranger: a land vast and spacious beyond any of their dreams, filled with air that seemed to move, and lit by a shining silver circle hanging in an immense black sky.

In front of their feet, the ground swept away in a long, gentle slope. It was not bare stone, as in Ember; something soft covered it, like silvery hair, as high as their knees. Down the slope was a tumble of dark, rounded shapes, and then another slope rose beyond that. Way off into the distance, as far as they could see, the land lay in rolling swells, with clumps of shadow in the low places between them.

"Doon!" cried Lina. "More lights!" She pointed at the sky.

He looked up and saw them—hundreds and hundreds of tiny flecks of light, strewn like spilled salt across the blackness. "Oh!" he whispered. There was nothing else to say. The beauty of these lights made his breath stop in his throat.

They took a few steps forward. Doon bent to feel the strands that grew out of the ground, almost higher than Poppy's head; they were cool and smooth and soft, and there was dampness on them.

"Breathe," said Lina. She opened her mouth and took in a long breath of air. Doon did the same.

"It's sweet," he said. "So full of smells."

They held their hands out to feel the long stems as they waded slowly through them. The air moved against their faces and in their hair.

"Hear those sounds?" said Doon. A high, thin chirruping sound came from somewhere nearby. It was repeated over and over, like a question.

"Yes," said Lina. "What could it be?"

"Something alive, I think. Maybe some kind of bug."

"A bug that sings." Lina turned to Doon. Her face was shadowy in the silver light. "It's so strange here, Doon, and so huge. But I'm not afraid."

"No. I'm not either. It feels like a dream."

"A dream, yes. Maybe that's why it feels familiar. I might have dreamed about this place."

They walked until they came to where the dark shapes billowed up from the ground. These were plants, they discovered, taller than they were, with stems as hard and thick as the walls of houses, and leaves that spread out over their heads. On the slope beside these plants, they sat down.

"Do you think there is a city here somewhere?" Lina asked. "Or any people at all?"

"I don't see any lights," Doon said, "even far off."

"But with this silver lamp in the sky, maybe they don't need lights."

Doon shook his head doubtfully. "People would need more light than this," he said. "How could you see well enough to work? How could you grow your food? It's a beautiful light, but not bright enough to live by."

"Then what shall we do, if there's no city, and no people?"

"I don't know. I don't know." Doon didn't feel like

thinking. He was tired of figuring things out. He wanted to look at this new world, and take in the scent of it and the feel of it, and figure things out later.

Lina felt the same way. She stopped asking questions, drew Poppy onto her lap, and gazed in silence at the glimmering landscape. After a while, she became aware that something strange was happening. Surely, when she had first sat down, the silver circle was just above the highest branch of the tall plant. Now the branch cut across it. As she watched, the circle sank very slowly down, until it was hidden, except for a gleam of brightness, behind the leaves.

"It's moving," she said to Doon.

"Yes."

A little later, it seemed to her that her eyes were blurring. There was a fuzziness in the sky, especially around the edges. It took a while for her to realize what was making the fuzziness.

"Light," she said.

"I see it," said Doon. "It's getting brighter."

The edge of the sky turned gray, and then pale orange, and then deep fiery crimson. The land stood out against it, a long black rolling line. One spot along this line grew so bright they could hardly look at it, so bright it seemed to take a bite out of the land. It rose higher and higher until they could see that it was a fiery circle, first deep orange and then yellow, and too bright to look at any longer. The color seeped out of the sky and washed over the land. Light sparkled on the soft hair of the hills and shone through the lacy leaves as every shade of green sprang to life around them.

They lifted their faces to the astonishing warmth. The sky arched over them, higher than they could have imagined, a pale, clear blue. Lina felt as though a lid that had been on her all her life had been lifted off. Light and air rushed through her, making a song, like the songs of Ember, only it was a song of joy. She looked at Doon and saw that he was smiling and crying at the same time, and she realized that she was, too.

Everything around them was springing to life. A glorious racket came from the branches—tweedling notes, peeps, burbles, high sharp calls. Bugs? wondered Doon, imagining with awe the bugs that could make such sounds. But then he saw something fly from a cluster of leaves and swoop down low across the ground, making a clear, sweet call as it flew. "Did you see that?" he said to Lina, pointing. "And there's another one! And there!"

"There there there there!" repeated Poppy, leaping from Lina's lap and whirling around, pointing in every direction.

The air was full of them now. They were much too large to be insects. One of them lit nearby on a stem. It looked at them with two bright black eyes and, opening its mouth, which was pointed like a thorn, sent forth a little trill.

"It's speaking to us," said Doon. "What could it be?"

Lina just shook her head. The little creature shifted its clawlike feet on the stem, flapped its brown wings, and trilled again. Then it leapt into the air and was gone.

They leapt up, too, and threw themselves into exploration. The ground was alive with insects—so many that Doon just laughed in helpless wonder. Flowers bloomed among the green blades, and a stream ran at the foot of the hill. They roamed over the green-coated slopes, running, sliding, calling out to each other with each new discovery, until they were exhausted. Then they sat down by the entrance to the path to eat what was left of their food. They untied Doon's bundle, and Lina suddenly cried out. "The book! We forgot about the book!"

There it was, wrapped in its blotched green cloth.

"Let's read it out loud while we eat," said Doon.

Lina opened the fragile notebook and laid it on the ground in front of her. She picked up a carrot with one hand, and with the other she kept her place on the scribbled page. This is what she read.

CHAPTER 20

The Last Message

Friday

They tell us we leave tonight. I knew it would be soon—the training has been over for nearly a month now—but still it feels sudden, it feels like a shock. Why did I agree to do this? I am an old woman, too tired to take up a new life. I wish now that I'd said no when they asked me.

I have put everything I can into my one suitcase—clothes, shoes, a good wind-up clock, some soap, an extra pair of glasses. Bring no books, they said, and no photographs. We have been told to say nothing, ever again, about the world we come from. But I am going to take this notebook anyhow. I am determined to write down what happens. Someday, someone may need to know.

Saturday

I went to the train station yesterday evening, as they told me to, and got on the train they told me to take. It took us through Spring Valley, and I gazed out the window at the fields and houses of the place I was saying goodbye to—my home, and my family's home for generations. I rode for two hours, until the train reached a station in the hills. When I arrived, they met me—three men in suits—and drove me to a large building, where they led me down a corridor and into a big room full of other people—all with suitcases, most with gray or white hair. Here we have been waiting now for more than an hour.

They have spent years and years making this plan. It's supposed to ensure that, no matter what happens, people won't disappear from the earth. Some say that will never happen anyhow. I'm not so sure. Disaster seems very close. Everything will be all right, they tell us, but only a few people believe them. Why, if it's going to be all right, do we see it getting worse every day?

And of course this plan is proof that they think the world is doomed. All the best scientists and engineers have been pulled in to work on it. Extraordinary efforts have been made—efforts that would have done more good elsewhere. I think it's the wrong answer. But they asked me if I would go—I suppose because I've spent my life on a farm and I know about growing food. In spite of my doubts, I said yes. I'm not sure why.

There are a hundred of us, fifty men and fifty women. We are all at least sixty years old. There will be a hundred babies, too—two babies for each pair of "parents." I don't know yet which one of these gentlemen I'll be matched with. We are all strangers to one another. They planned it that way; they said there would be fewer memories between us. They want us to forget everything about the lives we've led and the places we've lived. The babies must grow up with no knowledge of a world outside, so that they feel no sorrow for what they have lost.

I hear some noises across the room. I think it's the babies arriving. . . . Yes, here they come, each being carried by one of those gray-suited men. So many of them! So small! Little scrunched-up faces, tiny fists waving. I must stop for now. They're going to pass them out.

Later

We're traveling again, on a bus this time. It is night, I think, though it's hard to be sure because they have boarded up the windows of the bus from the outside. They don't want us to know where we're going.

I have a baby on my lap—a girl. She has a bright pink face and no hair at all. Stanley, who sits next to me, holds a boy baby, with brown skin and a few tufts of black hair. Stanley and I are the keepers of these children. Our task is to raise them in this new place we're going to. By the time they are twenty or so, we'll be gone. They'll be on their own, making a new world.

Stanley and I have named these children Star and Forest.

Sunday

The buses have stopped, but they have not allowed us to get out yet. I can hear crickets singing, and smell the grass, so we must be in the country, and it must be night. I am very tired.

What kind of place can this be, safe from earthly catastrophes? All I can guess is that it must be underground. The thought fills me with dread. I'll try to sleep a little now.

Later

There was no chance to sleep. They called us off the buses, and we stepped out into a landscape of rolling hills, in full moonlight. "That's the way we'll be going in," they told us, pointing to a dark opening in the hill we stood on. "Form a line there, please." We did so. It was very quiet, except for the squalling of a few of the babies. If the others were like me, they were saying goodbye to the world. I reached down to touch the grass and breathed deeply to smell the earth. My eyes swept over the silver hills, and I thought of the animals prowling softly in the shadows or sleeping in their burrows, and the birds standing beneath the leaves of the trees, with their heads tucked under their wings. Last, I raised my eyes to the moon, which smiled down on us from a long, cold distance away. The moon will still be here when they come out, I thought. The moon and the hills, at least.

The opening led us into a winding passage that ran steeply downhill for perhaps a mile. It was hard going for me; my legs are not strong anymore. We moved very slowly. The last part was the worst: a rocky slope where it was easy to miss your footing and slip. This led down to a pool. By the shore of the pool our group of aged pioneers gathered. Motorboats were waiting here for us, equipped with lanterns.

"When it's time for people to leave this

place, is this the way they will come?" I asked our pilot, who has a kind face. He said yes.

"But how will they know there's a way out, if no one tells them?" I said. "How will they know what to do?"

"They're going to have instructions," said the pilot. "They won't be able to get at the instructions until the time is right. But when they need them, the instructions will be there."

"But what if they don't find them? What if they never come out again?"

"I think they will. People find a way through just about anything."

That was all he would say. I am writing these notes while our pilot loads the boat. I hope he doesn't notice.

"It ends there," said Lina, looking up.

"He must have noticed," said Doon. "Or she was afraid he would, so she decided to hide it instead of taking it with her."

"She must have hoped someone would find it."

"Just as we did." He pondered. "But we might not have, if it hadn't been for Poppy."

"No. And we wouldn't have known that we came from here."

The fiery circle had moved up in the sky now, and

the air was so warm that they took off their coats. Absently, Doon dug his finger into the ground, which was soft and crumbly. "But what was the disaster that happened in this place?" he said. "It doesn't look ruined to me."

"It must have happened a long, long time ago," said Lina. "I wonder if people still live here."

They sat looking out over the hills, thinking of the woman who had written in the notebook. What had her city been like? Lina wondered. Like Ember in some way, she imagined. A city with trouble, where people argued over solutions. A dying city. But it was hard to picture a city like Ember here in this bright, beautiful place. How could anyone have allowed such a place to be harmed?

"What do we do now?" asked Lina. She wrapped the notebook in its covering again and set it aside. "We can't go back up the river and tell them all to come here."

"No. We could never make the boat go against that current."

"Are we here alone, then, forever?"

"Maybe there's another way in, some way that lets you walk down to Ember. Or maybe there's another river that runs the other way. We have candles now, we could cross the Unknown Regions if we found a way to get there."

This was the only plan they could come up with.

So, all day long, they searched for another way in. Under the brow of the hill, they found a hole where a stream wandered into the dark. The water was good to drink, but the hole was far too small for them to fit through. There were gullies full of shrubs, and Lina and Doon crawled among the leaves and prickly branches, but found no openings. Bugs buzzed around their ankles and past their eyes; brown earth stained their hands, and pebbles got into their shoes. Their thick, dark, shabby clothes got all full of prickly things, and since they were much too hot anyhow, they took most of them off. They had never felt such warmth against their skin and such soft air.

When the bright circle was at the top of the sky, they sat for a while in the shade of one of the tall plants on the side of the hill, in a place where the thick brush gave way to a clearing. Poppy went to sleep, but Lina and Doon sat looking out over the land. Green was everywhere, in different shades, like a huge, brilliant, gorgeous version of the overlapping carpets back in the rooms of Ember. Far away, Lina saw a narrow gray line curving like a pencil stroke across a sweep of green. She pointed this out to Doon, and both of them squinted hard at it, but it was too far away to see clearly.

"Could it be a road?" said Lina.

"It could," said Doon.

"Maybe there are people here after all."

"I hope so," said Doon. "There's so much I want to know."

They were still gazing at the far-off bit of gray when they heard something moving in the brush nearby. Leaves rustled. There was a scraping, shuffling sound. They stiffened and held their breath. The shuffling paused, then started up again. Was it a person? Should they call out? But before they could decide what to do, a creature stepped into the clearing.

It was about the same size as Poppy, only lower to the ground, because it walked on four legs instead of two. Its fur was a deep rust-red. Its face was a long triangle, its ears stood up in points, and its black eyes shone. It trotted forward a few steps, absorbed in its own business. Behind it floated a thick, soft-looking tail.

All at once it saw them and stopped.

Lina and Doon stayed absolutely still. So did the creature. Then it took a step toward them, paused, tilted its head a little as if to get a better look, and took another step. They could see the sheen of its fur and the glint of light in its eyes.

For a long moment, they stayed like this, frozen, staring at one another. Then, unhurriedly, the creature moved away. It pushed its nose among the leaves on the ground, wandering back toward the bushes, and when it raised its head again, they saw that it was holding something in its white teeth, something round and purplish. With a last glance at them, it leapt toward the bushes, its tail sailing, and disappeared.

Lina let out her breath and turned to look at Doon, whose mouth was open in astonishment. His voice shaky, he said, "That was the most wonderful thing I have ever seen, ever in my whole life."

"Yes."

"And it saw us," Doon said, and Lina nodded. They both felt it—they had been seen. The creature was utterly strange, not like anything they had ever known, and yet when it looked at them, some kind of recognition passed between them. "I know now," said Doon. "This is the world we belong in."

A few minutes later, Poppy woke up and made fretful noises, and Lina gave her the last of the peas in Doon's pack. "What was that, do you think, in the creature's mouth?" she asked. "Would it be something we could eat, a fruit of some kind? It looked like the pictures of peaches on cans, except for the color."

They got up and poked around, and soon they came across a plant whose branches were laden with the purple fruits, about the size of small beets, only softer. Doon picked one and cut it open with his knife. There was a stone inside. Red juice ran out over his hands. Cautiously, he touched his tongue to it. "Sweet," he said.

"If the creature can eat it, maybe we can, too," said Lina. "Shall we?"

They did. Nothing had ever tasted better. Lina cut the stones out and gave chunks of the fruit to Poppy. Juice ran down their chins. When they had eaten five or six apiece, they licked their sticky fingers clean and started to explore again.

They went higher up the slope they were on, wading through flowers as high as their waists, and near the top they came upon a kind of dent in the ground, as if a bit of the earth had caved in. They walked down into it, and at the end of the dent they found a crack about as tall as a person but not nearly as wide as a door. Lina edged through it sideways and discovered a narrow tunnel. "Send Poppy through," she called back to Doon, "and come yourself." But it was dark inside, and Doon had to go back to where he'd left his pack to get a candle. By candlelight, they crept along until they came to a place where the tunnel ended abruptly. But it ended not with a wall but with a sudden huge nothingness that made them gasp and step back. A few feet beyond their shoes was a sheer, dizzying drop. They looked out into a cave so enormous that it seemed almost as big as the world outside. Far down at the bottom shone a cluster of lights.

"It's Ember," Lina whispered.

They could see the tiny bright streets crossing each other, and the squares, little chips of light, and the dark tops of buildings. Just beyond the edges was the immense darkness.

"Oh, our city, Doon. Our city is at the bottom of a hole!" She gazed down through the gulf, and all of what she had believed about the world began to slowly break apart. "*We* were underground," she said. "Not just the Pipeworks. Everything!" She could hardly make sense of what she was saying.

Doon crouched on his hands and knees, looking over the edge. He squinted, trying to see minute specks that might be people. "What's happening there, I wonder?"

"Could they hear us if we shouted?"

"I don't think so. We're much too far up."

"Maybe if they looked into the sky they'd see our candle," said Lina. "But no, I guess they wouldn't. The streetlamps would be too bright."

"Somehow, we have to get word to them," said Doon, and that was when the idea came to Lina.

"Our message!" she cried. "We could send our message!"

And they did. From her pocket, Lina took the message that Doon had written, the one that was supposed to have gone to Clary, explaining everything. In small writing, they squeezed in this note at the top:

Dear People of Ember,

We came down the river from the Pipeworks and found the way to another place. It is green here and very big. Light comes from the sky. You must follow the instructions in this message and come on the river. Bring food with you. Come as quickly as you can.

Lina Mayfleet and Doon Harrow

They wrapped the message in Doon's shirt and put a rock inside it. Then they stood in a row at the edge of the chasm, Doon in the middle holding Poppy's hand and Lina's. Lina took aim at the heart of the city, far beneath her feet. With all her strength, she cast the message into the darkness, and they watched as it plunged down and down.

Mrs. Murdo, walking even more briskly than usual to keep her spirits up, was crossing Harken Square when something fell to the pavement just in front of her with a terrific thump. How extraordinary, she thought, bending to pick it up. It was a sort of bundle. She began to untie it.

THE PEOPLE OF SPARKS

Contents

The Message 285

PART 1: Arrival

1. What Torren Saw 289
2. Out from Below 298
3. Through the Village 308
4. The Doctor's House 320

THE FIRST TOWN MEETING 329

5. The Pioneer 334
6. Breakfast with Disaster 347
7. A Day of New People 363
8. The Roamer and the Bike 374
9. Hard, Hungry Work 389
10. Restless Weeks 402
11. Tick's Projects 414

12. Caspar Arrives with a Surprise 423
13. Taking Action 436

PART 2: Travelers and Warriors

14. What Torren Did 447
15. A Long, Hot Ride 456
16. The Starving Roamer 466
17. Doon Accused 478
THE SECOND TOWN MEETING 490
18. Caspar's Quest 493
19. Unfairness, and What to Do About It 498
20. The City Destroyed 506
21. Attack and Counterattack 514
22. Discoveries 524
THE THIRD TOWN MEETING 537
23. Getting Ready for War 541

PART 3: The Decision

24. What Torren Planned 551
25. Dread at the Last Minute 554
26. The Weapon 570
27. Firefight 582
28. Surprising Truths 590
THE FOURTH TOWN MEETING 600
29. Three Amazing Visits 612

"Darkness cannot drive out darkness;
only light can do that.
Hate cannot drive out hate;
only love can do that.
Hate multiplies hate, violence multiplies violence,
and toughness multiplies toughness
in a descending spiral of destruction."
—Martin Luther King, Jr.,
"Strength to Love," 1963

The Message

Dear People of Ember,

We came down the river from the Pipeworks and found the way to another place. It is green here and very big. Light comes from the sky. You must follow the instructions in this message and come on the river. Bring food with you. Come as quickly as you can.

Lina Mayfleet and Doon Harrow

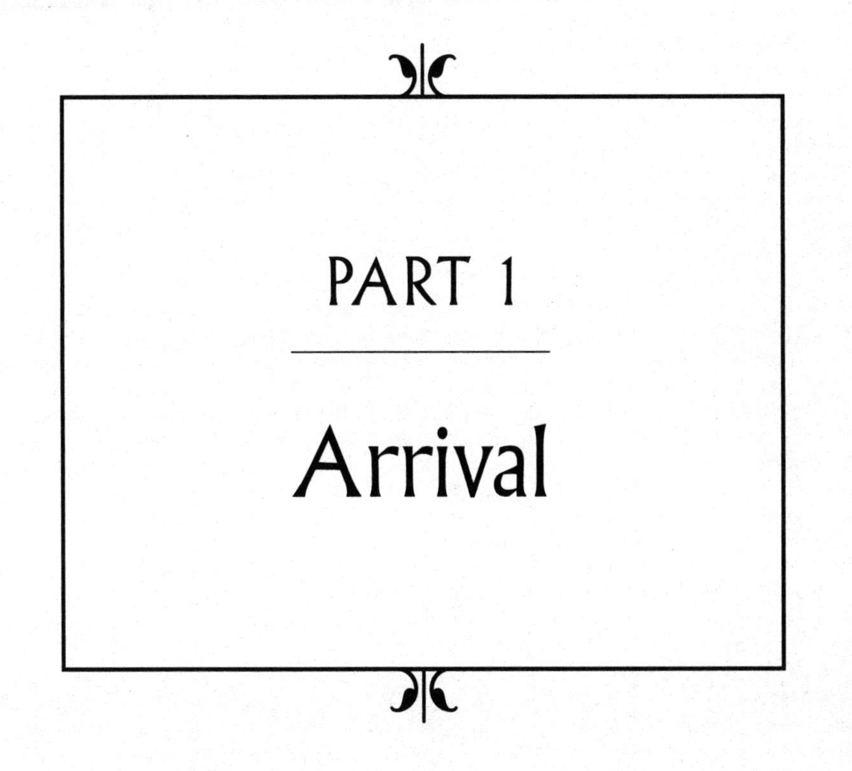

PART 1

Arrival

CHAPTER 1

What Torren Saw

Torren was out at the edge of the cabbage field that day, the day the people came. He was supposed to be fetching a couple of cabbages for Dr. Hester to use in the soup that night, but, as usual, he didn't see why he shouldn't have some fun while he was at it. So he climbed up the wind tower, which he wasn't supposed to do because, they said, he might fall or get his head sliced off by the big blades going round and round.

The wind tower was four-sided, made of boards nailed one above the next like the rungs of a ladder. Torren climbed the back side of it, the side that faced the hills and not the village, so that the little group of workers hoeing the cabbage rows wouldn't see him. At the top, he turned around and sat on the flat place behind the blades, which turned slowly in the idle summer breeze. He had brought a pocketful of small stones up with him, planning on some target practice:

he liked to try to hit the chickens that rummaged around between the rows of cabbages. He thought it might be fun to bounce a few pebbles off the hats of the workers, too. But before he had even taken the stones from his pocket, he caught sight of something that made him stop and stare.

Out beyond the cabbage field was another field, where young tomato and corn and squash plants were growing, and beyond that the land sloped up into a grassy hillside dotted, at this time of year, with yellow mustard flowers. Torren saw something strange at the top of the hill. Something dark.

There were bits of darkness at first—for a second he thought maybe it was a deer, or several deer, black ones instead of the usual light brown, but the shape was wrong for deer, and the way these things moved was wrong, too. He realized very soon that he was seeing people, a few people at first and then more and more of them. They came up from the other side of the hill and gathered at the top and stood there, a long line of them against the sky, like a row of black teeth. There must have been a hundred, Torren thought, or more than a hundred.

In all his life, Torren had never seen more than three or four people at a time arrive at the village from elsewhere. Almost always, the people who came were roamers, passing through with a truckload of stuff from the old towns to sell. This massing of people on the hilltop terrified him. For a moment he couldn't move. Then his heart started up a furious pounding, and he scrambled down off the wind tower so fast that he scraped his hands on the rough boards.

"Someone's coming!" he shouted as he passed the workers. They looked up, startled. Torren ran at full speed toward the low cluster of brown buildings at the far end of the field. He turned up a dirt lane, his feet raising swirls of dust, and dashed through the gate in the wall and across the courtyard and in through the open door, all the time yelling, "Someone's coming! Up on the hill! Auntie Hester! Someone's coming!"

He found his aunt in the kitchen, and he grabbed her by the waist of her pants and cried, "Come and see! There's people on the hill!" His voice was so shrill and urgent and loud that his aunt dropped the spoon into the pot of soup she'd been stirring and hurried after him. By the time they got outside, others from the village were leaving their houses, too, and looking toward the hillside.

The people were coming down. Over the crest of the hill they came and kept coming, dozens of them, more and more, like a mudslide.

The people of the village crowded into the streets. "Get Mary Waters!" someone called. "Where's Ben and Wilmer? Find them, tell them to get out here!"

Torren was less frightened now that he was surrounded by the townspeople. "I saw them first," he said to Hattie Carranza, who happened to be hurrying along next to him. "I was the one who told the news."

"Is that right," said Hattie.

"We won't let them do anything bad to us," said Torren. "If they do, we'll do something worse to them. Won't we?"

But she just glanced down at him with a vague frown and didn't answer.

The three village leaders—Mary Waters, Ben Barlow, and Wilmer Dent—had joined the crowd by now and were leading the way across the cabbage field. Torren kept close behind them. The strangers were getting nearer, and he wanted to hear what they would say. He could see that they were terrible-looking people. Their clothes were all wrong—coats and sweaters, though the weather was warm, and not nice coats and sweaters but raggedy ones, patched, unraveling, faded, and grimy. They carried bundles, all of them: sacks made of what looked like tablecloths or blankets gathered up and tied with string around the neck. They moved clumsily and slowly. Some of them tripped on the uneven ground and had to be helped up by others.

In the center of the field, where the smell of new cabbages and fresh dirt and chicken manure was strong, those at the front of the crowd of strangers met the village leaders. Mary Waters stepped to the front, and the villagers crowded up behind her. Torren, being small, wriggled between people until he had a good view. He stared at the ragged people. Where were *their* leaders? Facing Mary were a girl and a boy who looked only a little older than he was himself. Next to them was a bald man, and next to him a sharp-eyed woman holding a small child. Maybe she was the leader.

But when Mary stepped forward and said, "Who are you?" it was the boy who answered. He spoke in a clear, loud voice that surprised Torren, who had expected a pitiful voice from someone so bedraggled. "We come from the city of Ember," the boy said. "We left there because our city was dying. We need help."

Mary, Ben, and Wilmer exchanged glances. Mary frowned. "The city of Ember? Where's that? We've never heard of it."

The boy gestured back the way they had come, to the east. "That way," he said. "It's under the ground."

The frowns deepened. "Tell us the truth," said Ben, "not childish nonsense."

This time the girl spoke up. She had long, snarled hair with bits of grass caught in it. "It isn't a lie," she said. "Really. Our city was underground. We didn't know it until we came out."

Ben snorted impatiently, folding his arms across his chest. "Who is in charge here?" He looked at the bald man. "Is it you?"

The bald man shook his head and gestured toward the boy and the girl. "They're as in charge as anyone," he said. "The mayor of our city is no longer with us. These young people are speaking the truth. We have come out of a city built underground."

The people around him all nodded and murmured, "Yes" and "It's true."

"My name is Doon Harrow," said the boy. "And this is Lina Mayfleet. We found the way out of Ember."

He thinks he's pretty great, thought Torren, hearing a note of pride in the boy's voice. He didn't look so great. His hair was shaggy, and he was wearing an old jacket that was coming apart at the seams and grimy at the cuffs. But his eyes shone out confidently from under his dark eyebrows.

"We're hungry," the boy said. "And thirsty. Will you help us?"

Mary, Ben, and Wilmer stood silent for a moment. Then Mary took Ben and Wilmer by the arms and led them aside a few steps. They whispered to each other, glanced up at the great swarm of strangers, frowned, whispered some more. While he waited to hear what they'd say, Torren studied the people who said they came from underground.

It might be true. They did in fact look as if they had crawled up out of a hole. Most of them were scrawny and pale, like the sprouts you see when you lift up a board that's been lying on the ground, feeble things that have tried to grow in the dark. They huddled together looking frightened. They looked exhausted, too. Many of them had sat down on the ground now, and some had their heads in the laps of others.

The three village leaders turned again to the crowd of strangers. "How many of you are there?" Mary Waters asked.

"About four hundred," said the boy, Doon.

Mary's dark eyebrows jumped upward.

Four hundred! In Torren's whole village, there were only 322. He swept his gaze out over this vast horde. They filled half the cabbage field and were still coming over the hill, like a swarm of ants.

The girl with the ratty hair stepped forward and raised a hand, as if she were in school. "Excuse me, Madam Mayor," she said.

Torren snickered. Madam Mayor! Nobody called Mary Waters Madam Mayor. They just called her Mary.

"Madam Mayor," said the girl, "my little sister is very sick." She pointed to the baby being held by the sharp-eyed woman. It did look sick. Its eyes were half closed, and its mouth hung open. "Some others of us are sick, too," the girl went on, "or hurt—Lotty Hoover tripped and hurt her ankle, and Nammy Proggs is exhausted from walking so far. She's nearly eighty years old. Is there a doctor in your town? Is there a place where sick people can lie down and be taken care of?"

Mary turned to Ben and Wilmer again, and they spoke to each other in low voices. Torren could catch only a few words of what they said. "Too many . . ." ". . . but human kindness . . ." ". . . maybe take a *few* in . . ." Ben rubbed his beard and scowled. Wilmer kept glancing at the sick baby. After a few minutes, they nodded to each other. Mary said, "All right. Hoist me up."

Ben and Wilmer bent down and grasped Mary's legs. With a grunt they lifted her so that she was high enough to see out over the crowd. She raised both her arms and cried, in a voice that came from the depths of her deep chest, "People from Ember! Welcome! We will do what we can to help you. Please follow us!" Ben and Wilmer set her down, and the three of them turned and walked out of the cabbage field and toward the road that entered the village. Led by the boy and the girl, the crowd of shabby people followed.

Torren dashed ahead, ran down the lane, and got up onto the low wall that bordered his house. From there, he watched the people from underground go by. They were strangely silent. Why weren't they jabbering to each other? But they seemed too tired to speak, or too stupid. They stared at everything, wide-eyed and drop-jawed—as if they had never seen a house before, or a tree, or a chicken. In fact, the chickens seemed to frighten them—they shrank back when they saw them, making startled sounds. It took a long time for the whole raggedy crowd to pass Torren's house, and when the last people had gone by, he jumped down off the wall and followed them. They were being led, he knew, to the town center, down by the river, where there would be water for them to drink. After that, what would happen? What would they eat? Where would they sleep? Not in my room, he thought.

CHAPTER 2

Out from Below

The people from the dying city of Ember had come up into the new world only a few days before. The first to arrive had been Lina Mayfleet and Doon Harrow, bringing Lina's little sister, Poppy, with them. From a ledge high up in the great cave that held their city, they'd thrown down a message, hoping someone would find it and lead the others out. Then they'd waited. At first they'd explored the wonders around them. But as the hours passed, they began to worry that their message had not been found and that they would be alone in this world forever.

Then, in the late afternoon of the next day, Doon suddenly shouted, "Look! They're coming!"

Lina grabbed Poppy by the hand. All three of them ran toward the mouth of the cave. Who was it? Who was it coming from home? A woman emerged from the darkness first, and then two men, and then three children, all of them squinting against the bright light.

"Hello, hello!" Lina called, leaping up the hill. She saw who it was when she got closer: the family who ran the Callay Street vegetable market. She didn't know any of them well—she couldn't even remember their names—and yet she was so glad to see them that tears sprang to her eyes. She flung her arms around each one in turn, crying, "Here you are! Look, isn't it wonderful? Oh, I'm so glad you're here! And are more coming?" The new arrivals were too breathless and amazed to answer, but it didn't matter, because Lina could see for herself.

They came out from the cave, shading their eyes with their hands. They came in bunches, a few of them and then minutes later a few more, stumbling out into a light a thousand times brighter than any they'd ever seen. They stared in astonishment, walked a few steps, and then just stood, dropping the sacks and bundles they carried, gazing, blinking. To Lina and Doon, who felt already that they belonged here, the refugees from Ember looked strange in this bright landscape of green grass and blue sky. They were so drab and dingy in their heavy, mud-colored clothes, their coats and sweaters in colors like stone and dust and murky water. It was as if they had brought some of Ember's darkness with them.

Doon suddenly leapt away, shouting, "Father! Father!" He threw himself against his stunned father, who fell backward, sat down on the ground, and burst into a combination of laughter and weeping to see his son again. "You *are* here," he gasped. "I wasn't sure. . . . I didn't know. . . ."

All afternoon they came. Lizzie Bisco came, and others from the old High Class, along with Clary Laine from the greenhouses, and the doctor who had helped Lina's granny, and Sadge Merrall, who had tried to go out into the Unknown Regions. Mrs. Murdo came, walking in her brisk, businesslike way, but giving a cry of joy when she saw Lina hurtling toward her. People came whose faces Lina recognized but whose names she didn't remember, like the shoe repair man from Liverie Street, and the little puffy-faced woman who lived in Selverton Square, and the tall, black-haired boy with blue-gray eyes so light they looked like glints of metal. What was that tall boy's name? She spent a second trying to recall it, but only a second. It didn't matter. These were her people, the people of Ember. All of them were tired and all of them were thirsty. Lina showed them the little stream, and they splashed the water on their faces and filled their bottles there.

"What about the mayor?" Lina asked Mrs. Murdo, but she just shook her head. "He's not with us," she said.

Some of the older people looked terrified to be in such a huge place, a place that seemed to go on without borders in all directions. After they had stared nervously about them for a while, they sat down in the grass, hunched over, and put their heads to their knees. But the children ran around in ecstasy, touching everything, smelling the air, splashing their feet in the stream.

By evening, 417 people had arrived—Doon kept track. As the light began to fade from the sky, they shared the food they had brought, and then, using their coats as blankets and their bundles as pillows, they lay down on the warm, rough ground and slept.

The next morning they got ready to leave. Lina and Doon, when they first arrived, had spotted a narrow gray line that ran along the ground like a pencil stroke in the distance. They thought it might be a road. So the people of Ember, having no other clue about where to go, picked up their bundles and set out in that direction, a long, straggling line trailing across the hills.

It was on this walk that Mrs. Murdo told Lina and Doon about leaving Ember. The three of them walked together, Mrs. Murdo with Poppy in her arms. Doon's father walked behind them, leaning forward now and then to hear what Mrs. Murdo was saying.

"I was the one who found your message," Mrs. Murdo said. "It fell right at my feet. It was the day after the Singing. I was on my way home from the market, feeling sick with worry because you and Poppy had disappeared. Then there was your message." She paused and looked up at the sky. She was keeping a couple of tears from falling, Lina saw.

Mrs. Murdo composed herself and went on. "I thought it would be best to tell the mayor first. I wasn't sure I trusted him, but he was the one who could most easily organize the leaving. I showed him your message, and then I waited to hear the city clock ringing out the signal for a meeting."

Mrs. Murdo paused to catch her breath. They were going uphill, over rough clumps of earth—hard walking for city people, whose feet were accustomed to pavement.

"And was there a meeting?" Lina asked.

"No," said Mrs. Murdo. She plucked some burs off her skirt and shifted Poppy to her other shoulder. "Mercy," she said. "It's terribly hot." She stood still for a moment, breathing hard.

"So there was no meeting?" Lina prompted.

Mrs. Murdo started walking again. "Nothing happened at all," she said. "The clock didn't chime. The guards didn't come out and start organizing people. Nothing. But the lights kept flickering on and off. It seemed to me there was no time to lose.

"So I went to the Pipeworks and showed your message to Lister Munk. We followed the directions, and we found the rock marked with E right away—because people were there already."

"But how could they be, if they didn't have the directions?" Doon said. "Who was it?"

"It was the mayor," said Mrs. Murdo grimly, "and four of his guards. Looper was there, too, that boy who used to keep company with your friend Lizzie. They had huge, bulging sacks with them, piled up on the edge of the river, and they were loading the sacks into boats. The mayor was shouting at them to work faster.

"Lister yelled, 'What are you doing?' but we didn't need an answer. I could see what they were doing. They were going first. The mayor was making sure that he would get out, along with his friends and his loot, before anyone else."

Mrs. Murdo stopped talking. She trudged along, wiping sweat from her forehead. She frowned up at the hot, bright sky. Poppy whimpered.

"Let me carry the child for a while, Mrs. Murdo," said Doon's father.

"Thank you," Mrs. Murdo said. She stopped and passed the squirming Poppy to Doon's father, and they walked on.

Lina waited a minute or so, and then she couldn't wait any longer. "Well, what happened?" she said.

"It was awful," Mrs. Murdo said. "Everything happened at once. Two of the guards looked up at us and lost their balance and fell into the water. They grabbed hold of the loaded boats, which made the boats tip and dump their load into the river. The other guards and

Looper knelt down and tried to reach them, but they were pulled in, too. In the midst of all this, the mayor jumped onto the one boat that was still upright, but as soon as he hit it, it turned over and he plunged into the river." Mrs. Murdo shuddered. "He screamed, children. It was a horrible sound. He bobbed in the water like a giant cork, and then he went under. In just a few seconds, he and his guards were swept away. They were gone."

They walked in silence for a while, going downhill now. After a few minutes Mrs. Murdo went on.

"So Lister and I went back up into the city, and we had the Timekeeper ring the bell for a public meeting. We tried to explain what to do, but as soon as people heard the first bit—that a way out of Ember had been found, and that it was in the Pipeworks—everyone began shouting and rushing around. Things turned into a terrible mess. People were in too much of a hurry even to ask questions. Hundreds of them poured through the streets of the city all at once, and outside the door of the Pipeworks a huge crowd pushed and shoved to get in, so many people, so panicky, that some were trampled and crushed."

"Oh!" cried Lina. "How horrible!" These were people she knew! It was too awful to think about.

"Horrible indeed," said Mrs. Murdo. She frowned out across the vast landscape surrounding them, where there were no people in sight at all. "It was impossible to control them," she went on. "They rushed to the stairway—some people lost their footing and fell all the way down the stairs. Others ran right over them. And then when they realized that they were going to have to get into these little shells and float on the river, some people were so frightened that they turned around and tried to go up the stairs again, and some were so eager to get going that they jumped into the boats and capsized them and fell into the river and were drowned." She raised her eyes to Lina's. "I saw everything that happened," she said. "I'll never forget it."

Lina looked behind her at the citizens of Ember toiling across the hills. These were the ones who had made it out. "How many do you think were—left behind?" she asked Mrs. Murdo.

Mrs. Murdo just shook her head. "I don't know," she said. "Too many."

"And have the lights gone out forever now?"

"I don't know that either. But if they haven't, they will soon."

Hot as she was, Lina shuddered. She and Doon exchanged a look. They were thinking the same thing, she was sure: their city was lost in darkness now, and anyone left there was lost, too.

Later that day the refugees from Ember came to the road they had seen from afar. It was potholed and weed-cracked, but easier to walk on than the rough ground. It led alongside a creek that flowed swiftly over round, smooth rocks. In all directions, they saw nothing but endless expanses of grass. They shared the food they had brought with them, but it wasn't much. Some of them soon grew weak with hunger. They grew faint from the heat, too, which was hard to bear for people used to the constant chill of Ember. Poppy cried when she was set down on her feet, and her face looked flushed and hot.

Night came in the strange, gradual way so different from the sudden lights-out that signaled night in Ember. The travelers lay down on the ground and slept. They walked the next day, too, and the day after that. By then the food they had brought with them was gone. They traveled more and more slowly, stopping often to rest. Poppy was listless; her eyes were dull.

Finally, around the middle of the following day, they trudged up still another hill, and from there they saw a sight that made many of them weep with relief. Farmed fields lay below them in a wide valley, and beyond the fields, where the stream they'd been following joined a river, was a cluster of low brown buildings. It was a place where people lived.

Like the others, Lina was glad to see it. But it wasn't a bit like the city she had imagined, the one she'd drawn pictures of back in Ember, the one she'd hoped to find in this new world. The buildings of that city had been tall and majestic and sparkling with light. That city must be somewhere else, she thought as she started down the hill. She'd find it—not today, but someday.

CHAPTER 3

Through the Village

The woman who had greeted them led the people of Ember into the town. They went down a dusty street, past buildings that looked as if they'd been made out of the same brown earth that was underfoot. They were heavy-looking, imperfect buildings: their walls were fat and lumpy, rounded smooth at the corners. Lina saw cracks in the walls and crumbled places where bits of a window ledge or a step had fallen away.

Paths and alleys and strips of garden wound between the houses. It was clear that no one had planned this place, not the way the Builders had planned Ember. This town must have grown, one bit added to the next and another bit added to that. Plants grew everywhere. In Ember, the only plants were in the greenhouses—unless you counted mold and fungus, which grew on the trash heaps and sometimes in kitchens and bathrooms. Here, flowers and vegetables grew together beside every house. Plants sprang up alongside the streets, climbed walls, crawled over fences, pushed up through cracks in stairways, tumbled out of big pots and over windowsills and even down from roofs.

There were animals, too—huge, amazing, terrifying animals. In a fenced-in place at the edge of the town, Lina saw four brown animals much bigger than she was, with squarish heads and long, tasseled tails. Farther on, tethered to a post in front of a house, was a yellow-eyed creature with two spikes poking out of its head. When she walked by, it suddenly said, "Ma-a-a-a," and she skittered away in fright.

She turned to look for Doon, who had fallen a little behind. She found him stooping over, peering at some yellow flowers growing next to a wall. "Look at this," he said when she came up beside him. He pointed to a flower's tube-shaped center. "There's a spider in there the exact same yellow as the flower."

There was. Only Doon would notice such a thing. Tugging at the sleeve of his jacket, she said, "Come on. Stay with us," and she hurried him up toward the front of the line to join his father and Mrs. Murdo and Poppy.

These four people—Poppy and Mrs. Murdo, Doon and his father—were Lina's family now, and she wanted them close around her. Only Poppy was really related to her. But Mrs. Murdo was like a mother; she had taken Lina and Poppy into her house when their granny died, and she would have kept them with her if they hadn't had to leave the city. Doon's father was part of her family just because he was Doon's father. And Doon himself—he was the one who'd been Lina's partner in finding the way out of Ember. There was a tie between the two of them that could never be broken.

On they walked, down one street and up another, around curves and down through narrow passages. Everywhere, people stared at them. Some leaned from open windows. Some sat up on roofs, their legs dangling over the side. Some stood still in the midst of work they'd been doing, their shovels or brooms in their hands. These people were taller and browner than the people of Ember. Were they friendly? Lina couldn't tell. A few children waved and giggled.

After a while, the refugees came out from the narrow streets into a wide-open area. This must be like Ember's Harken Square, Lina thought, a place in the center of town where people gather. It wasn't square, though. It was more like a rough half circle paved in dusty brown brick.

"What is this place called?" Lina asked Mary Waters, who was walking just ahead of her.

"The plaza," Mary said.

Plah-zuh. Lina had never heard that word before. It was her first new-world word.

On one side of the plaza was the river. On the other side were stalls with thatched roofs and small buildings with display racks out in front holding faded-looking clothes, shoes with thick black soles, candles, brooms, pots of honey and jam, along with plenty of things that Lina didn't recognize.

A bigger building stood at the plaza's far end. It had wide steps in front, a double door, and a tower with windows up high that looked out over the plaza. Next to it was a tremendous plant of some kind—a great pole, much higher than the building, with branches like graceful, down-sweeping arms and leaves like bristles.

"What is that?" Lina asked a woman who was standing at the edge of the plaza, watching them go by.

The woman looked startled. "That's our town hall," she said.

"No, I mean the big plant next to it."

"Big plant? The pine tree?"

"Pinetree!" said Lina. "I've never seen a pinetree." Her second word: *pinetree.*

The woman gave her an odd look. Lina thanked her and walked on.

"Step this way, please," said Mary, who was trying to keep the unruly refugees in order. "There's plenty of water for you here—both in the river and in the fountain." She pointed to the middle of the plaza, where there was a pool of water circled by a low wall.

The water in the middle of the pool jumped up into a column of bubble and spray that splashed back down and jumped up again constantly.

The people of Ember surged forward. Dozens ran to the edge of the river and bent down to bathe their faces with water. Dozens more crowded around the pool. Children splashed their hands in it, crawled up on the rim, and tried to reach the leaping water in the middle. Some of the children jumped in and had to be hauled out by their parents. People at the rear of the crowd pushed forward, but people at the front weren't ready to be pushed. Suddenly there was yelling and jostling and water sloshing out onto the pavement. Lina slipped and fell down, and someone tripped over her and fell, too.

"Please!" shouted Mary, her deep, loud voice rising above the uproar.

"Order! Order!" shouted a man's voice. Lina heard other voices, too, as she struggled to her feet, the voices of the villagers crowding in at the edges of the plaza.

"Get back, Tommy, get away from them!"

"Where did you say they came from? Under the *ground*?"

"Are they people like us, Mama?" a child said. "Or some other kind?"

Of *course* we're like you, thought Lina. Aren't we? Are there more kinds of people than one? She got to her feet and wrung out the hem of her sweater, which was sopping wet. She spotted Mrs. Murdo on the other side of the plaza and headed toward her.

The commotion finally subsided. The people of Ember, their thirst quenched, gazed about them in wonder. Everything was strange and fascinating to them. They stood with their heads craned back, gazing at the towering plants and the peeping creatures that flitted around in them; they stooped down to touch the bright flowers; they peered in doorways and windows. Children ran down the grassy bank to the river, tore off their shoes and socks, and dunked their feet in the water. Old people, exhausted from their long walk, lay down behind bushes and went to sleep.

The three town leaders began moving among the people of their village, talking with them in low voices for a minute or two, then nodding and moving on. Lina saw these townspeople glance at the new arrivals with worried looks; they didn't seem to know what to say. Lina could understand why. What would the mayor of Ember have done, for instance, if four hundred people had suddenly arrived from the Unknown Regions?

By this time, the sky was beginning to darken. A few townspeople started calling the refugees together. "Come this way! Call your children! Please sit down!" They stood at the edges of the crowd with their arms stretched out and nudged people inward, until finally all four hundred people were squeezed into the plaza, gathered around the wide steps in front of the town hall, where the three leaders were standing.

Mary Waters raised her arms above her head and stood that way without speaking for several seconds. She looked powerful, Lina thought, even though she was very short. The way she stood, with her feet planted slightly apart and her back straight, made her seem almost to be growing out of the ground. Her black hair was streaked with gray, but her face was smooth and strong-boned.

Gradually people fell silent and turned their attention to her.

"Greetings!" she cried. "My name is Mary Waters. This is Ben Barlow. . . ." She pointed to one of the men standing next to her, a wiry man with a stiff, gray, box-like beard jutting from his chin. He had two wrinkles, like the number eleven, between his eyebrows. "And this is Wilmer Dent," she said, pointing to the other man. He was tall and thin, with wispy, rust-colored hair. He smiled a wavering smile and waggled a few fingers in greeting. "We are the three leaders of this village, which is called Sparks. Three hundred and twenty-two people live here. I understand that you come from a city three days' walk away. I must say, this is a . . . a surprise to us. We have not been aware of any post-Disaster settlements nearby, much less a city."

"What does 'post-Disaster' mean?" Lina whispered to Doon.

"I don't know," Doon said.

Mary Waters cleared her throat with a gruff sound and took a breath. "We will do our best for you tonight, and then tomorrow we will talk about . . . about your plans. Some of our households are willing to take in a few of you for the night—those with young children, and those who are old or ill. The rest of you may sleep here in the plaza. Those who go with the householders will share in their evening meal. Those who stay here will be given bread and fruit."

There was a scattering of applause from the people of Ember. "Thank you!" several voices cried out. "Thank you so much!"

"What's 'bread'?" Lina whispered to Doon.

He shrugged his shoulders.

"Will all those who most need shelter for the night please stand?" Mary Waters called. "As I said—those with children, and the elderly and ill."

A rustle swept through the crowd as people got to their feet. Voices murmured, "Stand up, Father," "You go, Willa," "No, I'm all right, you go," "Let Arno go, he's sprained his foot." Because of Poppy, Lina and Mrs. Murdo stood up. Doon remained sitting, and so did his father.

The brilliant yellow ball in the sky was traveling downward now, and the shadows grew longer. Night was coming, and with the gathering darkness Lina's spirits grew darker, too. She thought of the green-and-blue bedroom she'd moved into back at Mrs. Murdo's house in Ember, the lovely room she had been so glad to have. She was homesick for it. Right now, she would have been happy to have a bowl of turnip soup and then crawl between the covers of the bed in that room, with Poppy next to her, and Mrs. Murdo out in the living room tidying up, and the great clock of Ember about to strike nine, the hour when the lights went out. She knew that this place—the village of Sparks—was alive, and that Ember was dead, and she would not want to go back there even if she could. But right now, as the air grew chilly and whispered against her skin, and a strange bed in a stranger's house waited for her, she longed for what was familiar.

Mary Waters was calling out names. At each name, someone from the village stepped up and said how many people that household could take.

"Leah Parsons!"

A tall woman in a black dress came forward. "Two people," she said, and Mary Waters pointed at an old couple at the front of the crowd of refugees, who picked up their bags and followed the tall woman.

"Randolph Bonito," called Mary, and a big, red-faced man said, "Five." The Candrick family, with their three small children, went with him.

"Evers Mills." "Four."

"Lanny McMorris." "Two."

"Jane Garcia." "Three."

It went on for a long time. The sky grew darker and the air cooler. Lina shivered. She untied her sweater from around her waist and put it on. Light and warmth must go together here, she thought: warm in the day, when the bright light was in the sky, and cool at night. In Ember, the lights made no heat at all, and the temperature was always the same.

At the edges of the plaza, someone was raising a flame-tipped stick and lighting lanterns that hung from the eaves of buildings. They glowed deep yellow and red.

Mary was pointing at Mrs. Murdo now. "You, ma'am," she said. "Your child looks the sickest of anyone. We'll send you home with our doctor." She beckoned to a woman standing nearby, a tall, bony old woman with bushy gray hair chopped off just below her ears. She was wearing loose pants of faded blue and a rumpled tan shirt that was buttoned crookedly, so one side hung down lower than the other.

"Dr. Hester will take you," Mary said. "Dr. Hester Crane."

Lina stood up. She turned to Doon. "Will you be all right here?" she said. It made her uneasy to be separated from Doon and his father.

"We'll be fine," Doon said.

"No need to worry," said his father, spreading a blanket on the ground.

The doctor stooped down to look at Poppy, who drowsed in Mrs. Murdo's arms. She put a hand on Poppy's forehead—a big, knuckly hand, with veins like blue yarn. She pulled down the underside of Poppy's eye. "Um-hm," she said. "Yes. Well. Come along, I'll do what I can for her."

Lina cast an anxious glance at Doon.

"Come and find us in the morning," Doon said. "We'll be right here."

"This way," the doctor said. "Oh, wait." She scanned the mostly empty plaza. "Torren!" she called.

Lina heard the slap of footsteps on brick and saw a boy running toward them out of the darkness.

"We're going home now," the doctor said to him. "These people are coming with us."

The boy was younger than Lina. He had a strangely narrow face—as if someone had put a hand on either side of his head and pushed hard. His eyes were round blue dots. Above his high forehead, his light brown hair stood up in an untidy tuft.

He glared sideways at Lina and said nothing. The doctor headed up the road beside the river, walking with a long stride, her hands in her pockets and her head bent forward as if she were looking for something on the ground.

Staying close beside Mrs. Murdo, who was carrying the sleeping Poppy, Lina followed. The chilly evening air crept in through the threads of her sweater, and an insect hovering near her ear made a high, needle-like whine. The homesick feeling swelled so big inside her that she had to cross her arms tightly and clench her teeth to keep it from coming out.

CHAPTER 4

The Doctor's House

The sky had turned a deep blue now, almost black. At one edge shone a streak of brilliant crimson. In the houses of the village, one window and then another began to glow with a flickering yellow light.

They walked and walked. Each time they came to a doorway, or a gate in a wall, or stairs leading upward, Lina hoped this might be the house. Back in Ember, where she'd had the job of messenger, she'd been a tireless runner; running was her greatest joy. Tonight it was hard just to walk. She was so tired her feet felt like bricks. But Dr. Hester walked on and on, with the boy trotting ahead of her sometimes, and sometimes lagging back to stare at Lina and Mrs. Murdo and Poppy, until they came to the outer edge of the village. There, standing somewhat apart, was a low-roofed house. Except for a glimmer of light on its two windows, reflected from the reddening sky, it was in darkness, huddled beneath a great brooding plant the shape of a huge mushroom.

"Is that a pinetree?" Lina asked the doctor.

"Oak tree," the doctor said, so Lina understood that "tree" must mean all big plants, and they came in different kinds.

A path led to a wooden gate, which the doctor opened. They came into a shadowy, leaf-littered courtyard paved with uneven bricks. On three sides were the three wings of the house, like a square-cornered U. The eaves of the roof sloped down to form a walkway all around. In the failing light, Lina could just see that the courtyard was crowded with plants, some growing in the ground and some in pots of all sizes. Vines wound up the columns of the walkway and crawled along the edge of the roof.

"Come inside," the doctor said. She led the way to a door in the central part of the house. She and the boy went in. Lina stopped just inside the doorway, and Mrs. Murdo came up behind her, Poppy in her arms. They stood peering into the gloom. There was an odd pungent smell—like mushrooms or leaf mold, only sharper.

The doctor disappeared for a moment, and when she came back she held a lit candle. She moved around the room lighting more—two candles, three candles, four, until a wavery light filled the central part of the room. The corners remained in darkness.

"Come in, come in," the doctor said impatiently.

Lina moved forward. She felt grit beneath the soles of her shoes, and the tickle of dust in her nose. She was in a long, low room with clutter everywhere—clothes draped over the backs of armchairs, a shoe on a saggy couch, a plate with some bits of food on it sitting on the windowsill. At one end of the room were two doors, both of them closed. At the back, a stairway rose into a dark square hole in the ceiling. At the other end of the room, in the corner, was an open doorway—leading, Lina guessed, to the kitchen. Beside this doorway was a kind of hollow in the wall, framed by stones and containing some sticks and scraps of paper.

The doctor stooped down before this hollow place and held her candle to the sticks and paper there. In a moment, a flame leapt up. It was a bigger flame than Lina had ever seen, like a terrible orange hand, reaching up and out. Lina's heart knocked hard against her ribs. She stepped backward, bumping into Mrs. Murdo. They stood staring, Mrs. Murdo with a hand clutching Lina's shoulder.

The doctor turned around and saw them. "What's the matter?" she said.

Lina couldn't speak. Her eyes were fixed on the flames, which leapt higher and crackled.

Mrs. Murdo tried to answer. "It's, ah, it's—" She inclined her head toward the end of the room, where the first flame had become a dozen flames, licking upward, sending out flashes of orange light.

"Oh!" said the doctor. "The fire? You're not used to fire?"

Mrs. Murdo managed to smile apologetically. Lina just stared.

"It stays in the fireplace," the doctor said. "Not at all dangerous."

In Ember, there was never fire unless there was danger—someone's electric wiring had frayed and ignited, or a pot holder had fallen on a stove's electric burner. The only fire Lina had seen that wasn't dangerous was the tiny flame of a candle. This fire scared her.

In the window glass, reflections glimmered. The windows were set so deeply into the walls that there was a ledge at the bottom, wide enough to sit on. The boy, Torren, hiked himself up on one of these ledges and sat there, kicking his feet against the cabinet set in the wall below it. "Afraid of fire," he said in a low, scornful voice.

"Come in," the doctor said. "You can sit over there, if you like." She pointed to some chairs at the other end of the room, far from the fire, so that was where Lina and Mrs. Murdo sat. Poppy woke up enough to give a weak wail, and then she slumped into Mrs. Murdo's lap. "This will likely be the last fire of the season, anyway," said the doctor. "Nights will be getting warmer soon. We won't need one."

A creak sounded from outside, and then rapid footsteps. Someone pounded on the door. Lina clutched Mrs. Murdo's hand.

But the doctor only sighed and moved to answer the knock. "Oh, it's you, William," she said. "What do you need?"

"Some of that ointment," said a man's voice. "I need it right now. My wife cut her hand. It's bleeding all over."

"Come in, come in, I'll get it," the doctor said, and she went into another room and rummaged around while the man stood shyly just inside the door, looking out of the corners of his eyes at Lina and Mrs. Murdo.

The doctor brought him his jar of ointment, and he went away. No more than ten minutes later, another knock came, this time from a young woman who wanted some willow bark medicine for her sister, who had a pounding headache. Again the doctor rattled around in the other room. She came out with a small bottle, and the woman hurried off with it.

"Are you the only doctor here?" Mrs. Murdo inquired.

"Yes," said Dr. Hester. "It's a never-ending job." She suddenly looked worried. "Did I give William the right jar? Yes, yes, the one on the third shelf, I'm sure I did." She gave a frazzled sigh. "Now let's tend to your little girl. Put her down here." She patted the couch that stood against the wall. "And wrap her in this." She retrieved a knitted blanket that had fallen on the floor, gave it a shake, and handed it to Mrs. Murdo. "I'll give her a swallow of medicine."

Poppy accepted two spoonfuls of medicine—it was something reddish that Dr. Hester poured from a jar—and spit out the third, whimpering. Lina's heart ached to see Poppy so sick. Most of the time, Poppy was a ball of energy, so quick and curious you never knew what she'd do next. She might chew up a valuable document, for instance, or trot off on an exploration of her own at exactly the wrong moment. Now she was limp and pale, like a little sprout that hadn't been watered.

Mrs. Murdo laid her on the bed. Lina sat by her and stroked her hair, and quite soon she went to sleep. The doctor disappeared into the kitchen, and Torren climbed the stairs and vanished into the room above.

All at once Lina was overcome with tiredness. The disorderly house, the unfriendly boy, the fire . . . all of it was strange and disturbing. And Poppy was terribly sick, which worried Lina so much that she felt a little sick herself. She sat down by Mrs. Murdo and laid her head on Mrs. Murdo's lap. She was vaguely aware of clattering and chopping noises coming from the kitchen, and then she dozed off into a confusing dream of lights and shadows. . . .

"Dinner!" shouted Torren. Lina bolted upright,

and he laughed. "Have you heard of food?" he said. "Have you heard of eating?"

They sat at the table, all of them but Poppy, and the doctor ladled out something from a big bowl. Lina wasn't sure what it was. Cold potatoes, she thought, and something else. She ate it because she was hungry. But when she had eaten she suddenly became so tired again that she could hardly move.

"Quite tasty," said Mrs. Murdo. "Thank you."

"Well," said the doctor. "Certainly. You're welcome." She started to stand up, then sat down again, looking flustered. "Maybe you'd like to read? Or . . . walk around? Or . . ."

"We're a bit tired," said Mrs. Murdo. "Perhaps we could go to bed."

Dr. Hester's face brightened. "Bed, yes," she said, standing up. "Of course, why didn't I . . . Let's see. Where will we put you?" She looked around, as if an extra bed might be hidden in the mess. "The loft, I suppose."

"No!" cried Torren. "That's my room!"

"It's the only place with two beds," said Dr. Hester. Picking up a candle, she made her way through the clutter to the stairway.

"They'll touch my things! And Caspar's things!" cried Torren.

"Don't be silly," said Dr. Hester, starting up the stairs.

"But where will I sleep?" Torren wailed.

"In the medicine room," said Dr. Hester. Tears had appeared in Torren's eyes, but the doctor didn't notice. She disappeared into the loft, and for a few minutes Lina heard thumps and scrapes from above.

"Come on up," the doctor called.

Lina climbed the stairs, and Mrs. Murdo came after, carrying Poppy. By the light of the doctor's candle, Lina saw two beds under a sloping ceiling. There was a chest at the foot of each bed. Some clothes hung from hooks, and some boxes were neatly lined up on the sill of the one window.

"Two beds, but three of you," said the doctor, frowning. "We could . . . hmm. We could put the baby . . ."

"It's all right," Lina said. "She'll sleep with me."

And a few minutes later, she was in bed, Poppy in the crook of her arm, covers drawn over them. "Good night," Mrs. Murdo said from the other bed, and the candle was blown out, and the room went dark—but not as dark as the rooms in Ember at night. Lina could still see a faint gray rectangle where the window was, because of the lights in the sky, the silver circle and the bright pinpoints. What are they called? she wondered. And who is Caspar? And how can the doctor stand to have that huge, awful fire right there on the floor of her house?

Everything here was the opposite of Ember.

Ember was dark and cold; this place was bright and hot. Ember was orderly; this place was disorderly. In Ember, everything was familiar to her. Here everything was strange. Will I learn to like it here? she wondered. Will I ever feel at home? She held Poppy tight against her and listened to her snuffly breathing for a long time before she fell asleep.

The First Town Meeting

While Lina slept, the three town leaders were holding a meeting. They sat at a table in the tower room of the town hall, which looked out over the plaza. Mary's hands were clasped tightly in front of her. Ben scowled, his gray eyebrows bunched together, deepening the two lines between them. Wilmer pulled nervously on one ear and looked from Mary to Ben and back to Mary.

"They can't stay here," said Mary. "There are too many of them. Where would we put them? How would we feed them?"

"Yes," said Wilmer. "But where can they go?"

No one spoke. They had no answer for that question. Outside the settlement of Sparks, the Empty Lands stretched for miles in all directions.

"They could go up to Pine Gap," said Wilmer. "Maybe."

Mary snorted and shook her head. "Don't be

ridiculous," she said. "That's at least two weeks' walk away. How could these feeble people travel that far? How could they carry enough food with them? Where would they *get* enough food, unless we emptied our storehouse and gave them everything?"

Wilmer nodded, knowing she was right. The people of Sparks knew of only three other settlements, and they'd heard from the roamers that those places were smaller and poorer than Sparks. Their inhabitants wouldn't want extra mouths to feed, either.

The three of them gazed out the window and down at the moonlit plaza, filled with strange sleeping people from a city under the earth. Four hundred of them, with no food, no possessions to speak of, and nowhere to go.

"What I fail to understand," said Ben, "is why this particular misfortune has happened to us." He paused, looked into the air to his left, and frowned. This was a habit of his; he seemed to need a pause and a frown every now and then to put together his thoughts. Wilmer and Mary had gotten used to waiting through these pauses. "I don't see that we deserve it," Ben went on after a few seconds, "having labored as diligently as we have. And just when we are starting to prosper at last, after so many years of . . . well, adversity is a mild word for it."

The others nodded, thinking of the hard years. There'd been winters when people shivered in tents and ate chopped-up roots and shriveled nuts. There had been years of drought and plagues of tomato worms and devastating crop failures that meant people had nothing to eat for months but cabbage and potatoes. There had been times when people had to work so hard to stay alive that they sometimes died just from being too tired to go on. No one wanted to go back to those times.

"So what do we do," said Mary, "if they can't stay and they can't go? What is the right thing to do?"

The others sat silent.

"Well, there's the Pioneer," said Wilmer. "As a temporary solution."

"True," said Ben.

"A good thought," said Mary, and Wilmer beamed. "So what about this," Mary went on. "We'll let them stay in the Pioneer. We'll give them water and food—we do have some extra in the storehouse. In exchange, they work—they help in the fields, they help with building, they do whatever there is to do. We'd have to teach them how. As far as I can see, they know nothing. After a while, when they're stronger, and when they know better how to get along, they can move on. They can set up their own village somewhere else."

"We'll have to watch them carefully if we let them stay," said Ben. "They're strange. We don't know what they might do."

"They seem fairly ordinary to me," said Mary.

"Except for the business about living in a cave."

"You believed that?" said Ben.

Mary shrugged. "The question is, shall we let them stay?"

"How long would we have to keep them," asked Wilmer, "before they were ready to go?"

"I don't know. Maybe six months? Let's see. It's near the end of Flowering now." Mary counted out the months on her fingers. "Shining, Burning, Browning, Cooling, Falling, Chilling. They could stay through the summer and fall seasons and leave at the end of Chilling."

"That would mean they'd be on their own for the winter," Wilmer pointed out.

"That's right," said Ben. "Are you suggesting we should keep them even longer? We'll be stretching ourselves to keep them at all."

They fell silent again, considering this.

Finally Mary spoke. "Shall we let them stay for six months, then?" she said. "And teach them as much as we can?"

No one really liked this idea. They thought of the food the refugees would need, which would mean less for their own people, and the bother of teaching them all the skills they'd need to survive on their own. Each one—Mary, Wilmer, and especially Ben—wished the unfortunate cave people would simply vanish.

But they weren't going to vanish, and the leaders

of Sparks knew that they must for the sake of their consciences do the right thing. They wanted to be wise, good leaders, unlike the leaders of the past, whose terrible mistakes had led to the Disaster. So they would be open-minded. They would be generous.

With this in mind, the three leaders voted:

Mary voted yes, the cave people should stay.

Ben voted yes, reluctantly.

Wilmer voted yes.

So it was agreed: They would give them a place to stay. They would help them for six months. After that, the strangers would have to take care of themselves.

Mary, Ben, and Wilmer shook hands on this agreement, but none of them said out loud what they were thinking: that even after six months, the people of Ember would be hard-pressed to start a town. The founders of Sparks had known carpentry and farming, and even so it had taken them two years just to build rough shelters and get the rocks out of the fields. They had known how to manage animals and build good soil, but still their animals sometimes died of disease and hunger in the many years when the crops failed. They had known to expect harsh weather, wolves, and bandits, and still they suffered losses from all three.

The town leaders knew in their hearts that in this vast, empty country, where there were a thousand dangers the people of Ember did not understand, they would *never* be able to take care of themselves.

CHAPTER 5

The Pioneer

In the village the next morning, criers ran through the streets calling to the people of Sparks. They told them to bring out all their old blankets, pillows, towels, and rags, and any clothes they no longer needed. They were to heap these on the street in front of their houses. From the storehouse, people collected food—things that didn't need to be cooked, like apples from the prior fall, and dried apricots, and bread, and big hunks of cheese. Doon, who had gotten up at the first sign of light in the sky, watched these preparations with rising excitement.

By midday a caravan was moving southward out of the village. It was composed of strange vehicles that the villagers called "truck-wagons," or just "trucks." They were made of rusty metal and had four fat black wheels. At the front was a boxy part, like a metal chest with a rounded top, and behind that was a higher box with two seats in it where the drivers sat. The back of the truck was flat; this was where the crates of supplies were loaded. Attached to each of these trucks by sturdy ropes were two big, squarish, muscular animals, by far the most enormous animals Doon had ever seen. They made snuffling noises, and sometimes a low sort of groan.

"What are they?" Doon asked someone walking near him.

"Oxen," the man answered. "Like cows, you know? That milk comes from?"

Doon had never heard of cows. He had thought milk came as powder in a box. He didn't say this, of course. He just nodded.

"And what does 'truck' mean?" he asked. He understood the "wagon" part.

The man looked surprised. "It just means 'truck,'" he said. "You know—what people used to drive in the old times. There are millions of them, trucks and cars, everywhere. They used to run on their own, without oxen. They had engines in here." He rapped on the front of the truck. "You poured stuff called gasleen on the engine, and it made the wheels turn. Now, since we don't have gasleen anymore, we take the engines out, and that makes the trucks light and easy to pull."

Doon didn't ask what "gasleen" was. He didn't

want to show his ignorance all at once. He'd spread his questions around, find out just a few things from one person at a time.

He and his father walked along together beside one of the trucks. Doon had expected Lina to be with them, but by the time the caravan left she hadn't come. That was all right. She'd easily find out where they'd gone and come later.

Doon's father still had sore muscles from the long walk of the days before, so Doon soon went ahead of him. He was bursting with energy and joy and simply could not walk slowly. He took deep breaths of sweet-smelling morning air. Over his head, the sky was a deep, clear blue, a thousand times bigger than the black lid that had covered Ember, and around him the green-and-golden land seemed to stretch away without end. Doon kept wondering where the edges were. He made his way to the front of the procession and asked Wilmer, who was trotting along with his arms swinging jauntily.

"Edges?" said Wilmer, glancing down.

"Yes. I mean, if I were standing way over there"—he pointed to the horizon, where the sky seemed to meet the land—"would I be at the edge of this place? And what's beyond the edge?"

"There is no edge," said Wilmer, looking at Doon as if he must have something wrong with him. "The earth is a sphere—a huge, round ball. If you kept going and going, you'd eventually come back to where you started."

This nearly knocked the breath out of Doon, it was so strange and hard to comprehend. He thought at first that Wilmer was playing a joke on him, thinking he was a fool. But Wilmer's expression was plainly puzzled, not sly. He must be telling the truth.

There were a million mysteries here, Doon thought. He would explore them all! He would learn everything! That morning, he'd already learned the words *sun, tree, wind, star,* and *bird.* He'd learned *dog, chicken, goat,* and *bread.*

He had never in his life felt so good. He felt as huge as the land around him and as clear and bright as the air. No laboring in dank tunnels here; no running through dark streets to escape pursuit. Now he was out in the open, free. And he was powerful, too, in a way he hadn't been before. He had done something remarkable—saved his people from their dying city—and, along with Lina, he would be known for that deed all his life. He gazed around at this new world full of life and beauty, and he felt proud to have brought his people here.

The road passed the last houses of the village and ran along the river, which was wide and slow, with grasses bending along its banks. The trucks rattled. Clouds of dust billowed from their wheels. All around Doon rose a babble of voices as people pointed things out in tones of astonishment.

"Look—something white floating in the sky!"

"Did you see that little animal with the big tail?"

"Do you feel that? The air is *moving*!"

Children darted every which way, daring each other to touch the broad sides of the oxen, plucking blossoms from the brambles at the edge of the road, jumping onto the trucks for a quick ride until they were shooed off again.

And the sun shone down on everyone. The people of Ember loved the strange feeling of heat on the tops of their heads. They put their hands up often to touch their warm hair.

The road went up a gentle rise and around a clump of trees. "Here we are!" cried Wilmer, sweeping his arm out proudly. "The Pioneer Hotel!"

At the crest of the slope stood a building bigger than any Doon had ever seen. It was three stories high and very long, with a wing at each end perpendicular to the main part. Windows marched in three rows across its walls. In the center, overlooking a long field that sloped down to the river, was what must once have been a grand entrance—wide steps, a roof held up by columns, a double doorway. But the building was grand no more. It was very old, Doon could tell; its walls were gray and stained, and most of the windows were no more than dark holes. The roof had sagged inward in some places. Grass grew right up to the steps, and far down at the other end, Doon could see that a tree had fallen against the building and smashed a corner of it.

Ben Barlow strode across the wide, weedy field in front of the hotel and climbed the steps. Wilmer followed. He leaned against a column, and Ben took a position on the top step and waited for the crowd of refugees to assemble before him. Doon wove among the people until he found his father again, and they stood together.

Ben held up both hands and called, "Attention, please!" The crowd grew silent. "Welcome to your new home, the Pioneer Hotel," he said.

A cheer arose from the crowd. Ben frowned and held up both hands, palms out, and the cheer died away. "It is a *temporary* home only," he said. "We cannot, of course, keep you here in Sparks on a permanent basis. To do so would severely strain our resources and no doubt cause resentment and deprivation among our people." Ben cleared his throat and frowned into the air. Then he went on. "We have decided you may stay here for six months—through summer and fall, to the end of the month of Chilling. After that time, with the training you'll receive from us, you will go out into the Empty Lands and found a village of your own."

The people of Ember glanced at each other in surprise. Found their own village? Some of them smiled eagerly at this idea; others looked uncertain. The city of Ember had been constructed *for* them. All they'd ever had to do was repair work as the buildings got older. They'd never built anything from scratch. But, Doon said to himself, thinking about all this, I'm sure we could learn.

Ben went on. "The Pioneer Hotel has seventy-five rooms," he said, "plus a big dining room, a ballroom, offices, and a lobby. There will be adequate space for everyone."

Excited murmurs swept through the crowd. Doon started doing the math in his head. Four hundred and seventeen people divided by seventy-five rooms equaled five or six people per room. That sounded crowded, but maybe they were big rooms. And then there were the dining room and the ballroom, whatever that was, maybe those would hold ten or twenty people. . . .

"Now, of course this building is somewhat less than fully functional," Ben went on. "You won't have water pumps here, as we do in the village. But the river is close, just down this slope, and the water is clean. The river will provide water for drinking, bathing, and washing clothes. Your toilets will be outside—you'll start digging them tomorrow, once we've organized you into work teams. Today you'll settle into your rooms." He paused, frowning. The two lines between his eyebrows deepened. "There's not much furniture left in the rooms," he said. "Maybe a few rooms still have beds, but I think we've taken most of them by now. You'll be sleeping on the floor."

"Sleeping on the floor!" The voice came from somewhere behind Doon. Its tone was somewhere between outrage and amused disbelief. Doon turned around to see whose it was. In the middle of the crowd he spotted a tall boy, a young man really, who seemed to be standing up on something—maybe a rock or tree stump—so he could look out over people's heads. He was handsome in a sharp-edged way. His jaw was square-cornered. His shoulders were straight as a board. His dark hair was combed back from his face and slicked down, so his head looked neat and round and hard, and his eyes were as pale as bits of sky.

Doon recognized this boy, though he didn't know him—his name was Mick, or Trick, or Mack, or something like that.

"On the floor, yes," said Ben. "But we'll give you as many blankets as we can."

The boy's sharp voice came again, rising above the others. "One more question, sir: What about food?"

The question rippled through the crowd: Yes, food. What will we eat?

Ben raised his voice. "Please listen!" he shouted. "Listen!" All faces turned toward him again. Doon could see that Ben's eyes were fixed on the boy with the sharp voice. Ben had the look of a teacher speaking to a slightly unruly class. "Eating will work this way," he said. "You will be assigned to households in the village—four or five people to each house. At noontime, you'll go there for your main meal." He paused and frowned. "As for breakfast and dinner—your lunchtime family will give you food to take away with you, some to eat in the evening, and some to save for the next morning. They will be as generous as they can. But remember—we do not have an *abundance* of extra food. Your arrival means less for everyone." He gazed at the crowd for a moment and took a breath. "Is that clear?" he said. "Any questions?"

No one spoke for a moment, and then the tall boy said, "No, sir. Lead on."

So Ben led the way into the lobby of the ancient Pioneer Hotel. Doon and his father stayed close together, stepping carefully. It was hard to see. The only light came from the doorway behind them and from a hole in a great dirt-encrusted glass dome three stories above their heads. The floor was littered with chunks of fallen plaster and gritty with dirt that had blown in over the years.

"This place needs work," Doon whispered to his father.

His father brushed a spiderweb away from his face. "Yes," he said. "But we're lucky to be here. We could be sleeping on the ground."

Ben led them down a hall to the left, to a vast

room with high windows, where dusty sunshine slanted across the broken tiles of the floor. "This was the dining room," Ben called out. Doon saw only a few chairs, lying on their sides, most of them with a leg broken or missing.

Beyond the dining room was a room even more immense, with a raised platform at one end, a high ceiling, and a wooden floor. "The ballroom," Ben said. "In earlier years, before the Disaster, musicians sat up there on the stage. People danced out here." At the great high windows hung tatters of faded rose-colored cloth that had been curtains years ago.

"Smells moldy in here." It was that boy again. His clear, sharp voice carried over other voices even though it wasn't much louder. "Reminds me of home."

People laughed. It was true—the smell of mold was common in the underground city of Ember. There was a bit of comfort in it.

Doon suddenly remembered the name of this tall boy who kept speaking out. It was Tick—Tick Hassler. In Ember, Doon recalled, Tick had been a hauler. He had pulled carts full of produce from the greenhouses to the stores, and garbage from the stores out to the trash heaps. Doon hadn't known him then, but he remembered seeing him, pulling his loaded cart with his whole long body slanted forward and a fierce grin of effort on his face. He'd pulled his carts faster than anyone else.

Ben led them to the stairs, and they climbed to the floors above. Long, dim corridors lined with doors stretched the length of the building. Some of the doors were open. Doon looked through them as he passed. All the rooms were more or less the same: windows across one wall, a stained and faded carpet, a couple of broken lamps lying on the floor. A few of the rooms had beds, and several had other furniture—chests with their drawers hanging crookedly out, end tables, a chair or two. He stepped into some of the rooms and found that they had bathrooms as well, with rust-stained sinks and bathtubs that were homes to spiders.

For the next couple of hours, people swarmed through the corridors and up and down the stairs, calling to each other as they chose their rooms and decided who to share them with. People grouped together, chose a room, then changed their minds and teamed up with another group. Shouts rang through the halls.

"Jake! Down here!"

"No, this one is better, it has a chair!"

"Mama! Where are you?"

"This room's full! No more people!"

Doon heard Tick's voice ringing out over the others now and then. He wondered which room he was choosing, and who he was choosing to live with.

Finally everyone was settled. Doon and his father chose a room on the second floor, room 215, along with two other people. One was Edward Pocket, who had been Ember's librarian. He was a friend of Doon's, in a way. He was old and often crabby, but he liked Doon, who had been a frequent visitor to the library. The other was Sadge Merrall, the man who had tried to venture out into the Unknown Regions beyond the city of Ember. For a while after that experience, he'd gone out of his mind with fright and raved in Harken Square about monsters and doom. He'd recovered somewhat since then. In spite of his terror, he'd managed to climb into one of the boats that took people out of the city to the new world. But he was still a fearful, trembling sort of person. Nearly everything about this unfamiliar place scared him. He refused to go near the window of their new room. "Something might come in," he said. "There are things here that fly."

The four of them set to work fixing up the room. It was full of cobwebs, two of its three windows were broken, and bits of dry leaves and splinters of glass littered the carpet. It also had a dresser with three drawers, a padded armchair with a sunken seat, and two end tables with lamps.

They took their socks off and used them as dust rags to sweep away the cobwebs. They picked up the leaves and glass and tossed them out the windows. They put the lamps out in the hall—they were useless, of course, since there was no electricity—and they lined up the dresser and end tables in the middle of the room to make a sort of wall dividing the space in two. There was enough room for Doon and his father to spread their blankets on the floor on one side, and Sadge to spread his on the other. Edward Pocket, who was very short, decided to spread his blanket on the floor of the large closet, which had a sliding door. He said he didn't mind being slightly cramped; he liked the privacy.

That night, Doon didn't sleep much. He lay on his folded blankets and stared up through the window at the dark sky. His mind teemed with possibilities—so much to do, so much to learn! He felt suddenly older and stronger, though it had been less than a week since he'd left Ember. But he was a new person in this new world. He would do new things and be friends with new people. Maybe, he thought, remembering the voice that had stood out above the others that day, he'd be friends with Tick.

CHAPTER 6

Breakfast with Disaster

Lina's first morning in the doctor's house did not go well. Poppy was still sleeping when she awakened, and so was Mrs. Murdo, so she got up quietly, put on the same pricker-stuck clothes she'd been wearing the day before, and went down the stairs. The doctor was standing by the table in what must have been her nightgown—a patched brown sack that hung to her knees. The hair at the back of her head was sticking up. She was leafing through a big book that lay on the table.

"Oh!" said the doctor, seeing Lina. "You're up. I was just looking for . . . I was trying to find . . . Well. I suppose it's time for breakfast."

The doctor's kitchen looked like a complete mess to Lina. In Ember, the kitchens had been spare, stocked with only what was needed—some shelves, an electric stove, a refrigerator. But in Dr. Hester's kitchen there were a thousand things. Wide wooden counters ran along two sides, and on the counters was a jumble of jugs and pans and tubs and pitchers, big spoons and knives and scoops, and jars and bottles full of things that looked like pebbles and brown powder and tiny white teeth. There were baskets piled with vegetables Lina had never seen before. In the corner squatted a bulging black iron box. She thought it might be a cabinet, since there was a door in its front.

"We'll see if we have any eggs this morning," said Dr. Hester. "That would be a start."

Torren appeared suddenly from the other room. "Eggs!" he cried. "I want one!"

Eggs? Lina didn't know what that meant. She followed the doctor and Torren through a door that led outside. Beyond the door was a place like an open-air version of the Ember greenhouses, only the plants growing here were far bigger and wilder, curling and twining and shooting upward with tremendous energy. Lina recognized some of them: bean vines climbed up frames of netting, tomato vines grew on wooden towers, chard and kale plants spurted up like big green fountains.

In among the rows of plants, some fat, fluffed-up, two-legged creatures of the kind she'd seen on her way into town yesterday waddled along, poking at the ground with a sharp thing like a tooth that stuck out from their faces.

"What are those?" asked Lina.

"Chickens," said the doctor. "We'll check their nests and see if they've left us anything." She bent down and went through the door of a wooden hut in the back of the garden, and when she came out she had spiderwebs in her hair and a white ball in her hand—not a round ball, but one that looked as if it had been stretched sideways. "Just one today," she said.

"I want it!" cried Torren.

"No," said the doctor. "You've had plenty of eggs. This one is for our guest." She handed the egg to Lina, who took it gingerly. It was smooth and warm. She had no idea what it was. It felt more like a stone than food. Was it some sort of large bean? Or a fruit with a hard white peel?

"Thank you," she said doubtfully.

"See, she doesn't even want it!" Torren said. "She doesn't even know what it is!" He gave her a hard shove, making her stagger sideways.

"Quit that!" cried Lina. "You almost pushed me over!"

"Torren—" said the doctor, stretching out a hand. But Torren ignored her.

"I'll push you again," he said, and he did, harder.

Lina stumbled backward and caught herself just in time to keep from falling into the cabbage bed. She felt a flash of fury. She raised her arm and threw the egg at Torren, and it hit him on the shoulder. But instead of bouncing off, it broke open, and a slimy yellow mess dripped down his shirt.

"Now look what you've done!" Torren screamed. "It's ruined!" He put his head down as if to run at Lina and butt her, but the doctor grabbed his arm.

"Stop this," she said.

Lina was horrified. Disgusted, too. That yellow goop was something people ate? She was glad she didn't have to. But she felt stupid for what she'd done. "I'm sorry I wrecked the egg," she said. "I didn't know what it was."

"You wrecked my shirt, too!" shouted Torren, wriggling in the doctor's grasp.

"But you *pushed* me," Lina said.

"Well, yes," said the doctor in a weary voice. "That's how it goes, doesn't it? Someone pushes, someone pushes back. Pretty soon everything's ruined."

"Everything?" said Lina. "But can't his shirt be washed?"

"Oh, yes, of course," the doctor said. "I didn't mean that. Never mind." She let go of Torren. "I guess we'll have bread and apricots for breakfast."

Mrs. Murdo had come downstairs now, leaving the still-sleeping Poppy in bed. They all had breakfast together. Lina ate five apricots. She loved them for their taste and for the feel of them, too—their rosy-orange skins were velvety, like a baby's cheek. She also liked the bread, which was toasted and crunchy, and the jam, which was dark purple and sweet. Mrs. Murdo kept saying, "My, this is tasty," and asking questions about what bread was made of, and what a blackberry looked like, and why apricots had a sort of wooden rock in the middle. Dr. Hester seemed a bit flummoxed by these questions, but she did her best to explain. She was nice, Lina decided, but distracted. Her mind seemed to be elsewhere. She didn't notice that Torren was putting all his apricot pits into his pocket, for instance—or maybe she didn't care.

When breakfast was over, Torren went up to the loft and came back down carrying a bulging bag. "These are my *things,*" he said loudly. "I don't want anyone touching them." He knelt down and opened the doors of the cabinet under the window seat and thrust the bag inside. "Caspar gave them to me, and anyone who touches them gets in *big* trouble." He closed the cabinet doors and glared at Lina. What an awful boy, Lina thought. How could nice Dr. Hester have such a horrid son?

Lina had thought she'd go back to the plaza and find Doon right after breakfast. But she changed her mind when she went upstairs to waken her little sister. Poppy seemed so sick that Lina was frightened. She didn't want to leave her. She brought her downstairs, and all that morning, Poppy lay on the couch, sometimes sleeping, sometimes wailing, sometimes just lying much too still with her mouth open and her breath coming in short gasps. Lina and Mrs. Murdo sat on either side of her, putting cool cloths on her forehead and trying to get her to drink the water and the medicine the doctor provided. "I don't know what's causing this child's fever," the doctor said. "All I can do is try to bring it down."

After all the walking of the days before, Lina was glad to sit still. She settled into a corner of the couch, her legs tucked under her, and watched the doctor dither about. She seemed to have a hundred things to do and a hundred things on her mind. She'd stand for a second staring into the air, murmuring to herself, "Now. All right. First I must look up . . . ," and then dart over to her enormous book and shuffle through its pages. After a second or two, she'd suddenly set the book down and hurry off to the kitchen, where she would take a bottle of liquid or jar of powder down from a shelf and measure some of it into a pot. Or she'd dash out to the garden and come back with an armload of onions. Or she'd vanish out the back door and appear again with a sheaf of dried stems or leaves. It was hard to tell what she was doing, or if she was really accomplishing anything at all. Every now and then she would come back to Poppy and spoon some medicine into her mouth or put a cold, damp cloth on her forehead.

"What is that enormous book?" Lina asked her.

"Oh!" said the doctor. She always seemed a little startled to be spoken to. "Well, it's about medicine. A lot of it is useless, though." She picked up the book from the floor and riffled its pages. "You look up 'infection' and it says, 'Prescribe antibiotics.' What are antibiotics? Or you look up 'fever' and it says, 'Give aspirin.' Aspirin is some kind of painkiller, I think, but we don't have it."

"We had aspirin in Ember," said Mrs. Murdo, rather proudly. "Although I believe it had nearly run out by the end."

"Is that so," said the doctor. "Well, what we have is plants. Herbs, roots, funguses, that sort of thing. I have a couple of old books that tell about which ones to use. Sometimes they work, sometimes they don't." She ran a hand through her short, wiry hair, making it poke out on one side. "So much to know," she said, "and so much to do . . ." Her voice trailed off.

"I suppose your son is a help to you," said Mrs. Murdo.

"My son?"

"The boy, Torren."

"Oh," said Dr. Hester. "He's not my son."

"He's not?" said Lina.

"No, no," the doctor said. "Torren and his brother, Caspar—they're my sister's boys. They live with me because their parents were killed in an avalanche years ago. They were in the mountains, on an ice-gathering trip."

"And the boy has no other relatives?" asked Mrs. Murdo.

"He has an uncle," said the doctor. "But the uncle didn't want the trouble of bringing up the boys. He offered to have this house built for me if I'd take them on." The doctor shrugged. "So I did."

"What is an avalanche?" Lina asked. "What are mountains?"

"Lina," said Mrs. Murdo. "It's not polite to ask too many questions."

"I don't mind," the doctor said. "I forgot that you wouldn't know these things. You really lived underground?"

"Yes," said Lina.

Dr. Hester scrunched her gray eyebrows together. "But why would there be a city underground?"

Lina said she didn't know. All she knew was what was in the notebook she and Doon had found on their way out. It was a journal kept by one of the first inhabitants of Ember, who told of the fifty couples brought in from the outside world, each with two babies to raise in the underground city. "They thought there was some danger," Lina said. "They made Ember as a place to keep people safe."

"It was that long ago, then," said the doctor. "Before the Disaster."

"I don't know," said Lina. "I guess so. What disaster?"

"The Disaster that just about wiped out the human race," said Dr. Hester. "I'll tell you about it sometime, but not right now. I have to go and see to Burt Webb's infected finger."

"Can I ask one more question?" said Lina.

The doctor nodded.

"Why is this place called Sparks?"

"Oh," said the doctor, smiling a little. "It was the People of the Last Truck who gave it that name—our twenty-two founders. They were among the very few people who survived the Disaster. For a while they found food by driving around from one place to another in the old towns, using cars and trucks that still had a sort of energy-making stuff called gasleen—'gas' for short."

Cars and trucks? thought Lina. Gasleen? But she didn't want to interrupt, so she didn't ask.

"When food and gas began to run out," the doctor went on, "they decided it was time to start a new life somewhere else. They found one last truck that still had gas, and they loaded it up with supplies—food in cans and boxes, tools, clothes and blankets, seeds, everything useful they could find. Then they drove east, out across the Empty Lands, staying close to the river. Right here, the truck broke down. When they opened the hood, a great spray of sparks shot up out of the engine. So they decided to settle in this spot, and they named it Sparks." The doctor stood up and looked around for her medicine bag. "It turned out to be a fitting name in another way," she said. "Sparks are a beginning. We are the beginning of something here, or trying to be, the way a spark is the beginning of a fire."

"But fires are terrible," said Lina.

"Terrible or wonderful," said the doctor, who had found her bag behind a chair and was heading out the door. "They can go either way."

Lina never did go down to the plaza that day. She didn't think Doon would worry—he knew Poppy was sick, and he'd figure out that Lina had stayed with her. She would go and look for him tomorrow, she decided, and find out then what was happening to the people of Ember.

Late in the afternoon, Lina went outside and sat on a rickety bench in the courtyard of the doctor's house, waiting to see if anyone was going to make dinner. It seemed unlikely. The doctor was off treating someone's toothache, and Mrs. Murdo was up in the loft with Poppy, who had started crying an hour ago and still had not stopped.

A door opened, and Torren came outside. He sauntered over to Lina and stood in front of her.

"Your sister is probably going to die," he said.

Lina jerked back. "She is *not.*"

Torren shrugged. "Looks like it to me," he said. "Looks to me like she has the plague." He sat down on a wooden chair, where he could stare straight into Lina's face. He was wearing a sort of undershirt—it was white and looked like a sack with holes for neck and arms—and his thin legs stuck out from baggy shorts of the same material. He had combed his hair so that it stood up like a tuft of grass at the top of his forehead, making his long, narrow face look even longer.

"I don't know what you're talking about," Lina said.

"You don't know about the Three Plagues?" said Torren in a tone of exaggerated surprise. "Or the Four Wars? You've never heard of the Disaster?"

"I've heard of it," said Lina. "But I don't know what it is. I don't know about anything here."

"Well, then, I'll tell you," he said. "You can't go around being so ignorant."

She said nothing. She didn't like this boy's superior attitude, but she wanted to know everything there was to know. She would let him tell her, but she wasn't going to ask him to.

"It was a long time ago," he said. He spoke in a precise, teacherly voice. "There were millions of people in the world then. They were all geniuses. They could make their voices travel around the world, and they could see people who were miles away. They could fly."

He paused, waiting, no doubt, for Lina to be amazed.

She *was* amazed, but she wasn't going to show it. Besides, he was probably lying. She just nodded.

"They could make music come down out of the air. They had thousands of smooth roads and could go anywhere they wanted, really fast. They had pictures that moved." He waited again. He took a few apricot pits from his pocket and rattled them idly in the palm of his hand.

All right, she would ask. "What do you mean, pictures that moved?"

"Didn't think you'd know that one," Torren said with a tight little smile. "They were huge pictures, taller than a house. They were called movies. You'd look at a wall and see a story happening on it, with voices and other sounds."

"How do you know all this?" asked Lina. She thought he might easily be making it up.

"We learn it in school," said Torren. "They teach us *a lot* about the old times, so we won't forget."

"Have you seen a moving picture, then?"

"Of course not," he said. "You have to have electricity. There hasn't been any for a long time." He chucked one of the pits at a bird that was about to drink from the water dish. The splash scared it away.

"We had electricity," Lina said, glad to score a point over him. "We had it in Ember, until it ran out.

We had street lights, and lamps in our houses, and electric stoves in the kitchen."

For a moment Torren looked dismayed. "But did you have *movies*?" he said.

Lina shook her head. "Anyway," she said, "what does all this have to do with my sister?"

"I'm about to tell you, if you'd just let me." The important tone came back into his voice. "So there were all these billions of people, but there got to be too many of them. They messed up the world. That was why the Three Plagues came. But before the Three Plagues, they had the Four Wars." Once again he paused and looked at her in that infuriating way, lifting his thin eyebrows.

"Just tell me," she said. "Don't look at me like that."

"You don't know about the Four Wars?"

"No. War—what's that?"

"A war is when one bunch of people fights with another bunch, when both of them want the same thing. Like for instance if there's some good land, and two groups of people want to live there."

"Why can't they both live there?"

"They don't *want* to live there *together,*" he said, as if this were a stupid question. "Also you could have a war because of revenge. Say one group of people does something bad to another group, like steal their chickens. Then the first group does something bad back in revenge. That could start a war. The two groups would try to kill each other, and the ones who killed the most would win."

"They'd kill each other over chickens?"

"That's just an example. In the Four Wars, they were fighting over bigger things. Like who should get some big chunk of land. Or whether you should believe in this god or that god. Or who got to have the gold and the oil."

All of this was enormously confusing to Lina. She didn't know the meaning of "god" or "gold," and she wasn't sure what he meant by "oil." "You mean," she said, thinking of the jars that had once been stocked in the storerooms of Ember, "the kind of oil you cook with?"

Torren rolled his eyes. "You *really* don't know anything," he said. He flung the rest of the pits he was holding at three little red-headed birds pecking at the weeds between the bricks, and the birds scattered, cheeping. "This was really beautiful, valuable oil. Everyone wanted it, and there wasn't enough of it to go around, so they fought over it."

"They hit each other?"

"Much worse than that," said Torren. He leaned forward, elbows on his knees, and in a low, husky voice told Lina about the weapons they had had in those days, the guns that let you kill people without even getting near them, and the bombs that could flatten and burn whole cities at once. "They set the cities on fire all over the world," Torren said. His small eyes glittered. "And afterward came the plagues."

"I don't know what a plague is," Lina said.

"A sickness," said Torren. "The kind where one person catches it from another person, and it spreads around fast before you can stop it."

"We had one of those," Lina said. "The coughing sickness—it would come sometimes and kill a lot of people and then go away again."

"We had three," said Torren, as if three plagues were better than one. "There was the one where you wither away, like you're starving to death; the one where you feel like you're on fire and you die of heat; and the one where you suddenly can't breathe. No one knew where they came from, they just rose up and swept over the whole world like a wind."

Lina shuddered. She was tired, all at once, of listening to Torren, who took such pleasure in describing horrors and saying words she didn't understand.

"So," Torren said. "The Four Wars and the Three Plagues—those together were the Disaster. When it finally got over with, hardly any people were left. That's why we had to start all over again." He stood up and brushed away a twig that was clinging to his shorts. "We don't have war anymore," he said. "Our leaders say we must never have war again. And besides, there's no one to fight against. But if we ever *do* have to have one, we'll win, because we have the Terrible Weapon."

"The Terrible Weapon?" said Lina. "What's that?"

But just then Mrs. Murdo came out the door with Poppy in her arms. Lina jumped up and ran over to her. "Is she better?"

"She's a little better." Poppy lay against Mrs. Murdo's shoulder, her head turned sideways, her eyes dull. "Wy-na," she said in a small voice. Lina ruffled her fine brown hair.

Torren cast an indifferent glance at Mrs. Murdo and walked away across the courtyard. The gate clattered behind him.

"Poppy doesn't have a plague, does she?" Lina said.

"A plague? Certainly not," said Mrs. Murdo. "Whatever gave you that idea?"

"That boy," said Lina. "That horrible boy."

CHAPTER 7

A Day of New People

The next day, back in the plaza, Ben Barlow organized the residents of the Pioneer Hotel into teams. The teams would work together and eat lunch together. Each team would be led by someone from Sparks, who would decide where that team's labor was most needed each day. Some days a team might work with the people of Sparks at the bakery or the shoe workshop or the wagon yard; other days they might do a job on their own, such as repairing a fence or digging a ditch. Sooner or later, nearly everyone would have done nearly every kind of work. This was the best way for them to learn, Ben said.

Doon's team included his father, two teachers from the Ember school (Miss Thorn and Mrs. Polster), Clary Laine, the greenhouse manager, and Edward Pocket, the librarian, who would join them for lunch but not work with them because he was so old.

Doon found Lina in the crowd—the first time he'd seen her since they arrived. He told her about the Pioneer Hotel; she told him about the doctor's house and what she'd learned from Torren about the Disaster. Lina and Mrs. Murdo were told they'd be a team of two with the job of helping Dr. Hester, since they were staying at her house. They were sent home, and all the other work teams went off to their first project: digging the hotel toilets.

They went out into the scrubby woods behind the Pioneer. The work leaders had brought picks and shovels from town; they gave each person a tool. "You'll dig fifty holes," one of the leaders said, "each one six feet deep. Then you'll build a shelter of scrap lumber around each one."

But the people of Ember had never done much digging or picking. They had to be shown how to put a foot on the shovel's edge to drive it into the dirt, and how to lift the pick over their shoulders and bring it down hard. At first they scraped and hacked awkwardly at the hard, dry earth, grunting with effort, dislodging only a few crumbs of dirt with each stroke. After ten minutes of hard work, they'd made hardly more than shallow dips in the dirt. They were breathing fast. "Did you say six *feet* deep?" someone called out.

"That's right," came the answer.

So the Emberites set themselves to the task, which

was for most of them the hardest work they'd ever done. After an hour, Doon had blisters on both hands and a kink in his neck. Some of the others had given up entirely and had flopped down onto the ground, dripping with sweat and aching in every muscle. Doon made himself keep going, but he was glad when the work finally stopped at noon and the team leaders marched them back into the town. He heard people murmuring to each other as they walked. "Do you think we'll have to work like this *every day*?" "It'll make us strong, I guess." "Or else kill us."

Each team was assigned to a different household for lunch. Doon's team went with the Parton family. Through the streets of the village, they followed a stout, cheerful woman named Martha Parton, whose wide rear end wagged from side to side as she walked. "Here we are," she said after a few minutes. She opened an unpainted wooden door and ushered her six guests inside. "Welcome to our home," she said.

Doon looked around the low-ceilinged room. At one end was a long wooden table; at the other, a couple of benches stood before a niche in the smoke-stained wall. Sitting on the benches were two people, who got up and came forward as Martha introduced them. "My husband, Ordney," Martha said. He was tall and narrow, with a mustache like a brown toothbrush under his nose. "And my son, Kensington."

Kensington was a little younger than Doon, a

skinny boy with yellow hair, big ears, and a freckled nose. He kept his eyes on the floor, except for a couple of quick, curious glances. "Hi," he said to the floor in a soft, shy voice.

"And these," Martha Parton said to her family, sweeping her arm in the direction of the guests, "are the people from underground." She raised her eyebrows at them. "You're lucky to have found your way here," she said. "The only other settlements we know of are little miserable ones hundreds of miles away. Everything else is just hard, rocky dirt, and ruins, and grass."

"And you've not only come to the right place," added Ordney. "You've come at the right time. It's taken years of hard work, but Sparks is finally doing well."

"Now!" said Martha, clapping her hands. "Time to eat!"

They sat down at the big table, and Martha brought out dishes of food. "I suppose you've never tasted anything like this," she said, handing around a bowl of fresh peas. "Just picked this morning. And this is pumpkin bread, made from what I canned of last year's crop. Good, isn't it? Did you have pumpkin bread where you came from?"

"No, indeed," said Doon's father.

"We did have peas, though," said Clary. "Grown in our greenhouses."

"And very fine they were," said Mrs. Polster loyally. "Though slightly smaller than these."

"Probably you haven't had pickled carrots, either," Martha said, passing the dish around. "These are from my mother's famous recipe."

"We did have carrots," said Mrs. Polster. "A nice pale orange, some of them fully four inches long."

"Is that right," said Martha. "Ours are twelve inches, usually."

Miss Thorn picked delicately at her food, making a polite comment now and then. Edward Pocket ate with such a vigorous appetite that he had no time for talking. Kensington ate steadily and silently. Every time Doon glanced his way, he found the boy staring at him, but as soon as their eyes met, Kensington looked back at his plate.

Ordney Parton cleared his throat. Apparently this meant he was going to speak, because his family all instantly looked at him. "I never knew," he said, "that there was a kind of people who lived underground. Must feel strange to you here on the surface."

"Actually," said Doon, "we aren't a different kind of people. This place feels familiar, in a way, because we came from here originally."

"From here? Oh, I don't think so," said Martha. "You don't look a bit like us. You're so much—well, smaller, if you'll pardon my saying so. And paler."

"True," said Clary, "but I suppose that's because of

living in a dark place for so long. Everything is bigger and brighter here."

"But why do you think you came from here?" Martha asked.

"Because of a notebook we found," Doon said. "It was written by someone from this world who went to live in Ember right at the beginning. All the people of Ember came from this world."

"Is that so," said Martha, eyeing Doon skeptically. "Well, I must say, it's the strangest thing *I've* ever heard."

Doon's father changed the subject. "You have such a fine, solid house," he said. "What is it made of?"

"Earth," said Martha.

"Pounded," said Ordney. "Strong as stone."

"Thick walls," said Martha. "They make it cool in hot weather and warm in cold." She reached for another pickled carrot. "I suppose you lived in—what? Some sort of burrows?"

"Stone houses," said Edward Pocket, suddenly joining the conversation because his plate was empty. "Two stories. Extremely sturdy. Never too warm."

There was a silence.

"Such a lovely lunch," said Miss Thorn in a small voice.

"Perfectly delicious," Mrs. Polster declared. The others chimed in, and Martha beamed.

They all rose from the table. Martha scurried into

the kitchen and came out with a basket full of cloth-wrapped parcels. She handed one to each of her guests. "Your supper," she said, "and breakfast."

"Thank you," said Doon's father. "You're very generous."

They filed out the front door. Doon was the last to leave. Just as he stepped outside, he felt a light tap on his shoulder. He turned to see Kensington standing behind him, his eyes wide.

"Aren't you the one who found the way out?" he whispered.

Doon nodded.

"I thought so," the boy said. He made a curious gesture—stuck out his hand with the fingers curled and the thumb straight up. Doon didn't understand it, but he thought it must mean something good, because a shy smile went with it. "Call me Kenny," the boy said, and he darted back through the door.

Doon followed his father and the others down the street. He's heard of me, he thought. He felt a pleasant sort of glow. Of course, Kenny was just a little boy; it was natural for a young boy to admire an older one.

All afternoon, they worked on the toilet holes. Doon was ready to drop by the end of the day. When the work leaders let them go, he walked down the long slope of ground in front of the Pioneer Hotel to the river. Large stones bordered the water at this point; he found one that was flat on top and sank onto it, tired to his bones. The sun was setting; the western sky glowed pink. The trees on the other side of the river cast long, thin shadows across the ground. He sat for ten minutes or so, just gazing, his thoughts swirling slowly.

It was going to take the people of Ember—all four hundred of them—several days just to build their outhouses. And already they were exhausted. How long before they got used to doing this kind of work? Doon couldn't imagine feeling so tired day after day. He had blisters on his hands, his wrists and shoulders ached, and the back of his neck felt hot and sore, as if it had been burned. And he was strong and young! What about the older people and the younger children? Of course they'd all have to work if they expected to be fed, but—

His thoughts were interrupted by footsteps crunching behind him.

He turned. There was Tick Hassler, walking toward him across the field. Doon's pulse quickened a little. Tick moved through the grass with a long stride, and when he came to the rocks alongside the river, he stepped from one to the next easily, never slipping or losing his balance. He raised a hand in greeting, and Doon waved back.

"Thinking deep thoughts?" Tick said, coming up beside Doon and smiling down at him.

"Not really," said Doon. "Just watching things."

"Ah," said Tick. He put his hands on his hips and gazed out across the river. The setting sun shone on his face, making it glow, and draped his long shadow over the rocks. Doon wished he would sit down and talk. After a while, Tick said, "I'll tell you something."

Doon glanced up quickly. Tick's eyes were a blue so light it was almost startling.

"This is a very fine place you've brought us to," Tick said.

"Yes," said Doon, pleased at being given the credit.

"You deserve a lot of respect," Tick said. "You may be just a kid, but you took action when things got desperate. You were brave."

Ordinarily, Doon didn't pay much attention to what other people thought about him, but there was something about Tick that made it pleasing to have his good opinion. Somehow, he didn't even feel insulted at being called "just a kid." "Thank you," he said. He thought surely Tick would sit down on the rock next to him now, and they would talk, but instead he stepped onto another rock, closer to the water, so that he had his back to Doon.

They both gazed for a while at the reddening sky. Then Tick turned around and said, "Really a wonderful place. Just look at all this!" He swept his arm in a wide arc, taking in the groves of trees, the fields, the river, and the glowing red ball of the sun.

"Yes," said Doon. "It *is* wonderful."

"We just need to get ourselves a little more comfortable," Tick said. "I have ideas already. We could fix up this old building, first of all. Get people organized and working together. Get new glass for the windows, maybe. Pipe some water in from the river. What do you think?"

"Sure," said Doon.

"Chet Noam wants to work with me," Tick said. "Lizzie Bisco, too, and Allie Bright. How about you?"

"Sure," said Doon again, a little disappointed that Tick had talked to all these other people before him.

"You'll be great on the pipe project," Tick said, "because of your experience."

Doon nodded. Actually, there were lots of things he'd rather do than work with pipes again, as he had in the Ember Pipeworks. But it might actually be fun to work on a plumbing project with Tick. Energy blazed from Tick's keen blue eyes.

"There's so much we can do . . . ," said Tick, and Doon waited to hear the end of his sentence, to hear what else he thought they could do, but Tick didn't say any more. He just bent down, plucked a stone from between the bigger rocks, turned back to face the river again, and threw the stone with all his might. It sailed high up, a black dot against the scarlet sky, and came down with a splash in the shallow water on the far side of the river.

Then he twisted around and smiled at Doon, an exuberant, radiant smile. "See you," he said, and he stepped across the rocks, climbed up the riverbank, and went back toward the hotel.

When he was gone, Doon picked up a stone and flung it as hard as he could. It plunked down in the middle of the river—not a bad throw, but not as good as Tick's.

CHAPTER 8

The Roamer and the Bike

Several days passed. Poppy would get a little better and then a little worse, and Lina and Mrs. Murdo stayed with her nearly all the time, putting cool rags on her forehead and trying to get her to drink the medicine the doctor gave her. When Mrs. Murdo wasn't caring for Poppy, she was prowling around the medicine room, inspecting the doctor's jumbled collection of herbs and potions and powders, making notes in a tiny notebook, and rearranging things, trying to create some order.

Dr. Hester was often gone, seeing patients in the village, and when she was in the house she was doing ten things at once, or trying to, and being interrupted by patients who came to the door at all hours. It seemed to Lina that the people of Sparks were constantly cutting themselves, spraining their muscles, getting rashes, and falling ill. The doctor would give them medicine or bandage their wounds, and a few days later the patients would bring something in return—a basket of eggs, a jar of pickles, a bag of clean rags.

Lina had never seen anyone so disorganized as the doctor. She peeked into the medicine room once when the doctor was out and was amazed at the clutter in there—shelves and cupboards and tables piled with stuff in bottles and stuff in boxes and stuff in jars, all higgledy-piggledy. How Dr. Hester found anything she couldn't imagine.

It took the doctor a couple of days even to get organized enough to figure out how Lina could help her. But when she did, she began giving her one chore after another, and sometimes several all at once, often forgetting that Lina didn't know how to do them.

"Could you go and water the asparagus?" she'd say. Then before Lina could ask what asparagus was, and where to find it, and what to put the water in, she'd say, "And then can you rip some of those rags in the kitchen basket into strips for bandages? And when you've done that, maybe you could wipe the floor in the medicine room—I spilled something the other day, I think over by the window. And the chickens, the chickens—they need to be fed." And then she'd be out the door, leaving Lina to remember the string of tasks and figure out how to do them.

Everything here seemed extremely *inconvenient* to Lina. To get water, you had to go outside the gate to a pump and work a stiff handle up and down. To go to the bathroom, you had to go out in back of the house to a little smelly shed. There was no light at night except for candles, and at first she'd thought there was no stove to cook on. "Oh, yes," said the doctor, "that's the stove there"—she pointed to the thing like a black iron barrel in the corner of the kitchen—"but I hardly ever use it in the summer. Too much trouble to keep the fire going, and it's too hot anyway. We mainly eat cold food in summer."

When she did want to cook something—boil a pot of water to cook an egg, for instance, or make tea—the doctor had to squat down, stuff some dry grass and twigs into the stove's belly, and set them alight. Sometimes she used a match; sometimes she hit what looked like two rocks together until they made a spark and the grass caught fire. Then she had to feed in bigger and bigger twigs until the fire was finally hot enough. This fire seemed fairly safe to Lina, though she didn't like to get too close to it; at least it was contained in its iron box. It wasn't free to leap out at her like the fire in the fireplace. Fortunately, the doctor didn't make another fire in the fireplace after that first night. As the days grew hotter and hotter, the nights were no longer cool. Extra warmth was the last thing they needed.

One day—a week or so after Lina first came to the

doctor's house—a patient came with news to tell as well as a wound to bind. She was a scrawny young woman with brownish teeth. She had a bad scratch on her wrist where she'd scraped it against some rusty wire. "There's a roamer in the village," she said. "Just arrived this morning."

"What's a roamer?" Lina asked.

The doctor, tying a rag around her patient's wrist, said, "Roamers go out into the Empty Lands and bring things back."

"From the old places," added the patient. "The ruined places."

"My brother Caspar is a roamer!" said Torren. "And when I'm old enough, I'm going to be a roamer, too, and we're going to be partners."

This was the first time Lina had sensed real happiness in Torren. His little eyes shone with hope.

"That will be exciting," Lina said. "Is it dangerous to be a roamer?"

"Oh, yes. Sometimes you run into other roamers trying to get the same things you want. Sometimes you're attacked by bandits. You have to fight them off. Caspar has a whip."

"A whip?"

"A great long cord! As long as this room, almost. If people get in his way, he lashes them." He lifted his arm overhead and brought it down as if he were lashing something. "Whhhhtt! Whhhhtt!" he said.

"Now, stop that," said the doctor absently, tying the final knot in the rag. The patient left, and Lina and the doctor and Torren, along with Mrs. Murdo, carrying Poppy, went down to the market plaza to see the roamer.

A crowd had assembled in the plaza. Lina looked for Doon, but she didn't see him. She saw only a few Emberites, in fact; most of them must have been working in other places. But a great many villagers were there, clustered around a big truck. The truck was loaded with barrels and crates, and on it stood a brown-skinned woman with wiry muscles in her arms and legs. "I have been in the far north," she cried out in a shrill, strong voice, "out in remote corners of the Empty Lands. I have traveled roads where I saw no human being for weeks on end. And in these distant regions, I came across houses and farms that had never before been searched. I have treasures for you today." She beckoned with a long brown arm. "Step up and look."

The crowd pressed forward. Apparently this roamer was known to the villagers. Some people called out greetings and questions.

"Did you bring us any writing paper this time, Mackie?"

"What about seeds?"

"What about tools?"

"And matches?"

"And clothes? I'm so tired of wearing homemade patchwork!"

"I have all that and more!" the woman called. "Come close. Special things first." She bent over an open crate and rummaged around for a moment. When she stood up again, she was holding a blackened iron cooking pot, so big she had to use both hands to lift it. "What am I offered?" she cried.

"Half a bushel of dried apricots!"

"A bushel of peas!"

"Barrel of cornmeal!"

The woman listened, cocking her head, her eyebrows raised. She waited until the offers stopped, and then she pointed at a tall young woman with shiny black hair who had offered five loaves of apricot cornbread. "Done!" she said, and she lowered the pot into the young woman's hands.

For the next special thing, the roamer reached into a big cardboard box. She brought out a smaller box colored blue and held it high. "Soap flakes!" she cried. "Twenty-four boxes of them!"

Dozens of people bid for these. They were all gone in minutes. Then came more cooking pans, two thick jackets of shiny material, rolls of rope, garden tools, books, a pair of scissors, some doorknobs, some nails. There were a few odd, useless things, too. For half a dozen carrots, one woman bought a pair of faucets, one with an H and one with a C. "What will you do with them?" asked Lina. People here got their water from long-handled pumps that stood at certain spots in the village. No one had indoor running water. "I'll turn them upside down," said the woman. "They'll make good candle holders."

When the roamer brought out a handful of jewels, Lina gasped. She had never seen such things—necklaces and bracelets made of gleaming stones and silver chains. But only a few people seemed interested in them, and they bid hardly anything—one girl bid a couple of potatoes, but a man got them for a slightly used pair of sandals. "If my wife doesn't want them," he said, "I'll use them to pretty up my oxen."

The roamer brought out the last of her wares—packets of paper, boxes of safety pins, some spoons and forks. The doctor stepped up to buy a set of small glass bottles.

"Dr. Hester!" the roamer said. "Good to see you!"

"And you, Mackie," said the doctor. "It's been a long time."

"I was hoping you'd be here," the roamer went on. "I ran into your nephew the other day."

"Caspar?" cried Torren in a voice so piercing that several people looked up, startled. "Where is he?"

"He was up in the apple country," said Mackie. "I told him I was coming down here, and he said to tell you he's heading for home."

"Is that right," said the doctor. She was clearly not as excited as Torren. "We haven't seen him for quite a while."

"One year, ten months, and nineteen days," said Torren. "When will he be here? Did he say?"

"Should be soon," said the roamer. She was putting the little bottles into a cloth bag. "I'd guess within the next two weeks or so."

When the roamer's sale was over, Lina walked home along the river road with the doctor and Mrs. Murdo and Poppy, who was asleep in Mrs. Murdo's arms. Torren leapt ahead, his thin legs splaying out sideways. He bounced off steps, jumped onto walls, leapt up to grab branches of trees, and swung from them.

As they neared the doctor's house, Torren, who was way ahead of them by now, suddenly turned around and raced back. "You have to get out of our room!" he said to Lina and Mrs. Murdo. "My brother will want his own room, and he'll want to be with me. You all have to move."

"Fine," said Lina. "We will. We'll go live with our own people as soon as Poppy's well enough."

Torren's narrow face lit up. "Good, good, good!" he cried. "When are you leaving?"

"Not *today,*" said Lina. "Not right this *minute.*"

"But soon!" Torren cried. He skipped ahead of

them again, through the gate and across the courtyard.

The doctor said not to mind Torren, he was being rude because he was so excited. But it seemed to Lina that Dr. Hester didn't see clearly when it came to Torren. He wasn't rude just when he was excited, he was rude nearly all the time. The doctor was so preoccupied with her work that she hardly noticed him. Maybe if she'd pay him more attention, Lina thought, he wouldn't be so awful.

But he *was* awful, and Lina would be glad to get away from him. Two weeks, she thought. Then we'll meet Caspar the Great, and if Poppy is well by then, Torren can have his room back and we'll go and live with Doon and the others.

Now and then, Lina saw people on wheels going by on the road in front of the doctor's house. The only wheeled vehicles Lina had ever seen were the heavy wooden carts in Ember. But these people were riding beautiful, slender devices, two big wheels per person. They glided by, their feet going round and round. She wanted to do it, too! So *badly,* she wanted to. "What are they?" she asked the doctor.

"Bikes, of course," said the doctor. "You've never seen one?"

"No," said Lina, looking at a bike with longing. If she could have a bike, she thought, she could go even faster than when she ran. She could go so fast and so far. . . . She looked out toward the endless rolling hills. She could go everywhere. She could go to wherever the roads ended.

"I wish I could ride one," she said.

"Well, you can, if you want," said the doctor. "There's an old one out behind the toolshed. I suppose it still works."

"There is?" Lina nearly dropped the basket of eggs she had just gathered. "May I get it now?"

"I guess so," said the doctor. "But would you mind watering the parsley first? And if you could just shell these peas . . . and maybe wash that spinach . . ."

Lina did these tasks in a fever of impatience, and when she was finished she dashed out to the shed. The bike was leaning against the shed wall. It was old but beautiful—made of wires and slender pipes and rods, some of them silver under their coat of dust, and some of them red. Thin, weedy vines wove among the spokes of the bike's wheels, and cobwebs draped its seat. Lina took hold of the two handles and pulled the bike from its nest. She wheeled it out onto the road in front of the house and brushed the cobwebs and dry leaves and bits of grass off it, and then she swung one leg over and settled herself on the seat.

Now what?

She spent the rest of the morning figuring it out. She pushed on the pedals, rolled forward, tipped over sideways, and had to put her feet down. She rolled forward again but didn't know how to turn. She fell off. She heaved the bike upright and tried again. She fell off again. After an hour or so of this, she gave up and went inside for a while.

And later, when she tried again, something had changed. She had the feel of it in her legs now, or somewhere in her. She rolled forward, she put a foot on the pedal and pushed, she rolled farther, she brought up the other foot, and magically, her body understood for a second what to do. She was sailing; her feet were going round and round. A smile broke over her face. She held on, feet going round, breathless, breeze against her face—a whole long distance, maybe five yards, before suddenly she was nervous and dragged her feet along the ground to stop. She stood holding the handlebars, her mouth open in amazement.

And by the end of the day she had it. She could ride back and forth on the road, she could stop whenever she wanted to. She could even turn around corners without putting a foot down.

"I'm going to see Doon," she told Mrs. Murdo. She was longing to see Doon, longing to talk to someone she really knew. Mrs. Murdo was fine, of course, but she was a grown-up. Lina wanted to be with a *friend.* She got on the bike and rode, sweeping down the river road, into the plaza, where she asked someone for directions, and out the other side of the town to the hotel.

When she got there, she stopped for a moment just to stare. The enormous old building looked to her like a wonderful place to live. She felt a sudden longing to have her own room there, back among her old friends and neighbors.

It was nearly evening by then. People were sitting on the hotel steps in the last rays of the setting sun, eating their dinners from their food parcels and talking. Some were down by the river, cooling their feet, splashing water onto their faces. Over by the farthest wing of the hotel, a few boys were gathered around another boy, who was sitting on a fallen tree talking to them. Maybe Doon was over there.

She wheeled her bike toward them—the ground here was too rough and weedy to ride on. Her old friends and neighbors called out to her as she passed, and she waved at them, glad to be back among people she knew.

When she got closer to the group of boys, she saw that Doon was among them. He and a couple of others were listening to that tall dark-haired boy—what was his name, Tigg? Tim? He'd been a cart puller in Ember, she thought. He laughed as she came up, a ringing, confident laugh, and all the other boys laughed, too.

She went up behind Doon and tapped him on the shoulder. He turned around. She grinned at him. "Look, Doon!" she said. "I have a bike!"

He seemed astonished to see her. "Oh!" he said. "Lina!"

"Come and talk to me," she said.

His eyes shifted back toward the tall boy. "Okay," he said, but he didn't move.

"Come on!" said Lina, tugging at his jacket.

They walked down toward the river. Lina leaned the bike against a tree, and she and Doon sat facing each other on the ground.

"What a huge place!" she said, waving an arm at the Pioneer Hotel, and talking fast in her eagerness. "What's it like? Will you show me around? Poppy is a little better, and maybe in a couple of weeks we can come and live here, too. With you. And with everyone."

Doon nodded. "That would be good," he said.

"It's kind of lonely at the doctor's house," Lina went on. "There's a boy there who doesn't like us, and the doctor is so busy she can hardly think, and her house is a mess, and I have to do a million chores." She paused for breath. "Today we saw a roamer, Doon."

"A roamer?"

She explained what a roamer was. Doon listened, but she saw his eyes veer back toward the group of boys.

"Who is that boy?" she asked. "The one who's talking?"

"Tick Hassler," said Doon.

Lina turned around and looked at him. He was handsome, she thought. His black hair was thick and glossy, and his face was all sharp angles, as if it had been carved from wood. "Is he a friend of yours?"

"Sort of," said Doon. "I mean—I'm just getting to know him."

"Oh," said Lina. "Do you know which room Lizzie is in?"

Doon said he didn't. "I don't stay inside very much," he said. "It's kind of dark and dismal in there. What I like is being outside." He pointed up into the branches of the tree, where little fluttery things were hopping around. "Remember when we first saw those?" he said. "When we'd just come up from Ember? I learned that they're called birds. When you start really looking at them, you see there's all different kinds. I've seen ones with a yellow chest, and ones with stripes on their wings, and ones with red heads. There's even one that's bright blue." He gazed upward. "It's strange, isn't it? Why have all these different kinds, I wonder? Just for the fun of it?"

A burst of laughter came from the group of boys around Tick Hassler. Doon glanced over at them.

"Do you like it here, Doon?" Lina said. "In the village of Sparks, I mean?"

"I do," said Doon. "I like it a lot."

"Me too," said Lina. "Mostly."

"But it sort of worries me that we have to leave in six months," Doon said. "There's so much we need to learn."

"Well, I guess so," said Lina. "But maybe if we leave . . . I mean, I still wish . . ."

"Wish what?" said Doon when she trailed off.

"Oh, I don't know." She'd been going to say she wished they'd found the city she used to dream of. But she was afraid Doon might think that was silly.

The sun was going down. Shadows grew longer. "Show me your room before I have to go," Lina said, "so I'll know where to find you."

Tick was walking away, and the other boys were following him. Doon gazed after them. "I can't right now," he said. "I will next time you come."

"All right," Lina said. She got up from the ground and swatted the leaves off her pants. She picked up her bike. "I'll see you sometime," she said, and she rode back to the doctor's house feeling lonelier than she had before.

CHAPTER 9

Hard, Hungry Work

Instead of getting easier as the days went on, work for the people of Ember got harder. It wasn't just the work—it was the heat they had to work in. Every day was hotter than the last. Doon had never felt this warm in his life—it was like being cooked. All the people of Ember felt this way. They sweated, their skin turned red and stung and peeled off, and the brightness of the sky hurt their eyes. They got terrible headaches. Sometimes one of them would drop to the ground in a faint, just from being too hot. At times like these, people thought, This is a dreadful place we have come to. They put their hands over their eyes, missing the familiar darkness.

The team leaders tried to be understanding when their workers drooped and fainted. But the people of Sparks were used to the heat; beside them, the people of Ember seemed like weaklings. A few times, Doon saw the leader of his team press his lips together and drum his fingers against his leg when one of the Emberites had to sit down and rest.

Doon's team leader was Chugger Frisk, a big, stubble-jawed man who didn't talk much except to give directions. Every day he sent his team wherever it was most needed. Doon did all kinds of jobs over the next few weeks. He dug ditches for the pipes that conducted water from the river to the crops in the fields. He repaired the wagons that hauled the produce home from the fields. He milked the goats out in the goat pasture and made sure the water troughs for the oxen were full. He picked fruit, built fences, planted seeds, stirred vats of soap, and dug chicken droppings into the cabbage field.

Except for being so hot, he didn't mind the work. He was getting strong, and he *liked* being strong. He liked feeling the muscles in his arms getting harder, and he liked being taller (he knew he was taller, because his old pants were too short). The feeling of being a new person in this new world stayed with him. He would be thirteen soon—not a child anymore. Work was making him sturdy and ready for anything.

Besides, as he worked he was finding out all kinds of things he wanted to learn. How did the pumps work that brought water up from the river to the fields? How was cheese made, and shoes, and candles? Where did they get the ice that kept things cold in their big ice house? What were the bushy-tailed animals that scurried up trees, and the long, rope-like animals that he sometimes almost stepped on in the grass? He wanted to know how houses were built, and what glass was made of, and how bicycles worked. It was exciting, having so much to learn. But every time he remembered that he and his people had less than six months to learn it—less than six months to master all the skills they'd need to build a town of their own—a worm of fear twisted in his stomach.

Chugger wouldn't answer questions. He was too busy giving directions or working. So Doon often asked his questions at lunch. Sometimes Ordney answered him, sometimes Martha did. Ordney's answers were more like lectures, and Martha's were more like boasts. After a while it was clear that both of them were getting tired of questions, so Doon asked fewer of them. One day, Kenny followed him outside after lunch and stretched up to whisper in his ear. "I can show you where there's answers to your questions," he said. "Want me to?"

"Sure," said Doon.

"Right now?" said Kenny.

"Okay," said Doon.

Kenny led him through the streets of the village,

going first toward the river and then away from it, along a street that led out away from the houses and into a grove of oak trees.

"There," said Kenny, pointing ahead.

At first Doon saw only the long line of a roof above the trees. Then the street opened out into a big empty space that, he could see, had once been covered with pavement. Now the pavement was cracked and weeds grew up through it. To the left of this span of pavement stood a huge building—a rectangular structure so tremendous it could have held both the Ember school and the Gathering Hall. At the end facing them were two massive wooden doors, which Kenny walked toward. "In the ancient days," Kenny said, "you didn't have to open these. They were made of glass, and they had eyes and opened as soon as they saw you."

"That can't be," said Doon.

"It was, though," Kenny said.

Above the doors was a sign missing most of its letters. It was a long sign, so you could tell whatever it used to say was a long word, but now all it said was UPE ARK.

"What does that mean?" Doon asked, pointing to the sign.

"I don't know," Kenny said. "We just call it the Ark. It's our storehouse. We're going around to the back."

He led the way around the side of the building to a small door in the back wall, which he opened.

He had to push hard, because something was behind the door that had to be shoved out of the way.

Doon peered into the darkness. At first he couldn't make out what he was seeing. Lumpy mountains appeared to fill the room to the ceiling and spread from wall to wall. He took a step forward, but his foot jammed against something hard on the floor.

"There's answers to everything in here," said Kenny.

As his eyes adjusted to the dimness, Doon saw that the room was full of—was it boxes? No, they almost looked like books. They lay in toppling stacks, giant heaps, sliding mounds, as if they had been dumped in from an enormous bucket. Some of them lay open, with their pages crumpled. Some were so warped that their covers curved. A smell of ancient dust and mold arose from them. He reached down and picked one up. Its cover was furred with dust. He opened it and saw pages of tiny neat printing. It *was* a book, yes. Not like the books of Ember—these were much bigger and sturdier, and had much more writing. He riffled the pages—more dust flew up—but he couldn't tell what the book was about. One page said, "Chapter XV. The Thermodynamics of Aluminum." He had no idea what that meant.

"This is amazing," said Doon. "Can I take some back to the hotel?"

"I guess so," said Kenny. "No one will notice."

Doon set down the book about thermodynamics. He brushed his smudged fingers against his pants. He felt like a hungry person who had been led to an immense banquet, far more food than he could eat in his whole life. He was starving, all of a sudden, for the knowledge hidden in these books. He reached out and chose three of them blindly, not even looking at the titles.

"Don't you want some?" he said to Kenny.

"No," said Kenny. "I already read four books in school. That was enough. We learned about history. Pre and post."

"Pre and post?"

"Pre-Disaster and post-Disaster."

"Oh," said Doon. "What do you like to do, then?" he asked.

"Just poke around," said Kenny. "I poke around in the woods. You could come with me sometime," he said, looking up at Doon with hopeful eyes. "If you want."

"Maybe I will," Doon said, though he was thinking probably he wouldn't. He had so many other things in mind to do. Besides, Kenny was a little young to be his friend.

During the first week after the Emberites arrived, Martha Parton had showed off her cooking skills at lunch every day. She made mashed potato pie, fresh peas with chives, walnut croquettes, mushroom gravy, cheese popovers, red-onion-and-bean dumplings, scrambled eggs with tomato jam, apricot pudding, and apple butter cookies. Every time she brought in a new dish, she said, "I don't imagine you had these where you came from," or "This will be new to you," and the Ember guests would say, "You're right, we've never had this! We've never tasted anything so delicious! It's wonderful!" and Martha's mouth would crimp into a small, pleased smile.

As time went on, however, the food at lunchtime became plainer. Martha got tired of making something new every day to impress her guests. What they found in their dinner and breakfast parcels became less interesting, too—usually it was some chunks of cornbread, ten or twelve carrot sticks, and a few slimy bits of goat cheese. If they were lucky, there might be a hard-boiled egg. Martha took to mentioning, as if it were a little joke, that even though the Partons were given extra food from the storehouse because of the extra people, it *seemed* as if they had less! Wasn't that odd!

Doon started to feel hungry a fair amount of the time, and he knew others did, too. His father never spoke of it, but Edward Pocket griped about the food every evening. "I know I'm old and small," he'd say, polishing off the last crumbs of both his dinner and his breakfast, "but that doesn't mean I can live on air."

One day Ordney made a disturbing announcement. The cabbage crop, he said, was going to be smaller than expected. Worms had got into it. They'd have only about two-thirds of the cabbage they had last year.

After this, not only was the food at lunchtime plainer, but there was less of it. One week, they had string beans, last year's pickled cabbage, and goat's milk pudding for lunch four days in a row, and when they opened their baskets at dinnertime, they found only a bottle of cold potato soup to serve as both dinner and breakfast.

Clary had started a garden just a few days after the Emberites arrived at the Pioneer Hotel. She cleared a patch of ground about forty feet square not far from the riverbank and planted seeds that she had brought from Ember. Children who were too little to go to work in the village helped her pull weeds and fetch buckets of water from the river. Old people sat in the shade giving her advice. After a while, green shoots appeared in rows on the patch of dirt, and Clary was out there every morning and every evening, tending them. In several weeks, there would be a little extra food for the people of Ember out in their own front yard.

But it wouldn't be nearly enough. Some people were already grumbling about their skimpy dinner parcels. One night, when Doon was in room 215 eating with his father and the others, he heard voices in the hall and went out to see a cluster of people a few doors down. Lizzie was there—Doon spotted the red cloud of her hair. Tick was there, too. His voice carried above the rest. "Well, I got three carrots, a plum, and a chunk of sour cheese," he said. "Lucky me. That ought to keep me going for a while."

A few people laughed drily at this. Doon heard Lizzie giggle.

"It'll keep you going for maybe half an hour," someone said. "I don't know how they think we can work, with nothing but scraps to eat."

Along the hall, other doors opened, and other voices joined in.

"All I got was some limp green beans and a few clumps of porridge!"

"I've had carrot soup three days in a row!"

Some people counseled patience. "We shouldn't complain," someone said. "It's hard for them to give us food. We should be grateful for—"

"I'm tired of being grateful!" someone else broke in. "They promised to feed us, but they're starving us instead!"

"It seems to me," said Tick, "that we should do something about this. I think maybe I'll mention the problem at lunch tomorrow. Maybe we *all* should. Maybe we should tell them it's very hard to work when you're hungry."

"I'll tell them!" cried Lizzie's high voice, and other voices rose in agreement. An excited, angry babble filled the hallway, drowning out those who spoke for patience. "I'll speak up!" "We have to protest!" "Tick is so right!"

"Tick for mayor!" someone shouted, laughing.

For a second Tick looked surprised. Then his eyes glowed with pleasure. He raised a fist in the air. "We'll stand up for ourselves!" he said, and the people around him roared and raised their fists, too.

Doon turned to his father and Edward and Sadge, who had all come to the door to see what was going on. "We should tell the Partons," he said. "If we're working, we need enough to eat. It's only fair."

"Of course, they don't *have* to give us *anything*," said Doon's father. "They're giving what they think they can spare." He looked sadly at the dry chunk of cornbread in his hand. "But I suppose it can't hurt to mention it," he said, "without being rude, of course. I imagine they're doing the best they can."

Mrs. Polster agreed to be the one to bring the matter up. She did so at lunch the next day. They were having cold spinach soup.

"I have a request," she said firmly. She set down her soup spoon.

Everyone looked toward her. Doon felt a jitter in his stomach.

"We have noticed," said Mrs. Polster, "that the food parcels you so generously give us have become considerably *smaller* lately. We find that when we have eaten what is within, we are still, to be frank, *hungry.* This is a difficulty for us."

There was silence. Everyone stared at Mrs. Polster, who sat very calmly with her hands in her lap, waiting for an answer.

"What?" said Martha Parton at last. "Did I hear right?"

"I believe so," said Mrs. Polster, "unless you have ear trouble. I said we are not getting quite enough to eat."

Martha laughed a one-note laugh, a laugh of disbelief. Kenny stopped chewing and looked frightened. Ordney drew himself up and cleared his throat. "I am surprised," he said. "I had thought you people understood the situation."

"We do, indeed," said Doon's father hastily. "We're very grateful for what you've done for us. It's just that . . ."

"We're working quite hard," said Clary.

"It's a very small amount . . . ," said Miss Thorn timidly.

"For both dinner and breakfast," added Edward Pocket.

"Last night," said Doon, "I had a boiled egg and

three carrots for dinner. And nothing for breakfast this morning."

There was a silence again, a terrible, vibrating silence.

Then Ordney leaned forward, gripping the edge of the table with his fingertips. "Now, listen here," he said. "We're doing the best we can with what has been asked of us. And I must say, a great deal has been asked. Suddenly we're supposed to feed twice as many people as before! More than twice as many!" He glared at the Emberites, shifting his eyes to each one in turn. "And yet we do not have twice as much food as we did before. It's true that each family is being given a little extra from the storehouse for this emergency. But not much. *Sparks village just does not have enough for four hundred extra people.* Are we supposed to feed you instead of our own families? Why should we? Who *are* you, anyway, you strangers from some city no one's ever heard of?"

By the end of this speech, Ordney's face was a deep red and his voice was shaking with rage.

Doon felt frozen. All he could think was, *He's right. Of course he's right. But we're right, too.*

Everyone else must have been thinking the same thing. They finished their soup in silence. At the end of the meal, Martha dumped the food parcels on the table instead of handing them out. They each took one, but Doon's father was the only person who said thank you.

Later, when Doon opened his parcel, he found a wedge of cabbage leaves turning yellow at the edges and a hunk of some sort of bean cake. His stomach clenched. They're tired of helping us, he thought. What are we going to do?

CHAPTER 10

Restless Weeks

Poppy was now almost well. She still slept more than usual, but when she wasn't sleeping she tromped around the doctor's house pulling spoons off the table and spilling cups of water and crumpling pages of books. That is, she was almost her old self. So Lina often asked Mrs. Murdo if it wasn't time for them to go and live with the others at the Pioneer Hotel. Mrs. Murdo always said she wasn't quite ready. They'd wait until the brother came, she said. Lina had a feeling the real reason was that she liked helping the doctor. She was always poring over the doctor's big medicine books, and helping her pick her herbs and mix her remedies. So they stayed on.

And Lina worked for the doctor. It wasn't that she didn't like working. But in Ember, she'd had an adventurous job, an important job. She'd run with her messages all over the city—running the way she loved to run, so fast she almost flew. It was hard for her to stay in one place all day. She felt restless and bored.

She did a huge amount of cooking—well, not cooking exactly, since the doctor rarely wanted to bother making a fire in the stove, but chopping and peeling and slicing and mixing. She wiped up spilled medicines and herbal solutions from the counters, she swept dirt from the floor, she pulled down cobwebs from the ceiling. There were always rags to be torn into bandages. There were always herbs to be pounded into powder and bottles to be labeled and plants to be watered. While everyone else was out in the village, doing new, interesting things and meeting new people, Lina was stuck doing *housework.*

One day she asked the doctor if there was any extra paper she could use for drawing. There wasn't, the doctor said, but if she could find blank pages at the backs of books, she could use those. So Lina tore out eight blank pages, the doctor gave her a pencil, and she began drawing whenever she had a few minutes of free time.

Out of habit, she drew the city she had always drawn—she hardly knew how to draw anything else. But she thought that since she was here in the real world, she should be able to imagine the city much better than before. She remembered the first drawing she'd done with her colored pencils, back in Ember, when she'd made the sky blue instead of its normal black. She had thought it was just an imaginary thing, a little crazy, to draw a blue sky. But now look! The sky really was blue! She must have known it somehow, in some secret place in her mind. Something in her was a little bit magic, maybe—she could see beyond what was right in front of her eyes to things that used to be, or things that could be in the future.

So she shut her eyes and tried to look deep into her imagination. But the old version of the city, the one she'd drawn so many times, seemed to be stamped inside her eyelids. She kept drawing the same thing—the tall buildings, the lighted windows. She added a few extras: some trees, a couple of trucks with their oxen, a chicken. But it didn't look quite right. Would the buildings be taller than the trees? How much taller? Would there be chickens in the city? She felt discouraged. So she set aside her city drawings and tried to draw what she saw around her.

She drew the lemon tree outside the doctor's back door. She drew her bike. She drew the front of the doctor's house, and the gate, and the grapevine over the door. Once a truck parked a little way up the road to unload some crates, and she dashed out with her paper and pencil and drew the truck and its oxen.

But none of these gave her quite the same thrill as drawing the city. There was a feeling that went with drawing the city, a feeling of longing and excitement and mystery. It was as if her drawings of the city were a half-open window, a glimpse of something she couldn't quite see clearly.

Torren sometimes came up behind her when she was drawing and peered over her shoulder. Now and then he would point out some part of the picture that didn't look right, but most of the time he didn't comment at all. He was hopping with impatience these days, waiting for his brother to come home. "He'll be bringing me something," he said one day. "Every time he comes home, he brings me something." He went to the window seat and took his bag of treasures from the cabinet underneath. "I'll show you these," he said to Lina, "if you promise not to touch them."

Lina wandered over. She didn't want to appear too interested, since Torren was certainly never interested in anything *she* did, but she was curious about these prized possessions he'd been hiding.

He reached into the bag and took out one thing at a time, placing it carefully on the window ledge. There were six things, all different. Lina could not identify a single one of them.

"Caspar brought me these," Torren said. He lined them up, making tiny adjustments to their positions until he got them just right. "They're all extinct."

Lina took a step closer and bent down to look.

"Don't touch them!" Torren cried.

"I'm not," said Lina irritably. "Well, what are they?"

Torren pointed to the first thing, which was shaped like a T and made of scratched silver metal. "An airplane," Torren said. "It carried people through the air."

"Oh, come on," said Lina. "It's not even a foot long."

"Real airplanes did," Torren said. "This is just a *model* of a real airplane."

He pointed to the next one. "A tank," he said. "It runs over people and crushes them."

"What's the point of that?" Lina asked.

Torren sighed at Lina's stupidity. "It's for fighting enemies," he said.

The next thing looked like a short, chubby bike. "Motorcycle," said Torren. "It goes really fast." Then came a battered silver tube. "Flashlight. You push this button, and light comes out."

"Show me," Lina said.

"It doesn't *work,*" said Torren. "I told you, all these are extinct."

The next thing was a black rectangle with rows of small colored buttons. "Remote," said Torren.

"What's it for?"

"It makes things happen when you press the buttons."

"What kind of things?"

"Just things," said Torren. "I don't know. It's very technical."

The last thing was different from all the rest. It seemed to be an animal, made of some stiff grayish material. It stood about ten inches high, on four thick feet. "Elephant," said Torren. "As tall as a house."

"Tall as a *house*?" Lina tried to imagine it. "You mean if I stood next to one I'd only come up to here?" She pointed at the creature's knee.

Torren swatted her hand away. "It was the biggest animal on earth," he said. "If it wrapped its nose around you, you would die."

"I'd love to see one," Lina said.

"You can't. There aren't any more." Torren spread his arms out, hiding his treasures from view. "You have to go away now," he said. "You only get one look."

So Lina went out into the courtyard and picked a few green grapes, which turned out to be much too hard and sour to eat. Through the window, she could see Torren moving the tank and the motorcycle toward each other, and she could hear him making growling and crashing noises. What must the ancient world have been like, she wondered, with all these strange things moving around in it? Was it wonderful or terrible?

One afternoon, when Lina was in the village picking up some salt for the doctor, she saw a long line of people at a clothing shop. A few Emberites were among them. Lizzie was in the line, wearing the black scarf around her neck that she'd worn ever since she arrived, to show that she was mourning for Looper, her boyfriend back in Ember.

"Why are there so many people here?" Lina asked.

"They have eyeglasses!" Lizzie said. "A roamer brought in a special load of them yesterday."

"Glasses? But you don't wear glasses."

"These are *dark* glasses," Lizzie said. "They call them sunglasses. They make it so the light doesn't hurt your eyes as much."

Most of the people of Sparks already had sunglasses. A couple of the work leaders, understanding how much the light bothered the Emberites' eyes, traded some extra wooden crates for a couple of boxes of the glasses and gave them out for free. Lina tried some on but didn't like them because they made all the green look brownish. She also thought they made people look sneaky, as if they had evil secret plans.

Lina liked going to the market plaza. It was always alive with people and animals, and the markets had things she'd never seen before—sandals made of old truck tires, hats and baskets woven of straw. It was a noisy, bustling, interesting place. It was also very messy.

The animals made the mess. Goats and oxen, pulling carts in from the fields, left their big, smelly plops all over. These got cleaned up eventually—

someone came and scraped them into buckets and took them away—but often this didn't happen until halfway through the morning, and people had to step carefully until then and breathe in that powerful smell. This gave Lina a good idea. She would do a favor for the marketplace, she decided; everyone would appreciate it.

So the next morning, just at dawn, she rode her bike down to the plaza with a big bucket hanging from the handlebars. She scooped up a load of cow plops and goat plops and dumped it into the river. Back and forth from the plaza to the river she went, scraping up one smelly, squashy load after another, and when she was just about to dump the last load, one of the shopkeepers arrived. She smiled at him, expecting some words of approval. But instead his face twisted in rage.

"What are you *doing*?" he shouted. He started running toward her. "Dumping that good stuff in the river?" He seemed unable to believe his eyes. "What is the matter with you?"

Good stuff? thought Lina. What was he talking about?

He snatched the bucket out of her hand. "You people are—" He stopped. He pressed his lips together and closed his eyes for a moment. "All right," he said in a tight voice. "I suppose you didn't know. This stuff is precious. You do not throw it in the river!"

Lina took a step backward. She felt as if she'd been slapped. "Oh!" she said. "Then what do you do with it?"

"It goes out to the fields," the man said. "It goes into the rotting pile, and when it's ready they dig it into the ground. It's fertilizer. I guess you've never heard of it."

"No," said Lina. "I didn't know. I'm sorry. I was trying to be helpful."

"The most helpful thing you people could do would be to . . . well, never mind." He gave Lina a last disgusted look and walked away, leaving her with a half-filled bucket she didn't know what to do with. She carried it out of the village and up the road, and when no one was around, she dumped its contents at the side of a field.

It wasn't only Lina who got into this kind of trouble. As time went on, she heard about other people doing or saying the wrong thing and irritating the people of Sparks. Sometimes it was because they seemed stupid. People from Ember were frightened by chickens, had never seen a cloud, and didn't know the meaning of ordinary words like *storm* and *forest* and *cat* and *lemon.* They knew nothing about history. They'd never heard of other countries. They didn't even know that the earth was round like a ball. To the villagers, they seemed unbelievably dumb.

On the other hand, they sometimes acted a bit superior, boasting of the things they'd had in their underground city. The villagers didn't like hearing that in Ember people had had electric lights and flush toilets and hot and cold running water. Once when Lister Munk, who had been the Pipeworks supervisor, was telling a Sparks man about the generator, the man called him a liar. When Lister protested that he was telling the truth and implied that Sparks was a rather backward place compared to Ember, the man hit him. It took five people to break up the fight.

Worst of all was the ravenous hunger of the Emberites. The village families were pleased that these strangers were so impressed by their fruits and vegetables, but they were also worried. Their leaders had told them the newcomers were to be fed, and all households were being supplied with extra food for the purpose. But the people of Ember never seemed to get full. They cleaned every last crumb off their plates, asked for seconds, finished those off, and then sat there looking hungry. The villagers resented it. Lina sometimes overheard them talking in the markets. "It's too much to ask," she heard a woman grumbling. "And these cavepeople are going to be here nearly five more months! Am I going to have to give them some of my strawberry crop? I don't see why I should." And another woman was even more direct. "I wish they'd just get out," she said. "It's hard enough to feed your own family, much less a bunch of strangers."

Lina wasn't used to feeling unwanted. She didn't like it. There were plenty of things about this place she didn't like. The dust that coated her feet and legs, for instance, turning them a yellowish brown. The tiny bugs that bit her and made red itchy spots on her arms. The way the sun burned the back of her neck. This place wasn't so perfect, she wanted to tell those crabby villagers. In Ember, for instance, they didn't have so many mean, snotty people as they did here.

Lina sometimes rode down to the Pioneer Hotel to see Doon. He always seemed glad to see her, but it wasn't the same as it had been back in Ember, when they were involved in the desperate search for a way out of their doomed city. Doon showed her around the Pioneer, and he told her about the work he did and the people he ate his lunch with. But he seemed distracted, or troubled, as if he was trying to solve a problem that he wasn't telling her about.

Lina would ride back to the doctor's house after these visits with thoughts struggling against each other in her mind. She missed the old Doon, her clever, adventurous partner. And she herself felt different here, too. She didn't know what to do or how to be. Some of the people were trying to be kind, but there was so much unkindness mixed in with the kindness.

To the people of Sparks, the people of Ember were just a nuisance. How could they stay in a place where they weren't wanted?

This world was huge. There must be another place in it for the people of Ember.

CHAPTER 11

Tick's Projects

By the month of Burning, it was so hot that the people of Ember felt as if they were trapped in a huge oven. The sun blazed down, the grasses dried to a brownish yellow, the roads were deep in dust. People gasped and sneezed and wilted. All they wanted was to lie down in the shade, or wade deep into the cool water of the river. But the work went on as always—in the ferocious heat, they hauled garbage, cleaned out the goat pens, pulled weeds in the fields, shoveled manure. When they flopped down on the ground to rest or stopped every few minutes for a drink of water, the workers of Sparks glared at them and grumbled. They suspected them of being lazy, and that made the people of Ember angry. Resentment increased on both sides, until any little accident could flare up into a fight.

At the Pioneer Hotel, the mood grew more and more grim. At first, it had been rather fun to live there, especially for the smaller children, who explored the hidden corners of the huge old building, held races in the long corridors, and played colossal games of hide-and-seek. Lizzie Bisco liked going into the Ladies' Room on the ground floor, where there was still a large fragment of mirror attached to the wall. She could see almost her entire self in it, which pleased her on the days when she had just washed her hair in the river or found a bit of colored cloth to use as a ribbon.

But for the older people, the Pioneer Hotel quickly stopped feeling like a fine adventure. They didn't like sleeping on piles of pine needles and dry grasses wrapped in bedspreads. It annoyed them to have to go to the river for water, and to have no indoor bathrooms, only outhouses full of bad smells and spiders. They worried that the candles might set things on fire, and they wanted real windows, with glass, to keep the bugs out. Almost two months had passed since they'd arrived in Sparks. In about four months, they would have to leave. If they didn't like living in the hotel, they knew they'd like even less to start from nothing somewhere out in the wilderness. They imagined sleeping with no roof over their heads, having no protection at all from the sun or the bugs, and scratching through the grass for something to eat. No one liked the prospect. In the dim hallways, in the roofless, ruined lobby, and in the dusty ballroom, people gathered in little clusters and spoke to each other in worried tones, and sometimes their worry turned to anger and fear.

One person, however, did not stand around talking: that was Tick Hassler. When he saw a problem, he did something about it. He'd become a sort of leader around the Pioneer Hotel, just by the force of his personality. He started what he called the Pioneer Hotel Rehabilitation Project. He explained his ideas to anyone who would listen, and the way he explained them made them seem instantly exciting and fun.

"Here's what we'll do," he said, the night he announced the first project. It was late evening of a very hot day, nearly dark, and a few people were still sitting out on the steps of the hotel, hoping for a cool breeze. Tick never seemed much affected by the heat. Everyone else was disheveled and sweaty by the end of the day, but Tick always managed to look neat, his hair combed so flat it looked almost polished, his bare arms and legs smooth and brown, his clothes—a plain black T-shirt and black shorts—never torn or stained. He wore his sunglasses almost all the time, and they gave him a commanding and slightly mysterious look.

Doon was there the night Tick announced his first project. It was a relief, after a hard day, to be part of a group of people who were easy with each other, a group with a common purpose. Several of Doon's classmates from the Ember school were part of it, and some boys who had been cart pullers with Tick, and quite a few others. There were some girls, too. Lizzie was always somewhere around Tick, listening eagerly as he talked, or trotting off on an errand of some sort for him. She had stopped wearing the black scarf that signified her mourning for Looper. "I've been sad long enough," she told Doon. "Besides, Tick doesn't think black looks good on me." Now she wore her sunglasses all the time.

"What we're going to do," said Tick, sitting on the low wall that bordered the steps, leaning forward with his elbows on his knees, and speaking in a way that made you feel his words were meant just for you, "is get ourselves organized. There's a lot that needs to be done around here." People nodded. "The first thing we need," Tick went on, "is a gathering place, like the Gathering Hall back in Ember. And what's the perfect spot for it?" He held out his hands, palms facing the sky, waiting for an answer.

No one spoke.

"This field, of course!" He swept an arm out, taking in the whole of the big field in front of the hotel, with its rough, weedy ground, scrawny trees, and chunks of concrete and other rubble. "We're going to clear it out. We're going to make it into a grand plaza, better than the one in the village. We can have meetings here, with our leader speaking to us from these steps."

"We don't have a leader," someone said.

"But we will someday, once we decide who's best for the job," Tick said. "I'm going to start on it tomorrow—who wants to work with me?"

And although they had already worked a full day, nearly all of them flung their hands up and volunteered. Doon did, too. It wasn't so much that he wanted to clear the field and make a plaza; he wasn't sure they really needed such a thing. After all, they'd be leaving here before long. But he wanted to be part of this; he didn't want to be left out.

The project got off to a great start: twenty or thirty people were out there every evening, pulling up weeds, digging out rubble, and hacking down trees. Tick was always there, working twice as fast and hard as anyone else and telling them all what terrific progress they were making. It was hard work, but somehow it was fun, too.

Then one night Tick called everyone together and announced that he had a new idea. "We won't stop working on the field," he said, "but I'm going to take a team out to start on another project. We need to build a platform out over the river. It'll get us out toward the deeper part, where we can swim and catch fish and maybe even launch a boat someday. There might be lots of places to explore besides this one. Who wants to work with me?"

Of course everyone wanted to switch over to this

new project. It sounded much more interesting than clearing the field. And besides, people wanted to be on the project Tick was working on.

So a great many of them started helping with the new platform—the dock, Tick said it was called. They ripped boards off the old storage sheds behind the hotel, they piled up rocks in the river to make supports. The field project slowed way down. Hardly anyone was working on it anymore.

And as the weeks went on, Doon began to see that this was how Tick's projects went. He would have an idea and get everyone excited about it. They'd start in to work. Then after a while Tick would have an idea for a new project, and everyone would follow him to that one, while the old project withered away. What Tick seemed to like was the thrill of something new, and the power of being a leader. This slightly dimmed Doon's admiration for Tick. But no one was perfect, after all. Tick had far more energy than most people, and far more ideas, even though they weren't all good ones.

In addition to helping with Tick's projects, Doon had plenty of his own projects to keep him busy. In the early mornings, he helped Clary with the garden she'd put in near the river. He was working on a way to make watering easier for her. He'd seen a pump the villagers had constructed, which used the river's current to push water out into the channels that watered the fields. This pump was fairly simple—a deep hole in the riverbank, with an arrangement of pipes and valves at the bottom. He thought he could figure out how to make one.

In the evenings, by the last of the daylight, Doon read. He was choosing books from the room in back of the Ark every few days now. His choices at first were pretty random—he just grabbed whatever he could reach. But then he'd had a great idea for bringing some sort of order to this vast collection. One day, when he got back to room 215 after work, he'd found Edward Pocket standing by the window, frowning at the sky. Edward looked unhappy. His gnarled hands were tightened into fists, and his mouth was bunched up into a twisted knot.

"Are you all right?" said Doon.

"Oh, I'm fine," said Edward. "I just love sitting around all day doing nothing."

"You're bored," said Doon.

"Yes!" Edward cried. "Yes, yes, yes!" He raised both hands and grabbed wads of his frizzled gray hair and stretched his mouth into a mad grin. "They say I'm too old to work, but I'm not ready to freeze up and die. I don't want to spend my days *chatting.* Or *sleeping.*" He said the words with contempt. "What am I supposed to do with myself?"

And of course Doon had the answer. It was so obvious he didn't know why he hadn't thought of it before. "I know exactly what you can do," he said, and he told Edward Pocket about the books.

Now Edward spent all the daylight hours in the book room, sorting and organizing and arranging the books. He often picked out ones he thought Doon would like and brought them back to the hotel. In this way, Doon learned about bird migrations, cowboys, basketball, whales, mountain climbing, Egyptian history, dog training, French cooking, car repair, and dinosaurs, among other things. Edward even found a book called *Science Projects,* in which there was a chapter that explained how to do an experiment that made electricity. The experiment required things Doon didn't have, but he kept the book anyway, in case he ever got them. You never knew what was going to turn up in the loads the roamers brought to town.

In the meantime, Tick carried on tirelessly with his projects. The dock never did get built. It kept getting torn apart by the river's current. But other projects succeeded. One of Tick's ideas was to hoist the flag of Ember over the Pioneer Hotel. Lottie Hoover, who had worked in one of Ember's city offices, had rolled the flag up and tucked it into her bag just before she rushed down into the Pipeworks to leave. Doon didn't really see the point of flying Ember's flag over the hotel—everyone knew that it was the people of Ember who lived there—but he helped with the project, sawing the limbs off a tall, thin tree to make a flagpole. Soon the flag of the city of Ember, deep blue with a yellow grid, flapped above the Pioneer.

"Beautiful," said Tick, gazing up at it. He turned to the people gathered around him. "We have to show them," he said, "that we're *proud* of being the people of Ember. They have all the advantages right now. They control the food. They control the work teams. They're taller than we are, and stronger. But we can't let any of that matter. If we want them to respect us, we have to respect ourselves."

Several days later, as Doon was walking through the plaza, he noticed that a flag was also flying from the tower of the town hall. It was black with a spray of orange dots rising from the corner—sparks, Doon thought. He wondered if they'd had this flag all along, or if someone had made it and put it up after seeing the one at the Pioneer Hotel.

CHAPTER 12

Caspar Arrives with a Surprise

Lina was sweeping the floor of the kitchen when she heard the thump and shuffle of hooves outside. There was a shout, in a man's voice—"Hello-o-o! Where is everyone?"—and then a shriek from inside the house, running footsteps, and Torren's voice screaming, "Caspar! Caspar! You're home!"

Lina flung down the broom and dashed to the door. There was Torren, clamped onto the front of a very large man, who was rumpling Torren's hair and thumping him on the back. Behind the man was his truck, an especially large one, piled high with boxes and crates, pulled behind two huge oxen with curved horns. They stood breathing noisily, their sides going in and out.

"Well, small brother," said Caspar. "Glad to see me?"

"Yes!" said Torren. He unwrapped his arms from

around his brother's trunk and gazed up at his face. "You were gone so long this time."

"I had to extend my route," said Caspar. "Quite far, in fact. *Quite* far. The work of a roamer gets harder every year."

Lina could see Caspar's resemblance to his brother, Torren—they both had the same small eyes and the same wispy light brown hair. But while Torren was narrow, Caspar was wide. He had a wide, round, rosy-pink face, with a glistening, round chin. It was almost a babyish-looking face, except for the tiny mustache on the upper lip, twisted at both ends into points.

Dr. Hester, who had been picking peas, came out from the side of the house. "Welcome back, traveler," she said.

"Auntie Hester!" cried Caspar, flinging his arms wide. He stood that way while Dr. Hester walked toward him, and when she came close he gave her a hug that lifted her feet in their dusty slippers off the ground.

"Don't do that," she said, her face squashed against Caspar's shoulder.

He dropped her back down. "Can't help it," he said. "You're light as a feather."

"I'm not, either," said the doctor, rubbing her neck. "You're just showing off your muscles."

"Well," said Caspar, "it's true that being a roamer builds muscles." He made a fist and flexed his meaty arm back and forth. "Heavy things to lift, you know.

Some *exceedingly* heavy. Out near the Camp Range foothills a few months ago, I got stuck in the mud and had to lift the whole back end of the truck, which was loaded at the time with—"

Torren jumped up and down at Caspar's side. "Did you bring me a surprise?"

Caspar looked startled. "A surprise?"

"Yes, the way you always do. A surprise for me!"

For a second Lina felt sorry for Torren; the look on his face was so hopeful. She had a feeling that Caspar was more important to Torren than Torren was to Caspar.

Caspar laughed. He had the oddest laugh—*hih-hih-hih-hih,* all on one high, squeaky note. It was hardly a sound of pleasure at all. "Well," he said, "as it happens, I did bring one surprise. It's more of a surprise for everyone, though." He looked back toward his truck. "Are you there?" he called.

"Right here," answered a gruff voice. From behind the truck stepped a woman almost as big as Caspar himself—a massive tree trunk of a woman, with swirls and tangles of red-brown hair falling to her shoulders. She was dressed in faded blue pants and a huge brown shirt. She looked at them, smiling slightly. Her eyes were blue and fierce.

"This is Maddy," said Caspar. "She's my roaming partner."

From Torren there was silence. Dr. Hester held out

her hand and said, "Welcome." The big woman pumped the doctor's hand firmly up and down three times, and then Dr. Hester glanced toward the house and saw Lina standing in the doorway.

"Caspar," she said, turning back to him. "Have you heard about what's happened since you've been gone? About the people who came here from the underground city?"

"I heard some tale like that," said Caspar.

"Lina is one of them," Dr. Hester said. "Come here, Lina."

Lina walked out toward Caspar, who squinted at her and then thrust a hand into the pocket of his pants and pulled out a pair of slightly bent glasses, which he put on. He peered at her through their cracked lenses as she approached. When she got close, he held out an enormous hand. Lina shook it.

"Underground, eh?" said Caspar. The cloudy glasses made his eyes look bigger and dimmer. "Some sort of mole people? But you've got no fur!" He laughed his squeaky laugh again. "Hih-hih-hih!"

Lina smiled politely at this stupid joke. Something about Caspar seemed to be slightly off, she thought.

"Lina's sister, Poppy, is with us, as well," Dr. Hester went on, "and their guardian, Mrs. Murdo."

During all this Torren had been standing very still. His narrow face had closed down: his eyes looked like tiny stones, and his mouth was pinched small. He was staring at Maddy. Suddenly he cried, "But *I'm* supposed to be your partner!"

Caspar blinked at him, as if he'd already forgotten he was there. "You?" he said. "You're much too young."

"I'm almost eleven!" Torren yelled. "I'm big enough!"

"Not quite, little brother," Caspar said. He grinned at Maddy, who gazed back at him calmly. She was like a big rock, Lina thought. Her face didn't move.

Torren scowled. "Don't call me little!" he shouted. He turned and ran toward the house.

Caspar watched him go, lifting his eyebrows slightly. "It's hard for children to accept change," he said. "But they must learn, mustn't they?"

Dr. Hester said, "Our three guests have been sleeping in the loft, Caspar. They'll have to sleep in the main room while you're here." She paused. "How long do you think you'll stay?"

"Just a night or two," said Caspar. His face took on a serious look. "I'm on a particular mission this time. Heading for the city."

The city? thought Lina. What city?

The doctor echoed her thought. "The city?" she said. "Why in the world would you go there?" She seemed astonished, as if she'd never heard before of anyone going to the city.

"Because of this particular mission," Caspar said. "Of a secret nature."

"I see," said Dr. Hester. "All right, then. It's nearly time to eat. Take your beasts down to the barn, and then come on in."

That night, Caspar talked a great deal about his exploits as a roamer. "In the northern forest lands," he said, "I came upon some old cabins that still had glass in the windows. It was quite a trick to get the glass out without breaking it—took four days—but I managed. Did cut my hand a bit." He extended his large hand and pointed out a tiny scar on the palm. "Quite a lot of blood from that. Then up near Hogmarsh, I found a very valuable item." He gazed around at them, smiling slightly.

"What was it?" asked Torren, who had forgotten for the moment to be mad at his brother.

"An ancient statue," said Caspar. "It depicts some very rare sort of bird, with a long neck and only one leg. You can see that it was once painted pink." He paused to let the wonder of this sink in.

"Pink, tink, stink," said Poppy. "Pinky stinky." She stared at Caspar and giggled.

"Hush, Poppy," said Lina.

"Then in Ardenwood," Caspar went on, idly twisting his tiny mustache, "I had to fend off a few bandits."

"Bandits?" cried Torren. "Really?"

"Well, they might as well have been bandits,"

Caspar said. "Turned out they had no weapons, but they were set on stealing from me, that's for sure. I got rid of them fast with a few well-placed lashes." Caspar sliced his arm through the air, as if he were cracking a whip. "And a good thing, too," he went on, "because not far from there I located another special thing—several boxes of authentic, pre-Disaster artificial flowers. They are made of very fine cloth, hardly faded at all."

"Artificial flowers?" said Lina, wondering why the people of Sparks would want fake flowers when they had real ones growing everywhere.

"Yes," said Caspar. "I have a sort of knack for finding unusual things."

Maddy didn't join much in the conversation. Once Mrs. Murdo, being polite, asked her if she too enjoyed being a roamer, but she only smiled a little and said, "I don't mind it. There are worse things to be."

Mrs. Murdo waited to hear about the worse things, but it seemed that was all she was going to say.

When it was bedtime, Caspar went up into the loft and Torren dashed up after him. Maddy took Torren's place in the medicine room, saying a brief good-night and closing the door firmly after her. The doctor helped Lina and Mrs. Murdo make up beds of pads and blankets on the couch and on the floor.

"It sounds interesting to be a roamer," Lina said.

"I suppose so," said the doctor.

"And Caspar has a special knack for finding things?"

The doctor bent over and spoke softly into Lina's ear. "He has a knack for finding the *wrong* things," she said. "He's always bringing loads of things people already have, and not finding the things people really need. Artificial flowers," she said wearily. "What are we going to do with artificial flowers?" The bed being made up, she went around the room and blew out all the candles but one. "He's always been a bit odd," said the doctor. "Looks as if he's gotten even odder since he was here last. He tries hard, though, you can say that for him. He has high ambitions. He wants to be a famous roamer. He doesn't know that he's a bit famous already, among the other roamers—but not famous the way he'd like."

She handed the last candle to Lina and stumped off to her room.

The next day was strange and unpleasant. Caspar sat in the big armchair telling stories about his adventures while Torren hovered around him asking questions. Lina listened for a while. She was curious about this work of roaming—it sounded exciting, like something she might want to do herself. But she soon got bored, because it seemed to her that Caspar never said much about the really interesting parts of his adventures. She wanted to hear what the faraway places were like, and how the old buildings looked, and everything that was in the buildings, but all Caspar talked about was how brave and clever he'd been to find the things he found, and what injuries he'd suffered in finding them.

Maddy didn't listen to Caspar; she spent most of her time in the courtyard or the garden, motionless and silent, gazing at the plants, her arms folded across her wide waist. Every now and then she plucked a leaf or blossom, rubbed it between her fingers, and sniffed it. Once she asked Lina what a certain plant was. "I'm not sure," Lina said. "I only know a few of them."

"Then you know more than I do," said Maddy, flashing Lina an unexpected smile. But other than that, she said almost nothing to anyone. She didn't seem angry or unhappy, just off in her own world. Lina wondered about her but felt far too shy to ask questions.

After a while, Caspar shooed Torren away, sat down at the table, and pulled some scraps of paper from his pocket. He spread them out and bent over them, and his jovial, boastful manner changed. He ran his finger along the lines of writing on the papers. He wrote on them with a stubby pencil. And as he did so, he frowned and muttered and mumbled to himself, words that sounded like nonsense to Lina except for an occasional string of numbers. "Mmmbgl bblbble 3578," he would say. "Throobbm wullgm fflunnnph

44209." She wandered up behind him and tried to look over his shoulder. After all, she had experience with torn documents and hard-to-decipher bits of writing. But Caspar twisted around and scowled at her, holding his hands over the papers. "Private! Private! Keep away," he said. He wouldn't let Torren see, either, so Torren sat on the window seat and sulked.

Around midafternoon, the doctor rushed in the door looking even more frazzled than usual. Her shirt was smudged with blood, and her shirttails were half tucked in and half not. "I'm out of clean bandages," she said. "Lina, did you do them? I need some. And I need that lavender extract—a bottle of it. No, I'd better get two bottles." She hurried into the medicine room.

Lina had forgotten all about the bandages. She dashed into the kitchen, pulled some rags from the basket, and tore them into strips. She took these to the doctor, who was on her knees, rummaging through a chest.

"And," said the doctor, "I'm going to have to make some mustard plasters tonight. You'll need to go out into the orchard and gather me some mustard flowers. I'll need a lot. Get the leaves, too, and the roots. I want the whole plant." She found her bottles of oil, thrust them into her bag along with the bandages, and rushed out the door again.

Lina felt her spirits sink down into her shoes. She didn't want to gather mustard plants. It was too hot. It was *ferociously* hot. She was sick of being hot, having her neck damp beneath her long hair and her clothes sticking to her back. She was sick of doing chores. She shuffled out into the courtyard, where a few of the doctor's seedlings were drying up in their pots. She trudged to the pump, filled a bucket, and splashed some water on each limp plant. Then she sat down in the shade of the grapevine and leaned against the wall beneath the window and thought about everything that was wrong.

She was mad at the doctor for giving her so much work to do and hardly noticing when she did it. She was mad at Mrs. Murdo for not moving them out to the Pioneer Hotel. And she was lonely. She missed being with people she knew. Especially, she missed being with Doon in the old way, the way they'd been together when they were partners in Ember. Now he seemed to care more for his new friends than he did for her. Every time she thought about him, she felt a thud of pain, like a bruised place inside her.

From the window just above her head, Lina heard Caspar's voice. "Not now!" he said. "I have to do some planning. I need quiet."

The door opened, and Torren stormed out. He threw a furious glance at Lina but didn't speak. He ran through the gate and up the road. He's mad, too, thought Lina. Everyone's mad.

From inside, she heard Caspar's voice again,

startlingly near. He was talking to Maddy, who must have come in the kitchen door. Lina realized they were standing by the window, just behind her.

"We'll head out day after tomorrow," said Caspar. "Starting early."

"Uh-huh," said Maddy in her low, growly voice.

"All those stories about germs still lurking there," Caspar said, "they're nonsense, you know. Those germs died out long ago."

"No doubt you're right," said Maddy.

They were talking about the city! Lina sat very still and listened harder.

"People talk about other kinds of danger there, too," Caspar went on. "Bandits and so on. Doesn't bother *me*."

"Of course not," Maddy said.

"And anyway, even if there is danger," said Caspar, "it's worth the risk, because of what we're going to find."

"You sound very sure that we're going to find it," said Maddy.

"Of course I'm sure," said Caspar. "Aren't you?"

The answer to this was just a grunt.

They moved away from the window, and their voices grew fainter. Maddy spoke next. Lina couldn't hear all of what she said, but she caught the words "How far?" and in Caspar's answer she heard the words "day's journey." Then she heard steps clomping up the stairs to the loft, and the room went quiet.

Lina sat very still. Her bad mood faded. Other thoughts swirled in her mind. She was remembering the sparkling city whose picture she had drawn so many times, the great city of light, the city she had always believed in. Now Caspar was planning to go there. It wasn't dangerous anymore, and it was only a day's journey away.

She knew, of course, that the city Caspar was talking about had been damaged, like everything else, in the Disaster. The beautiful, shining city she had imagined must have been this city in the past, in the time before the Disaster. In her mind, she revised her vision of the city: some of the high towers would have toppled, and their windows would be broken. Stones from ruined buildings would have fallen into the street. Roofs would have caved in.

But the idea that struck her was this: maybe the people of Ember were meant to restore the city. Perhaps their great job—the reason they had come up into this new world—was to live in the city and rebuild it, so that once again it was the glorious, shining city of Lina's vision.

This was *such* a beautiful idea. That night, she lay in bed thinking about it, and the more she thought, the more sure she was, and the more excited.

CHAPTER 13

Taking Action

One evening Doon wandered off by himself toward the far corner of the hotel, where the trees grew thickly and the undergrowth beneath them was dense. He made his way into the woods, to a thicket of vines all woven together like thorny ropes. Little lumpy fruits, some red and some black, grew on these vines. Doon had already discovered that the red ones were hard and sour, but if left to ripen they turned black and sweet. He had been checking the vines regularly; each day there were more and more of the black ones. Today, he saw, there were more black berries than red. He began picking them. Some he ate right from the vine—they were sweet and juicy. Others he put in a basket he'd brought with him to take back to the others in room 215.

He heard footsteps behind him. A voice—he recognized it instantly—called out, "Doon!" He turned around, and there was Tick striding toward him, smiling his dazzling smile.

Doon stood up—he'd been squatting to reach for the berries on the lowest vines. "Look what I found," he said, holding out a handful of berries to Tick.

Tick took one and popped it into his mouth. His eyebrows shot up in surprise. "Terrific!" he said. He took the rest of them from Doon's palm. "So," he said, "are you going to save us again?"

"Save us?" said Doon, confused.

"Yes, from starvation. You're the hero of Ember. It's about time for you to save us again."

It flustered Doon to be called a hero. He wasn't sure if Tick was admiring him or making fun of him. He couldn't think what to say next.

Tick reached into the thicket and plucked a few berries for himself. "These are good," he said. "Mind if I take some?"

"They don't belong to me," said Doon. "Anyone can have them."

Tick hunted among the vines for a while, picking berries and popping them into his mouth. Then he said, "You know that building they call the Ark?"

Doon nodded.

"Ever been in it?"

"No," Doon said. "Just in the separate room at the back. They have books in there—you should see them, there must be thousands."

Tick didn't comment on the books. "I went in there the other day," he said. "They had me carry in a crate of pickled beets. It's their storehouse, you know. They say they're short of food. Hah!" Tick gave a laugh that was more like a bark. "That place is *full* of food."

"Really?" said Doon.

"Really," said Tick, tossing three berries into his mouth. "There's jars of preserved fruit, and sacks of dried fruit, and every kind of pickle, and bags of corn—loads and loads of food. And we get limp carrots for our dinners. I believe there's a bit of stinginess going on."

Doon frowned. He thought of his father, looking with dismay last night at the scanty contents of his dinner parcel. He thought about what Ordney had said at lunch the week before: *We just don't have enough for four hundred extra people.* Was this untrue after all?

Tick had moved a few steps away and found a patch that was thick with berries. He was picking them rapidly, eating each one. When he spoke, his words sounded a little juicy. "I don't know about you," he said, "but I don't like unfairness."

"I don't, either," said Doon. He walked over to Tick and offered him the handful of berries he'd just collected. Tick took them all.

"I believe an unfair situation needs to be corrected," Tick said.

"Corrected how?"

Tick wiped his red-stained fingers on his pants. "Well," he said, "that's something we have to figure out."

We, thought Doon. He liked that. Though he'd stopped taking part so often in Tick's projects, still he admired Tick's energy and felt his power. He was glad Tick had sought him out. He was glad that Tick seemed to consider him different from the others, smarter, more important. "You're right," he said. "We should do something."

Tick nodded. "I don't trust these Sparks people," he said. "In some ways, they seem very primitive. Do you know that they make fire by hitting two stones together?"

"They do?" Doon hadn't seen anyone starting a fire, since he was rarely in kitchens. He knew that the fire in the bakery was kept going all the time; he'd seen people going in there sometimes carrying candles that had gone out. "They don't have matches?" he said.

"Sometimes they do," said Tick. "But not always. Matches seem to be rare."

"We should give them some of ours," said Doon. All the people who'd come out of Ember had the matches that were supplied with the boats. The Emberites had hundreds of matches.

"Oh, I don't think so," Tick said quickly. "We need them. We have to keep those for ourselves."

Doon wondered why, when they had so many; but

he thought maybe matches figured somehow in Tick's plans.

"So you're with me?" said Tick.

"Sure," said Doon. Then he hesitated. "With you in what?"

"Action," said Tick. "You took action before, when there was an urgent situation. We may need to take action again pretty soon."

Doon still didn't know what Tick had in mind, but he asked no more questions. Tick had a way of letting you know that he'd given all the answers he was going to give. "All right," Doon said. "I'm with you."

"Good," said Tick. He held out his hand, and Doon shook it. Tick grinned and walked away.

Doon watched him lope across the field. For a moment he was lost in his thoughts—*food in the storehouse, stinginess, unfairness, figure something out, you're with me. . . .* When he came to himself again and glanced down at his hands, he was startled to see them streaked with blood. Had he scratched himself on the thorns of the vines? It took him a second to realize that what looked like blood was only berry juice, passed to his hand from Tick's.

Lina made a plan. She'd hide among the boxes and crates on Caspar's truck, and she would ride that way to the city. It was only a day's journey away. Surely she'd be able to find a way back. There must be other roamers on the roads.

Of course, she *could* just ask Caspar if she could go with him. But she was sure he'd say no. He was on some kind of important business. He wouldn't want to be bothered with her. It was best to go secretly. Once she had seen the city, she would know if it was the place where the people of Ember were destined to live. She was sure she'd know as soon as she saw it. Then she could hop out of the truck and find her way back. Caspar might never see her at all.

The next day, she tore part of a blank page out of one of the doctor's books and wrote this note:

> *Dear Mrs. M,*
>
> *I have gone with Caspar and Maddy on the truck. I will be back in two days or maybe three. There is something important I want to find out. Also I need a change from here. See you soon.*
>
> *Love, Lina*

Her plan was to wait until that night, when Mrs. Murdo was asleep, and tuck the note between the pages of the ancient, crumbling book she had been reading, something called *Charlotte's Web.* (She kept urging Lina to look at it, but Lina said she wasn't that interested in spiders—it would be better for Doon.) Mrs. Murdo read only in the evening, so Lina would have at least a day's head start before anyone knew where she was.

A few doubts about her plan lurked in the back of Lina's mind. She knew Mrs. Murdo would worry about her. Poppy would miss her. And Lina didn't really like Caspar, or trust him, and she knew that he and Maddy would probably be angry if they found that she had come along. It was a bit of a risky journey she was embarking on. But anything truly important involved risks, didn't it? She had taken a huge risk before, in the last days of Ember, and it had been the right thing to do. So probably this was the right thing, too. She was so sure the city was their destination, and she was so determined to see the city for herself, that she turned her mind away from her doubts. It would be an adventure, she told herself. She would be fine.

She got up before the sun the next morning. She crept out of her bed on the floor one tiny motion at a time. Poppy didn't stir, nor did Mrs. Murdo in her bed on the couch. In the half darkness, Lina put her clothes on and pulled the pillowcase bag she'd packed the night before from its hiding place in the window seat. She tucked her note between the pages of Mrs. Murdo's book. Then, carrying her bag, she opened the door so softly it made no noise and went out into the courtyard.

Just beyond the gate, the truck was standing ready. The oxen weren't attached to it yet; they were down the road, at the barn, to be brought later by the stablehand.

Lina climbed onto the back of the truck. Its metal bottom was gritty with dust and bits of dry grass. It was loaded with four large barrels, two bicycles strapped together, a box full of tubs and buckets, and four big wooden crates made of slats of wood spaced about an inch apart. The crates were taller than Lina and about four feet square—like small rooms, almost. Three of them were full of goods to be sold, but the fourth was empty—its contents had been sold in Sparks. That one would be Lina's hiding place.

Getting into it was easy. First she tossed her bag over the side, and then she climbed up the slats as if they were a ladder and jumped down in. The wood was rough and splintery, but she had prepared for that. She'd brought a small blanket from her bed. She spread this on the bottom of the crate and lay down on it, using her bag of supplies as a pillow. She was sure that if she lay very still, no one would see her.

And she was right. An hour or so later—she didn't know for sure how long, but the sun was now shining through the slats in the crate, and she could feel its warmth on her back—she heard the clatter of the gate latch, and voices. Torren's first:

"But I'd be helpful!" he said in a tearful, desperate wail. "I would! I know how to tie knots, and I can—"

"Now, that's enough," said Caspar. "You're not coming with us, get it through your hard little head. You're not old enough. Roaming is a dangerous business, it's not for children."

"She gets to go," Torren said.

"Of course. She's not a child. She's my partner."

Lina felt a jolt as the box holding Caspar's and Maddy's belongings was heaved up onto the truck. "Here comes Jo with the oxen, right on time," said Caspar.

The truck squeaked and trembled as the oxen were hitched to it. Lina heard the gate latch clatter again, and then the doctor's voice: "When will you be back this way?"

"Not for a while." The truck slanted as Caspar got on. "Several months, is my guess. We've got a big route planned out."

"You should be taking *me*!" cried Torren. "You'll be sorry you didn't! I'll tell on you! I'll tell Uncle!"

Caspar chuckled. "Uncle would not be interested," he said. "He's much too busy. Always has been." There was the crack of a whip. "Goodbye, little brother," Caspar called, and the truck jolted forward.

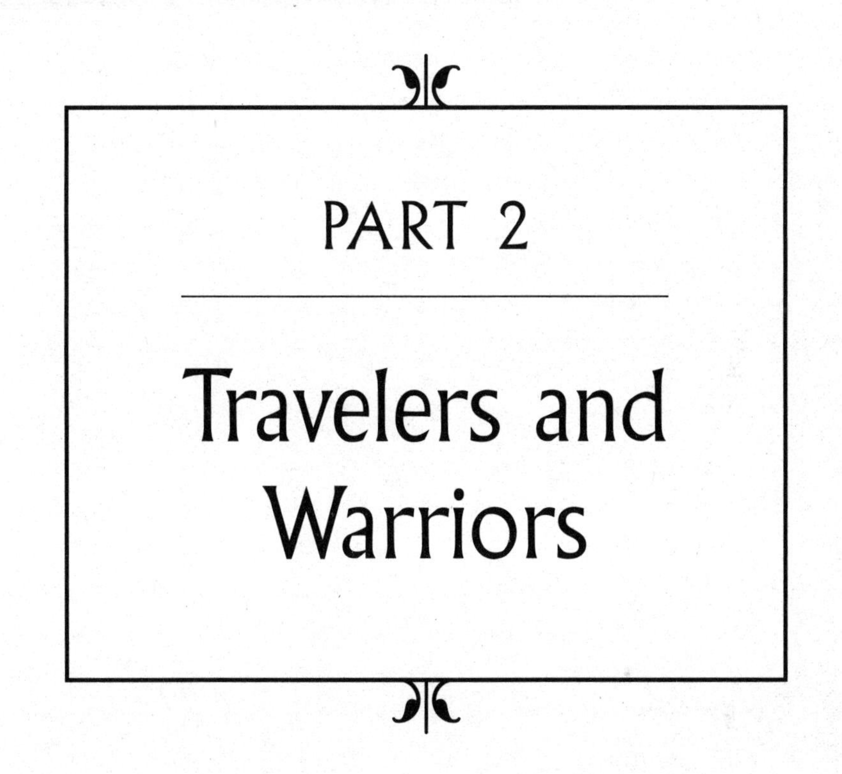

PART 2

Travelers and Warriors

CHAPTER 14

What Torren Did

All day, after Caspar and Maddy left, Mrs. Murdo wondered where Lina was. Had the doctor sent her on an errand? She asked, but the answer was no. Did Torren know where she was? He said he didn't know and he didn't care. Thinking maybe Lina had gone to the Pioneer Hotel to see Doon, Mrs. Murdo walked down there. But no one had seen her. By evening, when Lina was still missing, Mrs. Murdo was very worried.

She found the note in her book that night. She frowned as she read it. This didn't seem like a good idea to her. It was one of Lina's rash, impulsive acts, and probably it was dangerous. Mrs. Murdo went downstairs, knocked on the doctor's door, and showed her the note. "Can we send someone after them?" she said. "To bring her back?"

But the doctor shook her head. "They're a whole day ahead," she said. "No one could catch up. Even if you could find someone willing to go."

So Mrs. Murdo went back to bed and tried to sleep. She told herself that Lina had survived many dangers before. But still she lay awake worrying most of the night.

In the morning, at breakfast, Torren asked where Lina was and Mrs. Murdo told him. He jumped up from his chair. He threw down his piece of bread, which bounced on the table. "*She went with them?*" he cried. "She went with Caspar?"

"Calm down," said Dr. Hester.

"No!" yelled Torren. "I won't calm down! I hate her! I hate all you cave people! Why did you have to come here and ruin everything?" With a furious swipe of his hand, he knocked over Mrs. Murdo's cup of tea. He kicked backward at his chair, which fell over, and he ran out of the room. Through the window, Mrs. Murdo saw him racing across the courtyard and out the gate.

"Jealous," said the doctor. "He wants Caspar all to himself. Heaven knows why."

"That boy craves attention," said Mrs. Murdo. "I doubt that he cares who it comes from."

"I suppose you're right," said the doctor, looking at Mrs. Murdo with faint surprise.

Torren sped down the river road, full of boiling rage. *He* was the one who should be sitting beside Caspar, not that fat Maddy and not the stupid cave girl. *He* should be there, riding on the truck, going away to be a roamer. But she had snuck off and done it instead, and he hated her for it. It was the worst thing that had happened to him in his whole life.

He ran a long way, his feet pounding the dusty road, his fists pumping back and forth, furious tears streaming down his face. When he stopped, panting, he was way out in the tomato field, not far from the wind tower, where he had been the day the cave people came over the hill. He remembered how they had looked—like a swarm of horrible insects coming down toward the village.

Now the cave people had settled in as if they were going to stay forever. They were eating food that should belong to Sparks people. They were wearing clothes that Sparks people had given them. They walked around in the streets of Sparks as if they belonged here. Torren wanted them gone.

He stomped among the tomato plants, throwing punches at the air. "Get out of here, get out!" he cried, as if Lina and all the Emberites were there to hear him. His thoughts were like flames inside his head. He kept seeing Caspar on the seat of his truck with Maddy on one side of him and Lina on the other. The feeling that went with this picture was like a sharp stick in his stomach.

If only he had one of those giant bombs they had

in the old days! He imagined they were about the size of watermelons. He would shoot one at Lina! *Pow!* It would sail halfway to the city and drop right on Caspar's truck and blow them all up! Then he would shoot another one at the Pioneer Hotel. *Blam!* It would flatten the building and blow up every one of the cave people. He longed to throw that big bomb. He could almost feel it in his hands.

He'd come out at the end of the row of plants now, where a small whitewashed storage shed stood at the edge of the field. Crates of tomatoes were stacked nearby, ready to be distributed. Without thinking, Torren grabbed a tomato from the nearest crate and hurled it against the wall of the shed. It splattered. Red water dripped down the white wall. It felt so good to do this that he did it again. In a fury, he snatched up one tomato after another. *Wham, wham, wham,* he flung them with all his might, until the window of the shed splintered, the wall was a bleeding mess, and a long mound of broken red flesh lay on the ground.

He stopped and took a breath. What would the farmers think when they saw *this*? Two whole crates of tomatoes, smashed. They'd be angry. But they wouldn't know he had done it, would they? No one had seen him.

And that was when an idea floated into Torren's mind. A really excellent idea. He smiled, thinking about it. He threw one last tomato, aiming for the dark, glass-toothed hole of the broken window. There was a satisfying crash as the tomato knocked something over inside. Torren turned and ran, but he didn't go all the way home.

When Doon came through town that morning on the way to work, he found Mrs. Murdo waiting for him by the side of the road. She signaled to him with one finger, and he left the stream of workers and came over to her.

"Lina has gone off," she said. "I thought you should know."

"Gone off? Gone off where?"

Mrs. Murdo produced a scrap of paper from the pocket of her skirt. "Read this," she said.

Doon read. He scrunched up his nose in puzzlement. He remembered Lina telling him something the other day about these people, Caspar and Maddy. What had she said? He tried to recall. He looked again at the note. "'Something important,' she says. What would that be?"

Mrs. Murdo shrugged her thin shoulders. "She gets ideas in her head," she said. Doon could see that she was worried, though she didn't say so.

"Well, she says she'll be back in two or three days," said Doon. "That's not so long."

"The odd thing is," said Mrs. Murdo, "that Caspar, when he left, said he wouldn't be back for several months."

Doon frowned. What was Lina up to? He didn't understand it. But he didn't want to make Mrs. Murdo more worried than she was. "She must have some plan for getting back," he said, handing back the note.

"Of course," said Mrs. Murdo briskly. She folded the note and replaced it in her pocket. "There's no need to worry. I'll have her come and find you as soon as she returns."

She headed back toward the doctor's house, and Doon went toward the fields. He walked slowly to give himself time to think. He was upset about Lina. How could she be so foolish as to launch herself out into an unknown world with two unknown people? But in a way he wasn't surprised. Lina was always eager to investigate new places. Look how she'd gone up to the roof of the Gathering Hall on the first day she became a messenger in Ember. Look how eager she'd been to go down into the Pipeworks. She probably just wanted to see what was outside of Sparks. As soon as she'd satisfied her curiosity, she'd be back.

But Doon was upset about Lina for another reason, too, and it didn't have to do with her safety. He was upset that she had gone exploring without him. All through the last days of Ember, they'd been partners. Now she had gone off on her own, leaving him here.

He was annoyed, and he was hurt. He had to admit to himself that he hadn't been a very good friend to Lina lately. Maybe he'd hurt her feelings by paying so much attention to Tick. But still—it was *Lina* who was his partner in important things. If she had an urgent reason for hitching a ride with Caspar, why hadn't she told him? Why hadn't she asked him to come along?

He trudged toward the tomato field, head down, scuffing his shoes irritably in the dust, and so he didn't notice until he was right up to it that a commotion was going on by the storage shed. Everyone was crowded around it, and Chugger the team leader was yelling. Doon hurried forward to see what was going on.

"Wasted! Wasted!" Chugger was shouting. "Two whole crates, smashed! Who's done this? And the shed plastered with muck, and the window broken!" He glared at the crowd of workers. "Any of you know about this?" he demanded. "Anyone know what mad person did this?"

No one said a word. Doon stared with horror at the mess on the wall. It looked gory, as if it were smashed animals instead of just tomatoes. He could feel the rage of the person who had done it.

"I don't like this," Chugger said darkly. "Nothing like this ever happened before you people arrived. I want it cleaned up right away. Walls washed, window fixed, mess cleared away. Get on it."

"Listen," said someone. Doon turned to see—it

was Tick speaking. "We didn't do this. Don't get all tough with us."

Chugger whipped around. "Who else would do it? Who else but one of you, always griping and grumbling?"

"But we only just got here now—how could we have done it?" someone called out.

"Besides, we wouldn't!" cried someone else. "We would never waste food!"

More and more voices rose in protest. Doon added his, too, saying, "It wasn't us, it couldn't have been!" But Chugger just stood and scowled at them. Finally he yelled, "Quiet! Get to work!" Just after that Doon heard running footsteps behind him and turned to see Torren racing across the field. He was shouting in his shrill, high voice as he came.

"I saw!" he cried, waving his arms. "Last night I was out here, and I saw!" He ran into the midst of the workers and stood panting, his little eyes wild. "I heard a thump, thump, thump, so I snuck up to see, and I *did* see!"

"Well, then," said Chugger, "what did you see?"

"I saw who threw the tomatoes! I saw who made that big mess and broke the window!" He stood with his neck poked forward and his skinny arms held tight to his sides. His whole body was trembling with excitement. His eyes scanned the group of workers. "It was him!" he shrieked, pointing straight at Doon. "It was him that did it! I saw him!"

Doon was so shocked he couldn't make a sound. He stood with his mouth open, staring at Torren. Around him, a few people spoke up. "He did not!" said someone. "He couldn't have! Anyway, he wouldn't." "No," someone else said. "He would never do that."

But Chugger seized his arm and pulled him roughly aside. "What do you have to say for yourself? Is this your doing?"

Doon shook his head. "No," he said. "No. That boy is lying."

"And why would he do that? Why would he take the trouble to come out here first thing in the morning to point to you and lie?"

"I don't know," said Doon.

Chugger released his arm with a push. "I'll be keeping a special eye on you from now on," he said.

"But why?" said Doon. "I didn't do this."

"How do I know that?" said Chugger. "It's your word against his. And he's one of us."

CHAPTER 15

A Long, Hot Ride

Lina lay very still—or as still as she could with the jolting of the truck over the rutted road. Her eyes were at the level of the space between the two lowest slats of the crate, so she could see out just enough to guess where they were—along the road by the river first, and then turning to go around the outskirts of the village. Occasionally she heard someone call a greeting to Caspar, and she heard Caspar's voice returning it. Maddy never said anything that Lina could hear.

After a while there were no more voices. The sun beat down on Lina's back and she began to get terribly hot and uncomfortable. She thought it might be safe to sit up now. The sound of the wheels would muffle any sounds she made, and she was far enough toward the back of the truck so that Caspar and Maddy wouldn't see her moving. So she unfolded herself. She peered out and saw emptiness—vast stretches of dry, brown-gold grass, no people, no houses. It was an enormous space; she had not realized any place could be so big.

Sometime in the afternoon, because of the heat and the rocking motion of the truck and because there was nothing else to do, Lina went to sleep. When she awoke, she could tell right away that it was nearly evening. The air was cooler, and the sun was so low in the sky that she could no longer see it overhead; its slanting rays came between the slats of her crate.

A cramp gripped her stomach. It was partly hunger—she hadn't thought to bring any food with her. But it was mostly fear. They must be close to the city. And when they arrived, what would she do? And what would Caspar do when he found her?

The truck slowed and came to a stop. Lina felt Caspar and Maddy jump down.

"This looks like a good enough place," said Caspar's voice. "Near the water, anyhow."

"Looks all right to me." That was Maddy's voice.

"I'll take the animals down to the stream," said Caspar. Lina heard clanking and slapping sounds as he unbuckled the harness, and then the slow thud of hooves as the oxen were led away.

What was Maddy doing? Lina heard a few footsteps, some rustling among the grasses. Then there was silence. She had to move. Her legs were cramped and she had a pain in her back. Cautiously, she stood up.

She stepped onto the first slat of the crate and then the second, and when she got high enough to look over the top edge, the first thing she saw was Maddy, sitting on the ground a few feet from the end of the truck, leaning against a tree and staring right at her.

"Well, well," said Maddy. "Look who's here."

Lina just stared. She couldn't move.

Maddy heaved herself up from the ground and came over to the truck. She regarded Lina with a look that was half puzzled and half amused. "What in the world are you doing here?"

"I want to see the city," said Lina.

"Don't you know it's a five-day journey? How did you expect to ride in a crate all that time? And not be discovered?"

"Five days? I thought it was one day."

Maddy just shook her head. "What are we supposed to do with you?"

"I don't know," said Lina. She felt a trembling start up in her stomach. She should never have come.

There was a long pause before Maddy spoke again. Then she said, "Listen. It would suit me fine if you came along to the city, if you're sure you want to."

"I do want to," Lina said, though she wasn't really sure.

"Good," said Maddy, "because it looks like you have no choice." She smiled. It wasn't an unfriendly smile, but there was a quirk in it that seemed to say,

What a situation. "Stay there, then," she said. "I'll be back." She stamped away.

Lina watched Maddy heading toward a strip of green grasses and low trees that must border the stream; at the edge of this strip she could see Caspar and the oxen. In all directions, the landscape was the same she'd seen that morning—gently rolling, empty of buildings, covered with brown-gold grass. Here and there stood low, dark green, mushroom-shaped trees. Three of them stood near the truck, their leaves dusty, their trunks thick and gnarled. The sun had gone down behind the hills in the west, and the sky there was scarlet. Though the air was still warm, Lina shivered. She sat back down in the crate, pulled her knees up to her chest, and wrapped her arms around them. Somewhere a bird sang its going-to-bed song.

Then suddenly there were loud footsteps and Caspar's voice coming toward her, and in a moment Caspar's fist thudding against the crate. "Come out!" he said.

Lina climbed out and stood on the truck looking down at him.

"Jump down!" he said.

She jumped down.

Caspar glared at her. "So," he said. "A stowaway. What were you trying to do? Cause trouble? That's your idea of fun?"

"No," Lina said. "I want to see the city."

"What for?" A look of suspicion passed over Caspar's face. "What do you know about the city?"

"Nothing," said Lina. She wasn't going to tell Caspar about her vision of the city, or what the city might be for the people of Ember. "I just want to see it."

"Well, too bad," said Caspar. "Why should I take you there? Why would I want an extra person to feed? A kid to look after? Your ride stops right here. You can go back where you came from."

"One second," said Maddy. "Listen to me before you decide. She could be useful to us."

"Don't be ridiculous." Caspar whacked his two big hands together as if to dismiss the subject.

"Yes, she could," said Maddy. "When you're looking for something in a ruined place—you know how it is. Small spaces, sometimes. Tippy rubble where you need to step carefully. A small, light person could go where we couldn't."

Caspar took a step back and studied Lina, still glowering. Lina tried to look as small and light as she could.

"As for food," said Maddy, "she can share mine."

"Ridiculous," said Caspar again. But he kept his eyes on Lina. She could see he was thinking.

"Come on, Caspar," Maddy said. "Let's take her. We don't have much choice, after all. The only other thing we can do is leave her out here by herself." She turned to Lina. "If we let you come," she said, "you'll have to work for us. You'll have to do what we say."

"All right," Lina said, though she wasn't sure it was all right at all. Maybe it would be better to give up seeing the city and try to get back to Sparks from here. But how would she do that? She'd never be able to find her way. And the Empty Lands frightened her; she didn't want to be alone in such a vast, wild place. "But how will I get back again? Will you take me?"

"You should have thought of that when you climbed onto the truck," said Caspar. "That's your problem, not ours." He turned to Maddy. "Right, partner?"

"Certainly," Maddy said. "Now let's get settled for the night. The first thing we need is some kindling. Lina and I will go and gather it."

Lina followed her out toward the trees. Once they were in among them, Maddy bent down and spoke to her in a low voice. "Don't worry. You were foolish to do this, but I won't let harm come to you. And I'll see you get home again, somehow." She straightened up again. "Now," she said. "Gather up some dry twigs and sticks and a few tufts of dry grass."

They carried the sticks and grass back to where the truck was parked. There Maddy scraped out a shallow hole in the ground with the heel of her shoe. In the hole she set the smallest splinters of wood, arranging them in a sort of square. Over these she placed some sticks, and on top of those she added larger branches. She tucked in some handfuls of dried grass at the bottom of this stick building.

Until this point, Lina did not understand what she was doing. But when she pulled from her pocket a little cloth-wrapped package, unwrapped it, and took out a short blue-tipped stick, she knew. She took in a quick breath and stepped backward.

Maddy held up one of the matches and said, "Have you ever seen one of these?"

"Yes," said Lina.

"You're lucky, then," said Maddy. "They're rare."

She struck the match across a rock and the blue tip burst into flame. She held it to the grass, and the grass sizzled and flared up.

"Come and stand close," she said to Lina. "We need to shield this from the breeze until it gets going."

But Lina stayed where she was, staring. The little flame at the heart of the stack of sticks flickered. It reached for the splintered end of a stick, caught it, set it aflame. The sizzling grew to a hissing, and then to a crackling. Flames jumped, and jumped higher, and there again was the orange hand stretching upward with its pointed fingers, waving, leaning toward her.

Lina stumbled backward. She didn't want to be afraid—Caspar and Maddy weren't. Caspar had come back now and was crouching right beside the fire, feeding it with sticks and grass. But for Lina it was as if the flames were shrieking a message at her: Run, run, run! She stood twenty feet away, staring at the fire with a pounding heart. The wind blew a ribbon of smoke at her, and when she breathed, it stung the back of her throat.

Maddy noticed, after a while, that she was out there. "Come closer, Lina," she called. "It won't hurt you."

But Lina could not get her feet to walk toward that hissing, snapping blaze. It might not hurt Maddy and Caspar; but if she were to stand near it, she was sure it would reach for her with that orange hand, flick its fingers against the ends of her hair or the hem of her shirt, and she too would flare up. "I'm all right here," she said. "I don't want to be near it."

Caspar laughed. Maddy lumbered to her feet and came beside Lina. She put an arm around her. "You're shaking," she said. "Well, never mind. You don't have to be by the fire if you don't want to."

From a box on the truck, she took what they called "travelers' cakes"—lumps a little smaller than a fist, made of Lina knew not what—and she and Caspar stuck them on the end of long sticks and roasted them over the flames. "You have to get fond of these if you're a roamer," Caspar said. "They keep well, that's their best quality. You need them for those long stretches where there's no other food to be found."

They were dry and tasteless, but Lina was hungry,

so she didn't mind much. She ate hers standing up, and she licked her fingers when she was through.

She wondered where they were going to sleep. There was no room on the truck, so she supposed they'd have to lie on the ground. It was quite dark now. A breeze had come up. From somewhere far away, she heard an animal noise: *yip-yip-yip,* then a long wail, then an eerie chorus of wails. "What's that?" she asked Maddy.

"Wolves," Maddy said. "Out hunting. They're not very close, don't worry."

Lina shivered. The darkness here was so enormous, and so full of terrible things. In Ember, except when there was a blackout, people were almost always safe in their beds when darkness came. Lina wasn't used to being outside at night. She thought about Mrs. Murdo, who would be getting into bed in the doctor's attic room right now. Mrs. Murdo would be worried about her. Poppy would be saying, "Where Wyna?" No one would imagine that she was out in this great emptiness, with nothing between her and the sky.

Maddy took some rolled-up blankets from the truck and spread them on the ground. She put two of them close to the fire. The third she offered to Lina. "Put this wherever you want to sleep," she said.

Lina walked over to take the blanket, and as she did, Caspar tossed a big branch onto the fire. Sparks sprayed up. Some flew sideways, caught by the wind.

Lina jumped away, but a few sparks landed on her sock. She stamped her foot frantically, but this only made the sparks burn brighter. The threads of her sock glowed. On her ankle she felt a pain like a fierce bite. "No!" she cried. "Get it off me!" She shook her leg and clawed at her sock with her hand. Panic rose up in her, and she would have taken off running if Maddy had not blocked her path and grabbed her in strong arms. Once she'd stopped her, she bent down and put a hand over the burning place in Lina's sock, and when she took her hand away the glow was out.

But the pain was still there. Maddy took off Lina's shoe and sock and poured cold water on the burn, but it didn't help much. All night, Lina huddled on the ground under the thin blanket, gritting her teeth against the pain on her leg and wishing she had never come on this awful journey.

CHAPTER 16

The Starving Roamer

The next morning, after a breakfast of plums and coarse bread, they set out again. Maddy made Lina a place to sit at the back of the truck, between two of the crates. She took the blankets they'd slept on and spread them on the rough floor of the truck. Lina could sit on the blankets, lean against the nearest crate, and dangle her legs over the truck's back edge. The burn still hurt this morning; it was a reddish, angry-looking blister. After a while, as the sun came up and sweet grassy smells arose from the earth, Lina began to enjoy herself again. She watched the countryside fall away behind the truck, stretches of brown-gold grass as big as the sky, trees like hairy spikes, rocky slopes.

And this is how it was for four more days. At night they would find a place by a stream to sleep, if they could find a stream. They passed other ox-pulled cars and trucks on their way, both going their direction and coming back. They would stop and talk with these roamers and sometimes trade with them for food. Caspar always asked if they'd been to the city. Very few of them had. The ones that had been there just shook their heads when Caspar asked if they'd found anything interesting. "It's a waste of time to go there," they said. "Don't bother." Most of the roamers they met had been scavenging in what they called the suburbs, which Lina understood to mean towns that lay around the city.

Caspar and Maddy hardly spoke to her at all during the day. Around noon they would stop the truck and get something to eat from the chest of provisions they had brought. At first there was dried fruit, but they soon used that up. After that it was travelers' cakes, morning, noon, and night.

Caspar always went to sleep right after he'd filled his belly. He lay back on the ground and snored. Then Maddy would beckon to Lina with a tilt of her head, and they would walk away from Caspar and find a place to sit, often beneath a tree, one of those trees that spread their branches out like the top of a big mushroom. They would sit in the soft grass and look up at the sky through the tree's branches. Sometimes a breeze swept across the land and brought them the scent of dusty earth and dry weeds.

After lunch on their second day of traveling, Lina asked Maddy where she came from.

"A horrible place," was all she said.

"Horrible in what way?"

"Small, cold, and poor. Houses made of old boards. Bad soil for growing things, never enough food. A place that was withering."

"What does that mean, withering?" Lina asked.

"It means shrinking and dying. Things were getting worse there. There was too much sickness, too much hunger, too much unhappiness. People were always quarreling, and a lot of them were leaving. It was ending, the place where I came from. I wanted to be somewhere that was beginning."

"Our city was ending, too," said Lina. She looked up at the blue sky and thought about the sky in Ember: utter blackness, not a speck of light. No lights shone anywhere in Ember now. "There's no one left in our city," she said.

"Sparks is a place that's beginning," said Maddy. "If it can get past the hard spots."

"Hard spots?"

"Yes, like suddenly having to take in four hundred people."

"Oh," said Lina, remembering the conflicts in the village and all the reasons she'd wanted to get away from there. Her heart sank. "Maybe by the time we get back, that will all be over, all that trouble," she said.

"Maybe," said Maddy. "I hope so. Sparks is a whole lot better than where I came from."

"I can understand why you wanted to leave that place," said Lina.

"Pretty badly," said Maddy. "Bad enough to take up with a fool."

"Fool?"

Maddy just tipped her head toward the sleeping Caspar.

"You came with him just to get away?" Lina whispered.

Maddy nodded. "Roamers hardly ever came to our little settlement," she said, "mainly because we had nothing to trade. Caspar was only the second one I'd ever seen. I thought I might never see another, so I grabbed the chance."

"Why couldn't you just leave by yourself?"

"I thought of it," Maddy said. "But I didn't know where to go. I didn't know the roads, or where the settlements were. I didn't know how I'd get food. I guess I wasn't quite bold enough to go alone."

"When you got to Sparks, you could have stayed there," Lina said. "You didn't have to keep traveling with him."

"I would have stayed," said Maddy, "if I hadn't promised to help him on this quest of his. I try to honor my promises, if I possibly can."

That afternoon, as they traveled on across the rolling hills, Lina thought about places that were ending and places that were beginning. She knew about endings. Now she wanted to be part of a beginning. Maybe the people of Ember could begin again in the city. If not . . . well, she wouldn't think about that until she had to.

On the second night, they pulled up beside the ruins of a town. Not much was left of it, but you could see that once there had been hundreds of houses. The concrete foundations, overgrown with weeds, lined up along curved streets. Here and there a wall or a chimney was still standing. Caspar stopped the truck just beyond the outer row of ruins, and Maddy went around to the back and opened the trunk that held their dwindling supply of food. They had stopped beside a ditch where a trickle of water ran. It was green, scummy water, but Lina drank it anyway. It was all there was.

Caspar seemed especially grouchy. His pink face was splotched and damp, and his eyes looked inflamed. He had forgotten to twist his mustache into points, and it hung down at the corners of his mouth. He dug a crumbling travelers' cake from the trunk and glowered at Maddy. "What's the matter with you, anyway?" he said. "You haven't been very chatty lately."

"I'm never chatty," said Maddy calmly.

Caspar took a savage bite of his cake. "It's like traveling with a tree stump," he said. "I thought you were going to be a pleasant and helpful companion."

Maddy did not reply to this. She chewed serenely,

gazing out over the acres of fallen houses. Lina realized there was a certain beauty in Maddy that she hadn't seen before. Her back was straight, she held her head high, and there was something unswayable in her. The bones of her face were strong, and her gaze was firm. There was nothing fluttery about her. You could see that Caspar was finding out that she was not what he'd taken her for at first. She was more than he'd bargained for.

On the third day, near evening, they saw a truck coming toward them from a great distance away. They were on a long, straight road with few trees or buildings to block their view, just the dry brown grass and a few ancient fences leaning over and flocks of birds rising, swooping through the air, and fluttering down again. Up ahead came this dark dot, toiling forward. In twenty minutes or so, the two trucks drew near.

Lina stood behind Caspar and Maddy, looking forward. This roamer looked poor. He had only one ox, a shaggy, swaybacked animal, and on his truck there were only two crates, not four as on Caspar's. The man himself was almost as shaggy as his ox. His hair was long and his beard lay like a hairy brown bib against his chest. As he came closer, he stood up on his truck and shaded his eyes with his hand, peering at them.

"Watch out for this one," Caspar said. "Could be a bandit. Looks bad and mean and dangerous."

When the other truck was twenty or thirty feet away, its driver suddenly hauled on the traces. His ox veered, and the truck turned sideways so that it blocked the road. Lina couldn't tell if he'd done this on purpose. His movements were jerky, as if something was wrong with him. He climbed down from his truck and stood in front of it, his neck tucked down and his shoulders hunched as high as his ears. His eyes glittered in his hairy face. He stood there like that, saying nothing, waiting for them.

Caspar stopped the truck. He stood up and leaned forward. "Out of my way, you ragged wretch! Move that flea-bitten rig!"

The roamer came a few paces closer. His mouth opened—a hole in the tangle of beard—but no words came out.

Lina could see the back of Caspar's neck flush deep red. "I said, *Out of my way!*" He snatched up his whip and sent the long lash curling out toward the man and snapped it a few feet from his face. The roamer let out a howl. He lurched toward them.

All this happened in only a minute or so. Lina's heart was beating wildly. *Was* this a bandit? Was he going to attack them? She ducked down behind a crate and peered between the slats.

Caspar raised the whip again. "Come any closer and I'll cut you to shreds!" he shouted.

But before he could lash out, Maddy grabbed his

arm. "Wait," she said. Caspar tried to shake her off, but she yanked at him so hard he lost his balance and sat down again. "Why not find out what the man wants before you attack him?" she said.

Caspar struggled against her, but she was strong. She managed to wrench the whip out of his hand. Then she jumped down and confronted the other roamer, who had halted just in front of the truck.

"What do you want from us?" she said to him, standing squarely in his path, her hands on her wide hips. "Why have you stopped us like this?"

The roamer backed up a step. He looked at her with his mouth hanging open. He was grubby, Lina saw. His hands and his bare feet were nearly black with dirt. He mumbled something.

Maddy bent closer to him. "What?"

He mumbled again.

She turned to Caspar, who had climbed down from the truck and was approaching with his fists clenched. "He says he's out of cakes." She turned back to the man. "How long since you've eaten?"

The man stared at his hands. He had long, filthy fingernails. His fingers twitched. "Three days," he croaked. "Just crumbs . . . three days."

"Well," said Caspar, "if you think we're going to supply you with food, you're very mistaken."

"Surely we can spare a couple of cakes," Maddy said.

Caspar's face was dark red. "We can*not,*" he said. "We are on a special mission, extremely important. We need that food for ourselves—*all* of it."

Lina thought this was unreasonable. "He can have one of mine," she said.

Caspar whirled around. "No!" he said. "You're going to need your strength."

"You're being ridiculous," said Maddy, but Caspar reached out and pushed her. "Back in the truck," he said. "And you"—turning back to the roamer —"get your rattletrap out of my way, if you want to stay alive."

From the roamer came a sound Lina had never heard before from a human being—a hoarse hissing sound, as if he were spitting a stream of fire straight at Caspar's face. He did this twice, and then he turned away and scuttled back to his truck. He pulled on the ox's traces and it moved a few feet along, just far enough for Caspar to drive his truck past it. Caspar yelled at him one more time as he passed: "You shouldn't *be* a roamer if you can't feed yourself!" He cracked his whip at the man and drove on.

Lina climbed into a crate and sat with her head on her knees for a while after this. She was horrified by the starving, filthy roamer. How did he come to be in such a state? Was it his own fault? Was he a madman? But Caspar could have given him *something,* couldn't he? Or were they so low on food that losing any of it really would harm them? Her stomach lurched; she felt queasy. But she didn't know if it was hunger or horror at what she'd just seen.

That night, Lina woke up for a moment and heard the oxen making unsettled noises. She heard a creaking sound, too. But the sounds stopped, and she went back to sleep. In the morning, Maddy discovered they had been robbed.

"Well, well," she said, opening the food chest. "Look here."

"What?" said Caspar, who was wetting his mustache with spit and twisting it into points.

"Someone's been into our food," said Maddy. "I wonder who."

Caspar jumped to his feet. "Into our food?"

"He didn't get much," Maddy said. "Just three or four, I'd guess." She put her hand in the chest and felt around. "But he left us something."

Sputtering with rage, Caspar hauled himself up onto the truck. When he looked into the food chest, he let out a string of furious swear words.

Lina crept out from under her blanket and stood up. "What is it?" she said. "What happened?"

"Our friend from yesterday has been for a visit," said Maddy. "We wouldn't give him what he wanted, so he took it. And left something for us, too."

"Left what?" said Lina. Caspar was shaking with fury. His face was dark red.

"Looks like dirt," said Maddy. "I think he took

what he wanted and dumped a bag of dirt on the rest." She wrinkled her nose. "Might be some ox droppings in here, too."

"The skunk!" Caspar cried. "The miserable rat!"

"In my opinion," said Maddy, "you should have given him a couple of cakes in the first place."

"I didn't ask for your opinion," said Caspar.

"You're going to get it anyway," said Maddy, suddenly fierce. "You turned a crazy old guy into an enemy in less than two minutes. *You* did it. You've done it over and over, I've seen you: you approach people like an enemy and *bam!*, they turn into one, whether they were to begin with or not."

"It's my policy to be ready to defend myself," Caspar said, scowling. "At any moment."

"Fine," said Maddy. "So now, because of your policy, we're out four cakes instead of two, and we have a lot of dirt on the rest." She closed the chest, stood up, and glared at Caspar with a mixture of anger and scorn. "If you ask me, making friends is a better defense than making enemies."

"I didn't ask you," said Caspar.

On the fourth day, they went uphill hour after hour. The heat was terrible. The only water they found was at the bottom of a deep ravine. All three of them scrambled down, half stepping and half sliding, carrying Caspar's biggest pots, and, sweating and gasping, they lugged the filled pots back up so that the oxen could drink.

Then they went uphill some more. It was late afternoon by the time they came to the top of the ridge. Lina was so tired by that time and so hot that she felt like a boiled vegetable, limp and runny. She was a bit dazed, too, only half awake, and so she was startled when the truck jolted to a stop and she heard sharp exclamations from Caspar and Maddy. She jumped down and went around to the front. A tremendous view of land and water lay before her. Such immense water she had never seen—green-blue, glinting in the rays of the late sun, white ripples racing across its surface. To her right, it stretched as far as she could see, but straight ahead she could see the shore on the other side—green trees covering the ground, and hills rising beyond.

"The bay," said Caspar. "This means we're almost there. We go around the end of it and then north."

"When do we get to the city?" Lina said.

"Tomorrow," said Caspar. His wide face broke into a grin, and he laughed his high, weird laugh. He opened and closed his fingers, stretching and gripping, as if he were imagining taking hold of something. "We'll be there tomorrow, and then our work begins."

CHAPTER 17

Doon Accused

Word of the tomato throwing, and Torren's accusation of Doon, spread quickly through Sparks. Some people believed Torren, some didn't. But no one could prove who was telling the truth. Torren said he'd seen what he'd seen in the middle of the night, when he couldn't sleep and took a walk to the field to look at the stars. Doon said he'd been home all night, sleeping, and that his father and the others in his room knew it. But people said he could have slipped quietly out without anyone knowing, couldn't he? He could have gone down there and done his mischief and come back, and they all would have thought he'd been sleeping the whole night.

At noon that day, when he and the others showed up at the Partons' house for their midday meal, no one spoke to them. Martha let them in, and they sat down at the table, where places had been set for them as usual. Doon's father said, "Good day," and Mrs. Polster said, "How are you?" and Miss Thorn and Edward Pocket looked around at the family's stony faces and tried to smile. Ordney put food on their plates (was it an even smaller amount than usual?) and passed the plates to them. Kenny ate tiny mouthfuls. His eyes darted nervously from face to face. But no one spoke.

Finally Doon's father said, "Excuse me, but perhaps there's been a mistake."

Martha looked at him coldly. "I don't believe so," she said.

"Perhaps you're thinking," Doon's father went on, "that my son Doon actually did what he has been accused of."

"In this household," said Martha, "we do not approve of wasting food."

"Neither do we!" cried Doon. "I would never do such a thing! I *didn't* do it." All eyes turned toward Doon. He could feel a red flush rising in his face. "Really," he said, keeping his voice calm. "I didn't."

"Who did, then?" said Ordney.

"I don't know," said Doon.

"No one knows," said Mrs. Polster in her firmest voice. "Certainly we aren't going to believe the word of one unhappy little boy against the word of this young man, who has proved himself so outstanding."

"Why not?" said Martha. "Torren Crane is a decent boy, as far as I know. I don't see why you call him unhappy."

"All you have to do is look at him," Mrs. Polster said.

Miss Thorn nodded. "I do think she's right," she murmured.

"Well, *one* of you people must have done it," Martha said. "Certainly none of *us* would have."

"Nothing has been proved one way or the other," said Doon's father. "It would be unfair to draw any conclusions."

There was an uncomfortable silence. Everyone focused on eating. When it was time to leave, Kenny passed out the food parcels, and as he handed one to Doon, he silently mouthed three words: *I believe you.*

At least one person was on his side, Doon thought. It made him feel better, but only a little.

In the end, because it was one person's word against another's and there was no proof either way, nothing was done. Officially, the identity of the tomato thrower remained a mystery. But the effect of all this was to make the people of Sparks and the people of Ember even more resentful and suspicious of each other than they had been before.

Doon felt unfriendly eyes following him wherever he went. At first he tried to explain when people glared at him that way. He spoke reasonably. "Why would I get up and walk all the way into a field in the middle of the night to throw tomatoes at a wall?" he said. "It doesn't make any sense." But people didn't seem interested in reason. He was one of *them,* and that meant he was strange and might do anything. So Doon stopped trying to explain. He kept his eyes on the ground and ignored the people who muttered darkly as he passed by.

It wasn't just Doon who suffered from the tomato incident. It was all the refugees from Ember. Sometimes the villagers called them names right out loud on the street. It was as if those smashed tomatoes had brought all the quietly rumbling resentments out into the open. The town simmered like a pot about to boil over.

One morning Doon found a crowd gathered in the plaza when he came into town for work. Both Sparks people and Ember people were clustered together, looking at something. He edged between them to see what it was. Across the pavement, someone had scrawled a message. It looked as if it had been written in mud. The sloppy, runny letters said:

THEY MUST GO!

The crowd stared at it silently. A few of the villagers seemed embarrassed. They looked sideways at the Emberites and shook their heads. "Mean," someone muttered. But others scowled. One man, noticing

Doon, glared at him so angrily that Doon felt as if he'd been punched in the stomach. This message was there because of him; he knew it. He put his head down and hurried away.

At the hotel that night, people were upset. They clustered in buzzing groups out by the front steps, talking about the words painted on the plaza. Doon saw Tick striding among them, speaking with everyone, his face flushed and his eyes glittering. When he came toward Doon, he paused. "They've turned against us," he said. "I knew they would. We mustn't stand for it." And he plunged back into the crowd.

A day passed, and then another. The sun blazed down, but Doon felt as if darkness had invaded him. Protests and questions raged through his mind. Why had Torren pointed at him? Was it just at random, or had he singled him out for some reason? Why did Chugger believe Torren and not believe him? Who had written the muddy message on the bricks of the plaza?

Lina did not return, and this added to Doon's glumness. According to the note she'd left Mrs. Murdo, she should have been back by now from wherever she'd gone. Doon's feelings about her were divided between worry and anger. He tried not to think about her, since there was nothing he could do.

Whenever he had a free moment, he holed up with a book and tried to forget about what was happening in the village. Edward Pocket brought him a steady supply. Edward was obsessed with his job. Every now and then Doon would ask him how it was going, and Edward would get a feverish look in his eyes and say, "Ah! It goes by inches, young Doon. By millimeters. I've done this much"—he held his thumb and forefinger a tiny distance apart—"and this much remains to be done." He stretched his arms as far apart as they would go. "It's a gargantuan task. I press forward, but will I finish in my lifetime? It is doubtful." His fingers black with dust, he often came home in the evening later than the workers who went into the village, and he was so tired by then that he usually went straight to bed right after dinner, even though it was still light. Doon would hear him mumbling in his sleep inside the closet. He could make sense of only a few words. "Caterpillars," Edward would say. "Cathedrals. Cattle. Chemistry. Christmas." Then he'd groan and thrash about, banging his bony limbs against the closet door, and go silent for a while. When he muttered again, he'd be on to a different letter: "Hamlet. Harry Potter. Hawaii. Heart surgery. Hippopotamus. Hog farming." Doon imagined that Edward's mind was so stuffed with information by now that there wasn't room for any more, and the excess had started leaking out in the night.

Sometimes Doon passed the Sparks school on his way to work in the morning. It was a small building with a wide, open porch all around it, where the students often sat to do their lessons. The children of the village—there weren't very many of them—went to school only a few hours a day, and only until they were ten years old. Kenny Parton went there. He would wave to Doon when he saw him going by, and before the trouble with the tomatoes, the other children would look at Doon curiously, a few of them smiling. But the first time Doon passed the school after the tomato trouble, he saw fifteen or twenty cold-eyed faces turned toward him. Someone shouted, "Get out of here!" and someone else threw a crumpled wad of paper over the porch railing at him. He walked faster, looking straight ahead. A moment later he heard the teacher scolding the class for rudeness, but not very sternly.

The next day, as Doon and the others arrived at the Partons' for lunch, Kenny peeked out from behind a corner of the house and beckoned to Doon. His eyes wide, his voice even softer and more timid than usual, he said, "You know at school yesterday?"

Doon nodded.

"I was sorry they yelled at you," Kenny said. "They shouldn't. You didn't do it."

"How do *you* know?" said Doon, who was feeling crabby just then at all residents of Sparks. "Maybe I did."

Kenny shook his head. "No," he said. "I don't think so."

"Why not?" said Doon.

"I can just tell," said Kenny. "I can tell about people. You wouldn't." He gave Doon a quick, shy smile.

Doon was touched. Kenny looked like a timid little wisp, but there was something strong inside him.

"I wish you didn't have to leave," Kenny said.

Doon smiled. "We'll be here for a few more months," he said.

"Then what?" Kenny asked.

"We go away and make our own town."

"Where?" asked Kenny.

Doon shrugged. "I don't know. Out in those empty places somewhere."

Kenny looked down at his feet. He stood for a minute in silence. Then he said, "That will be really hard. How will you get food?"

"Grow it, I guess. Just the way you do here."

"But you'll be leaving in the month of Chilling. That's the beginning of winter. You can't grow food in the winter," Kenny said, looking up at Doon with worried eyes.

"Winter?" said Doon. "What's winter?"

"You don't have *winter* where you came from?" Kenny's eyes grew very round. "You mean it's always *summer* there?"

Doon was confused and slightly alarmed by Kenny's tone. "I don't know those words," he said.

Kenny stared at Doon, his face blank with surprise. "Seasons," he said. "They're the seasons. In summer it's hot. In winter it's cold."

"That's all right, then," said Doon, relieved. "We're used to cold."

"But you can't grow food in the winter. It's *really* cold. And clouds come over the sun. And it rains."

"Rains?"

Kenny was so amazed that his mouth dropped open. He flung his arms up and wiggled his fingers like drops sprinkling down. "Rain! When water comes from the sky! And the river rises, and sometimes it floods! And the dirt turns to mud!"

Doon felt as if his mind had suddenly stopped. He stared at Kenny's wiggling fingers and tried to grasp what he was saying. Water dropped from the sky? But—people's clothes would get wet. Everyone would have to stay inside. And if they couldn't grow food . . . "Wait," he said. "You mean the town leaders *know* it will be winter when we leave? They *know* it will be cold and wet?"

"I guess so," Kenny said. He lowered his eyes, then looked up again. "Probably they mean to send food with you," he said. "To get you through the winter. That must be it." He gave a small, hopeful smile. "That must be it," he said again, and he darted away toward the front door and went into the house.

Doon followed. His vision of the future, already shadowed by anxiety, had just grown several shades darker.

One morning a week or so later, as Doon came out the door of room 215, he nearly bumped into Tick Hassler, who was running at full speed down the hall. "Something's happened!" Tick called to him.

"What?" said Doon, breaking into a run himself to keep up with Tick.

"I don't know," Tick said. "But I heard people out in front, shouting."

Tick must have jumped out of bed and not taken time to do anything but throw on his clothes, Doon thought. He hadn't combed his hair, he hadn't tied his shoes, he hadn't even washed his face—there were gray smudges on his neck and below his ear. In the usually well-groomed Tick, these were signs of serious alarm. Doon's heart beat faster. He took the stairs three at a time, crossed the lobby, and, still following Tick, pushed through the front door.

Outside, a crowd stood in the field, staring up at the hotel. Doon ran out to join them and turned around to see what they were seeing.

Someone had scrawled words on the walls of the Pioneer—tremendous black letters, rough and scratchy, as if written with burnt wood. "GO BACK TO

YOUR CAVE," said the message, over and over. "GO BACK TO YOUR CAVE. GO BACK TO YOUR CAVE." The few ground-floor windows that hadn't already been broken were broken now.

Doon stood staring for a minute, feeling sick, and then anger rose in him. This was the work of whoever had slopped that mud message onto the plaza—another ugly message, bolder this time. Around him the others were rushing forward, shouting, staring at the scrawled words. Some of them stood silent and glum, with arms folded or hands in pockets. Others shook their fists in the air and vowed revenge. Tick was more furious than anyone, but he didn't yell. Doon watched him weaving through the crowd, seizing one person after another by the arm, talking in a voice as sharp as a blade but low and steady. His light blue eyes glinted like steel.

"It's what I thought," Tick said. "This shows it. They've pretended to be kind, but their kindness isn't real. Here's what we can know from now on: they hate us." He narrowed his eyes, lowered his voice almost to a hiss, and said it again. "*They hate us.* They want to get rid of us. Well, I'll tell you what." People all around turned toward him. "They want us to leave, but I'm not leaving. Are you?" He scanned the crowd.

"No," said someone.

Doon thought about what Kenny had told him:

winter, cold, rain. Maybe Tick is right, he thought. They *do* hate us.

"Do you *like* being called cavepeople?" Tick cried. "Do you *like* being told to crawl back into a cave?"

And angry voices, twenty, fifty, a hundred of them, cried, "No, no!"

Doon went up close to the wall of the hotel and examined the words scratched there. He pictured the people who had done it, clutching their burnt chunks of wood, writing with big, angry strokes in the dark of the night. Yes, Tick was right. Hatred seethed in those jagged letters. He felt almost as if their strokes had scraped open his skin.

The Second Town Meeting

The three town leaders called a meeting after these unpleasant incidents—the tomato-throwing, and the graffiti on the plaza and on the hotel wall. They met in the tower room of the town hall to talk.

"This is unfortunate," Mary said. "I'm afraid these spiteful deeds will cause bad feelings to get worse on both sides."

Wilmer nodded. "Feelings are already bad," he said.

"These cavepeople," said Ben, "are not as civilized as we are. People who will destroy two whole crates of tomatoes might do anything."

"We don't know for sure that one of them did it," Mary said.

"Come now, Mary," said Ben. "I think it's safe to assume."

"And what about the people who wrote 'Go Back

to Your Cave' on the hotel walls?" said Mary.

"The problem is," said Ben, "we don't know who did that. But I must say that I think they were expressing an understandable frustration. These cavepeople have adversely impacted our way of life. The food we give them comes out of the mouths of our own people."

"We do have a bit of a surplus in the storehouse," said Mary.

"But why should we use it for *them*? It's our protection against hard times." Ben smoothed his beard and went on. "I have a rule to suggest," he said. "I think it would be best if the cavepeople didn't eat in the homes of families anymore. I think it's too hard on our families to have strangers eating with them every day. It would be better if the families simply hand them their food parcels when they arrive. They can eat somewhere else."

"Where?" asked Mary.

Ben waved a hand in the direction of the river. "On the riverbank," he said. "Or at the edge of a field. Or on the road. I really don't care where they eat," he said, "as long as they don't intrude on our households."

"Quite a few people have complained of the inconvenience," said Wilmer. "The Parton family seems the most unhappy."

"That's because they have that evil boy," said Ben. "The one who threw the tomatoes."

"We don't know that he's the one who threw them," said Mary.

"We are as sure as we need to be," said Ben.

So they voted: should they make that rule?

Mary voted no.

Ben voted yes.

Wilmer hesitated for several seconds, his eyes darting between Mary and Ben. Finally he voted yes.

"I suppose this will make things better," said Wilmer.

"I'm sure it will," said Ben. "We need to make it clear that this town belongs to us. This is *our* place, and these people are only here because of our generosity."

"I think we *have* made it clear," said Mary. "We went to all that trouble to make a flag and put it up on the town hall."

"No doubt that will help," said Ben. "Still, we must constantly reinforce the message: if they don't behave themselves, they can't expect to stay here even as long as six months."

"They've just begun to get used to things," said Mary. "They're not ready to leave."

"That," said Ben, "is not our problem."

CHAPTER 18

Caspar's Quest

On the last night of their journey to the city, the travelers stayed in a real house. It was roofless, but most of its walls still stood, providing shelter from the wind that blew strongly off the water. There was no furniture in the house, of course. They sat on the bare floor.

Caspar was excited that night. He talked so much that he almost forgot to eat—his third travelers' cake sat on his knee getting cold. At one point, he turned to face Lina. "Now, listen," he said. "I'm going to tell you something, so you'll understand the importance of what we're doing." He paused. Then he spoke in a low, vibrating voice. "I happen to know," he said, "that there is a treasure in the city."

"There is?" said Lina. "How do you know?"

"Old rhymes and songs speak of it," said Caspar.

"The trouble is," said Maddy, "those old rhymes and songs don't make sense anymore. If they ever did."

"They make sense to me," Caspar said. "But that's because I've studied them carefully and have found out their deeper meaning."

"What do the old rhymes say?" Lina asked.

"Various things," said Caspar, "depending on what version you hear. But they're always about a treasure in an ancient city." He looked into the air and sang tunelessly: "'There's buried treasure in the ancient city. Remember, remember from times of old. . . .' One of them starts like that."

"Why hasn't anyone searched for the treasure before?" asked Lina.

"I'm sure many people have," Caspar said. "But no one has found it."

"How do you know?" Lina asked.

"Because obviously, if someone had, we would have heard about it."

Lina thought about this. She saw some holes in Caspar's logic. Someone could have found the treasure, taken it away, and never said a word.

"Another problem," said Maddy, "is that these rumors never say what city the treasure is in. It could be some city a thousand miles away."

Caspar gave an exasperated sigh and set down his cup of water. He raised two fingers and pointed them at Maddy. "Listen," he said. "Be logical. It's *here* that the rumors are passed around. I've never heard them in the far north, where I was last year. I've never heard them in the far east, either. This talk of treasure in a city—I hear it *here,* and within a hundred or so miles of here."

"Still," Maddy said. "There are at least three ancient cities within a hundred miles of here."

"But only one *great* ancient city," said Caspar. "That's the one we're going to."

"A city is big," Lina said, remembering the myriad streets and buildings of Ember. "How will you know where in the city to look for the treasure?"

A crafty look came over Caspar's face. He smiled, with his lips pressed together and his eyes narrowed. "That's where my careful study comes in," he said. "Many, many hours of study. I've written down every version of the rhyme I've heard—which is a great many, forty-seven to be exact. I've compared them, word for word, letter for letter. *Then*—" Caspar paused. He looked at them in a way Lina recognized—it was the same way Torren looked when he was about to make a big impression. "*Then* I applied my skill with numbers."

"Numbers?" said Lina.

"That's right. What you do is, you count the letters in the words. You count in all different ways, until you start to see a pattern. The pattern is the key to the code, and the code tells you the secret of the message." He sat back, looking highly pleased with himself.

"And the secret of the message . . . ," Lina said, confused.

"Is the location of the treasure, of course!" Caspar slapped a hand on his big thigh. "It's obvious, once you've figured it out. Street numbers, building numbers—it's all there."

"Well, then," said Maddy, "what is the location of the treasure?"

Caspar jerked his head back. "You think I'd tell you?" he said.

"I thought I was your partner in this," said Maddy.

"You'll know when it's time," said Caspar. "Until then, the information stays strictly with me."

Lina glanced at Maddy in time to see her rolling her eyes toward the sky.

That night, Lina couldn't sleep. Animal sounds kept her awake—scrambling and snuffling just beyond the walls, and a strange hooting in the distance. Dark thoughts troubled her, too. Caspar's search sounded all wrong somehow. She didn't want to help him. The thought of it filled her with dread. She lay on the hard floor of the house, staring at the black sky, feeling worse and worse, until finally she decided she must try to think about something else. So she said to herself, over and over for a long time, "Tomorrow I'll see the city, tomorrow I'll see the city."

They traveled the next day, mile after mile, along a road that was nearly straight, though they had to trace a winding path around the places where the pavement was pitted or thrust up or crumbled away. On their right was the vast green sheet of water, bordered by waving grasses where great white birds stood knee-deep in pools and rose like floating paper, and flocks of black birds flew up trilling into the air, their shoulders red as blood. On the left was a forest of trees so thick they hid all but the briefest glimpses of the ruined buildings among them.

Lina's excitement was rising. She rode standing up now. She'd climbed back into the crate and stuck her feet between the third and fourth slats of the side, which put her at the right height for holding on to the top edge and looking forward. She could see over Caspar's and Maddy's heads to the rear ends of the oxen, their sharp hip bones sticking up, left-right, left-right, their tasseled tails switching back and forth. The sun sank lower in the sky until it was directly ahead, blazing straight into Lina's eyes. "We'll be there before night," Caspar said.

The road began to slope upward. Hills rose on either side, and soon Lina could no longer see the water, just the brown humps of the hills, spotted with clumps of trees and scarred here and there by the remains of old roads and buildings. The air was cooler. They rounded a curve—and all at once the city lay before them.

CHAPTER 19

Unfairness, and What to Do About It

In the days after the hateful words had been scrawled on the wall, Doon went to work grudgingly. He didn't want to work with people who did such awful things. He had to remind himself that they weren't *all* ignorant brutes, and that they *were* still giving the Emberites shelter and food—even though they were no longer allowing them to eat with their lunchtime families, and even though they were planning to send them out to fend for themselves in the winter. But the people who had written those words—no one was trying to find out who they were, no one was punishing them. Who was the one getting the evil looks and being called bad names? *He* was, he who had done nothing! He couldn't stand the *wrongness* of it. He felt it physically, as if he were wearing clothes that were too tight, a shirt that pinched him under the arms, pants that were too short and too snug. Unfair, unfair, he kept thinking. He couldn't *bear* unfairness.

One day he was assigned to clean the fountain in the center of the plaza. Chugger handed him his tools for the job: a bucket, a long stick with a metal scraper on one end, and a pile of rags.

Chugger lifted up one of the bricks in the pavement near the fountain. Under it was a round handle. "You turn this off first," he said. "It shuts off the water coming in from the river." He gave it several turns, and the spouting water in the middle of the fountain dipped and vanished. "Now the water in the basin will drain through the outflow pipe," Chugger said. "It goes back into the river. When the basin is empty, you climb in there and scrub. I want this thing clean as a drinking glass when you're through."

Chugger left, and Doon watched the water level slowly going down. The lower it got, the more green scum was revealed. It coated the inside of the fountain like slimy fur.

He plunged his stick into the water, scraped it along the fountain's inner wall, and pulled it out again. Wet green strings swung from the end of it, and he shook them off into the bucket. He thrust the stick in again, scraped again, brought up more muck. Into the bucket it went. For the next ten minutes, he scraped the bottom and sides of the fountain with his stick and filled the bucket with slippery strands of scum, along with a few apricot pits, dead bugs, and rotting leaves.

The water was about half gone now, but it seemed to be draining very slowly. Probably, Doon reasoned, this was because the outflow pipe was getting blocked up with all the loosened scum being drawn toward it. But because the water was so murky, he couldn't see where the outflow pipe was.

At that moment, Chugger came up behind him. "What the heck is taking you so long?" he said. "If you had any sense, you'd have figured out the drain is clogging up." He grabbed the stick out of Doon's hands and began probing in the water.

"I *did* figure that out," Doon said, "but I couldn't see where it was because—"

"There!" said Chugger, who wasn't listening. He'd pried loose a clump of soggy crud, and the water level was once more going down. He thrust the stick toward Doon again. "Now get busy. And try using your brain once in a while, if you have one." He stalked off.

Doon clamped his teeth together to hold in the rage that boiled up in him. He glared at the retreating back of Chugger and imagined throwing his stick so that it hit him right between the shoulder blades.

I hate being talked to that way, he thought. As if I'm a moron. Why does he get to talk to me like that?

When the water had all drained out of the fountain, Doon took his shoes off, grabbed a handful of rags, and climbed in. On his knees in the green slime that covered the bottom, he wiped and scrubbed. Now and then people came by and peered in at him. "Ugh," they'd say as they passed, or "Yuck." It felt as if they were saying ugh and yuck about him—not surprising, since he was now just about as filthy as the rags he was using. No one said, "Good job!" or said they were pleased the fountain was getting cleaned.

When he finally finished, he opened the inflow valve and plugged the outflow valve, and once again the water leapt from the central pipe and the fountain began to fill. Doon sat down on the rim and put his bare feet in the water to rinse them off. He stayed there for a minute, resting. The cool, clean water felt good.

Chugger came around the corner. "What are you *doing*?" he yelled. He strode toward Doon. "I don't know how you do it where you're from," he said, "but here when we work, we work. We don't sit around gazing at the sky."

Doon started to say he was not gazing at the sky, he was taking a one-minute rest. But when he opened his mouth to speak, the rush of anger that came up through his body was so volcanic that he closed his mouth again and sat there shaking, his face flushed and burning, afraid he would explode if he tried to say a word. *Do not get angry,* he told himself, remembering the advice his father had given him so many times. *When anger is in control, you get unintended consequences.*

"You don't speak when you're spoken to?" said Chugger. "Maybe you didn't hear me. Maybe I need to make it clearer." He took a deep breath. His voice came out in a hoarse bellow: "Get moving, you stupid barbarian! Now!" He seized Doon by the arm and yanked him backward.

That was when Doon felt his rage shooting up like steam, unstoppable.

"Let go of me!" he screamed. "I'm not the barbarian! You are! *You* are!" He tried to jerk away from Chugger, but Chugger held on. Doon pulled harder, wrenching his whole body sideways and slamming against the bucket, which was next to him on the rim of the fountain. The bucket went flying, spewing its slimy contents over a girl who happened to be passing by. She screamed and slapped at the stinking green sludge running down the front of her shirt. People rushed up to her and shouted angrily at Doon, who gave one more frantic pull and finally freed himself from Chugger's grasp.

For a second he and Chugger stood glaring at each other. Doon knew how he must look to the people around him: clumsy, filthy, wild-eyed, and, worse than that—a violent boy, the kind of boy who would waste good food, the kind of boy whose ugly, fiery temper could cause real damage.

He turned and stalked away. No one tried to stop him. He realized when he'd gone a short distance that he'd forgotten to pick up his shoes, but he wasn't going to go back for them. He ran barefoot all the way to the Pioneer.

I've done it now, he thought. I've made everything worse. And yet none of it is my fault. I was trying hard to do my job, and trying even harder not to get angry. But look what happens.

The unfairness of it, the tremendous injustice, felt like a stone in his heart.

"We will do something about this," Tick said to Doon that night. They were standing by the hotel's back stairs, where they'd encountered each other on the way in from the outhouses. "You are being abused. We all are. We mustn't stand for it."

Doon nodded. He had told Tick about winter, and now Tick was more outraged than ever. The look on his face was hard and determined. Doon admired Tick's strength, and the way he always seemed to know what to do. He himself was never so absolutely clear. He saw too many sides of things; it confused him.

"What should we do?" he asked.

"Strike back," said Tick. "They have attacked us, more than once, in many ways. It's time for them to find out that if they hurt us, they'll get hurt, too."

They'll get hurt. Was this the right thing? But it did seem fair. After all, wrong should be punished. "How do we do it?" said Doon.

"Many possibilities," said Tick. He leaned against the wall beside the stairs. He had a red patch on his arm, Doon noticed, that he kept scratching at; it was the first time Doon had seen that Tick, too, suffered from the bites and scrapes that plagued the rest of them. He isn't perfect, Doon reminded himself; he isn't always right about everything.

"We could refuse to work," Tick went on. "But everyone would have to refuse, and I'm not sure everyone would. It would be better to take direct action."

"Action about what?" asked Doon.

"About food. We don't get enough. This is an injustice *all* of us feel. So what about this: we storm the storehouse and take what we need by force."

"Steal food?" said Doon.

"It isn't stealing. It's evening things out. It's getting what should rightfully be ours." There was not a hint of uncertainty in Tick's voice.

Doon thought about this. It did make sense. You had to act against injustice, didn't you? You couldn't just let it happen.

"I know lots of people who'll join us," Tick said. "I'll call them together. We'll have a meeting and make a plan." He started up the stairs and then turned around and looked down on Doon. "But first," he said, "we have to arm ourselves."

"We do?"

"Of course. We need to make sure we'll defeat our enemy."

"What do we arm ourselves with?"

"I'll tell you," Tick said, "when we meet. Tomorrow night, after dinner, out at the head of the road."

CHAPTER 20

The City Destroyed

When the city came into view before them, the three travelers stood speechless, gazing out over ranges of hills standing dark against the western sky. They could see that this had once been a city—to the right, a cluster of tall buildings still stood, tall beyond anything Lina had imagined. But they were no more than shells of buildings, hollow and broken, their windows only holes. Through some of them Lina could see the sky, turned scarlet by the sunset.

All else was a windswept wasteland. Whatever buildings had once been here had long ago fallen and crumbled into the ground. Earth and dust and sand had blown across them, and grass had grown over them, softening their outlines. Here and there traces of ruins remained—they looked from this distance like outcrops of stone, hardly more than jagged places on the smooth slopes. Faint lines of shadow showed where streets must once have been.

Lina stared, trembling. This was far, far from the city she had imagined. Not even the version she'd revised for the Disaster had looked like this. This couldn't be called a city at all anymore. It was the ghost of a city.

Even Caspar seemed daunted. He craned forward, his hand shading his eyes. "It looks somewhat destroyed," he said.

"It looks completely destroyed," said Maddy.

They got down from the truck and stood beside the oxen.

"A trick of the light," said Caspar, squinting harder. He pulled his glasses from his pocket and put them on. "When we get closer, no doubt it will look different."

"How do you plan to get closer?" Maddy asked him, and for the first time Lina saw that a few yards in front of them, the road came to an end. There was an edge of broken pavement, and beyond it a great slab of roadway slanted downward. It had stood on pillars once; you could see a few of the pillars still standing, and rods of thick wire twisting out of them. From here on, the road was a chaos of concrete, gigantic chunks leaning against each other. There was no way the truck could go on.

The sun was nearly down now, and the brilliant red of the sky was fading. Between the ruined buildings drifted a gray mist, and the wind blew more sharply. Some white birds soared high above, screaming.

"It used to be so beautiful," said Maddy. "I've seen pictures of it in books." There was a tremor in her voice. Lina looked up and saw that tears stood in her eyes. "I knew it was destroyed," Maddy said. "But not like this."

"What happened to it?" Lina asked.

"It was the wars," said Maddy. "They must have been . . ." She shook her head. "They must have been terrible," she said.

"What were they about?" Lina asked.

Maddy shrugged. "I don't know."

"And the people who lived here? What happened to them?"

"All killed, I suppose," said Maddy. "Or most of them."

Caspar was frowning at the shadowy wilderness that lay below. "In the daylight," he said, "I'll be able to see how to proceed."

"Proceed!" Maddy grabbed Caspar's arm and wrenched him around to face her. "Are you out of your mind?"

Caspar yanked his arm away. "No," he said. "I am not."

Maddy swept her hand out toward the city. "It's miles and miles of buried rubble!" she cried. "Streets buried under fallen bricks and broken glass! Mountains of concrete and melted metal! Sand and earth blown over it all, and grass growing on it!"

Caspar nodded, his face grim. "Right," he said. "A challenge. You were right about bringing this one along." He tipped his head toward Lina. "Someone small and light, that's what I'll need. Going to have to do some tunneling."

"No, Caspar," said Maddy. "You must give up this idea. You can't find anything there."

"I can," said Caspar. "I can find it, I have the numbers, I have it all worked out." He plunged one hand into his pocket and scrabbled around and brought out a scrap of paper. He snatched his glasses off, put the paper up close to his eyes, and squinted at it. Lina took a step closer to him and peered sideways. The paper was black with scribbling, a tangle of words and numbers and cross-outs. "Forty-seven east," muttered Caspar. "Three ninety-five west." His eyes flicked back and forth between the paper and the dark hills before him, flicked faster and faster. "Seventy-one," he mumbled. "It's just a matter of . . . In the daylight . . ." He caught sight of Lina. "What are *you* staring at?" he said.

"Nothing," said Lina. She felt suddenly sick and frightened. Maddy was right. Caspar *was* out of his mind.

The sun disappeared behind the farthest hill, and darkness fell. Maddy turned back toward the truck. "We'll camp right here tonight," she said. "We still have enough water in the buckets."

They set their blankets on the side of the truck away from the wind, but Lina shivered and couldn't sleep. After days of longing to arrive at the city, she wanted nothing now but to leave. This was a terrible place, full of angry ghosts and sad ones. When she closed her eyes, she seemed to hear their voices—shouts and screams and a dreadful sobbing—and to see flashes of fire in the smoky sky, and sheets of flame sweeping through the streets.

A wail escaped from her. She couldn't help it, she felt so afraid and miserable. A moment later, she heard Maddy's voice close to her ear. "Let's talk for a while," Maddy said.

"Okay," said Lina. She sat up, wrapping her blanket around her. Caspar was pacing up and down on the other side of the truck, muttering to himself. "What about him?" she said.

"Don't worry," answered Maddy. "He's lost in his calculations."

A gust of wind shook the truck. Its loose fender clattered.

"I hate it here," said Lina.

"Yes," said Maddy. "Terrible things happened in this place. You can still feel it."

"Were the people in those old days extremely evil?" Lina asked.

"No more than anyone," Maddy said.

"But then why did the wars happen? To wreck your whole city—almost your whole world—it seems like something only evil people would do."

"No, not evil, at least not at first. Just angry and scared." Maddy was silent for a moment. Caspar's footsteps came closer, crunching on the gravelly ground, and then receded again. Lina inched a little closer to Maddy. "It's like this," Maddy said at last. "Say the A people and the B people get in an argument. The A people do something that hurts the B people. The B people strike back to get even. But that just makes the A people angry all over again. They say, 'You hurt us, so we're going to hurt you.' It keeps on like that. One bad thing leads to a worse bad thing, on and on."

It was like what Torren had said when he was telling her about the Disaster. Revenge, he'd called it.

"Can't it be stopped?" said Lina. She shifted around under her blanket, trying to find a place to sit where rocks weren't digging into her.

"Maybe it can be stopped at the beginning," Maddy said. "If someone sees what's happening and is brave enough to reverse the direction."

"Reverse the direction?"

"Yes, turn it around."

"How would you do that?"

"You'd do something good," said Maddy. "Or at least you'd keep yourself from doing something bad."

"But how could you?" said Lina. "When people have been mean to you, why would you want to be good to them?"

"You *wouldn't* want to," Maddy said. "That's what makes it hard. You do it anyway. Being good is hard. Much harder than being bad."

Lina wondered if she was strong enough to be good. She didn't feel strong at all right now.

"Time to sleep," said Maddy.

Lina pulled the blankets over her head, but still she could feel the wind and hear the oxen making low, uneasy sounds. She heard Caspar still pacing, too, and muttering under his breath.

I want to go home, she thought. And for the first time, the picture that arose in her mind was not of the dark, familiar buildings of Ember but of Sparks under its bright sky. She thought of Dr. Hester's house, and the garden blooming in the sun, and the doctor puttering with her hundred plants. She thought of Mrs. Murdo sitting in the doctor's courtyard, basking in the warmth, and Poppy playing with a spoon beside her. Even Torren was in the picture, proudly arranging his possessions on a window ledge.

And of course there was Doon. He should have

been her partner on this journey. If he were here with her, she'd feel less afraid. She missed him. Maybe when she got back to Sparks, he'd be tired of hanging around that boy named Tick and be ready to be her friend again.

CHAPTER 21

Attack and Counterattack

The morning after the trouble at the fountain, Doon awoke to a clamor rising through his window from the front of the hotel. He looked out, but he could see only the tops of people's heads, all clustered around the front steps. He ran downstairs with his shirt still unbuttoned, flapping around him, to see what was happening.

The doors of the hotel stood open. Through them, he saw that a heap of trash had been dumped on the front steps. He went closer and looked. The pile seemed to consist of rotten vegetables and filthy rags, scattered all over with shiny green leaves and sharp twigs and long creepers pulled up by their dirty roots.

Doon stared at it with the same sick feeling he'd had when he saw the black words on the hotel walls. It wasn't so much the pile itself that made him feel sick; it was that whoever did this hated the people of Ember, and hated Doon himself in particular. This was an act of revenge.

He went outside, edging around the pile. Clary was standing on the step just below it, peering down at the leaves and branches. "Why would they bother to scatter leaves on everything?" she said. "And they're all the same kind, too." She picked up a sprig and looked closely at the bright green leaves, rubbing them between her fingers, sniffing them. "Strange," she said.

But most people were too upset to pay attention to the contents of the pile. An angry buzz filled the air, and now and then one voice or another rose above the rest. "This is an outrage!" It was a clear, sharp voice—Tick's, Doon was sure. Then a high voice: "I hate them, I hate them!" That must be Lizzie—and sure enough, there she was, standing near Tick, dunking her shoes in a bucket of water to get the dirt stains off.

After a while, Tick climbed the steps and clapped his hands. "All right, everyone!" he called. "We've been attacked again—and this is worse than the first time. It's a disgusting insult, and it fills us with rage. But all we can do right now is get this mess off our doorstep. Let's get busy and clean it up."

Everyone did. They picked up armloads of the leafy vines and carried them away. They shoved the garbage down onto the ground and kicked it into the bushes. They brought buckets of water up from the river and sloshed them over the steps until everything was more or less clean. Tick supervised all this, calling out directions—though he didn't do any of the actual work himself, Doon noticed. Doesn't want to get his clothes dirty, thought Doon rather grumpily.

When the cleanup was done, people stood around and argued. Some were for marching down to the town that very minute, confronting the town leaders, and demanding that the vandals be punished. Other people said no, it wasn't good to cause trouble, it would just make everything more unpleasant, and anyway, it wasn't the *whole* village that was against them, only *some* of them.

"But which ones?" someone yelled. "And how do we stop them? They have to be stopped!"

"I'm tired of being blamed and punished!" cried someone else.

"I'm tired of being starved!"

"And what about winter?" someone yelled. The word had spread, and people had added this to their list of grievances.

"Are we just going to sit here and take this treatment?"

"No! No! No!"

Doon could see Tick moving through the crowd, bending to speak into the ear of one person and then another. As people listened, their eyes narrowed and their lips tightened, and they turned to Tick and nodded.

The shouting died down after a while, because people couldn't agree on a course of action. If they didn't go to work, they wouldn't get any lunch. So most of them went back to their ordinary routines: they washed their hands and faces in the river, they ate what remained in their parcels for breakfast, and they headed up the road toward the village.

Doon and his father went, too, though Doon went reluctantly.

"Father," he said, "this is the third time they've attacked us. Don't you think we have to do something?"

"What do you propose to do?" his father said.

"I don't know," said Doon. "But we have to do *something.* We can't just let ourselves be *trampled,* can we?"

"Son," said Doon's father, "I don't know the answer. We're in a tough situation here." He clasped his hands behind his back and walked for a while looking down at the road. "It does seem that something is called for," he said finally. "The trouble is that violence just leads to more violence. So I don't know."

Doon's team was assigned to the cornfield that day. He and his father spent hours on their knees, yanking prickly weeds out of the ground. Doon's arm itched. He kept having to stop and scratch it. Was a mosquito biting him? He scratched and scratched again. It felt like fifty mosquito bites, not one. He had them on his other arm, too. Both arms itched like crazy. Finally he stopped working and held his arms out in front of him. From wrist to elbow, they were carpeted with red lumps.

"Look, Father!" he cried. "I have a rash! What *is* it?"

"I don't know, son," his father said, "but I have it, too."

The itchy rash spread over the arms and hands and faces of all the Emberites who had helped with the cleanup that morning. "What *is* this?" people said as they worked in the bakery and the bike shop, the brickyard and the tomato fields. They itched, they scratched, and the rash spread and oozed and itched still more.

The villagers knew what it was. "Poison oak," they said. They explained about the oil on the leaves, how you only had to touch it to get the rash. "You must have been out scrambling around in the woods," they said. But the Emberites had not been scrambling in the woods. They knew how they'd been poisoned. Someone had done it to them on purpose.

Fury spread among the Emberites like a fire. Those who'd heard about the poison oak raged about it to those who hadn't, and before long everyone knew. Diggers threw down their shovels. Fruit pickers pushed the ladders to the ground and stalked out of the orchard. Someone in the bakery flung a great clump of dough at the supervisor, and someone in the egg shop hurled three eggs at the wall. The terrible itching aggravated everyone's anger, and before long the people of Ember began to gather in the streets and in the plaza, and the gathering became a crowd, and the crowd became a mob.

Doon ran into the village with the other field workers, and he found himself in the middle of this mob. He heard Tick's voice from somewhere nearby: "They gave us poison! What shall we give them?" When there was no response but a confused babble, the question came again, louder: "What shall we give *them*?"

This time an answer came: a crash, and a tinkling of shattered glass. Someone had thrown a rock through the window of the town hall. Cheers arose, and all around him Doon saw people suddenly bending over, looking for rocks to throw. More crashes. More yells.

People started snatching things from the stalls. A jar of jam came sailing overhead. Arms reached up to catch it, but it fell past them and landed a few feet from Doon, smashing open and splattering his legs with sticky red goo and splinters of glass. He saw people stuffing muffins into their pockets, and he saw Tick with his arm stretched backward, ready to throw a rock at the windows of the tower. He saw Miss Thorn running with her hands shielding her head, and the Hoover sisters backing up into the egg shop, trying to get away. He was frightened, suddenly.

At that moment, the doors of the town hall opened, and Ben Barlow strode out. His face was twisted with rage. "Stop them!" he shouted. "Stop these thieves and vandals!"

"You poisoned us!" shouted someone in the crowd.

"We've had enough!" shouted someone else, and threw a potato right at Ben. It hit him in the stomach, and he bent over, his mouth dropping open.

A roar came from the crowd. Tick's voice rose above the others: "Fill your pockets!" he screamed. "Fill your pockets and run!"

There was a mad scramble, and then the Emberites pushed their way out of the plaza and raced down the streets to the river road. Doon ran, too. He saw Tick up ahead of him, sprinting fast, his shirttails flying.

Now we really are thieves and vandals, Doon thought. Was this a bad thing? Or was it exactly what the people of Sparks deserved?

That night, Tick went up and down the corridors of the hotel, knocking on doors and urging people to come to his meeting. They did come—at least a hundred of them, by Doon's count. They gathered at the head of the road as the daylight was fading. Doon saw Chet and Gill and Allie and Elvan from his old class at the Ember school, along with people he knew from the Pipeworks, people he knew from Ember's shops, and others. Most of them were boys and men, but there were women and girls, too. Most were silent, but some whispered excitedly to each other. They formed a semicircle in front of Tick, who had climbed onto a tree stump. Doon saw Lizzie standing near Tick, gazing up at him wide-eyed. The moon shone behind Tick's head; it gave a silver edge to his hair but left his face in darkness.

"All right," Tick said. His voice was quiet, but instantly the whispering stopped. "Our time has come. They have attacked us three times now. Today we showed them a little of our anger. We made them understand that we won't be taken advantage of any-more. They must know that if they hurt us, they will be hurt, too. We will strike back. We are warriors now."

Murmurs of approval rumbled through the crowd. Doon, who was standing at the rear, heard several people echo Tick's words: "Strike back, yes, we have to strike back. We are warriors."

"We must be ready," Tick said. "When the next confrontation comes, we won't be as disorganized as we were today. We'll have a plan. And we'll be armed."

More murmurs, and a ripple of excitement.

"How will we arm ourselves?" Tick asked. He

answered the question himself. "We have what we need right here where we live," he said. "Look in your bathrooms. You'll find strong metal rods there, just the right length, and enough for everyone."

People looked at each other in puzzlement. Metal rods in the bathroom? But Doon knew immediately what Tick meant: the towel racks. Take them off the wall, and you have a sturdy weapon that could do real damage—bruise soft flesh, even break hard bone.

Tick waited until the word was passed through the crowd and everyone understood about the weapons in the bathrooms. Then he said, "There are other ways to arm yourself, too. Did you bring a knife with you from Ember? Are there still slivers of glass left in the windows of your room? Have you noticed that some of the stones by the river are just the size to fit in a fist?"

Again, he waited. All around Doon, people were nodding and whispering. Doon tried to imagine what the uprising earlier that day would have been like if the rioters had been swinging steel rods and striking out with knives and broken glass. People would have been hurt; there would have been blood. But think of the hurt the villagers had inflicted on the Emberites—the pangs of hunger, the humiliation, the name calling, the terrible itchy rash. Didn't one hurt deserve another? Wasn't he simply being squeamish to shrink from it? He would have to strengthen himself, he thought—not just his body, but his spirit, his will.

It would take a kind of strength he didn't have yet to strike another person with the intent to harm.

Tick was bending forward now and speaking in a softer voice. People shushed each other and listened. "Go back now and sleep, my warriors," Tick said. "In the next days, prepare your weapons and prepare your will. Remember how you felt when you saw those ugly words scrawled on our walls. Remember how you felt when the poison rash crawled up your arms. The people of Sparks will wrong us again, we can be sure of that. When it happens, we'll be ready."

After the meeting, Doon walked back to the hotel feeling vaguely uneasy. Tick must be right, but somehow Doon couldn't feel wholehearted about being a warrior. Was it because he was a coward? He didn't want to be a coward. He didn't really think he was one. What was his problem, then?

CHAPTER 22

Discoveries

When Lina awoke the next morning, she thought there was something wrong with her eyes. Everything had gone gray. She sat up and looked around. No, it wasn't her eyes—it was the air that was wrong. It was so thick she could hardly see through it. The truck was merely a dark shadow. The buildings of the city had vanished entirely.

From somewhere in the murk, she heard Caspar's voice. He was muttering to himself, as he had been the night before, but she could hear only a low, growly sound, no words.

A dark shape appeared and moved toward her. It was Maddy. She bent over and whispered, "Don't get up yet. Lie back down."

"What's wrong with the air?" Lina asked her.

"It's called fog," Maddy said. "It comes in off the water. Now lie down. Curl up."

Lina lay down and pulled the blanket up under her chin. Maddy knelt beside her and whispered, "Pretend you're sick. Moan and groan a little. Refuse to get up. I'll explain later."

Lina followed instructions. She stared up into the swirling grayness and whimpered a little. It wasn't hard to pretend she didn't feel good. She'd rarely felt so cold and miserable in her life.

She saw Maddy and Caspar huddling together, two shadowy humps in the fog. They were talking, and their voices rose, but she couldn't make out what they were saying.

She must have gone to sleep again. When she opened her eyes, the fog was thinner. A pale sun like a circle of paper shone through it. Without sitting up, she looked around for Maddy and saw her sitting on the back of the truck, eating. She didn't see Caspar anywhere.

"Maddy," she whispered.

Maddy jumped down and came over to her. "You can get up now," she said. "He's gone."

Lina sat up. "Gone?"

Maddy nodded. "Into the ruins. He won't give up this notion of finding treasure. Something in his mind has slipped, I think. He wasn't all that steady to begin with, and now he's lost his balance." She took Lina's hand and pulled her to her feet, and together they folded the blanket. "He wants you to help him with his search—go into the small spaces where he can't go. I told him you'd help tomorrow but today you weren't well. So he went off to look around by himself. 'Preliminary exploration,' he called it."

"I don't want to help him," Lina said.

"You aren't going to," said Maddy. "We're leaving."

"We are? When? How?" Lina asked.

"Now," said Maddy. "Come and help me."

Maddy climbed up onto the truck, unstrapped the two bicycles, and handed them down to Lina. She opened the food chest and took out some of the remaining travelers' cakes, along with two water bottles, and she wrapped these in blankets and tied them with rope.

"Here," she said to Lina. "This pack is yours, and this bike."

"You mean we're going to ride all the way back to Sparks?" Lina thought with horror of the vast, empty distance, and the blazing heat.

"We won't have to ride all the way," Maddy said. "There are lots of roamers. Someone will help us."

"And we just leave Caspar here by himself?" Lina wasn't sure that even someone as unlikable as Caspar should be abandoned in this terrible place.

"He'll be fine," said Maddy. "He has his truck and all his supplies. He doesn't need us."

So they tied the packs onto their backs. They

walked the bikes across the rubbly part of the road until they came to the place where it opened out into the long downhill curve. Just then the fog lifted and the air came clear. Lina turned around to take a last look at the city, the city she'd had such hopes for, the city she thought might be a home for the people of Ember. In the sunlight, it looked more sad than terrible. Over the rolling, grass-covered mounds, the skeletons of the old towers stood like watchmen. The trees bent their backs before the wind, and the wind swept ripples across the surface of the green water that wrapped around the city's edges. Maybe, thought Lina, the sparkling city she'd seen in her mind was a vision from the distant future, not the distant past. Maybe someday the people of Ember—or the great-great-grandchildren of today's people of Ember—would come back here and build the city again.

"All right," said Maddy. "Let's ride."

Lina flung her leg over the bike and settled herself on the seat. This was a bigger bike than the one she was used to. She gripped the handlebars, gave a push with her foot, and she was off.

From the start, the bike moved so fast she hardly had to pedal. She zoomed forward, going far faster than even her fastest running. The wind in her face swept her hair out behind her, shot through her clothes, nearly peeled back her eyelids. The bumps in the road made the handlebars buck like something alive—she held on with a steel grip. It was absolutely terrifying and absolutely joyful. Down the long hill they went, she and Maddy alone on the wide, empty highway, no need to pedal at all, only steer around broken places or bits of debris. The fast air came into Lina's mouth and buffeted down into her lungs, and she laughed out loud, it was such a glorious freedom. When the slope leveled out a little, she steered the bike in big curves, back and forth, and Maddy did, too. They whooped and laughed and raced each other, and alongside them the white birds swooped, too, screeching in their shrill voices.

Then came a long stretch of flat road and hard pedaling. With many stops for resting and eating and drinking water, they rode all day. Lina's seat was sore and her legs grew tired. Blisters rose on her hands from holding so tight to the handlebars. But Maddy said, "Just a little farther, a little farther, and then we'll stop," and Lina kept going, finding strength when she thought it was gone, until at last, at the end of the day, they came to the place where the water ended and they could begin to turn eastward toward the hills.

Here they stopped for the night. They found a creek with a trickle of clear water running along the bottom. Maddy said the round green leaves that grew on the creek's banks were good to eat, so they had those with their travelers' cakes, along with some wild onions and a few blackberries they found deep in a thicket of bramble. There was no cold wind here, as there had been near the city. The evening was warm and still, except for the chirping of frogs in the creek. They spread their blankets on the ground. Somewhere in the dark, an owl hooted softly and another answered. Maddy was lying on her back with her hands clasped over her wide stomach. To Lina, gazing at her profile against the sky, she looked like a small range of hills, solid and comforting. So Lina dared to ask a question that had been troubling her.

"Maddy," she said, "could there ever be another Disaster like the one that came before? Or even worse? What if every single person and every single animal was killed?"

"Don't worry," said Maddy. "People didn't make life, so they can't destroy it. Even if we were to wipe out every bit of life in the world, we can't touch the place life comes from. Whatever made plants and animals and people spring up in the first place will always be there, and life will spring up again."

Maddy turned over and tugged her blanket around her neck. "Time to sleep now," she said. "More hard riding tomorrow."

In the morning, they were on their way as soon as the sun rose. Lina groaned as she got on her bike again—her muscles were sore from yesterday. But she soon warmed up, and for a long time the road was flat and the riding was easy.

After an hour or so, Lina spotted something moving up ahead of them, a dot in the distance. "Look!" she called to Maddy, who was a little way behind her, and she pointed. "I think it's a truck! Maybe a roamer!"

In ten minutes or so, they had caught up to it. The man driving the truck turned when he heard them calling. Surprise lit up his face, and he halted his oxen and jumped down.

"Greetings!" he cried. "Glad to see some travelers! Haven't met anyone on the road for four days."

He was a short, stocky man with a wild fuzz of black hair that stood out several inches all around his head. Pelton Moss was his name, and he was indeed a roamer, as was easy to see from the crates and barrels on his truck. All his containers were nearly empty, though. He had sold his most recent load of goods to a remote south-bay settlement. Now he was heading back in the direction of Sparks. "I'll take you with me," he said, "if you'll help with my collecting on the way."

And so for five days, Lina got to be a roamer. At every ancient abandoned town, they stopped and combed through the derelict houses. Not much was left; these houses had been picked nearly clean in the last two hundred years. But sometimes, if they looked carefully, they found things the previous roamers had overlooked, or things they had thought worthless.

Lina loved these searches. In some ways, it was like being a messenger back in Ember—she could go everywhere, look in every forgotten corner, and if she was lucky make discoveries. And she was lucky.

She found a silver locket with a picture of someone inside, though the picture was so old and stained she couldn't tell if it was a woman or a baby. She found a small, round pane of glass with a handle. The glass made whatever you looked at appear bigger. "A magnifying glass," said Pelton. "Nice." She found a tiny red truck with wheels that still turned. She found a strip of leather with a buckle and two round metal pieces attached to it. It was too short to be a belt. There were words on the metal circles, but they were so worn she couldn't read them. "That's a dog collar," Pelton told her. "Not very useful, but interesting."

At a house that stood by itself far out in a field, she opened a cabinet on a back porch, where the screen was hanging in brown flaps. In the cabinet was a box that said "Monopoly" in faded letters on its lid. Inside were tiny dotted cubes and tiny bits of wood shaped like houses. "Wonderful!" Pelton exclaimed. "Extremely rare!" There was another box in the cabinet with a picture of a garden on top and a heap of oddly shaped pieces of cardboard inside. And at the back of the cabinet, in a clutter of broken dolls, torn pages from books, and little jars of dried-up paint, Lina found a bar of metal about three inches long that Pelton said was a magnet. "Put it up against the truck," he said. "It'll stick right on there."

Even as she enjoyed the searching, though, Lina couldn't help imagining how it would be for the people of Ember to come out into this empty land and try to start a town. How would they turn the hard, cracked earth into fields of crops? What would they build houses with? What would they eat while they chopped at the soil and put together their shelters? A picture rose in her mind of Ember's four hundred people scattered across the brown fields like a flock of lost birds, scratching in the dry grass for seeds or bugs, huddling for shade beneath the few trees, trying to build shelters of sticks or straw. She shuddered and made the picture go away. It was best to keep her attention on searching.

Maddy didn't do much searching. She didn't care for bending over and creeping underneath things and wedging her large self into small spaces. While Lina and Pelton hunted, she walked around in the fields and the overgrown gardens behind the houses, looking for old fruit trees, wild grapevines, and the kinds of leaves, roots, nuts, and mushrooms that were all right to eat. Lina would look out the window of the house she was poking through and see Maddy wading through knee-high grass toward a gnarled old apple tree. Or she'd see her wide back in among the bushes as she picked berries. Sometimes Maddy simply sat. Lina would see her settled into an ancient lawn chair, gazing across a field or up a street, not moving at all. What was she thinking about? Lina wondered at those times. She looked so serious.

On the evening of the third day, they stopped by a wide, slow part of the river. As the sun went down, they sat on the riverbank, drinking cool tea that Pelton made with mint leaves, and they talked. Pelton told about the places he'd seen, and Maddy and Lina told about Caspar's quest in the city, his mad study of the old songs about treasure.

"Oh, yes," said Pelton. "I've heard those old rhymes all my life, and my father before me heard them, too. It's an old verse, or a song, I think, come down from years ago and scrambled, probably, in the process. Everyone says it in a different way. Something like this." He sang in a sweet but off-key voice:

"There's buried treasure in the ancient city.
Remember, remember from times of old.
What's hidden will come to light again.
It's far more precious than diamonds and gold.

"That's the way I heard it, from an old man who lives up in the mountains near Angel Rock. Then I heard another version from Maggie Pierce, over by Falter. She sings it like this:

"Remember the city, the city remember,
Where treasure is hidden under the ground.
The city, the city, always remember,
That's where the treasure will be found."

Lina stared at him. Her mouth dropped open, her eyebrows flew upward, and her heart thudded in her chest.

He laughed. "What are you looking so amazed at? Think you're going to go find this treasure? Nobody believes those old things anymore. They're nursery nonsense, old jingles made up to put babies to sleep."

"Some still believe it," said Maddy. "But it's only those with a bit of madness in them. And a good measure of greed."

"That's right," said the roamer. "I've known a few like that. One of 'em was sure it was in the old city of Sanazay and spent his whole life digging through the ruins, looking for it. Finally died when a chimney fell on him."

Maddy snorted. "Such nonsense people believe," she said.

Lina was shaking her head. She began to smile. "No, no," she said. "No, you have it wrong." She laughed, she couldn't help it. "It isn't nonsense, it's true. I'm sure, I'm sure!" What she suddenly knew seemed so wonderful and astonishing that she leapt up and clapped her hands and laughed again.

"You're a silly one," said the roamer.

"I'm not silly! The city in that rhyme—it's the city I come from!"

The roamer cast a sideways glance at Maddy. "What's the matter with her?" he said. "Has she got a fever?"

Maddy reached up for Lina's hand. "Calm down now," she said. "Tell us what you're talking about."

So Lina explained. "Sing the first line again, the first line of the second song," she said.

Pelton eyed her strangely, but he sang: "Remember the city, the city remember, where treasure is hidden under the ground."

"That first line," said Lina. "I'm sure it's meant to be 'Remember the city, the city of *Ember.*' That's the name of my home. It was under the ground."

"Not sure I believe *that,*" said Pelton.

"I think it's true," said Maddy. "They all say it, all the ones who came from there."

"And what about the treasure, then?" Pelton asked.

"It was *us*!" cried Lina. "We were the treasure, the people of Ember!" She felt a swell of love all of a sudden for her old city. "Sing that first song again, the last lines of it."

Pelton sang: "What's hidden will come to light again. It's far more precious than diamonds and gold."

"You see?" said Lina. "Come to light! We came up into the light! And we were more precious than diamonds and gold because they thought we might be the last people—the only ones left."

The three of them gazed at each other in wonder. "I believe she's right," said Maddy at last.

"Maybe so," said Pelton. He stared curiously at Lina. "You lived *underground*?"

So then for the rest of the evening, Lina told about the city of Ember, and how she had been a messenger there, and how she and Doon had found the way out. It was late when they finally lay down for the night. Lina couldn't sleep at first, thinking of the old songs and what they meant. Someone, long ago, had hoped that at least a few people would survive and had wanted them to remember her city and the treasure it held, the treasure that was most valuable of all—herself, her family, and all the generations of people who had lived in that secret place, their purpose, though they didn't know it, to make sure that human beings did not vanish from the world, no matter what happened above.

The Third Town Meeting

After the rampage in the plaza, the three town leaders went up to the tower room for an urgent meeting. They flopped into their chairs and sat without speaking for a few moments, staring down at the mess below.

"What do we do now?" said Wilmer.

Ben curled both hands into fists and set them on the table in front of him. "The cavepeople," he said, "must leave."

"Leave?" said Mary.

"Leave," said Ben. "They must go away from here."

"But they haven't been here six months yet," said Wilmer.

"They must go now," said Ben. "It's better for them anyhow, to leave before winter really sets in."

"They won't want to leave," said Wilmer, tugging anxiously at a strand of his hair. "I think they understand now that there's nowhere for them to go."

"They *must* go," said Ben. "We can never feel safe while they are here. If they refuse to go, we will force them to. We have the means to do it."

There was a long silence. Ben and Mary glared at each other. Wilmer's eyes darted anxiously between them.

At last, Mary set the palms of her hands on the table and took a long breath. "You are speaking of the Weapon," she said.

"That's right," said Ben. "We have it for situations of dire emergency. I think we have an emergency now."

"We've never used it before," said Wilmer. "We don't even know how to work it."

"I think it is unwise to use it," said Mary. "We have always tried our best not to repeat the mistakes of our ancestors. Using the Weapon would be the first step down the path they took."

"We may not actually have to *use* the Weapon," said Ben. "All we have to do is threaten them with it. Just the sight of it will make them do what we say—that is, leave."

"What you are proposing," said Mary, "is sending four hundred people to their deaths."

"Not necessarily," said Ben. "The village of Sparks started with almost nothing, why shouldn't they?"

"It's not true that we started with nothing. The founders of Sparks came here from the old cities, in a truck loaded with enough food and supplies to keep them going for months. These people have nothing at all."

"We will send a truck with them, then," said Ben. "With barrels of water, some food, and some basic supplies."

"That would last them about a week," said Mary. "Besides, they have no skills. They haven't had time to learn them."

Ben sighed impatiently. "Are we supposed to subject our own people to hardship and danger because of a bunch of refugees from a cave? Isn't it our job to *protect* our own people?"

"But if they rebel against this order," said Wilmer, "then what?"

"I thought I had made that clear," said Ben. "We use force. It is our only option." He pondered for a moment, frowning into the air above Wilmer's head. "We'll put the Weapon on a truck and take it to the hotel. If they put up any resistance, it'll be right there, ready to use." He thumped a fist on the table. "I say we give them a day to prepare. The day after tomorrow they will leave Sparks. All of them. For good. Shall we vote on it?"

They nodded.

"I vote yes," said Ben. "They must leave."

"I vote no," said Mary.

Wilmer stared down at his hands. He swallowed.

He took a shaky breath. "I . . . ," he said. "I vote . . . I vote yes."

So it was decided. They would make the announcement that very night, calling the people of Ember together after they were through with work and before they went back to the hotel. Ben would be the one to tell them. He would make it clear that the decision was final.

CHAPTER 23

Getting Ready for War

The announcement shocked the people of Ember. That evening, they swarmed through the halls of the Pioneer Hotel in an uproar. People wept and shouted and moaned. In the lobby, Doon encountered a group of people embroiled in a huge argument.

"It's the fault of that Hassler boy," shouted someone. "He was the one who started the riot. He was egging people on."

"No! He stood up for us! He gave them what they deserved!" cried someone else.

"He's a troublemaker!"

"He's a hero!"

Doon started up the stairs. Halfway up, he passed Lizzie. Her face was flushed with excitement. She grabbed his arm. "He won't let them kick us out," she said, "will he?"

"Will who?" said Doon.

"Tick. I'm sure he'll save us. He's so brave, isn't he? He'll make them change their minds." She hurried on down the stairs.

It was many hours before people went to sleep that night. The noise in the hallways went on and on, as some people wailed that they were all going to die, and others vowed to fight, and others gathered up their belongings and stuffed them into sacks. Sadge was so frightened by what was happening that he curled up in the corner with his blanket over his head. But Doon and his father and Edward Pocket sat talking for a long time.

"I don't see how we could make a town from nothing out in the Empty Lands," said Doon. "I don't believe they ever thought we could. We'd starve trying to do it. We *can't* go—they can't make us."

His father, who sat leaning against the wall with his knees up, shook his head sadly. "I don't know," he said. "This Weapon they have—they could use that to force us out."

"But what could it be?" Doon said. "Just one weapon? I don't understand it."

"To be effective," said Edward Pocket in his most learned tone, "a weapon must come into contact with the person or persons it is used against. The question is, how can one weapon be effective against four hundred people? My guess is that it's something very large that could be made to fall on us and crush us."

"But where could they hide it, if it's that large?" asked Doon. "It would have to be as big as a mountain."

"It could be an animal," said Doon's father. "They might have it in a cage in the basement of the town hall. Something very fierce that they would let loose on us."

"Or it might be something like the poison oak, only worse," said Doon. "Some sort of poison that they could spray at us."

His father nodded thoughtfully. "Yes," he said. "That could be it."

"But Father," said Doon, "we have to fight them, don't you think? No matter what the Weapon is. We can't just leave. It's so unfair!"

Edward Pocket, who had been sitting cross-legged on the floor, scrambled to his feet. He clenched both fists and raised them as if ready to pound someone. "I'm not leaving!" he shouted. "Let them try and make me! I'll chain my leg to their big old tree!"

From under his blanket, Sadge moaned.

"Besides," Edward went on, "I have work to do here. They need me. They need all of us!" He sat down again. "Probably tomorrow they'll change their minds."

"I don't think so," said Doon's father. "That Ben sounded serious to me."

"So what do we do, then, Father?" asked Doon. "We fight, don't we?"

Doon's father sighed. He stretched his long legs out in front of him and stared down at his knees. "Think about what it would mean to fight," he said. "Say we barricade ourselves here in the hotel and refuse to leave. They come at us with their Weapon, whatever it is. Some of us are hurt, some die. We go out to meet them with whatever weapons we can find—sticks, maybe, or pieces of broken glass. We battle each other." He ran his hand across his head and sighed again. "Maybe they set fire to the hotel. Maybe we march into the village and steal food from them and they come after us and beat us. We beat them back. In the end, maybe we damage them so badly that they're too weak to make us leave. What do we have? Friends and neighbors and families dead. A place half destroyed, and those left in it full of hatred for us. And we ourselves will have to live with the memory of the terrible things we have done."

Doon pictured all this as his father spoke. He hadn't really imagined before what fighting would be like. "But still," he said. "At least some of us would survive and have a place to live. If we go out into the Empty Lands, we'll all die."

His father just shook his head. "I don't know, Doon. I have to admit, I just don't know what we should do."

"I know what *I'm* going to do," said Edward Pocket.

"What?" asked Doon.

"Go to bed," said Edward. He stamped over to his closet and crawled in. "Wake me up," he said, "when you've got all this figured out."

An hour or so later, the noise of marching sounded in the hallway, and the *thump-thump* of knocks on doors, one after the other. Tick's voice rang out: "Calling all fighters!" he shouted. "All fighters! All those who refuse to be banished! Meet at the head of the road. We must make our plan!" The footsteps passed, and Doon heard the same message repeated farther down the hall, and again farther yet.

He put his clothes and shoes back on. In spite of what his father had said, he still didn't think the people of Ember should agree to go quietly out into the wilderness. Somehow, they must resist—and Tick was the only one with a plan.

The hall was full of people, a few of them murmuring quietly to each other, most of them silent. All were heading for the stairs. Outside, the night was warm, but a restless wind stirred in the trees and scraps of cloud flew across the stars. With the others, Doon headed for the meeting place.

Tick stood in a patch of moonlight, the dense shrubbery behind him. When people had gathered around, he held up his rod, and all whispering died away.

"Listen carefully," Tick said. He spoke in a level voice, not loudly, but every word was sharp and clear. "The day we've been ordered to leave—the day after tomorrow—we will assemble at dawn, at the front of the hotel. Have your weapons with you. There are still many people who haven't made up their minds to fight, and a few who are ready to go meekly into the Empty Lands, following orders. We want to change their minds. Flash your weapons! Shout our battle cry: 'We will not go!' Remind them of the black words of hatred scrawled in mud on the plaza and on the walls of our hotel, and the poison leaves on the doorstep. We will make those cowards ashamed of their weakness. We will make them understand that obedience to evil commands is a disgrace. Most of them, maybe all of them, will join us. And once they have, we will march into the village, loud and defiant and strong, and in the plaza we will confront the town leaders and make our demands."

A few people raised their fists and shouted approval.

"What are our demands?" Doon asked. He was standing at the front of the crowd, just a few feet from Tick.

"They are these," said Tick. "We demand to be made full citizens of this town, not cast out into the wilderness. We demand to be properly fed. We demand decent places to stay. We demand the end to unfair rules and insults."

These seemed reasonable things to ask for, Doon thought. "And if they refuse to agree to our demands?" he asked.

"Then of course we fight."

"But they have this Terrible Weapon they talk about," said Doon. "What about that?"

Others echoed his question. "Yes, what about it?"

Tick smiled. His teeth showed white in the moonlight. "They have one weapon," he said. "We have many. And each weapon, in the right hands, is an engine of power." His voice grew louder. "We will attack them," he cried, "like this!" He raised his steel rod and brought it slashing down so that the air whistled around it. The end cut into the ground. He raised it again and whipped it back and forth, striking tree trunks so hard he gashed their bark. He whirled around and battered the bushes behind him. "You cannot defeat us!" he cried to an imaginary enemy. "Right is on our side! We will have your blood! We will break your bones!" He went into a frenzy of stabbing and slicing, thrashing wildly among the bushes. Leaves flew, twigs snapped.

Something fluttered and fell. Doon saw it. So did Tick. He stopped for a moment and glanced down. At his feet was a half-grown baby bird that must have been huddled deep within the bushes. It flopped onto its side, its beak gaping.

"You see?" Tick cried. "The enemy falls at my feet!" He raised his rod. "With one blow I—"

Doon stepped forward and grabbed Tick's arm. "Don't," he said.

Tick tried to pull away. Then he relaxed and lowered his weapon. He grinned. "Okay," he said. "I think it's dead anyhow." He stuck the toe of his shoe beneath the bird and flipped it away, into the grass. "But you get the idea," he said, turning back to his warriors. "Imagine *hundreds* of us doing that! We'll be unbeatable." His face was alight with glee.

And that was when Doon's vague, uneasy feelings came together into one clear understanding: Tick *wants* war. The thought of war excites him and makes him happy. But not me. The thought of war makes me sick.

Doon's way parted from Tick's that night. He walked back to the hotel and up the stairs slowly, his heart heavy. He still didn't know what he was going to do the day after tomorrow. All he knew was that he did not want Tick for his commander. He would command himself.

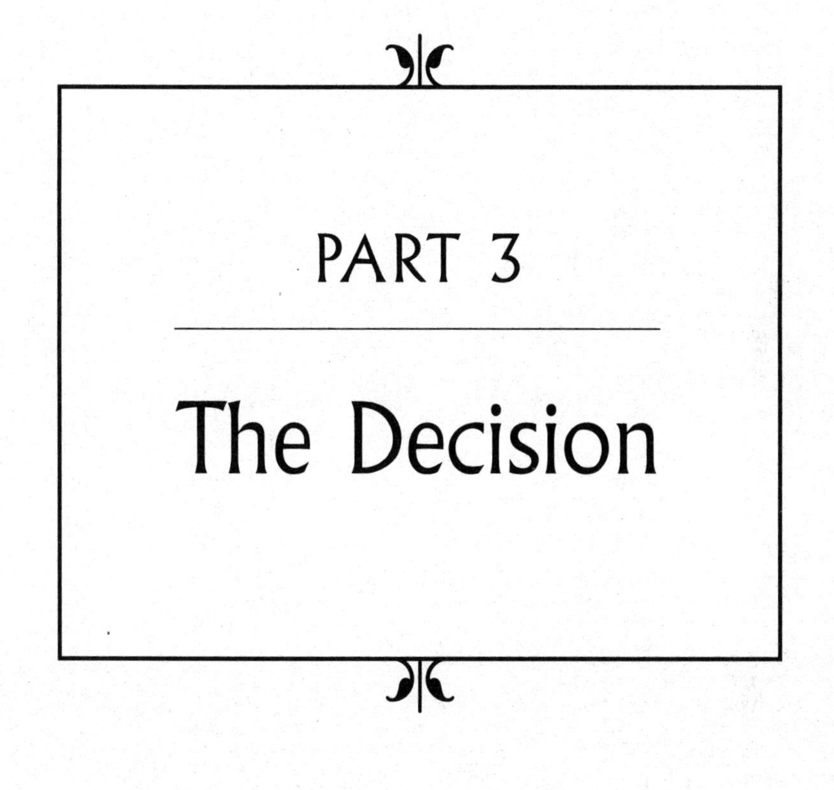

PART 3

The Decision

CHAPTER 24

What Torren Planned

Torren heard the news from old Sal Ramirez, who came in the evening to have the doctor look at his infected eye.

"They've been ordered out," said Sal as Dr. Hester stood over him, pulling his eyelid down. "The cave-people. They have to leave. Day after tomorrow."

"That can't be true," said the doctor. She dipped a spoon into a small glass jar full of clear liquid. "Tip your head back," she said. She dripped drops into Sal's eye.

"It is true," said Sal. "Ben told 'em to go."

"But how can they?" said the doctor. "There's no *place* for them to go."

"Some of 'em refused," said Sal. "They said they'd fight." He wiped his eyes. "Ben said he'd bring out the Weapon if they did."

"The Weapon!" The doctor set the jar down on the

table and stared at Sal. "Has Ben gone out of his mind?"

"Don't know," said Sal.

Torren listened from his place on the window seat, shivering with excitement. There was going to be a war, right here in Sparks! And the terrible Weapon would be used at last—on the cavepeople! He had always wanted to know what it was. Now he'd find out.

Sal left, with a bandage pressed to his eye. The doctor sat down at the table and stared out the window at the flame-colored streak in the western sky. "How have we come to this?" she said, but she didn't seem to be asking Torren.

The look on her face caused a little fear to mix with Torren's excitement. He didn't want to be *in* the war, he thought. He could get hurt. The Weapon might accidentally get *him* instead of the cavepeople. He just wanted to *see* the war, not fight in it.

"Where will the war be?" he asked the doctor.

"What?" She looked at him as if she'd forgotten he was there.

"The war," he said. "Day after tomorrow. Where will it be?"

"You're talking nonsense," said the doctor. "If there's a war, it will be everywhere." She stood up slowly, hoisting herself with an arm on the table. Her face looked heavy, and she shuffled to her room without saying good night.

Torren went to bed and lay there a long time with his mind racing. He decided he would get up before anyone else the day after tomorrow, the day the war would begin. He would get dressed. He would take a hunk of cornbread from the kitchen and put it in his pocket. He would take a knife, too, in case the war came close to him. Then he would go down to the plaza and climb to the top of the big pine tree, so high up that he'd be hidden from below. From there, he would be able to see everything.

CHAPTER 25

Dread at the Last Minute

As Pelton's truck drew near the village of Sparks, Lina was more and more impatient. She longed to see Poppy and Mrs. Murdo and Doon. "Another day's travel," Pelton said. "We'll be in Sparks by tomorrow morning."

Lina was too excited to sleep much that night. Her mind galloped forward to the people she would see tomorrow, and backward to everything she'd seen on her journey. She finally fell asleep a few hours before morning, and when she awoke, she could feel immediately that something in the air had changed. A wind had arisen, a warm, gusty wind that bent the brown grasses and rattled in the leaves of the trees. The blue of the sky had faded to a hazy gray, and the heat seemed more fiery than ever. She felt something unsettling in the air, a warning, like the first traces of fever when an illness is coming on.

"Could be nearly a hundred degrees today," said Pelton. "But in a week or two the heat will start to slack off. The season's changing. You can feel it in the wind."

They started out early. After only an hour or so, Lina could see the fields and buildings of Sparks in the distance. She stood up—she was sitting on the front seat of the truck between Maddy and Pelton—and shielded her eyes with her hand to see better. There it was—and now it looked like home to her, the solid little brown houses, the tidy fields around them. When they came to the road that led to the Pioneer Hotel, Lina had a sudden idea. "Let me off here," she said. "I want to tell Doon I'm back. I'll walk the rest of the way."

She thanked Pelton for all his help, and he thanked her in return. "Take a few of the things you found," he said, "whatever you like." She rummaged through the crate until she found the magnifying glass, the magnet, and the little red truck, and she tucked these into her pack.

"I'll go into town and help Pelton with the trading," Maddy said to Lina. "I'll meet you later at the doctor's house."

Lina jumped down from the truck. Her legs strong and springy, her hair flying in the wind, she ran up the road toward the hotel.

She expected to see people at the river, washing, and people sitting on the hotel steps eating their breakfasts, getting ready for work. But the grounds of the hotel were empty, and when she went inside, she found people milling about the lobby in confusion. Some of them were crying—she saw the two Hoover sisters, one wailing, the other trying to comfort her, and she saw old Nammy Proggs sitting on a rolled-up blanket, grumbling to herself. People were arguing with each other—she heard angry voices, and questioning voices, and voices full of fear.

For a second she just stood looking, wondering what was happening. Then someone spotted her. "Lina!" Her name rang out over the hubbub. Faces turned toward her, and people rushed up to her and crowded around her. "You're back! Where have you been? We thought you'd disappeared forever!" She saw Clary's face, smiling, and she heard the voices of friends from school, and Captain Fleery of the Ember messengers, and someone who used to work in the shoe store. "Are you all right?" they said. "What a time to come back! Why did you leave? Where have you been?" Hands reached for her, arms wrapped her in hugs. She saw a red head bouncing up and down as Lizzie jumped in the air, trying to see over the crowd, and she saw Mrs. Polster beaming at her, and Miss Thorn at her side.

"I'm fine, I'm fine!" she said. "I'm so happy to be back! But what's going on here? And where's Doon?"

"I'm here!" It was Doon's voice. There he was, just

coming down the stairs. She broke away from the welcoming crowd and ran over to him. He didn't speak, just reached out an arm and grabbed her hand. The look on his face startled her. Was he angry?

"Come outside," he said.

She followed him down a passage and out a door in the back of the hotel. There was a small concrete terrace there, bordered by a low wall. Behind the wall, the drooping branches of a dusty tree stirred in the wind. Doon sat down on the wall and pulled her down next to him.

For a moment he said nothing. When he spoke, his voice came out in a rough shout. "*Where have you been?*" he said. "Don't you know how everyone has worried about you? Don't you know everyone has thought you were *dead*?"

Lina shrank back. "I didn't mean to be gone so long," she said. "It was a mistake. I thought—"

"Nearly a month you've been gone!" Doon said.

"It was because of the city, Doon. I thought the city would be like those drawings I made. I thought maybe we could go there, all of us, and live there, and . . . and be happy," she finished weakly.

"You could have told me you were going," Doon said. "I might have wanted to go, too. Did you think of that?"

"I didn't really think at all," Lina said, "I just saw the chance and went. But if I *had* thought about it"—

she frowned, remembering—"I'd probably have figured you wouldn't *want* to come. Because you were too busy with that . . . that Tick."

Doon's face fell. "Oh," he said. "Well, you're right. I guess I was . . . I thought Tick might be . . ." Doon stopped, looking flustered. "I'm sorry," he said.

"I'm sorry, too," said Lina. They were silent for a moment. Then Lina said, "Shall we forgive each other?"

"All right," said Doon. He smiled.

Lina smiled back. "But what's going on *here*?" she asked. "Why is everyone so upset?"

"They've ordered us out, Lina! They've told us we have to leave tomorrow morning!"

"What?" Lina could not take this in. "Who has to leave?"

"All of us! All the people of Ember!"

"And go where?"

"Out into the Empty Lands. We have to make a new life for ourselves, they said. On our own."

Lina's mouth dropped open. A wild confusion filled her mind. "But how can we? What would we eat? Where would we live?" Again the frightening picture rose in her mind—the people of Ember scattered like fallen birds across a vast, dry landscape. "There are wolves out there," she said, "and bandits!"

"I know," said Doon. "And it will be winter soon. Have you heard of winter?"

Lina shook her head. When Doon explained, her eyes widened in shock.

"All this time you've been gone, Lina, they've done terrible things to us. The first thing was that boy Torren." He told her about the smashed tomatoes that Torren blamed on him.

"He said he saw you?" Lina said, outraged. "Why would he do that?"

Doon shrugged. "Ask him. I don't know." He went on to tell her what else had happened. "They've thrown us out of their houses! They've written hateful words on our walls. They've poisoned us with leaves!"

"But why? What did we do to them?" Lina said. The wind blew her hair forward over her shoulders. She clutched a handful of tangled strands to hold them still.

"We ate their food," said Doon. "That was the main thing. But other things happened, too." He told her about the riot in the plaza, and about what happened at the fountain. "Now," he said, "they've threatened to use their Weapon on us if we don't leave. So Tick says we'll use our weapons on them."

"Our weapons? What weapons?"

Doon sighed. For the first time, Lina noticed how thin he was. She saw the shadows beneath his eyes.

"There's so much to tell you," Doon said. "And we only have today."

"But I haven't even been home," Lina said. "I have

to see Poppy, and Mrs. Murdo. Are they still at the doctor's? Is Poppy all right?" A scattering of dry leaves blew against her legs. The wind whipped her hair. The whole world had changed suddenly, just in the last half hour. Her throat tightened, and she felt tears threatening.

"Yes, they're still at the doctor's," Doon said. "Come on, I'll go with you. We'll talk there."

"Wait," said Lina. "I brought you a present. Two presents." She unrolled the pack she'd carried all the way from the city, took out the magnet and the magnifying glass, and handed them to Doon. "This one is a magnet," she said. "If you put it against metal, it sticks there. I guess it isn't very useful, but it's interesting. The other one is for making things bigger—I mean, making them look bigger."

"Thank you," Doon said. He examined his presents curiously. He held the glass up and peered through it at the back of the hotel.

"Look at something small," Lina said. "Like a leaf or a bug."

Doon riffled among the leaves on the ground and found an ant, which he set on the palm of his hand. Holding the glass above the ant, he looked through it. "Oh!" he said. "Look! You can see its knee joints! And even . . ." He trailed off, absorbed in looking. Then he raised his eyes to Lina. "It's like a miracle!" he said. He blew the ant from his palm and looked around until he found a beetle. "Look at this!" he cried. "You can see it chewing!" He tried a feather, and a bit of moth wing, and a blade of grass.

"This is such an amazing world," he said finally, putting the glass and the magnet into his pocket. "I love it here, except for the troubles with people."

Lina and Doon went through the village and up the road to the doctor's house. It was still early morning when they got there—when they came through the door, they saw everyone at the table, eating breakfast. Mrs. Murdo was facing the door, so she saw them first. She stood up, her spoon still in her hand. She stared for a second, her eyes round, her mouth open, words trying to come out of it. Then she rushed toward Lina and wrapped her in a hug. At the same time, Poppy jumped down from the bench, dashed toward Lina, and hugged her knees. The doctor stood up and watched this reunion wide-eyed.

Torren leapt up, too, but not to hug Lina. He ran to the door and looked out, and then he cried, "Where's Caspar? Isn't he here, too? Where is he?" But no one paid attention to him. They were too busy fussing over Lina, asking questions and not giving her a chance to answer. "Where have you been? Are you all right? Why didn't you *tell* us . . . Do you know what's happening here?"

Poppy yelled, "Wyna, Wyna, pick me up! Pick me

up!" And the doctor, thrown into a state of even more confusion than usual, murmured, "Some tea? Or . . . let's see. Why don't we all . . . So glad you're . . ." And all around the edges was Torren, pulling at Lina's sleeve, saying, "But why *isn't* he here, where is he? When is he coming?" and getting no answers.

When things calmed down a little, Lina said, "Maddy will be coming soon. She stayed in town to help the roamer for a while."

Mrs. Murdo stopped smiling and grew stern. "Lina," she said, "how could you go off like that and not talk to me first? And just leave that careless little note, which was not, I would point out, true. Three days, you said. It's been twenty-eight! That was a thoughtless, foolish thing to do."

"I know," Lina said. "I'm really, really sorry. I didn't know I'd be gone so long." She explained how, when she overheard Caspar, she'd thought he'd said "a day's journey" when really he'd said "five days' journey." "And then," she said, "other things happened, and . . . it took a long time."

"Yes," said Mrs. Murdo. "And we had a long, long time to worry about you." She picked up Lina's pack, which Lina had dropped on the floor, and set it on the window seat. "And you know what's happened here? You know we've been ordered to leave tomorrow?"

"I know," Lina said. "But I can't believe it's true."

"It's true," said Mrs. Murdo. "It doesn't please me

a bit, but what to do about it I don't know. Come and have some breakfast."

Lina and Doon sat down at the table, where the others had been eating raspberries and cream. Though Lina was so thoroughly sick of travelers' cakes that all real food should have looked good to her, she had no appetite. Her stomach was in a knot.

"I can't eat," she said. "I'm not hungry. I have to—Doon and I have to talk."

"At least take an apple," said Mrs. Murdo.

"First of the season," the doctor added. "From up north."

Lina took the hard red fruit, and she and Doon went outside. The heat was baking now. They went through the courtyard, where the doctor's plant pots were mostly empty, the plants having either been put into the ground or died. The ones still there struggled in the heat, limp or brown. They crossed the road and walked down to the riverbank. Even the river was suffering in the heat—it no longer flowed deep and smooth but ran in streams between the exposed stones. Its edges were yellow-green and smelly.

They sat on the ground. Lina said, "It would take me hours to tell you everything I've seen. But listen, this is the main thing: people had a beautiful city, and they wrecked it."

"On purpose?" said Doon.

"With wars. With fighting. It was horrible, Doon!"

She shuddered, remembering. "That war—it sort of whispered to me. There was a moment when I could hear screams. I could see flames."

"And there's nothing left?"

"Almost nothing."

"And all across the Empty Lands—are there houses?"

"Some. But they're old and falling down. Mostly it's fields and fields of brown grass. There's howling animals. If we had to go out there and try to live—well, we couldn't."

"That's why some people—a lot of people—want to fight." Doon told her about Tick, and the weapons he and his warriors had gathered. He explained the plan—how they would go into the village tomorrow, refusing to leave, prepared to fight. And he told her about the Terrible Weapon the town leaders had threatened to use.

"Yes," Lina said, "I've heard about the Weapon, too. Torren mentioned it one time. But what is it?"

"We don't know," Doon said.

"If it's from the old times," Lina said, "then it is so terrible that Tick's little weapons would be like—like twigs against it. The old weapons could burn whole cities." She clasped her arms across her stomach and bent forward. Everything inside her felt cramped, knotted up. Her hands were slick with sweat. "There can't be war," she said.

"But we can't leave, either," said Doon.

They sat watching the water struggle along between the rocks. The sun blazed down, burning the backs of their necks.

"Don't you think," said Doon, "that fighting would be better than just giving in? At least it's *doing* something."

"I don't know," said Lina. "It scares me." She ran her finger over the glossy red skin of the apple Mrs. Murdo had given her. "I talked a lot to Maddy on my journey," she said at last. "She's wise, Doon. She told me how war gets started. It's when people say, 'You hurt me, so I'll hurt you back.'"

"But that's just how people are," said Doon. "Of course when people hurt you, you want to get back at them."

"And then they want to get back at you. And then you want to get back at them again, only worse. It goes on and on, unless someone stops it."

"Stops it how?"

"You have to catch it soon, Maddy said. As soon as you see it starting, you have to stop it. Otherwise, it can be too late."

"But *how* do you stop it?"

"You have to reverse the direction," said Lina. "That's what Maddy told me. She said that if someone had been brave enough, the wars might not have started in the first place."

"But Lina!" Doon slapped his hand down on the ground next to him. "What does that *mean*? How do you *do* it?"

Lina wasn't entirely clear about this. She took a bite of the red fruit the doctor had handed her. It looked as hard as a polished stone, but the juice that burst into her mouth was sweet. "I think it's this," she said. She chewed and swallowed. "Instead of getting back at the other side with something just as bad as they did to you—or something worse—you do something *good.* Or at least you keep yourself from doing something bad." She took another bite of the apple. "I think that's it. One bad thing after another leads to worse things. So you do a good thing, and that turns it around."

Doon sighed. "That's not very helpful," he said. "How are we supposed to do something good for these people who have done so many bad things to us? Why would we even want to?"

"Well, that's it," said Lina, wiping apple juice off her chin. "You don't want to, but you do anyway. That's what makes it hard. Maddy said it was very hard. It's much harder to be good than bad, she said."

"So what do we do, then?" said Doon. His tone was bitter. "Say we'll be happy to work without food? Say we'll always be nice no matter what they do to us?"

"No," said Lina. "That can't be right."

"Or should we just go quietly out into the Empty Lands and not bother them anymore?"

"No," said Lina. "That can't be right, either." She stared at the water rippling by. She was thinking hard. "We don't want to leave," she said. "And we don't want to fight. Do you think those are the *only* two choices?"

"What else could there be? If we don't fight, they'll make us leave. If we don't leave, we'll have to fight."

Lina discovered a tough part in the center of the apple, surrounding some brown seeds. She picked at the seeds with her fingernail. "There must be some other way," she said. "What if we all just sit down in front of the hotel and refuse to move? We don't leave, but we don't fight? They wouldn't use their weapon on us if we weren't fighting, would they?"

"I don't know," said Doon. "They might."

"I don't think they would," Lina said. "They're not *bad* people."

"But we couldn't sit there forever," Doon said. "Sooner or later, they'd make us leave. They'd pick us all up one by one and load us onto trucks and drive us away."

"Maybe they wouldn't," said Lina. "Maybe we could talk, and work something out."

"I don't think so," said Doon. "Tick and his warriors would never just sit. They *want* to fight."

Lina drew up her knees and rested her chin on

them. Something good, she thought. What good act would turn things around?

"We could volunteer to be roamers," she said. "A whole lot of us, so they wouldn't have to feed us, and we could bring things back to them."

"We don't know how to be roamers," said Doon. "We don't have trucks. Or oxen. We wouldn't know where to go."

"We could say we'll do all the worst jobs," Lina said.

"But that wouldn't be fair," said Doon impatiently. "Why should we? That's no good." He stood up, slapping the dry grass from his pants. "I think it's too late for any of that. None of it's going to work."

Lina stayed where she was, still thinking. She desperately wanted to find an answer, but no answer came to her. Her spirits sank, and she suddenly felt tired. "Well, then, we just have to be on the lookout," she said. "Some chance might turn up. We have to watch for it. I don't know what else to do." She knew how weak and silly this sounded.

But to her surprise, Doon smiled a little. "That's like what my father told me when I was working in the Pipeworks. 'Pay attention,' he said. It was a good idea then. I suppose it still is. Anyway, I guess it's the best we can do."

Lina dropped her apple core on the ground and scuffed some dirt over it, and they trudged back to the doctor's house. Doon stayed there for lunch instead of going to the Partons', and then he headed back to the hotel. Lina meant to spend the rest of the day thinking as hard as she could about the choice she'd have to make tomorrow. She sat on the window seat, sideways, her legs stretched out, and she tried to get her mind to produce ideas. But she kept coming up against the two walls: fight (she didn't want to fight) or leave (she didn't want to leave). A slow fly buzzed against the window. Wind stirred in the grape leaves outside. Think, thought Lina. Pay attention. And then she fell asleep.

CHAPTER 26

The Weapon

Morning came. Doon got up. He had to be ready for anything. So he rolled up his blankets and made a pack for all his clothes, everything he had. His father and the others did the same. Downstairs, out in front of the hotel, the people of Ember were gathering and swarming about, loud and distressed and confused. Tick roamed among them, urging courage, inspiring them to stand up for their rights, telling them the time had come for battle. His eyes flashed with a cold light. His voice rang out like the high, urgent tone of a bell. Very often, the people he spoke to seemed to catch fire from his words and be filled with the burning desire to fight.

Over half the people of Ember joined with Tick to be warriors. Some of them had wrenched the towel racks from their bathroom walls; others grabbed rocks or branches to use as weapons. They started down the road to the village, and the rest of the Emberites followed in a confused mass.

Doon went, too. The morning sun, already hot, blazed down on him; wind riffled his hair and his shirt. His mind was in turmoil, his heart thudding like a fist in his chest. Tick and his warriors, carrying their towel racks, their sink pipes, their shards of glass, strode along roaring their battle cry: We will not go! We will not go! More and more people picked up the chant as they came into the streets of the village, and at doors and windows faces appeared, shocked faces, and people still in their nightgowns. They shouted to each other—Look, the cavepeople are coming! They're coming into town! Other windows flew open, and doors, and people stepped out into the streets, unsure whether to be angry or afraid.

All the people of Ember had come. No one stayed behind to wait for the trucks that would take them out into the Empty Lands. All of them had to know what was going to happen. They had to be there, whatever it was.

They poured into the plaza and stood packed together, the warriors roaring and the others nervous, some of them half hiding in doorways or behind trees, afraid of what was going to happen, not sure if they wanted to be part of it or not.

Tick roared out his challenge. "People of Sparks! We refuse to leave! We are here to make our demands, and if you will not meet them, we will fight!"

"We will fight!" roared the warriors.

Others looked at each other fearfully. Will we?

From a side street Ben Barlow appeared, running. He bounded up onto the steps of the town hall, faced the crowd, and yelled back. "What are you doing here? This is an outrage, this is unacceptable! You are leaving today, leaving here for good."

"We will not go!" screamed the crowd.

"Wilmer! Mary!" shouted Ben. The other two leaders followed him up onto the steps.

"Clear out, now!" they shouted. "Back to the hotel! Move back, move back!" They stood in front of the crowd and tried to press them backward, but it was no use. There were simply too many Emberites. Ben darted at Tick and tried to grab him, but Tick struck him with his rod, and he lurched sideways, clutching his arm. No one had expected the Emberites to have weapons.

Doon was standing on the river side of the plaza, slightly apart from the main crowd. He had the feeling things were right on the edge of chaos, right on the edge between being in control and being out of control. It was frightening—the yelling, the waving of weapons, the people of Ember filling the plaza and the people of Sparks crowding in around the edges, their faces full of rage and fear. Maybe, thought Doon, the leaders will be willing to discuss our demands. Maybe we can talk, and everything will be all right. It was the only ray of hope he could see.

"These are our demands!" cried Tick. "Listen carefully!"

But Ben just screamed back. "We've heard enough from you! We're finished talking to you! No more talking. No more demands!"

When he heard that, Doon felt a jolt of fury. It launched him into action. He sprang up onto the bench next to him and shouted at the top of his lungs at Ben: "At least *listen*!"

That drew the attention of Chugger, who was standing near him. He lunged at Doon, but Doon leapt away. He heard Ben's voice shout, "Catch that boy!" Angry faces turned toward him, arms reached to grab him. He ducked and swerved and wove his way along the edge of the crowd, and as soon as he was in the clear, he ran.

But he didn't go far. He had to stay close to the plaza; he had to know what was going to happen. He ran up the river road and darted behind the town hall, where a few garbage barrels stood by the back door. He paused for a moment. Was anyone following him? From the plaza came a roar and then a voice shouting. What was happening? Doon *had* to know.

He pushed against the town hall's back door. It opened easily and he slipped inside. A hallway led toward the front of the building. On his right was a flight of stairs. Surely, he thought, no one was in here. They were all outside, dealing with the army of Emberites. He ran up the stairs, and at the top, he found himself in the tower room.

It was a square room with windows on all sides. A table stood in the middle, with straight-backed chairs around it. Down below was the plaza, swarming with people. The noise was like the roar of water. Tick was at the front of the crowd—Doon could see the top of his head, like a shiny black stone, and his steel rod glinting in the sun.

Straight below were the steps of the town hall and the tops of the heads of the three leaders. To his right, the windows were partially blocked by the branches of the great pine tree that stood next to the town hall. When he looked out the windows toward the rear of the building, he saw the town hall roof below.

This was perfect. He could see what was going to happen; he could hear, too, because the windows were open. And, he realized, if he stayed here, he wouldn't have to decide whether he was going to fight or not. This seemed a bit like cheating—but it was a relief, too. The thought of taking part in a bloody brawl had filled him with dread.

Standing to the side of the front window, Doon looked down. Right below him was Ben Barlow—he could see the wiry gray hair on the top of his head, and his hands waving furiously in the air. Mary Waters and

Wilmer Dent had stepped up behind Ben. Mary tried to take him by the arm, but he shook her off. He made his hands into a megaphone for his mouth. "We will not be threatened!" he shouted. "We are in charge of this town! It is our place, we built it, we own it!" He yelled so loudly that his voice rasped and cracked. "You are destroying our way of life. You must go!"

The crowd rumbled. They pressed forward. Clouds came over the sun, and a vast shadow swept across the plaza.

"You may try to make us leave!" shouted Tick. "But we are here to stay!"

The air seemed to quiver with rage. Or was it just the wind? Everything was moving—the clouds raced overhead, the branches of the trees thrashed, the Emberites raised their motley weapons. Up on the roof of the tower, the flag of Sparks whipped and snapped on its pole—Doon could hear it, though he could not see it.

He felt the wind whirling through his mind as well. His father's words came back to him. *When the fight is over, what do we have? A place destroyed. People who hate each other.* Standing above it all in the tower, he had the strange feeling of being separate, belonging neither to one side of the fight nor the other. Whose side was he on? Not on Ben's, certainly. But not on Tick's, either, with his warriors calling out threats, eager for a fight.

Ben held up his hand and shouted again. "We warned you! And we're ready for you." His voice was hoarse. "I'll give you one last chance. Will you leave or not?" With his head thrust forward and his hands tightened into fists, he waited for an answer.

"No!" screamed Tick.

His army bellowed it out with him. "No!" "Never!" "No, no!"

Ben dashed to the door of the town hall. Wilmer went with him, and together they darted inside. Doon froze, afraid they might climb up to the tower. But they came out onto the steps again right away, pulling a thing of black metal that ran on wheels. For a moment the clamor of the crowd ceased as they craned their necks, trying to see over each other's heads. Doon had a good view from where he stood, but still he had no idea what the thing was. He knew it must be the Weapon, but it looked almost like a great black insect. It stood on black iron legs. It had a complicated black iron body nearly as long as a truck, studded with hooks and boxes and points. A narrow scarf of ridged metal hung across it. It was ugly, Doon thought, like the skeleton of a monster.

Ben turned the thing so that it pointed out over the crowd. He stood behind it, his feet planted wide apart. "This is your last chance," he shouted at the crowd. "Disperse! Or take the consequences."

Mary Waters dashed toward him. “No, Ben!” she cried. “We can’t do this!”

Ben pushed her away. “We agreed!” he cried. “Stand back, Mary!”

Now the crowd in the plaza sensed danger and began to push backward. Tick cried, “Stand your ground!” but Doon saw him take a step back, too.

Ben squatted at the rear end of the Weapon. “Leave now, and take your gang of hoodlums with you!” he shouted. “Or I fire!”

Fire? thought Doon. What does he mean?

It was clear that Tick didn’t know, either. “You have one weapon,” he shouted, “but we have many!” And he raised the rod in his hand, and behind him his warriors did the same.

Ben gave a furious shout. He was crouched over the Weapon. Doon saw his bent back, and his arm jerking at the machine. Nothing happened. His arm jerked again, harder, and at the same time Mary rushed forward. She aimed a powerful kick at the nose of the Weapon, bumping it upward, and the Weapon, in a harsh machine voice, began to chatter. *Uh-uh-uh-uh-uh-uh-uh-uh-uh-uh-uh-uh-uh,* it went, turning its snout back and forth. People in the crowd began to scream.

Doon couldn’t see at first what the Weapon was doing. What was the point of its loud, furious shuddering? The noise was horrible, but the Weapon was staying in one place, not flying out into the crowd. Was it shooting something out of its— Yes! Across the plaza, over the heads of the people, Doon saw a line of holes punching into a wall, splintering a window—

But the Weapon suddenly stopped its chattering. Doon looked down and saw Ben give it a furious shake, and shake it again, pounding on its nose to aim it lower as the crowd yelled in panic and scrambled backward, and Mary shouted and tried to rush toward Ben, but Wilmer grabbed her arm—

And then the Weapon exploded.

No chattering this time, just a spurt of fire that shot from the Weapon's rear end, knocked Ben flat on his back, and toppled the Weapon forward so that it stood on its nose. This made the fire shoot straight upward, a column of bright orange, scattering sparks and reaching toward the branch of the pine tree that hung over the town hall steps.

From his place in the tower, Doon watched, horrified. Where was his father in that frenzied crowd? Where was Lina? Below him, the pine tree was on fire. The building would be on fire, too, in a minute, because the tree stood right up against it. Smoke was already curling through the windows. He had to get out.

And that was when he heard a scream—not from the plaza below, but from somewhere above him. A bird? An animal in the pine tree? A second later, an echoing scream arose from the crowd. Doon heard someone cry, "The tree! Up in the tree! Someone's there!"

Doon was at the door, ready to flee down the stairs. But he heard the scream again, and it sounded close. He darted back into the tower room and ran to the window that faced the tree. The lower branches of the pine tree were a mass of flame. He could hear the rush and roar as the fire raced among the dry needles. When he turned his gaze upward, he saw what the screaming was about: a boy was clinging to a branch a little higher up than the tower roof, hugging the trunk of the tree and screaming in terror as the fire swept upward.

Kenny! Doon thought. Was it? He couldn't tell for sure. But he knew he couldn't leave him there. Maybe somehow he could get him in through the window. He opened it as far as he could—it was the kind of window that swung outward on hinges—and then he grabbed one of the chairs from around the table. Holding it by its back, he thrust it out the window as far as he could.

"Climb down!" he shouted to the boy in the tree. "Climb down, quick!"

The boy saw him—and with a start Doon realized who he was. It wasn't Kenny at all. It was Torren, the one who had started so much trouble, the one who had pointed a lying finger at Doon. For one furious second, Doon felt the urge to leave Torren to his fate and get himself out of the tower as fast as he could. But he pushed that thought away and shouted louder: "Hurry! Get down here!"

Torren clambered down through the branches, down toward the flames beneath him. When he was opposite the tower window, he was still too far away to reach the legs of the chair. He edged out along a branch, but it was a slender branch and bent under his weight.

"Jump!" Doon yelled. "Jump! And catch the chair legs! I'll pull you in!"

Torren crawled backward to where the branch was sturdier. He stood up. Then he froze. He stood clutching the tree trunk, staring down at the flames, his mouth a dark O.

"Jump!" screamed Doon again. Smoke was pouring into the tower room now. "Hurry! You can do it!"

A gust of wind. The flames leapt. Now the branches just below Torren's feet were blazing, and suddenly he made up his mind—Doon could see the moment of decision in his face. He clamped his lips tight. He fastened his gaze to the chair dangling out the window. And then he pushed himself away from the trunk with his hands and flung himself toward the tower. His hands caught the rung between the chair legs, and Doon's whole body was yanked forward. He almost lost his grip on the chair, but not quite. "Hang on!" he yelled. With all his strength, he hauled the chair upward, and when Torren's hands were within reach, he grabbed one of them, and then both of them, letting the chair topple back into the room. One last heave, and Torren was in the tower room, shaking so violently he could hardly stand.

"Now," said Doon, "let's go."

He headed for the door. Over the sill of the window Torren had just come through crept a row of flames like sharp orange claws.

CHAPTER 27

Firefight

Lina was on the side of the plaza farthest from the river when Tick called out his demands and Doon yelled, "At least *listen*!" When she heard his voice, she tried to make her way toward him, but the crowd was so dense and turbulent that she couldn't get through. Tick's warriors were everywhere. The sun flashed off their steel rods and pipes and jagged pieces of glass. She was worming her way among the dozens of shoving and shouting people when Ben fired the Weapon.

She heard the sound, a chain of loud pops, and the people in front of her screamed and scrambled backward. Lina ducked and put her hands over her head. She stayed that way as people pressed past her and stumbled over her, and in a moment the popping noise stopped. Then there was a bang, and more shouts, and when she dared to stand up and look, she saw that the pine tree was on fire.

The flames were small at first, creeping along just one branch, with sudden flashes as dry bunches of pine needles caught fire. But in seconds the flames grew bigger. They leapt and crackled. Black smoke rose in a pillar into the air. The crowd pressed backward, crashing against each other. The people of Ember, for whom fire was a rare and terrible danger, stared upward with their eyes wide and their mouths gaping. Some of them screamed. Some were too frightened to make a sound.

Such a terror came over Lina that she couldn't move, except to stagger a few feet back along with the crowd. Her eyes were fixed on the flames—the terrible orange hands, reaching up into the branches of the tree. A voice in her mind screamed, "Run! Run!" but she couldn't run. Her legs wouldn't work. It was all they could do just to hold her up.

A voice cried out, "Someone's in the tree!" and Lina looked up through the smoke just long enough to see the upper branches thrashing and get a glimpse of something white moving among them. Then she was surrounded again by struggling people. She tripped over a piece of pipe rolling on the pavement and fell to her knees. When she managed to get to her feet again, the mass of people had pressed back behind her, and she found herself near the front of the crowd.

On the steps of the town hall, she saw Ben lying motionless, sprawled on his back. Wilmer bent over him, and Mary Waters shouted, "Fire truck! Fire truck!" The fire had leapt from the pine tree to the town hall tower—flames licked up its wall.

That was when Lina heard a wild laugh from behind her. "Let it burn!" someone cried. "Let it burn! It's their punishment! They deserve it!" She recognized the voice. It was Tick. Others took up the cry. "Let it burn!" they shouted, and a chorus of voices raised a harsh, triumphant cheer.

The people of Ember were packed together at the far south end of the plaza now, as far from the town hall and the fire as they could get. A few ran into the streets to get away, but most of them waited to see what was going to happen. They stayed at a safe distance, hovering between terror and fascination, and watched as the flames streaked up the sides of the tower.

The people of Sparks were running in all directions. Shopkeepers grabbed buckets and ran to the river and filled them with water, but most of the fire was high above their heads, impossible to reach. They flung the water into the air and then stood with empty buckets, watching the tower burn.

The two fire trucks arrived, their drivers standing up and lashing the oxen to make them trot. Water sloshed from the big barrels on the trucks' beds. As soon as the trucks stopped, people jumped up onto them, grabbed buckets, and began dipping buckets in the water.

"Fire line! Fire line!" the cry went up, and the villagers, who must have practiced this many times, formed straggling lines stretching out to the fire from the truck at the edge of the plaza. Burning twigs broke from the pine tree and blew in the wind, and new fires started up here and there. The people in the fire lines flung water in all directions, but for the few flames each bucket of water doused, it seemed ten new ones sprang up.

Lina's heart was beating so hard it drowned out all her thoughts. She wanted to run, to get away from here, but something paralyzed her. Part of it was fear of the fire. Part was fear of something else, fear of an idea that was trying to come to the surface of her mind. She didn't want to hear it. *Pay attention,* a voice whispered to her. She tried to push it away.

Faster and faster, the people on the truck dipped the buckets into the barrels, dipped, filled, and handed the buckets to those in the line, who passed them along from hand to hand. The last person in line, the one standing nearest the flames, flung the water, which hissed and steamed and put out a few flames.

Tick and his warriors, along with the rest of the people of Ember, watched all this as if it were a frightening but fascinating show. Tick and a few others cheered. But most people just gazed goggle-eyed as the flames blackened the town hall. When the wind blew sparks toward them, they shrieked and pressed back farther.

Lina scanned the crowd. Where was Doon? Where was Mrs. Murdo? She didn't see either of them—she could hardly see anything. Smoke filled the air. All she could see was a shadowy tumult of people. Only the flames were bright. The pine tree was a column of fire—within it, Lina could see the tree's black skeleton. When a great branch broke off and fell, crashing into the shrubbery below and setting it alight, a terrified clamor arose from the people of Ember, and now instead of pressing backward many of them turned and ran.

Lina stayed where she was. She felt as if she were being gripped by two huge hands. One pulled her backward, away from the fire, back toward the streets of the town, through which she could run to safety. The other pulled her forward into danger, urging her to do what she suddenly knew was right. It was the good thing. It was what she'd been waiting for. But she didn't want to do it. *I can't,* she thought. *I don't want to. I'm too afraid. Someone else will do it. Not me, not me. I can't.*

At that moment, the tower collapsed. Its walls crumpled, the roof caved in, and flames shot up from the hole. The flagpole came hurtling down like a spear. The blackened walls leaned and toppled.

And then the fire was everywhere. Flaming branches and tufts of needles, blown by the wind, landed in the dry grass at the edge of the plaza, and in the trees by the river, and on the thatched roofs of the market stalls. "There!" cried the people in the bucket line, pointing. "There! And over there!" The lines twisted around, the buckets traveled faster and faster from hand to hand, and those at the front of the lines tossed the water this way and that. But there were too many fires, and not enough people to keep up with them.

It's now, thought Lina. I have to do it. I *will* do it.

Quickly then, before she could change her mind, she ran. She ran with a hammering heart, with her head down and her hands in fists. She ran as if fighting a powerful wind, out across the plaza by herself, and when she reached the nearest bucket line she pushed her way in.

"Traitor!" shrieked a voice behind her. It was Tick's voice, that voice like a cutting blade. Lina heard it, but she paid no attention. "Traitor, traitor!" Tick cried again, and his warriors echoed him. "Traitor!" they yelled, jumping backward when the sparks flew too close.

Doon got out of the tower just in time. He'd had to almost throw Torren down the stairs and then take them three at a time himself. Torren ran off somewhere as soon as he went out the back door, but Doon dashed around to the plaza, staying close to the market stalls, and joined the crush of Emberites at the south end. Panting, he stared back at the ruin he had escaped from—the black spine of the pine tree, the smoldering boards of the town hall. He watched as the flames consumed the building and the tower collapsed. He saw the fire lines snaking among the scattered blazes, and he heard Tick's laugh ringing out over the clamor. "Burn, burn!" yelled Tick, and other voices chimed in with his. "Let it burn! Serves them right!"

For a moment Doon stood there, stunned, his mind a blank. It seemed that war surged around him, but not the war he had imagined. Where did he belong in this battle? Who was his enemy, where were his friends? Noise and confusion assailed him. His eyes stung. His legs were shaking.

And then he saw Lina break away from the crowd and run across the plaza. He heard Tick and his warriors screaming, "Traitor!" And he felt as if suddenly his eyes had opened (though they hadn't been closed) and he had awakened from a bad dream. The air around him seemed to become clear. Strength returned to his legs. He edged between the people in front of him, burst out of the crowd, and ran the same direction as Lina—toward the fire lines.

And seeing what Lina and Doon had done, others

followed. Clary pushed through the crowd and ran forward, and Mrs. Murdo went after her, taking long, quick strides and holding up her skirts. Then came the Hoover sisters, and Doon's father, and fragile Miss Thorn, and five more people, and three more after that. They ran with their hands before their mouths or their arms over their heads, shielding themselves from smoke and falling embers, and they added themselves to the bucket brigade and began hauling water.

More and more of the people of Ember followed. At last the only ones not fighting the fire were Tick and a few of his men. Wearing half-stubborn, half-frightened expressions, they clustered at the far end of the plaza, shouting, "Traitors!" now and then, with their useless weapons dangling from their hands.

CHAPTER 28

Surprising Truths

Fighting the fire was so hard that Lina forgot to be afraid. Everything but firefighting was erased from her mind. Her hands reached for the next bucket, over and over and over, and when a warning cry arose she would look up to see where the danger was and dart out of its way. The water in the barrels soon ran out, and the rear ends of the lines had to move back to scoop water directly from the river, which meant a longer distance for the buckets to travel. The lines snaked left and right, moving to follow the fires, which sprang up in the dry grass like a crop of terrible weeds.

In the smoke-dimmed air, people looked like ghosts, swarming every which way, shouting at each other. Once Lina caught sight of Doon. He had jumped into the fountain and was bent over, as if fishing with his hand for something at the bottom. He jumped out again, soaking wet, and in a moment the fountain began to overflow, and the water spread, running toward the flames in the grass at the plaza's edge. Oh, Doon, hooray! Lina thought.

She saw Maddy, too, several times, appearing and disappearing in the swarm of firefighters, sometimes calling out instructions or warnings, sometimes just passing along the buckets, her hair flying in the wind.

It was the wind they fought against as much as the fire. It blew in unruly gusts, and the flames leaned and stretched before it, reaching for new things to burn. But there were twice as many people fighting the fire now, and before long the people began to win. The flames became flickers, put out with a shovelful of dirt or a splash from a bucket, and finally no trace of orange remained in sight. The plaza was a landscape of ashy puddles and smoldering black heaps, looking strangely open without the town hall and the pine tree.

Then for a few moments, people just stood and stared at each other. All of them had smoke-darkened faces and ash-dusted hair and damp, grimy clothes. The people of Ember were just as grubby as the people of Sparks; everyone looked more or less the same.

Lina went searching for Doon. She couldn't find him, but she did find Mrs. Murdo sitting on the ground at the north end of the plaza. Her bun had slid all the way off the top of her head and was hanging beneath one ear. Her skirt was dotted with burn holes. "Are you all right?" Lina asked her.

"I believe so," Mrs. Murdo said. "And you?"

"I'm fine," said Lina.

"Yes, you are," said Mrs. Murdo, giving Lina a long look. "Very fine indeed." She held out an arm. "Help me up," she said, "and we'll go back to the doctor's house and get ourselves decent again."

When the fire was out and all the firefighters were exhausted and wet and dirty, Doon discovered that his legs felt shaky again, and he went down through the village streets until he found a shady place under a tree where he could sit for a while. People trudged by him, heading for their homes, and the people of Ember passed, too, going back to the hotel, which that morning they'd thought they might be leaving forever. Doon didn't call out to anyone. He felt too tired even to talk. He just wanted to rest a minute before facing whatever was going to come next.

But he hadn't been sitting there very long before he saw Kenny coming up the road, and when Kenny spotted him he came over and sat down. "I saw you," he said. "You pulled Torren in from the tree."

Doon nodded.

"I knew you were that kind of person," Kenny said. Bits of ash sprinkled his blond hair, as if someone had shaken pepper on his head.

"What kind?" said Doon.

"The brave kind," Kenny said. "The good kind. Not like that other boy."

"What other boy?"

Kenny leaned back against the trunk of the tree and stretched out his legs. "The one who was yelling for people to fight. That one with the pale eyes."

"Tick," said Doon.

"Yes. I knew he wasn't a good one, ever since I saw him in the woods that day."

"What day?" Doon said.

"That day when he was out there with bags on his hands," Kenny said.

Doon turned to stare at Kenny. "Bags? Why? What was he doing?"

"Cutting vines," said Kenny.

"What kind of vines?" Doon asked. His heart was starting to pound.

"Well, I wasn't close to him. I'm not sure. But it was something he didn't want to touch, I guess. Like poison oak."

"Poison oak? Why would he cut poison oak vines?"

"I heard what happened," said Kenny. "About the leaves on the hotel steps. They thought we did it, but I don't think so."

Doon's thoughts were racing. He was remembering things: how Tick had an itchy patch on his arm days before the stuff appeared on the hotel steps; how he led the cleanup but didn't participate himself; how he had smudges on his neck the morning that "GO BACK TO YOUR CAVE" was written on the hotel walls; how he stirred everyone up, fed their anger, by reminding them of those two attacks over and over again.

And as if his mind had been full of clouds but now was clear, he understood. Tick *needed* all that anger and outrage. The more upset people were, the more of them would want to fight. And the more fighters there were, the more people for Tick to lead. Tick wanted power. He wanted glory. He wanted war, with himself in command. He had raised his army by attacking his own people.

Doon was breathing fast. His hands were cold and shaky. He knew, suddenly, that this changed everything. It meant that the people of Sparks had not attacked the people of Ember after all. Their fears and suspicions had made them unkind and selfish, but—except maybe for the muddy words in the plaza—they had not attacked. And if there hadn't been the writing on the wall and the poison oak, there probably wouldn't have been the riot in the plaza. And if there hadn't been the riot, the town leaders might not have decided that the Emberites had to leave.

Doon jumped to his feet.

Startled, Kenny said, "What's the matter?"

"You've told me something important," Doon said. He held out a hand and pulled Kenny up. "I have to—I have to—" What *did* he have to do? He had to talk to someone. He had to explain. "I have to get going," he said to Kenny, and he headed back up the road toward the village center again, thinking about whom he should talk to, and what he should say.

The doctor was standing out in front of her house with Poppy at her side when Lina and Mrs. Murdo arrived. Poppy came galloping toward them. "Wyna!" she yelled. "I saw fi-oh! I saw fi-oh!"

"Are you hurt?" Dr. Hester asked.

"Just tired," said Lina.

"And dirty," said Mrs. Murdo.

"Dirty, dirty," said Poppy, tugging at Lina's shirt and trotting along beside her.

Torren was sitting on the sofa with his feet in a tub of water.

"What happened to you?" asked Lina.

"I got burns on my feet," Torren said.

"On your feet? How did you do that?"

"You didn't see?" said Mrs. Murdo.

"See what?" said Lina.

So Mrs. Murdo told her. "I don't know why Doon was up in that tower to begin with," she said, "but it was a lucky thing for Torren that he was."

Lina raised her eyebrows at Torren. "Doon told me

what you said about him. Aren't you ashamed, now that he's saved your life?"

Torren didn't answer. He stared down at his feet.

"You lied," Lina said. "You blamed Doon for something he didn't do."

Torren slumped down into the sofa pillows.

"He didn't throw those tomatoes!" said Lina. "He would never do such a thing. Why did you say he did?"

"It was a mistake," said Torren in a muffled voice.

"Well, who did it, then?"

"Someone else."

"Who?"

"Just someone. I'm not telling."

"You *are* telling something, though," said Lina. "Maybe you won't tell who *did* do it, but you have to tell that Doon didn't." She shuffled through the clutter on the table and found a scrap of paper. "Here," she said, handing it to Torren with a pencil. "Write on here that you told a lie about Doon. Sign your name."

Scowling, Torren wrote. He handed the note to Lina, who headed for the door. "I'm going back to the village," she said. "Just for a little while. I'll be home by dinnertime."

After dinner that evening, Lina did a lot of talking. Mrs. Murdo and the doctor wanted to know what was out there in the Empty Lands, and how it was to be a roamer, and what the city was like. Maddy, sitting on the window seat with a cup of tea, put in a word now and then, but mainly she let Lina tell the story. Torren sat on the couch with his feet stretched out—the doctor had wrapped them in rag bandages—and pretended not to listen, but every now and then he couldn't help asking a question. Usually his questions had to do with Caspar.

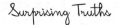

"I don't understand," he said, "why *you two* came back and not Caspar."

"He hadn't finished what he wanted to do," said Lina. "His mission."

"What *was* his mission?" cried Torren. "You must have found out."

"We did find out," Lina said. She glanced uncertainly at Maddy.

"Your brother," said Maddy, "is looking for something he will never find. When he realizes that, he will come home."

"But *what* is he looking for?" Torren said. He reared up on his elbows and glared at Maddy.

"He is looking for a treasure," said Maddy. "But he doesn't recognize it even when it's right in front of him."

"Did he forget his glasses?" Torren said.

"No, no. But he has trouble seeing even with his glasses on."

Lina didn't like Torren any better than she ever had, but she did feel a little sorry for him. So she fetched glasses of honey water for him that evening, and she gave him the little red truck she'd found as a roamer. Poppy seemed to think all this was a kind of party for Torren. She joined in by bringing him things to play with—spoons, socks, potatoes. When it was bedtime, they carried him into the medicine room, and then Lina went with Mrs. Murdo and Poppy up into the loft.

Mrs. Murdo unpinned her hair, which fell around her shoulders in strands clumped together with soot. "I have something to say to you," she said to Lina.

Lina's heart sank. Whatever it was, she was sure she deserved it.

"I saw what you did," Mrs. Murdo said. "You did a remarkable thing, running out alone like that. Quite courageous."

"Well, I had to," said Lina.

Mrs. Murdo raised her eyebrows questioningly.

Lina was too tired to explain about trying to do a good thing to change the direction, and how she had hoped that someone else might do it so she wouldn't have to, but nobody did. So she just shrugged her shoulders and said nothing.

Mrs. Murdo ran a comb through her hair. "I believe a great many of us were thinking of doing the same thing," she said. "But no one quite had the courage. Only you."

"I didn't feel courageous," said Lina. "I felt afraid."

"That makes it all the braver," said Mrs. Murdo.

Lina felt a glow, like a little flame inside her—no, not a flame, a light bulb, that was better. A little light bulb was glowing in her heart.

"I believe I'm more tired than I've ever been in my life," said Mrs. Murdo. "And tomorrow there's more to face."

"Tomorrow?" For a moment Lina couldn't remember what had to be faced tomorrow.

"Well, yes," said Mrs. Murdo. "I suppose tomorrow we'll find out if they're still planning to make us all leave."

The Fourth Town Meeting

That night, the wind cleaned the smoke from the air, and in the morning the sky was a brilliant blue and the air felt tingly. The sunlight was warm, but it had a new quality, thinner and sharper. The season was changing.

A messenger from town arrived at the hotel that morning. Doon, who happened to be the first person up, ran into him on the hotel steps. "Tell your people," said the messenger, "that the leaders of Sparks wish to meet with the people of Ember at noon today. They will come to the hotel ballroom."

Doon conveyed this message to the next several people he saw, and they told others, and soon everyone knew. At noon, they assembled in the ballroom. Doon stood with his father in the midst of the crowd. All around him, he heard uneasy murmurings. Would this be more bad news? He heard Miss Thorn whisper to someone, "I'm so nervous, I have a stomachache."

He was nervous, too; his hands were damp.

At a few minutes after twelve, Mary Waters and Wilmer Dent came into the ballroom. With them were four men carrying a stretcher on which Doon saw a blanket-draped figure. The stiff gray beard jutting up from the chin told him it was Ben Barlow. Dr. Hester walked beside him, and with her were Mrs. Murdo, Lina, and Poppy. Other townspeople followed, lining up around the edges of the room—Doon recognized storekeepers and team leaders (including Chugger), along with many of the families of Sparks. The Partons were there; he saw Kenny trotting behind his parents.

Doon raised his arm and called to Lina, and she came to stand beside him. "Is Ben badly hurt?" Doon whispered.

"I think so," Lina whispered back. "The doctor says he was hit in the shoulder. She said the blast almost blew off his arm."

"Listen," Doon said. "I have to tell you something important." And in the next few minutes, as the town leaders and the men carrying Ben mounted the steps to the stage, he whispered to Lina what he'd discovered about Tick.

"Really?" she kept saying. "*Really?* How *could* he? I can't *believe* it!"

"And last night," Doon whispered, "I went and found Tick, and I told him I knew, and he said—"

But at that moment, Mary Waters held up her

hands for quiet. Doon stopped whispering and turned his eyes to the stage. The men had set the stretcher down and propped one end of it on a chair, so that Ben lay at a slant. A bandage covered one of his eyes. He glared out at the audience with the other.

When Mary spoke, there was a slight quaver in her deep voice.

"We are here to talk of serious matters," she said. "Ben was badly injured yesterday, but he has insisted on coming. We all wish to speak with you face to face." She paused. "First of all, I must tell you this."

Doon felt his stomach lurch.

"We have realized," Mary said, "that we cannot ask you to leave here. Your generosity yesterday has helped us remember our own."

No one spoke, but the people of Ember glanced at each other and let out breaths of relief. Doon bumped his shoulder against Lina's, and they grinned. "Yesterday," Mary went on, "when our Weapon exploded and the fire went out of control, a child of Ember crossed the line that divided us from each other. We are grateful to her for leading the way."

"Lina! Lina!" cried a few scattered voices—Lina thought she heard Maddy's voice among them. Doon startled her by yelling, "Lina the brave!" right in her ear.

"I want to say," Mary continued, "that we have made mistakes and we are sorry for them. We had good intentions, at the beginning. We did our best to help you. But when it got hard, we closed our hearts."

Wilmer Dent smiled apologetically. "We were worried—" he began.

Ben interrupted him. His voice was hoarse and weak, and he seemed to be having trouble breathing. Doon strained to hear him. "We were justifiably . . . concerned," he croaked. "About critical . . . food shortages. Attempting to ensure . . . the safety of . . . our own people." He made a kind of wheezing, gasping sound. "Under . . . standably," he added.

Wilmer shrugged his shoulders, still smiling nervously. "It was just that we were—"

"Afraid," said Mary. "We were afraid, let us say it right out. We were afraid that you would ruin everything for us. We were almost on the edge of prosperity. We feared that you would push us back into deprivation."

There was a silence then in which no one knew what to say.

"So we tried to get rid of the problem instead of solving it," Mary went on. "Fortunately, both our plans and yours were thwarted." She stepped forward and gazed out at the crowd. Her eyes met Doon's and held them for a second. "Just last night," she said, "I learned two things that have changed my picture of what has happened here. The first is this: we still don't know who wrote the muddy words on the plaza—we may never know—but the other attacks on the people of Ember, the ugly writings on the walls of the Pioneer and the poison oak on the doorstep, were not carried out by Sparks villagers at all."

The Emberites turned to each other with puzzled looks and murmured confusedly. "But how could—" "But who would—" "What does she mean?"

"It was young Doon Harrow who explained it to me," said Mary. "I'd like him to explain it to us all, if he will." She nodded to Doon and gestured upward with her hand.

So Doon stood up. He told the assembled people the same thing he'd told Mary the night before when he came to her house late in the evening.

"It can't be true!" someone cried out—Doon thought it was Allie Bright, who had been Tick's right-hand man.

"It *is* true," Doon said. "Tick told me himself last night. He said it was just good strategy. He said he knew there was going to be war, and he needed to raise a strong army. When people are attacked, he said, they get mad, and angry people are the best warriors. So he decided to *make* people angry. He told me he got a good idea for how to do it when he saw those muddy words in the plaza."

At that, a roar swelled up and filled the ballroom. People shouted, "Where is he?" and twisted around to look for Tick. A few of them began barging through the audience trying to find him.

Doon called out, "Wait! Listen! He isn't here."

The commotion quieted down. People turned toward Doon.

"Last night when I talked to him, Tick was stuffing everything he owns into a sack," said Doon. "He told me he was leaving. He said he couldn't live anymore with cowards and traitors. He'd heard a roamer was coming through the village today, and he planned to catch a ride with him. Some others are going, too. They're going to the settlement in the far south, Tick said, where they hope to have a better welcome than they got here."

A great clamor greeted this announcement. Some people laughed, some shouted, "Good riddance," and some just grumbled and shook their heads.

Finally Mary raised her hands again and called, "Please! Quiet! I have more to say."

People grew silent again and listened.

"I said that I had learned *two* things," she said. "The second is this: the incident that set off this chain of violent events did not happen as we thought. It was not Doon Harrow who destroyed those crates of tomatoes."

This came as no surprise to the people of Ember, who had never believed Doon guilty in the first place.

But the villagers at the meeting looked startled. Doon saw Martha Parton flick her eyes toward him, her eyebrows flying upward, and he saw Ordney give him a quizzical look. Behind them, Kenny smiled a sunny smile.

"Torren Crane has taken back the statement he made," Mary said. "He did not, after all, see Doon Harrow throw those tomatoes. He still refuses to say who *did* throw them. We must make up our own minds about that. But I believe we can be sure that it was not a person from Ember."

At that, a cheer arose from the crowd, a loud, disorderly cheer, and Doon was so astonished that he nearly fell over. Lina grabbed his arm. "I made him write it down on paper!" she yelled into his ear. "I took the paper to Mary last night!"

When the cheering subsided, Mary continued. "We should take note," she said, "of how easy it is to bring out the worst in us. The actions of a few troubled individuals fanned resentments into violence. Only an accident kept us from murdering each other."

She turned around to face Ben, whose head was lolling sideways, his eyelids drooping. "Ben has something to say now. Ben? Are you able?"

The doctor, standing next to Ben, nudged his shoulder gently, and Ben opened his eyes.

"Can you make your statement, Ben?" asked Mary.

Ben frowned at the ceiling. The audience waited.

Finally he spoke. "I have been told," he said, ". . . that Doon Harrow . . ." He stopped. Frowned again. "I wish to thank . . . young man named Doon Harrow . . ." He took a shaky breath. "For rescuing . . . foolish nephew."

What? thought Doon. What's he talking about?

Ben scowled. He appeared to be gathering his strength. "Foolish nephew Torren Crane," he rasped, "in the . . . pine tree. Who could have been killed . . ." Ben's voice sank to a whisper, and the audience strained to hear. ". . . By my foolish actions."

Doon stood stunned. Torren was Ben's nephew? That was a surprise. But it was even more of a surprise to hear Ben almost apologizing for what he'd done.

Lina was thumping Doon on the back. Someone behind him cried out, "Three cheers for Doon!" and three cheers rang out in the ballroom. Doon just stood there, with what he thought was probably a silly smile on his face.

Then Mary stepped forward and called for quiet again. Her voice grew steady and businesslike. "Now," she said, "we must look to our future. You will not get everything you want. Neither will we. All of us will suffer, perhaps even be in danger. There will be more mouths to feed—but more hands to do the work, too. And though we may have a shortage of food, we have no shortage of work." She paused. She smiled a little. Her eyes passed over the people in the room, and Doon felt her gaze almost like a reassuring touch. "The main thing," she said, "is this: we will refuse to be each other's enemies. We will renounce violence, which is so easy to start but so hard to control. We will build a place where we can all live in peace. If we hold to that, everything is possible."

Someone clapped. Doon turned around and saw his father, clapping with his hands held high in the air.

"There is much to be worked out," Mary said. "It won't be easy, but we'll talk about it together." She paused for a second, and a change came over her face—the beginning of a smile. "One more thing," she said. "We will no longer speak of 'the people of Sparks' and 'the people of Ember.' From now on, we are *all* the people of Sparks."

A rustle swept through the crowd. Both Doon and Lina felt a pang of sorrow. To call themselves people of Sparks meant leaving behind the last trace of their old home—its name. The villagers, too, felt a pang; for them it was a pang of fear. These were their people now? Could they really live peacefully together?

But the sorrow and the fear lasted only a few seconds. Everyone was tired of sorrow and fear. Whatever lay ahead, they thought, would probably be better. They were willing to try it.

After that, they turned to the practical details.

"Actually," said Alma Hogan, the storehouse manager, "there's a fair amount of food in the storehouse.

It's just that we never like to use it all up. This year, we'll expect to use it all and hope we can replenish it next year. I'm afraid a great deal of it is pickles, though. By the end of winter, we may all be eating more pickles than anything else."

Doon's father mentioned politely that the hotel residents would have to have decent houses sooner or later. Mary said they would start building some of them now out behind the meadow. The best of Sparks's builders would be in charge, and they would teach the Emberites construction. "The houses will be small," Mary said, "and we'll be able to build only a few before the rains come. Most of you will have to spend the winter in the hotel."

Clary stood up to announce that her garden was producing well; in addition to cucumbers, melons, and peppers, she had grown nearly a hundred butternut squashes, which would keep well through the winter. That would help a little. The villagers looked at her curiously. Butternut squashes? They had never heard of them. "I grew them from seeds I brought from Ember," Clary said. "I brought all the seeds I had, all kinds. Next year I'll be able to grow more."

Mrs. Murdo said she had learned a great deal in her time with the doctor. She would like to be Assistant Doctor. "It's clear that this community needs more than one," she said.

"I know something about plants," said Maddy,

speaking up for the first time. "I wish to be Assistant Hotel Gardener, with Clary Laine."

Edward Pocket said he demanded to be made Official Librarian. Mary looked surprised. "We don't have a library," she said.

"Exactly right," said Edward. "You have a disorderly heap of books. I have made great progress with them, however. I invite you to come by and see."

Ben Barlow kept muttering dire warnings about crop failures and vitamin deficiencies and epidemics, but Mary said they would cope with those problems when and if they actually occurred.

Little by little, people began to feel interested in how this new arrangement was going to work. There were endless questions. What if there were arguments? How would they be settled? Would the Emberites go back to eating with their lunchtime families? Would they get enough for dinner and breakfast? What would happen when they needed things other than food, like shoes or soap or hats?

"The trouble is," said Mrs. Polster, "we don't *have* anything. We can't trade for the goods at the market because we don't have anything you'd want."

But Doon saw the solution to this right away. "We do!" he said. Mrs. Polster raised her eyebrows at him. She wasn't used to being contradicted. "We have *one thing* that you need," said Doon. "Matches! We still have a lot left. We could use them to trade with, at least for a while. Two matches for a pair of shoes, say."

People laughed and clapped—it was perfect. Ben said in his opinion a pair of shoes was worth at least *five* matches, but no one paid much attention.

"All of this has to be worked out," Mary said. "It's going to involve disagreement, and it's going to involve hardship. But we have endured hardship before. We can do it again."

Wilmer sighed. "It's just that we hoped we wouldn't have to," he said.

Mary shot him a stern look. "We can do it again," she repeated. "And we will."

CHAPTER 29

Three Amazing Visits

Lina gave up on trying to persuade Mrs. Murdo to move to the hotel. Since they'd all have their own houses sooner or later, they might as well stay at the doctor's house until then. Besides, Mrs. Murdo was so intent on learning to be Assistant Doctor that it seemed unkind to take her away.

Lina and Maddy took on the job of harvesting and preserving the produce from the doctor's vegetable garden. Every morning they picked baskets of tomatoes and beans and peppers and corn and squash. Every afternoon, they sliced tomatoes and laid them in the sun to dry; they took dried beans out of their pods and put them in jars; they cooked peppers and packed them in olive oil; they tied bunches of herbs with string and hung them up to dry. Poppy puttered around their feet, "helping" by sprinkling dry leaves here and there or banging spoons on pots. Even

Torren, whose feet were healing, often chose to hang around with Lina and Maddy. He said he knew how to make a garlic braid, so they gave him a basket of garlic, and he made one.

One afternoon, as she and Maddy were cutting green beans for dinner, Lina heard wheels crunching on the road outside. The next moment, she heard the whuffling of an ox, and then Torren sprang up and limped as fast as he could to the front of the house. Uh-oh, thought Lina. Is it who I think it is?

It was. There was Caspar's battered truck, and there was Caspar just climbing out of it. He looked grubby. His mustache drooped. Torren ran toward him, crying, "Caspar! Caspar!" And Caspar smiled in a tired way.

"Hey, brother," he said. He thumped Torren's back a couple of times. Then he started toward the house. Lina and Maddy went out to meet him.

When he saw them, he stopped and glared. "Deserters," he said. But he didn't seem to have the energy to berate them further. He trudged into the house and plunked down on the couch. Torren plunked down beside him.

"I've been waiting and *waiting* for you," Torren said. "Why didn't you come back with them?" He flicked his hand toward Lina and Maddy.

"I had important work to do," said Caspar. "Which they didn't want to help with."

"And what happened with your work?" asked Maddy, standing by the door. "Did you find what you wanted to find?"

Caspar didn't even look at her. He closed his eyes and slumped against the back of the couch. "My numbers," he said, "need readjusting. They were completely right except for one thing."

"What thing was that?" asked Maddy.

"Wrong city," said Caspar, still without opening his eyes. "I have reworked the numbers. Tomorrow I head north."

Maddy and Lina exchanged a look.

Caspar turned his head toward Maddy and squinted at her. "I don't suppose you want to come," he said.

"No, thank you," said Maddy. "I plan to stay here, where something with real potential is beginning."

Torren tugged on Caspar's arm. "Did you bring me something this time?" he asked.

Caspar opened his eyes. He looked at the ceiling for a while. "Well, yes," he said. "I did."

"What?" shrieked Torren. "What is it? Can I have it now?"

"It's out in the truck," said Caspar. "I found a whole crate of them, very unusual. You can have one."

"One what? Let's go get it!" Torren darted to the door.

Caspar heaved himself up and they went outside. Lina watched as Caspar rooted around in one of his crates. He came up with something she recognized with a start. She hadn't seen one for a long time—it was like seeing something that belonged to an old friend, now dead.

"What is it?" said Torren.

"A light bulb," said Caspar. "I found a case of forty-eight of them, all unused."

"But what does it do?" Torren asked, peering into the light bulb as if he expected to see something alive in there. He tapped the glass with his fingernail.

"It gives light," said Caspar. "If you have electricity."

"But we don't have electricity."

"That's right," Caspar said wearily. "So you hold on to it, in case someday we do."

Torren went to the window seat and sat there turning the bulb around and around in his hands. Lina watched him, thinking about Ember. People had figured it out once, she thought. They could figure it out again.

A few days after Caspar left, there was another visitor to the doctor's house. Lina was out in the courtyard at the time, cracking walnuts with a rock. She saw someone approaching the gate, a bent figure walking slowly and somehow crookedly. She stood up. The person seemed to be having trouble with the gate latch, so she went to help, and that was when she realized it was Ben Barlow. His injured arm was bandaged and strapped to his side, and the jacket he wore was draped over it with the sleeve hanging empty. That was why he looked lopsided.

"Good afternoon," said Ben. "I wonder if Torren is here."

"He is," said Lina. "I'll get him."

She found Torren out in back of the house, sitting under a tree, eating a hunk of bread. "Your uncle has come to see you," she said.

Torren stared at her. "My uncle?" He sounded both excited and scared. He jumped up, shoving the bread into his pocket.

When Ben saw Torren coming toward him, he frowned. Then, as if catching himself, he changed his expression to a smile. "Hello, nephew," he said. "How are you getting on?"

Torren looked wary. "Fine," he said.

"Good," said Ben. He stroked his beard. Lina wondered if that was all he had to say.

Torren filled the silence. "Is your arm still attached to you?" he said.

"Yes," said Ben. "Just barely." He started to frown into the air again and then thought better of it. He sat down on a bench. "Well," he said. "I thought I'd just come and see you. Haven't seen you for a while."

"Years," said Torren.

"Well, yes. Busy life, you know, being a town leader. Many decisions to make. Matters of right and wrong to . . . to grapple with."

"Oh," said Torren. Lina could tell he was thinking the same thing she was: Why has he come?

"Sometimes one makes the right decision," said Ben. "Sometimes not."

"I guess so," said Torren.

Ben readjusted his bandaged arm. Lina saw that his beard was not as neatly trimmed as usual. Probably he had a hard time doing it with his left hand. She was pretty sure Ben didn't have a wife—she'd never heard mention of one.

"Well," said Ben. "You were fortunate, weren't you, getting pulled out of that tree?"

"Yes," said Torren.

"I am forced to acknowledge," said Ben, "that it was my fault. That fire."

"I guess so," said Torren.

"An accident," said Ben, "but one that did not have to happen."

"Uh-huh," said Torren.

Ben got to his feet with painful slowness. "So," he said. "Enjoyable talking with you. No doubt we should get to know each other. You must come by for a visit sometime, though of course I'm rarely home."

"You're very busy," said Torren.

"That's right," said Ben. He made his way toward the gate with his limping step. As he went out, he waved over his shoulder with his good hand, but he didn't turn around. Slowly, he started back toward the village.

"That was an apology," Lina said to Torren when Ben was gone. "He's sorry for doing what he did. I guess he's sorry for not being a good uncle, too—for not taking you to live with him."

"*Live* with him?" said Torren. He made a horrible face.

"Well, I thought you weren't happy living with Dr. Hester," Lina said. "You never *seem* very happy."

"I am *too* happy," said Torren crossly. He sat down on the bench that Ben had just left and pulled the hunk of bread from his pocket. A few little birds were hopping nearby. Absently, Torren tossed them some crumbs. He seemed to be thinking. "I *like* it here," he said to Lina, and he looked up at her with his eyes all round, as if he had only just discovered this himself.

The next day, Doon came to the door of the doctor's house carrying a sack. Kenny was with him, standing slightly behind Doon and peering curiously past him into the room.

"I have to show you this," Doon said to Lina. "I made it with the present you brought me."

"He's kind of a genius," Kenny said. "He already showed me."

Doon set the sack on the window seat. It was only just after dinnertime, but the days were shorter now, and the sun was nearly down. Dr. Hester had already lit two candles. She and Mrs. Murdo and Maddy were sitting at the table shelling lima beans. Poppy was sitting with them, tearing the bean pods into little pieces. All four came over to see what Doon had brought.

Torren came, too. He was actually more interested in showing Doon what *he* had than in seeing what was in the sack. "I got a present from Caspar," he said.

"Great," said Doon, but he wasn't really listening. Lina could see how excited he was about whatever he had in the sack. His eyes shone in the candlelight, and his hands fidgeted impatiently with the string around the sack's neck. When he got it untied, he reached into the sack and brought out a small device made of wood and metal—some sort of machine, Lina thought. It had a coil of wire, and inside the coil she saw the magnet she'd given Doon. There was a handle that looked as if it would make something turn. Lina, not being much interested in machines, was a little disappointed.

It was clear that Torren was disappointed, too. "Want to see my present from Caspar?" he said.

"In a minute," said Doon. "Let me show you this first."

"What does it do?" Lina asked.

"Is it some kind of a can opener?" asked Mrs. Murdo.

"Or maybe it's a sort of mixer?" said the doctor.

"Or a drill?" said Maddy.

"Nope," said Doon happily, and Kenny, his face shining with the shared secret, whispered, "Nope," too. "You won't believe it," Doon went on, "but it makes electricity. I found the directions for it in a book called *Science Projects,* but I couldn't try it out before because I didn't have a magnet. I didn't even know what a magnet was. But then you brought me one, Lina! And just the other day I remembered about this project." He took the machine over to the table and set it down. "What you do is, you turn this crank, and that turns the magnet, and that generates the electricity and runs it down these wires. It's supposed to be enough to light a light bulb. The trouble is, I can't test it because I couldn't find any light bulbs that weren't broken."

Torren started jumping up and down. He pounded on Doon's arm. "My present from Caspar! My present from Caspar!" he yelled. He bolted into the medicine room.

"What's the matter with—" said Doon, but Lina broke in.

"Doon!" she said. "His present from Caspar was a light bulb! Unused!"

Torren came out of the medicine room carrying

the light bulb encased in both hands, walking now, fast but with stiff legs, being extremely careful. "You won't break it, will you?" he said to Doon. "Your experiment won't blow it up, will it?"

Doon gazed at the light bulb as if it was the most wonderful thing he'd ever seen. Gingerly, he reached for it. "I'll be very, very careful," he said. "You can help me, Torren. Hold the light bulb right here." He showed Torren where to put the bulb, and he wound two loose wires around its metal end.

"Now," he said. "Blow out the candles."

Lina blew them out. The room went dark.

Doon began turning the crank of his machine.

At first nothing happened except that the magnet turned around. Doon cranked faster. And faster. And a glimmer appeared in the light bulb, first a glimmer and then a glow, and then the bulb shone with a faint but steady white light.

Lina shrieked. Poppy shrieked, too, because Lina had, and both the doctor and Mrs. Murdo gasped and broke into applause. Kenny beamed, glancing between the light bulb and Doon's face. Torren was being too careful to make a noise, but his eyes grew wide and his mouth dropped open.

For almost three minutes, until his hand got tired, Doon turned the crank of his machine around and around. The doctor wagged her head in wonder, Mrs. Murdo turned her face away to hide her tears, and

Torren held on tight to the light bulb even though it was getting very warm. Lina gazed at the light shining on everyone's faces. Full to the brim with hope and love and joy, she watched the little light bulb shining like a promise in the night.

THE PROPHET OF YONWOOD

Contents

The Vision	633
1. The Inheritance	637
2. The Third Floor	647
3. The Girl in the Closet	653
4. Break-In	663
5. The Fiery Vision	671
6. Mrs. Beeson's Idea	682
7. The Short Way Home	695
8. A Crack in the Sky	704
9. At the Prophet's House	709
10. The Photograph and the Journal	719
11. Trouble Spots	729
12. Inside the Backyard Shed	739
13. The Perfect Living Room	746
14. Someone in the Basement	756
15. Up to the Woods	768

16. The Snake's Dinner 774
17. Hoyt McCoy's Horrible House 783
18. What Grover Saw 789
19. Blue Envelopes 800
20. Orders 813
21. Getting Ready for the Open House 819
22. An Indoor Universe 826
23. The Emergency Meeting 835
24. The Bracelet 841
25. The Open House 850
26. Catastrophe 861
27. The Chase 870
28. One More Trip to the Woods 877
29. The Last Day 889
30. Nickie and the Prophet 895
31. Love 903
What Happened Afterward 914

The universe is not only stranger than we imagine,

it is stranger than we can *imagine.*

—J.B.S. Haldane

THE PROPHET
OF
YONWOOD

The Vision

On a warm July afternoon in the town of Yonwood, North Carolina, a woman named Althea Tower went out to her backyard to fill the bird feeder. She opened her sack of sunflower seeds, lifted the bird feeder's lid—and that was when, without warning, the vision assailed her.

It was like a waking dream. The trees and grass and birds faded away, and in their place she saw blinding flashes of light so searingly bright she staggered backward, dropped her sack of birdseed, and fell to the ground. Billows of fire rose around her, and a hot wind roared. She felt herself flung high into the sky, and from there she looked down on a dreadful scene. The whole earth boiled with flames and black smoke. The noise was terrible—a howling and crashing and crackling—and finally, when the firestorm subsided, there came a silence that was more terrible still.

When the vision finally faded, it left Althea stunned. She lay on the ground, unable to move, with her mind all jumbled and birds pecking at the spilled birdseed around her. She might have lain there for hours if Mrs. Brenda Beeson had not happened to come by a few minutes later to bring her a basket of strawberries.

Seeing Althea on the ground, Mrs. Beeson rushed forward. She bent over her friend and spoke to her, but Althea only moaned. So Mrs. Beeson used her cell phone to call for help. Within minutes, four of her best friends—the doctor, the police chief, the town mayor, and the minister of the church—had all arrived. The doctor squatted beside Althea and spoke slowly and loudly. "Can you tell us what's wrong?" he said. "What is it?"

Althea shivered. Her lips twisted as she tried to speak. Everyone leaned in to hear.

"It's God," she whispered. "God. I saw . . . I saw . . ." She trailed off.

"Merciful heavens," said Brenda Beeson. "She's had a vision."

Of course they didn't know at first what her vision had been. They thought maybe she'd seen God. But why would that frighten her so? Why would she be muttering about fire and smoke and disaster?

Days went by, and Althea didn't get better. She lay

on her bed hardly moving, staring into the air and mumbling. Then, exactly a week later, a clue to the mystery came. The president of the United States announced that talks with the Phalanx Nations had reached a crisis. Their leaders would not give in on any of their demands, and the leaders of the United States would not give in on theirs. Unless some sort of agreement could be reached, the president said, it might be necessary to go to war.

Brenda Beeson made the connection right away: War! That must be what Althea Tower had seen. Mrs. Beeson called her friends, they told their friends, the newspaper wrote it up, and soon the whole town knew: Althea Tower had seen the future, and it was terrible.

All over Yonwood, people gathered in frightened clusters to talk. Could it be true? The more they thought about it, the more it seemed it could be. Althea had always been a quiet, sensible person, not the sort to make things up. And these were strange times, what with conflicts and terrorists and talk of the end of the world—just the kind of times when visions and miracles were likely to happen.

Brenda Beeson formed a committee to take care of Althea and pay attention to anything else she might say. People wrote letters to the newspaper about her and left flowers and ribbons and handwritten notes in front of her house. The minister spoke of her in church.

After a few weeks, nearly everyone was calling her the Prophet.

CHAPTER 1

The Inheritance

Nickie Randolph's first sight of the town of Yonwood was a white steeple rising out of the pine forest that covered the mountainside. She leaned forward, gazing through the windshield of the car. "Is that it?"

Her aunt Crystal, who was driving, put one hand up to shield her eyes from the rays of the setting sun. "That's it," she said.

"My new home," said Nickie.

"You have to get that notion out of your mind," said Crystal. "It's not going to happen."

I'm going to *make* it happen, thought Nickie, though she didn't say it out loud. Crystal's mood was already bad enough. "How long till we get there?" she asked.

"We'll be there in twenty minutes, if nothing else gets in our way."

A lot had gotten in their way so far. The Streakline

train was closed down because of the Crisis, so they'd had to drive. They'd been on the road for seven hours, though the trip from Philadelphia should have taken no more than five. But long lines at gas stations, detours around pot-holed or snow-covered stretches of highway, and military roadblocks had slowed them down. Crystal didn't like delays. She was a fast-moving, efficient person, and when her way was blocked, she became very tense and spoke with her lips in two hard lines.

They came to the Yonwood exit, and Crystal turned off the highway onto a road that wound uphill. Here the trees grew thick on either side, and so tall that their bare branches met overhead, making a canopy of sticks. Drops of rain began to spatter the car's windshield.

After a while, they came to a sign that said, "Yonwood. Pop. 2,460." The trees thinned out, and the rain fell harder. They passed a few storage sheds, a collapsing barn, and a lumberyard. After that, houses began to appear on the side of the road—small, tired-looking wooden houses, their roofs dripping. Many of them had rockers or couches on the front porch, where people would no doubt be sitting if it weren't the dead of winter.

From a small brick shelter at the side of the road, a policeman stepped out holding a red stop sign. He held it up and waved it at them. Crystal slowed down, stopped, and opened her window. The policeman bent down. He had on a rain jacket with the hood up, and rain dripped off the hood and onto his nose. "Hello, ma'am," he said. "Are you a resident?"

"No," said Crystal. "Is that a problem?"

"Just doing a routine entry check, ma'am," the man said. "Part of our safety program. Had some evidence lately of possible terrorist activity in the woods. Your purpose here?"

"My grandfather has died," Crystal said. "My sister and I have inherited his house. I've come to fix the house up and sell it."

The man glanced at Nickie. "This is your sister?"

"This is my niece," said Crystal. "My sister's daughter."

"And your grandfather's name?" said the man.

"Arthur Green," said Crystal.

"Ah, yes," the policeman said. "A fine gentleman." He smiled. "You be careful while you're here, now. We've had reports indicating there may be agents of the Phalanx Nations traveling alone or in small groups in parts of the area. Have you been spoken to by any suspicious strangers?"

"No," said Crystal. "Just you. You seem very suspicious."

"Ha ha," said the man, not really laughing. "All

right, ma'am," he went on. "You may go. Sorry for the delay, but as you know there's a crisis. We're taking every precaution."

He stepped away, and they drove on.

"Terrorists even *here*?" Nickie said.

"It's nonsense," said Crystal. "Why would a terrorist be wandering around in the woods? Pay no attention."

Nickie was so tired of the Crisis. It had been going on now for months. On TV and the radio, it was all you ever heard about: how Our Side and Their Side had come almost, but not quite, to the point of declaring all-out war. In the last week or so, the radio had started broadcasting frightening instructions every hour: "In the event of a declaration of war or a large-scale terrorist attack, cities will be evacuated in an orderly fashion. . . . Residents will be directed to safe locations. . . . Citizens should remain calm. . . ."

It seemed to Nickie that everything in the world had gone wrong—including her own family. Eight months ago, her father had left on a government job. He couldn't tell them where he was going or what he was supposed to do, and he warned that he might not be able to get in touch with them very often. This turned out to be true. She and her mother had had exactly one postcard from him. The postmark had been smudged, so they couldn't tell where the card came from. And the message was no help, either. It said, "Dear Rachel and Nickie, I am working hard, everything is fine, don't worry. I hope you're both doing well. Love, Dad."

But they were not doing well. Nickie's mother missed Nickie's father and couldn't bear not knowing where he was. She worried about losing her job, and so she worked too hard, and so she was always tired and sad. And Nickie hadn't felt happy or safe for a long time. She hated Philadelphia. Something awful seemed always about to happen there. The emergency sirens blasted night and day. Government helicopters circled overhead. In the streets, where trash blew in the wind, dangerous people might be around any corner. And school—a tall, grim building with stinking bathrooms—was just as bad. The books were older than the students, the teachers were too tired to teach, and mean kids prowled the halls. Nickie hated being at school.

But she didn't much like being at home, either, in the big tenth-floor condo where she and her mother lived, with its dusty, unused rooms and its huge plate-glass windows that gave a frightening view straight down to the tiny street below. She was home alone too much lately. She was nervous and restless. She'd read half a book and set it down. She'd work on her Amazing Things scrapbook and get bored after pasting in just one picture. She'd gaze through her binoculars at people going by on the street below, which she used to do for hours, but even her endless curiosity seemed to have faded, and she'd turn away after a few minutes. When she was really desperate, she'd turn on the TV, even though there was almost nothing on but news, and the news was always the same: grim government spokesmen, troops in camouflage dashing around in foreign places, and the skeletons of blown-up cars and buses. Sometimes the president would come on, his white hair always brushed perfectly smooth, his neat white beard giving him a look of wisdom. "These are dangerous times," he would say, "but with the help of God we will prevail."

She was lonely at home, with her father gone and her mother always at work, and she was lonely at school, because *both* her best friends had moved—Kate to Washington last year, and Sophy to Florida two months ago. Sometimes, late at night when her mother still wasn't home, Nickie felt like someone in a tiny lifeboat, drifting by itself in a big, dark, dangerous sea.

That was why, as soon as she heard about Greenhaven, her great-grandfather's house in Yonwood, before she'd even seen it, she decided it would be her home. She loved its name; a haven was a safe place, and that's what she wanted. The trouble was, Crystal and her mother wanted to sell it.

"But why can't we sell *this* place instead?" Nickie had said to her mother. "And get out of the horrible city and go live in a beautiful, peaceful place for a change?"

Nickie had actually never been to her great-grandfather's house in Yonwood, except for one time when she was too young to remember. But she'd made up a picture of Yonwood in her mind that she was sure must be close to the truth: it was rather like a Swiss ski village, she decided, where in the winter there would be log fires in fireplaces and big puffy comforters on the beds, and the snow would be pure white, not filthy and gray as it was in the city. In summer, Yonwood would be warm and green, with butterflies. In Yonwood, she would be happy and safe. She desperately wanted to go there.

After days of arguing, she finally convinced her mother to let her at least see the house before it was sold. All right, her mother said. Nickie could take a couple of weeks off school, drive down with Crystal (her mother couldn't leave work), and help her get the place fixed up and put on the market. Nickie agreed, but her real plan was different: somehow she would persuade Crystal to keep the house, not sell it, and she and her mother (and her father, when he came back) would go and live there, and everything would be different, and better.

That was her Goal #1. But since she was sure this was going to be a life-changing trip, she thought she might as well add other goals as well. Altogether, she had set herself three:

1. To keep her great-grandfather's house from being sold so she could live in it with her parents.
2. To fall in love. She was eleven now, and she thought it was time for this. Not to fall in love in a permanent way, just to have the experience of being madly, passionately in love. She knew she was a passionate person. She had a big love inside her, and she needed to give it.
3. To do something helpful for the world. What that would be she had no idea, but the world needed help badly. She would keep her eyes open for an opportunity.

They were driving now up the town's main business street. It was in fact called Main Street—Nickie saw the name on a sign. They passed the church whose steeple Nickie had seen from the highway. In front of it was a two-legged wooden sign that said, in hand-painted letters, "Church of the Fiery Vision." Nickie could tell, though, that the sign used to say something else; the old name of the church had been painted over.

Beyond the church, the shopping district began. Probably it was pretty in summer, Nickie thought, but now, in February, it had a gray and shuttered look, as if the buildings themselves were cold. Some stores were open, and people walked in and out of them, but others looked permanently closed, their windows dark. There was a movie theater, but its ticket booth was boarded up. There was a park, but its swings and picnic tables were wet and empty.

Crystal turned left, drove uphill for a block, and turned right on a street lined with old houses. On one side of this street—it was Cloud Street, its sign said—the ground sloped upward, so that the houses stood up high, at the crest of their lawns. They were huge houses, with columns and wide porches and numerous chimneys. The people in there, Nickie thought, would be sitting beside roaring fires on an evening like this, probably drinking hot chocolate.

"It's this one," said Crystal, drawing in toward the curb.

Nickie gasped. "*This* one?"

"I'm afraid so." Her aunt stopped the car, and Nickie gaped at the house, stunned. Rain poured down, but she opened the window anyway, to get a better look.

It was more of a castle than a house. It loomed over them, immense and massive, three stories high. At one corner was a tower—round, with high windows. The steep slate roof bristled with chimneys. Rain ran down it in sheets, glistening in the last of the daylight.

"You *can't* sell this house," Nickie said. "It's too wonderful."

"It's awful," said her aunt. "You'll see."

A gust of wind dipped the branches of a pine tree that grew close to the house, and Nickie thought she saw a light in a high window.

"Does anyone still live here?" she asked.

"No," said Crystal. "Just the mice and cockroaches."

When Nickie looked up again, the light was gone.

CHAPTER 2

The Third Floor

They put up the hoods of their jackets and dashed through the pelting rain, along the path, up the steps, and across the stone terrace to the wide, wooden door. The Yonwood real estate office had sent Crystal a key; she fitted it into the keyhole, turned it, and pushed the door open.

They stepped into a wide hall. Crystal groped for the light switch, and a light came on, revealing walls hung with gilt-framed paintings of old-fashioned people, such old paintings that they were nearly black. At the end of the hall was a flight of stairs curving up into the darkness.

Through an archway to the left was the dining room, where chairs stood around a long table. Through an archway to the right was the living room. "The front parlor," Crystal said, turning on a lamp. It was a gloomy room: dark red curtains at the windows, floor-length; walls lined halfway up with bookcases, and above the bookcases red fuzzy wallpaper; Persian rugs on the floor, thin as sheets of burlap, patterned in dusty blue and faded red. And beside the window, a long couch with three bed pillows and two blankets neatly folded.

"This must have been where Grandfather spent his last days," Crystal said.

"Who took care of him?" Nickie asked.

"He hired a girl, I believe. For those last few weeks, he wasn't able to cook for himself, and he needed help to get around." Crystal reached out and picked something up from a side table. "Look," she said. "Here he is. Grandfather." It was a silver-framed photograph of a smiling, silver-haired man. "You would have liked him," Crystal said. "He was interested in everything, just like you."

Nickie studied the man in the photograph. He was very old; his skin sagged, but his eyes were lively.

Crystal strode to a window and swept back the curtains. "What I need to do," she said, "is make a list of the valuables." She took a notebook out of her big purse. "I may as well start on it, as long as we're here. I think there might be some first editions among the books."

"I'm going to look around, okay?" said Nickie. "I want to see everything."

Her aunt nodded.

Nickie went back through the dining room and through a swinging door that led to the most ancient kitchen she had ever seen. It had a smell so indescribably repellent that she hurried away down a passage that led behind the front parlor.

There she found two bedrooms, each with a towering four-poster bed of black carved wood and a great black chest of drawers topped with a mirror in a heavy frame. Up on the second floor were four more bedrooms. She pulled open a few drawers, expecting to find them empty. But they were filled with folded clothes and jewelry boxes and hairbrushes and old bottles of dried-up perfume. It looked as if no one had ever cleaned these rooms out after their occupants had gone away or died.

There was a study on the second floor, too, where a computer sat on a desk, and a lot of file folders and papers and books lay scattered around the room. Her great-grandfather must have worked here. He'd been a college professor before he retired, but Nickie wasn't sure what he'd been a professor *of.* Some sort of science.

It was strange, she thought. Until just a few days ago, this house had been lived in continuously for over 150 years. It was never vacant, and it was never sold—her ancestors had always owned it. Children had grown up here. Old people had died. The house had been so full of life for so long that it probably felt like a living thing itself—and now, in its sudden emptiness, knowing its family no longer wanted it, she imagined it must feel frightened and lonely. Well, *I* want you, she thought. I think you're wonderful.

Remembering that there was a third story, Nickie looked for another stairway. She found it behind a door to the left of the big front stairs—these weren't broad and polished but narrow and plain. There was no handrail along the wall.

At the top was a closed door. She opened it to find herself in a hall with two doors on each side. She looked into all the rooms. Two of them were crammed full of stuff: suitcases and boxes and hatboxes, enormous old trunks with leather straps, stacks of papers and portraits in broken frames and mildewed books and paper-wrapped packages and grocery bags stuffed with who knows what, all of it draped in swags of dusty cobwebs.

The third room was a tiny bathroom that hadn't been cleaned for a while.

But the fourth room was wonderful. It was big and airy, with windows on two sides. The tower formed one corner of it, making a circular alcove with windows all around and a wide window seat running beneath them—the perfect place for sitting with a book on a sunny day, or with lamplight over your shoulder on a dark day like this one. Nickie guessed that this room had been a nursery, because old toys were jumbled into cabinets along one wall. A rolled-up rug lay at one end of the room, and by the windows was a rocking chair. At the far end of the room stood an iron bed, neatly made, as if just waiting for her.

This would be her room, she decided. She loved it already.

As she was about to go back into the hall, a sound stopped her. It was a sort of squeak, or cry, cut short as if someone had clapped a hand over the squeaker's mouth. Nickie stood still and listened. At first she heard nothing—just the patter of the rain on the windows. She was about to move on when she heard it again—two squeaks this time, and a bump. It seemed to be coming from the closet.

She froze, suddenly remembering the light she'd seen from the street. What if someone dangerous was hiding in the closet? A burglar surprised in the middle of a burglary? Or a homeless person who'd sneaked into the house? Or even a terrorist? She hesitated.

There was another squeak—very faint, but definitely coming from the closet. In a choked voice, Nickie said, "Who's in there?"

No answer.

Nickie's curiosity took over. This happened to her a lot. Her hunger for finding things out was so strong that it overcame caution and even common sense. So now, although she was afraid, she dashed to the closet, flung open the door, and leapt back.

Inside, pressed up against the rear wall, half hidden by shirts and dresses dangling from hangers, was a tall, thin girl with wide, terrified eyes. Her hands were wrapped around the muzzle of a small, wildly squirming dog.

CHAPTER 3

The Girl in the Closet

Nickie stared. The girl stared back. The dog wriggled in her arms and paddled its hind legs frantically.

"Who are you?" Nickie asked.

The girl hunched up her shoulders and craned her head toward Nickie. She had a long face and thin brown straggly hair. Her front teeth were a little crooked. "Please," she said in a hoarse whisper. "Don't tell that I'm here. Please don't tell." The girl stepped cautiously out of the closet. "I'm not supposed to be here," she said. The dog wrenched its muzzle out of her hands and yelped. She grabbed it again. She was wearing jeans and a limp green sweater. Nickie could see that the girl was older than she was—a teenager.

"But why *are* you here?" said Nickie.

"I took care of the old man," the girl said. She spoke in a trembly whisper. "For the last six months, till he died. But now I don't have nowhere to go, and if they find me, they'll put me in a home. And take him away." She ducked her chin toward the dog. "So I need to stay here till I can figure out what to do next."

"What's your name?" Nickie asked. She spoke in a whisper, too.

"Amanda Stokes," said the girl. "What's yours?"

Nickie told her. "Arthur Green was my great-grandfather," she said. "My family owns this house now."

"Oh, Lord," said Amanda. She had a worried-looking face, as if she'd been worrying all her life. "Are you going to come and live here?"

"Yes," said Nickie firmly. "But not right away."

"So you won't tell that I'm here?"

Nickie considered. Would it be wrong to keep this girl a secret? She didn't want to do anything wrong. But it seemed to her that telling on Amanda would cause more harm than not. What would it matter if she stayed here a few days longer?

"I can live here real quietly," Amanda said. The dog jerked in her arms and tried to yelp. "Even with him. He's pretty quiet, usually."

"What's his name?"

"Otis. I found him a couple days ago out by the dump. I know he doesn't have no owner, because he didn't have a collar and he was real dirty. I washed him in the laundry sink."

Nickie scratched the dog behind his small, pointed ears. He was a light-colored dog, a sort of strawberry blond, with round brown eyes. His fur grew in a way that made his face look like a ragged sunflower.

From somewhere downstairs came Crystal's voice. "Nickie! Where are you?"

Nickie dashed into the hall and shouted down. "Upstairs!"

"Come on down!" called her aunt. "Let's get settled in."

She went back into the bedroom. "Okay," she said. "I won't tell about you, but you have to be really quiet. Stuff some rags under the door—this door and the hall door both. I'll try and keep my aunt from coming up here. If she's going to, I'll try to warn you."

"Oh, thank you," Amanda said. "Thank you a lot. It's just for a couple days. I'm looking for a job, and when I get one I'll find me a place of my own."

Nickie nodded. "Goodbye," she said, and she dashed back down the stairs.

For dinner that night, they had tomato soup from a can Crystal found in a cupboard. They sat at the big dining room table and ate while the rain beat on the windows. On a pad of paper, Crystal started making a list of all the things she'd have to do to get the house ready for sale: *Call cleaning service. Call auction house.*

Call salvage place. Talk to lawyer. Call painters. Call plumbers. It was clear to Nickie that Crystal would be spending a lot of time on the phone.

"Crystal," Nickie said. "I don't see anything so awful about Greenhaven. Why do you say it's awful?"

"It's huge and dark and impossible to clean. The kitchen is unspeakable. The plumbing is ancient. The whole place smells like mice. That's just for a start."

"But it could be repaired, couldn't it?"

"With great effort and expense." Crystal went back to her list. *Schedule open house,* she wrote. She tapped a long red fingernail on the table, thinking.

Crystal wasn't exactly beautiful, but she always wore stylish clothes and fixed herself up—nail polish, earrings, makeup. Her hair was a sort of streaky blondish color that required frequent visits to the beauty salon. She'd been married twice. First there'd been Uncle Brent, and later there'd been Uncle Brandon. Now there was no one, which was probably one reason Crystal was more snappish and impatient than usual.

"Crystal," said Nickie, "if you could live in any kind of house, what kind would it be?"

Crystal looked up. She gazed at Nickie blankly for a second, her mind elsewhere. Then she said, "Well, I can tell you what it *wouldn't* be. It wouldn't be an old pile like Greenhaven. And it wouldn't be a dinky, tacky little apartment like the one I live in now."

"What, then?" said Nickie.

"A gracious house," said Crystal. "Big rooms, big windows, a big garden. And—" She leaned forward and smiled a wry little smile. "A nice big man to live in it with me."

Nickie laughed. "*Another* husband?" she said.

"The first two weren't quite right," said Crystal.

"Would you want to have a dog?"

"A *dog*? Heavens no. Dogs ruin furniture."

"But if a dog just showed up and needed a home, would you keep it?"

"Certainly not. It would go straight to the pound to wait for a happy life with someone else." She spooned up the last of her soup. "Why are you asking about dogs?"

"Just wondering," said Nickie, with a sinking heart. "I like dogs."

After dinner, Crystal went to take a bath and Nickie dashed up to the third floor. She tapped on the door of the nursery, and Amanda, in her pajamas, opened it. Otis stood on his hind legs to greet Nickie, and she hugged and petted him. "Everything okay?" she asked Amanda.

"Yeah," Amanda said. "I'm being real quiet."

"Good," said Nickie. "Because I found out Crystal doesn't like dogs. We have to be extremely careful."

"Okay," said Amanda. "I'll put him under the covers with me tonight."

Nickie gave Otis one more pat and hurried back downstairs. For a while, she and Crystal sat in the front parlor and watched the news.

A local announcer was talking. "Several residents in Hickory Cove and Creekside," he said, "have reported signs of unusual activity in nearby wooded areas. A hiker claims to have caught a glimpse, in a remote part of the woods, of a man wearing a white or light tan coat. Residents of the area are advised to be alert to anything out of the ordinary, including unknown persons arriving in town; evidence of tampering with buildings, pipelines, or electrical equipment; and strange behavior of any kind."

Then the president came on. Nickie didn't like listening to him because his voice always sounded too smooth. He said something about the Phalanx Nations and missile deployment and fourteen countries and Level Seven alerts. Crystal frowned. "It gets closer every day," she said.

"What does?"

Crystal just shook her head. "Big trouble," she said.

The president ended with his usual sentence: "Let us pray to God for the safety of our people and the success of our endeavors." Nickie always wondered about this. The idea seemed to be that if you prayed extremely hard—especially if a *lot* of people prayed at once—maybe God would change things. The trouble was, what if your enemy was praying, too? Which prayer would God listen to?

She sighed. "Crystal," she said, "I'm so sick of the Crisis."

"I know," said Crystal. She flicked off the TV. "We all are. But it doesn't help to worry. All we can do is keep our wits about us. Not let fear take over. And try to be good little people and not add to the badness." She smiled at Nickie and stood up. "Tired?"

Nickie nodded.

"Which room would you like to sleep in?" Crystal asked. "You can have first pick."

The room she really wanted was the one on the third floor, but right now it was occupied. So Nickie chose one of the bedrooms on the first floor, and Crystal took the one next to it. They found sheets and blankets in a linen closet and made up the beds, and they unpacked their suitcases and hung their clothes in the closets. Nickie put her nightie on and slid between the sheets of the enormous bed. She thought about Amanda and the little dog, hidden away upstairs. They would be going to bed now, too. It would be nice, she thought, to sleep with a dog curled up next to you.

The bed's black posts rose toward the ceiling; in the darkness, they looked like two thin soldiers standing guard. Nickie wondered who this room had belonged to in years past. Who else had lain here looking at those posts, and at the violet-flowered wallpaper, and the stains on the ceiling? She wished she could know about their lives—not just her grandfather's but all the lives of this house, all those ancestors she'd never known.

This is how Nickie was: she wanted to know about everybody and everything—not just encyclopedia-type information, but ordinary things like what people did at their jobs and what their houses looked like inside and what they talked about. When she passed two or three people walking together on the street, she always hoped to catch an intriguing bit of conversation, like "I found her lying there dead!" Or ". . . and he left that very day without telling a soul and was never seen again!" But almost always, all she heard were the dull, connecting bits of the conversation, things like "And so I said to her . . ." and "Yeah, I think so, too," and "So it's really kind of like . . ." And by the time they said whatever came next, they were out of earshot.

She also wanted to know about things that weren't so ordinary, strange *extra*ordinary things like, Were there people on other planets? Was ESP real? Were there still places on Earth where no one had ever been? Were there animals that no one had yet discovered? In a magazine, she had come across a photograph of a dust mite taken with an electron microscope. A dust mite was much too small to see with the naked eye, but when you took its picture and magnified it many times, you could see that it was as complicated and weird as a monster in a science-fiction movie, with fangs and feelers and bristles.

When Nickie saw this picture, she suddenly understood that a whole other world existed right alongside the world of things she could see. In the dust under the furniture, in between the strands of the carpet, even crawling on her very own skin and inside her guts were creatures of unbelievable strangeness. She loved knowing this. She took the dust mite picture with her everywhere she went.

Now she listened to the rain pattering steadily at the windows and closed her eyes. She thought about the spirits of all the people who had lived here. Maybe they were still hovering around, wondering who was coming next. It's going to be me, she told them silently. *I'm* going to live here. And this reminded her of something she'd forgotten to do. She sat up and turned the light back on. In the drawer of the bedside table, she rummaged around until she found a stubby pencil and a scrap of paper. On the paper she wrote:

1. Keep Greenhaven.
2. Fall in love.
3. Help the world.

Her three goals. She was determined to accomplish them all.

CHAPTER 4

Break-In

Sometime in the middle of that night, as the rain fell and Nickie slept, someone—or something—came out of the forest above the town. The night was dark and moonless, and whoever it was came so quietly that no one heard him. Wayne Hollister, who ran the Black Oak Inn at the north end of town, glanced out the window when he got up to go to the bathroom around 2:00 a.m., and he was pretty sure he saw something moving on the road, but he didn't have his glasses on, so he couldn't tell what it was. Maybe a man in a raincoat.

Early the next morning—it was a Friday—a boy named Grover Persons was walking up the alley in back of the Cozy Corner Café, hunting for a particular kind of wildlife on his way to school, when he noticed that the glass window next to the café's back door was broken. He stopped to investigate. He could see that the window must have been punched in from the outside. A few fragments lay on the ground below the window, but most of the glass was inside, scattered across the restaurant's kitchen counter. Some jagged shards remained in the window frame, and something else was there, too: it looked like a white dish towel snagged on the broken glass. On the towel was a dark stain. Grover peered at it. It looked like blood.

He went around to the front of the restaurant, where Andy Hart, the manager, was just opening up.

"Andy," said Grover, "someone broke your back window last night."

Andy stood stock-still and gaped at him for a second. Sunlight, which shone through gaps in the leftover rain clouds, flashed on his glasses and lit up his high, shiny forehead. Then he charged around to the back, with Grover behind him. When he saw the broken window and the stained cloth, he let out a shriek that brought people running from all around. In minutes, the entire four-man police force and ten or twelve other people had gathered behind the Cozy Corner. They stared at the broken window, which looked like a great snaggle-toothed mouth with a bloody tongue hanging out the bottom.

"Stay back," said Chief of Police Ralph Gurney. "Don't touch anything. This is a crime scene."

People moved back. Grover could hear them murmuring to each other in worried voices.

"Andy, you in there?" called Officer Gurney through the window. "What's been taken?"

From inside, Andy called, "Nothing much. It looks like just a package of chicken."

"So," said Officer Gurney. "This must be either a prank or a threat."

Again came the uneasy murmurs from the crowd.

At another time, this broken window might have seemed like a minor incident. After all, no one was hurt; not much was stolen. But people were already on edge. It had been more than six months since Althea Tower had had her terrible vision, and every day that vision seemed closer to coming true. Just last night, the Phalanx Nations had announced that they had missiles deployed in fourteen countries. The United States had replied by raising the alert level to Seven. Everyone knew that terrorists were all over the place. It seemed that the evils of the world were coming far too close for comfort.

Officer Gurney ran a strip of yellow tape around the back area of the café, roping it off so no one could disturb the site. Then he scanned the crowd. His eyes lit on a comfortably plump woman wearing a red down jacket that made her look even plumper. She had a short brownish-blond ponytail that stuck out through a hole in her red baseball hat.

"Brenda," said Officer Gurney. "What do you think?"

Grover was in danger of being late for school by this time. He'd already been late twice this month. If he was late again, he might get a note sent home to his parents. But he had to risk it. This was too interesting to miss.

The woman stepped forward. Grover knew her, of course; everyone did. Mrs. Brenda Beeson was the one who had figured out the Prophet's mumbled words and explained what they meant. She and her committee—the Reverend Loomis, Mayor Orville Milton, Police Chief Ralph Gurney, and a few others—were the most important people in the town.

Officer Gurney raised the yellow tape so Mrs. Beeson could duck under it. She stood before the window a long time, her back to the crowd, while everyone waited to see what she would say. Clouds sailed slowly across the sun, turning everything dark and light and dark again.

To Grover, it seemed like ages they all stood there, holding their breath. He resigned himself to being late for school and started thinking up creative excuses. The front door of his house had stuck and he couldn't get it open? His father needed him to help fish drowned rats out of flooded basements? His knee had popped out of joint and stayed out for half an hour?

Finally Mrs. Beeson turned to face them. "Well, it just goes to show," she said. "We never *used* to have people breaking windows and stealing things. For all our hard work, we've *still* got bad eggs among us." She gave an exasperated sigh, and her breath made a puff of fog in the chilly air. "If this is someone's idea of fun, that person should be very, very ashamed of himself. This is no time for wild, stupid behavior."

"It's probably kids," said a man standing near Grover. Why did people always blame kids for things like this? As far as Grover could tell, grown-ups caused a lot more trouble in the world than kids.

"On the other hand," said Mrs. Beeson, "it could be a threat, or a warning. We've heard the reports about someone wandering around in the hills." She glanced back at the bloody rag hanging in the window. "It might even be a message of some sort. It looks to me like that stain could be a letter, maybe an *S*, or an *R*."

Grover squinted at the stain on the cloth. To him it looked more like an *A*, or maybe even just a random blotch.

"It might be a *B*," said someone standing near him.

"Or an *H*," said someone else.

Mrs. Beeson nodded. "Could be," she said. "The *S* could stand for *sin*. Or if it's an *R* it could stand for *ruin*. If you'll let me have that piece of cloth, Ralph, I'll show it to Althea and see if she has anything to say about it."

Just then Wayne Hollister happened to pass by, saw the crowd, and chimed in about what he'd seen in the night. His story frightened people even more than the blood and the broken glass. All around him, Grover heard them murmuring: Someone's out there. He's given us a warning. What does he mean to do? He's trying to scare us. One woman began to cry. Hoyt McCoy, as usual, said that Brenda Beeson should not pronounce upon things until she was in full possession of the facts, which she was not, and that to him the blotches of blood looked more like a soupspoon than an *R*. Several people told him angrily to be quiet.

But Grover had lost interest now that he'd heard Mrs. Beeson's verdict. If he ran really fast, he might not be late after all. He took off.

When he got to school, he told the first person he saw about the break-in, and then he told the next person, and pretty soon kids were crowding up around him. His friend Martin handed him a piece of paper and told him to draw the blood blot on it, exactly the way it was.

"I can't remember it *exactly,*" he said. "But it was more or less like this." He drew a gloppy string of blotches.

"That's supposed to look like a letter?" Martin frowned, peering at Grover's drawing through his thick-framed glasses.

"Well, I'm not drawing it perfect. Maybe it was

more like this." He drew a different blob. "That's not it, either." He laughed.

But Martin frowned again. "Do it right," he said. "I don't appreciate the way you're clowning around."

Grover drew it again, as well as he could remember.

"And she said it was an *S* or an *R*?" Martin wanted to know.

"She wasn't sure which," said Grover.

"And what did she say it stood for?" someone asked.

He told them, and he answered a lot of other questions, too, showing how Officer Gurney had strung the yellow tape, and repeating what Mrs. Beeson had said, and imitating, with a few high-pitched screams thrown in, the sobs of the woman who'd been so frightened. He imitated Hoyt McCoy, too, copying his gloomy look so well that everyone laughed. "Hoyt McCoy said it looked like a soupspoon," he said.

"Yeah," said Martin, "but Hoyt McCoy is a weirdo."

"Maybe so," said Grover, "but Mrs. Beeson doesn't know everything."

"Grover!" said Martin. His voice rose, and his face turned almost the same red as his hair. "*She* took the Prophet's vision seriously, even if *you* didn't."

The bell rang. Grover was late after all, and so was

everyone who'd been listening to him. "Gotta go," he said.

Martin scowled at him. "This will be my first late mark of the whole year," he said.

"It's not *my* fault," said Grover. "You didn't have to stand around talking to me."

But Martin just turned away. He'd changed, thought Grover as he hurried toward his classroom. He used to be nicer than he was now.

CHAPTER 5

The Fiery Vision

That morning, Crystal poked around in the kitchen cupboards and found just about nothing fit to eat. "Would you feel like walking downtown and getting us a few groceries?" she asked Nickie. "I'll start cleaning up this foul kitchen."

So Nickie put on her jacket and went downhill two blocks to Main Street, thinking how nice it was to be out by herself, as she couldn't safely be in the city. The stores were just opening. It was cold, but the sun came out sometimes from between the clouds, and the town looked washed clean. Quite a few people were already out. She noticed that nearly all of them held cell phones to their ears as they walked. Of course she was used to seeing cell phones in the city; there, half the people you passed were jabbering away. But here people weren't *talking* into their phones; they were just listening. It was odd.

She passed a small restaurant called the Cozy Corner Café, where several people were standing outside, talking in excited voices, and a police car was just pulling away. Something must have happened there—maybe a customer had taken sick.

She passed a drugstore, a bakery, and a shoe store. She passed a closed-up movie theater, where a sign stuck over the ticket window said, "Pray instead!" In the window of a clothing store, she saw a display of white T-shirts that said, "Don't Do It!" in big red letters on the front, and after that she kept noticing people on the street wearing these T-shirts. Don't do what? she wondered.

As she passed an alley between a hardware store and a computer repair shop, she heard a strange sound. It was a kind of hum with a rhythm to it—*MMMM-mmmm-MMMM-mmmm*—a sound that a machine might make. She stopped and looked around, but she couldn't see where it was coming from. She could tell that other people on the sidewalk noticed the sound, too. They frowned, but they didn't seem puzzled by it, just annoyed, or maybe a little frightened—a few of them started walking faster, as if to get away. The sound faded after a moment. Nickie decided it must be some gadget in the computer shop.

Farther on, she found the Yonwood Market, and there she bought some bread, milk, eggs, and powdered cocoa. She bought a small box of dog biscuits, too, and tucked this under her jacket.

Nickie was just turning off Main Street on the way back to Greenhaven when, from high overhead, there came a distant roar that quickly rose to a piercing scream, and five fighter jets streaked across the sky. Jets came often these days; they scared her. She stopped walking, set down the bag of groceries, and put her hands over her ears until the jets were gone.

Then she felt someone touch her shoulder. She looked up to see an elderly woman standing over her. "It might be starting," the woman said in a shaky voice. "It might be starting right now—you never know—but it's best not to be scared if you can help it. You need to have faith; that's what I say. We'll be all right here because of what we're doing, as long as we have faith, that's the main thing." The spidery hand patted Nickie's shoulder. "So don't worry, little girl, and remember to pray, and . . ." The woman glanced upward. "We'll be all right, because . . ." She trailed off and tottered away, leaving Nickie feeling the opposite of reassured. Maybe people here were just as scared as they were in the city. That made her heart sink a little. But on the other hand, the woman had said, "We'll be all right." It was confusing.

Once she got back to Greenhaven, though, she forgot about it. She hid the dog biscuits in her bedroom and then went into the kitchen, where Crystal made hot chocolate for them. They sat at the huge, elegant dining room table. Crystal got out her to-do list.

"This room is so . . . majestic," Nickie said. She had decided to point out good things about Greenhaven as often as she could, to change Crystal's mind about selling it.

"I suppose so," said Crystal, glancing up. "Certainly this table is very fine. It should fetch a good price." She went back to her list. "I'll start by talking to the real estate agent," she said. "Then I'll go make arrangements at the auction house and find a cleaning service. I should be back by noon."

"I'll stay here," said Nickie. "I can start going through stuff."

"You'll be all right? You won't fall down the stairs or lean out high windows?"

"Of course I won't," said Nickie. "I'll just take stuff out of cupboards and boxes and look at it. I'll separate it into Stuff to Keep and Stuff to Throw Away."

"Throw Away will be the big pile," Crystal said.

When Crystal had gone, Nickie fetched the dog biscuits and dashed up the stairs. "Amanda!" she called. "It's me!" She heard barking when she came to the door at the top. When she opened it, she saw Otis rocketing toward her. He skidded to a stop in front of her and rose to his hind feet, stretching his front paws up as if he wanted to pat her face. She knelt down and scratched his ears. "Hi, Otis," she said. "You sure are cute."

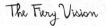

Amanda came out into the hall. She was still in her bathrobe.

"I heard Otis barking when I came up the stairs," Nickie said. "I don't see how we can keep him a secret if he barks. Crystal will hear him."

"Oh, Lord," said Amanda. "Maybe I could get him a muzzle."

"That seems kind of cruel," Nickie said. "There must be a better way."

Nickie went into the nursery room and looked around. The long tube of rolled-up rug gave her an idea. "We could soundproof this room," she said. "I'm sure we could."

They spent the next two hours doing it. They unrolled the big rug. They found small rugs in other rooms, brought them up to the nursery, and spread them out to cover the entire floor. From bathrooms and linen closets they brought towels and blankets, which they hung over the windows and the door with thumbtacks. Every now and then Nickie would go downstairs, Amanda would get Otis to bark, and Nickie would listen hard. Finally, after four tries, Nickie couldn't hear a thing.

"It works!" she said when she came back up. She

surveyed what they'd done. It was more than a soundproof room: it was also a strange and beautiful room, almost like the inside of a tent, with its carpeted floor and walls hung with blankets. It glowed with patterns and colors—faded blue and faded red on the floor, rose and lavender, pale green and gold on the walls. The light was dim now, because they'd covered some of the windows, so they brought up a lamp with a parchment shade from one of the rooms below, and more cushions for the window seat, and another rocking chair.

"If only we could make a fire in the fireplace," Nickie said, "this would be the coziest room in the world."

"It's real nice," Amanda agreed. "Otis might chew these rugs, though."

"I'll buy him some toys," Nickie said. "You can teach him to chew those instead." She bent down and rumpled Otis's ears. "Now," she said, "I'm going to start looking through stuff."

"Looking through what?"

"Everything in the house. I want to see it all," Nickie said. "Have you noticed any scrapbooks while you've been here? Or diaries, or photograph albums?"

Amanda pondered. "Maybe in the front parlor cabinet," she said.

So Nickie went downstairs, filled a box with stuff

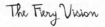

she found in the parlor cabinets, and took it back up to the nursery. She and Amanda sat on the window seat beneath a lamp and looked through it. A great deal of it was boring: old packs of bent playing cards, a calendar from 1973, a photo album containing eighteen faded photos, every one of them of a black cocker spaniel. But there were also some old letters, some *National Geographic* magazines, and quite a few albums with pictures of people. Jammed way in the back, she found three very old-looking cards with black borders. They were from different people, but all of them were dated 1918, and all of them, in old-fashioned handwriting, said more or less the same thing: "We send heartfelt condolences for your tragic loss." What was the tragic loss? she wondered. None of the cards said.

"Hey, I thought of something else you'd probably want to look at," Amanda said. "I'll go get it."

She went downstairs and came back up in a minute with a little brown notebook. "The old man wrote in this sometimes when I was taking care of him," she said, handing it to Nickie.

Nickie opened the notebook. Her great-grandfather's name was written inside the front cover: Arthur Green. She leafed through it. It looked more like a series of jottings than a real journal. He'd made the first entry at the beginning of December, just a couple of months ago. It said:

12/7 Some odd experiences lately. Might be my failing mind, but might not. Will note them down here.

Interesting, Nickie thought. She put the notebook in the Stuff to Keep pile. She'd look at it later.

Otis, in the meantime, chewed quietly on a chair leg. By the time they realized it, he had made some rather deep tooth marks. Fortunately they were on the back leg of the chair and didn't show too much.

Amanda took one of the *National Geographic* magazines and leafed through it. "Oh, Lord, look at this," she said. She held out the magazine, open to a picture of a volcano erupting, with flames and billows of black smoke. "This is kind of like what the Prophet saw."

"Who?"

"The Prophet!" said Amanda. "Althea Tower! You haven't heard of her? She's famous! Everybody in this whole town follows her! Or just about everybody."

"Why do you call her the Prophet?"

"Because she is one," said Amanda. She propped her elbows on her knees and leaned forward. She spoke in the hushed voice people use for imparting awesome information. "She saw the future in a vision."

"What did she see?" asked Nickie.

"Well, she couldn't exactly tell, because it was so

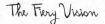

awful it made her sick. She could only give hints. Like she said 'fire' a lot, and 'explosions.' It musta looked sort of like this"—Amanda tapped her finger on the volcano picture—"except all over the world. Anyway, she took to her bed and she's been there ever since."

"That's amazing," said Nickie. "But I don't understand. What did it mean? Was it like a bad dream?"

"It wasn't a *dream*," Amanda said scornfully. "It was the *future*. It was a warning. Mrs. Beeson figured that out."

"Who's Mrs. Beeson?" Nickie asked.

"This lady who lives down the street from here. She's a real sweet, smart lady, used to be the school principal. She has a dog named Sausage; you'll probably see her walking it sometimes." She leaned forward again. "So anyway," she said, "what happened is, people have strayed from God's way, so that's why everything is so awful and heading for doom. But God wants to save us, so he gave the vision to Althea. If we do right, we'll be saved, and what she seen in her vision won't happen. At least not to *us*."

"So what are we supposed to do?" Nickie asked.

"Everything the Prophet says, because it's God's orders coming through her. She tells us what things to give up."

"Give up?"

"Yeah. Like one thing she says a lot is 'No sinnies,' which Mrs. Beeson says means 'No sinners.' We have to be real careful to be good. Also she says 'No singing,' so we don't listen to the pop radio anymore, or CDs, or movies that have singing. And on TV we only watch the news." Otis wandered over, and Amanda reached out absently to scratch him.

"But why?"

"It's to practice not being selfish. So you have more love to give to God." Amanda sat back, looked at Nickie in a satisfied way, and closed the *National Geographic* with a slap.

Nickie pondered. It was true that giving things up was something that holy people often did. She knew that some monks and priests gave up marriage. Some of them even gave up talking and lived their lives in silence. In other countries, there were holy people who gave up comfortable beds and slept on nails. People like these, she supposed, were totally devoted to God. Maybe she herself should give something up, just to see how it felt.

"Did *you* give anything up?" she asked Amanda.

"I did," Amanda said. "I gave up romance books. Mrs. Beeson says they're a waste of time anyway, so it was good to give them up."

"Hmmm," said Nickie. This was just the sort of thing that fired her imagination. It was like something out of a book, the kind of book where dark forces are trying to take over the universe and only a few valiant people know how to defeat them and are brave enough to do it. She thought of her Goal #3—to do something helpful for the world. Maybe giving things up was one way to do it. She wanted to ask more questions, but Amanda set down the *National Geographic* at that point and stood up.

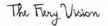

"I'm gonna get me a piece of toast," she said. "Want to come?"

Nickie nodded. They left Otis closed into his room and went downstairs. In the kitchen, Amanda sliced the bread, and Nickie, thinking about how interesting it would be to have visions and what she would do if she had one, put on the teakettle for more hot chocolate. But just as Amanda was getting the peanut butter out of the cupboard, though they hadn't heard a single footstep or a knock, a face appeared at the window of the back door. A voice cried, "Hello-o!" in a yoo-hoo sort of way, and before they could move, the door opened.

CHAPTER 6

Mrs. Beeson's Idea

"Excuse me, dears," said the woman at Greenhaven's back door. "I thought I'd stop by and say hello." She stepped inside. "I'm Brenda Beeson," she said.

Nickie stared. Brenda Beeson, the friend of the Prophet! But she didn't look especially holy. She was a middle-aged woman, not exactly fat, but sort of pillowy, with round rosy cheeks. She had on a quilted red jacket, and her blue eyes gleamed out from beneath the visor of a red baseball cap. She looked like a mixture of a grandmother and a soccer coach, Nickie thought.

"You must be Professor Green's granddaughter," Mrs. Beeson said.

"Great-granddaughter," said Nickie. She told Mrs. Beeson her name.

"Nickie?" said Mrs. Beeson. "Short for Nicole?"

"Yes." Nickie never used her real name, Nicole. It was a pretty name, she thought, but it felt *too* pretty for her, since she was rather stocky and had a round chin, a short nose, and straight, unstylish brown hair. She considered herself a smart person with a good imagination but sort of ordinary-looking, and so Nickie felt like a better name.

"Pleased to meet you," said Mrs. Beeson. "I'm your neighbor. I live three houses down, across the street." She took off her cap and stuffed it in her pocket, and Nickie saw that she had caramel-colored hair pulled back in a jaunty ponytail, and she wore little bobbly earrings. Mrs. Beeson turned her gaze on Amanda. "I didn't expect to see *you* here, dear," she said.

Amanda had backed up against the sink. She had a piece of bread in one hand and a jar of peanut butter in the other, and she looked scared.

"Why haven't you left," said Mrs. Beeson, "now that Professor Green has passed?"

"I'm about to go," said Amanda. "Soon as I find a place."

"Find a place? You have no family to go to?"

Amanda just shook her head.

"No parents?"

"My mom died," Amanda said. "My dad took off."

"No one else?"

"Just my cousin LouAnn," Amanda said miserably. "I don't like her."

"Well, dear, this won't do at all," said Mrs. Beeson. She unzipped her jacket with one quick pull and sat down at the kitchen table, ready to handle Amanda's future. Nickie noticed a round blue button pinned to her sweater. The picture on it looked like a little building. "I'm sure I can help," Mrs. Beeson said. "I have several friends in social work. I'll contact them right away. They'll be able to place you in a home." She pulled a little phone out of her pocket—a cell phone, Nickie guessed, though it had a different shape from the ones she was used to.

Amanda took a step forward. Terror was written on her face. She dropped the piece of bread and clunked down the peanut butter jar and raised her hands like stop signs in the direction of Mrs. Beeson. "I don't want to go to any home," she said. "I'm seventeen, I can get a job, I can find—"

"Nonsense," said Mrs. Beeson kindly. "Everyone needs a home." She paused, her mouth half open. An idea seemed to be forming behind her eyes. Her eyebrows rose. "In fact," she said, "I know someone who needs a helper right now. A dear friend of mine."

"What kind of helper?" asked Amanda suspiciously.

"A household helper," Mrs. Beeson said. "A live-in helper."

"I don't know," said Amanda. She hunched up her shoulders and scowled at the floor.

"The friend I am speaking of," said Mrs. Beeson with a little smile, "is Miss Althea Tower."

Amanda's eyes went wide. She stood up straight. She said, in a voice that cracked in the middle, "The Prophet?"

"That's right. You know she's very unwell, and the girl we hired to take care of her is leaving. You could stay with her, couldn't you? You were so good with the professor."

In just five seconds, Amanda had become a whole new person. Her face shone with eagerness. She straightened her shoulders, hooked a stray lock of hair behind her ear. "I could do it," she said. "I'd really *like* to!"

"Wonderful," said Mrs. Beeson. "If you can get ready, I'll take you over there right now and see if we can make an arrangement."

Nickie could see that Mrs. Brenda Beeson was the kind of person who moved fast and made firm decisions. She seemed nice, too. So after Amanda went upstairs, Nickie decided to ask some questions. But before she could say anything, there was a sudden pealing of tiny bells. Mrs. Beeson put her phone to her ear.

"Hello? Yes, Doralee, what is it?" She listened. "No, dear, I'm afraid not." A pause. "I know you're anxious, but, honey, Althea cannot see people's futures on demand. No. She is a prophet, not a fortune-teller." Another pause. "I'm sorry, Doralee dear, but it's out of the question. Please don't ask me again." She put down the phone and sighed. "I get these requests all the time," she said. "People are so nervous."

Nickie plunged ahead with her question. "Mrs. Beeson," she said, "do you think something terrible is going to happen? Like in the Prophet's vision?"

"Well, I don't want to scare you, honey," said Mrs. Beeson, "but I'm afraid it might. There's a lot of people in the world right now who want to hurt us. The forces of evil are strong. But our country is standing up against them, and here in Yonwood we are, too." She picked up the peanut butter jar and the loaf of bread and put them back in the cupboard. She brushed some crumbs off the table. "Our Prophet," she said, "is helping us."

"I know," said Nickie. "Amanda told me."

"Did she tell you about the hotline?" Mrs. Beeson asked. "It's a recorded phone message. Every day, people can call seven-seven-seven to hear her latest words and learn what to do about them. If there's something urgent, I can buzz their phones so they all get the message immediately. I arranged it all with my DATT phone." She showed Nickie the little phone, which had more tiny screens and buttons and sliding bits than any phone Nickie had seen. "I love high-tech gadgets, don't you? DATT stands for Do A Thousand Things. It doesn't really do quite a thousand, but just about." She pressed a button. "Wait a sec, that's the temperature." She pressed another button. "There we go. Nearly eleven. Where is that girl? I need to get going."

But Nickie wasn't through asking questions. She spoke quickly. "You know what, Mrs. Beeson?" she said. "I really want to do something to help the world."

"Then you've come to the right place," said Mrs. Beeson, putting her phone back in her pocket. She smiled. "Everyone here is trying to help the world. We're all quite passionate about it. We've had so many town meetings and church discussions and special votes—well, dangerous times bring people together. There are still a few who cling to their selfish ways, though, and that's very troubling. Even one can ruin everything, just the way one moldy strawberry in a basket can mess up all the rest."

Amanda's steps sounded on the stairs, and Mrs. Beeson stood up. But Nickie had to ask one more question. "What should I do?"

Mrs. Beeson was pulling on her jacket. She stuck her red cap on her head and pulled her ponytail out through the gap in the back. "Do?" she said. "Well, let's see. You might let me know if you happen to notice any trouble spots."

"You mean," Nickie said, "a trouble spot might be like—like what?"

Amanda came into the kitchen. "Here I am," she said. She had on nice clothes, and her hair was carefully combed.

"You look lovely, honey," said Mrs. Beeson. "I'll go and get my car. Meet me in front of the house."

"But Mrs. Beeson," said Nickie urgently. "What would a trouble spot be?"

Mrs. Beeson paused in the doorway. Her eyes grew serious. "You look for sinners, Nickie," she said. "It's one of the things the Prophet says most often: 'No sinners,' she says. 'No sinners.'"

"Sinners?" said Nickie. "You mean like lawbreakers?"

"Yes, but not *only* them," said Mrs. Beeson. "Sometimes they're not actually breaking a law, and still you have a sense of wrongness about them. You can just *feel* it." Mrs. Beeson paused for a moment to zip up her jacket. "Do you know of the man named Hoyt McCoy? Who lives down on Raven Road?"

"No," said Nickie. "I don't know anyone."

"No, of course you wouldn't. But he's an example. There's something about him—a whiff of wrongness. It's very strong." She started down the hall but stopped and looked back. "Do you love God?"

Nickie was surprised. "Sure," she said. "I guess so." The truth was, she had never thought about it. Her parents hadn't taken her to church, so she didn't know much about God.

"Excellent," said Mrs. Beeson. "We have to love God more than anything else. If you do, then you'll do fine. You can help us build a shield of goodness."

With another beaming smile, she turned and headed out the door.

"Isn't this just amazing?" Amanda said when Mrs. Beeson had left. "I was so scared when she came to the door. I mean, she's a real nice person, but I thought sure she was going to send me to a home. I never thought something like *this* could happen. Me taking care of the Prophet! Whoo! Do I look all right?"

"You look fine," said Nickie. "But what about Otis?"

"Oh, Lord, Otis," Amanda said. "Can you take care of him? He might hurt my chances to get hired. Can you feed him? And take him outside a couple times a day? Just for a little while? Please, please, *please*?"

And of course Nickie said she would.

As soon as Amanda had gone off with Mrs. Beeson, Nickie found a pencil and a scrap of paper and wrote down these words: *Sinners. Wrongness. Forces of evil. Shield of goodness.* Those were the things to remember. It was so perfect—she could accomplish her Goal #3 by helping to battle the forces of evil and build the shield of goodness. Just the very words made her feel like a warrior. Maybe she should give something up, the way everyone else was. If she did, would she have more love to give to God? She thought probably her love for God was a little weak, since she didn't know much about him and hadn't really thought about whether she loved him or not. It was hard to love someone invisible that you'd never met. Giving up something might strengthen her devotion. What could she give up? She'd think about it.

Then she ran up to the nursery to see Otis. She knelt down and held him up by his front paws so that they could look at each other eye to eye. "Otis," she said, "Amanda had to go away. I'm taking care of you now. Okay?" Otis gazed back at her. His eyes were like shiny deep-brown marbles. He cocked his head, as if trying to make sense of her words.

It was going to be a little tricky, taking care of Otis. She'd have to keep Crystal from coming up to the third floor. And she'd have to feed Otis and take him outside without letting Crystal see him. She hated leaving him all alone in the nursery room with nothing to do but chew things up. Did dogs get depressed from being alone too much? She didn't want Otis to be depressed. Luckily, it looked as if Crystal had so many errands to do and people to talk to that Nickie could probably be alone at Greenhaven for hours every day.

She pulled Otis onto her lap and hugged him. He wiggled out of her arms—his small blond body was amazingly strong—and then he sort of danced in front of her, his front paws stretched out straight and patting the air. "Woof!" he said, and Nickie instantly understood that *woof* meant *play*.

In the closet she found a little brown shoe that must have belonged to a child years ago. "Watch *this,* Otis!" she cried, and she threw the shoe across the room.

Otis hurled himself after it. He snatched up the shoe and raced back to her. He gave it a shake to make sure it was dead, and then he dropped it and waited, his round brown eyes on hers, shining with expectation.

They played Retrieve the Shoe for a long time, until Otis got distracted by a spider on the floor. Nickie went downstairs for another cup of hot chocolate and got back to find Otis in a squatting position, his back humped and his tail up and a faraway look in his eyes. Just in time, she seized an old magazine, put it under his rear end, and caught what came out before it could stain the rug.

Take him outside twice a day, Amanda had said. She'd forgotten. She found a leash hanging in the closet, hooked it to Otis's collar, and led him downstairs and out the kitchen door.

While he trotted among the bushes, she looked around. There was a clothesline back here and a concrete terrace bordered by a low stone wall. In the back of the house was a door that probably led to the basement. She tried it, but it was locked.

Once Otis was emptied out, they went back upstairs to the nursery. Nickie wondered if Amanda was having her interview with the Prophet at this very moment. She was so curious about the Prophet. She longed to meet her.

It was almost noon, but Crystal wasn't back yet, so Nickie went into the next room, one of the rooms crammed with trunks and boxes. Moving aside a stack of old magazines, she opened the biggest, oldest-looking trunk and saw a great jumble of stuff—mostly papers—inside. She scooped up an armful and took it back to the nursery room to look through.

No one had bothered to put any of these things in order, or even to store them neatly so they didn't get bent and crumpled. There were a lot of old Christmas cards, some faded snapshots of babies, and bunches of ancient bills and report cards and school papers. Toward the bottom of the pile, she found an envelope so old that its edges had come apart. Inside was a photograph on cardboard backing. She had just time to glance at it, and to notice that something about it was odd but she wasn't sure what, when she saw Crystal's car pull up outside. Nickie put the photograph back in its envelope. She scooped her piles off the window seat and put them in the toy cabinet, where Otis couldn't get at them. "Now, you sleep," she said to Otis. She left the room, closed the door behind her, and crammed some rags under it. Then she raced downstairs.

Crystal was just coming in the front door. She took her coat off and hung it on the coatrack in the hall. "Well, I met the real estate agent," she said. "Len Caldwell, his name is. Quite nice and helpful. He's very tall and has a funny little mustache." She smiled at Nickie. "And what's been happening here?"

Nickie opened her mouth and then quickly closed it. "Oh, I've just been wandering around," she said. "I love how big and spacious this house is, don't you?"

"It's big, all right," said Crystal. "There *is* something nice about having space to spread out. Of course, it's just more space that has to be cleaned."

Nickie was about to mention the beautiful curving staircase and the view of mountains from the back windows—but just then the phone rang.

Crystal picked it up. "Hello?" she said. "Rachel! How are you?"

It was Nickie's mother.

"Uh-huh," said Crystal. "Uh-huh, uh-huh. I know, it's really hard."

"I want to talk to her!" Nickie whispered loudly.

"You did?" said Crystal. "What did it say?"

"What did *what* say?" Nickie said.

"Huh," said Crystal. "Odd. Here, tell Nickie; she wants to know."

"Mom!" said Nickie into the phone. "Are you okay?"

"I'm okay," said her mother's weary voice. "I got a postcard from your father."

"You did? What did he say?"

"Not much. I hope he's all right. I just wish I knew where he was."

"Read it to me," Nickie said. "But wait a sec—I need to find a pencil. I want to write it down."

So her mother read her the postcard, and Nickie wrote down what she said. Then they talked for a while about her mother's job, about bomb alerts in the city, and about how cold it was. Nickie said how much she loved Greenhaven, and what a terrible mistake it would be to sell it. When they said goodbye, Nickie would have felt sad if she hadn't had the words of the postcard to study:

Dear Rachel and Nickie,

All is fine here. Work is going well. Wish I could tell you where I am, but it's strictly forbidden.

My love to you both, Dad

P.S. Three sparrows came to the bird feeder today!

Her mother was right. It didn't say much. Though it did tell her something new about her father—she hadn't known he was interested in birds at all.

CHAPTER 7

The Short Way Home

Grover couldn't concentrate at school that day. The classrooms were alive with whispers about the terrorist in the woods, and the bloody letter, and what Brenda Beeson said it meant. Even his teacher seemed nervous, Grover thought. She kept glancing out the window, and twice she came up with the wrong answers to the problems she was explaining.

After school, still more kids surrounded Grover and asked him to describe what he'd seen. He wished he could tell them that the Prophet herself had come to examine the bloody cloth. She was the one they were curious about. But no one had seen her since she'd had her vision—besides the doctor, no one but Mrs. Beeson and her small, devoted group. Grover remembered seeing Althea Tower in the bookshop sometimes before her vision, but she hadn't been interesting then—just a sort of fluffy-haired woman with rimless glasses and dust on her fingertips from handling used books. She'd always smiled at him when he went in there, but she never said much. She was pale, as he recalled, and wispy, and had a quiet voice.

But now he'd like to get a glimpse of her, to see if her eyes looked scorched and her hair frizzled like electric wires, to see if her face looked blasted, or frozen into astonishment, or whatever look there might be on the face of a person who had been shown a vision by God. If it really was God—Grover didn't know, and mostly he didn't care, as long as the results didn't affect him.

He ended up spending so much time talking to the kids in the schoolyard that he was in danger of getting home late. He was supposed to be home by three-thirty to help his grandmother with the kids; if he got home after his mother did, she'd tell his father, and his father was sure to yell at him. So he decided to do something he rarely did, because it was a bit of a risk: take the short way home.

The short way home was through Hoyt McCoy's backyard. Actually, *backyard* was too small a word for it; Hoyt McCoy's house lay within a large and brambly acreage. He had two or three times more land than most of his neighbors. At the rear part of it, a few slats of the fence had fallen sideways, making a hole big enough for a skinny boy to get through. Grover, holding his schoolbooks close to his chest, was just skinny enough.

Crossing Hoyt's yard cut a good five minutes off the time it took to get home. Grover knew this because he'd done it a few times before. The only risky part was at the back corner of the property, where the house stood. Here he would be within view of some windows, if anyone happened to be standing by them. But so much overgrown shrubbery grew up the back of the house, and the windows were so coated with dust and grime, that he didn't think the chance of being seen was very great.

This time, though, he was wrong. As he came up behind the house, staying as close to the fence as he could and trying not to crunch too much on the fallen leaves, an upstairs window flew open. The deep voice of Hoyt McCoy rang out.

"Halt, trespasser! I have you in my sights! Vacate these premises instantly!"

Grover stopped so fast that he dropped his books. He froze, hoping the bushes would hide him. He waited, watching the open window. Did Hoyt mean he had a rifle trained on him? Would he actually shoot it? Grover didn't know. So he stayed where he was until finally the window closed. Then he waited a little longer, and at last he bent to pick his books up and moved on, staying in the shadows, setting each foot down with great care, until he came to the gravel drive that led out to the street. Then he ran.

Hoyt McCoy was one of Yonwood's oddities. He'd moved there about ten years ago from a university town somewhere. For a year or so after he'd bought the house, workers from out of town had come every day, and sounds of drilling and sawing and hammering had issued from inside. People thought maybe Hoyt's family was coming to live with him—but no. Hoyt lived alone. Sometimes he went away for weeks at a time, leaving the gate across his driveway padlocked. When he was at home, he seemed almost never to have visitors, although a few times Grover had seen a dark green sedan turning in at his driveway, in which there were always two men in suits. They were probably tax collectors, Grover thought. It wasn't likely Hoyt McCoy would have friends. He was tall and gaunt, with caved-in cheeks and dark hollows around his eyes. He walked with his shoulders stooped and his head craned forward, as if he were looking for something to pounce on—and in his way, he did pounce on things. Everything met with his disapproval. On days when Hoyt showed up at the market or the post office or the drugstore, Grover had seen him tut-tutting at loud children, shaking his fist at cars that came too close to him, and scolding clerks for being rude. He also scoffed at everything Mrs. Beeson said about the

Prophet's vision. "Orders from heaven," he would say, pursing his lips. "Nonsense. *She* doesn't know. I'm the expert on heaven, not her. If you want to know about celestial matters, ask me." But no one ever did ask him, as far as Grover could see. Hardly anyone ever spoke to him at all, if they could help it.

When Grover got home, only a little bit late, he found his grandmother in the living room in her usual spot, the armchair by the heater, with a baby on her lap. All around her, little kids of various ages crawled and toddled, babbled and cried and screeched. The TV was on. A newsman was saying that the president had set a deadline of one week, exactly seven days, for the Phalanx Nations to deactivate their missiles. Otherwise, the United States would have no choice but to—

His grandmother aimed the remote and flicked off the TV. "Heard there's more trouble in town," she said.

Grover dumped his books on a side table. "I was the first one there, Granny Carrie," he said. "I was the one who told Andy."

"Good for you," said his grandmother. "On top of things as usual."

One of Grover's little brothers whacked his sister with a stuffed animal. The little girl wailed. The baby on his grandmother's lap started to cry.

This was how it always was at Grover's house. He

had six brothers and sisters, all younger, who created a constant uproar. His father worked as a handyman, and his mother worked at the dress shop, so his grandmother was the one who minded the children. Grover had to mind them, too, when he came home from school. All of this meant he was always short of time—time for homework, and time for other things that were more important to him than homework.

"Look here, Grover," Granny Carrie said. "I found some good ones for you." She leaned over and picked up a stack of magazines from the floor. "There's one that gets you ten thousand dollars. Another one gets you a car, but you could trade that for cash."

"Great," said Grover. He took the top magazine and opened it to the page his grandmother had dog-eared. "The Fabulous Dorfberry Sweepstakes!" it said in big red letters. "Hundreds of Prizes! Grand Prize $10,000!" He read the fine print. All you had to do was collect five box tops from Dorfberry's Cornmeal Products and fill out an entry blank. Easy. His family ate a ton of corn muffins and cornbread. He could collect five box tops in less than a week.

"For this one here," said Granny Carrie, opening another magazine, "you have to write a paragraph." She showed it to him. "Why buy Armstrong Pickles?" said the ad. "You tell us! One hundred words or less." The grand prize was five hundred dollars, which would be more than enough.

"This is good," said Grover, moving the magazine away from the reaching fingers of his littlest brother. "Thanks. I'll probably win a whole lot of these and have money left over. I'll buy you a Cadillac."

"You better not," said Granny Carrie. "You can buy me some new slippers. These ones are getting worn out." She stuck out her feet, on which she was wearing yellow slippers with duck heads on them. They were a little ragged around the edges.

"Okay," said Grover. He'd be happy to buy his grandmother anything she wanted.

At five-thirty his mother came home, looking tired and carrying a bag of groceries. "Somebody's lurking around in the woods," she said, setting the bag down and taking off her coat.

"I know it," said Grover.

"Don't you go up there," she said. "You stay around here for a change." She started taking boxes and cans from the bag and putting them away.

A little later, Grover's father came home. He came in the back door, leaving his toolbox on the porch. "Hear about the break-in?" he said.

"Yes," said everyone.

"Gurney and his men ought to get up there in the woods and flush that guy out," said Grover's father. "Take their rifles with them."

"Don't talk about rifles," said Grover's mother. "It scares me."

His father just shrugged. "Serious times call for serious solutions," he said.

"A shield of goodness is a better protection," his mother said.

"Fine," said his father. "You work on being good; I'll keep the gun loaded."

"It could be just some poor wandering tramp up there," said his grandmother.

"Trouble is," said his father, "we don't *know.* He could be a tramp; he could be a guy scoping out bomb sites. Do you want to take the risk?"

Grover noticed a smear of grease on the side of his father's neck. Probably he'd been doing a plumbing job today. He could do just about anything—plumbing, carpentry, electrical work. He always had a lot of jobs, and he always came home tired and slightly grumpy in the evening.

"I'm going down to the shed," said Grover. There was still at least half an hour before dinner, and he wanted to use it.

"Now, listen here," said his father. "You waste a lot of time fooling around in that shed. What about your homework? Don't tell me you don't have any."

"I do, but I can do it later," Grover said.

"What comes first, getting ready for your future or fiddling with your little hobbies?" Grover's father put one foot up on a chair and untied his shoe. "If you're going to do something useful with your life, you've got to get started."

"I *am* going to do something useful," Grover said.

"Not the way you're going, you're not," said his father, untying the other shoe and letting it thump to the floor. He started in on the rant Grover had heard a thousand times. "You have to think *practical.* The world is headed for disaster; I think we can say that for sure. But afterward, assuming the human race survives, there's going to be a big need for builders, architects, engineers. Study a little harder, and you could be one of them."

But Grover had other ideas. He picked up his books and went back to his room. He flopped onto his bed. Instead of going down to the shed, he'd put the finishing touches on his application tonight, the one that was going to change his life. It was in the slim blue notebook he carried with him everywhere.

But where was the notebook? He had his English book, his math book, his history book—but not his blue notebook. Had he left it at school? He wouldn't have done that. Could he have—? A terrible thought struck him.

His blue notebook—he suddenly knew—was lying in the weeds behind the horrible house of Hoyt McCoy.

CHAPTER 8

A Crack in the Sky

He was going to have to go tonight, while it was dark. Otherwise, Hoyt would see him and try to shoot him again. This gave Grover a queasy feeling in his stomach, which made it hard to eat his dinner. When dinner was over and the little kids were in bed, his parents settled on the couch and flicked on the TV. A government spokesman was talking about the deadline the president had set for the Phalanx Nations to agree to the United States' demands, and that if the demands weren't met, the consequences would be serious, but no one should be alarmed, because emergency measures were planned, and—

"I'm going outside for a while," Grover said.

"All right," his mother said without looking at him. "Be back in by nine-thirty."

Grover went out the back door as if he were going across the yard to his shed, but instead he circled around the side of the house and headed down the street. Lucky it wasn't raining, he thought. Rain would turn his blue notebook into a soggy rag. And lucky the moon was just a sliver in the sky, shedding hardly any light. That would help him hide from Hoyt's sharp eyes.

Grover hurried downhill. He wanted to get this over with. If he hadn't already filled in so much of the application form, he could just leave it there and send for another one. But he'd put in hours trying to get it just right. And besides, the deadline was only a week away. He wouldn't have time to send for another one, get it done, and turn it in on time. He had to find the one he'd lost.

He passed the last house on his street and turned left onto Raven Road. It was darker here, because there were fewer houses shining the light from their windows out into the night. In less than five minutes, he came to the drive that led back into Hoyt's land and started walking up it. His shoes crunched on the gravel, a sound that seemed much too loud. He tried to walk on the edge of the drive, where the gravel merged into dirt, but his feet kept getting tangled in the brambles that grew there.

He crept along to the left, moving toward the back of the house, staying as close to the fence as he could. The house loomed tall and dark—only one window on the top story was lit. With thorns and stickers catching at his sleeves, Grover made his way through the thickets of brush to the place where, that afternoon, he'd frozen at the sound of Hoyt's voice. He was sure this was where he'd dropped his books; his notebook should still be right there on the ground, as long as Hoyt hadn't found it and thrown it in the trash, or some animal hadn't taken it away to shred for its nest. There was a straight line of sight from here to the top window of the house, the one that now glowed yellow around the edges of the drawn shade.

He dropped to his knees. Where was the darned thing? The shadows of the trees and bushes were so thick here that he could hardly see at all. He'd have to find it by feel. He ran his hands over the ground. Pebbles, clumps of cold dirt, scratchy weeds, dry fallen leaves. But no notebook. He held back a groan of frustration. He *had* to find it, because if he didn't find it, he wouldn't be able to go, even if he *did* get the money, and he *had* to go, because his whole future depended on it, and he was *furious* with himself for dropping it, and—

At that moment, his fingers touched something smooth. He reached farther and felt the spiral wires. His notebook. He grabbed it and stood up. Carefully, he riffled the pages, feeling for the loose one. Yes, it was there, tucked into the middle, just where he'd put it. All right. Now to get out of there.

He turned back toward the driveway and felt his

way forward between the tree trunks and the brush. He crept behind Hoyt's black car, parked near the corner of the house. At the spot where he'd have to go out into the open, he paused and checked the house again. It was still all dark except for the rectangle of light around the top-floor window. But as he watched, the light went out. Startled, Grover stepped back into the shadows and stood still for a moment. It might just be that Hoyt had turned off his light to sleep. Or it might be that he'd heard something and was about to peer out his window. Grover waited and watched—and an odd thing happened.

At first he thought he was imagining it, it was so faint. A light seemed to be growing behind the curtained and shuttered windows on the ground floor. It was a bluish light, like moonlight. It gleamed very faintly around the edges of the windows, in the gaps between the shades and the frames, until a narrow, pale-bluish rectangle appeared around all the ground-floor windows. What was it? Did Hoyt have twenty televisions that went on all at once? Was he doing some weird sort of experiment? Whatever it was, it gave Grover an eerie feeling.

He stood still for a moment, staring. Then, as if his ears had suddenly been stuffed with cotton, the whole world seemed to go silent, and in the sky over Hoyt McCoy's house, a brilliant line, thin as a wire, shot across the darkness. It was there for less than a second.

It vanished, and the sounds came back—rustling leaves, a distant calling bird. But Grover had seen it—it wasn't his imagination. It had looked like a long, narrow crack, as if the two great round halves of the night sky had slid apart just for a second, just enough to let through a light that was on the other side. It was the strangest thing he had ever seen.

But nothing else happened. The blue light continued to shine behind the windows; the house was silent; the sky stayed black. After another few minutes, Grover clutched his notebook tightly and moved toward the driveway, quiet as a cat and slow, until he got far enough from the house. Then he dashed along the driveway's edge down to Raven Road, where he set out for home.

CHAPTER 9

At the Prophet's House

Saturday morning, Crystal bustled everywhere, checking on things, adding items to her list. Plumbers arrived and began clanking away in the kitchen and in the bathrooms. Painters arrived and started sanding down windowsills and spreading out tarps in the parlor. Crystal marched from room to room, giving directions.

Now and then people stopped by to tell her how sorry they were about Professor Green. Some of them stood chatting for a long time. Nickie could see that they were curious about Crystal and maybe a little suspicious. They asked her all kinds of questions—"Are you married, dear?" "Will you be coming to live in Yonwood?" "What church do you attend?" "Have you met our Mrs. Beeson yet?"—until Crystal said it was lovely talking with them, but she had so much to do that she must say goodbye.

"I'm off to see some antique dealers," she said to Nickie when they were gone, "about selling some of this ghastly furniture. After that I have a meeting with the real estate agent. I'll see you sometime this afternoon."

As soon as Crystal had left, Nickie ran past the painters and up the stairs. She opened the hall door, then the nursery door, and there was Otis waiting for her, looking up with his round brown eyes and wagging his rear end, his short comma-shaped tail pointing at the ceiling. She took him downstairs and, when he was finished, brought him back inside. In the kitchen, she made herself a cup of hot chocolate. As she was doing that, the telephone rang.

She hardly ever answered the telephone here, since it was never for her. The answering machine answered if Crystal wasn't home. Usually the voice on the answering machine belonged to someone talking about house repairs. But this time the voice was Amanda's.

"Hello," it said. "Um . . . uh . . . Well, this is Amanda Stokes, and I . . . uh . . ."

Nickie snatched up the receiver. "Amanda!" she said. "It's me."

"Oh, good," said Amanda. "I didn't know what to say if it was your aunt getting the message."

"Did you get the job? With the Prophet?"

"I did!" said Amanda. "I am so lucky! But I'm calling up because I need my stuff. Can you bring it to me?"

"Sure," Nickie said. "Just tell me what to bring."

"It's all in my suitcase, under the bed. Except don't bring the books that are in there. Those are the ones I gave up. You can have them."

"Okay. I'll come right now. What's the Prophet's address?"

"It's 248 Grackle Street," Amanda said. She explained how to get there and said thanks, and Nickie hung up and did a little dance of excitement right there in the hall. She was going to see the Prophet's house! She was going to meet the Prophet herself!

She took Otis upstairs. She pulled out Amanda's suitcase from beneath the bed and opened it up, then rummaged through it to find the books (and also because she was curious). Underwear, socks, a striped flannel nightgown, some T-shirts, and a few pairs of pants. A floppy pink stuffed kitten, so old its fur was mostly worn away. A battered postcard with a picture of a beach. Nickie couldn't resist reading it. In big round handwriting, it said, "Dear Pumpkin, What a great place! Lots of beaches! See you soon, Your Mama." The date on the postcard was twelve years ago. Nickie wondered if this was all Amanda had of her mother.

She found the books underneath everything else. There were four of them, all paperbacks. She picked one up. On the cover was a woman with hair like a black waterfall, swooning in the arms of a man who was gazing at her hungrily. It was called *Heaven in His Arms.* Another one was called *A Heart in Flames.* Its cover showed a clasped-together couple standing on a windswept cliff with a blazing sunset in the sky behind them. All the books were like that. They looked interesting. She would read them herself. They might help her with Goal #2.

She put everything else back into the suitcase, went downstairs, edging past a carpenter repairing the front door, and set off for the Prophet's house.

It was a blustery morning. Big heaps of cloud rushed across the sky, and the wind was chilly. A few dead leaves skittered along the sidewalk. Nickie turned onto Main Street. Downtown, something seemed to be going on. Clusters of people stood here and there on the sidewalks, talking excitedly. As Nickie passed the drugstore, she saw that the TV inside was on, and people had gathered around it and were listening to the news. There were more people around the TV in the video store and also at the Cozy Corner Café. The president must be making some kind of announcement—she could see his solemn face and white hair on the screen—but she didn't want to stop and listen to him right now. She wanted to get on to the Prophet's house. Later she could find out what he'd said.

She walked four blocks up Grackle Street to number 248. It was a neat white house with a front porch, more or less like the other houses on the street, except that there were some bunches of limp flowers tied to the fence, along with a Christmas tree angel, a couple of holy-looking pictures, and a couple of handwritten signs. One said, "Althea, Our Prophet!" and the other one said, "We believe!" A bird feeder hung from the porch roof, but there were no seeds in it. The curtains in all the windows were closed.

Nickie rang the bell, and after a moment Amanda opened the door. "Oh, hi," she said, reaching for the suitcase. "Thanks for bringing this."

"You're welcome," Nickie said.

"Well," said Amanda. "See you later." She took a step back and started to close the door.

"But can't I come in?" Nickie said. "Can't I meet the Prophet?" She tried to look past Amanda into the room. Were there people in there? She thought she heard the sound of voices.

"Oh, gosh, no," said Amanda. Her eyebrows bunched into a worried line, and she backed up another step. "There's strict rules."

"Even if I just peeked in her door and said hello in a really soft voice?"

"Oh, yeah, even that. I can't let you," Amanda said. "I'd get in trouble."

"Well, who gets to visit her?"

"Just Mrs. Beeson and her committee. You know,

Reverend Loomis, and the mayor, and the police chief, and the others. One or two of them's here most of the time, sitting with her, in case she says something important," said Amanda. She glanced back over her shoulder. "A couple of 'em are here right now."

"Right now?"

"Yeah, having a meeting about stuff she's said."

"You mean she talks to them?"

"She sort of mumbles," Amanda said, "and then they hover over her and listen and whisper about what they think she said. And then they tiptoe out, and sometimes, like now, they stand around in the living room arguing about what she meant."

At that moment, a car pulled up at the curb.

"Uh-oh," Amanda said. "Mrs. Beeson is here. I got to get back to work."

Mrs. Beeson got out of her car and bustled up to the door. "Excuse me, dears," she said. "Urgent business." She pushed past them and disappeared into the house.

"I have to go," Amanda said. "But listen—how's Otis?"

"He's fine," Nickie said.

"I'm getting up my nerve to ask Mrs. Beeson if I can have him here," said Amanda.

Nickie's heart sank. She'd already forgotten that Otis wasn't hers.

"But I don't think she's going to let me," Amanda went on. "So I don't know. Do you think you—?"

"Oh, yes," said Nickie, relieved. "I'll take care of him. I don't mind at all. Don't worry about it." Her heart sprang up again. She said goodbye and headed down the path.

Clouds sailed across the sun, turning the day dark. She hurried to keep warm, down Grackle Street and past the park to Main Street. Maybe she could find out now what the president's announcement had been.

She made her way toward the Cozy Corner Café, thinking she could go in and ask someone there. But before she got there she heard a sort of buzz in the air, like a distant swarm of bees, and all around her people stopped in their tracks and pulled cell phones from their pockets and purses.

What was happening? It must be news from Mrs. Beeson, maybe about the "urgent business" that had taken her to the Prophet's house. She had to know. Who could she ask?

She spotted a red-haired boy wearing glasses with heavy frames. He was coming out of the café, carrying a doughnut, and had his phone pressed to his ear. He looked about her age, or a little older. She'd ask him.

She stepped up beside him and said, "Excuse me," into the ear that didn't have the phone against it.

He turned and looked at her.

"What's going on?" Nickie said. "Can you tell me?"

He frowned. "Wait," he said, holding up the hand with the doughnut. He was still listening intently. She waited. Finally, he folded up his phone.

"Who are you?" he said. "I don't know you."

She explained who she was. He stared at her suspiciously for a moment, but he must have decided she couldn't be a terrorist, because he said, "I'm Martin. Did you hear the president's announcement?"

"No," said Nickie. "What did he say?"

"Well, look," said Martin. "I've got it on my DATT." He flicked a tiny switch on his phone, and on a tiny screen the tiny face of the president appeared.

He looked grim. His face was grayish, as if he hadn't slept or eaten well for a while. "Six days remain," he said in a tiny version of his usual voice, "before time runs out for the Phalanx Nations. They have remained uncooperative. Therefore I am asking all directors of defense to activate their emergency plans, in case an attack is imminent." He went on about evacuations and shelters and troop movements, and he ended in the usual way: "Let us pray to God for the safety of our people and the success of our endeavors."

Nickie gulped. She looked up from the little screen. "So is that why—," she began. But she stopped, because something strange was happening. All up and down the street, the lights in the stores were going off.

One after another, the windows went dark. "What's going on?" she said.

"It's because of Mrs. Beeson's bulletin," said Martin. "She's just figured out a new instruction from the Prophet. See, for a long time the Prophet has been saying 'No lies,' or 'No lines,' or 'No lights,' but no one could tell which. Mrs. Beeson thought it was 'No lies,' because it's bad to tell lies. But now she realizes it must be 'No lights,' because that matches up with what the president just said."

"It does?"

"Obviously," said Martin, folding up his phone and putting it in his pocket. "The president is warning us about an attack. It might come any minute. If we turn our lights out, we won't be seen from the air."

Nickie looked up and down Main Street. It seemed almost like night, with all the windows dark and the sky clouded over. For the first time, she felt a real shiver of fear at the war that might come. It must have shown, because Martin said, "You shouldn't worry too much. There *is* destruction coming, but we're probably safe here."

"You mean because of the Prophet?"

"That's right. It's like having a phone line direct to God. As long as we follow directions, we should be okay. Even though there's a terrorist in the woods."

"There is?"

Martin nodded. "He broke into the restaurant just yesterday morning."

"That's awful," Nickie said. She had thought she'd escaped all that by coming to Yonwood. Clearly she'd been wrong.

Martin was peering at her as if trying to decide what kind of creature she was. "Do you love God?" he said.

Having been asked this question once before, Nickie was prepared. "Oh, yes!" she said. "I really do."

Martin smiled. His teeth were white and even, and Nickie noticed that his eyes, behind his glasses, were hazel, an interesting color that went well with his red hair. "That's good," he said. "Well, I have to get going. See you." He strode away, leaving Nickie standing there on the strangely darkened street, beneath the darkening sky. She felt excited and uneasy at the same time. She'd met a boy—that was progress on Goal #2. But the danger to the world had just gotten worse—which made Goal #3, doing something to help, more urgent than ever.

CHAPTER 10

The Photograph and the Journal

Nickie walked back to Greenhaven, thoughts zooming around in her mind like bees. So much had happened in just two days. She felt a little dizzy with it all. She would read for a while, she decided, to get calmed down.

Her plan for that afternoon was to go through the Look at Later pile. She went into the kitchen to make herself a cup of hot chocolate—and it occurred to her all at once that hot chocolate was the perfect thing to give up. It was something she really liked, so it would be *hard* to give up; and doing something hard would strengthen her goodness, just the way exercise strengthened muscles.

So she made a cup of mint tea instead and carried it up to the nursery, where she took her Look at Later pile from the toy cabinet and set it on the window seat. The light was dim there because of the blankets she and Amanda had hung over the windows, and because of the cloudy sky. She pushed one of the blankets aside a little and settled down with a big red pillow at her back. Otis jumped up next to her.

The first thing she wanted to check was that envelope she'd begun to look at yesterday. She picked it up and slid out the photograph. It was brownish and had a cardboard backing. It showed six people—two men and two women, seated, and two children sitting on the floor in front of them. They wore old-fashioned outfits and had sour looks on their faces, as if they were annoyed with the photographer for making them sit still so long.

The Mssrs. Bunker and Their Wives, visitors to Greenhaven on June 4, 1868.

There was something odd about the two men, who sat next to each other in the center of the group. At first Nickie thought one of them was sitting in the other one's lap. She looked closer. The two men, who looked just alike, seemed to be stuck together. Yes! They were joined by what looked like a thick finger of flesh that went from the stomach of one to the stomach of the other. That was why they were sitting in that odd way. They were twins—connected twins, or something like that. There was another word for it that she couldn't remember.

Under the picture, someone had written, "The Mssrs. Bunker and Their Wives, visitors to Greenhaven on June 4, 1868."

Visitors to Greenhaven! They had been here, in this house. She gazed at the picture a long time. How would it be to live your life attached to someone else? You could never get away from each other, not to go for a walk, not in bed at night, not even in the bathroom! If one was sick, the other would have to lie there, too. If one wanted to go downtown and the other wanted to stay home and read the newspaper, they'd have to negotiate about it and try to agree. Each one would always hear everything the other one said. It was the strangest kind of life she could imagine.

She put the picture back in its envelope and took up the small brown notebook that Amanda had brought to her, the one her great-grandfather had written in.

She read the first entry again, where he said he'd been having odd experiences, and then she read on.

12/10 It's the second-floor bedroom, I think, the one at the west end of the hall. Why there? Some memory being triggered? Can't figure it out.

12/13 Darn hip giving me trouble. Stayed in bed most of the day.

12/19 Althea T. still not speaking much after nearly six months. Brenda B. very worried about her.

He was writing about the Prophet! But then the next entry was about something quite different:

12/27 Could past, present, and future all exist at the same time? And certain people slip around between them? See theories set forth in recent sci. journals. Ask M.

Hmmm. What was that about?

A movement on the sidewalk below caught her attention. She looked out the window. There was Mrs. Beeson, wearing a rain jacket with the hood up over her baseball cap, walking a long-bodied, short-legged dog on a leash. That must be Sausage, Nickie thought. She watched as Mrs. Beeson passed, walked on, and turned in at a house across the street. It was a brick house, old but well cared for, with a straight path that led to a white front door with a tall, narrow window on each side. Two bushes flanked the door, both of them trimmed into neat round shapes like green beach balls. It was a perfect-looking house, Nickie thought, just right for Mrs. Beeson, who was aiming to get rid of all the wrongness in Yonwood. If only the whole *world* could be that way!

She watched until Mrs. Beeson and Sausage had disappeared into the house. Then she lay back on the big red pillow to think for a while, and the next thing she knew, it was twilight outside and Crystal's voice was calling from downstairs.

She leapt up and rushed out of the room, not forgetting to cram the rags under the door, and she sped downstairs before Crystal could come up looking for her.

"What a day!" Crystal said. She hung her coat on the coatrack that stood in the hall. "I've been all over the place. What have you been doing? Just reading?"

"Mostly," said Nickie.

"Found anything interesting?"

"Lots," Nickie said. "This house is just full of interesting stuff. I don't see how you can stand to sell it!"

Crystal just shrugged. "Interesting stuff like what?" she said.

"I found a really strange old photograph, for one thing. Wait a second and I'll show you."

She dashed upstairs again. Otis trotted over to her when she went in. Feeling sorry that he'd be alone from now till morning, she knelt down and patted him for a while. She rumpled his ears and, when he rolled over, scratched his stomach. Then she took the picture of the twins from its envelope and hurried back downstairs, where she found Crystal talking on the phone.

"Try not to worry," Crystal said. "I'm sure he's fine. Okay. Okay. Bye." She hung up. "That was your mother," she said.

Nickie cried, "But I wanted to talk to her!"

"She was exhausted," said Crystal, "too tired to talk. She just wanted to let us know that she's had another postcard from your father. I wrote it down for you." She handed Nickie a scrap of paper.

Nickie read:

Dear Rachel and Nickie,

We are working hard here on a big project.

I am well, and I hope both of you are, too. I miss you.

Love, Dad

P.S. Sure would like to have one of Rachel's peanut butter cookies right now!

Again, not much news. But also again, a puzzling P.S. She couldn't remember her mother *ever* making peanut butter cookies. What was going on in her father's mind?

Crystal had gone into the kitchen, and Nickie followed her. "Here's the picture," she said, putting it on the table.

"Oh, yes!" Crystal said. "I remember hearing about this! These men are Chang and Eng, who came from Siam—that's what we now call Thailand. They were the original 'Siamese twins.' They came to the United States and traveled around being exhibited for years, and then they retired to North Carolina, not far from here. Grandfather told me they'd visited this house once—it was at the time of his great-grandfather, sometime after the Civil War. They must have given this photo to the family as a sort of thank-you gift." She turned the photograph over. "Look at this!" she exclaimed. "They've written on the back."

Nickie peered at the old-fashioned handwriting. It

said, “With gratitude for your hospitality,” and it was signed with two names.

“If this is authentic,” said Crystal, “it could be worth something.”

“How much?” said Nickie.

“I have no idea. Not a great deal, probably, but something.”

Nickie took the photo and turned it over again. “I guess those two boys are their children,” she said.

“Yes,” said Crystal. “In fact, I think they had something like ten children apiece.”

“Wouldn’t it be hard to be married to Siamese twins?” said Nickie, looking at the grumpy faces of the two big women.

“I surely think so,” said Crystal. “In fact, as I recall, the two women were sisters, but they didn’t get along. After a while, the twins got themselves two houses, one for each wife, and the husbands alternated between them.” She shook her head. “Amazing, isn’t it, that they managed to work things out at all? I tried twice, under much easier circumstances, and failed both times.” She opened up a cupboard and took down a can of soup. “Can you bear to have soup again for dinner?” she said. “I’m too tired to do anything else.”

“That’s okay,” said Nickie. She wondered if she should tell Crystal about the Prophet, and Mrs. Beeson, and how Yonwood was battling the forces of evil by building a shield of goodness. But she hesitated. Crystal might decide that Nickie shouldn't be getting involved in that battle. She might decide that Nickie needed more supervision. Nickie didn't want that at all. So all she said was, "Crystal, do you think there's going to be a war?"

"I don't know," Crystal said. "Fortunately, I'm too busy to think much about it." She cast a quick look at Nickie. "Don't *you* think about it, either," she said. "There's not much we can do."

"Just live good lives, right?" Nickie said. "Not add to the badness. That's what you said before."

"Uh-huh," said Crystal. She opened the can and scooped the soup into a pot.

"So if *everyone* lives good lives, then maybe bad things won't happen," Nickie said. "At least not to us." But she could tell Crystal wasn't really listening. She was holding the soup can under the faucet to fill it, but only a feeble trickle of water was coming out.

"Something is wrong with the water pressure," she said. "We must have a leaky pipe somewhere. And the plumbers were just here! They've made it worse instead of better. And of course tomorrow is Sunday, so a plumber will be hard to find." She sighed. "There's *so* much to do. I suppose I should face the third floor. I haven't even been up there."

Nickie's heart jumped into her throat. "It's just

rooms full of boxes," she said. "You don't need to see it."

"No, I really should." Crystal stirred the soup with one hand and ran the other hand wearily through her hair. "I need to see what I have to deal with. Not tonight, though. I'll do it first thing tomorrow morning." Crystal reached for two bowls. "It's getting dark," she said. "Would you switch the light on?"

That was when Nickie remembered. "We have to close all the curtains and blinds," she said.

"We do? Why?"

"So we can't be seen from the air," said Nickie. "In case there's an attack." She pulled down the kitchen blinds.

"Oh, I don't think that's necessary," Crystal said. "But if it makes you feel better, go ahead."

Nickie went from room to room, closing curtains and blinds all over the house.

CHAPTER 11

Trouble Spots

The next morning after breakfast, as soon as Crystal had washed her dishes and disappeared into the bathroom, Nickie raced upstairs. She hooked Otis to his leash and flew down the stairs again. She tiptoed past Crystal's room, where she heard the roar of the hair dryer, and zipped out the back door.

At the far end of the garden, she looped Otis's leash around the trunk of a tree. "Now, Otis," she said, "try to be quiet. I'll come back for you as soon as I can."

Inside again, past Crystal's room (this time she heard the *pssst-pssst* of the hair spray), up the stairs to the nursery. She hid the dog dishes and the dog food in a box of old toys in the closet, tore down the blanket that they'd hung over the door—and then came Crystal's steps on the stairs, and her voice calling, "Are you up there?"

Nickie showed her the two storage rooms first. "Oh, horrors," said Crystal, looking at the cobwebby trunks and boxes and suitcases. "It's *true* that they never threw anything away. Just looking at it gives me a headache." She went toward the nursery. "What's in here?"

"I've been sort of staying in here," Nickie said.

Crystal strode in. She gazed at the rugs, the blankets hung on the walls, the rocking chair and lamps.

"I did it," Nickie said. "I wanted to make it cozy."

Crystal smiled at her. "Well, it is cozy," she said. "It's actually quite a nice room. It smells a little funny, though." She wrinkled her nose. "Probably there are rats up under the roof. Let's let some air in." She went to the window and thrust it open. The sound of barking and whining floated up from below, but Crystal paid no attention. "When we get ready to put the house on the market," she said, "we can sell this as a perfect space for a home gym. Or maybe a media center. Screen over there"—she raised her hands, measuring a wall-sized screen—"theater seats here. Could be quite lovely. What do you think?"

But she didn't pause to hear what Nickie thought (which was that she didn't like any of those ideas). She went right on to say that she would decide what to do about all this later, but today, since it was Sunday and she couldn't do much shopping, she was going to take a drive with Len. "I don't suppose you want to come," she said.

"Who's Len?" said Nickie.

"The real estate agent."

"Oh," said Nickie. "No, I don't want to come."

Once Crystal had left, Nickie rescued Otis from the back garden and played with him a long time to make up for his exile. The shoe they'd been using for a toy had turned into a shapeless wad by now, so Nickie found an ancient yellow tennis ball in the closet. Otis adored it. He had to stretch his jaws wide apart to hold it, which made him look as if he were trying to swallow a grapefruit.

When Otis lost interest in chasing the ball and settled down to gnaw on it, Nickie decided that today would be her day to explore Yonwood. It was going to be her home, after all, if she accomplished her Goal #1. And while she was at it, she would keep her eyes open for sinners and trouble spots and anything that had a feeling of wrongness. If she was going to accomplish Goal #3, she needed to understand all this. She would keep her eyes open for Martin, too. She might happen to run into him somewhere, and they might happen to talk to each other. She needed to find out if he was someone she could fall in love with (Goal #2). So far, she couldn't tell. He was nice-looking. He was friendly, sort of. That was enough for a start.

She walked to the upper end of Main Street, where the school was, empty today because it was Sunday. Though it was still cold and windy, the sun was out. Some boys were shooting baskets in the schoolyard. She looked to see if Martin was one of them, but he was not.

A few blocks farther on and she was in downtown Yonwood. A few stores were open, but their lights were still off. They looked uninviting, like dim caves. Small clusters of people gathered in places where a TV was on, showing the news. Nickie heard snippets as she passed: "Five days remaining until the deadline . . . ," said the president's voice from the Cozy Corner Café. "Ambassador has been assassinated," he said from the newsstand. "Group calling itself the Warriors of God has claimed . . . ," he said from the drugstore. The familiar nervous feeling started up in Nickie's stomach as she heard these words, and she could tell that other people were nervous, too. A woman behind her was talking about how the tension was just killing her, and another woman answered that it was killing her, too, but that they had to have faith that they'd be all right, and the first person said, Yes, she did believe that, but she just wished everyone did. . . . Nickie hurried on, not wanting to hear any more.

Half a block down, she suddenly heard the strange

hum she'd heard before: *MMMM-mmmm-MMMM-mmmm.* Where was it coming from? A machine inside a building? Some kind of car or engine on the street? She looked around but saw nothing. The hum grew slightly louder. Was it behind the grocery store? She peered up a narrow alley and thought she saw someone darting across the other end—but she wasn't sure. The hum faded.

Nickie turned around. Behind her were two of the people who'd been watching the president at the drugstore a minute ago: a short bald man and a gray-haired woman. "Did you hear that funny sound?" she said. "Do you know what it was?"

Neither one answered. They kept on walking. The man cast a suspicious glance at her, and the woman pressed her lips together and shook her head.

"I just wondered—," Nickie said.

The woman stopped and glared at her. "You should *know,*" she said. "Why don't you know? Whose child *are* you?" But she didn't wait for an answer. She reached for the man's arm, and they hastened away.

Nickie felt as if she'd been slapped. She wasn't supposed to ask about the hum; that was clear. But why not? How was she supposed to find out if she didn't ask?

She went on. Toward the end of Main Street she came to the grocery store, and beyond that was the church she'd seen when she and Crystal had first arrived. "The Church of the Fiery Vision," the sign said, but she could also make out the old name that had been crossed out: "Yonwood Community Church." Today the sign also said, "Today's Sermon: Pulling Together in Dark Times." A lot of people were gathered here, milling about and greeting one another in low voices. Many of them were wearing the round blue button she'd first seen on Mrs. Beeson. The doors of the church stood open, and beside them was a thin-faced man dressed in a sort of robe, dark blue with a white border. Was that the Reverend Loomis? Nickie wondered. She saw Mrs. Beeson standing near him, though she almost didn't recognize her at first, because Mrs. Beeson was wearing a woolly gray hat like an upside-down bowl, and her hair was brushed and fluffy instead of in a ponytail. She spoke to all the people as they went inside. Nickie waved to her, and Mrs. Beeson flashed her a smile.

Nickie turned around and walked back the way she'd come, but on the other side of the street this time. She noticed a few things that might be examples of wrongness. By the park, she saw an old man spitting on the sidewalk. Surely that was a wrong thing to do. She also saw an angry little boy pulling a cat's tail. She told him not to, and he scowled at her. It was wicked to hurt animals, but was it wicked if a six-year-old did it? She wasn't sure. In an alley beside the boarded-up movie theater, she saw three teenage girls smoking. She wasn't sure about that one, either. Was it bad to smoke? Or only bad before a certain age? She would ask Mrs. Beeson.

For a few minutes, she followed along behind a group of kids to see if they were being cruel to each other, the way kids sometimes were. She saw some teasing, and a little roughhousing, but nothing much. She looked for Martin in this group, but he wasn't there.

When she was back where she had started, at the north end of Main Street, she headed downhill. The houses were farther apart here than in Greenhaven's neighborhood, and smaller. She saw a woman sitting on her front porch, reading the paper. A few children played ball in the street. No one was doing anything wrong, as far as she could tell. Really, Yonwood seemed like a very good town, so much better than dirty, crime-riddled Philadelphia. Following the words of the Prophet must be working.

Farther on, she came to what looked at first like a big, wild vacant lot. A high fence ran alongside it, and beyond the fence grew tall, unkempt trees. After a hundred yards or so, she came to a gravel drive with a mailbox beside it. "H. McCoy, 600 Raven Rd." was printed in black paint on the mailbox, and a "No Trespassing" sign was nailed to a tree. She recognized the name McCoy. Mrs. Beeson had mentioned this person. He was the one she was worried about, for some reason. She peered up the driveway. At the end, rising from a tangle of trees and rangy shrubs, she could just glimpse the peak of a roof. Tree branches threw shadows across it, and the shadows danced in the wind like long, thin ghosts. Should she go in there and see what H. McCoy was up to? Not today, she thought. Some other time. She walked on.

A block or so farther on, an alley led off Raven Road—really more of a wide path, rutted and unpaved. It went behind the houses on Trillium Street. Curious, Nickie turned that way.

From the alley, she could see into backyards. Most of them were empty and quiet. At one house she heard loud voices through an open window. She paused a moment to listen. The people inside were insulting each other and swearing. Surely that was bad. Did it mean they counted as sinners?

At the next house, a wire fence bordered the alley. Beyond the fence she could see the gnarled bare branches of fruit trees, and beyond those, the back of a house that badly needed a coat of paint. Just inside the fence, so close to the alley that she could have touched it if she'd wanted to, stood a shed made of weatherworn planks.

At this place, there was a lot going on. Two small children charged around among the tree trunks yelling at each other. One of them had a toy truck that the other seemed to want, and he chased his brother wildly, falling down on skids of slippery leaves, shrieking the whole time. A window in the back of the house opened, and an old woman stuck her head out and cried, "You kids quit that!" but the kids paid no attention.

Nickie watched them, peeking out from behind the shed so she wouldn't be noticed. The shrieking boy finally grabbed the truck away from the other boy, and that boy wailed furiously. Another child appeared, a girl maybe four or five years old, and scolded the boy who was crying. And then a bigger boy, closer to Nickie's age, burst out the back door. He had curly blond hair, big ears, and a strong, skinny body.

The boy leapt down the porch steps. "Hey, Roddie, lost your truck?" he called. "Want an airplane instead?" And he took hold of the little boy's hands and whirled him around so that he flew off the ground, squealing with laughter.

"Fly me!" said the other boy, and the big boy did. He flew the girl, too. Then he said, "Now, all of you quit making such a racket. There's plenty of toys inside. Go on."

"But I want—" the little boy started to wail.

"*Go on,*" said the big boy. "And leave me alone."

Nickie expected that he'd disappear back into the house, but instead he came toward the shed at the end of the yard. She ducked down quickly. He fiddled with the door for a moment—maybe it was locked, she couldn't see—and then opened it and went inside.

Nickie should probably have left at this point. She had no reason to think this was a trouble spot. But, as usual, curiosity took hold of her. What was the boy doing in this falling-down shed? Because the shed backed up against the fence, and because there was a dusty window in the back of the shed, just the right height for looking into, she might be able to see in without being noticed. She put her eye to the glass.

CHAPTER 12

Inside the Backyard Shed

It was Sunday morning and for once a sunny day. Grover's father was in the garage, getting ready to change the oil in the car. His mother had gone to church. Grover finally had some time to himself.

When the little kids had finished their breakfast, he shooed them outside. "Get out there and tear around," he said. "There's sun today, but it might be gone tomorrow." They charged into the backyard, and he sat with Granny Carrie at the kitchen table while she finished her cup of coffee. He contemplated his grandmother. She was wearing a plaid flannel shirt this morning, with an old green sweatshirt over it, and orange sweatpants with thick, fuzzy socks and her duck slippers. Her short white hair was so wispy that her pink scalp showed through.

"Going to sit out on the porch this morning," she said. "Take in some sun."

"You'd better wear a hat," Grover said. "It's chilly out there."

"I will," she said. "I've got that nice green-and-yellow one your mother knitted me."

Grover smiled to himself. His grandmother didn't care a bit what she looked like. She'd happily wear fifteen different colors, all clashing with each other. She sometimes looked like a heap of bright laundry with a little wrinkly walnut head on top. His mother was always trying to get her to spiff up, but Grover thought she looked fine the way she was: completely different from every other old lady in town.

From outside came five or six piercing shrieks. Granny Carrie rose from the table and hoisted up the window by the back door. "You kids quit that!" she yelled.

More shrieks followed, and then a wail.

"I'll go deal with them," Grover said. "I'm going out there anyway."

He took his jacket from its hook by the back door and went out into the yard. For a few minutes, he fooled around with the kids, and then he shooed them back into the house and went down to his shed. If the kids behaved, and if his father didn't call him to help with the car, he'd have at least an hour, maybe more, all to himself.

The shed's door was fastened with a combination lock, its combination known only to him. He twirled it, opened it, and went inside, closing the door behind him.

And as soon as he was in there, he became, as always, a different Grover. Not the funny Grover, not the big brother Grover, but the serious, brilliant, totally focused Grover, pursuing his passion.

A few rusted garden tools still hung on one wall of the shed, but he'd cleaned out all the old broken flowerpots and half-empty boxes of plant food and bags of moldy potting soil that used to be in here. Along one side of the shed he had built a wide shelf, and on the shelf were the two glass tanks, each equipped with lights and sitting on a heating pad, where he kept his prized possessions: his snakes.

He bent down and peered into each tank in turn. "How're you doing, my beauties?" he murmured. Both snakes were barely visible. They'd burrowed under the dry leaves and bark he'd put in the tanks for shelter. All he could see was a small patch of patterned scales pressed against the glass in one tank and the narrow tip of a tail lying across a twig in the other.

He checked the temperature in the tanks—86 degrees for one, 80 for the other. Just right. Then he raised the glass top of the tank on the left and set it down on the shelf. He reached inside in a slow, unstartling way, and he took hold of the snake gently, a few inches behind its head, and raised it up into the air.

It curved and whipped, looping itself into an *S*

and then a *J* and then an *S* again, flowing like a moving rope between Grover's hands. It was a gorgeous creature, nearly two feet long. Rings of black and yellow and rusty red alternated all down its slim body. It looked like a beaded belt, except that at the top end was a head with glittering black eyes and a darting tongue like a sliver of black paper.

"Pretty soon," said Grover, "I'll have some dinner for you. Maybe tomorrow or the next day. Something delicious." He held up the snake and looked it in the eye. "Okay?"

This snake's name was Fang. He'd found it during the summer, sleeping at the base of a rock in the woods. It was the first milk snake he'd captured, and he was very pleased with it. For nearly eight months now, he'd kept it alive and healthy. Fortunately, it didn't have to be fed very often during the winter. Finding food for it wasn't easy, and he couldn't always afford to order from the reptile supply company. Of the dozens of snakes he'd captured in the last three years or so, he'd kept this one the longest. If he couldn't find food for his snakes, or if they started to look sickly, he always let them go.

Grover was on his way to being a snake expert. Four years ago, a snake had come out of the bushes and crossed the path in front of him as he was walking in the mountains. He had stopped and watched as it slithered along, moving without legs, swimming without water, a creature built all in one line, strange and beautiful and, to him, thrilling rather than frightening. He'd been nine years old at the time. The whole rest of that summer, he'd scrambled around in the woods, looking under rocks and logs and in holes in the ground, hoping to find a snake to take home with him so he could see it up close and watch it live its life. He went to the library and got out books about snakes, and on the library computer he went on the Internet and found endless pages of information and pictures. Before long his head was packed with snake knowledge.

For a while, he talked to everyone about this new passion—his parents, his grandmother, his friend Martin. But his parents were too busy to be very interested, and Martin didn't understand how he could care about such dirty, slimy things. Only his grandmother really listened. She thought it was a fine idea to collect snakes as long as he didn't ever show them to her. She said she would scream like a fire engine if any snake got close to her.

So now Grover kept his snakes to himself. He fixed up the shed (his father didn't have time for gardening anymore, so he didn't mind), and he used every penny he could earn on snake supplies. So far, he had found, kept, and released thirty-seven snakes. Only two had died in his care. He knew all the kinds of snakes around where he lived. Now his ambitions had grown.

He had a plan. All he needed to make it happen was money, and he was working on that. Success was near.

He told this to his snake. "Success is near, Fang," he said. "Really. No doubt about it. You'll see."

With the hand that wasn't holding Fang, he took the lid off the other tank. This tank held Licorice Whip, his young red belly snake. He'd had it only a few weeks. It was the thickness of a slender cord, about a foot long. He lifted it out. He held the two snakes up, one in each hand, and gazed at them as they wove among his fingers and coiled around his wrists, sliding their cool dry skin against his skin, raising their small, elegant heads and staring back at him, almost as if they were about to speak.

Then suddenly he heard a noise: a soft thump against the wall of the shed, and a rustling. He shifted his gaze to the dusty window just in time to see something move quickly on the other side. Someone was out there. As fast as he could, he set the snakes back in their tanks and put the lids on. Then he dashed out and ran along the fence to the gate that led out to the alley. Up ahead, going around the curve, someone was running, but it was too far away to see who. He didn't try to give chase. Probably it was Martin, who used to be his friend, trying to catch him doing something forbidden. He didn't bother to run after him. He went back to the shed.

"What is the *matter* with that guy?" he said to Fang and Licorice Whip. "Seems like he's out to get me."

He took Fang out of his tank, draped him around his shoulders, and started in on the task of cleaning tanks. But after he'd been working twenty minutes or so, he heard footsteps outside. The door of the shed opened, and his father leaned in. "Got an emergency job to do," he said. "Leaky pipe. I'm going to need your help."

Grover sighed. He put Fang back in his tank and, after locking up the shed, followed his father back to the house.

CHAPTER 13

The Perfect Living Room

Nickie had bumped against the shed by accident when her foot slipped on a stone. She'd seen the boy's face turned toward the window, and she'd dashed away, going up the hill toward town, running until she was sure no one was following her.

What she'd seen in the shed had given her a chill: the boy holding the snakes up in both hands and gazing at them so ardently, the snakes twisting in the dim air, their black tongues flicking in and out. She'd never seen a live snake before. Weren't most snakes poisonous? Wouldn't it be dangerous to have snakes in a place where there were little children? She felt a surge of excitement. This might truly be a trouble spot. She reminded herself of Mrs. Beeson's words: A sense of wrongness. Sometimes you can just *feel* it. The boy with the snakes definitely gave her a strange, creepy feeling. She walked faster. Mrs. Beeson would be home from church by now. She would go straight to her house. She had a lot to ask her about.

Mrs. Beeson's doorbell had three bell-like notes—*ting, ting, tong.* After Nickie rang it, she waited nervously. Maybe you were supposed to have an appointment to talk to Mrs. Beeson.

But the door opened, and there she was. She had no hat on, but she was still in her church outfit, and she had her DATT phone clapped up against her ear. Sausage came trotting up behind her and sniffed at Nickie's shoes.

"Just a sec, Ralph," Mrs. Beeson said into the phone. She smiled at Nickie. "Come on in, honey," she said. "I'll be off the phone in a jiff."

Nickie walked in. As she waited, she noticed again the round blue button pinned to Mrs. Beeson's sweater. What *was* that little picture on it? It seemed to be a tall, narrow building, like— Of course. It was a tower. And the Prophet's name was Althea Tower.

"So Ralph," Mrs. Beeson said into the phone, "you just have to trust me on this. We have to get everyone behind us, and if we need to use unusual measures, well, then we do. These are unusual times." She paused. "I know, I know, but that's what she said. I'm sure. Uh-huh. All right. See you later." She set down her phone and turned to Nickie. "Come right in here," she said, leading the way into the living room.

Nickie was curious to see if Mrs. Beeson's house was as perfect on the inside as it was on the outside. It was. Mrs. Beeson had the coziest and neatest living room Nickie had ever seen. A fat white couch sat opposite fat blue armchairs. A coffee table held a plate of cookies and three books, neatly stacked, the top one black with gold letters on the front—probably a holy book of some sort. Three pictures hung on the walls: one was a beautiful scene of a mountain lake, one was a color photograph of Sausage, and one was a photograph of a freckle-faced young man in a soldier's uniform. "My husband," Mrs. Beeson said. "Killed twenty-two years ago in the Five Nation War, fighting against our enemies." A vase of artificial roses stood on the mantel and next to it a box in the shape of a heart. There was no mess at all. No sweaters draped over chair backs, no flopped-open magazines, no shoes left on the floor. No *stuff* scattered anywhere. It was just the opposite of Greenhaven.

A jingly tune was playing softly, but Nickie couldn't tell where it was coming from.

"Mrs. Beeson," she said. "I need to ask you about some things."

"Very good!" said Mrs. Beeson. "Have a seat. Help yourself to a cookie."

Nickie sat on the white couch. Mrs. Beeson was about to sit down across from her when suddenly a soft roar started up, and a little dome-shaped machine rolled into the room. Sausage skittered frantically and jumped onto Mrs. Beeson's lap.

"Don't mind the robot vacuum," said Mrs. Beeson. "Just lift up your feet when it comes close. It makes Sausage a bit nervous, but I think it's marvelous. I've programmed it to do the whole house every other day."

Nickie watched, fascinated, as the vacuum trundled back and forth across the floor. "It's cute," she said. She took a cookie from the plate.

"It is, isn't it?" said Mrs. Beeson. "I've found many of the new gadgets so helpful. Like my little DATT phone. It can take pictures, send e-mail, record TV, get instant news, identify poisonous substances, tell one fingerprint from another . . . all kinds of useful things. Now if it could just detect wrongdoing!" said Mrs. Beeson, laughing. "What a help that would be." She scratched Sausage's ears. "So. You have something to ask me?"

"Yes, I do." Nickie set down her half-eaten cookie and told Mrs. Beeson about the old shed and the boy with the snakes twining around his arms. "I wasn't sure if he would count as a sinner or not."

"Snakes?" said Mrs. Beeson. She lifted a foot as the robot vacuum rolled beside her chair. "Where was this?"

Nickie told her.

"Interesting," said Mrs. Beeson. "I've been reading a great deal of spiritual literature these last months, and I haven't come across one good word about snakes."

"Some other things, too, I wondered about," Nickie said. "Spitting on the sidewalk, and pulling a cat's tail, and smoking. I wasn't sure about the cat or the smoking. It was a little boy hurting the cat, and some teenagers in the park smoking." Mrs. Beeson nodded, frowning. "And some people were yelling in a house on Trillium Street," Nickie went on. "It sounded like a bad fight, but I didn't hear what it was about."

"What address?" Mrs. Beeson asked.

Nickie described the house. "*And,*" she said, suddenly inspired, "you know that man Hoyt McCoy?"

Mrs. Beeson leaned forward. The vacuum had moved on to another room now, so she set Sausage back down on the floor. "Yes? What about him?"

"When I passed his house," Nickie said, "I kind of peeked up the drive, and I saw strange shadows. Like black ghosts or something, hovering around outside. It made me feel creepy."

"Um-*hmmm,*" said Mrs. Beeson. "Very interesting indeed."

"I know it was bad to spy," Nickie said. "And bad to eavesdrop, and to look in the window at the boy with the snakes. I probably shouldn't have done it, but—"

Mrs. Beeson held up a hand. She looked Nickie straight in the eye. For a moment she didn't speak, and

Nickie heard again the jingly tune that the noise of the vacuum had covered up. "You did well," Mrs. Beeson said. Her voice was solemn. "Listen, honey. I want you to remember this. When you know that you're doing God's work—then you're willing to do anything. I mean *anything.*"

A shiver like a miniature lightning bolt shot through Nickie's middle, right beneath her ribs. *Anything* if it's God's work, she thought. Yes, that's what it is to be a holy person: you're willing to do anything. She thought of stories she'd heard about saints who let themselves be killed in awful ways. She thought about the brave characters in the books she loved, how they faced monsters and crossed flaming mountains and did not live by the rules of ordinary people. And it wasn't out of the question for someone as young as herself to be like them. Often, at least in books, it was a child who vanquished the darkness. She could be like that. She felt a great fierce desire to bring goodness to the world—or at least to Yonwood.

Mrs. Beeson stood up. Sausage got up, too. "What a help you are, honey," Mrs. Beeson said. "I think you and I have the same thing in mind—a bright, clean world where everyone knows how to behave! Wouldn't it be splendid?"

Nickie nodded, imagining it: everyone kind, everyone good, no creepiness, no wars.

"So the more of these trouble spots we can find,

the better off we'll be," Mrs. Beeson went on, her voice becoming very stern. "Remember what I said about how one moldy strawberry can ruin the whole basket? We're not going to let that happen. We're going to make this a good and godly town through and through." She bent over and swept the crumbs of Nickie's cookie into her hand. "And I'll tell you frankly, honey, I'm the one to get it done. I may look like a dumpling, but I have a spine of steel."

"Are you a preacher, Mrs. Beeson?" Nickie asked.

"No, no. I'm retired. But I can't just sit around, can I? That's not my way." She laughed. "I coach girls' baseball in the spring. I lead a study group at the church. Organize Yonwood's spring cleanup. Might even run for mayor someday. I like to wear a lot of different hats."

They headed for the hall, where several of Mrs. Beeson's different hats hung from a tree-shaped hat rack. "I keep hearing music," Nickie said. "Where's it coming from?"

"Oh!" said Mrs. Beeson, smiling. "It's my music box!" She darted back into the living room and picked up the heart-shaped box from the mantel. "It's very high-tech—powered by some new kind of tiny everlasting battery. Plutonium, I think. It just goes and goes. Isn't it charming?"

"Yes," said Nickie.

Mrs. Beeson opened the front door and ushered her out. “Thank you so much,” she said. “Anything else you notice, you just come and let me know.” She beamed at Nickie, and Nickie glowed.

Afterward, though, she felt a tiny bit guilty. She hadn’t really seen ghosts hovering around Hoyt McCoy’s house, or anything bad at all. She’d just had a *feeling* about the place. But everything else she’d said was true; maybe that made up for one small fib.

As she came through Greenhaven’s front door, the telephone rang. She picked it up and said hello, and Amanda’s voice answered. “Oh, good, it’s you. I just remembered something. I still have the house key. I oughta bring it back.”

“Okay,” Nickie said. “Come whenever you want. And Amanda—anything new about the Prophet? Is she better?”

“No, she’s just the same. Really sad and quiet. Keeps on saying stuff you can’t figure out. Sometimes she wanders off.”

“Wanders off?”

“Yeah, it’s almost like she’s walking in her sleep. She goes out in the yard, or even out the front door, and I have to quick go get her and bring her back.”

“Is she trying to go somewhere?”

“I don’t know.”

"And I *still* can't come and meet her? Because I'm *so interested,* Amanda. Maybe *I* could tell what she's saying."

"I doubt it," said Amanda. "If Mrs. Beeson can't tell, I don't see how *you* could."

"Well, okay, maybe not," Nickie said. "But I'd like to just *see* her sometime. What does she look like?"

"She looks sick. All shadowy around the eyes." Amanda sounded impatient. "I have to go."

Nickie spent the next hour or so roaming around Greenhaven. She loved being alone here. She burrowed through the silent rooms like a miner hunting for gold. What she wanted was anything old, and especially anything written. From desk drawers and closet shelves and the backs of cabinets, and from the trunks and boxes in the third floor rooms, she pulled out packets of letters, programs from long-ago theater performances, journals and ledger books and guest lists and postcards. She sat on the floor reading until the air around her felt thick with the past. All these words, written so long ago, seemed to say to her, Remember us. We were here. We were real.

She kept Otis nearby. If she was sitting on the floor, he pushed his nose against her arm, wanting to be petted. He tugged at the leg of her pants, wanting to play. Sometimes he slept, stretched out, belly to the rug, his rear legs flopped behind him like a frog's. Now and then he would wander off, and when Nickie remembered to look for him, she'd find him chewing happily on the corner of a curtain, or trying to dig through the hardwood floor. He was all the company she needed.

Around two-thirty, when Crystal still wasn't back, she decided to take Otis for his afternoon outing. She heard banging as she went down the hall, probably coming from one of the bathrooms. The plumber must be here. She went out through the kitchen to the back garden.

To her surprise, the basement door was slightly ajar. The plumber must have gone down there to get at the pipes under the house. Good. She'd been curious about the basement—she could have a look. She picked Otis up, pulled open the door, and peeked in. The plumber had turned on the light. It was dim, just a bulb in the ceiling, but it showed her a flight of stone steps. Holding Otis tightly, she went down.

CHAPTER 14

Someone in the Basement

The basement was huge—a low-ceilinged room that stretched out into shadowy darkness ahead of her and to the left. It wasn't an empty darkness—she could see what appeared to be low hills lurking in the shadows. Another light bulb shone dimly in a far corner. Did that mean someone was down here? One of the workmen, maybe? She thought of calling out, "Anyone here?" But there was something still and heavy about the silence that made her afraid to break it. She would just look around a little, quietly, and then she would climb up the stairs and leave.

The air had a smell like the damp, earthy underside of rocks. Once her eyes had adjusted to the dimness, she saw that the hills were piles of furniture, a great crammed-together mass with just a narrow passage winding through it. Tables lay with their feet in the air, and between the feet were other tables, and dining room chairs and stools and chests of drawers, and on top of the chests were more chairs, upside down, making a nest for footstools and mirrors and lamp bases and unidentifiable things covered in sheets. Far back against the wall stood four-poster beds, some piled with three or four mattresses, and great looming wardrobes with mirrored doors. All of it had turned the same dirt-gray color because of the dust that coated it. Cobwebs drifted in long strings from the ceiling, brushing Nickie's face as she walked by. Otis squirmed in her arms.

She followed the passage that twisted through all this—it was like walking down a tunnel, almost, because the furniture was stacked shoulder-high. She moved toward the light.

She heard a scrape, and then a rustling sound.

She stopped, held her breath, and listened. Was someone in here? She bent down and peered through the forest of furniture legs, but it was too dark to see.

Something stirred over by the wall. Wood knocked against wood, a head rose from the jumble of furniture, and a voice spoke.

"Pa?" it said. "Is that you?"

"No," said Nickie. Her heart jumped, but curiosity kept her from running away.

The head ducked down again. There was more

scraping and rustling, and then someone crawled out from beneath a big table: a boy with cobwebs in his hair.

"I know who *you* are," the boy said. He held his hands cupped together as if protecting something. "The old guy's granddaughter."

"Great-granddaughter," said Nickie.

"And who's *that*?" He nodded at Otis, who was squirming in Nickie's arms.

"It's Otis," she said. "I'm taking care of him for somebody. Who are you?" She couldn't see the boy's face; the light was behind him. It cast his huge, blurry shadow onto a cabinet that leaned against the headboard of a bed.

"Grover," said the boy. "My pa is fixing your pipes."

"But what are you doing down here?"

The boy sprang toward her all of a sudden. "Lying in wait!" he cried. "For unwary creatures to fall into my trap!"

Nickie shrieked and then instantly regretted it, because he laughed to see that he'd scared her.

"I already caught one unwary creature," he said. He held up his clasped hands. "It's a prisoner now, awaiting its fate."

"What is it?"

He stepped toward her and she stepped back. She couldn't help it. He might have a spider in his hands, and he might be the kind of boy who would suddenly throw it at you.

"I'll show you if you're brave enough to look," he said. He stretched out his hands and opened them so she could see what he held. It was not a spider. She couldn't tell what it was. Something small and pinkish. Otis strained forward, sniffing madly. She put her hand around his muzzle.

"An infant mouse!" the boy cried. "There's eight of them in a nest down there by the heating pipe."

"Let me see," said Nickie. "Hold it in the light."

He did. It had hairless, almost transparent skin, tiny, twitching paws, and little blind eyes. It was about as big as a quarter. "Why did you steal it?" she asked him.

"I need it," he said. "For my snake."

"What?"

"For my snake to eat."

She looked up at the boy's face, which was framed in blond curly hair. His ears stuck out. She knew, suddenly, who he was.

"You don't believe me?" he said.

"I believe you," she said. "But I don't like it." She turned around and started back the way she'd come.

He followed her up the stairs and out of the basement. She set Otis down, and he sniffed Grover's shoes with great interest.

"Where'd the dog come from?" Grover asked.

"I'm just taking care of him for a little while," Nickie said. "He's a secret—don't tell about him, all right?"

Grover tilted his head upward and yelled, "Hey, everybody, guess what, there's a—"

Nickie shouted, "Stop it!"

He laughed. "I'll keep your secret," he said. "Now you owe me a favor."

"Are you really going to give that baby mouse to a snake?" Nickie asked.

"Yep." Grover stretched his mouth into a wicked grin. "Because I'm *meeean* and *eeeevil,*" he said, and gave a maniac laugh. "Worse than"—he lowered his voice to a gruesome whisper—"Hoyt McCoy. Have you heard of him?"

Nickie nodded, feeling a lurch in her stomach.

"Well, I'm much worse than him," Grover said.

"You have spiderwebs in your hair," said Nickie. She turned and walked away from him, through the back door and into the house. What terrible luck, she thought. A boy right here where she could get to know him—and he turns out to be the boy with the snakes. And on top of that, a kidnapper and murderer of baby mice. She couldn't possibly fall in love with someone like him.

She went upstairs again, planning to read until Crystal got home. She switched on the lamp and picked up her great-grandfather's notebook. On the floor beside her, Otis went to sleep and dreamed, making soft little *wip-wip* noises and fluttering his paws. Nickie read:

1/2 Legs very weak and painful. Spent the day reading the scientific journals. Intrigued by this notion of extra dimensions—other worlds right next to ours? Had a chat with M but of course can't understand a word.

What might that mean? She knew about three dimensions—up, down, and sideways. What were extra dimensions? Who was M? She read on:

1/4 Extraordinary experience last night: Went into the back bedroom to look for the scissors, thought I saw someone in there, over by the bed—dark-haired figure, transparent swirl of skirt. Dreadful feeling of sorrow hit me like a wave. Had to grab the doorknob, almost fell. Figure faded, vanished. Maybe something wrong with my eyes. Or heart.

He was ninety-three when he died. Maybe he was losing his mind a little bit, thinking he was seeing ghosts. She read on:

1/19 Brenda B. came by today. All worked up, trying to figure out what Althea is saying and what to do about it. Kept talking about how she's studying every holy book she can get her hands on, aiming to understand God's word. I quoted St. Augustine to her: "If you understand it, it isn't God." Gave her a cup of chamomile tea.

That was interesting. But then came another mystifying one:

1/30 String theory—M theory?—eleven dimensions—gravity waves—alternate universes? Possible leakage between one universe and another? Amazing stuff. M says his research is very promising.

Maybe he thought he'd slipped into an alternate

universe in the back bedroom and seen a ghost, somehow. Which one was the back bedroom, anyhow? Nickie left the sleeping Otis and went down to the second floor, hoping to catch sight of the ghost herself. It was clear which one was the back bedroom: its window looked out over the backyard. She saw no ghost in that room, but through the window she saw Grover, who was probably waiting for his father. He was walking along the low wall that bordered the concrete terrace and crouching down every now and then to study the ground, maybe looking for more creatures to capture. She watched him for a minute. He was definitely good-looking. She liked the springy way he moved, and his floppy hair more or less covered up his sticking-out ears. She couldn't fall in love with him, of course, because of the snakes and the baby mouse, but she decided to go down and talk to him again anyhow.

When Grover saw her come outside, he beckoned to her, and she went over to him.

"Listen," he said, in an urgent whisper. "I want to show you something amazing. No human eye has ever lit on it before."

Nickie was wary. "Is it about snakes?"

"No, no," said Grover. "I told you, no one has ever seen this."

"Not even you?"

"Not even me."

"Well, what is it?" Nickie said.

Grover reached into his lunch bag and brought out a small green apple.

"I've seen apples before," Nickie said.

"Yeah, but watch this." Grover took out his pocket-knife, pulled the blade out, and sliced the apple in half across the middle. He pointed to the inside—the white flesh oozing juice, the five little seeds in a star shape.

"I've seen that, too," said Nickie.

"No, you haven't," Grover said. "No one has. Not a single person has ever seen the inside of this apple until now. It is a completely new sight to the human eye." He took a big bite out of one half of the apple and stood there chewing, with a wide, satisfied smile across his face.

"Oh, you think you're so clever," Nickie said. She grabbed the other half of the apple out of his hand. She was annoyed at being tricked, but she couldn't help smiling a little, too. What he'd said was true, after all.

An idea popped into her head. "I know something *you've* never seen before," she said. "No human eye has ever seen it, or ever *will* see it."

"That doesn't make sense," said Grover, munching on his apple.

"Yes, it does. I'll show you."

"But if you show me, then I will have seen it."

"No, you won't," said Nickie. "Just wait here. I'll go get it." She ran inside, went to her bedroom, and came back out clutching a piece of paper. She held it out. "Do you know what this is?"

Grover peered at it. "It's some fake monster out of a science-fiction movie," he said.

"Nope," said Nickie. "It's a dust mite. In this picture, it's magnified many, many zillion times. You will never see it in real life, because it's smaller than the eye can see."

"Hah," said Grover. He looked up at her and quirked an eyebrow. "Where'd you get it?"

"I cut it out of a magazine. I like strange, interesting things."

"You don't like snakes, though," Grover said. "Probably you're afraid of them."

"I am not."

"You'd never want to see a snake eat a mouse."

"Maybe I would." As soon as she said this, she realized it was true. It would be a horrible thing to see, but interesting. And it might help her decide if there was something evil about this boy or not.

"Really?" Grover looked surprised.

"Really."

"I don't believe you. You're just saying that to sound big."

This was somewhat true, but Nickie wasn't going to admit it. "Just tell me when," she said. "I'll come and see it."

So he said she should come the next day about three-thirty, and he told her how to get to his house. Just in time, she remembered not to say she already knew where he lived.

Crystal got back around five. She came in the front door, her cheeks red with cold and her eyes sparkling, talking and talking about the lovely scenery in the surrounding hills. "This really is a gorgeous area," she said. "I had *such* a wonderful time."

"Good," said Nickie, not really listening.

"And Len told me some interesting things about Yonwood," Crystal said. "A woman here has had some kind of religious experience, apparently. People think it means Yonwood is a sort of chosen place, and they'll be safe even if there's war."

Nickie started paying closer attention. "Does Len think that?"

"He doesn't know what to think," Crystal said, flinging her coat on a chair. "He was in school with this Prophet person. She was a shy, bookish little girl, he said, not the type to grab for attention. So he thinks maybe what happened to her was real. Have you heard anything about it?"

"A little," Nickie said, trying to look uninterested.

"Tomorrow," said Crystal, "I'm going to have my hair done at the local beauty shop. I'll probably come out looking like a dandelion, but at least that'll be better than *this* mess." She swatted at her bangs.

"Good idea," said Nickie, though she thought Crystal looked fine as she was.

"After that," Crystal went on, "I'm going into Asheville for some shopping. I don't suppose you want to come."

"No," Nickie said. "I don't want to come."

"What are you going to do?"

"Oh, nothing much," Nickie said. She didn't think it was a good idea to mention snakes or mice.

"You're such a good girl," Crystal said. "All this time on your own, and you never get bored or get into trouble. It's amazing."

Nickie just smiled.

CHAPTER 15

Up to the Woods

A few times during the next day, which was Monday, Grover found himself thinking about Nickie as he sat in his desk at school. He wasn't thinking about her in a boy-girl sort of way. The notion of "being in love" never entered his mind. He was thinking about her in an interesting-person sort of way. It wasn't often that he met anybody, especially a girl, who cared about things like dust mites. He was looking forward to showing her his snakes later on, after school. It would be fun to see if she was scared after all.

But first he had to do some hunting. Just before two o'clock, he filled in the last answers on his English test and then staged a highly realistic coughing fit. "Can't breathe! Nurse's office!" he gasped, and he staggered, choking, out of the classroom. Then he slipped out a side door and trotted up Fern Street to the path that led into the woods.

The forest was his second home. He knew all the trails that threaded up the mountainside. He knew the creeks and the outcroppings of rock and the places where salamanders were likely to be hiding under rotting logs. In the summer, he spent hours up here. Sometimes he scrambled through brush and waded down streams, but other times he just found a good spot and sat still. He had learned that if he sat without moving for a long time, he would see things. Animals would come out from their hiding places and potter around in the open, not realizing he was there. Once, at dusk on a summer evening, a spotted skunk walked past him, so close he could see the long, curved nails on its front feet.

Today he was after some dinner for his red belly snake. The milk snake would get the baby mouse, which he was trying to keep alive so that Nickie could watch it being eaten. For the red belly, a few good-sized slugs and maybe a small salamander would do. Actually, he could get these in his own backyard pretty easily. But he *wanted* to go into the woods. He hadn't been for a while, because of homework and bad weather and working on jobs with his father. He missed it.

He was aware that people had been talking lately about someone lurking up there, maybe a terrorist planning dark deeds. But Grover wasn't worried about him. He didn't think about him much. Talk about terrorists and war was the sort of talk that just slid off his brain. He was too occupied with his own concerns to pay much attention to it.

He started along a steep uphill trail, which would take him, in fifteen minutes or so, to a place where a stream rushed between shallow banks. He could get down to the water's edge easily there and find a few of the things that liked living in damp places. He'd brought a plastic jar with him to take them home in.

The rhythm of his steps said, Happy to be here, happy to be here. Rays of sunlight shot between the clouds, making spots of light like polka dots on the ground. On either side, the woods were thick—everything close in, dense, stickery, twined with vines, here and there a bare-twigged mountain ash with red berries like decorations. The whirr of bird wings rushed up from bushes as he passed. He was always looking beside the trail, which grew narrower as he climbed higher, for the holes and burrows that an animal might be living in. Holes, rotting logs, sun-warmed rocks—all those were places favored by snakes and therefore favored by Grover.

As he walked, he hummed a little tune—an ambling, careless tune that went with being happy and trotting along and knowing what he was doing—and his eyes scanned the woods and the ground for anything of interest, and his mind traveled off where it usually did, to his plan to join the Arrowhead

Wilderness Reptile Expedition this summer. It was perfect for him—Addison Pugh, a famous herpetologist, was leading it, and it was out in Arizona, where he'd never been and where the snakes would be all different from the ones here. He would have a great time, he would learn a huge amount, and he would meet people who could help him on the way to his career. He had to go. How could something as trivial as $375 stand in the way? It was very inconvenient that his family didn't have any spare money. On the other hand, it had forced him to be creative. He felt pretty confident about the cereal jingle he'd made up, and he'd solved the cryptogram and sent it in quickly. Sweepstakes weren't so promising, because winning was just luck. But he'd entered so many of them—at least fifty just in the last few weeks—that he *had* to win something. It wouldn't take much—just a few small prizes from three or four different contests, and he'd have enough.

All these thoughts swirling through his mind kept him a little less observant than he usually was. He was up fairly high on the mountainside now, and the trail turned into more of a dotted line up here, blocked every now and then by overgrown bushes or a fallen tree. This didn't matter to Grover. He climbed over or went around whatever was in the way; he always knew where he was. But it meant he had to watch his feet more, stepping over stuff and being careful not to trip, so at first he didn't see that something was moving farther up the mountainside, where the trees were denser. The sound of his own footsteps covered up the sound that anyone else's footsteps might have made. A few yards farther on, he came to the place where a muddy path led down the stream bank to the place he wanted to go, and there he paused for a second. That was when he heard a distant rustling, the sort of rustling that only something big makes.

He froze. Without moving any other part of himself, he turned his head toward where the sound seemed to have come from. The trees and the thick undergrowth beneath them made it impossible to see very far, or at least to see clearly. All he could see was a patch of paleness far off in the distance. It moved, paused, moved again, and disappeared. He stood still for another three or four minutes, but he heard no more rustling and saw nothing, either. So he went on down the stream bank and sat on a rock by the water.

Nothing large and pale lived in the woods, as far as he knew. He couldn't think what it could possibly be. Maybe some huge white bird? A stork? But why would there be a stork in the woods? There wouldn't. A ghost? He didn't believe in ghosts. Anyway, a ghost wouldn't make a rustling sound, would it?

So maybe the talk about someone lurking up here was worth paying attention to after all. Grover felt a small shiver of fear. Maybe this terrorist was up here just waiting for someone to kidnap. Give me a million dollars to fund my terrorist organization, or else I'll slice this boy up and scatter him in the pines.

Grover put his arms across his knees and hunched down, bending his face toward the water. The stream rushed by, carrying leaves and bits of twig, making the weeds at the water's edge flow sideways. He stayed that way for a while, imagining what he would do if a terrorist stepped suddenly from behind a tree and grabbed him. The best thing would be to have a snake with him at the time, so he could terrify the terrorist with it and startle him into letting go. A venomous snake would be best. If he didn't happen to have a snake, he'd have to struggle. Too bad he didn't know karate or any of those other martial arts. He could kick, though. He was strong and agile, and he could bite. He pictured himself twisting like a giant boa constrictor around the terrorist and biting him in the back of the neck.

It would be best, though, not to get caught in the first place. So he got busy with what he'd come for. He turned over rocks, dug the toe of his shoe into crumbling logs, lifted up sodden leaf litter, and poked sticks into holes. Before long he had some nice grubs, a millipede, five water snails, two good-sized slugs, and a small purplish salamander with gold spots on its back. He put these all in his jar and started down the trail.

CHAPTER 16

The Snake's Dinner

Shortly before three-thirty, Nickie set out for Grover's house. She'd seen it from the back—at least a glimpse of it beyond the shed and the fruit trees—but now she saw the front for the first time. It was a one-story yellow house with two battered tricycles standing out in the yard and three saggy steps leading up to a porch. On the porch was a couch covered in green material worn almost to white on the seat and arms, and on the couch sat a very old woman wearing a red housedress with a zipper up the front and a baggy lavender sweater. As Nickie came up the walk, the old woman peered at her.

"You're not from here," she said.

"No," said Nickie. "I'm just visiting."

The old woman nodded. She was wearing, Nickie noticed, yellow bedroom slippers with ducks on the toes.

"I'm looking for Grover," Nickie said.

But Grover must have seen her coming. The door opened, and there he was. "You *did* come," he said. "Amazing."

"Got yourself a girlfriend," the old woman said to Grover.

"She isn't my *girlfriend,* Granny," Grover said. "Just a girl."

Inside, the house was dim and crowded. The TV was on—it was the president, announcing that only four days remained before the deadline he'd set for the Phalanx Nations. But no one was paying attention. The living room was full of sagging furniture, and every piece of furniture seemed to have a child climbing on it, or curled up in it, or crawling out from under it. They all stared at Nickie when she came in.

"My brothers and sisters," Grover said, waving a hand at them.

"How many are there?" Nickie asked, spotting another one toddling up the hall.

"Six. The twins and four more. Plus me—I'm the oldest."

He led her down a short hall that went right through the house. The walls were covered with photographs—school pictures, wedding pictures, baby pictures, some in frames and some stuck up with thumbtacks.

They went out the back door, and Grover led the

way across the sloping yard, over the dead grass and brown rain-plastered leaves, between the gnarled trunks of the fruit trees, down to the shed beside the alley.

Nickie began to feel nervous. Her stomach clenched.

Grover twirled the dial of a combination lock on the latch and opened the shed door. She followed him in. The air had an earthy smell. A few garden tools, mostly broken, hung on hooks on the walls. On a shelf across one wall were the two snake tanks, and on other shelves, and on the floor, and on a small table and a chair were piles and piles of magazines and flattened cereal boxes, soap boxes, and cake mix boxes. The whole mess was sprinkled here and there with little bits of bent cardboard.

"What's all that?" Nickie asked.

"Contests," said Grover. "Sweepstakes, lottery tickets, stuff like that. There's gobs of dollars out there being given away. I enter everything I can find."

"Why?"

"Because I need money, *obviously.*" He made a "how can you be such a moron" face at her. "I want to go on the Arrowhead Wilderness Reptile Expedition this summer, which costs three hundred seventy-five dollars, which I don't have. So I'm going to win it."

"People hardly ever win contests," Nickie said. "I don't know anyone who has."

"Well, you will pretty soon," Grover said. "Look at

this one." He held up a page torn from a magazine. "You write one paragraph, no more than a hundred words, saying why Armstrong Pickles are the best. Want to hear my paragraph?"

"Okay," said Nickie. She glanced uneasily at the two glass tanks on the shelf, but she didn't see anything inside, only dry leaves.

Grover rummaged around on the table and came up with a sheet of binder paper. He read: "Last Sunday night, I was studying for my math test. It was late, and I was tired. My eyes kept closing so I couldn't see the numbers in my book. I thought, How am I going to pass this test if I can't stay awake? Then inspiration hit me. I needed an Armstrong Pickle! I jumped up from my chair and ran to the refrigerator. I pulled one of those big, green, pimply pickles out of the jar. The first cool bite made my brain go ZING! And the next day I got an A on the test." Grover looked up, grinning. "Only ninety-eight words."

Nickie laughed. "It's great," she said. "What do you get if you win?"

"You get five hundred dollars plus a whole free crate of pickles," said Grover. "There's all kinds of contests. Ones where you think up a slogan, and ones where you make as many words as you can out of some product's name, and ones where you solve a cryptogram, and—"

"Have you won any of them yet?" Nickie asked.

"Oh, yeah," said Grover. "I won six free boxes of Oat Crinklies, and I won a bunch of coupons for Rosepetal laundry soap. Just no money yet, but that will come."

He turned to the snakes. "All right," he said. "Time to get down to business. First the milk snake. He hasn't eaten for a few weeks."

"A few *weeks*!"

"Yep. They don't eat much in the winter. Snakes out in the wild around here crawl down underground and hardly eat at all till spring. Hey, you know what I saw when I was up in the mountains looking for snake food?"

"What?"

"I saw that terrorist. The one who broke the restaurant window."

"You *did*? Weren't you scared?"

"Nah. He was far away. Big, though. Huge. I just caught a glimpse of him."

Grover took the top off one of the tanks. Inside it, the snake stirred, lifting its head and then more and more of itself from the bark and dry leaves that covered it. Rings of black, yellow, and reddish-brown striped its long body.

"It doesn't look a bit like milk," Nickie said.

"I know it," said Grover, gazing fondly at the snake. "It's called that because people used to find them in their barns and think they'd come to milk the cows."

From a small cardboard box next to the snake tank, he took out the tiny mouse he'd shown Nickie before. It was pink and wet-looking, with a tiny head and bulgy bluish eyes, and tiny legs with tiny toes like fringe at the ends. It was moving slightly in Grover's palm, but it looked limp and weak.

"Bye-bye, baby," Grover said. He picked up a long pair of tongs, the kind people use to turn meat on a barbecue grill. His teasing manner was gone now. He moved carefully. All his attention was on what he was doing. He gripped the tiny mouse with the tongs and waved it back and forth before the snake's head. The snake lifted the front half of its body into the air. Its tongue flicked in and out.

"I don't know," said Nickie. "Maybe I don't want to watch."

But it was too late. The snake struck out and snatched the mouse. It withdrew into the tank and wrapped a coil of itself around the mouse's body to hold it still, and then it opened its mouth extremely wide and began to stuff the mouse's head into it.

"They always eat things headfirst," Grover remarked. "And they have expandable jaws."

Nickie froze in horror, but she couldn't take her eyes away. It took only a few seconds for the pink body of the mouse, still wriggling, to disappear down the snake's throat. For a second, a bit of tail hung over the snake's lower jaw. Then the whole mouse was gone. The snake stretched out on the sand again. Behind its head was a mouse-sized bulge.

Nickie breathed out. She hadn't realized she'd been holding her breath. She felt ill. "It's horrible," she said.

"Not really," said Grover. "It's how the snake lives. If I didn't give him a mouse, he'd catch one himself."

"How can you stand to do it? The poor little mouse."

Grover shrugged. "It's nature," he said. "Nature likes the snake just as much as the mouse."

"I guess so," Nickie said.

"Well, that's it," said Grover. He set down the tongs and put the lid back on the tank. "At least you didn't faint."

"I've *never* fainted," said Nickie. She felt upset—somewhere between sick and angry.

"Want to see the red belly eat?"

"No. It's too weird."

"It's not weird at all," Grover retorted. "It happens every day, hundreds of times. If you want to see something *really* weird, go over to Hoyt McCoy's house in the middle of the night. He cracks the sky open. I saw it."

"Come on," said Nickie. "You're making that up."

"No! I really saw it. A long, skinny line in the sky. He's doing *something* weird over there. Maybe he's sending signals to enemy nations! Or he opens the sky, and aliens and demons ooze through!" Grover wiggled his fingers in a creepy, oozing way.

Nickie just shook her head. With Grover, she didn't know how to tell the difference between truth and kidding. "I have to go now," she said. So Grover led her back across the yard and into the house, down the hall among the toddlers, and out onto the front porch, where the grandmother was still sitting on the old couch.

"Going already?" the old woman said.

"I showed her the milk snake," said Grover.

"No wonder she's leaving in a hurry."

"Fed him his dinner," said Grover.

"It was gruesome," Nickie said.

"No kidding," said the grandma. She eyed Nickie with interest. "You going to introduce me to this young lady?" she asked Grover.

"This is my grandmother, Carrie Hartwell," Grover said to Nickie. "We just call her Granny Carrie." He turned to his grandmother. "And this is Nickie," he said.

"Nickie Randolph," said Nickie. "My great-grandfather lived here. His name was Arthur Green."

"Ah," the grandmother said. "He was on the side of the angels."

Nickie wasn't sure what this meant, but it sounded all right. She said goodbye and walked back out to the street. Her legs felt shaky and her stomach churned. Was it good, she wondered, to feed a baby mouse to a snake? It wasn't good for the mouse, but it was for the snake. Was it evil for Grover to do it? She just didn't know.

CHAPTER 17

Hoyt McCoy's Horrible House

Nickie headed back toward Greenhaven by way of Raven Road. She hadn't really planned to go that way; her mind was on what she'd just seen in Grover's shed. But when she found herself passing the gravel drive that led back into Hoyt McCoy's overgrown acres, she hesitated. She thought about what Grover had said—that Hoyt McCoy cracked open the sky. Surely that couldn't be true. But whatever he'd seen might have been a sign of wickedness. Mrs. Beeson thought there was something strange about this man, that he was probably a trouble spot. And Nickie had promised to help her. So maybe, while she was here, she should check on Hoyt McCoy. She didn't really want to; even her strong curiosity didn't extend to creepy isolated houses and people with a whiff of wrongness about them. But if she was going to do her part to root out badness so that goodness could win, she had to be brave.

She gritted her teeth and took a deep, shaky breath. She would just dart in and have a quick look around, hoping to see something that would let her take back a clear report to Mrs. Beeson.

She started up the driveway. Brown, shriveled blackberry vines grew along the edges; weeds sprouted up through the gravel. Tall pine trees on the left cast a spiky line of shadows, and Nickie stayed within these shadows as much as she could. She rounded a curve, and there, up ahead, was the house, a mud-colored two-story building tucked back among great looming oaks and pines, its paint worn off, drifts of old leaves on its peaked roof. She stopped and looked for signs of movement. Three birds shot up from a clump of grass, but other than that, she saw nothing stirring, either outside the house or behind its windows. So, cautiously, she moved forward again.

What was she looking for? She didn't really know. Something truly awful, like freshly dug graves or human bones? Signs of craziness, like Hoyt McCoy dancing around naked? Disgusting filthiness, like a smelly outhouse or rat-swarmed garbage? She didn't see anything like that—nothing but a dusty black car parked at the head of the drive. Maybe bad things happened inside that dark, silent house, but she certainly wasn't going to go close enough to peer in the windows. She would go up to the beginning of the brick path that led to the front door, she decided, and if she didn't see anything notable by then, she'd leave.

So she crept away from the protective shadow of the trees and tiptoed across the open space in front of the house. She stood at the foot of the path. Her gaze scanned the front door, the windows to the left and right of the front door (heavily curtained), the windows on the second floor (where the blinds were closed), and a window in a gable above them, where—she took a sudden step backward, and her knees went weak—the barrel of a gun pointed at the sky.

And as she stood there, frozen with fear, the gun angled downward until it aimed straight at her. From inside the house, a voice called out, "Stop right there, trespasser, intruder, spy! Don't move, on pain of dire consequences!"

But Nickie was not going to stand there and get shot. She dashed toward the shadow of the trees as fast as her jelly-like legs would carry her. Any second, she expected to hear a bang and feel the punch of a shot between her shoulder blades. At the edge of the driveway she stumbled and fell, and she lay there for a second, shaking, and looked back at the house. The gun was still pointing downward, but no one was shouting; no one was coming out the front door. So she staggered to her feet again. This time her legs worked, and she ran.

She knew Crystal wouldn't be home yet. So she ran straight to Mrs. Beeson's house, leapt up the steps, and rang the doorbell. When Mrs. Beeson answered, Nickie was breathing so hard she could barely speak. "Mrs. Beeson!" she gasped. "That McCoy man tried to shoot me!"

Mrs. Beeson's eyes grew so wide that the whites showed all the way around. "What? Shoot you!"

Nickie told about the gun pointing out of the window and the voice that had bellowed at her.

"Oh!" Mrs. Beeson grasped Nickie by the arm and pulled her inside. "This is even worse than I thought. I must get the police—must get them out there right now—" She hurried away down the hall, leaving Nickie quivering by the door. In a moment Nickie heard her speaking to someone on the phone. "Raven Road," she said. "Yes, McCoy. Be careful—he has guns. I'll meet you out there."

When she came back, she was pulling on her coat. "We'll bring him in," she said. "Don't worry. You poor, brave little thing." She gave Nickie a quick, sweet-smelling hug. "I should have known—that feeling I had. Why didn't I—?" She clasped her hands and took a deep breath. "Slow down, Brenda," she told herself. "Be calm."

But Nickie wasn't calm at all; she was terribly excited. "There's more!" she said. "The boy with the snakes—he feeds them live baby mice! And that terrorist up in the woods—he saw him! And he told me that Hoyt McCoy cracks the sky open and sends signals to enemy nations!"

Mrs. Beeson snatched her purse from a table by the door. "I have to get out there right away," she said. "You go back home now and keep yourself safe. Who knows, he might be—But we'll get him, don't worry. I'll come and talk to you when it's all over."

Nickie went back to Greenhaven wishing, for once, that Crystal was around so she could tell her about what had happened. But the only sign of Crystal was a note she'd left on the hall table by the phone:

Nickie—

Your mom called. Sounded pretty tired and worried. Another postcard came from your dad. It said:

Dear Nickie and Rachel,

Everything here is going well. We're working hard and making good progress. I hope both of you are taking excellent care of yourselves.

Love, Dad

P.S. Stayed up till midnight last night reading Shakespeare!

I didn't know your dad read Shakespeare.

Back by dinnertime—C.

I didn't know he did, either, Nickie thought. There was something odd about these postcards. She needed to think about them. Was he trying to send a message of some kind? He'd always liked codes and puzzles. He'd explained a lot of different ones to Nickie, and they'd had fun working on them together. Could these postcards be in code?

She went up to the nursery and laid the three postcard messages in a row on the window seat. She studied them for a while, but if they were in code, she couldn't figure it out. So she gave up for the moment and played with Otis for a long time. His happy spirit made her feel better. Everything about him made her feel better, in fact—his damp black nose, the way the wavy hair grew on the top of his head, the five little pads on the bottoms of his feet, even his doggy smell. They played all their favorite games, and Nickie pondered her father's odd messages, and thoughts of horrible Hoyt McCoy gradually faded from her mind.

CHAPTER 18

What Grover Saw

Something was going on at Hoyt McCoy's. Grover, who was out by the street getting the mail just before dinnertime, saw two cars—one of them a police car—streaking down Trillium Street and veering left up Raven Road, and of course he followed to see where they were going. They turned in at Hoyt's driveway. Obviously they weren't just stopping for a friendly visit. They were going fast. Their wheels skidded on the driveway's gravel.

Had Hoyt had a heart attack or something? Had he maybe shot himself in the foot with that rifle of his? Maybe he had shot someone else and they were going in to arrest him. Whatever was happening, Grover had to see it.

He ran up Hoyt's driveway in the wake of the cars and stepped in among some trees at the side of the drive so he could watch without being seen. Both cars had pulled up in the open space in front of Hoyt's awful-looking house, and from them sprang Yonwood's policemen and Mrs. Brenda Beeson. The cops had taken their guns from their holsters and were pointing them at the front door of the house. The chief, Officer Gurney, roared in his chest-deep voice, "Hoyt McCoy! Come out with your hands up! We have you surrounded!"

Actually, they didn't have him surrounded. They were all in front of the house. But when Gurney said that, a couple of police scurried around to the back. Mrs. Beeson, in her red baseball cap, stood behind the other two. Her fists were clenched at her sides, her nose slightly wrinkled, as if she were sniffing the air, and her eyes fixed like searchlight beams on the front door of the house.

In a moment, the door opened. The tall, stooped figure of Hoyt McCoy appeared. He had on a baggy olive green sweater and black pants, and his shaggy hair stuck together in bunches, as if he hadn't combed it for several weeks.

"Hands up! Hands up!" yelled Officer Gurney, who must have learned his lines, Grover thought, from watching cop shows on TV.

But Hoyt did not put his hands up. He came out onto his front step and stared at the crowd in his driveway as if he thought he must be having a nightmare. Then he raised one hand, but not in surrender. He pointed a finger straight at Officer Gurney. "Off . . . my . . . property!" he shouted. "All of you. *Out!* What do you think you're doing here?"

"You're under arrest!" yelled Officer Gurney, though he didn't take a step closer to Hoyt. "Attempted murder!"

At this, Hoyt lowered his arm and smiled. Smiled? Grover crept a little closer to make sure. Yes, he was smiling, a strange look on that long, bloodhound face of his. He smiled and shook his head slowly. He came down his front steps and approached Officer Gurney, apparently not worried that he was about to be shot. Gurney raised his other arm and took hold of his gun with both hands, as if a tank or an enraged rhinoceros were charging at him.

"Officer," said Hoyt, "a mistake has been made, and I see the source of it standing just behind you." He nodded at Mrs. Beeson, who didn't move. "For some reason, this lady is determined to *hound* me. She sends her spies to trespass on my land. Now she accuses me of murder, which is so ludicrous that I can only smile." He smiled again, a thin, grim smile that had no humor in it.

Mrs. Beeson stepped forward, and Grover stepped forward, too, to hear what she was going to say. It didn't seem to matter if he came out a little from among the trees; no one was paying any attention to him.

"*Attempted* murder," Mrs. Beeson said in a voice that quivered with outrage. "I have always known that you were a bad one. But now we have found you out before you could—"

"Attempted murder of *whom*, madam?" said Hoyt.

"A child! A little girl who had strayed onto your land and was perfectly innocently gazing at your dreadful—"

"Now, wait just a moment, dear lady," Hoyt said. His smile vanished. His face grew dark with anger. "This is really too much! Lately my estate has been *crawling* with prowlers. A boy, a girl, and no doubt others I have not spotted."

Grover knew who the boy prowler had been. But who was the girl? He didn't know any girls who would even think of setting foot on Hoyt McCoy's land.

Hoyt railed on. "*Why,* a person would like to know? *Why?* I happen to be intensely busy at the moment—busy with matters of great importance, matters that could alter the world's future—and yours, madam. And yet you send spies to pester me." He shook his finger at Mrs. Beeson. "And when I call out at them, when I rightfully demand that they leave the premises, I am accused of attempted *murder*? It is quite beyond belief."

All this time, the police remained in a half-crouching position, like runners at the start of a race, ready at any second to leap forward and wrestle Hoyt McCoy to the ground. Hoyt didn't seem to be alarmed by this. He glared straight past them and fixed his eyes on Mrs. Beeson.

She glared back. "You trained a rifle on a little girl," said Mrs. Beeson in a breathless, furious voice. "A *rifle.* She saw it, and she saw you lower it—to point straight at her! She heard you—you threatened her. You—" Here she seemed to run out of both words and breath. Her face was as red as her cap.

Officer Gurney took a bold stride forward. "Come quietly now," he said to Hoyt. "We're taking you in."

But an expression of great amusement slowly spread across Hoyt's face. "Ah," he said, ignoring Gurney. "Now I understand. Look up there, ladies and gentlemen." He pointed upward and backward, over his shoulder. "There's your murder weapon."

Grover looked up. So did the cops, and so did Mrs. Beeson. In a gable window above the second story, the barrel of a rifle pointed at the sky. At least, it looked to Grover like a rifle, although it was bigger than the rifle his father had, and its shape was slightly different. Maybe it was actually a shotgun. That would explain why it was pointed at the sky—Hoyt was using it to shoot birds, when he wasn't shooting trespassers.

"That," said Hoyt, "is not a gun. That is the telescope with which I scan the skies." He turned back to glare at Mrs. Beeson again. "And also scan my property for trespassers. I wish to be left alone. But you, Brenda Beeson, send one spy after another. Why? *Why?* Why cannot a person be left in peace?"

It was an interesting moment. Grover held his breath, waiting to hear what Mrs. Beeson and her men would say. Everyone waited. Mrs. Beeson, too, seemed to be waiting, perhaps for a cue from God. Grover could see her face tightening—eyes narrowing, forehead furrowing. Really, he thought, she ought to be relieved. She ought to be saying, Oh, good, no crime has taken place after all! My mistake! Very sorry!

Instead she told Officer Gurney to take one of his men and go upstairs to make sure that Hoyt McCoy was telling the truth. "And look around as you go," she added. "In case—you know—there might be—"

"Absolutely," said Officer Gurney.

"What!" cried Hoyt. "You assume you may come barging into my house without a search warrant?"

"It's a matter of security," Officer Gurney said. "In times like these, a threat to security changes the rules."

"Outrageous," said Hoyt. "But I won't take the trouble to stop you. You will find nothing in my house that has the faintest whiff of criminality."

He went inside with the two men, and they were gone for about fifteen minutes—a very boring fifteen minutes for Grover, who didn't want to draw attention to himself by walking away. The cold from the ground was seeping up into his feet. Mrs. Beeson got into her car and sat there waiting. She looked cross and huddled, as if *she* were the suspect about to be taken in. Grover thought this was rather funny. He didn't really favor one side over the other in this dispute. He hadn't enjoyed being yelled at and scared by Hoyt McCoy the day he crossed his property. But he didn't care much for Mrs. Beeson, either. These days she was seeing something wicked everywhere she looked.

The police came out of the house, finally, and Hoyt stood on his step with his hands on his hips and watched them triumphantly as they got back into their car.

"Your timing was excellent," he said. "If you'd come tomorrow, you'd not have found me here, as I am about to go away for a few days on a mission of more importance than you can imagine. You might have tried to interfere with my trip, which would have been a very bad decision. As it is, we've got this little matter out of the way and I hope never to have the pleasure of your company here again."

The men weren't bothering to listen to him. "Weirdest place I've ever seen," Grover heard Officer Gurney say before he slammed the car door. "Messiest, too. The guy's a nutcase."

The cars started up their engines and drove off down the driveway. Hoyt stood where he was, watching until both cars had turned onto Raven Road.

Grover waited for him to go back inside, but he kept standing there, and finally Grover realized that Hoyt was looking right at *him*.

"I see my trespasser is back," Hoyt said. There was no anger in his tone.

"I'm leaving," said Grover. "I just wanted to see what was going on."

"Since you're here," said Hoyt, "let me tell you something."

Uh-oh, thought Grover. Now I get yelled at. But he stood his ground. At least no one was shooting at him.

Hoyt came down the steps, stalked over to Grover, and stood right in front of him. There were grease stains on his sweater, Grover noticed, and his pants were unraveling at the cuffs. He smelled like burned toast. "What Lady Brenda doesn't know," Hoyt said, "is that she has the wrong information. Heaven is *my* territory. I know what goes on there. I know what the universe has in store for us."

"You do?" said Grover. Not being yelled at surprised him so much that he answered as if they were having a normal conversation.

"As well as anyone," said Hoyt.

"Well," said Grover, "what *does* the universe have in store?"

"Ceaseless marvels," said Hoyt McCoy. "Infinite astonishment. But only for those who care to pay attention."

"I saw a crack of light over your house," Grover said.

"Aha," said Hoyt. He narrowed his eyes and looked hard at Grover. "Never mind about *that,*" he said.

"Why?" said Grover. "Is it a secret?"

Hoyt McCoy ignored his question. "If you were to simply ring my doorbell like a civilized person instead of sneaking around my property, I might show you a few things. Assuming you were interested."

But Grover wasn't nearly interested enough for that. "Maybe sometime," he said. "But right now I have to go." He moved backward a few steps.

"Let me tell you one more thing," said Hoyt, raising his voice. "You may tell this to your Mrs. Beeson, if you like, who likes everything to be neat and clean and normal. I am *not* particularly neat or clean; I am certainly *not* what anyone would call normal. But I am as *good* as anyone else."

And very loony, thought Grover. He murmured a few more polite words and made his exit, trotting down the gravel drive and heading home with a great sense of relief.

Grover couldn't sleep that night. Thoughts swarmed through his mind; he couldn't shut them off. So he got up, being quiet so he wouldn't wake his brothers. He put his clothes on and went outside. He would take a short, fast walk—just up the hill to Main Street, down a few blocks, and back home. He'd done it before when he couldn't sleep, and it usually helped.

He wasn't afraid. There was nothing in Yonwood that could hurt him, unless that terrorist was roaming around town again. And if he was, Grover could watch him from some safe place and see what he was up to and turn him in. The thought was invigorating. Grover started off. He climbed the hill at a rapid pace, breathing in cold night air, looking up at the stars, wondering why he didn't do this more often. Being out alone at night made him feel free.

He went up Trillium Street, around behind the Cozy Corner (no terrorists there tonight), and down Main Street, where the streetlamps were out, as they were all over town. He saw nothing stirring—not a night watchman or an alley cat or even a spider—until, as he passed the dark windows of the grocery store, he happened to glance up Grackle Street and saw someone about a block away. Whoever it was didn't walk purposefully but drifted a little this way, a little that way, as if lost or looking for something. Was it a sleepwalker? Grover stopped and stared. He was too far away to be sure who he was seeing, but suddenly he thought he knew. It must be her; it was the right street. Why would she be outside? She seemed to be wearing—what? A nightgown? Something pale and floaty. He started in that direction. But before he'd gone more than a few steps, another figure appeared, a skinny girl, who dashed up behind the lost-looking one and took her arm and led her back into the house.

Grover turned downhill and headed for home. What he'd seen had given him a sad, shaky feeling. Poor Prophet, he thought. It must be awful to have God speak to you and turn your mind to ashes.

CHAPTER 19

Blue Envelopes

Nickie woke on Tuesday morning to the sound of rain roaring on the roof and slashing against the window glass, coming in gusts as the wind blew one way and then another. It was the sort of day when you want to stay inside, make a fire, and sit by it with your cup of hot chocolate. But of course Nickie had given up hot chocolate, so she drank mint tea that morning instead. She actually felt quite virtuous doing it, because it was so hard. She could tell that her willpower was being exercised, like a muscle. This didn't make her *happy*, exactly. She missed the chocolate. But it made her feel strong. Could it be that the more things you gave up, the stronger you would feel?

Crystal went out early to talk with Len about plans for the open house. "Meet me at the café at six," she said as she went out the door. "We'll have dinner together and you can tell me all about your adventures."

Otis's outing was very short that morning. He stood on the threshold of the back door and looked doubtfully at the rain. Nickie had to push him outside. Once there, he did his duty in record time and dashed back in. Nickie took him upstairs.

The nursery room was especially cozy that morning, with the sky so dark outside, and the sound of the rain on the windows, and the pools of golden light from the lamps. Nickie set Otis up on the window seat and gave him a new bone to chew. She propped up some cushions to lean against, and then she looked around for something to read. Her eyes fell on the books that Amanda had left behind. Why not try one of those? She picked the one with the dark-haired beauty on the cover and opened it at random:

> *In the candlelight, Blaine's eyes glittered like jewels. Clarissa caught her breath as he leaned toward her. What a magnificent man he was! His square jaw, his thick glossy black hair, his wide shoulders—her heart raced. When he reached out and stroked her cheek, she trembled all over. "Blaine," she said. "You must never leave me. I want to be with you always."*

Nickie raised her eyes to the rain-spattered window. She tried to imagine feeling this way about someone. First she pictured Martin, with his hazel eyes and short red hair. Did she think he was magnificent? Not really. He seemed nice, and he was on the side of goodness. But he didn't make her heart race. She pictured Grover instead. His hair was cute, in a floppy sort of way. He was smart and interesting. He had a sense of humor, if you liked that kind of humor. But he was also a bit peculiar. She had no idea if he was on the side of goodness or not. And she certainly wouldn't say he was magnificent. If he stroked her cheek, would her heart race? No. She would think it was weird and creepy. Did she want to be with him always? Definitely not. It was hard to imagine wanting to be with anyone *always.* There'd be times when you wanted to be alone, or with someone else.

She turned a few pages and read some more:

> *Clarissa fled down the stone steps to the windswept beach, her raven tresses flowing out behind her. She scanned the empty sands, and when she saw no sign of Blaine, a great cry of anguish escaped her lips. She could not live without him! She would sooner die!*

Nickie shut the book. There was no doubt about it: if that was love, she was not in love with Martin *or* Grover. She could live without either of them perfectly well.

She looked out the window, where the rain was still pelting down. At the end of the block, she noticed someone approaching, wearing a wide-brimmed pink rain hat and carrying a canvas tote bag. When the person came closer, she saw who it was: Mrs. Beeson! How perfect. If she ran fast downstairs, she could catch her and ask her what had happened to horrible Hoyt McCoy.

She didn't bother to grab an umbrella—she just threw on her jacket and ran out into the rain. Rivers of water streamed through the gutters. All along the street, bare tree branches flailed against house walls and shut-tight windows. She ran to meet Mrs. Beeson, who smiled when she saw Nickie coming.

"Hi!" said Nickie. "I saw you from the window, and I was wondering—"

"I was just thinking of you," Mrs. Beeson said. She looked a little frazzled around the edges. Her lipstick was slightly crooked, and her ponytail, beneath the rain hat, was damp and drooping. "You've been such a help. Walk with me, if you'd like. I'm delivering a few notices."

"Notices?" said Nickie.

"Yes, urgent ones. I'm getting a little impatient. Here we have such a miraculous chance to save ourselves, and a few people are about to ruin it for everyone. Such selfishness! I have to make them understand.

We have a terrorist in the woods! The Crisis gets worse all the time! In three days we might face war!" Mrs. Beeson shook her head at people's foolishness. "So I've decided it's time to take some drastic action. I've done the downhill ones and most of the uphill; only one more to go." She drew Nickie in next to her, under the umbrella. Her sugary smell enveloped them both.

"What are the notices about?" Nickie asked.

But Mrs. Beeson was already on a different subject. "It was just too bad about Hoyt McCoy," she said, "wasn't it? About your mistake, I mean, honey. But I still feel sure that he has something to hide. Don't you?"

Nickie was puzzled. "I don't *know* what happened with Hoyt McCoy," she said. "That's what I wanted to ask you. Didn't you arrest him? Did I make a mistake?"

Mrs. Beeson looked at her in surprise. "You didn't know?" She explained about the police action and the rifle that was really a telescope. "However," she said, "I'm sure we were right *essentially.* He just reeks of wrongness. I can *feel* it, and doing this work makes me trust my feelings more every day. It's just a matter of catching him in the act, that's all. But never mind. Here's the last house."

Nickie was so stunned by this news about Hoyt McCoy that she could hardly breathe. A telescope! And the police had gone out and aimed guns at him! Because of her.

They had stopped at a brick house with a collapsing woodshed next to it. Mrs. Beeson opened the mailbox. She reached into the canvas bag and took out a blue envelope. In the upper left corner were the words "Urgent: From B. Beeson." She put it in the mailbox, and they moved on.

Nickie started to ask again what was in the envelopes, but Mrs. Beeson was already talking. "Sometimes I'm sorry this ever happened," she said. "That vision of Althea's, and then the instructions afterward. Some parts of it are very hard. The punishment part, for instance."

"Punishment?" said Nickie.

Mrs. Beeson turned a corner and headed up Fern Street, walking so quickly that Nickie kept getting left behind. "Yes, for people who just won't cooperate," Mrs. Beeson said. "We can't allow that, can we? It would be letting down everyone else in Yonwood."

"What's the punishment?" Nickie asked.

But Mrs. Beeson must not have heard her over the splash of the rain. "It's such a responsibility," she went on. "I've agonized over it, I must admit. Some of the things she says—I don't know. I hate to think she really means—" She shook her head, staring down at the wet sidewalk. "I just hesitate to—"

Then suddenly she stopped, and a little rush of water flowed off the top of her pink hat onto Nickie's head. Her voice became strong again. "What am I saying? I hesitate? Just because something is hard? Just because it means making a sacrifice? No, no, no. That's what faith is, isn't it? Believing even when you don't understand."

Nickie looked up at her. She was gazing at the sky, her eyes shining, paying no attention to the rain falling on her face. "It is?" Nickie said.

"Yes," said Mrs. Beeson. "It is." And with that, she hurried away.

Back at Greenhaven, Nickie went upstairs, passing some men who were polishing the floors with a roaring machine. Mrs. Beeson, she thought, seemed more fired up than ever, like an engine revved to a higher level. Nickie had the feeling something was going to happen.

In the nursery, Otis greeted her energetically. "Oty-Oty-Otis!" she cried. She rolled him over and scratched his pink tummy, and he paddled his feet and stretched his head out so she could scratch his throat, too. "You are a darling, Otis," she said. She lifted him up onto the window seat, and she turned on the lamp. As the rain pounded down outside, she started in again on the stack of papers she'd taken from the big trunk.

She found some letters written to "Mommy and Daddy" from a girl at summer camp in 1955, and an article cut from a newspaper's social pages about an elegant birthday party held at Greenhaven in 1940. After setting aside still more bent postcards and ancient Christmas cards and faded photographs, she came upon a fragile old envelope with a strange-looking letter inside that she thought at first was just a page of crazy scribbling. But when she looked at it closely, she could see that it was writing after all. It was a sort of *double* writing. The letter writer (someone named Elizabeth) had written on the page in the usual way and then had turned the paper and written right *across* what she'd written before! The result looked totally unreadable—like two barbed-wire fences laid on top of each other. But she found that if she held the paper in a certain way, slightly tipped, the writing going one direction faded into the background, and the writing going the other direction became clear.

The letter was dated January 4, 1919. Most of it wasn't really worth the trouble it took to read. Elizabeth wrote about ordinary things: visitors who'd arrived, a party, new clothes, a new horse. One bit was intriguing, though: "I hope your dear mother is not so terribly sad as she was. I see as I write this that it's been a year today since the fever took darling baby Frederick. Such a great sorrow! But time must have healed her a little by now."

Nickie imagined the mother, young and beautiful and wearing one of those long, slender dresses she'd

January 4, 1919

My Dearest Amelia,

Samuel arrived this afternoon with his new wife, Sarah. She is such a darling. She was wearing a brown traveling dress, but later she changed into a beautiful mauve wool from Paris. I long to wear Paris fashions! There is to be a large dinner party on Saturday. All the Porter cousins are coming, and I'll wear my green silk with the lace trim.

Have I told you about Father's new horse? He's a very fine one, coal black with a white star. Father let me name him. I chose the name Galahad. I long to ride him, but Father won't allow me to. He says Galahad is too spirited, and I am not yet an experienced rider. I know I could do it though. I'd like to ride him up to Greenhaven to visit you!

I hope your dear mother is not so terribly sad as she was. I see as I write this that it's been a year today since the fever took darling baby Frederick. Such a great sorrow! But time must have healed her a little by now.

Please give my kindest regards to all your family and my special love to you.

Elizabeth

seen in the photographs, sitting in anguish at the bedside of her baby, not able to give him the right medicine because it hadn't been invented yet. It would be dreadful to watch your baby die. No wonder she was still sad a year later.

She decided to keep this letter because of the strange way it was written. She set it on the shelf with the picture of the twins.

It was time to meet Crystal for dinner. Nickie walked toward downtown. Overhead, she heard the fighter jets again, roaring across the sky, above the clouds. She shivered, thinking of the president's deadline. Only three days left.

The whole town had a gloomy, closed-in look tonight. Nearly all the houses were dark, their blinds and curtains drawn. A small house on Birch Street had lighted windows, though, and as Nickie passed she saw a police car draw up in front of it. Good, she thought. They're going to make those people follow the rules.

When she got to the Cozy Corner and pushed open the door, warm food-scented air greeted her. The restaurant was dim because its lights were off, but candles on each table made it seem cozy anyhow. She spotted Crystal right away: she was sitting with her back to Nickie, at a table beside the window, and across from her sat a tall man with a little mustache. It must be Len, the real estate agent. Why was *he* here? Crystal hadn't said she was meeting Len for dinner. She'd said she and *Nickie* would have dinner together and Nickie would tell about her adventures. Not that she had any adventures she wanted to tell about.

Len saw her standing there. He said something to Crystal, and she turned around and called, "Nickie! Here we are!"

When Nickie sat down, Crystal said, "I talked to your mother today. She got a card from your father. Didn't say where he was or what he was doing, but he said he might have a surprise for her pretty soon."

"He must be coming home!" Nickie said. "Oh, I hope he is." She missed her father with a terrible ache all of a sudden. He called her his chickadee and made paper airplanes for her. She wished he were here right now.

She wanted to ask if her mother had said anything else, but Crystal had moved on to another subject. "We've been planning," she said. "We're thinking this Saturday for the open house."

"Crossing our fingers for good weather," said Len, grinning, and holding up two sets of crossed fingers and wagging them at Nickie.

"That means a lot of work has to get done during the next three days," said Crystal. She sounded quite cheerful about it. She took her notebook out of her purse, and she and Len started in on still another to-do list as if it were the most fun thing in the world.

Nickie ordered her soup and stared out the window. The last of the sunlight edged the top of the mountain in gold. Someone in a "Don't Do It!" T-shirt walked by, and someone else with a cell phone clapped to her ear. Across the street, a black car pulled into the gas station. Hoyt McCoy got out of it. Just the sight of him made Nickie feel guilty. She watched as he filled up his gas tank, and she was glad when he drove off, heading down the road that led to the highway.

Dinner took forever. Crystal's to-do list got longer and longer, and every item had to be discussed in tedious detail. Now and then Nickie commented on something, but no one paid attention to her. She was just about to say she was going back to Greenhaven when there was a loud tap on the window next to her. Startled, she turned. Outside stood Grover, his eyes round and worried-looking.

"Who's *that*?" said Crystal.

"The handyman's son," Nickie said. "I sort of know him." She laughed, thinking he was joking around as usual. But instead of breaking into a smile or a maniac face, Grover shook his head and beckoned to her. His mouth moved, making exaggerated words: "Come out." Nickie's smile froze on her face. What was wrong?

She stood up from the table. "I have to go ask him something," she said, and before Crystal and Len could say a word, she dashed out the door and hurried after Grover.

CHAPTER 20

Orders

He was waiting for her a few steps farther up the block, outside a shoe store.

"What's the matter?" she said. "Why were you looking at me like that?"

"Something bad has happened," he said. "You know my snakes?"

She nodded.

"They told me I have to get rid of them."

"What? Who told you?"

"Brenda Beeson. I went home for lunch and there was a note for me in the mailbox. It said snakes are touched with evil and it isn't good to keep them and I have to get rid of them."

"Oh," said Nickie, with a shock of dismay.

"Someone must have told her," Grover said. "I think I know who: my so-called friend Martin."

Nickie didn't answer. She stared at a man taking

the display tables of on-sale shoes inside for the night. She didn't want to meet Grover's eyes.

"He was lurking around outside my shed a few days ago," Grover went on. "Someone was, anyway. He ran away before I could see who it was." He scowled. "I don't *want* to get rid of my snakes."

Nickie felt a sickening dizziness. She couldn't remember, all of a sudden, whose side she was on. Was she God's helper or Grover's friend? Her mind went numb. She didn't know what to say.

"I had to tell someone," Grover said. "I saw you in there, so . . ." He shrugged, looking at her curiously, probably wondering why she was standing there like a dummy.

Without her even wanting it to, the truth pushed its way out of her. "It wasn't a he," she said, looking down at the sidewalk.

"What? Who wasn't?"

"It was me. Outside your shed. It was me who told her about the snakes."

Grover's mouth dropped open. "You? *You?*"

"I've been helping her," Nickie said. "Looking for things that are bad, you know, helping her root them out. I didn't *know* if keeping snakes was bad. I just asked her about it. That's all I did."

"Why are you *helping* her?" Grover said. He flung his hands out and looked at her with an "I can't believe this" expression.

"Because I want to fight against evil," Nickie said. "Find trouble spots. Help keep everything on the side of good, so we'll be safe."

"You know what they're going to do if I don't get rid of my snakes?" Grover said.

"What?"

"Put one of those bracelet things on me. Hah!" he cried out suddenly. A woman passing by gave him a startled look. "Let 'em try it. They're never gonna touch me."

"What bracelet things?" Nickie asked.

"You don't know about them?" Grover circled his wrist with his thumb and forefinger. "They hum. They go *MMMMmmmm-MMMMmmmm*. Some little non-stop battery thing powers them. You can't get them off, even with a hammer or a hacksaw, because they're made of something incredibly hard. Anybody they say is a sinner gets one. Nobody can talk to a person with a bracelet, and they won't take it off till you either quit sinning or leave."

"Leave?"

"Leave town. Move somewhere else."

"That must be what I've heard, then," Nickie said. "Twice I heard it."

"There's three or four people who have them right now. They don't come out much. They don't want to be seen. Jonathan Small has one. So does Ricky Platt."

"What did they do wrong?"

"I don't know about Ricky, but Jonathan sings," said Grover. "No one is supposed to, since the Prophet said 'No singing.' But he sings these loud show tunes in the shower every morning. His neighbors heard him, and the cops came and snapped the bracelet on him. He said he wouldn't quit singing, but I think he's about ready to change his mind. That bracelet thing drives a person crazy." He twisted his lips in a disgusted way. "A whole lot of people got these letters in their mailboxes. I heard about two of 'em already: The Elwoods got one for yelling at each other. Maryessa Brown got one for smoking. And you should have seen what happened to old Hoyt McCoy. They brought out the whole police force and tried to arrest him. I saw it—I was there."

Nickie's heart had started beating rapidly. "Maybe you should let the snakes go," she said.

"Why should I?" he said. "What harm are they doing?"

"They could bite someone," Nickie said weakly.

"There's a lock on the shed! No one goes in there but me!" Grover was shouting now, and people passing by were frowning at him. His face took on its wild-eyed look. "And anyway," he yelled, "they're *not venomous snakes*!"

Nickie stepped back. "I'm sorry," she said. "I was just trying to . . . I don't know, to do the right thing."

She took a deep, shaky breath. "If they try to put one of those bracelets on you, what will you do?"

"Run. They won't catch me." Grover's chin jutted out, and his lips pressed together in a hard line. He pointed a finger at her and shook it in her face. "You should *think* about what's the right thing to do. Not just take someone's word for it." And with that he turned around and stalked away, leaving Nickie standing beside the door of the shoe store, with dark feelings swirling through her like storm clouds.

The storm in her mind got worse when she tried to sleep that night. She couldn't stop thinking about the blue envelopes. Mrs. Beeson must have given one to every person who was doing something they'd decided was wrong. How many of them were people Nickie herself had talked about? And were they all going to do what they were told? Or were there others like Grover, who would refuse? And what *was* the right thing to do?

She didn't feel well. Her stomach was all unsettled. She lay in bed for a long time, not sleeping, thinking about Grover's snakes, and the humming bracelets, and the Prophet, and the president, and God, and about good versus evil, until her mind was a swirl of confusion. Finally, she crept out of bed. She felt her way down the hall in the dark to the back stairs, and she tiptoed up to the third floor and into the nursery.

Otis, who'd been asleep on the bed that had been Amanda's, jumped down and ran to her, wagging his rear end, and Nickie picked him up and got into the bed herself. She could feel the warm spot where he'd been lying—it was right by her knees. She put him back there and laid one arm across his furry body, and after that she felt better. But she didn't sleep soundly that night. A dark feeling stayed with her. She wasn't sure if it was guilt or dread.

CHAPTER 21

Getting Ready for the Open House

For the next two days, Wednesday and Thursday, Nickie worked with Crystal at Greenhaven, helping her get ready for the open house. Crystal gave her the assignment of cleaning and neatening the rooms on the third floor. "We won't bother to make those rooms beautiful," she said, "but they can at least be presentable. Get rid of mess and cobwebs, sweep up the dead bugs, take extra furniture down to the basement, that sort of thing." She cast her critical gaze around the front parlor, where they were standing. "The rest of the house," she said, "has to be as elegant as possible. I think we can manage it. The house has good bones."

Once each day, Crystal came up to the third floor to see how the work was going, and Nickie had to quickly close Otis into the hall closet and put the radio on loud to disguise any sounds he might make. Luckily, Crystal wasn't very interested in the rooms on the third floor. All she wanted was for them not to look too awful. She glanced in, said Nickie was doing a good job, and went back downstairs.

As she worked, Nickie turned over the problem of goodness in her mind. On Thursday evening, as they were sitting in the kitchen having a dinner of canned soup and soda crackers, and listening to the news on the radio, she asked Crystal her question.

"Crystal," she said. "How do you tell if something is good or bad?"

Crystal was exhausted from rearranging furniture and hauling boxes of stuff down to the local thrift shop. "You mean like a good or bad book?" she said. "A good or bad movie?"

"No," Nickie said, "I mean like something you do. How do you know if it's a good thing to do or not?"

On the radio, the news announcer broke off in the middle of a sentence, and there was a sudden silence. Then he said, "We have a bulletin from the president. One moment."

The president's voice came on, not quite as smooth as usual. Instead of answering Nickie's question, Crystal held up one finger and said, "Listen."

"One day remains," the president said, "before the deadline we have issued to the Phalanx Nations. I regret to say no progress has been made. Our resolve is firm: we will not back down in the face of threats from godless evildoers. Citizens should prepare for possible large-scale conflict. Please refer to the Homeland Security website at www . . ."

Crystal turned down the radio. She frowned and broke a few soda crackers into her soup. "It sounds bad," she said. "We ought to be all right here, but I'm worried about your mother in the city."

"Let's call her, then," said Nickie, "and tell her to come."

"No, I wouldn't want her traveling right now. I'm not really sure what to do." She turned up the radio again, but the president was finished, and the newsman was reporting on a terrorist group that had taken a hundred hostages and was refusing to release them until they swore to follow the one true faith.

"Could you answer my question now?" said Nickie. "About how you tell if something is good or bad?"

"It's a deep question," Crystal said, "and I'm deeply tired. I guess if I had to answer, I'd say that you look to see if what you're doing causes harm. If it hurts anyone. If so, it's probably not good."

"What if it doesn't hurt any *people,*" said Nickie, "or even any animals, but it hurts God?"

"Hurts God? How can God be hurt?"

"Well, I mean if what you do goes against what God says."

"You'd have to know what he says, then, wouldn't you? Assuming he's up there saying anything." Crystal swallowed a spoonful of soup. "It's too deep for me," she said. "I just want to eat my dinner and go to bed. And by the way, your mom called again and read me another one of those odd postcards from your dad."

Nickie jumped up. "Did you write it down? Where is it?"

"It's here somewhere." Crystal went out to the hall. "Here." She handed Nickie a scrap of paper.

It said:

Dear Rachel and Nickie,

How is everything with you? Here it's work as usual. I am doing all right, though I miss you both.

Love, Dad

P.S. Nickie, I was thinking about that movie we went to for your ninth birthday. Wasn't it called "Snowblind"?

Nickie thought back to when she turned nine. She remembered it well. She and Kate and Sophy had gone ice-skating. There was no movie. So this confirmed it:

either her father was losing his mind, or he was sending a message in some sort of code. She would crack it. She was sure she could. She took the postcard messages into her bedroom, spread them out on the bed, and began to study them in earnest. And after a while, she had an idea about what the key to the code might be.

On Friday morning, Nickie awoke and instantly knew that she had to find out what had happened to Grover and his snakes. If he was still mad at her, too bad; she couldn't bear not to know.

Crystal said she was meeting Len for breakfast so they could discuss last-minute open-house details. "Want to come?" she said, and of course Nickie said no. As soon as Crystal had left, she ran upstairs to feed Otis and take him outside, and when that was done she headed for Grover's house.

It was very cold. Iron-gray clouds hung like a ceiling over the town. Main Street was strangely quiet. As usual, small clusters of people stood inside the stores with TVs on, but when Nickie glanced in, she didn't see the president on the screen. She couldn't tell what was on—it looked like an old movie of some kind. But she didn't stop to wonder about it. She was in a hurry.

Granny Carrie saw her coming. "You won't find him here," she said as Nickie came up the steps.

"I won't? Where is he?"

"Up in the woods somewheres. They came and clamped one of them bracelets on him this morning early, and he took off."

Nickie stood still where she was, with one foot on the porch and the other on the step. "A bracelet?"

"Yep," said Granny Carrie. She pressed her lips together. "*MMMMMM-mmmm-MMMMM-mmmm,*" she said, "Nasty thing."

"He didn't go to school?"

"I doubt it," said Granny Carrie. "With the noise that thing was making, they'd-a probably thrown him out."

"So he didn't let his snakes go, then," said Nickie.

"Said he didn't see why he should."

"How did they catch him? He said he'd run."

"Ambushed him," said Granny Carrie. "Teddy Crane and that old Bill Willard jumped on him from behind the garage when he set out for school. Then he ran off, and the two of them came here and told us what they'd done."

"I'm going to go find him," said Nickie.

"Better not," Granny Carrie said. "His pa's already gone up there after him. No point in you going. You don't know your way around in the woods. He could be anywhere."

"But that terrorist is in the woods," Nickie said.

"So I've heard," said Granny Carrie, frowning and rocking. "It does make a person worry. We've got a lot to worry about today." She waved a hand toward the window, from which came the sound of the TV. "That deadline the president set is up. We're waiting to hear if there's going to be war."

CHAPTER 22

An Indoor Universe

Nickie turned away from Grover's house with her mind whirling. The president's deadline! That's why people were gathered in the stores. They were waiting to hear his announcement. Why was an old movie on, though? Had they started the war without telling anyone? She glanced at the sky, almost expecting to see bombers streaking overhead.

She didn't know what to do. It was true that there was no point in trying to find Grover. Even if she did find him, how could she help? And she certainly couldn't keep a war from happening. Her Goal #3 seemed silly now—how could she possibly do anything to help the messed-up world? She was just a kid.

She walked down the road, hardly noticing where she was going, staring down at the pavement, kicking now and then at a rock. She thought of Grover, a humming bracelet clapped onto his wrist, fleeing up into the mountains, where probably a dangerous person was hiding out. She thought of Hoyt McCoy, accused by police of something he hadn't done. These things were her fault. Somehow she had done wrong by trying to do right.

She trudged on until she came to Raven Road, and there she turned left. She hadn't planned to go this way; her feet just seemed to carry her. When she got to Hoyt McCoy's driveway, her feet stopped. She stared at his "No Trespassing" sign. She gazed up the driveway, past the row of looming trees to the place where the drive curved around toward the house. Part of her wanted to hurry on past. But another part thought she should go in there and tell him she was sorry for what had happened. Was she brave enough? The very thought of it made her stomach shift and her hands get clammy. But she started up the driveway anyhow. She would just knock on his door, apologize very fast, and come away. She was brave enough for that.

The house was as dark and silent this time as it had been before. From a distance, she checked the gable window. It was closed. Nothing that looked like a gun or a telescope stuck out of any of the house's windows. This gave her courage. When she got closer, she realized Hoyt's car wasn't there. Good! Now if she just had a bit of paper and a pencil stub in her pocket, as she usually did—

But behind her she heard the sound of an engine

and the crackle of gravel. She turned, and there was Hoyt McCoy in his black car, coming toward her. He'd seen her, of course; she couldn't leave. So she waited, with her heart thudding.

"Ah," said Hoyt, getting out of the car. "The other trespasser."

Nickie managed to speak. "I—I came to say I'm sorry," she stammered, "about what happened."

"You mean the invasion of the Beeson Police?"

"Yes. Well, it was because . . . I thought you were going to . . . to shoot me."

"I do not shoot people," said Hoyt. He opened the rear door of the car and took out a battered suitcase. "I may not *like* people, but I do not shoot them."

"I just thought," said Nickie, "that you had a gun . . . you know, aiming out your window."

"And my question for *you* is this." Hoyt set down the suitcase, put his hands on his hips, and glared at her. "Why were you here, on my property, looking at my windows in the first place?"

Nickie had no answer for this question. It was no good to say she was trying to do the right thing. Deep down, she'd suspected that looking in windows and snooping around people's houses was probably more wrong than right, no matter what the reason for doing it. So she just stood there, staring down at the ground.

"But of course I *know* why," Hoyt McCoy went on. "Brenda Beeson sent you. Did she send the boy, too?"

"What boy?"

"The boy who sneaked behind my house a week ago. The boy who was lurking about when those cops tried to snatch me. Skinny boy, hair falling in his face."

"Oh, Grover. No, she didn't send him." For a second, the thought of Grover in the woods came to her; she pushed it away. "Well, I have to go now," she said. She'd done what she came to do.

"Wait one moment," said Hoyt McCoy.

Nickie's heart gave a bump.

"I have just returned from a tense encounter which I believe has had the result I hoped for. That puts me in a rather generous mood, rare for me." He walked up his front steps and turned to face her. "I'd like to show you," he said, "that a person may be gruff and somewhat on the sloppy side without being a madman or a criminal. But probably you would decline to step inside my house."

"Well, thank you very much," Nickie said, with her heart beating harder, "but I really have to go."

"I thought so," said Hoyt. "A wise choice, in general, though in this case unnecessarily cautious. Still, you might be willing just to look in from where you are." He took his keys from his pocket, opened the door, stepped in, and stood to the side, so that Nickie could look past him. She saw a wide hall. On either side was an arched opening that led to a room, and down at the end, the hall opened into still another room. Even though it was daytime, the windows were all covered with blinds and curtains; dim electric light bulbs filled the rooms with a yellowish gloom. Signs of careless housekeeping were everywhere: in the hall she saw stacks of books on the floor, clothes hanging from doorknobs, a table strewn with loose change and bits of hardware and scraps of paper. From what she could see of the other rooms, they were just as messy.

But why was he showing her all this? Shouldn't she turn around and run? She took a few steps backward—but somehow, curiosity held her there.

"I am not interested," said Hoyt, "in the dull daily world of chat and tidiness, of keeping up appearances, of being nice and polite and well groomed. No one who doesn't like my looks or my house need ever come near me, and that will suit me well. My world is the heavens, both by day and by night." He raised a hand and turned slightly. "Watch," he said.

Nickie heard the snap of a switch. Instantly, the lights in the house went out, leaving a darkness that would have been complete except for the light from the open front door. Again a bolt of fear shot through her, and she skittered backward a few more steps. Was he going to come out from his strange den and grab her? But a moment later she stood still again, because she saw something happening in the darkness.

The walls and the ceiling had begun to glow. Gradually, they changed from black to a deep midnight blue, as if they were made not of plaster but of glass, like a television screen. Tiny points of light appeared, first just a few here and a few there, and then more and more, until the signs of an untidy daily life receded into shadows, and the rooms of Hoyt McCoy's house became star-spangled chambers of night.

"The effect is better, of course, if the front door isn't standing wide open," said Hoyt. "You may come in and see if you like, but if you're still afraid of me I won't insist."

Nickie just stood there, staring and speechless.

"It took quite a while to customize this house," Hoyt said. "People used to peer over the fence wanting to see how I was remodeling. They were dismayed when the house looked exactly the same after the work was done as before." He laughed—a dry *heh-heh.* "The heavens are my habitat," he said. "Also my job, though as a rule I do not speak of it."

This reminded Nickie of what Grover had said. "Do you crack open the sky?" she asked.

Hoyt raised his eyebrows. "Who told you that?"

"Grover. He said he saw it."

"Ah, yes, so he did." Hoyt smiled dryly. "He's an observant sort. Most people simply write it off as lightning."

"What is it, then?"

"Not something I choose to speak of at this time," said Hoyt. "I have been extraordinarily busy these last few days, involved in some very delicate, high-level conversations. Right now I am satisfied but exhausted. Far too exhausted to explain anything."

"Well," said Nickie, pointing in through the door, "all that is really beautiful." It was. It was as if Hoyt's front door had become a porthole to the universe. She longed to step inside and see it up close, have it surround her, as if she were floating in space. But she still didn't feel quite brave enough. If only Hoyt had been like a kindly old uncle, then she would have. But he was so big and rumpled and shaggy and grouchy—she was still afraid of him, though it did begin to seem that she needn't be.

"Thank you," she said. "I love seeing it. Is it the whole universe?"

"Oh, no," said Hoyt. "Just a small portion of one universe, ours. If I had several billion more houses, I might have room for a few other universes as well."

Other universes. Nickie thought of her great-grandfather's notes. But she could barely get the idea of one universe into her mind, to say nothing of others. "I'd like to see it," she said. "But . . . maybe I'll come some other time."

"Simply ring the bell," said Hoyt. "Trespassers are not welcome. Certain selected visitors are. You may include yourself among them." With a brief nod—no smile—he closed the door, and the universe disappeared.

Back at Greenhaven, Nickie wandered through the house, too stirred up to settle to anything. She gazed at the ancestors in their gold frames; she ran her fingers along the curves of the banister; she stared at her reflection in the great dining room mirror. Up in the nursery, she rocked in the rocking chair beneath the glow of the lamp, holding Otis on her lap and running her hand from his head to his tail, over and over.

Around four-thirty, when Crystal still wasn't back from wherever she was, she took Otis down for his afternoon outing. To her surprise, there were people on the street, walking as if they had an appointment somewhere.

Quickly, she took Otis back upstairs and came down again. As she went out the front door, she saw Martin among the people passing. She ran up to him. "What's happening?"

"You didn't hear?" Martin looked down his nose at Nickie. "There's a meeting. Mrs. Beeson called it. She wants to speak to everyone. It's urgent. You should come—it's at the church."

"Do you know what it's about?" Nickie asked.

"No," said Martin. "But it must be important." He set off down the sidewalk again. "You should come," he said again, over his shoulder. "And your aunt, too."

Crystal wouldn't be interested; Nickie was sure of

that. But she herself would go, of course. She had to know what the meeting was about. She dashed back into the house to get her jacket—the sun was down now, and the temperature was dropping—and then she joined the flow of people moving toward the church.

CHAPTER 23

The Emergency Meeting

From the uphill and downhill neighborhoods, people converged on Main Street—frowning, worried-looking men, mothers holding the hands of young children, older children following along, unusually quiet. Everyone was unusually quiet, in fact; when they spoke at all, it was in low voices, just to exchange a few questions: What's this about, do you know? Have no idea. Must be something serious. Maybe something new from the Prophet. Maybe so. They hurried past the dark windows of the stores, which had closed early, down past the deserted park, down toward the very end of Main Street—a stream of people, almost all the citizens of Yonwood. Though not quite all, Nickie remembered. Hoyt McCoy wouldn't be here, and Grover wouldn't, because he was up in the woods somewhere, and no doubt there were a few other

Yonwood citizens who didn't come when Brenda Beeson called.

But certainly most of the town was now pouring into the narrow, upright building that was the Church of the Fiery Vision. Once Nickie got past the crush of people at the door, she saw a long room filled with rows of wooden pews. High in the walls were windows of stained glass, but because the sky outside was growing dark, she couldn't make out the pictures in them. The light inside the church was dim, too. It came from candles placed in dozens of spots around the room. They lit up the aisles and the seats, but the space above, up to the ceiling, was a gulf of darkness.

Quickly and quietly, people filed into the pews and sat down. Nickie sat toward the back. Then came long moments when nothing happened. People whispered and rustled, waiting. At last a door opened behind the pulpit, and Mrs. Beeson came out. She climbed up the steps to the pulpit and stood there looking out at the crowd. The whispering immediately died down.

There was no hat of any kind today. Mrs. Beeson's hair was fluffed out in a cloud around her head, and she wore a red dress with her round blue Tower button pinned to the front. She stood looking out at them in silence for a long time, her eyes flitting from one face to another. At last she spoke. There was a wave of creaks and rustles as everyone leaned forward to hear.

"Well, friends," she said, "we're in a dark time."

There was a murmur of agreement from the crowd.

"Our Prophet has seen a dreadful disaster in the world's future. It could be the war that might be coming. It could have to do with the terrorist in our woods."

The crowd murmured again.

"But she's also tried to tell us how to be safe from this disaster. I call that a miracle. It's like being taken under God's wing."

Mrs. Beeson smiled, and Nickie could tell that the people in the room were feeling that smile's warm glow.

"And so most of us," Mrs. Beeson went on, "have done our best to do what our Prophet tells us to do. It's not always easy to know what that is. Sometimes the Prophet says things that even I can't interpret. She says 'No words,' for example. Unless she means swear-words, which we don't say anyhow, I must admit I'm mystified. And there's something else she says that until now I've thought I must be hearing wrongly. But as danger comes closer, I'm forced to believe she means exactly what she says."

Mrs. Beeson paused. She stood still, her blue eyes scanning the crowd. She looked like a queen, Nickie thought, in her ruby red dress, with the light from the candles gilding her hair. The people in the church seemed to hold their breath.

Finally, Mrs. Beeson squared her shoulders and

spoke. "What I am about to say is for the good of us all," she said. "We must be obedient, whether we understand or not. God's ways are beyond our knowing." She paused again, for a long time. Tension twisted in Nickie's stomach. People sat so still that the whole room was utterly silent.

When Mrs. Beeson spoke next, her voice was hardly above a whisper, but it was so fierce that you could hear every word. "Althea has said it over and over, but I haven't wanted to hear it. 'No dogs,' she says. 'No dogs.' It's quite clear. Somehow, our dogs are standing in the way."

"What?!" cried a woman a few rows up, but someone else shushed her.

Mrs. Beeson's voice rose. "Yes," she said. "I see it now. I see it in myself, in my own feelings for my little Sausage." She leaned forward, gripping the pulpit with both hands. "Why should we give an animal love that should go to our families? Why should we give an animal love that should go to God? We have to act, my dear friends. I know it's hard, but the dogs—all of them—must go."

Nickie's heart started rapid-fire beating. Dogs must go? What was she saying?

A clamor arose from the people in the church. Voices cried, What? and No! but Mrs. Beeson spread her arms out and stood like an angel about to rise. "Listen!" she cried.

Everyone grew silent again.

"It's painful, I know," she said. "But terrible times demand extraordinary sacrifices. Seems to me what the Prophet is saying to us is this: the more we say no to the things of the world, all those things we're too attached to, the more we can say yes to God. It's what I've told you before: when you have faith that you're right—you *know* it from the bottom of your soul—you're willing to do anything for it. Anything."

At that, the people grew silent again. A few stood up and left the church—one man shouted "She's wrong!" as he went out the door—but all the rest stayed. Nickie saw some of them look at each other with stern, brave looks and nod. Then they looked back at her again, waiting for instructions.

"It will be like this," she said. "The day after tomorrow, I will send a bus to all dog-owning households. You will put your dog aboard the bus, and the driver will take the dogs to a wild place many miles from here, where the dogs will be free to go back into nature, where they belong. No animal will be harmed, and we here in Yonwood will have followed our instructions to the letter. We will be free to love God with all our hearts."

Nickie felt as if she'd been set on fire. They won't take Otis, she thought. Never.

But she realized after a moment that she didn't have to worry about Otis. No one knew that Greenhaven was "a dog-owning household." The only people besides herself who knew about Otis were Amanda and Grover, and they wouldn't hurt him. She would keep him safe—she'd be extra super careful when she took him out to pee—and when the house was sold, she'd take him away with her, back to the city.

Because she knew now that she would fail at her Goal #1, which was to live at Greenhaven with her parents. She still loved Greenhaven, and Yonwood, too, but she no longer wanted to live in a place where Mrs. Beeson and her Prophet delivered instructions from God.

CHAPTER 24

The Bracelet

On Friday morning, as Grover was on his way to school, two men had jumped him as he passed the car-repair garage. They'd been standing behind a gate that led into an alley beside the building, and when Grover came past they simply stepped out into his path and blocked his way. Before he realized what was happening, each of them grabbed one of his arms. One of them whipped the bracelet out of his pocket, snapped it around Grover's right wrist, clicked a button on a remote control, and the bracelet was activated. It started up its noise: *MMMM-mmmm-MMMMM-mmmmm.*

He wrenched free and ran, but by then, of course, it was too late. The noise screamed from his wrist. He shook his arm as if the thing were a scorpion biting him, as if it were a cloud of bees attacking, but there was no stopping it. Get away, get away, was all he could think. He ran around the far side of his house and down Woodfield Road, where there were fewer people, though the few he passed stared at him in horror. He didn't look at them. Get away, get away. He ran past the school, staying far out at the edge of the playing fields, past the end of Main Street, where the windows of the Cozy Corner Café were still dark, and then, all the time with the noise streaming out behind him like a kite tail, he ran up the path into the woods.

When he'd run uphill for ten minutes or so, he stopped. The whine of the bracelet—*MMMM-mmmm-MMMMM-mmmmm*—zinged around his head like a monster mosquito. He had to do something about it. Though the morning was cold, he was warm from running. So he took off his jacket and the sweatshirt he was wearing underneath it. He put his jacket back on, and he wrapped the sweatshirt around his wrist, tying it as tightly as he could by the sleeves. It made his arm into a sort of club, with a great lump at the end. The sound was deadened, but not silenced. He could still hear it, and of course anyone walking in the woods—human or animal—would be able to hear it, too. So he unwound the sweatshirt. He took off his jacket and his T-shirt, put his jacket back on (because he wouldn't be able to once he'd made his hand into a club), and wrapped the T-shirt around the bracelet as a first layer. Then he wrapped the sweatshirt around that. This made a wad as big as a soccer ball. His arm looked like a giant lollipop. It might make a good weapon, he thought. Too bad Teddy Crane and Bill Willard weren't around for him to clobber.

The double wrapping muted the noise of the bracelet down to a faint hum. It was good enough. Grover strode on.

What he was going to do he didn't know. He had no plan, other than to escape the town and all the pitying, tut-tutting faces that would be trained on him—people on the street, his teachers, the other kids at school. No. He would figure out a way to get the thing off. He wouldn't go home until he had.

He climbed fast, fueled by rage. After half an hour or so, he came to the place he'd been a few days before, where the path led down to the stream. This was a good spot to stop for a moment, he thought. He was thirsty. He'd have a drink.

As he knelt by the stream and splashed water into his mouth with his left hand, he remembered the person he'd seen moving through the woods when he was last here—the pale patch off in the distance. For a second, with water dripping down his chin, he stopped moving and listened for footsteps. But as soon as he wasn't making the noise of footsteps himself, crunching over twigs, rustling in the leaves, all he could hear was the thin whine of the bracelet, sounding through its wrappings: *MMMM-mmmm-MMMMM-mmmmm,* like a faraway siren.

So he wiped his wet hand on his pants and walked on. He thought of singing really loud to cover up the noise. But if there *was* some evil person lurking up here, singing would just attract his attention. He tried to tune his ears to the tweeting of the birds instead.

The path wound up the mountainside. Every now and then he came to a place where the trees thinned out and he had a view over the town below. School would have started by now. They'd notice he wasn't there. Would Bill and Teddy have gone to his house after they'd clapped the bracelet on him and told his parents? Would anyone come looking for him?

By midday, he was close to the top of the ridge, and he was starting to feel hungry. He happened to have a couple of stale crackers in his jacket pocket, so he ate those. But it wasn't much of a lunch. At this season of the year, he wouldn't be able to find much in the woods that he could eat. The berries would be gone, and although there were lots of mushrooms, he didn't know enough about them to tell the edible ones from the poisonous. He'd just have to be hungry for a while, that's all. Good thing he'd had a big breakfast.

When he came to a small open field, he decided to stop for a while and attack the bracelet. There was a shelf of rock at the edge of the field, large and low. Here he sat down. He unwrapped the sweatshirt from around his wrist, and then the T-shirt. The hideous noise wailed out into the air. Grover winced. It was like having skewers poked in his ears.

The bracelet was a flat metal band about a quarter of an inch thick, a dull silver color. There was a small hinge at one point on it, and a couple of grooves that went all the way around. The sound came from inside, but Grover couldn't see any way of getting at it—no switch or slot or sliding panel.

Maybe he could just slip the thing off. He curled his hand into a tube shape and tried to work the bracelet over his knuckles—but it wouldn't go. He slipped the fingers of his left hand under it and pulled as hard as he could, hoping to break the hinge, but all he accomplished was to make the edge of the bracelet dig into his skin. In furious frustration, he banged the bracelet against the rock, but the silver surface of it was barely even scratched. The noise went on without a pause, *MMMM-mmmm-MMMMM-mmmmm,* making him want to scream.

One more try. He found a rock about the size of a baseball and, placing his wrist on the bigger rock, smashed at the bracelet over and over. After five minutes of pounding, he'd made a tiny dent in the bracelet's surface and a sizable scrape on his hand. With a yell, he flung the rock away and gave up. He put the wrappings back on his wrist. Failure.

He lay back on the warm rock and stared at the

sky, where a hawk was circling far, far above. What had he done wrong? Nothing. Who was he hurting? No one. So why was he being tortured? He didn't know. Had Althea Tower muttered something about snakes? Was there a law against snakes in some holy book? He didn't know. And he didn't know what he could do about any of it.

Stymied, he closed his eyes. The sun shone on him, and he grew sleepy and dozed off.

When he woke up, he could see that it was late afternoon. The shadows of the trees crept across the field, and the air had grown chillier. Grover felt bleak. What was he going to do when night came? What would he do tomorrow? He was hungry, and he was cold, too, because with his T-shirt and his sweatshirt wrapping up his wrist, all he had on was a flannel shirt and his jacket. Which was better, to be warm and have that noise screaming at him, or be cold and without the noise? He decided to be cold, at least for the moment.

For the first time, he realized that he was going to spend the night up here. He hadn't really thought about it before, when all he wanted was to get away. But he saw that he would have to. Darkness would fall before he could get down the trail—and he didn't want to be back in town anyway.

So he'd better use the daylight that was left to get ready. He'd make himself some sort of den to sleep in, and he'd look as hard as he could for some nuts or shriveled-up berries to eat.

First the den. He wanted to be in among the trees, not out in the open. So he crossed to the west side of the field and made his way into the thicket of undergrowth, stamping down brush and breaking off twigs that got in his way. It was like burrowing through barbed wire, he thought, so many stickers and scratchers. Underfoot, the ground was leaf-littered and rocky and uneven. And damp. It wasn't a great place for a campout.

But after creeping around for a while, he found a sort of scooped-out place in the ground surrounded by a group of pines. The pine needles were thick on the ground, and he mounded them up to make a mattress. This wouldn't be too bad, he thought. Now for food.

A few rays of sunlight still fell across the top of the mountain and lit up the trees on the other side of the field. Grover started to make his way out of the woods, back through the brush the way he'd come. But just as he got to the edge of the clearing, he saw, within the trees on the opposite side, something white moving.

He stood still. The trees would hide him, he thought, if he didn't move. If only he had binoculars! His heart began a quick, steady thudding. Could the terrorist hear the faint hum of the bracelet?

The white patch moved slowly. It seemed to be coming toward the clearing. Grover held his breath. He squinted, trying to see more clearly in the failing light. The white patch moved, stood still, moved again, and at last came out from the shelter of the trees and into the field.

And Grover's heart gave a great lurch. This terrorist was not human. And it was not a terrorist, either. It was a bear. A white bear—something Grover had never seen nor heard of.

The bear came out into the field. It walked with a lopsided motion, as if maybe one of its feet hurt. Its nose was down; its head swung slightly from side to side. Its coat, Grover could see, was not pure white at all. It was a dirty cream color, smudged with gray.

It came closer. Grover held his breath. He didn't really think the bear would attack him. He'd caught sight of bears up here before, and he knew that the main thing was not to take the bear by surprise. Make a noise, let it know you were there, and it would turn around and shuffle off. Still, he was nervous. It was almost night, he was all alone, and he was making a strange noise the bear would soon start to hear.

And as soon as he had that thought, the bear lifted its head. It stopped moving and looked straight toward Grover. The last rays of the sun shone on its small round ears, turning them pink.

So Grover did what he knew he should do. He stepped out from the trees and stood in the open. He raised his right arm, so that the humming ball at the end of it stood up in the air like a stop sign. In as strong a voice as he could muster, he called out: "Bear! Here I am! I'm your friend, not your dinner!"

They stared at each other. Grover saw that the bear's nose was a pale tan, and its eyes shone in the slanting sunlight like little rubies. He called out again, waving his arm. "I see what you are!" he said. "You should get away from here! You're not safe!"

And as if it understood, the bear turned away. It didn't hurry. It turned around and trundled back the way it had come. In a few minutes, it had gone into the woods and disappeared.

Grover slept that night on his cushion of pine needles. He covered himself with more pine needles, and he used the wad around his wrist as a pillow. The bracelet whined in his ear and, when he finally fell asleep, made its way into his dreams as a screaming jet plane diving toward him and swooping away, over and over. When he awoke in the morning, he was very cold and very hungry, and he knew there was nothing to do but go home. At least it was Saturday; no one would try to make him go to school.

CHAPTER 25

The Open House

The house looked beautiful on Saturday morning. Its floors were polished, its paint was bright, and the pieces of furniture that remained were the finest antiques of the lot, and dust-free. Big vases stood here and there, with artistically arranged pine branches and bare twigs arching out of them.

Now Crystal was scuttling among the downstairs rooms, looking for anything that might discourage a buyer. Was there a crack in the plaster? Cover it with an antique portrait in a gold frame! A scuffed place on the floor? Put a Persian rug there! She puttered and fussed, fixed and fidgeted, talking the whole time. "The Tiffany lamp! Here would be the perfect spot. And wait, these cushions . . . Nickie, would you get those green ones from the middle bedroom? That's better. Really, it's looking good. Except for . . . hold on a sec . . . maybe the leather-topped game table over here . . . Help me move it, Nickie."

Over an hour went by, during which Nickie could not stop thinking about Otis two floors above, needing his breakfast, needing to go outside, ready any second to start whining or barking. But Crystal, for once, wasn't in a hurry.

At ten o'clock, she turned on the radio. "There ought to be some news," she said. She stopped dashing around and sat down to listen. Nickie listened, too. "We are expecting an announcement from the White House at any moment," said the newscaster. "The president's deadline ran out yesterday, but so far there has been no word on the status of the situation."

They kept listening, but no announcement came. There was a report about an earthquake somewhere, and a riot somewhere else, and then something about two movie stars getting married, and finally the announcer came back on and said that there was still no news about the tense international situation and that people should stay tuned.

"It's odd," said Crystal, flicking off the radio. "But at least it's not war. Not yet."

She went back to work. For another half hour, she wandered around adding final touches here and there. Finally she flopped down on the red plush sofa in the front parlor and surveyed what she had done. "Not bad," she said. She checked her watch. "Ten forty-two. We open at eleven. Len should be here any minute."

"Do you need me anymore?" Nickie asked.

"No, no," said Crystal, waving a hand. "You go off and play."

"Okay," Nickie said. "I just have to get some stuff from upstairs first."

Crystal nodded. She reached for a spray bottle and squirted a fine mist at a potted fern.

Nickie dashed up the stairs. Poor Otis, poor Otis; if he'd made a puddle on the floor, she wouldn't say a single scolding word. She burst through the door at the top of the stairs, closed it behind her, flung open the nursery door, and there was Otis scrambling backward, yelping and squealing with a desperate tone in his voice. He'd been standing right there, she could picture it, nose to the place where the door would open, waiting for her. She scanned the room. Only one small puddle, which she quickly mopped up.

"Okay, Otis," she said, "just a couple more minutes. I'll be really quick." Otis jumped up and down beside her leg. "I know you're hungry, but we have to get out of here first. You have to be *incredibly quiet.*"

She hooked Otis's leash to his collar and wound it once around his muzzle so he couldn't bark. Then she picked him up and carried him down the hall and down the stairs. She paused at the second floor, listening for Crystal. Heard nothing. Went down the next flight to the door that led to the hall behind the kitchen. Listened again. This time she heard voices.

"Looks great!" said Len's voice. "You do, too."

"Well, thanks! You're such a sweetie."

That was Crystal. They were by the front door, Nickie thought. Good. She darted into the kitchen, grabbed an apple and a muffin from a bowl on the table, opened the door to the back garden, and shouted, "Bye, I'm leaving! Good luck!" Before anyone even answered, she shut the door behind her and took off.

It was not a beautiful day for a walk. Gray clouds hung low and dark in the sky, and the air was cold enough to bite. Nickie had on her warmest jacket and a thick knitted scarf around her neck and a knitted hat that came down over her ears, and she was still chilly. She'd warm up as she walked, probably, but it would be nice if the wind would die down. She snuggled Otis's head up under her chin.

At the end of the block, she went around the corner, turned onto Fern Street, and started up the path that led in among the trees. A few yards along, she stopped and set Otis down on the ground. Instantly, he pulled the leash tight, making a beeline for the base of a tree, where he lifted his back leg and sent a stream of pee against the bark. "Good boy," said Nickie. Suddenly she felt happy and free. The cold didn't matter. The woods stretched before her, mysterious, unexplored. No danger of running into the dog-napping Prophet out here, or any of her spies. And if there was a terrorist wandering around in the woods—well, if she saw him, she'd just hide, that's all.

So they hiked, Nickie striding along on legs that felt strong and glad to be exercised, and Otis zigzagging across the path from one fascinating smell to the next. The ground crackled underfoot—icy dead leaves, brittle twigs, dirt hardened by cold. In all directions stood the endless ranks of gray-brown tree trunks, their bare branches making a dense weave that reminded her of the crosshatched writing on the old letter. Wind rattled the branches against each other, and here and there a few last rags of leaf fell down.

It was a little after eleven o'clock. In a while, she'd find a place to sit, and she'd eat the muffin and the apple she had with her. But now all she wanted to do was walk, and walk fast.

The trail wound back and forth, always sloping upward, but never very steep. Most of the time, all Nickie could see was the deep forest on both sides, but after a while she came to a clearing where the trees thinned out on the downhill side, and she could look down the mountain and see the roofs of the town below. It looked small and peaceful from here. No people were visible. She tried to make out which house was Greenhaven, but she couldn't tell. It made her a little sad, this view of Yonwood, the place where she had been sure she wanted to live. In her imagination, it had been so perfect—peaceful and beautiful, safe from the troubles of the cities. If someone had told her then that Yonwood was working to battle the forces of evil by building a shield of goodness, she would have been happy to hear it. Those things were exactly what she wanted. How strange that it could all turn out so differently.

She walked on. It wasn't a steady walk, because Otis had to stop every few yards and thrust his nose beneath a bush or into the leaf litter that covered the ground. Some spots were so interesting that he had to snuffle in them for quite a while. During these times, Nickie stood still and gazed around her. Birds flitted among the branches, twittering in a muted way. Overhead, clouds moved slowly across the sky, so the forest was sometimes in shadow, sometimes in sunlight. When the sun shone down, crystals of frost and patches of ice glistened like glass.

When she'd walked for an hour or so, she started thinking it was time to rest, and time to eat. She looked for somewhere to sit down. A few yards farther on she came to a fallen tree that lay alongside the trail, covered in a tangle of brown stickery vines and furred with green moss along the top. She tore the vines away to make a clear space, and she tied her end of Otis's leash to the stump of a branch sticking up from the log. Then she sat down, took the muffin and the apple out of her paper bag, and ate them both, except for the last chunk of muffin, which she gave to Otis. She crushed the paper bag into a ball and stuck it in her pocket.

That was when she heard the footsteps. There was no mistaking them—firm and steady, a tramp, tramp, tramp that came from above her on the trail, not far distant. Nickie's heart started racing. Could she duck behind a tree? Crouch down behind this fallen log? But Otis had heard the footsteps, too, and after a moment of cocking his head and pricking up his ears, he let out a string of loud barks. So there was no use hiding. Whoever was coming would have heard them already. He would come around the bend in a moment and see them, and Nickie would just have to hope that if it was a terrorist or some other sort of wild person, he would have more important things on his mind than a girl eating lunch.

So she sat frozen on the log and waited, and in a few seconds the person came around the bend, and it wasn't a terrorist; it was Grover.

"Hey!" he cried when he saw her. He stopped and stared. Then he made a face of extreme horror, pulling down the corners of his mouth and making his eyes bulge out. "Aaaaaiiieee!" he yelled. "It's a terrifying terrorist! And a savage monster! Save me, save me!"

"Stop that," said Nickie. Relief swept through her, and she grinned.

Otis bounded over to Grover and stood up against his legs, and Grover stooped to pet him—with his left hand, because his right hand was bundled up in a clump of clothes. When he came closer, Nickie could hear the hum of the bracelet: *MMMM-mmmm-MMMMM-mmmmm.*

"Can I see it?" she said.

"Five dollars per view," said Grover.

"Come on."

So he unwrapped his wrist, and the noise came out loud and shrill in the cold air. Nickie peered at the thing. "It's awful," she said. "You can't break it with a rock or anything?"

"Not without breaking my arm, too. I tried." He wrapped it up again. "What are you doing here?"

"It's the open house today," Nickie said. "I have to keep Otis away. Not just because of the open house, but the Prophet, too."

Grover sat down on the log. "Why?"

Nickie told him what Mrs. Beeson had said. "It's tomorrow. She's going to take all the dogs away."

Grover responded to this by rearing backward and nearly falling off the log, as if knocked off balance by astonishment. "I am stunned," he said.

"Me too," said Nickie. "You don't think she could be right, do you? That dogs take up too much love? Which should go to God?"

"I don't think so," said Grover, sitting up straight again. Otis sniffed at his wrist, which hummed faintly. "I really don't think so."

"But Otis is all right because nobody knows about him. Hardly anybody. You do, but you wouldn't tell, would you?"

"Nope," said Grover. He rumpled Otis's ears. "Guess what?" he said.

"What?"

"I saw the terrorist."

"Not *really,*" said Nickie. "Did you?"

"I did." He told her about the bear. "It was an albino," he said. "I'm pretty sure it was, because I've never heard of a white bear. Except polar bears, and there aren't any in North Carolina." He looked thoughtful, and a little sad. "I told it to go away," he said, "for its own good. People here don't like things that are different."

"Was it beautiful?" Nickie said.

"Not really. It was sort of dirty-looking. It had smudges on it. And it was limping."

"Were you afraid?" Nickie asked.

But Grover didn't answer. He was staring into space with his eyebrows raised. "I just thought of something," he said.

"What?"

"The broken window. I bet it was the bear. Put its foot through the glass."

"You mean at the restaurant?"

"Right. Snatched up that chicken and snagged the napkin with a claw, I bet. And that blood. She said it was an *R*, but I always thought it was just a blot. It was bear blood. Bet you anything."

He explained, and Nickie listened. "Bear blood," she said wonderingly. "No one guessed."

They sat without talking for a few moments. The bracelet hummed beneath its wrappings.

"You have to get that thing off you," said Nickie. "What are you going to do?"

Grover stood up. The wind was blowing harder now, and dark clouds were coming in from the east. "It doesn't matter about my snakes, I guess. I can let them go. I studied them a lot already. And in the summer, when I leave, I was going to let them go anyway."

Nickie looked up in surprise. "You mean you made enough money?"

"I will," said Grover. "I made ninety-seven words out of 'Sparklewash for Dishes.' That ought to be enough to win."

They walked back down the trail together. Grover talked about albino animals most of the way—how rare they were, how he'd never heard of an albino bear before, how some people had considered them sacred in other times and places. Nickie listened with half her attention. A sadness had come over her. She was sad that Grover probably wasn't going to win his contest and go on his expedition, and she was sad that Greenhaven might have a new owner by now, some stranger who wouldn't love it as she did. She felt tired, and sad, and cold.

Overhead, the clouds had gathered and darkened, filling in the whole sky.

"Looks like it's going to snow," said Grover.

CHAPTER 26

Catastrophe

“How was the open house?” Nickie asked.

“Lovely,” said Crystal.

“And did anyone want to buy the house?”

“Well, we have an offer,” said Crystal. She didn’t sound as happy as Nickie thought she would.

“From who?”

“A couple named Hardesty. Retired, children grown. Looking to start a senior health center. Vitamins, herbal remedies, exercise equipment. A library with books about how to cope with hair loss and stiff joints and swollen ankles and that sort of thing.” Crystal looked dispirited. “I don’t love the idea,” she said. “But they offered a good price, and they’re ready to sign as soon as they sell their house in the city. I called your mother about it. She thinks we should accept.”

So it was over. Goal #1 lost—no hope at all. Once again, that night Nickie crept upstairs after Crystal had gone to sleep and spent the night in the nursery with Otis. He curled up close under her chin. His fur smelled of the woods.

In the morning, Nickie got up while the sky was still dark. She took Otis out, stood with him in the cold while he did what he needed to do, and took him back upstairs. Then she climbed into the bed in her regular room to wait for the light.

As soon as a gray streak showed in the gap between the curtains, Nickie got up and got dressed. She moved quietly. In the chilly kitchen, she made herself some toast and drank a glass of milk. Then she went out to see what was going to happen when Mrs. Beeson's helpers came to get the dogs.

She didn't know when or where the dog pickups would start—but as it turned out, it was easy to find them. As soon as she got down the hill, she saw a school bus moving slowly down Main Street. There were no children in it. At Trillium Street, it turned right. A blue van behind it made the same turn; on the van's side, in white letters, was printed "Church of the Fiery Vision." In the front seat, next to the driver, Nickie saw Mrs. Beeson. Other people were in the van, too. It was full.

Nickie followed the bus, walking fast.

The bus and the van pulled up at a small brown house. Out of the van climbed Mrs. Beeson and several men, including all four of Yonwood's police officers. One of the policemen knocked on the front door of the house.

A man came to the door, leading a medium-sized brown-and-white spaniel. He patted the dog twice and then went quickly back inside and shut the door. The policeman led the dog to the bus and lifted it inside. Everyone got back in the van, and it moved on.

This is how it went—Nickie followed and watched it all. Other people trailed after the bus, too; she saw Martin among them, nodding sternly as he watched the dogs being collected. How could she ever have thought she liked him?

All around her, people commented on what was happening. Most of them had decided, it seemed, that Mrs. Beeson was doing the right thing. "It's hard, of course," said a stout middle-aged woman in a green knit hat. "But doing the right thing just *is* hard sometimes, isn't it? I don't have a dog myself, but if I did, I'd give it up in a heartbeat."

A bald man in round glasses nodded. "I know a lot of people who had trouble with this," he said, "but once they made the decision, they were proud of themselves. They felt *strong,* you know what I mean?"

Nickie thought of how giving up hot chocolate had made her feel: strong, yes, and proud of herself for doing a hard thing. But how could you feel that way about your dog, who was going to be thrown out into the cold? It wasn't just *you* giving something up; you were making the dogs give up their home, and maybe their lives.

The woman in the green hat nodded. "We have to trust in our Prophet and put aside our own selfish feelings," she said. "For the good of all."

But it was hard for Nickie to see the good in what was going on. At each dog-owning household, the bus stopped, the police went to the door, knocked, and then waited while the people inside put the leash on their dog and brought him or her out. Some people put on a brave or saintly face like the first man: they simply patted the dog once or twice on the head and then went back inside and closed the door and did not watch the men lead the dog away. At other houses, there were scenes, especially if children lived there. Loud crying came from inside, and some children even broke away from their parents and ran out and grabbed their dog's collar, screaming, "No, no, you can't take him!" and the policeman had the sad duty of uncurling the fingers from the collar, and the parents had to wrestle the child back inside. A very few families refused to open their doors at all. Mrs. Beeson wrote down their addresses.

After about an hour, when a second and third bus had been added to the first to hold all the dogs, and a chorus of barking, whining, and howling came from the bus windows, Nickie began to tremble, as if she had a hard-beating heart in every part of her body. Her teeth chattered, but not just from the cold. Suddenly she couldn't stand it anymore. She ran, heading back home to get Otis and hide him where no one could find him, just in case, just in *case,* somehow the dog bus came to Greenhaven.

As she ran, she kept saying to herself, It's all right, it's all right, no one knows he's there, I have plenty of time, he's safe, no one knows about him, only Amanda and Grover, so he's all right. But still, the sound of barking and shouting followed her as she ran.

Crystal would probably be there. But Nickie didn't care anymore if Crystal found out about Otis. She'd have to find out soon anyway. It was time for her to know. And Crystal would help her hide him—wouldn't she? She wouldn't let him be taken away.

But when she got to Greenhaven, Crystal's car wasn't there. Where could she have gone? Out to breakfast? It didn't matter. Nickie raced up the path and bounded up the stone steps. She opened the front door and dashed inside and started up the stairs. And stopped short just before reaching the second floor, because there was Amanda, standing at the top of the stairs with Otis in her arms.

Nickie stared—but then relief swept through her. "Oh!" she said. "You thought of it, too!"

Amanda didn't move. "Thought of what?" she said. Otis licked her neck, and she lifted her chin to get away from his tongue.

"To hide Otis," said Nickie. "So they won't find him. Even though nobody knows he's here, it would be better—"

"They do know he's here," said Amanda. She still didn't move.

"Oh, no! They do? Then we have to hurry! How do they know? Come on, let's—"

"I told Mrs. Beeson," said Amanda in a cool, flat voice.

"You what?" Nickie's heart seemed to stop.

"I called her up and told her. Course I did. Did you think I'd want to mess up everything? Did you think I'd go against the Prophet?"

Nickie ran at Amanda and grabbed at Otis with both hands. Amanda pulled him away. "No!" she cried. "She said no dogs! I have to take him!"

"You can't take him!" Nickie reached again for Otis, who was now thrashing wildly in Amanda's grip, but Amanda darted to the side and turned her back, clutching Otis close to her chest, and when Nickie came at her again and grabbed her arm, she made a sudden ferocious twist, sending Nickie staggering across the floor, and turned back toward the stairway. Nickie got her balance and came after her.

When Amanda reached the top of the stairs,

Nickie was close behind. She could have pushed her. It would have been easy. Amanda would have dropped Otis, who'd have scrambled away, and she would have fallen down the whole length of those hard, polished steps. She might have broken bones. She might have been killed. The urge to push her was so strong that Nickie just barely kept herself from doing it. Instead she grabbed for Amanda's shirttail, Amanda jerked away, and Nickie fell back and sat down hard on the top step.

Before she could get up, Amanda was halfway down the stairs. Nickie followed, but Amanda was too far ahead. When Nickie reached the bottom step, Amanda was at the front door, throwing it open. When Nickie got to the front door, Amanda was racing down the path toward the sidewalk. And when Nickie made it to the sidewalk, Amanda was running as fast as she could toward the corner of Cloud and Trillium streets, where the blunt yellow nose of the school bus was just coming into view.

That was when the sobs came up in Nickie's throat and the tears flew from her eyes, and she kept running and crying, but only for half a block, because she could see the man coming down from the bus and Amanda running up to him and holding out Otis, and the man taking Otis into the bus. At that point Nickie stood still and screamed. Someone came out of a house and scowled at her. She screamed again. The bus moved on, turning a corner. She ran after it, crying so hard she could scarcely breathe, but it turned another corner and disappeared.

Two desperate urges arose in her: one was to find Amanda and choke her to death, and the other was to find Crystal and make her drive after the school bus, so she could get Otis back.

Finding Otis was more important than choking Amanda. But where was Crystal? Nickie stood in the street looking wildly around, rooted to the spot, trying to think what to do. Maybe Crystal had left her a note. She ran back to Greenhaven and dashed from room to room, but no note was there. Maybe Crystal was at the restaurant. With trembling hands, she fumbled through the phone book and found the number, but when she asked if Crystal was there, the person who answered said no. Finally she ran outside again and stood in the street. Could she run downtown and try to find the school bus and somehow bash her way into it and rescue Otis? She didn't know. She couldn't think. Her breath came in hiccupy sobs, and her heart was running like an engine out of control. She wailed; she couldn't help it—a long, wavery wail.

And at that moment, Crystal's car came around the corner. It drove up the street and pulled in at the curb, and instantly Nickie was beside it, pounding on the window, which Crystal rolled down.

"They've taken Otis!" Nickie cried. "Amanda—she

came—she *betrayed* me and stole Otis and he's in the bus with all the dogs! You have to help! Please, please! If we follow the bus, we could get him—"

Crystal gaped at her. She had a paper cup of coffee in her hand. A white bakery bag was on the seat beside her. "What in the world are you talking about?" she said.

"They're taking the *dogs*!" Nickie cried. "There's no time to explain! Please, please, can you just drive me? And I'll tell you about it while we go."

Nickie's frantic face must have persuaded Crystal. "All right," she said. "Jump in."

CHAPTER 27

The Chase

As fast as she could, in a few short sentences, Nickie told Crystal everything.

Crystal kept interrupting, turning to Nickie with wide eyes and a dropped jaw.

"You mean you've had a *dog* up there all this time?"

"There was a *girl* in the *closet*?"

"You've been *battling* the forces of *evil*?"

"She says dogs are doing *what*?"

But all Nickie wanted was to find out where the buses had gone. "Never mind, never mind," she said. She was still having trouble talking because of breathing so hard and shaking. "I'll tell you later. Go that way." She pointed down Cloud Street. "That's where Amanda gave— But then it turned the corner, I think onto Birch Street—and that was maybe five minutes ago, or ten, so I don't know where the bus is now."

Crystal headed down Cloud Street. "Where did this Prophet woman say they were going to take the dogs?"

"Into the woods, she said. Far away, into the woods where they belong, and then let them go so they can be wild the way they're supposed to be."

"Odd," said Crystal, driving through the neighborhood as fast as possible without actually squealing the tires. "Dogs haven't been wild for several hundred thousand years. Not most dogs, anyway. They need us."

"And we need them!" Nickie wailed. "I need Otis!"

They curved up onto Spruce Street but saw nothing. No one was in the street. A few snowflakes sifted down from the sky and landed on the car's windshield. Crystal put on the wipers. She headed down Grackle Street and turned onto Main Street.

Nickie shouted, "Look!" and pointed ahead. Far down at the other end of Main Street was a patch of bright yellow. "The bus!"

But a moment later it turned off Main Street and was gone.

"It went to the right," said Nickie. "That's High Peak Road; it goes up the mountain. So that means they've finished collecting the dogs, and they're taking them away. Can we go faster?"

Crystal stepped on the gas. "If we *do* catch up to the buses," she said, "what happens next?"

"We just follow them till they stop." Nickie was

leaning forward, both hands gripping the dashboard. "Then when they let the dogs out, we grab Otis."

"What about everybody else's dogs?"

"I don't know. I wish we could save them, too."

"What if the people on the bus refuse to let us have Otis?"

"I don't know, I don't know," said Nickie. "Let's just go really fast."

They turned up High Peak Road. It was a narrow, winding road, with the ranks of trees standing close on either side. The snow was falling faster now, whirling toward them, making it hard to see. Crystal slowed down. There was no sign of the buses.

"I don't know," said Crystal. "This might not be a good idea."

Nickie said nothing. She kept her eyes glued forward, staring through the spinning whiteness. How would Otis survive in a snowstorm? He was little. He didn't know how to get his own food.

Crystal glanced over at her. "Why didn't you tell me about this dog before?"

"I thought you'd take him to the pound. You said you would."

"I did?" Crystal shook her head. "So you've been getting fond of him all this time, haven't you?"

Nickie nodded. Tears came to her eyes again, and she couldn't speak.

"I don't get it," Crystal said. "This Prophet woman

says the love you give a dog is subtracted from the love you give God. Have I got that right?"

Nickie nodded. The sky was growing darker as afternoon turned to evening. The shadows in the woods were so thick she could no longer see between the trees.

"So would that apply to cats, too, I wonder? Parakeets? Hamsters? Undeserving people? How do you decide what's okay to love, according to the Prophet?"

"I don't know," said Nickie. She didn't want to talk about this now. She just wanted Crystal to hurry up. The car was going slowly around the curves. Crystal had turned on the headlights, but they brightened the spiraling snow more than the road ahead. Nickie's neck hurt from craning forward, trying to see.

"Love is love, seems to me," said Crystal. "As long as what you love isn't armed robbery, or bombing airplanes, or kidnapping little children."

"Can we go faster?" Nickie asked.

"Not without sliding off the road." Crystal shook her head. "We're going to have to give this up, I think. It's dangerous." She slowed down even more to go around a bend in the road, and then suddenly she stamped on the brakes and the car slid sideways. Careening toward them out of the blinding whiteness was something big and yellow.

"The bus!" screamed Nickie. "It's coming down!"

Crystal pulled over and stopped. Behind the first bus was another one, and another, each one furred with white on top. They passed by and trundled on downhill.

"But are the dogs still in there?" Nickie said. "Or did they let them out?"

Crystal pulled the car back out onto the road. "My guess is that those bus drivers didn't want to drive in this weather any more than I do. I bet they just dumped the dogs and turned around."

"Then let's keep going!" Nickie cried, bouncing frantically in her seat. "We can find them!"

Crystal drove on, but she was frowning at the road and going slower than ever. After about ten minutes, they came to a place where the trees thinned out, and on the right was an open field, lightly dusted with snow. Nickie could see a dark mush of tire tracks here. "Stop!" she cried. "I think this is where the buses turned around. Can we get out and see?"

"We're turning around, too," said Crystal, but she stopped the car. Nickie flung the door open and jumped out. She ran toward the tire tracks and scanned the field. At the far edge, where the forest resumed, she saw something moving. A dog—no, two dogs, or three—leaping across the snow-dusted ground, heading for the trees.

"Otis!" Nickie shouted, though the dogs she saw

were too big to be Otis. "Otis, Otis, come! Come back!"

But the dogs disappeared into the woods. If they heard her at all, they paid no attention. It was just an adventure to them, a thrilling freedom—at least at first. They didn't understand yet that there were no food bowls in the woods, no warm fires, no people.

Crystal came up and stood beside her.

"I want to go after them," Nickie said. "Will you wait for me? I'll just run across there and call Otis again from where he can hear me—"

"We've got a snowstorm starting up," Crystal said, "and it's almost dark. I can't let you go plunging around in the woods. I'm afraid we're too late."

"No!" cried Nickie. "It's just over there," she said, pointing across the wide field to where the trees made a dark line in the distance. "Otis!" she screamed again.

But nothing moved out in the field, and the snow whirled faster, filling the air, until the trees had vanished behind a blur of white.

"We have to go," said Crystal. Her voice was sad and kind.

All the way back down the mountain, Nickie said hardly a word. She sat staring through the passenger-side window at the tree trunks ghostly in the snow, knowing it was too dark to see anything moving among them, but unable to make her eyes look anywhere else. She felt as if a hundred stones had collected inside her.

Crystal pulled up outside Greenhaven. "I'm sorry about this, sweetie," she said. "I just had no idea any of this was going on. How could I not have known it?"

"You were busy," said Nickie. "With other things." She was so tired all of a sudden. She barely had the strength to open the car door.

But even after they got inside, Crystal kept asking questions, and Nickie kept having to explain things, and then they had to have something to eat, which Nickie wasn't hungry for at all, and Crystal had to talk about how strange it was that no word had come from the president about whether there was going to be war. It seemed like forever before Nickie could get into bed and close her eyes. And of course by then she wasn't sleepy anymore. She lay there thinking about Otis out in the snowstorm, cold and hungry and alone. She thought about the white bear, which might eat small dogs. She thought about Mrs. Beeson, who was trying to do good and was causing so much pain, and about Althea Tower, the Prophet, whose vision had started everything. And she thought about what she herself had done, and at that she buried her face in the pillow and tried not to think at all. "I want my mother," she whispered, "and my father. I want to go home."

CHAPTER 28

One More Trip to the Woods

In the morning, a white cloak of snow lay across the ground. Rooftops and tree branches wore caps of white, and from the bedroom window, Nickie saw that the mountainside had turned from gray to silver. The sun shone down on this white world and made it glitter.

It was beautiful. If she hadn't been so sad, Nickie would have rushed outside to make snow angels and snow caves. But she didn't have the heart for it this morning. Besides, Crystal had plenty of work for her.

Nickie begged Crystal to drive her up High Peak Road again so she could look for Otis. But Crystal said no. This was a busy day. They'd never find the dog—the woods were vast, and besides, everything was buried in snow. And anyhow, they'd be leaving soon, and what would Nickie do with a dog?

Nickie's orders were to clean out the nursery—put

the lamps and furniture back where they came from, pack up the toys and games and other things, throw out anything old and useless. All morning she worked on this. It was awful not having Otis there. When she picked up his food bowl and his water bowl, a lump of sorrow rose into her throat. She put the bowls in a big plastic bag so she wouldn't have to look at them.

She was going to keep the picture of the Siamese twins. Crystal had told her she could have it, either to keep or to sell. She'd called an antique expert and asked about it, and he offered to pay $350 for it, sight unseen. But Nickie wanted to keep it, along with the cross-written letter. After all, these were among the few souvenirs she'd have from this whole trip. She put them carefully at the bottom of her suitcase.

She'd asked Crystal if she could keep her great-grandfather's notebook, too. She felt as if he'd kept her company, a little, while she was here in his house. Now she picked up the notebook and riffled the pages, thinking again about the mystery they contained. The professor had encountered a pool of sadness in the west bedroom, and he had seen something there, too, or thought he had. She sat down on the window seat and flipped through until she found that entry:

1/4 Extraordinary experience last night:
Went into the back bedroom to look for the

scissors, thought I saw someone in there, over by the bed—dark-haired figure, transparent swirl of skirt. Dreadful feeling of sorrow hit me like a wave. Had to grab the doorknob, almost fell. Figure faded, vanished. Maybe something wrong with my eyes. Or heart.

Reading this again, she remembered something: the long-ago death of a child, and the mother's grief. And the dates: January 4 for the death, January 4 for the echo her great-grandfather had felt. If that's what he'd really felt, an echo.

Could it be? When the child died, the mother would have felt such a knife-like sorrow that it might have left a scar somehow beside the bed in the west bedroom, a scar so deep it could last through a hundred years and more. And the old professor, near death himself, might have felt it, might even have caught the merest glimpse of the grief-stricken mother as she had stood there on that awful day.

Or, thought Nickie, closing the notebook and staring outside at the light on the snow, maybe the professor had read about this tragedy somewhere and forgotten that he knew it. Maybe he'd just imagined what he saw and what he felt. Or maybe he'd made it all up to go with the theories of "parallel worlds" that he was interested in, those "leaks" between the past and present, present and future.

Had he really caught a glimpse of the past? Did the Prophet catch glimpses of the future? There was no way to know.

She put the notebook in her suitcase with the photograph of the twins and the crosshatched letter, and she went back to work on the nursery. When she was finished, the room looked just the way it had when she'd first seen it: empty except for the rolled-up rug and the rocking chair and the iron bed, with a slanted rectangle of sunlight on the wooden floor. What would this room be when the new owners moved in? She hated to think of it filled with dumbbells and stationary bicycles. It wasn't meant to be that kind of room; she just knew it. It wasn't meant to be someone's office, either, full of humming computers and gizmos with little flashing lights. It was meant for children.

After that, she went down to Grover's house to say goodbye. A snowplow had cleared the streets, pushing the snow in lumpy banks to either side. Already, the snow was starting to melt; trickles of water ran down into the street.

Nickie heard bits of conversation as she passed people. Mostly it was about the silence from the White House. No declaration of war. No declaration of peace, either. Just nothing. The nothingness seemed to upset everyone. They argued about what it meant. Good news or bad news?

Nickie couldn't worry about it. Her mind was full of so much else that the question of war seemed far away. She headed down Trillium Street.

No one was sitting on the porch when she got to Grover's house—it was much too cold. She knocked on the door, and Grover's grandmother opened it.

"Hi," Nickie said. "Is Grover here?"

"Down in his snake shack," said Granny Carrie. "They came and took that thing off of him," she added.

"Good," said Nickie.

"That woman has her notions," Granny Carrie said.

Nickie figured she meant Mrs. Beeson. "She wants the town to be perfect," she said.

"In this life," said Granny Carrie, "you don't get to have things perfect. Life is messy, no way around it." She beckoned Nickie into the house, and Nickie went down the hall and out the back door and across the slippery yard to the shed. Inside, Grover was stacking the empty glass cases.

"Hi," said Nickie.

"Hi," he said. For once he didn't make a comic production out of it.

"I came to say goodbye," Nickie said. "We're leaving the day after tomorrow."

"Wish I was," said Grover. He put the cases on a lower shelf and started to spread out some magazines in the empty space. "Did your dog get taken?"

Nickie nodded. She still couldn't talk about it without crying, so she changed the subject. "Did you find out yet if you won any of those contests?"

"Not yet."

"I hope you did."

"I probably didn't. I'll probably be stuck here forever."

"You don't know. Anything could happen."

Grover made a round-eyed, open-mouthed, fake-excited face. "Right!" he said. "All kinds of possibilities! I could get a great job waiting tables at the café! Or I could go be a soldier! Or—oh, boy—the world could blow up!"

"I don't think any of those will happen," Nickie said. Actually, it seemed to her that any of them might; but she could see that Grover was discouraged, and she wanted to cheer him up. "I think you're going to get to go on your trip."

"Hah," said Grover. "You're just saying that to cheer me up."

"No, I'm not," said Nickie, because an idea had hit her, a really good idea, and all at once she was telling the truth. "I can see into the future," she said, "and I *know* it's going to happen."

"Well, fine," said Grover. "And you're going to be president of the world."

Nickie just smiled. "You'll see," she said. "It's been nice knowing you." And she walked back to Greenhaven feeling, for the first time in two days, a little bit good.

The next day the sun shone brightly again. Nickie stood on the sidewalk in front of Greenhaven and watched as a crew of burly men carried one piece after another of heavy, dark, carved-wood furniture down the steps and down the path, grunting and swearing, and heaved the beds and sofas and sideboards into the truck bound for the auction house. She saw the lamp go, the one with the parchment shade. The rocking chair went, too, piled into the back of the truck like a prisoner being carted off to jail. When that truck was full, another one arrived. This time the burly men went down into the basement, where decades' worth of beds and chairs and dining tables were stacked on top of one another. It took hours just to empty out the basement.

When the trucks were finally gone, Nickie and Crystal wandered through the house. Their footsteps thudded hollowly on the bare floors, and their voices, when they called to each other from room to room, shivered with echoes. Strangely enough, though, the house didn't seem sad. Nickie had the feeling it was glad to be emptied out and unburdened. It was taking a deep breath of fresh, cool air, looking out through its clean windows, ready for whatever was coming next. Even Crystal seemed to sense this.

"Really," she said, "it's a fine old place. Without all that ghastly Victorian furniture, it's much improved. You could put, for instance, a white couch right there by the front parlor windows, and a glass-topped coffee table . . ." She held out her arm and tilted her head to one side, imagining it, and then wandered into the dining room. "And then of course a total kitchen remodel. A slate floor would tone in well, and maybe cabinets in birch or white pine to lighten the look. . . ." She stopped in the kitchen doorway, and her arm dropped to her side. "But what am I thinking? It's going to be Senior Haven." She sighed. Nickie sighed, too.

It was sad the way things had turned out. Losing Otis was the worst, but she hadn't achieved a single one of the goals she'd set for herself, either. She wasn't going to live here with her parents after all; she hadn't fallen in love; and she hadn't done a single thing to make the world a better place.

She'd be going away from here next morning, probably forever, so she decided to go up into the woods and look for Otis one more time. And say good-bye to Yonwood.

With the last of her money, she bought herself a snack at the café: a bag of corn chips, two peanut butter cookies, and a bottle of grape juice. She put these in her backpack, along with a small plastic bag full of dog crunchies and Otis's food and water bowls, just in case. She set off up the trail and was soon in the woods, where the sun striped blue tree-trunk shadows across the snow. The sun was warm on her face. She walked with stubborn energy, and every five minutes or so, she stopped and called for Otis. But she heard no distant barking—no sound at all, except for the patter of melting snow dripping from the branches.

She came to the log where she'd sat with Grover three days before. Here she looked out over the view of the town. The sky was deep, deep blue, an upside-down ocean of air. Was God up there somewhere, looking down on the whole world at once? Deciding who was good and who wasn't, figuring out what was normal, planning to sweep everything clean? She wanted to know. She wanted to be sure. But this was one area where her overactive imagination didn't seem to work. She simply could not figure out how a being in the sky, no matter how vast he was, could see everywhere. She didn't see why God would say one thing to the Prophet of Yonwood and another thing to another prophet halfway across the world. Because clearly not all these people who said that God spoke to them heard the same thing. All the fighting nations said God was on their side. How could God be on everyone's side?

Nickie could only think that either there were lots of different Gods all saying different things to different people, or that God didn't really speak to people at all, or that people *thought* they were hearing God speak when really they were hearing something else.

A bird flew across the sky, level with her line of sight. It lit on the top branch of a pine tree, pointed its beak upward, and sang out a long, warbling burble of notes. Did God speak to birds? Or were birds speaking to God?

She called Otis one more time, shouting his name out into the vast air. No answer. Just the bird, singing its heart out. Suddenly she felt finished here. She was ready to go, ready to get out of this place that made her heart hurt. She took off her backpack and got out Otis's bowls. From her water bottle, she filled his water dish. She poured the crunchies into his food bowl. Both of these she set at the side of the trail, next to the end of the fallen log. Maybe he would find them, or maybe one of the other dogs would, and remember its home, and go on down the trail back to its family.

The bag with her snack in it was still in her backpack. She realized she wasn't hungry. The very thought of food made her stomach clench. So she set the bag on the log. She liked the look of that—a present for a dog, and a present for a person. An offering to whoever might need it. Why not make it even nicer? She walked a little way off the trail, poking around in the leaf litter, looking up into the branches. Some pinecones lay beneath a tree, and she picked up the best one, a perfect fat sturdy shape, all its little wooden tabs lined up in a spiral. She went farther, though in the deep shade of the pines the snow still covered the ground, and her shoes sank into it and got wet. She found a bush with red berries and broke off a branch of it. She found a smooth, plum-sized stone patterned with veins of white. She brought these things back to the log and arranged them around the bag of snacks. The branch was like an arm around the bag; the berries were jewels. The stone was for her heart, which was heavy and hard. And the pinecone was just a pinecone—something nature had made that looked nearly perfect.

She stepped back and gazed at what she'd done. Very nice, but it needed a finishing touch. What did she have that she could add to it? She put her hands in her pockets and felt around. In her left pocket was a piece of paper. She pulled it out. It was the picture of the dust mite, a little bent. She stuck it between the pinecone and the stone, so that it stood up. It added a note of strangeness that was exactly right. It seemed to say, "Remember, I am here, too, along with other things you can't see. The world is full of endless strange surprises."

She started back down the trail. If no dogs find the

food, she thought, maybe squirrels will. Or that white bear. Or if no one finds it, then it can all be for God. Only not for the Prophet's God, her mean, picky God who dislikes so many things. It's for *my* God, the god of dogs and snakes and dust mites and albino bears and Siamese twins, the god of stars and starships and other dimensions, the god who loves everyone and who makes everything marvelous.

CHAPTER 29

The Last Day

The next morning, Crystal had a great deal of business with the post office. There were twenty or thirty boxes of stuff she'd decided to save from Greenhaven that had to be shipped back to her house in New Jersey, so much of it that she couldn't fit it all in the car at once. It took her three trips.

While Crystal was at the post office, Nickie roamed around the empty, gleaming house. She went into every room and said goodbye to it—the front parlor, the dining room, the cleaned-up kitchen, the bedrooms, all swept and empty. In the west bedroom, she waited to see if she might feel a trace of the sadness that had washed over her great-grandfather, the grief left there from all those years ago. But all she felt was her own sadness at leaving this house behind.

Finally she went up to the third floor. Here the two trunk rooms were still crammed with the things of the past, waiting for Crystal's decisions. The nursery was empty, but as she stood by the window seat, she could almost feel the presence of the beings she'd encountered there—the letter writers and journal keepers, those who had taken pictures and had their pictures taken, those who had made scrapbooks and saved postcards and lived their lives in this place. And, with an ache, she felt the bouncing, wriggling, eager spirit of Otis.

Down below, the doorbell rang. She was the only one here, so she'd have to answer it. She went downstairs to the front hall, and when she opened the door, there stood Amanda with her suitcase. She looked terrible. Her hair was falling out of its barrettes, her skin was broken out. On her face was the look of someone expecting to be shot in the next three seconds.

"I don't want to talk to you," Nickie said.

"No, you have to let me," said Amanda. Her mouth wrinkled as if she was going to cry. "I have to tell you something."

"*You killed Otis!*" Nickie said. She swung the door hard, but Amanda put her hand out to stop it and took a step in through the doorway.

"But listen," she said, and now she really was starting to cry. "I thought it was right. It was a sacrifice! It was *so hard* to do it, but Mrs. Beeson said the harder the better. If it's real, real hard, you know it's right! That's what she said." She looked imploringly at Nickie, but Nickie glowered at her. “And,” Amanda added, “everybody else was givin’ up *their* dogs, so I thought it must be right.”

Nickie turned her back on Amanda, but she didn’t try again to close the door. She went into the front parlor and sat down on the bare floor with her back to the wall beneath the windows. Amanda followed.

“I wish I hadn’t-a done it,” she said. “I been thinkin’ about him all this time, out there in the snow.” She actually said “snow-ow-ow,” because a sob came up inside the word. She lifted up the hem of her sweater to wipe her nose.

“Well, how come you changed your mind?” Nickie said.

“Because I couldn’t stop thinking about Otis,” said Amanda, “and because I found Mrs. Beeson’s list.”

“What list?”

Amanda sat down on the floor facing Nickie. She took off her jacket—the sun was warming the room now—and Nickie saw that she looked thinner than ever. “It was this piece of paper in Althea’s kitchen,” Amanda said. “A little edge of it stickin’ out from under the telephone book. So I looked at it. I shouldn’t’ve. But I did.”

“So what was it?” Nickie kept her voice cold and hard so Amanda wouldn’t think they were friends. But she was interested.

“Names,” said Amanda. “About fifty of ’em. At the

top of the list it said 'Sinners'—just that one word. Then there was names, and by each name a couple words. Like 'Chad Morris, defiant, surly.' And 'Lindabell Truefoot, sluttish.' And 'Morton Wilsnap, queer.' And then 'Amanda Stokes.'"

"You?" Nickie forgot to stay cold and hard, she was so surprised.

"Yeah. And after my name it said, 'disobedient.' How could that be true?" Amanda's voice rose in a wounded wail. "I always did every single thing she told me to do."

"You sure did," said Nickie, going hard again.

"Except for one thing, which was I bought a couple of those romance books I like to read. She found 'em and scolded me. They'd sway me in evil directions, she said."

"What's supposed to happen to the people on this list?" Nickie said.

"Bracelets. It said that at the bottom. They're all supposed to get those bracelets. Even *me*!" Amanda crossed her arms over her thin chest. "Well, I'm not havin' one. I'm leavin' on my own, goin' to my cousin in Tennessee. I don't much like her, but it's better than being here. But I had to come to you first and tell you I'm sorry. About Otis. I wish I hadn't-a done it, I really do."

She looked so miserable that Nickie almost felt

sorry for her. But she thought of Otis out there in the melting snow, his feet wet and cold, his belly empty, and she tried to steel herself against Amanda.

"So do you forgive me?" Amanda said.

"If you could get Otis back, I might," said Nickie.

"But I can't. I'm catchin' a bus in twenty minutes." Amanda actually clasped her hands together and held them up under her chin like someone in an old-fashioned picture. "*Please,*" she said.

And Nickie remembered that she, too, had wanted to do whatever Mrs. Beeson told her, that she, too, had wanted very badly to be right. And also that she'd been just a hair away from pushing Amanda down the stairs. So she looked at Amanda's tear-stained face and hauled up forgiveness out of herself. "All right," she said. "I guess I forgive you." It was a grudging forgiveness but the best she could do.

Amanda sprang up. "Thank you," she said. "I'm goin' now."

"Right now?" said Nickie. "You mean you left the Prophet by herself?"

"It doesn't matter," Amanda said. "They'll find someone else to take care of her."

"But you left her alone? She's alone right now?"

"She is, but it's okay. She's just sleeping." Amanda picked up her suitcase and went to the door. "Bye," she said, and she walked away.

Nickie watched as she went down the sidewalk, moving with a sideways tilt because of the suitcases. And as soon as Amanda was out of sight, she threw on her jacket and dashed out the door, heading for the Prophet's house.

CHAPTER 30

Nickie and the Prophet

Nothing was moving around the house on Grackle Street except for a bird that fluttered around the empty feeder and then flew away, disappointed. Nickie tried the front door and found it open. She stepped into the silent house. No one was in the living room, so she went down the hallway, looking into all the rooms. A kitchen. A study. A bathroom. No one was in any of them. At the back of the hall was a flight of stairs, and she went up them. At the top, she found herself facing two doors. She hesitated a moment. Then she chose one of the doors and pushed it open.

She saw a room full of books. Shelves to the ceiling, books on every shelf, and at the end a big soft armchair by a window. Books on the floor, books on a desk. The chilly light coming in through the glass. Outside the window, another empty bird feeder. But no one there.

So she backed out and tried the other door, and when it opened, she saw that she had found the Prophet's room.

What had she expected? A dark den? Something like a church, with holy paintings and statues of angels? It wasn't like either of those. It was an ordinary room, with a bed beside a tall window. The window was closed; the air was stale. In the bed was a woman with ripply light brown hair spread out against a pile of white pillows. Her face was small and pale, and her huge frightened-looking gray eyes seemed to be staring past Nickie, or through her. Her mouth was partly open, but she didn't speak.

Nickie stepped in. Her heart was pounding like a drum. She hadn't thought about what she would say when she saw the Prophet, and now her mind went blank for a moment.

"Ms. Prophet?" she said. "I have to ask you . . . ," she began. The Prophet didn't move. Was she listening to her? Did she even see her? Nickie started again, louder this time. "Ms. Prophet! I'm Nickie! I have to talk to you!"

The Prophet's hands fluttered on the covers, but she said nothing.

So Nickie hurried on. "It's about the dogs," she said. "Why did you say 'No dogs'? I have to know."

The Prophet's eyebrows came together in a puzzled frown, as if she were hearing a foreign language.

She gazed down at her hands. Her lips moved, but no sound came out.

Nickie spoke more loudly. "They took the dogs!" she said. "Did you know it? It was because of you! They took Otis—he's up in the mountains, he's gone—and they took Grover's snakes! Why? I have to know why!"

The Prophet's mouth opened. She looked confused, or afraid. Strands of hair fell across her face, but she didn't brush them aside.

Suddenly Nickie couldn't bear it. All her grief and anger rushed up in her like hot steam, and she took three fast steps toward the Prophet and grabbed her by the arm and shouted right into her face: "Talk! Talk! You have to tell me why they took the dogs! You *have* to!"

At that, the Prophet finally spoke. "Dogs?" she said in a feeble voice. "Dogs?"

"Yes!" cried Nickie, shaking the Prophet's arm. "Mrs. Beeson told us the dogs had to go! She said we shouldn't love dogs, we should love only God. I don't understand it. I want you to explain it!"

For a second the Prophet gazed at her with burning eyes. Then she sank back onto her pillows and went silent again.

Nickie let go of her arm. It was hopeless. Maybe the Prophet's mind had been vaporized by her vision. Maybe she couldn't communicate with human beings anymore, only God.

So Nickie turned away. She went to the window and looked down. There was the backyard where, she'd heard, the Prophet had had her vision. It was such an ordinary backyard—a small brownish lawn, a chair, some trees, a few birds fluttering around. Nickie pushed the window open, and a draft of cool air flowed in, along with a few notes of birdsong. She stood there staring down, breathing the fresh air, feeling sort of empty, like a sack that everything's been spilled out of.

Behind her, the bed creaked.

Nickie spun around. The Prophet was sitting up. Her hair fell over her white nightgown, tangled and long. She pushed her covers away, swung her legs over the side of the bed, and stood next to it, trembling all over. She was hardly taller than Nickie. When she spoke, her voice was soft and raspy, as if she hadn't used it much for a long time, but her words were clear. "I forgot to fill the bird feeders," she said. "When did I last fill them?"

"I don't know," Nickie said. "Months ago."

"Months?" The Prophet passed a hand over her eyes. "How could it be months?"

"It was," said Nickie.

The Prophet just shook her head. "You were saying something to me," she said. "I didn't understand. Tell me again."

So Nickie explained again about how they'd taken the dogs.

"And what else?"

"They stopped the church choir, and radios, and movie musicals, because you said, 'No singing.' It was God's orders, Mrs. Beeson told us."

"God's orders?" said the Prophet.

"Yes," Nickie said. "And you said, 'No lights,' so people turned all the lights off."

The Prophet swept tangles of hair away from her face, stared at the floor, wrapped her arms around herself, and shivered. She stood without speaking, and Nickie thought maybe she had gone back into silence. But abruptly she raised her head again, and this time when she spoke her voice was stronger. "Listen," she said. "I've been ill. I have been ill and heartbroken and drowned in my vision. It's time for me to come back. Will you help me get dressed?"

So Nickie did. She brought clothes from the dresser and the closet, gray pants and a thick white sweater, and she helped the Prophet put them on. When she was dressed, the Prophet sat back down on the edge of her bed, tired. "Explain it again," she said. "Brenda Beeson—what has she been saying?"

Nickie explained again about Mrs. Beeson figuring out what the Prophet meant, and looking for anything that was wrong or evil, and how people were supposed to love only God, not singing or snakes or dogs. . . .

And while she was talking, the Prophet's great gray eyes filled with tears, and the tears rolled down her pale cheeks. "I understand now," she said. "She made a mistake. It was what I was *seeing,* that's what I was talking about. The vision—I couldn't stop seeing it. It was dreadful beyond words. A world burned and ruined. A world with no cities. Everything gone! All gone, all gone."

"You said 'sinnies.' Mrs. Beeson thought you meant 'sinners.' But you meant cities?"

"Yes, yes. The cities all destroyed. People gone. No singing or dancing. No lights. No animals. No dogs, even. All gone! It was what I *saw.* It wasn't orders from God."

Nickie was so astonished that her mouth fell open and she forgot to close it for a second. "It wasn't?" she said when she could find her voice.

The Prophet shook her head. "It was just me."

"Oh!" Nickie stood still, feeling stunned, to let this sink in. She thought of something else. "Why did you say, 'No words, no words'? That was one Mrs. Beeson couldn't figure out."

"No words?" The Prophet put a hand to her forehead. "I don't know. Why would I say that?" She murmured, "No words, no words." Then she looked up, and tears sprang to her eyes again. "Oh!" she cried. "It must have been 'no birds'! *No birds!* Think of a world without birds! It's not bearable." She picked up the nightgown lying next to her and wiped her eyes.

"Maybe your vision wasn't true," Nickie said. She felt sorry for the Prophet, who seemed so frail and sad. She wanted to comfort her. "Maybe it won't happen."

"Maybe not," said the Prophet. "I don't know. I keep having these terrible dreams where my vision starts up all over again. I see the leaders about to begin the war, and I cry out, 'Don't do it!' but they don't hear me." She shuddered.

Nickie came and stood close to her. "I just want to make sure," she said. "You didn't say we shouldn't love dogs?"

"No," said the Prophet. She reached out and took both of Nickie's hands in hers. "Oh, no," she said, softly but very clearly. "No, I would never say that. I love dogs. I love the whole world—all of it." For the first time, she smiled.

"Well, good," Nickie said. "I guess I'll go, then. If you're all right, Ms. Prophet."

"Oh, please," said the Prophet. "Call me Althea. I don't want to be a prophet. And what shall I call you?"

Nickie said her name.

"Thank you, Nickie," said Althea. "I believe you've wakened me up." She stood up rather unsteadily and immediately sat back down again. "Maybe if I got some fresh air," she said.

Nickie walked with her to the window, and Althea took a long, deep breath. "It feels so good," she said. "And listen—birds."

But Nickie was listening to something else. It was a faint sound, off in the distance, but clear. It was the sound of barking.

CHAPTER 31

Love

Nickie's heart gave a huge thump. "Dogs!" she said. "It sounds like dogs! I have to go."

"Yes, yes," said Althea. "Go! I'm so glad you came, but go now—quick!"

Nickie ran down the stairs and outside. The barking was louder, a yipping and yelping, with some ruffs and woofs mixed in, a chorus of dog noise. Where were they?

She ran toward the park. Other people were coming out of their houses, too, shouting to each other. When Nickie got to Main Street, she joined a stream of people. Cars on the street slowed down to see what was happening—and among them, Nickie suddenly saw, was Crystal.

"Crystal!" shouted Nickie. "Stop! Come here!"

Crystal rolled down her window. "What?" she called. "What's going on?"

Nickie just pointed—because at that moment she saw the dogs coming from the uphill end of the road, a jouncing, prancing, jostling gaggle of dogs pouring around the bend and down toward the town, ten dogs or twenty or thirty. She ran toward them, and in just a few seconds the pack was all around her, streaking by, and she turned to race after them. "Otis!" she screamed, trying to make out his small body among the flail of legs and tails. "Otis, where are you?"

They were coming through downtown now, and people burst out of the stores and halted, open-mouthed, on the sidewalks. The dogs ran down the middle of Main Street, and it looked to Nickie, pounding after them, as if they might just run on through the town, out the other side, and back into the woods. But instead they swept around the corner when they came to Grackle Street, raced through the little park, and whirled in a circle, the lead dogs veering around to chase the dogs at the rear, around and around like a tornado, until finally a few dogs broke away, and then more did, until most of them had stopped running and were nosing around the garbage cans or raising their legs against the trees.

By now a crowd of people had rushed down the street to the park. Nickie was among them. Their voices flew all around her. "I see Max!" someone cried joyously, and someone else called out, "Look! There's Missy! Here, girl! Come on!"

Right in front of Nickie, a few people wearing "Don't Do It!" T-shirts halted at the edge of the park. They stood there with their shoulders hunched and arms folded, as if to ward off any dog that might come near. "This is a bad sign," one of them said. The other muttered something that Nickie didn't stop to hear.

She pushed past them. Where in that swirl of dogs was Otis? Was he there? She didn't see him. A boxer had knocked over a garbage can, and five or six dogs rushed to paw through the contents. A black dog was on its hind legs at the drinking fountain, lapping water from the stopped-up bowl. People rushed every which way, calling dogs' names, clutching them by the collar, and the dogs leapt up, licked faces, thrashed tails back and forth.

But where was *her* dog? A dread seized her. What if he wasn't—?

But he was. There, under a picnic table, nose to the ground, sniffing at a scrap of paper, tail pointing straight up. "Otis!" Nickie screamed, and he looked up in surprise. When he saw her, he cocked his head, stared a moment, and then ambled toward her with the scrap of paper sticking to his nose.

She caught him up in her arms, squeezed him tight, rumpled the top of his head, and told him how happy she was over and over. He wiggled. He licked her chin. Twigs and burrs were tangled in his coat, and his feet were wet and packed with mud between the pads.

He smelled like earth and rot and dog doo. He was a mess.

Then a sharp voice rang out above the noise of the crowd. "Wait! Wait!" it cried. "This is wrong! We mustn't do this! We can't take them back!" And Nickie saw Brenda Beeson standing at the edge of the park, wearing her red baseball cap and waving her arms above her head.

A few people turned to look at her; a few of them paused. Then a dark-haired woman bent down, scooped up a small dog, and took it over to Mrs. Beeson. It was Sausage, Nickie saw—with her droopy ears all stuck with burrs.

Mrs. Beeson stared at Sausage. She reached out—and then she pulled her arms back. She turned away, she turned back again, and finally she just stood frozen, with a look of desperate confusion on her face.

And at that moment, a gasp arose from the Grackle Street side of the crowd, and all heads turned. Down the sidewalk, slowly and slightly tippily, came Althea Tower. She was wrapped in a voluminous gray cape, and although she had tried to fasten her hair back with a ribbon, most of it had come loose, and the breeze made it float around her head. She was so short and slight that she looked almost like a child—a frail, excited child, hurrying toward the place where something was happening.

Love

People were so amazed to see her that they just stared as she came closer. At last, two young men ran forward to help her. They led her into the park. People crowded around her, and Nickie heard her say, "Yes, thank you, yes, I'm all right. A girl came and shouted at me—that girl right there"—she pointed at Nickie, smiling—"and, well, I woke up." Then she murmured something to the young man on her left and tilted her head in the direction of Mrs. Beeson. They walked with her to where Mrs. Beeson stood flabbergasted, her eyes darting back and forth between Althea coming toward her and Sausage squirming in the arms of the dark-haired woman. Althea took Mrs. Beeson by the arm, and the two of them went apart from the crowd to talk.

Nickie, who knew what they would be talking about, saw no need to stay any longer. She left the park and the chaos of people and dogs behind and carried Otis back toward Greenhaven. When she was halfway there, Crystal, who had driven home and parked the car, came running toward her. "What in the heck is going on?" she said.

"The dogs are back," said Nickie. "Look. This is Otis."

Crystal stooped over and looked Otis in the face. He opened his long pink mouth and yawned at her.

"Cute," she said.

"I'm keeping him," said Nickie.

"I don't know," said Crystal. "Does the building you live in allow—"

"It does," Nickie said, though she didn't know if this was true. She didn't care. She'd make them change the rules if she had to. If they wouldn't, she'd make her mother move.

"Well," said Crystal. "Hmm." But she didn't argue.

Back at Greenhaven, they put the last of their belongings into their suitcases and carried them out to the street. The sun blazed down, glinting off the car and the scraps of snow still left from three days before. They put their suitcases in the trunk. "I have to stop at the real estate office on our way out," Crystal said. "Just for a second."

While Crystal was in there, Nickie sat in the car with Otis on her lap and picked the stickers out of his fur. Dirty as he was, and smelly, she adored the feel of him leaning against her. After a while he got sleepy and lay down with his head hanging sideways over her leg, and she adored the way his mouth looked upside down, with his black lips and the tips of his teeth showing. She picked the dried mud out from between the pads of his feet and didn't mind at all that she got dirt under her fingernails.

Crystal came out of the real estate office quite a while later, just as Nickie was starting to wonder what was taking her so long. Len was with her. When she got into the car, she rolled down the window, and he bent over, curling his hands over the windowsill. "So I'll let you know," he said. "It should be tomorrow or the next day."

Crystal nodded. "I don't even know how to feel about it," she said. "But you'll call me."

"Oh, yes," said Len. He looked at her in a meaningful way. "Oh, yes, I'll call you. Never fear."

Crystal smiled. She put one of her hands over one of his. "Goodbye, then," she said, looking up at him, and quickly he poked his head a bit farther through the window and kissed her on the mouth. It was just a peck, but even Nickie, with her limited experience of being in love, could feel that it was quite thrilling to both of them.

Crystal pushed the Up button to close the window. She put on her sunglasses. She stepped on the gas. They sailed down Main Street and out of Yonwood.

"What's he going to call you about?" Nickie asked as they rounded the curve toward the highway.

"The offer on the house. Looks like the Hardestys are vacillating. They've found another place they think might be better for their purpose. They might withdraw their offer."

"Then what?" said Nickie.

"I'm not sure." Crystal accelerated and merged with

the traffic on the freeway. "It depends on . . . I don't know. We'll see."

They rode in silence for a while. Nickie worked on getting a twig untangled from Otis's ear hairs. Then she said, "Len sure likes you."

A small smile appeared on Crystal's face. "I know," she said. "I like him, too."

"Is he going to come to New Jersey and be your boyfriend?"

"Oh, heavens," said Crystal. "I don't think so." She stepped hard on the accelerator and passed two slow trucks. Still smiling that small smile, she glanced over at Nickie, who was working very slowly on the twig, trying not to pull Otis's hair. "I think you're in love," she said.

Nickie looked up, startled.

"With that pup," said Crystal.

And with a sort of shock, Nickie realized it was true. She had definitely fallen in love with Otis. This *was* being in love, wasn't it? Looking forward to seeing him every day, feeling like a hole was ripped in her heart when he was gone, jumping for joy when he came back, not minding if he smelled bad, wanting to take care of him, actually *liking* the dirty and funny-looking parts of him? Surely it was being in love. It was true that she hadn't fallen in love with Grover, the obvious candidate. She'd fallen in love with a dog instead of a person. But that didn't matter. It was still love. She'd apply it to a person later on.

They drove back to the city. There Nickie carried out the good idea she'd had. With Crystal's help, she sold the photograph of the Siamese twins for $350. She added $25 of her own, and she sent that money to Grover. She put it in an envelope with a note that said, "Congratulations! You have won first prize in the Grand Amalgamated Products Association Sweepstakes!" A few days later, she got a postcard from Grover that said, "A very nice specimen of the Triple-Fanged Magenta-Spotted Rat Snake will soon be on its way to you in the mail. Thank you." Fortunately, no rat snake arrived.

It turned out that their building in the city did *not* allow dogs. But it also turned out that this didn't matter, because of the letter that came from her father the very day Nickie got home. Her mother opened it and gave a joyful shout. "He says his job has been made permanent, and he wants us to come and join him!" she said. "You'll never guess where he is!"

"Oh," said Nickie. "I forgot to tell you. I know where he is—California."

"You're right," her mother said. "But how did you know?"

"He told me, in those postcards," said Nickie. "I

figured it out. I knew he wouldn't be writing those strange P.S.s for no reason."

"They made no sense to me at all," said her mother. "What did they mean?"

"If you'll get the postcards," Nickie said, "I'll show you."

Her mother brought her the postcards, and Nickie laid them on the table. "Look," she said. "It took me a while to get it, but I finally did. Each one of these messages has a number in it. 'Three sparrows.' 'One peanut butter cookie.' 'Midnight'—that's twelve. And 'ninth birthday.' It's the very simplest code—Dad taught it to me. The numbers stand for letters in the alphabet. Three is *C*. One is *A*. Twelve is *L*. Nine is *I*. By the time I got that much, I knew where he was."

"Aren't you clever!" said her mother. "And isn't it wonderful—California!"

"Yes!" Nickie threw an arm around her mother's waist and hugged her. She knew what California meant to her mother, who'd grown up there and whose family had lived there for generations. For her mother, going to California would be going home.

They spent the next week packing, and as they packed Nickie told her mother everything about what had happened in Yonwood—about Otis and Amanda, about the Prophet, about Grover and his snakes, and about the three goals she'd set for herself.

"What happened with those goals?" her mother asked. "Did you reach them?"

"No," said Nickie. "Not really, except for falling in love with Otis. I didn't reach a single one."

But she was wrong about that. Sometimes it takes much longer than you think it will to reach the goals you set for yourself. And sometimes—as it happened with Nickie—you reach your goals in strange and unpredictable ways.

What Happened Afterward

The house in California was on a farm that spread out at the foot of low green hills. There were acres of land for Nickie and Otis to wander in. Nickie loved living there. Snow fell in the winter, and in the summer the fields were full of butterflies.

Crystal went back to New Jersey. Len came to visit her there, and she went to Yonwood sometimes to visit him, and it didn't take long for them to decide they were meant for each other and should get married. Luckily, the Hardestys decided to withdraw their offer on Greenhaven, giving Crystal the chance to make the decision that had been slowly growing in her mind. She took Greenhaven off the market, and she and Len moved into it themselves, filling its rooms with the kind of plushy pale furniture Crystal liked. Four children followed, a girl and three boys, who used the third-floor nursery room for games, puppy training, movie watching, and bouncing on a small trampoline. Two parakeets lived there, and one hamster. For the next five summers, Nickie flew across the country and spent a month at Greenhaven with her small cousins, and in this way she fulfilled, more or less, her first goal.

The summer Nickie was twelve and Grover was fourteen, the two of them paid a visit to Hoyt McCoy, and he showed them the universe that shimmered on the walls of all his downstairs rooms. Then he took them upstairs and showed them his telescope and whole rooms full of astronomical equipment. "I search for signs of extraterrestrial life," he told them. "It's difficult to search in this universe because everything is so far away. Fifty years for light to get here even from the *nearest* star—ridiculous! But other universes—which might be right next to ours, closer than that chair there—that's something else again." His eyes gleamed. "Imagine a rift, a crack in our universe that gives us access to another one. Only for an instant, just long enough to see that it can be done. Would you believe such a thing possible?"

They said they didn't know.

"*I* know," said Hoyt. "Not that I can begin to explain it to you. But that winter you were here, Nicole—well, I will just say that certain people in Washington were astounded by what I told them."

"Washington?" said Grover. "Astounded?"

"Quite. Astounded enough, at a crucial moment,

to put aside certain dire plans. Astounded enough to think that perhaps it was better to explore the world than destroy it. But I am saying too much. Never mind, never mind."

They pestered him with questions, but he would say no more.

Nickie always wondered, after that, if Hoyt McCoy had had something to do with preventing the war. People had waited for over a week after the president's deadline, with nothing but rumors in the news. Finally there came an announcement: an agreement had been reached with the Phalanx Nations after all; war had been averted. No country set off its arsenal of bombs, and the terrorists seemed to fade back into whatever dark corners they had come from. For a while, there were wild rumors that the government had received messages from an alien starship that taught the leaders how to solve their problems. But that was never proven, and hardly anyone believed it. Most people thought that they'd come through all right because God was on their side.

Brenda Beeson was extremely upset to discover that the Prophet's blurry words had not been orders from God. In fact, she couldn't quite believe it. She warned people not to lose faith, and to keep up their battle against evil. She pointed out that although war hadn't come, the terrorist was still up there in the woods. Then one day that spring a young photographer named Annie Everard took her camera up the trail to take pictures of wildflowers and came back instead with a fairly clear shot of a white bear. Everyone was relieved. Now that the danger was past, they decided to go back to following regular laws made by people rather than commands that might or might not come from God.

Mrs. Beeson found this extraordinarily frustrating. She ran for mayor the next year, but when she lost, she took up a life of study instead. She set up an office in her house, equipped with a powerful computer that had a lightning-fast Internet connection and all kinds of software for finding and reading and organizing information, and there she pored over holy writings from every place and time, trying to figure out, once and for all, what God was really saying.

Althea Tower asked everyone *please* not to call her the Prophet. She was sorry for all the things that had been done in her name, especially the episode of the dogs, even though it wasn't her fault. So she set up a place in her backyard where people could bring their dogs when they went away on trips. She also led birdwatching walks around town for anyone who wanted to come, and she kept her birdbaths and bird feeders full both winter and summer. She tended to have nightmares, though, and she never completely recovered her health.

Grover was in Yonwood only occasionally in those

years. After the Arrowhead Wilderness Reptile Expedition, he spent the next year living with his father's sister in Arizona so he could work with the Young Herpetologists program there on the weekends, and when he was seventeen and had graduated from high school, he went to study in Thailand. His life turned out to be the very one he'd wanted: adventurous, interesting, and useful. He traveled through the swamps of Malaysia, the forests of Kashmir, and the deserts of northern Africa; no one knew more than he did about the strange, endangered creatures of those lands.

Years later, Crystal sent Nickie two newspaper articles from the *Yonwood Daily.* One was about Grover. He had become, the article said, a world-renowned expert on a previously unknown Amazonian snake called the flame-tongued boa. He'd discovered that a gland in its throat produced a chemical that could be used to make a powerful painkiller, and the painkiller was now used by doctors all over the world. When Nickie heard this, she smiled to herself, remembering her Goal #3. On that first trip to Yonwood, she *had* done something to help the world after all: she had started Grover on the road to his discovery.

The other article was about Althea Tower. It was simply a brief notice of her death. She had caught a bad flu that developed into pneumonia, and she'd died at the age of sixty-four.

And so the Prophet wasn't around when it began

to look as if her terrible vision might be coming true after all.

The problem was, the conflicts that threatened the world when Nickie was eleven had never really been resolved. For a while, leaders turned to the quest for knowledge, putting their efforts into finding out what secrets the universe might hold, and the world changed in many ways. But time passed, the leaders of one era were succeeded by the leaders of the next, and the old fears and differences arose again, fiercer than ever.

And so, long after Nickie had grown up and married and had children, after her children were grown and gone, after her husband (who'd fulfilled her Goal #2) had died—that was when the world once again plummeted down toward darkness. Perhaps, Nickie thought, the Prophet really *had* seen a glimpse of the future—just a more distant future than anyone had thought. What was happening certainly matched the horrors that had frightened her so badly.

All over the world, people who believed in one truth fought against people who believed in a different truth, all of them believing theirs was the only *real* truth, and all of them willing to do anything—absolutely anything—to defend it. Nations readied and aimed their missiles. They sent their soldiers to take over cities and fight for land, and as the fighting swarmed across deserts and jungles and seas, new diseases broke out, and warring troops and fleeing refugees carried them to one country after another; hundreds of thousands died. Fear ran like a pack of wolves across the planet, and people were afraid for the survival of the human race.

That was when the enormous project that Nickie's father had worked on fifty years before was at last put to use. It was an entire city, built beneath the ground, stocked with supplies and sealed off from the surface so that its inhabitants could live there as long as necessary, safe from whatever was going to happen above. When the human race seemed truly threatened, the government contacted a few carefully selected people and asked if they might be willing to volunteer for this enterprise. Nickie, being the daughter of one of the Builders, was among them.

She was torn. She hesitated a long time before making up her mind. She loved the world and didn't like the prospect of going down into a dark place and remaining there, probably, for the rest of her life. But *because* she loved the world, she finally decided to go. She was sixty years old, after all; she'd had many good years of life. But she wanted to make sure people were still around after she was gone to keep on loving the world. Who would appreciate its beauty and wonders and strangeness if people were gone? So she volunteered. And as she sent off her letter of acceptance, she remembered again her long-ago Goal #3: to do something good for the world. She'd tried her best to help the world during her life, doing the small things that came along. Maybe this was a big thing for her to do—the biggest, and the last.

Besides, she was curious. What would it be like to live in an underground city?

When the day came, she was both sad and excited. On the train, she began keeping a journal, but when the travelers got to the cave entrance and had gone down a long tunnel to the river that would take them to the city, she was afraid the leader would catch her writing (it was against the rules), so she wrapped her journal in a green plastic rain hat, wound a narrow belt around it a couple of times to hold the plastic on, and stashed it behind a rock. Maybe someone will find it someday, she thought. It will be a sort of letter to the future.